THE IRREGULARS

THE IRREGULARS

THE NORTHWEST UPRISING: BOOK TWO

NADYA SIAPIN

The Irregulars/Nadya Siapin—1st ed.

The Travelling Storyteller Press

Cover art by MIBLArt (miblart.com)

Maps by @Saumyasvision/Inkarnate

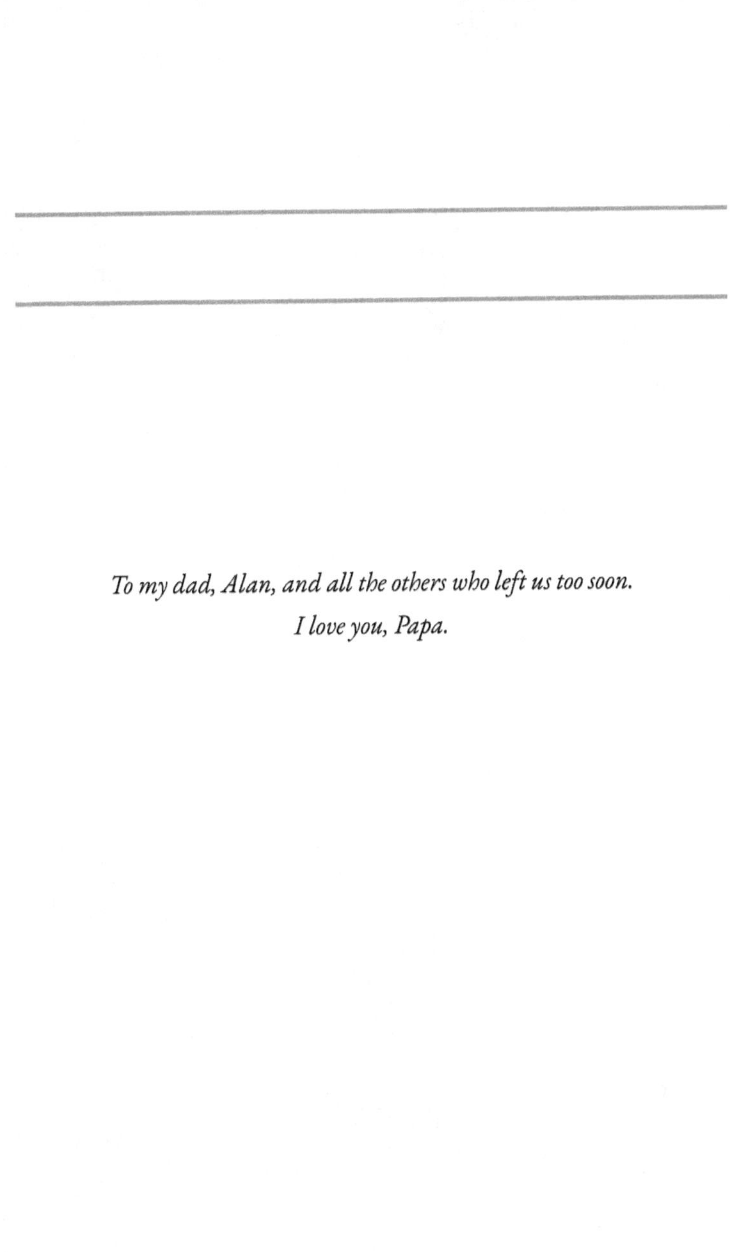

To my dad, Alan, and all the others who left us too soon.
I love you, Papa.

CONTENTS

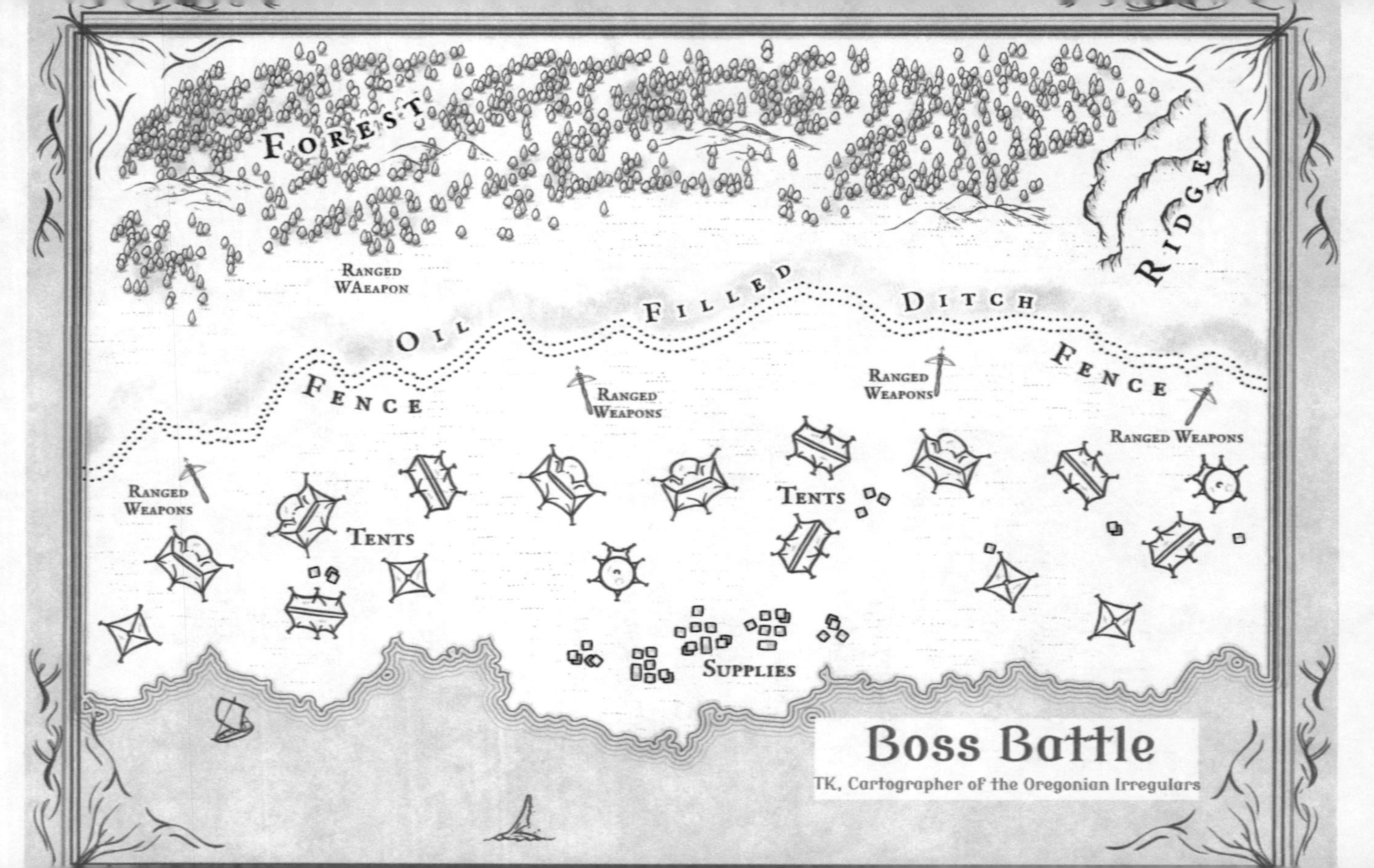

Boss Battle

TK, Cartographer of the Oregonian Irregulars

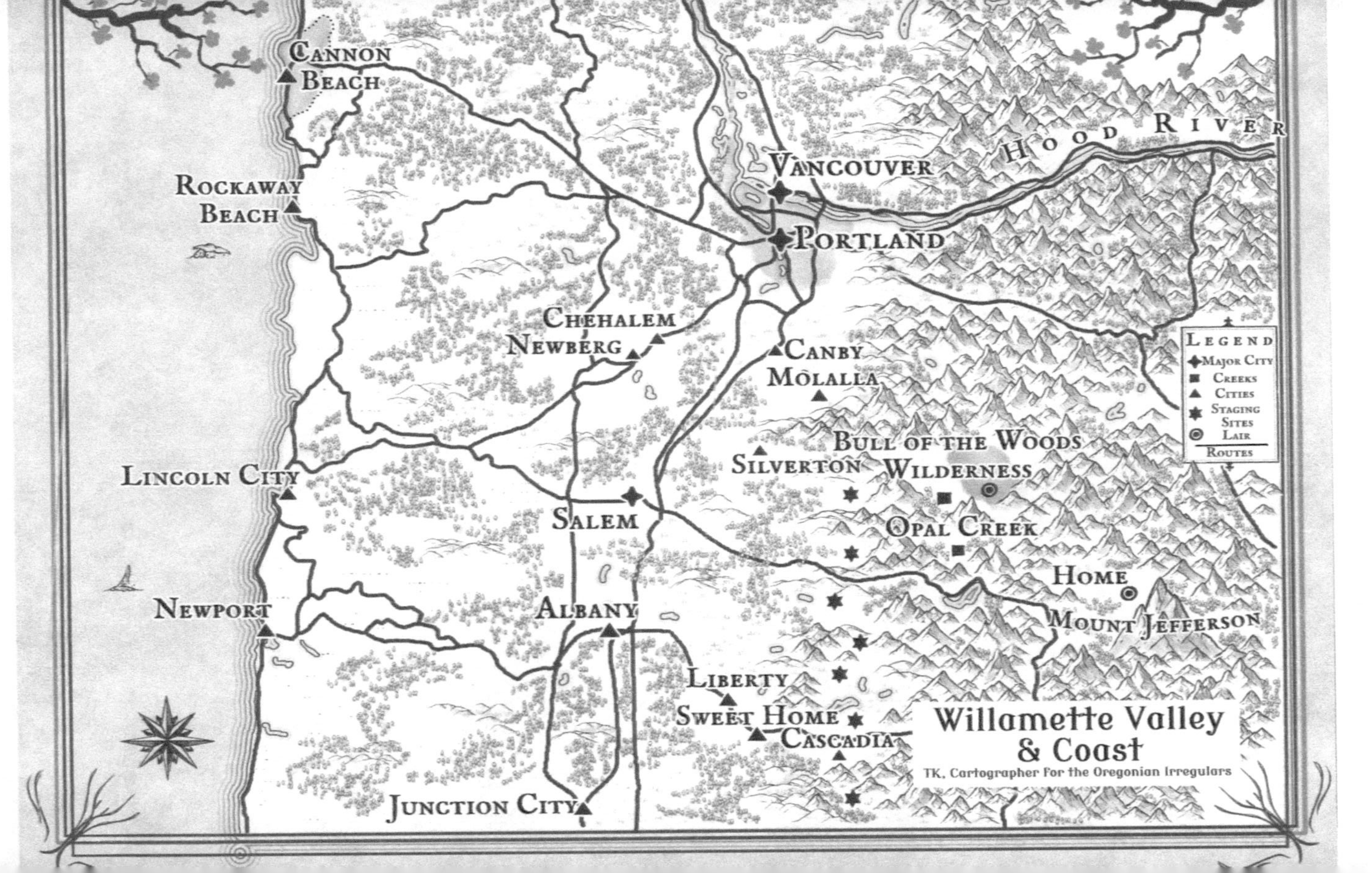

Cannon Beach
Rockaway Beach
Vancouver
Hood River
Portland
Chehalem Newberg
Canby
Molalla
Bull of the Woods
Silverton Wilderness
Lincoln City
Salem
Opal Creek
Home
Newport
Albany
Mount Jefferson
Liberty
Sweet Home
Cascadia
Junction City
Legend
Major City
Creeks
Cities
Staging
Sites
Lair
Routes
Willamette Valley & Coast
TK, Cartographer For the Oregonian Irregulars

PROLOGUE: THE PRESENT

Hope Sanders paced across the stage like a caged animal as the crowd watched with bated breath. Already, they'd learned more about the reclusive leader and her role during the Invasion, the West Coast's occupation by a foreign power, and the uprising. Starting with the fact that Captain, as she was known during the uprising, was a woman.

"A lot changed for us," Hope told the audience as she paced, "that summer after we lost Thunder and Lightning. We founded Home and relocated all our civilians and livestock up there."

The relocation had taken weeks to accomplish, between dodging or drawing away Steve, which is what they called the invaders, and hiding the tracks hundreds of people had made.

In the front row, Alex Carrington smiled, reminiscing about Home. Sonya Gatens had found the place orignally when she'd taken time off after two young fighters, Thunder and Lightning, had been killed. Alex had taken her kids up to Home two summers ago to visit the place. It'd become something of a pilgrimage for those who survived. A way to try to open up about the Invasion in a kinder way.

Motions had been made recently—partly at Alex's instigation—to ensure no construction ever happened up there, not even a memorial. The one at the Lair was sufficient. No, Home would remain untouched by civilization and remain a place of rest for hikers, park rangers, and firefighters as a tribute to those who had lived there.

"The soldiers' arrival changed everything," Hope continued. Her twins, sitting between Alex and Tom, perked up when their mother mentioned the soldiers. "Who knows how things would have turned out without their help and influence? I know my life would be vastly different."

Hope, still moving—always moving—swung back to face the crowd. "We spent a lot of time wishing the military would rescue us. When they finally showed up, I cussed more in those first days than I have before or since." Laughter rippled through the crowd. A faint smile played about Hope's lips but failed to warm her cold, tired eyes.

Hope chuckled suddenly, the sound catching the audience by surprise. For a moment, they saw her as she had been—a young woman delighted by all life had to throw her way.

"Those motherfuckers were almost more trouble than they were worth.

"Almost."

Chapter 1

"Fuck those fucking assholes who can't walk into a fucking occupied fucking valley without getting fucking captured. Fucking twats." I stalked back and forth just outside our camp on the edge of the foothills near Eugene. I'd been fuming for over a day, and my mood wasn't made any better by the dreary day in late fall. The sky hadn't let loose yet, but in Oregon, all you had to do was think of rain to summon it.

For over a year, I'd been running around with my cousin Sonya—everyone knew her as Sirius—Phoenix, and a pair of siblings, Dereva and Anansi, fanning the flames of a rebellion. We'd been invaded by the North Korean Liberation Army, who had taken over the entire West Coast.

After disabling our technology (we still didn't know how), they'd rounded up the inhabitants of California, Oregon, and Washington, turning them into slaves. Oregon had been turned into a giant farm, with animals and crops all over the Willamette, everything and everyone heavily guarded. We couldn't even rescue anyone because the families of the enslaved were kept separate as hostages so the enslaved would return each day.

Motherfuckers.

In all this time, the only thing we'd wanted was the US Army, riding to our rescue. We were less than a hundred fighters holed up in the Bull Run Wilderness, with nearly three times that in non-combatants stashed in the mountains. Sirius had come back from mourning her friends with the location of a cave system large enough to hide all our non-coms with room to spare in the Jefferson wilderness.

Just us, against an entire army.

Then, last week, a man showed up on the edge of our camp, telling us the army had arrived. He was an advance scout, and he'd stood in the middle of a camp full of angry, armed women while keeping an admirable level of respect and calm. I could work with that, and it didn't hurt that he was easy on the eyes.

Well, handsome as fuck was more accurate, but I conveniently forgot the way my heart jumped when I'd seen him.

Then I met his commander. A more self-righteous son of a bitch I'd never met. He'd taken one look at us, said "Collaborators and unimportant," and fucked off on some secret mission to the Valley. The asshole in charge, Major Hendricks, refused to tell us anything.

"Your...*fighters*," he'd managed to say as he looked down his thin, autocratic nose at me, despite being a couple inches shorter, "have...fraternized...with the enemy. We simply can't trust them. Or you." Then they'd promptly gotten captured.

Morons.

Based on how much I trusted Hendricks (not at all), we packed up and moved camp as soon as they were out of sight. Then, I'd sent my cousin to take a few scouts and follow them. I found out they'd been captured the day after it happened.

Normally, I'd be inclined to leave them, but my baby brother, Peter, was one of the idiots who got his ass caught. Now, four of us risked death, or worse, to spring these dumbasses from prison. I'd even had to send a vehicle back to the Lair, our home base and a former secret military outpost, to get additional support.

Who's the idiot now? my inner asshole taunted. *Fuck you, too,* I told it.

Taking five slow, deliberate breaths, I headed back into camp. "All right. I'm ready," I announced.

As Seahorse had predicted all those months ago, the girls weren't overly thrilled with the plan. Who could blame them? One thing goes wrong, and we're all either sex slaves or on the torture rack. To give ourselves our best chance of blending in, we'd brought the Fates—non-combatants who hadn't left the area around the Lair in months—into the field.

The Three Fates, former beauticians who'd been freed in one of our earlier rescues, circled me, plucking at my clothing and clucking. Going by the noises, they didn't approve of my fatigues, plain T-shirt, boots, sweatshirt, and plethora of weaponry that passed as our uniforms.

The First Fate, a woman who neither confirmed nor denied when I asked her if she was from Europe, snorted. "You aren't ready yet, but you will be."

Around us, fighters—mostly women but a scattering of men—prepped for the coming fight, giving their weapons a final check, tightening laces, and making sure they had plenty of ammo. I wished desperately to be a part of their number, but instead I faced the Fates, who were armed with the tools of their trade—makeup, scissors, hair dye, and...clothing.

Calling the tiny slip of cloth *clothing* was being generous. Sirius, Phoenix, and I had gone into Salem nearly a year ago, just to see what the hell was happening. While there, we broke into a brothel, killed a bunch of soldiers, stole a bus, and rescued some women who had been forced into prostitution. On our way out, we'd sacked the place, taking anything that might be useful, including the clothes.

That piece of foresight finally came in handy. I now sat on a tree stump in my bra and underwear while the three women worked over and around me, patting, trimming, primping, and coloring to make me look presentable.

Occasionally, they called for another bucket of water. Then they called in another fighter, Ink. The teen had a keen eye for art and tattooing. She drew designs over my scars with henna.

When they'd all finished and got me into the slip of a dress, I surveyed the expanse of visible skin, and how much of it was covered in henna tattoos, including around my left eye, where a cougar had given me a memento.

I stood and twisted experimentally, the cold wind blowing up my nether regions. "You know, I don't think I've been this naked in public since I was born."

They laughed, then the Second Fate brought over a pair of six-inch platform heels. "Your shoes, my dear."

I eyed them dubiously, but obediently sat down on the stump to pull the shoes on. "When did we get shoes?" I grunted, struggling to get a foot into the strappy contraption of torture.

"They came in an hour ago." Phoenix folded her arms, scowling down at the shoes she already wore. "They suck."

The First, seeing me struggle, knelt and brushed my hands aside to work the shoe on herself. "It won't fit?" She sat back, surprised.

I held up the other shoe, squinting at the text on the bottom. "Heh. It's a normal width shoe. It'll never fit," I informed the nonplussed beautician.

She looked at my trapped foot, my toes not even passing the halfway mark, her lips compressed in a thin line. "This was the only pair they found in your size. Now what?"

"I go barefoot." I wrenched the wretched thing off and flexed my foot, stretching my toes before standing. "If I walk right, I should be okay. I'm doing a natural thing." I wrinkled my nose, grimacing.

The First stood up, dusting off her knees. "It will have to do. We do not have shoes for another girl, so we cannot replace you. You must make the best of it. Now, you learn to walk!"

This declaration received some notice from the fighters surrounding us.

"But I already know how to walk!" I said. Women huddled around Dereva, who had a pad and pencil out, swirling apart and coming together again, their grins swiftly hidden at my glances.

"Hah!" The First brought my attention back. "No. You stride. Every move conveys violent intent. Now, you must learn to *seduce* with a step."

"Fuck me." More than one person had to hide a reddening face or outright laughter. I scowled. "Whose dumbass idea was this, anyway?" I asked the air.

"We only have one person who could come up with something as *bold* as this," Dereva piped up. The word *stupid* hung unspoken in the air. She looked like all she needed was a bowl of popcorn to be all set. Her pencil hovered over the pad. "You."

"The peanut gallery can shut up," I groused.

Nobody tried to hide their laughter anymore.

"You realize I'm about as seductive as a pineapple, right?" I looked at the Fates as if they would save me.

"Spiky on the outside, sweet and tart on the inside, and will dissolve you in acid if given enough time," Phoenix chortled, happy now that someone was more uncomfortable than her.

"...Okay. I'll give you that one. Asshole."

"Now, Captain." The First Fate interrupted our Roast The Captain session. "What you must do is this..."

***

Sung Ki's black eyes met mine as the truck slowed at the last checkpoint before town. Steep hills covered in fir trees held the mist barely above our heads, revealing the town at the last minute. *Only four of us.* I pressed my lips together, then remembered the lipstick and immediately softened them. Phoenix, Storm, and me sat in the back, dressed in tiny bits of nothing. In front, Sung Ki drove the only military truck we'd stolen that didn't have bullet holes in it.

"Lucky you, avoiding the shoes," Storm whispered.

"Big feet." I grinned.

"Shit." Phoenix pulled our attention around to see the compound. "Look at the security here."

"Well, at least we're in the right place."

Out of the whole town, only the industrial area had tall chain link fencing and curled barbed wire with guards walking their rounds. It was a small section, maybe a square mile. Steve even included a few houses from the neighboring suburbs inside their compound.

We were silent, conscious of our lack of weapons and clothing. "Not like we didn't know about this," I muttered, shifting in my excuse for a dress.

Sirius had brought word back that the place was like Fort Knox, which is why we'd brought the Fates in to tart us up like high-priced call girls, ready for a day or three's worth of debauchery. The Fates had assured me that women were often sent out to one of these bases for "entertainment" and that getting in wasn't the problem. What straight man is going to complain about scantily clad women showing up?

Leaving would be difficult, which is why we had friends on the outside.

The truck rolled to a stop at the gate and Steve whisked the door open for us. I was last out, and my eyes widened when the other two wobbled on the uneven asphalt. I let out a slow breath when they caught their balance.

Around us, Steve broke into excited chatter, and three stepped forward to frisk us, groping and fondling where they could. We gripped each other's hands in a mixture of courage and "we can't kill them yet" as we stood in a row. One Steve hiked up my skirt, but Sung Ki bulled through the soldiers, snapping and pushing them away.

They settled in a loose ring around us, several of them eyeing the sleeve work Ink had done on my leg to hide the scars that that mountain lion had given me.

Impatiently, Sung Ki waved at them to unload the bags and lead the way. Before moving out, the soldiers searched each bag. All they found were short lengths of solid steel pipes, meant to be fitted together, bases and ceiling attachments, wooden sticks, and a few more costumes as well as curtains and rope. Grunting, they finally led the way into a building a couple hundred yards away.

Sung Ki turned away from the men, and I saw her hands tremble until she clenched them into fists. Catching her eye, I nodded. Squaring her shoulders, she took a deep breath and followed Steve towards what looked like the offices for the warehouse complex, brusquely waving us after her.

I checked out the buildings we passed, hissing and hitching my stride when I stepped on a sharp rock. Grunting, I remembered what the Fates had said about walking. Rising onto my toes, I stepped carefully, my hips automatically swaying from side to side. *Fuck this shit.*

Once inside, Steve led us to a large central room with doors and interior windows along two walls. Sung Ki shooed them out, snapping orders at their retreating backs. With no time to lose, we ransacked the bags, pulling out the pipes, cloth, and ropes Steve just checked.

I stood on a chair to attach the ropes to the ceiling, stringing the cloth on it to make a curtain and stage area. The others began assembling the pipes into floor to ceiling poles, carefully setting aside a few extra pieces.

I flipped a ratchet out and started tensioning the first pole to the floor near the center of the room while Storm held it steady. We needed to make this look good.

"All set?" Sung Ki asked.

Glancing around, I nodded. "All set. Good luck."

She left through the only door that led to the outside, laughing quietly with the guard stationed there.

"Hey." Phoenix jolted me back into the room. "Where's the piece with the hooky thing?"

"Um…" I flailed around behind me, my questing fingers finally latching onto it. "Here." I held it out gingerly.

Phoenix took it and carefully peeled back the layers to reveal a gray center. Sparrow had spent hours disguising bits of explosives as pipes. Though she assured us they shouldn't go off on their own, I didn't find *shouldn't* particularly comforting.

She bustled around the main room, setting out the chairs stacked against the wall into neat rows. Some of the chairs had a bit of the soft explosive molded to the bottoms. Others had the extra pipes taped to them. We used the only stuff Sparrow could find that was moldable: some old, volatile acetone triperoxide putty.

"Here." Storm set the slightly curved wooden sticks at my side and shook small components out of a bag. I didn't know how they worked, but Sparrow, our former beauty queen and resident explosives expert, assured us they would form not only operable but semi-reliable timers.

I took a screwdriver and scraped out the (non-exploding) putty we'd used to keep extra items inside the pipes in the second bag. Mostly throwing daggers and a couple of disassembled handguns. Phoenix, done with the chairs, slipped all the knives into a bandolier and set it by Storm, then began putting the guns together.

"I wish it was more than just us to start," Phoenix muttered.

"Not a snowball's chance in hell," I grunted, jerking the wrench to ensure the connection was as tight as possible. The Fates had been clear. The fewer women who went in, the better chance we had of not being raped by the common soldiers. We were entertainment for the officers first.

Once they were done, the usual was for the girls to be passed around to the soldiers.

A soldier opened the door, whistling appreciatively. Storm raced over, shooing him out, blowing kisses as she shut the door. "Impatient bastards," she snorted, coming back to help place the third, and last, pole.

***

The curtains were drawn, and the room began to fill with officers. The murmur of their conversation was broken with the clink of glasses, slurping drinks, and the scrape of chairs against linoleum. Every time a slurping noise carried over the other sounds, I growled. Each noise piled on top of the others, fogging my mind until I was ready to walk out there and slaughter the lot.

Someone began shouting, then more joined in, whistling and catcalling in their native tongue. I didn't speak much of it, but catcalling sounds the same in every language. I braced my back against the wall while Phoenix used me as a ladder to get into the air duct near the ceiling. Storm pulled the curtain back and posed seductively in the narrow gap.

"Coming soon!" She blew kisses and flipped the curtain closed again.

Phoenix, finally in the damn duct, held her hands out. I passed her the bags and waved urgently to Storm. She snatched up her bandolier and slung it over her head and practically ran up me, her bare feet flexing as they pushed off my limbs. Their discarded shoes littered the floor, thankfully.

After passing my sticks to Storm, she scooted further into the duct to give me room. Sweat gathered in my armpits and upper lip despite the cool day. Sparrow had been quite clear that her timers had a good five-minute window to go off, and we were already too close. The damn officers had begun gathering earlier than we'd thought, and the last of our preparations had been hounded and plagued by them, slowing our exit.

Taking three fast steps, I ran up the side of the wall, barely catching the edge of the duct. As soon as I had a grip, Storm wriggled forward, grabbing the harness I'd added to my ridiculous outfit. We'd planned on putting on sensible clothes before shit hit the fan. The officers' early arrival screwed that. Now, the only thing she could grab was the harness.

As soon as I got my upper body in, Storm reeled backwards. I pulled my legs up—and the world exploded, everything turning red, then black.

***

I floated, randomly back in the foothills. It'd been a bit of work getting Peter alone without anyone noticing. I'd had to wait until he left the camp to find a tree, then I had to wait until he finished peeing before I could ambush him and drag him away. I'd cried. He'd tried to be manly before putting his head on my shoulder and sobbing. Sirius found us and we sat down to talk.

Peter, naturally, wanted to know if I'd found Papa and Sean, my younger brother. I hadn't. I asked him if he'd heard from Grace, and his news nearly gave me a heart attack.

"Grace and Charlie decided they're sneaking into occupied territory to get people out." He'd hunched his shoulders, waiting for my outburst, but I was so stunned I couldn't even move. "They're only going to Washington, though," he hastily reassured me. "Because that's the only place they can find soldiers to let them through."

I whimpered. Sirius snorted. "What? Now I know she's your sister. I sometimes wondered, considering she's so sweet and you're an asshole, but it turns out you guys have flaming recklessness in common." She shook her head, pointing at Peter. "All three of you."

"Pot, kettle," I taunted her.

***

"Fuck. Fuck." I coughed, rolling over, slowly returning to the present. I was on...what? I looked around groggily, my ears ringing. Crawling forward, I crossed over a low broken wall. What? Further in, I narrowly missed a piece of metal sticking up in front of me. Feeling it, half blinded by dust, I followed it up until it ended in jagged shards. Ah. Right. A pole

Twisting around, I barely made out Storm's head and arms reaching down. The conduit hung tenuously from the ceiling, shaking every time her or Phoenix shifted. Her mouth moved and she stretched her hand down urgently. Light finally dawned. The explosives had gone off early.

I think.

Time was relative when you didn't have any working timepieces. I don't know why we kept using hours and minutes. Habit, maybe.

"Captain! You idiot, get moving!" Storm's voice finally made it through the ringing in my ears.

I shook my head. The dust settled enough for me to see the bits and chunks scattered around. Staggering to my feet, something squished underfoot. Taking a deep breath, I resolutely did not look down and went to the fighters.

"Keep going," I said, my voice swimming as if through water. "We'll meet up at the pickup. Just...find some folks along the way, yeah?"

Storm disappeared briefly, then her head reappeared, her blonde hair hanging over her eyes. Shoving it back with one hand, she dropped my sticks and a pair of moccasins with the other. "You'll need these."

Nodding, I flexed my jaw, trying to pop my ears. Goddamn explosives.

I pulled the moccasins on before I had a chance to step on anything even more objectionable than I already had, grabbed the sticks, and staggered to the doors. Well, to the doorway. There was a large, gaping hole where the doors had been. Their remains littered the room beyond.

My ears cleared enough to hear the moans and weak cries of the wounded. The soldiers rushing in weren't interested in a filthy woman, no matter how little she wore, so I made it out unmolested. Exiting the building was as simple as stepping over the windowsill, making sure I didn't cut myself on the broken glass stubbornly clinging to the frame.

I lurched, slamming into a wall and bouncing off it in a moment of dizziness, weaving my way along. Sirius had given us a decent idea where the soldiers would be, and I made my slow way there. I passed a barrel filled to the top with rainwater and took a moment to dunk my head, trying to clear the dust from my eyes and ears. Seeing the difference in color between my hands and arms, I practically climbed in to wash off. By the time I finished, my slip was soaked but I didn't have dust filling various crevices anymore.

Scooping my sticks up, I pondered my dress as I walked. Which did I want to cover, my boobs or my crotch? This dress didn't give me an option for both. Sighing, I tugged it down. I felt a bit more secure that way.

Every building I passed, I checked the windows for occupants. After the third one, I hissed impatiently. Where were they?

At the fourth, I peeked through the window perfunctorily, prepared to pass as quickly as I had the others. Ducking under the window, I paused, frowning. Edging back, I looked again. A dim red glow deep inside a nearly black interior. Nothing else had been quite so dark. And that glow...a fire?

Seizing it as my best option, I circled the building, passing huge loading docks until I found a people-sized door on the far side, then went up a narrow set of stairs. At the top, I was high enough to see another billow of black smoke, followed by reaching flames. A second later, the concussion from the explosion hit me, and I smiled.

Trying the doorknob gave me no results. Locked. Pounding on the door, I screamed. "Help! Help me! Please let me in."

I sobbed loudly, my mouth pressed to the crack. Coughing, I spat some dust and sobbed hysterically. *How long can we do this?* I wondered. Acting panicky was hard work, and every second that passed left me sounding less like a scared woman and more like a pissed off bitch.

The door cracked open, and a suspicious eye glared at me. I sniffed and wiped my hands over my face to hide the lack of tears. The eye looked down, up, and down again. Then the door opened wide, and a leering soldier gestured me in. Like a lamb to slaughter, I gave him a trembling smile and stepped in.

Four guards lounged around the former office, which stank of unwashed people, fear, and blood. Any doubts I had about this being the right building disappeared. The office looked out over the warehouse, and now I could clearly see a sullen fire smoldering in a brazier set in the middle of the warehouse floor next to a table.

Cages lined the walls, filled with listless men in ragged clothing. I couldn't see how many men were in there. They wouldn't be able to move very fast. Doc would have her hands full with this lot. Turning, I smiled at the soldiers eyeing me hungrily, ignoring their predatory gazes.

"What those for?" one man asked, pointing to the sticks in my hand.

"It's part of my routine." I smiled brightly through clenched teeth. "I'm an entertainer." I used a sideways glance the Third Fate had spent half a frustrating hour teaching me just this morning with a shard of mirror. I got it right, if the rise in his pants was any indication. "Would you like me to show you?"

Enthusiastic nods all around. Smiling slightly, I stepped lightly into the middle of the room. This wasn't something I'd learned from the Fates. This, I'd learned from Sarge. Holding a stick in each hand, I spun them around, to the side, in a figure eight. Still spinning the sticks, I moved into the beginning steps of a dance, flowing high, then low, never stopping, always moving.

Giving the sticks an extra flick, I spun, whacking a soldier across the face, knocking the lower three-quarters of the stick loose. He cried out in shock as he fell, and the others scrambled to get their hands out of their pants. Another twist, then the blade was completely revealed. I slashed a man, opening a gash across his torso while the sheath flew off the second blade.

It was over quickly, and none of the enemy had gotten off a shot. Cleaning the blades took a moment, then I sheathed them and clipped the sticks onto the harness so their hilts protruded over my shoulders. It was the best place for them when I needed to run. Going to the desk, a quick search revealed three bunches of keys. I checked Steve's pants next, hoping for *something* to cover my legs, but they were all fouled by the men's deaths.

"Fuck. Oh, well." Snatching the keys up, I ran to the stairs, skipping down to the warehouse floor. Down here, the stench was even worse, and I gagged. An unwashed person in the wild doesn't really smell much. More like our scents blended into the forest. We smelled of dirt, leaves, and leather. Animals scarcely paid attention to us, and we barely noticed each other.

This was different. If despair had a scent, this was it.

The table had straps hanging from it and was marked with black blotches. From it rose a stale, metallic tang that clashed with the sweet smell of death. I didn't care to look more closely than that. Instead, I focused on the cages. What if Peter were already...?

Biting my lip to keep from shouting for my brother, I went to the closest cage, trying keys. They shivered and clanked in my hand while I tried key after key. Caged soldiers struggled to their feet, some limping to the bars. While some had less damage than others, none of the prisoners were uninjured.

"Hi!" I smiled and nodded. "Um...is this all of you?"

"All that's left." The man's voice was hoarse, raw, but when he walked over to me, he seemed steady enough. "Do we know you?"

"Last time you saw me, I had more clothes on." Moving onto the next keyring, I started fresh. "I'm Captain."

"Well, at the risk of sounding sexist, I can honestly say you're the best thing any of us have seen all week." I glanced up at him, startled. His eyes moved down my dress to my moccasined feet and back up. I blushed, glad it was hidden by the darkness. "But shouldn't you have brought stuff to shoot the bad guys with?"

I couldn't hold back a grin when the lock clicked open and I moved to the next. "What, you think this dress isn't enough to blind the enemy?" I looked down quickly at my legs, which shone like a beacon. "And if the dress doesn't, my glow-in-the-dark legs should. There's some extra guns up there." I jerked my head to the office, my hands already busy with the new lock.

Some of the men limped up the stairs, but the one talking followed me. "I spoke to you, back at your camp."

I made a non-committal noise. "Talked to a lot of people there." A quick glance from the corner of my eye caught his eyes at the right angle. Deep blue, they were the same shade as an early fall sky. Memory dawned. He was blond under the dirt, sweat, and blood.

He'd been the first one to walk into our camp. Storm had found him scouting for his unit, and he'd managed to convince her to not kill him. He'd stood in the center of a circle of armed women, cool as a cucumber. He didn't threaten, posture, or impress us with how great he was. He'd just stood there, his hands out to the side, fascinated by us.

The second cage's lock gave way under a key, and I moved to the last lock. Deciding to risk it, since it was too dark for him to see if I turned red. "I remember you, you know. Pretty Boy."

He groaned while those who followed our conversation chuckled. Under the bruises, grime, and swelling, his features were defined. He was young, unscarred. Anyone would consider him handsome with his strong jaw and straight nose. Many of the fighters had gossiped about the scout with the butter blond hair and respectful demeanor.

Now that I was on the last cage, my anxiety ratcheted up another notch. I hadn't seen Peter yet. The scout noticed how I tried to get a good look at every man there. "You're looking for the boy. Private Wilkins. I remember seeing you talking to him at your camp. Is he a friend of yours?"

"No," I lied. Shit! I hadn't thought anyone had seen me talking with Peter. "I just hate to see someone so young going into a war zone. I wanted to check with him and see if him and the others his age were okay with this shit."

The scout grunted, pulling me back to the present. "They signed up to fight."

"Yeah." I snorted. "Not the first time kids get caught up in shit that shouldn't have anything to do with them. I guess I just hoped the kid would be okay. He seemed like a nice boy." I bit my lip and hoped the tremors hadn't come through my voice.

The last lock opened and the men who could walked out. Squinting, I barely made out a shape still on the floor in the corner.

The scout jostled past me, heading to the long bundle. "Whether he'll be okay depends on what kind of care he gets," he said. The soldier flipped back the thin blanket, revealing Peter's face. He twitched, sleeping restlessly.

The ground shifted under my feet when I saw him, and I clutched the cage bars to keep from going over. "What happened to him?"

"He got shot when we were taken." The scout grunted, pulling Peter up and over his shoulders in a fireman's carry. "He's the only one who's lasted this long. Kid's a tough little bastard. He'll be fine with care."

The words "with care" snapped me out of my funk. "Right," I snapped, swinging around, raising my voice so they could hear me. "There should be another boom any—"

The ground rocked under us, then came the boom. "There they are. We've got a doctor coming, so we need to get to the meeting point. The bus will be here soon."

The scout stared at me, mouth open. "Bus?"

The sharp report of gunfire reached my ears. "Time to go! Where's that pain in the ass Hendricks?"

Their commander, a Major Hendricks, had refused assistance, been insulting, and tried to convince my fighters to walk away from me so that he could put his own second, Lieutenant French, in command. My people hadn't had any of it, but he'd still tried.

"He was executed, ma'am," another soldier reported, saluting. His left arm was crudely bandaged, and he leaned on a young giant for support, but he was up. He was a man of medium height, a little shorter than me, and slender. I reckoned the giant supporting him could carry him with one hand, but he stayed on his two feet. "His second, French, was a spy for the enemy. That's how they caught us so easily. I'm Sergeant Perry, by the way."

"Gah!" I held up my hand, as if trying to ward off a blow. "Haven't we told you we don't use names?"

He merely shrugged his good shoulder. "Doesn't matter to me." Well. It was even better that we'd moved on the moment they left our camp.

Walking quickly to the door, the men fell into a ragged formation behind me. Those who had weapons walked on the outside, the wounded and those supporting wounded in the middle.

"How many soldiers are with you, ma'am?" Perry asked.

"No soldiers," I replied, checking that my swords were loose in their sheaths. "But I've got every fighter coming in." At a ground floor door, I poked my head out, then pulled back swiftly. I held up three fingers, pointing to the left. The men readied their handguns, fingers trembling in anticipation. "Save your bullets," I whispered. "And for God's sake, don't shoot any women."

Drawing my swords, I stood poised in the doorway, the vibrations of marching feet running through the ground. As soon as they drew close enough, I spun out into the middle of the small patrol. The ecstatic agony of being extremely good at something I didn't want to be good at rolled through me. Sarge's training was...effective.

When it was done, a helmet spun gently on the ground near my foot, the chin strap neatly cut. After wiping the blades clean on the dead men's uniforms, I straightened to see the soldiers staring, mouths open. "What?" My free hand automatically went to my chest, then the hem, checking that the damn dress was in place.

"That was...fast," one pasty-faced soldier choked out.

"And bloody," another muttered.

"What it was, was efficient," the scout carrying Peter corrected. He watched me closely, faint crinkles showing at the corners of his eyes. He'd begun sagging under my brother's weight but straightened with a groan. "Which way now?"

"That way." I pointed west, away from the sounds of fighting.

"Isn't the entrance there?" Perry asked, pointing east.

"Yeah, but that's not where our ride's coming in. That's just where Steve *thinks* they are. Now, let's go."

"Move 'em out," Perry said, just loud enough to be heard, circling his uninjured hand in the air.

Peter shifted over the scout's shoulders, groaning and waking slowly. The man lowered my brother and handed him off to two other men. The men who didn't have guns quickly found things to arm themselves with, one man taking off his shoe and sock and putting half a brick in his sock.

I led the way, seventeen men in various stages of health following closely.

Roughly halfway to our destination, a ululating shriek echoed on my left. I snapped around, listening intently. Snarling, I turned to the scout, who walked next to me. "Gotta go. My people are in trouble. Keep heading that way." I pointed. "You can't miss our bus."

"Right." The scout nodded to the men. "You heard the Captain. Keep heading west. We'll see you there." I opened my mouth to tell him to go with his men, but he didn't give me time. "We've got enough men to protect them. One man more or less won't make a difference here."

Shutting my mouth with a snap, I nodded. These guys would be okay. We'd seen a couple more Steve along the way, and the soldiers had been more than eager to get a bit of their own back.

"Go," Perry said. "That's an order."

"You can't order me," the scout laughed. "I was barely in, anyway."

"Hey, Squirt." I nodded to the giant soldier supporting Perry. "Keep him in one piece. This dude's okay."

The soldier gaped at me while his buddies laughed. "How the fuck do you call a brother my size 'squirt'?"

I shrugged. "Fine. Goliath. Don't worry, at least I won't have to worry about you keeling over like Grandpa, over there." I pointed to a soldier, barely more than a boy, who hadn't managed to grow any stubble after several days without shaving. The kid walked unsupported but stumbled a bit when I pointed at him.

I headed out, closely followed by the scout. "Need a weapon?" I asked him as I headed north at a slow jog.

"Nah. I'll be fine." He managed to match my pace, but I could see he wouldn't be able to keep it up for long. Maybe just long enough.

Smoke drifted between the buildings, fresh bits of rubble scattered over the streets. Here and there, flames could be seen above the buildings. To the east, the rattle of guns moved slowly away. Seahorse was letting them drive her off. Soon, they'd disappear into the forest, getting as many soldiers as they could to chase them.

Through the general din, I could make out specific sounds of fighting. Shouts, screams, and individual gunshots cut through the air. "You go left, I'll go right." I spoke in a low voice, even though the chances we'd be noticed with the party up ahead were slim.

The scout gave me a nod and a thumb's up, then disappeared silently into the smoke.

"Huh." I stared, bemused, at the swirling smoke left in his wake. "No arguing, no 'I wanna do it my way!'" I sniggered. "I could do with more of that. Hope he survives."

Another shriek got my ass in gear. For the millionth time, I wished I had a pair of pants. Almost anything would do. I absolutely would not wear pants that a dead man had shit in, though. I hadn't sunk that low. A gust of hot air wafted up my dress, reminding me that if I made it out of this with no major cuts or burns, I should enter the damn lottery.

I stuck close to the walls, walking quickly through the haze. At the sound of running feet, I ducked down behind some barrels, holding my breath. The footsteps were definitely coming closer. I waited, counting the soldiers who ran past my position. A few seconds after the eighth one passed and no one else appeared, I jogged after them. Collaring the last man in line, I stabbed him in the back, just under the lowest rib.

I sighed, looking down at that young face, frozen in surprise and pain. "I'm sorry," I whispered to his sightless eyes, wiping the blade clean. "I wish like hell you lot had never come here."

Keeping a wary distance, I scooped up Steve's rifle, checking its magazine before continuing. A short, sequined, damp dress is not the sneakiest thing in the world, so I had to keep my distance.

The new last soldier in the line, showing a flash of intelligence and creativity, looked behind. I didn't have time to hide. The best I could do was collapse where I stood and hope he didn't see me. I bit my hand, a short squeal choking in my throat when broken rubble gouged my butt and back.

The soldier shouted and the running paused, but apparently their commander had his priorities and figured a single man didn't matter, because they moved on.

"Mother*fucking* son of a bitching piece-of-shit bricks," I muttered once they were gone. Getting up took a bit of doing, what with needing to pick chunks of rubble out of my ass. They hadn't drawn blood, but I'd have a polka-dot of bruises tomorrow.

The soldiers weren't in front of me anymore, but a breeze cleared the smoke enough to see the sidewalk I was on ended soon at a loading bay. All the warehouses around opened into a large square, the east side open for trucks to enter and exit.

At the corner, I took a quick peek around and swore. The troop hid behind a low wall just ten feet from me. On the far side of the loading square, Storm and Phoenix hustled across, slowed considerably by the row of people following. Steve prepared to mow them down, making sure to stay low and out of sight. It would be like ducks in a shooting gallery. My fighters would be dead meat in five, four, three...

I popped around the corner, firing rapidly until the magazine emptied. Once that happened, I ran into the middle of them, swinging the rifle like a club. Alerted by the fighting, Storm had the rescued down on the ground while Phoenix raced across the space between, taking advantage of Steve's distraction.

I broke the rifle over one man's head, then threw the remaining piece in another's face. By now, I was in the middle of them, and they didn't dare risk shooting or they'd hit their own. As I flicked out my swords, Sarge's words whispered in my mind: *Don't stand still, don't give them an easy target. Focus. Breathe.*

Duck, turn, slash, never stop moving. A face loomed in front of me, mouth open. I slashed and his face disappeared in a shower of red. A turn, the stock of a rifle was coming my way, one arm up to deflect...I punched him—*Oh, God, the blade was still in my hand*. He choked, drowning in his own blood. I kicked him off the blade.

And there were no more opponents to meet me. Phoenix vaulted the low wall, Storm led her group over at a ragged run, and I slumped to the ground, just missing a puddle of blood. Gasping, I cleaned my blades again. I'd have to sit down with a cloth and mineral oil when this was all done. Sheathing them, I rolled the nearest body over and started sorting through his weapons.

"You look like a bus ran over you," Phoenix said by way of greeting. "Twice."

Civilians crawled over the wall, some with more grace than others. Shouting heralded a new lot of enemy. "Where'd you get a pair of pants?" I demanded.

"Stole 'em," Phoenix said promptly. "Why didn't you?"

I growled. "Pants from dead men are full of shit. Literally." Phoenix snorted a laugh while the civilians looked appalled. "Where did you find this lot, anyway?"

"Some warehouse over there." She jerked a thumb over her shoulder, more concerned with reloading her rifle. "Didn't see any American soldiers."

"Oh, I found those." I had a small pile of guns growing next to me. "They should've met up with Sirius by now. Are there lots after you?"

"Yup."

"Are you people drunk?" a woman demanded in a high-pitched shriek.

"I wish I was," Storm muttered, peering over the wall.

The scout crossed my mind. I hoped he was alright. I liked him and the fact that he didn't try to undermine me. It was refreshing, after some people.

A man's voice broke into my thoughts. "You think you're going to take on an army?"

"We have been," I said, taking a gun off the top of my pile, readying it.

A man with a bushy black beard whistled. "Fuckin' 'ell! Would you look at that?" I stared for a moment. I'd never heard a British accent in real life before.

The sounds of fighting drew my attention and I turned to see what had the Brit so impressed. The blond scout was in the middle of another group of Steve, a pair of sticks in his hands, swinging and jabbing with the broken ends. He turned, ducked, stabbed another man and continued, moving with the power and grace of a dancer, his arms a symphony of motion.

Phoenix, her chin resting on the wall, whistled low and long. "Give the man a sword and a girl could be forgiven for mistaking him for an avenging angel."

"I think they called those ones 'archangels.'" I clutched the top of the wall, eyes wide. An explosion in the compound reminded us of what we were doing here. "Oh, right. Yes. Rescue."

Phoenix began picking off the soldiers surrounding the scout. Taking advantage of the break, he took a running dive through a broken window, disappearing from view. *Good luck, pretty archangel.* As soon as he was out of the way, Storm and me joined in, sending Steve running back to their lines. More enemy poured into the far side of the square, taking up positions.

After a year of covert war, guerilla fighting, and desperation, I'd have thought I'd be used to battle by now. Smoke drifting across the square, flames licking the sky—all of that should be second nature, shouldn't it? Shouts and screams, the moans of the injured and dying...Above all that, the rattle of gunfire, deafening, concussive, but somehow still surprising. The knowledge of imminent death combined with the heady rush of living made me glad I wasn't so inured to a fight that I felt nothing.

"C'mon, Sirius, get here." Storm's plea turned into a constant litany, a prayer for deliverance.

"Are we going to die here?" a man asked shakily.

I frowned. He looked familiar. Examining the rest of the rescued, most of them seemed vaguely recognizable. Looking back at the first man, an impression flitted across my mind. "Didn't you used to do the weather?" I asked.

"Yes!" The man reached out, thought better of touching me, and pulled back. He vibrated with barely restrained joy to have a modicum of his old life back. "But...are we going to die?"

"Better here, with a fighting chance, than in those cages," the Brit snarled.

I raised my eyebrows and glanced at Phoenix. She grimaced. "Weatherman wanted to stay put. English made him move," she muttered.

I looked at the Brit. There was something about him that looked familiar...I snapped my fingers. "I've got it. You're that actor, aren't you?"

His teeth flashed white through the black beard. "I am. Although you could say the same for most of us here."

"No shit—" A fresh spate of gunfire ripped over our wall and into the concrete building guarding our backs, making everyone kiss the ground. Tom Carrington, action superstar and Hollywood heartthrob, in our humble neck of the woods. Who'd a thunk a famous actor would end up in Nowhere, Oregon? "Stay down!" I shouted over the screams of terror and shock. "Ready?" I asked the fighters. They nodded and Phoenix shoved spare magazines into her pockets. "Why is it," I asked the air, "that women's clothes never have pockets?"

We looked down at our skimpy clothes, then at the pants the two had stolen, and cracked up. Still giggling, I twisted around, gun in hand, preparing to stick my head up over the low wall. Just as I was nerving myself up, more firing came from my right, from the west. Too many to be the scout. Masculine shouts, jeers, and catcalling along the lines of "How do you like me now?" drifted over.

I laughed. "The soldiers. After all this time, we're finally gonna have someone pull our asses out of the fire."

"We're still fucked," Phoenix said in a low voice.

"I hear something, I hear something!" a young woman cried, her ear pressed to the ground, tears streaming down her face. "There's something coming."

"We're going to die," the weatherman moaned piteously.

Storm, who had the best view down the road, whooped. "No, we're not. *She's here!*"

I took in the situation and began snapping orders. "Storm, man the doors. Make sure everyone gets on."

"Yo!"

"Phoenix, you and me have the rear. The rest of you," I glared around at the rescued, "get your asses onto the bus ASAP."

I'd barely finished when a monstrosity barreled into the loading square, pulling a tight U-turn to stop with its butt towards Steve and the door closer to us. Armored, painted in blotchy browns and greens, the result of mixing every paint we could get our hands on, with the engine generously enhanced to take the extra weight, our heavily modified school bus roared to a stop, the door flung wide.

Sirius leaned over, grinning widely. "Do you know how hard it was to find you? Not very," she said without waiting for a response. "You guys are really noisy for a covert op, you know that?"

I vaulted the wall with Phoenix hot on my heels. "I could kiss you," I bellowed even as I began firing. I had handguns loosely hooked through my sword harness, and rather than reloading, I simply discarded the empty guns and grabbed fresh. Gotta make Steve keep their heads down.

Storm shoved people towards the doors when there was a lull in bullets flying our way, while Steve realized, too late, that this was our salvation, not theirs. Our soldiers, the ones I'd just rescued, cut across the docks to meet the bus, all of them running. I choked on a breath. There weren't as many as there had been, and all I could think of then was Peter.

A sudden round of firing from the bus made me duck. That one motion gave me a chance to look over my shoulder. A rifle rested on the windowsill, and it certainly wasn't a woman manning the gun. Past the soldier, I saw more shaved heads through the windows and relaxed slightly. They'd already loaded the wounded.

The majority of our boys were still a good twenty feet away from the rear of the bus, so me and Phoenix charged out to meet them. Steve must've worked their way around, because from my left—the space we'd just occupied, another group leapt out, charging us with...fucking *bayonets*.

What. The. Fuck.

I hurled an empty gun into a screaming face and drew my swords—the ones I'd taken from dead officers. A man appeared in front of me, screaming and slashing wildly with a bayonet. I bellowed back, blocked and riposted. He disappeared in a shower of red. I turned, elbowing a soldier in a ragged uniform behind me, towards the bus.

I snarled. Protect the people behind you. Kill the ones in front. That was the plan now. I hurled back into the fray, bulling through Steve.

They're so lightweight, like bowling pins...

No. I'm heavy.

Unstoppable but not invincible. A thin line of fire cut across my ribs, and I shrieked my rage. A whirlwind fought next to me, a short woman with sandy hair, her wild green eyes incandescent with fury.

Phoenix.

Yelling behind. My name. Captain. The only name I knew anymore.

Reluctantly, I turned from the fight. As we pulled back, so did Steve, retreating to the cover of the buildings. Respite. I grinned fiercely and spat blood.

"Move your asses," Storm bellowed. "It's time to go!"

We turned and ran, Phoenix a couple steps behind me. The big, bearded Brit shouted, waving. He leaped out of the back of the bus, running towards us. I turned to look when someone slammed into my back and spun as we fell. I landed solidly on top of him. I squirmed, bringing my swords around when the shouting penetrated.

"It's me! It's me. Stop fighting!" It was the pretty blond. He let go and I rolled to my feet, closely followed by the scout.

"Go, go!" I shouted. Two steps and a bunch of shooting from the bus later, it dawned on me that Phoenix wasn't there. Spinning back to the fight, my jaw dropped. If the scout hadn't yanked me sideways, it would've all ended right there as a bullet whipped past my face.

Thankfully I didn't die in a nowhere town like Mohawk.

The sight that stopped me nearly dead was the Brit actor, running like a track star, a bleeding Phoenix slung over his shoulder, bouncing like a sack of potatoes.

"MOVE!" Storm bellowed.

I sheathed my swords as I ran, so the four of us arrived at the bus door simultaneously and piled through all at once in the miracle of physics that only occurs in high adrenaline situations. If we'd tried that in normal circumstances, it would never have worked.

"That's it," Storm cried, and Sirius stomped the gas.

I clambered out of the tangle first, using the nearest seat to pull my-self free. I had to squint to see through the armoring, but I finally knew why Steve had pulled back in the first place. Reinforcements had shown up—with a damn big gun towed behind a Chimera, one of the souped up, Hummer-style vehicles they preferred.

"Phoenix." I automatically looked for my best sniper. She lay half-con-scious on the floor, blood pooling around her leg. The Brit had his hands clamped over it to slow the flow while the scout kept her from sliding around. "Doc! Phoenix is getting my bus dirty!"

Doc popped her head above a seat. "How bad?"

"*Your* bus?" Sirius objected, taking a corner faster than was technically wise.

"Free flow of blood, and it's spreading fast. Sirius, they're still following. Turn!"

"Straight is how we get out," she protested, bracing her feet and cranking the wheel.

There were shouts of surprise as people tumbled into the aisle or were flattened against the wall. I winced when bullets pinged off our rear, but the armor held. For now. Phoenix cried out as a civilian tried to climb off her. The Brit braced protectively over her injured leg and the scout shoved the other woman off the injured fighter.

"Doc!"

"Here." A hand waved above the seats. Wading through the aisle, I lifted and shoved people back. By the time I reached her, she'd struggled to her feet. I barely moved aside before she stepped on me in her haste to get to Phoenix. "Nice dress," she said on her way past.

"It was," I agreed. The blue sequined dress was ruined. The cut over my ribs sagged, showing a thin red line. The remainder was bloody, dirty, and sooty with dozens of tiny tears just waiting for the right moment to fall apart. The fighters would be delighted, not only that it hadn't survived but that it had been destroyed at something like this.

"You're bleeding." The scout appeared behind me. A sudden lurch threw me back, into him. He caught me automatically. My heart stuttered and he held me for a moment before setting me on my feet and holding out a pad of cloth and a roll of bandages. "For you."

"Make it quick." I watched the back. The Chimera pulling the gun rounded the corner, slower than us but still coming. He lifted my arm and pressed the pad against my side, tying it firmly. I hissed, disinfectant stinging through the cut.

"Hey, we've got company," a soldier at the back called.

A woman shrieked and cried, clutching the man next to her. A collective groan filled the bus, and the atmosphere was grim. "I know." I sighed, then said, "Someone should have a nice, long suitcase at their feet. Pass it to the back, would you?" Two cases met me at the back door, and I flipped open the larger one. Lying inside, in all its polished and oiled glory, was Phoenix's big rifle. "Hello, baby," I crooned, scooping it up.

Kicking the lid shut, I shoved it back under a seat and swayed to the rhythm of the bus. Bracing the rifle in the open window, I aimed for the engine block. Nice, straight stretch...I fired three times, working the bolt between each shot. The Chimera slewed to a stop, smoking and steaming, to cheers from the bus.

"Wait!" a woman cried. "There's another one!"

Ominous silence filled the bus, broken only by Doc's cursing and orders. Peering through the scope, I focused on the driver, and...laughed. "She's one of ours," I called.

"But it's one of those damn Koreans," a civilian protested.

"Asian she may be. The enemy she is not." When the man tried to argue more, the scout made as if to intervene, but I waved him away. "You're new here, so here's how it works. I tell you she's good, you say 'Yes, Captain.'

Because only one of us has been doing this for over a year and it's not you. Understand?"

He tried staring at me defiantly, but it only lasted a few seconds before he looked away. "'s, Cap'n," he muttered sullenly.

"Good." Sirius's next turn nearly threw me, and only a desperate grab at a seat prevented me from being flung into a stranger's lap. "What the hell, woman?"

"We're running out of time!" she shouted back. "You remember that thing you wanted Sparrow to find?" She paused, and I could practically hear the wheels turning in her head as she assessed the road in front of us. Settling on a route, she gunned the engine. "Well, she found it. We really don't have long."

People screamed as the bus accelerated towards the chain link fence, closely followed by Sung Ki and Sparrow. The explosion began as a low rumble in the earth. Looking out the rear, the first of the warehouses in the center of the compound disappeared in flames and smoke.

***

We set camp high in the foothills that night. All we could see of Mohawk was a red glow through the low-hanging clouds. The fighters moved around, helping the wounded get settled. We spread out, pulling meals out of the vehicles. Every one of them carried extra MREs for just such an occasion. Tiny campfires sprouted across the slopes, each one giving light to three or four people.

"Well," Thorin said cheerfully, "at least we don't have to deal with—"

"Shh!" Sirius clapped a hand over his mouth while the rest of the fighters glared at him.

"Deal with what?" Phoenix's rescuer, the Brit, asked.

"You know." Thorin fluttered his fingers, starting high and bringing them low. "Water. From the sky."

"Oh, rain?"

"No!" Phoenix burst out. "You never say the 'R' word." She glared balefully at the man she'd just been sighing over.

Grumbling, the fighters dispersed to find their bedrolls. Everyone made it obvious they were putting their woolen blankets on top. Those who were still using sleeping bags shook their tarps out in an admirable passive-aggressive display.

"But why?" he asked, bewildered. "I'm English. We get plenty of rain. It's gloomy, but not that bad."

People had barely settled into their bedrolls and the first watch had pulled their hoods up when a heavy drizzle started. "That's why you never say rain," Storm said loudly.

While they talked, I stood off to the side with Seahorse. "How many of them followed you?" I asked.

"Virtually none." She shook her head, grinning wryly. "I think the whole 'lure them into a trap' thing will have to rest for a while."

I shrugged. "It couldn't last forever. They had to learn sometime. The number of guys they brought to the last one showed they were learning."

"The plus side is most of them would've died in the explosion. Though it doesn't make up for the ones we lost."

Three. We'd lost three. Shaking my head, I touched her shoulder and went to my bedroll. Listening to Peter's labored breathing at the next campfire, I bit my lip. We'd done everything we could for him, but we needed to get him and the other wounded back to the Lair, where they would be warm and fed and Doc could care for them better.

"Excuse me," a woman called, her voice muffled by the blanket over her head. "How long has all this been going on? I was taken from a movie premiere in San Francisco, and they refused to tell us how long."

"It's been over a year," Dereva said. "Not entirely sure how long. My guess is it's around November, but I could be wrong."

"Oh…" She was silent for a while. "I guess my job's not waiting for me. Is…Does it go…very far?"

"Covers the whole West Coast, as far as we know." Dereva continued her role of educator. Guess she took after her dad more than I thought. "We know that in Oregon, they're mostly in the Valley. Eastern Oregon was bombed and is lightly patrolled. Well," she amended, "it was lightly patrolled when a scouting team went through. Might not be true anymore."

"Why aren't we getting out of here?" a man asked. I couldn't be sure, but I thought it might be the weatherman again.

"You will be," I interjected. "The soldiers are here to take you folks out."

"We'll die going out that way, won't we?" the man continued, talking over me. "That's why you're all still here, isn't it? If it was safe, you'd have left by now."

Snorts and laughter mingled with the rain. I rolled my eyes. "This might be hard for you to get, so I'm gonna talk slow. We live here. Our friends and family are still here. We want to find them. We're all volunteers, dude. Not only do you not have to stay, we won't mind at all if you don't."

Sniggers silenced the man and I turned to my other side. He'd been a nice distraction from thinking about the fallen. We'd lost three—Amaretto, Maple, and Ducky. The soldiers had two more who'd died on the bus during our escape. The survivors had been surprisingly accepting.

"We knew we were dying in there," the scout said quietly. "And then…we weren't. Bobby told me he was glad he'd seen the trees one more time. Don't beat yourself up about it."

I chewed a hangnail on my middle finger, trying to get my teeth around it. I didn't beat myself up when people died. Well, not as much, anyway, but that didn't mean I wasn't going to go over every minute of it and try to figure out what I could do better next time. At the Lair, we'd all sit down and go over every step of the operation to see what could be improved in our training or thinking anyway, but I always repeated it with just myself, too.

The sergeant agreed to have his men buried in our meadow. There was no point in trying to get their bodies out. Five burials at once…I closed my eyes and let the tears flow. I usually waited until we were safely back at the Lair, but this one…Maybe it was because Peter's life was on the line, but the emotions just wouldn't be ignored.

"Are you still awake?"

Hastily wiping my face, I lifted the edge of my blanket to see the scout lying a couple feet away. "I am now."

"Sorry." His whisper was soothing, but he didn't turn over. Instead, he kept watching me. "You seemed fairly calm through all of this, but I wanted to ask how you're holding up to losing people? Actually, everyone seems very chill about it."

Pulling my pack closer, I rested my head on it. "When you see the size of our graveyard…" I swallowed, another tear escaping. "We have a process, and it doesn't start until we're safely back at the Lair. There, we can grieve."

"From what I've seen of your fighters, our boys will be in good company."

I nodded, biting my lip. "You should get some sleep. It'll be a long trip back."

"Good night," he said softly.

"Good night." I pulled my blanket back over my face. It wouldn't keep me dry, the rain was too hard for that, but it would keep me warm.

Sleep still eluded me, so I went over plans for our return to the Lair. We needed to avoid patrols as much as possible. Doc worried about jostling or crazy driving hurting some of the wounded even more, and she was adamant that the bus shouldn't go faster than thirty miles an hour, except in dire circumstances.

Eventually, I put those thoughts aside and listened to the rain in the pine needles. I fell asleep to the steady patter.

***

Four days later, we finally arrived back at the Lair. I limped from a slightly infected puncture in my leg. The ointment Doc and Wildwood, our herbalist, had concocted was doing its job, but not before I'd managed to get a little fever. The perimeter guard, still run by Mouse, sent a sentry back to the Lair to get help for the injured.

"I don't know what you're limping for," Phoenix grumbled, hobbling between the Brit and the scout. "I'm the one who got shot. *You* just had a little splinter."

"That 'splinter' was two inches long," I said dryly. "It was a freaking spear. You're just jealous I can still walk."

The welcoming committee, led by Amana, interrupted us. "*Capitán,*" she said, stopping in front of me, placing her hands on my shoulders. I rested mine on her elbows and we pressed our foreheads together. "I am happy jou are no dead," she whispered. "I would hate to train another."

"I'm glad I'm not dead, too. Although you would have enjoyed this trip."

"Really?" She fell into step next to me. "I look forward to hearing about it."

Anansi raced past us and threw himself into his sister's arms. They rocked back and forth, hugging each other tightly. The rest of the non-combatants at the Lair streamed past, finding the wounded and helping them inside. Anansi bounced over to me and threw an arm over my shoulders. A spurt of alarm shot through my chest. He didn't have to lift his arm too high anymore.

"Did you grow while we were gone?" I wrapped an arm around his waist and kissed his cheek. His tight, kinky black hair tickled my skin.

"You *were* gone for nearly a month," he reminded me, leaning against me for a moment. "Though I don't remember there being this many people when you left."

"*Sí, Capitán.*" Amana made a show of counting on her fingers. "So many more mouth to feed."

We stopped near the bunker door, waiting for everybody else to go inside. The soldiers had nearly identical looks of amazement. They gaped at the people around them, all the help, and especially at the bunker.

"Sorry about that." I sighed. "We did find some army boys, though! And they even did a bit of rescuing."

"Oh, *sí? Muy* exciting."

"And...there's the food!" I pointed. We'd managed to find and kill a big steer. He'd been happily munching on grass, but tonight, we'd be happily munching on him.

"*Muy bien.* Jou are useful after all."

It was good to be home.

Chapter 2

Man 1: Can't we stop Cooper from passing these gun control laws?
Peace is killing my business.
Man 2: Stop being so shortsighted. This can be a good thing.
Transcript of phone recording, 11:23 pm March 23, 2049

I spent the afternoon holed up in the Useless Room—a central command center with banks of dead and dark computers, monitors, and electronics—with Seahorse, Amana, Eleanor, Sarge, Driver, Lavender, Dereva, Anansi, Storm, and Sirius. The only thing we could use in the Useless Room were the large maps on the walls and a 3D map table to the right.

Amana laughed herself sick when we told her how we managed to get into the compound, demanding details from Dereva and Storm. "Show me how she walk again," she demanded.

Dereva, more than happy to comply, tottered across the room on her tiptoes in an exaggerated parody of my lessons. "And then," the girl chortled, "they decided to teach her how to *look*!" She puckered her lips and made a duck face at Amana, who slumped across the table, howling.

I buried my head in my hands with a whimper. I should've known this would happen.

Seahorse thumped the table, calling their attention. "Come on, let's get this done." Though she struggled to hide a smile. Traitor.

She stood in front of a detailed map of Mohawk hanging on the wall, marking points and locations as we ran through the fight. Normally, Phoenix would be with us, but with her leg, Doc declared her out of action. Those who hadn't fought followed the narrative, occasionally asking questions. Those questions were some of the most useful things we had, forcing us to consider our actions from different angles.

"Wait, where were the soldiers again?" Seahorse ran a finger over the buildings. I examined the map and put my finger on the one. "Gotcha." She pushed a pin in. "Okay, now that we have everything marked, let's run through it again."

While we planned to the best of our ability, things always went ass-up, so we used these sessions to figure out what went wrong. They always led to additional trainings and simulations to create muscle memory. We looked at every action and decision, not with the intent to blame, but to figure out what we could improve or see what skills we needed to be more effective. Not having Phoenix in the room left me twitchy, like there was something important I was forgetting.

This time, Seahorse decided people needed to work on their marksmanship and that uphill running would improve everyone's stamina. I grimaced and Sirius groaned. She'd never done anything that could be classed as exercise before the Invasion. While she was in much better shape now—a stocky tank of a human being—she still hated running. Unfortunately for her, running proved too useful to ignore.

"We should also find out what we can about the civilians," Eleanor said. "I don't think we've heard anything about this installation."

Apparently, no one had. Somehow, despite having a spy—Shrike—at the heart of Steve's command structure, we'd never known this place existed

"I have to wonder how the army heard about them." I leaned back in my chair, spinning slowly. "We need a soldier and a civilian."

"Let's get them now," Seahorse said. The ex-soldier folded her arms. "Sooner we know, the better. Though it's unlikely the soldiers will know where their intel came from."

"I'll ask." I waved. "I've probably spent the most time with the soldiers by now." Between their arrival in our camp, dealing with their ass of a major, and the fact that I'd busted them out, they'd probably be more willing to accede to a request if it came from me.

I heaved myself up and headed down to the section where Doc had her infirmary set up, the concrete cooling my bare feet. Being barefoot might put me at a disadvantage if a fight suddenly happened, but wearing shoes all the time just messes your feet up. It leads to infections, fungus, and painful calluses. After a man had lost a leg to a blister gone bad, we didn't take any chances.

The halls all looked the same, so newbies relied on the stenciling on the walls at the intersections. Doc's space was down the hall and the first right. I stuck my head into the barracks Doc had turned into her infirmary. "Hey, Doc! How's Phoenix and the rest?"

Doc stood, wiping her hands on a cloth. The man lying in front of her sat up slowly, holding his arm until Squirrel tied a sling around it. "Phoenix had a through and through. As long as we keep infection out and she gets rest, she'll be fine."

We'd kidnapped our doctor when Jewel, one of the first ones we'd rescued, got shot. Doc had decided to stay with us to escape an abusive husband. The petite woman was only a resident and hadn't let us forget we'd accidentally kidnapped a beginner doctor, though she'd grown into her role, as we all had. Do or die in this camp, unfortunately.

"Keeping her down will be a full-time job," I sighed.

She nodded. "In the others, we've got dehydration and malnutrition all the way up to broken bones that were never set and have begun healing wrong. There's also a load of burns, cuts, and infections in between. Plus, an outbreak of lice. One of those famous people," she glared balefully in their general direction, "didn't bother to mention they were itching everywhere until they'd already mingled with others."

I grimaced, but I had come here with another purpose. "Do you think we've got one of each who's able to walk and talk? We had a few questions and we hoped to get as much info as we can while it's fresh. Maybe see if they know about other compounds like this one."

"I can help." A hand waved, followed by a man rising to his feet. It was the British man who'd saved Phoenix. Tom Carrington, freshly shaved and handsome as hell. Holy shit. I still couldn't believe the hottest actor today was in my bunker.

"I think I can handle a bit of debriefing." Another volunteer stood. It was the pretty scout. I bit my lip to keep from smiling or blushing. "Just be gentle with me," he deadpanned, a wicked gleam in his eye.

The soldiers chuckled. One opened his mouth, ready to make some comment. I caught his eye and glared. He reconsidered and shut his mouth. I gave a short nod. "Thanks. We're back this way. You guys okay to walk?"

"I'm not dead yet," the blond soldier murmured as he caught up.

"I noticed," I said, then flushed. "I mean, you were kicking ass pretty good the other day and..." He grinned and I shut my mouth and took a deep breath, blowing it out in frustration. "You know what I mean."

"I'm not sure I do," he said mildly, blue eyes sparkling so close to mine as we made our way through the hallways, closely followed by Phoenix's savior.

"You're still standing," I snapped, and he muffled a laugh.

***

Heads swiveled to examine us when we made it into the Useless Room. Seahorse looked up from reading the notes Eleanor took. "Ah, good. You found two. We don't do names, so we can skip those, though your rank would be acceptable," she said to the soldier.

"I think I got busted back to private. They didn't give us a lot of time before we left." The soldier eased into a chair, sighing as he settled in. I bit my lip. I'd walked too fast for him, hadn't I? Shit.

"Honestly, I'm not sure there's much point in me trying to hide who I am," the other man interjected. "Unless nobody has watched a movie in the last ten years?"

I sat forward, eagerly watching to see how they'd react. Storm gave a little squeal, while Dereva flushed a deep red. Fortunately, her skin was dark enough to mostly hide it. For the rest, their reactions were a bit of a letdown. A couple minor exclamations and that was it. Then again, I hadn't gone jumping around asking for his autograph, either. Maybe after fighting like this for so long, no one cared as much about famous people.

The soldier grinned at the actor's nonplussed expression and hooked a chair around for the taller man. "Here, have a seat. Don't want you falling down from shock that they're not too impressed by you."

"You know what I want to know?" Seahorse sat forward. "What did you mean when you said you didn't have much time. These things are usually planned to the last inch."

The soldier grimaced. "I was supposed to be discharged, but after the nuke hit, all discharge papers were revoked, but my..." He stopped short at our expressions.

"What..." I croaked and cleared my throat. "What do you mean by 'nuke'?"

"I second that." Carrington raised a finger. "Who was bombed?"

The scout leaned back, then looked around the table, eyebrows raised. "You...Hendricks never told you?" I shook my head. He ran a hand over his unshaven face. "Shit. Dammit, Hendricks, I knew you were useless." He sighed. "Less than a month after they took the coast, a nuke was dropped on Atlanta with a warning not to interfere with their business. When the government kept poking and planning, a MOAB was dropped on Portland, Maine. Everything stopped, and most of the country has been dealing with the fallout from those two events. They slapped up a barrier at the new border..."

"Been there, seen that, got the t-shirt," Sirius muttered. "What's a MOAB?"

"Mother of all bombs," Seahorse murmured.

"Then, there's LA TV..."

"What's LA TV?" several of us asked at once.

The scout leaned back, his blue eyes troubled. "Oh, shit. Fuck. Beg pardon. Shit..."

What spilled out was hard to swallow. Cameras were operational in LA and were constantly live streaming onto the internet. They'd seen people murdered, raped, tortured. More still died of starvation and dehydration. It'd become a pastime, watching it. Bets were frequently placed.

"Some compounds have grown up in there. Religious fanatics, political factions, whatever. Very few areas that you might consider 'free.'" He rubbed a hand over his mouth, then continued with the rest.

"Six weeks ago, my pending release was canceled, and they dumped me on Hendricks. We weren't given any details until Oregon, and that was pathetic at best. Just that we were heading to Mohawk to get civilians out. Gotta say, getting a few miles inside Oregon and having all our tech die freaked some of the boys out. Lightened our loads by a few pounds, though.

"Hendricks spilled a few more beans before he was killed." He waved at Tom. "They've been blackmailing your families and using the money. Our job was to get you all out to remove their leverage. Then, French led us into a trap." He grinned crookedly and looked at me. "I'm glad they didn't get you, too. French told them where to find your camp. They dragged him into our warehouse and strapped him to the table. Seems like when they couldn't find sign of you, they thought he was lying. The Captain had disappeared like a ghost and they were pissed."

"Yeah." I scratched a scar on my arm. "I didn't really like your major, so as soon as you guys left, we packed up. I also sent Sirius after you just to see what you were up to." Sirius gave him a little wave.

"I'm glad you did." He watched me intently, a smile dancing around the corners of his mouth. "I really didn't like the idea of dying in there. No offense to your state, it's nice and all, but that's not how I plan on going out."

"Oh, you've got a plan, have you?" I grinned. "I have one, too. My plan is 'don't die.' So far, it's working pretty well."

Throwing his head back, candlelight turning his blond hair red, he laughed, leaning back in his chair. I bit my lip to hide a smile, but if Eleanor's knowing look was any indication, I didn't do too good a job.

"As much fun as talking about dying is," Sirius interjected, "I've got a question: Why the hell didn't they drop another nuke if they knew you guys were coming?"

The scout slowly settled into giggles and snorts and shook his head. "I haven't got a clue. Until recently, I had other things on my mind."

"Maybe they didn't know. It's probable that French only contacted them once he got in here," Driver said, sitting forward.

"Maybe, but..." I waved. "That would be leaving way too much up to chance. They've got a whole country outside of the no-tech zone. He could just as easily have sent a message to them, and they'd go and send it in with a boat or some shit."

"Either way," Lavender leaned forward, "this is all just speculation, which is the exact opposite of what we try to do here. So, back to facts?"

"Yeah." I grinned and turned to the scout. "French is dead, right? We don't have to worry about him showing up like the boogeyman, do we?"

The scout scratched his neck. "I mean, he could, but only if he was the Headless Horseman."

"Ooh." Steve wasn't messing around. They killed their own spy for one failure? Geez. "Remind me not to get on Steve's bad side," I muttered.

Sirius threw a piece of jerky at me. "What the hell are you talking about? You're already on their bad side."

I picked the dried meat out of my lap and chewed on it thoughtfully. "Okay, lemme rephrase that: remind me not to get *caught*."

"That's better." My cousin settled back into her seat, her arms crossed comfortably.

Carrington's story held little to help us in the fight, but what I found most interesting was that nobody had come from LA. He'd pondered that one a lot, though like he said, he had the time for it. "Since Steve controls LA, why avoid it?" I asked. "That's the largest population of rich people. Why didn't some of them end up with us?"

"Unless there's another compound," Eleanor said, tapping her pen on her notepad.

"If that's the case, it could be anywhere." I ran a hand over my tangled, still-damp hair. "Washington or California, even. But I'll have River ask Shrike to keep an ear to the ground." I sighed.

"You do realize it's bloody annoying when you say cryptic things like that, right?" Carrington asked.

My mouth dropped open, and I widened my eyes dramatically. "What?! Really? Nooo!"

His lips twisted and he leaned away, as if unsure what to make of me.

"Give the poor man a day before you start pulling that shit out, will you, Captain?" Seahorse looked at me wryly. "Try to ease them into it. You'll have to forgive her," she said to the men. "She was literally raised in a barn and it's too damn late to do anything about it."

***

In the brief time between the meeting and the memorial, the news of the cities being bombed in the East spread like wildfire through the Lair. A person could stand in the corner and follow the relationships in the bunker, hearing humanity swirl and eddy. Dereva talked with Kestrel, Hightide, and Sweetpea. They moved away, met up with their other friends, and so it went, right up to dinner.

Similar meetings happened with everybody who attended. That was another reason for having those particular people in all the Useless Room meetings. Between them, I never had to speak in public, make announcements, or give updates. I sat back and watched information spread without ever opening my lips.

I loved that.

After dinner, we had the funerals. Phoenix attended, leaning heavily on a cane and Tom Carrington's arm, glaring at anyone who tried to give her sympathy for her injury. I watched the soldiers as they entered our meadow, the cemetery where all our people were laid to rest. The Meadow had cairns rising in neat rows, the soil too shallow to dig six feet down. Some of the men looked like they'd been gut punched when they saw the line of cairns.

All the men who could stand on their own were part of those carrying the biers, though a couple of ours supplemented them. Once all the bodies were laid in their graves and memories shared, I stood with my back to the trees, facing the occupants of the Lair.

"Hail the victorious dead!" I shouted, the words echoing off the mountains.

"Hail!"

Hail. Praise those who died for a cause. Hail, all those who were kicked and still got up, again and again, until they couldn't. Hail, those men and women who laid their lives down for another, even over their drive to live.

Dereva raised her voice, singing "Amazing Grace," and those who could sing through their tears joined in. I relaxed, seeing the tears on the soldiers' faces. Men who refused to cry could be holding back a lot more shit than grief, and I didn't need to deal with emotional outbursts in the days ahead.

Once the song finished, flasks and bottles were produced and passed around while the graves were filled in. We made our way to the edges of the meadow, forming smaller clusters. Hightide went to Fox's grave, like she always did, and sat down next to the simple wooden marker, talking quietly.

The pretty blond scout found me sitting off to the side. I leaned back against a tree, trying to decide whether it was worth getting up for a refill. Or even if I should have a refill, considering it was Anansi's special concoction. The scout approached slowly, holding a small bottle out as an offering. My smile was a bit watery, but I held out my cup.

"Thanks." I toasted him.

"Alright if I join you?" he asked.

I gestured to the ground, and he settled down slowly, crossing his legs comfortably. He'd found time to bathe and shave more thoroughly, and the corner of my mouth twitched. So, we both smelled better than the first time we'd met.

Phoenix leaned more heavily on the actor's arm than her cane, though that could be due to the nature of her 'pain-killers.' However the hell Anansi made it, it earned the name Dirt Hugger. A few people were already staggering, and one woman slumped against her friend, drunkenly sobbing a story. Some funerals, she was me. She was all of us, at one point or another, really.

Finally, unable to avoid it any longer, I looked back at the scout. He watched me, his blue eyes tired but intent, lit by the last rays of sunlight. "You've got an impressive operation." He nodded toward the bunker. "Is this everyone you've managed to free?"

My lip curled. Didn't he realize how difficult it was to do anything, living like this? What did he expect? That we'd have half the Valley freed? I opened my mouth to give him a piece of my mind when his tone trickled through my booze-hazed hearing. He wasn't accusing. That heaviness in his eyes, the slump in his shoulders, was sorrow. If this was all we'd managed in a year, then how long and how many more lives would this take?

"No," I said gently. "This isn't everyone. We have a safe place set up in the mountains for families and non-combatants."

Hope blossomed slowly. "How many?" he asked hoarsely.

"There's more than three hundred at Home."

His mouth dropped open, and I smiled, eyes watery again. Home, a series of caves deep within the Jefferson Wilderness, housed all those who wouldn't, or couldn't, fight. Sirius had found it while she'd been away after Lightning and Thunder's deaths last summer. Moving the civilians had been an exercise and a half. Most of the fighters were down in the Valley and the edges of the foothills, keeping Steve occupied while they moved as quickly as they could into the caves.

Anybody who wasn't essential to the running of the Lair or the fight went up. Driver and Lavender, Dry Eyes, and Sarge elected to remain with us, but they sent their younger children to safety. Olivia and Sam, the daughter and son-in-law of our previous spy in Salem, ran Home and took care of the kids. We even sent a horse with them. They fished in the numerous lakes, hunted, gathered, and had plans to plant in the spring.

It would be a hard life, but quieter and safer than the Lair.

The scout closed his eyes and tipped his face towards the sky. A tear left a silver track down his cheek, shining in the moonlight. "We...I didn't think you had that many." Taking a deep breath, he let it out slowly. "When I first heard I was coming into Oregon, I thought there might be a couple of small groups that managed to slip between the cracks. Never that there would be a large, organized uprising."

"Don't sound so impressed." I nodded to the graves. "If I was better, we might not have lost so many."

"Loss is inevitable." He watched me intently, his eyes gleaming faintly. "An incompetent commander would have gotten everybody killed in the first couple months. It's about learning and doing better every chance you get. If you'll let us, we can help you with that. We've got a pyromaniac on board, and once he's better, he can work with your explosives person."

My lips quirked at his reference. Sparrow's detonation of the gas tanks had come a little close for comfort. "Good luck. Once you see what we're working with, you all might just be running for the hills. We know enough to know how much we don't know."

"I guess that's something." His teeth flashed in a quick grin. "So, since I'm sticking around, does that mean I get a new name?"

"We do it to protect family and friends in the Valley, but it does have the added benefit of confusing the hell out of Steve, so...sure." Safe in the dark, I stared back at him, ignoring the drunken singing, the full moon shining down on our service, and the stars shining more brightly than they ever did Before. "What do you want to be called?"

He leaned in and my stomach flip-flopped. "You choose. You're more used to this than I am."

"I have been calling you Pretty Boy in my mind," I admitted.

He laughed. "So, you think I'm pretty?"

"Objectively speaking…"

"And absolutely not. I refuse to be known as Pretty Boy. Keep thinking."

Chewing on my lip distracted me from his face, so close to my own, while I tried to think. What continually ran through my mind was the pure artistry of his performance in Mohawk, twin sticks spinning around him, and Phoenix's comments. "Okay, I've got one. Archangel."

"Bit presumptuous, don't you think?"

"It's what Phoenix thought you looked like." I shrugged, then twisted, scratching my arm. "An avenging angel. Suits you." *More than you know.* Cleaned up, his thick, golden hair, cropped short for the military, and deep blue eyes could have been in a classic painting, although his features weren't as soft as those looked.

"It really doesn't," he assured me, thankfully breaking my train of thought. "But I'm happy you think it does."

He studied me even more closely than I did him. What did he see? What I'd seen in the mirror was nothing to write home about. I was passably pretty, once, long before the scars. The only reason I'd passed muster to go into Mohawk was because of the Fates' talents.

Conditioner gave my dark, honey blonde hair a softness and shine that it hadn't had in months, but it wouldn't last long. Makeup to enhance and conceal, to soften what I even had to admit was my resting bitchface. The truth was, my eyes were pale blue, almost gray, and most people wouldn't look me in the eyes anymore. I'd look in a mirror to try to see what it was that always made them look away, but I couldn't tell.

Would he still look at me like I was pretty once the newness of the situation wore off? I frowned. Why was I worrying about what a man thought? Huffing a tiny laugh, I looked away from him, unable to deal with the new emotions roiling through me.

Coward.

Damn straight.

CHAPTER 3

Over the next few weeks, we had to send out more hunting and gathering parties for...everything. The newly rescued were malnourished at best, half-starved at worst, and constantly hungry. Books and movies sure didn't cover this part of apocalyptical shit.

In desperation, I took a small group, just two vehicles, north and west, heading to stores firmly in occupied territory—the Woodburn Outlets. There, I stood in the doorway of an overpriced outdoor store in the outlets in the dark hours just after midnight, hands on my hips, surveying the fighters as they browsed.

"Take it all," I called. "Steve might not see a need for these things yet, and I'd rather not leave them anything."

"Would you also like me to find another car?" Sirius asked, sarcasm dripping from her voice.

"Yeah, thanks. Two would be better, but I'll settle for one. Get it all, people! Olivia says they need more bedding at Home, too."

I joined the women loading packs and bags, handing them off to others to run them to the trucks. Freeze-dried food looked and tasted like shit, which might be why Steve passed on it, but we were at a point of wanting it. Screaming started at the far end of the store.

"Bras!" Storm cried. "They've got *bras*!"

The screaming turned into wild laughter when Sweetpea broke into the back room and triumphantly emerged with boxes loaded with dried food, snacks, and chocolate. Hightide, Jewel, and Legs joined her, pulling out bags of clothing and bedding.

Done with the food on the shelves, I stood in the center of the chaos, cackling madly as we loaded both vehicles to the brim. Sirius returned with a minivan just when I thought we'd have to abandon some loot. The minivan was half-full by the time we finished.

"Captain!" Dereva leaned out of the driver's side window.

"Yo!"

"There used to be a flour mill a few miles that way." She waved west. "Wanna see if it's got anything we can use? It's a bit hard to find, so Steve might've missed it."

I crawled into the bed, sprawling across our booty and sighing. Tonight was a good night. "Do it. I need to get back in Amana's good graces after all the extra people."

The girl laughed and pulled out, closely followed by the other vehicles. Wriggling and squirming, I managed to move enough stuff to make space to stand at the machine gun. A fighter's work never ended.

***

Amana's face when we triumphantly entered the Lair carrying our booty made the extra miles and danger worth it. Phoenix limped out of the common room, her cane thumping the floor with every step, and stuck her tongue out at me.

"Assholes went and had fun without me," she muttered as I passed.

Sirius sniggered, carrying three twenty-five-pound bags of flour over her shoulder that she carefully dumped on a table in the common room. Even with gathering every able-bodied person in the place, it still took us several trips to get the loot into the Lair from where the vehicles were hidden nearly a mile away.

A soldier, barely more than a boy, gave us a doubtful look. "You people seriously run around stealing shit? What about the rightful owners?"

"Dude." Sirius stopped in front of him, a sack of flour over her shoulder and another in her free hand. "Did you happen to look around while you were in the Valley? It's a fucking miracle Steve hasn't found and burned this shit yet. Man, we've been stealing since day one. We need supplies constantly and we don't have any way to make more flour. Better us than Steve and Dorothy." She stumped down the hall without waiting for a reply.

The soldier gaped after her, his mouth opening and closing like a fish. "I really hate these nicknames," he shouted after her.

"It's easier than saying 'Those assholes with the red armbands,'" she called without looking back.

He shrugged, still confused. "I guess, but...damn."

***

Regular rounds through the infirmary barracks became a thing for me. Eleanor approved, said it meant they "can get to know you as a person and a leader." I thought them getting to know me better might make them run screaming for the hills, but so far, they hadn't. I'd talk with the younger soldiers and bring a deck of cards with me every time.

Peter spent most of his time sleeping, waking up just long enough to eat, but I played a lot of Go Fish with the huge guy, Goliath, and a couple others, including Archangel and their demolitions man, Chaos. Goliath barely forgave me for my earlier joke, since some of the soldiers still called him 'Squirt' when I came around. Whenever my brother was awake, I stayed back, unsure whether he'd remember our conversation before they got caught.

Even then, I could observe him and the camaraderie he had with them. Though leaving one day, I ended up counting on my fingers—how often had I seen Dereva sitting with him?

Now, I watched from the sidelines while Doc and the army medic took care of Peter, unable to get too close. I'd already pissed off enough people, both within the Lair and in the Valley, to risk them finding out his importance to me. The judge I'd banished with his son flashed through my mind. I never knew his name, but if he'd survived long enough to find other people, I was glad he didn't know mine.

Most of the soldiers insisted on staying, a full ten of them. I couldn't hide a smile when Archangel was one of them. The other seven either saw it as their duty to finish the mission or didn't want to stay in a place run by women. Two of the celebrities, out of twenty, also decided to stay. One of them was Tom Carrington.

I smirked when Phoenix named him Gryphon.

Sergeant Perry, who felt compelled to complete the mission and report on French's treason, hoped to leave before winter set in, but it was already too late in the mountain passes. He resigned himself to waiting for spring with gentlemanly grace.

"I'd swear it hit earlier this year," I said to Perry. "But you don't want to cross those mountains until it's nearly thawed. Good news is, an early snow might make an early thaw."

"I'm not worried about that." He glanced over his shoulder. He was older than most of his men, in his early thirties, slender and neat. "Two of the boys think we shouldn't mingle. I'll beat that stupid thought out of them," he assured me, "but they're going to be shits about it."

"If they hurt anyone here, I swear to you, I will geld them myself. Tell them that." My voice sounded cold, even to my ears.

Perry flinched, reflexively cupping himself. "Yes, ma'am." He saluted automatically, then held it deliberately.

Awkwardly, I saluted back. "Don't go doing that regularly. Seahorse will never let me hear the end of it."

A commotion down the hall caught our attention. Amana stood nose-to-nose with a burly man in his mid-twenties, her head tipped back to meet the gaze of a man a good six inches taller than her. Which still made him short, because she's tiny.

"Jou can leave anytime jou want, *pendejo*," she snapped. "*Por favor*, leave. Jou stay in my Lair, jou work. *Comprendes?*"

"What if we leave and...accidentally tell the North Koreans where to find you? What if we 'accidentally' hurt a couple of you on our way out?" he sneered at her.

Perry started forward, fire lighting his eyes, but I held him back and shook my head. "Give her a moment." She'd assert dominance in her own way, as she had so many times with people who assumed a girl still in her teens didn't have anything worthwhile to contribute.

Amana snorted. "Yes, jou very brave. Maybe jou hurt us? Hah! Do jou know what we do to men like jou? Here, I am told jou are a soldier, that jou are supposed to protect us. Instead, jou threaten. Jou will tell Steve? Do it! We will die, and jou can live a *cobarde*. No better than jou man, French."

Deliberately turning her back on him, she walked slowly away, giving him every opportunity to attack her. He stared after her, tense as a bowstring until he relaxed slowly. I nodded. Good. I wouldn't have to kill him today.

"What the fuck?" This was the first time Perry had cussed around me, but the poor man looked dazed. "She made Bruiser back down?"

I sniggered. "Bruiser? His name is *Bruiser*?"

"Your woman's got balls." Archangel stepped around the corner, where he'd watched the whole thing. "He's got a temper, which is why command sent him in here."

"She ain't got balls, man. She's got *ovaries*." I watched Bruiser wander away. "Besides, she's mean enough that if she got into a fight, she'd fuck him up bad. I've seen what's left over of men who try to push her around. She doesn't fight because she doesn't want to, not because she can't." I didn't even try to keep the admiration from my voice. That girl was the biggest badass I knew.

"Dinner!" Optimus Prime raced down the hallway, shouting. "Dinner's ready!"

***

While some soldiers—like Bruiser—took a while to find their way around, Archangel leaped into our routine, helping Anansi with the garage doors and going to the gym with Sarge. He was of average height, about six feet tall, so he'd frequently gone up against larger men and had a few tricks to teach the fighters. I watched unobtrusively from the gym door while he showed Dereva a move.

When she threw him, he popped back to his feet, grinning and clapping her on the back. Then, he demanded she do it again, visibly delighted when she did even better. I sighed irritably. He was damn near perfect and a perfect freaking distraction.

When it came to Gryphon and Triskele, the only two rescued civilians to stay, the residents of the Lair displayed the same lack of give-a-fuck that the people in the Useless Room debrief had shown. As Mouse put it, "So they're famous. But can they shoot?"

This mentality met Gryphon the first time he stepped into the gym. "Apparently, being a bloody movie star doesn't get you any points in here," he said to Archangel. "I had one tiny girl ask me if I could really shoot a gun like I did in the movies. She didn't stop glaring until I did. Bloody hell, these girls don't mess about."

Dereva also gave Peter a name. The two of them and Sweetpea cornered me in the common room, piling onto the benches and hemming me in. The girls walked on either side of Peter, helping steady him while he struggled with his crude crutches, the best we could do under the circumstances.

"Guess what?" Peter puffed his chest in mock pride. "I'm official now. I have a name."

I smiled and took a sip of the weed water we called tea. "And that is?"

"Hot Fuzz." He grinned.

I laughed, inhaled my tea, choked and spent the next minute coughing while Dereva helpfully pounded my back. "Why?" I wheezed when I finally got my breath back. "Because your hair's fuzzy and you're a little cute?"

"No," Dereva said dryly. "It's because he's a skinny, American PC Butterman. He actually asked me if I'd ever 'fired a gun whilst flying through the air.'"

I snorted. "So why not call him Butterman? Nobody would ever think that was a real name."

"What? No!" Peter protested. "Hot Fuzz is way cooler. Don't do this to me!"

"Watch me." I smirked.

"Yeah," Sweetpea chimed in. "She likes the sound of men crying. It's one of the few things that gives her joy."

I put a hand to my chest. "Ouch." The kids piled off the benches and took off—to see where else they could cause chaos, presumably—and I shook my head. "Those ones are trouble," I called to Amana, where she shredded vegetables in the kitchen.

"Perfect. They do well in the field, then."

***

The addition of all the testosterone in the Lair, attached to young men who found all the beautiful women very interesting, gave me a permanent scowl and caused Eleanor to write more copies of the Rules for Relationships out and post them throughout the bunker. Same-sex relationships already abounded and were much easier to manage, both parties already having a healthy respect for the trials their partner had undergone.

Hetero relationships seemed to have more issues built in, starting with the fact that a couple of the younger soldiers were just looking for a 'good time.' The Rules were created to protect the women and prevent misunderstandings. Many of the women didn't have good boundaries and the men might think they were...Oh, fuck it. Too many men were entitled pricks, and here that would get them shot or castrated. Eleanor wrote the rules to reduce those chances.

Sadly, this didn't happen until three young men went on a spree last year, raping a few of the girls and causing one to commit suicide. The civilians tried to condone their actions and spare the rapists. It'd gone so far that Amana, who had defended herself against them and killed one, was standing at the foot of a tree with a rope around her neck when we returned from a trip.

Since the Rules, only one woman had been kissed against her will. Seahorse, who discovered them, hadn't gone easy on the man. We did give him another chance, with the understanding that a second mark would result in banishment. He'd elected to go Home, and Olivia said he was very useful and courting a woman.

Respectfully.

Using the Rules and with every female fighter on alert, we managed to impress on the young idiots the seriousness of their actions. It only took one boot perfectly delivered to a young man's groin. Sadly, I was not the person to deliver the boot.

Until Archangel wandered into the common room one day, supporting a dazed young soldier, Grayman. Archangel, unusually pale, set Grayman carefully on one of the couches and made his way to me. Moving with extreme precision, he seated himself across from me.

Thoroughly concerned, I set aside my mending. "What happened?"

He rubbed a trembling hand across his mouth. "We were out exploring and familiarizing ourselves with the area…"

"And?" I prompted when he looked lost in thought.

"Huh?" He started. "Oh, we, uh, we found some tracks, military boots. Not familiar." He fell into the familiar patterns of a report. "We followed them. Six men. Then, we heard the sounds of a fight. When we investigated, your perimeter guards were just…cleaning up. You have a bunch of kids manning the perimeter?" he demanded.

I held my hands up. "It was either make them the perimeter guard or let them participate in quelling a mob. It seemed like a good idea at the time."

"They killed a full patrol! Like it was nothing! Then hid the bodies. These kids were professional. Scattering leaves…There was hardly a fight. And their commander, Mouse…"

I shook my head. "Trust me, we didn't do that to her. We found her in a Dorothy hellhole. I wanted her to stay out of the fight, but she won't do it. Besides, they're careful. Wildwood and Anansi made some poison darts or something. I mean, these kids stay well away from actual fighting…"

I trailed off. Something I'd said shook Archangel even more. "What?" I demanded.

"Your herbalist and another kid made poison darts?" he said in an overly controlled voice.

"You say that like it's a bad thing."

He buried his face in his hands. "Oh, my God. Grayman!"

"Yessir!" Grayman sat up automatically, habit breaking through his daze.

"Tell all the boys to stay away from the women unless they talk to..." He glanced at me.

"Eleanor, Lavender, Kestrel, and the girl in question," I supplied helpfully.

"Them." He pointed at me. "Tell them to keep their hands to themselves."

***

About two months after the rescue, in the middle of the usual chaos of games, meals, and gear, Ink danced into the common room, back from a scavenging raid. She carried two small cases close to her heart, clutching them tightly as she spun.

I nudged Sirius. "Check her out."

Twisting, Sirius squinted. "That's the happiest I've ever seen her. Well, we know it's not a man."

"Or woman."

Ink spurned all attempts at a romantic attachment, preferring her art. Kestrel told me privately that she wasn't sure the fighter would ever be ready for a relationship. After the dump I'd found her in, I almost wasn't interested in men. Well. Not men.

One man.

A shine of gold at the next table over, where Archangel showed Gryphon how to care for his weapons, temporarily derailed my line of thought, but Sirius's knowing grin brought me back. So, I waved to Ink. "Hey, Ink. Show us what you got."

Ink set her packages carefully on the table, biting her lip and wriggling with excitement. "It's ink! I've finally found ink."

I stared at her, confused. "But we have ink. All those pens...?"

"*Tattoo* ink. And in this section," she opened a smaller compartment, "there's needles and stuff. I'll have to practice, but I can give people tattoos!"

By this time, a small crowd gathered around us, and Doc pushed to the front. "You said you need practice?"

"Well. Yeah." Ink shrugged. "I've never used tools quite like these, so...yeah."

Doc pursed her lips, nodding thoughtfully. "Then I've got practice for you. I want," she had to talk over Ink's squeal of excitement, "I want everyone's blood type tattooed somewhere, in the same spot on everyone, where I can easily see it if they're wounded or unconscious. Those who don't know their blood type can see me and we'll get you tested."

"Um..." I looked from the serious doctor to the tattoo artist barely staying inside her skin. "Shouldn't we...ask people if they want a tattoo first?"

Doc snorted. "We can, but if they say no, then I'll have a much harder time treating them, especially if they need blood. Do you know how many people we could save if I was able to check people's blood type instead of having to wait until they're conscious? It's the difference between living and dying, and if they refuse, they're a hell of a lot more likely to die."

I frowned, trying not to laugh. "Have you been hoping for something like this to show up?"

Doc rolled her eyes. "Since we haven't got a way to make dog tags or whatever...Let me think about it. Yes! I need to know."

Sirius shifted so she straddled the bench. Holding her right arm to Ink, she tugged up her sleeve. "Get your shit together. I'm A+."

***

"I just want to go hunting for a few days." I whipped around, throwing my hands up. "I've been cooped up in here for two weeks!"

Eleanor folded her arms, not budging an inch. "You're not going."

I'd thought I could just grab some gear and go hunting, hopefully bringing back some fresh meat. If not, I'd have a chance to breathe and try to work through emotions that were piling up. Instead, I'd been blocked by Eleanor, who now stood in my doorway, effectively stopping me from reaching freedom.

"Why not?" I asked plaintively. I say 'plaintively.' I mean 'whinily.'

"Because these soldiers are too new. They need to get used to you as a leader. Those two who don't like following orders from a woman could all too easily stir up trouble."

I snorted. "As if. If we still had civilian types here, maybe. But with you guys? I'm safe with you." I fluttered my eyelashes.

She choked back a laugh. "Enough! Every time I let you out of my sight, things go to pot."

"What?! When?"

"Mohawk. Your first hunting trip. Cascadia wasn't exactly great..." She started ticking off times on her fingers.

My mouth dropped open. "That's dirty fighting."

"I learned it from you, dear."

"Fine." I dropped my pack. "What do you propose?"

"Things would be a lot smoother if you got those garage doors working."

I sighed. "'Nansi's been working on that for ages with some of the boys and got nowhere."

"So, they can benefit from a woman's perspective." Eleanor's tone brooked no argument. "Now, go."

"Yes, mom," I muttered. Eleanor gave me a slight smack on the rump. I leaped away, laughing, holding my butt as I went to find the boy.

***

"Fuck me," I whispered, staring at the ground. Twenty feet doesn't look too high when you're firmly planted, but when you're hanging from a rope...I held it a little tighter.

I hung from the rafters, suspended by a climbing harness and rope we'd recently found with Anansi. Checking out the detailed workings of the door apparently required two people to be suspended. Anansi'd had a reason he needed me up here, but in the moment, I couldn't register anything except that the ground was entirely too far away.

He'd brought his recruits, who currently worked in teams of three to keep us in the air, including the former actor and current scout. The men holding me strained more than the ones holding the boy, and Gryphon gave me an inscrutable look.

"You're heavier than I thought you'd be," was all he said.

Shaking my head, I latched onto the beam spanning the top of the door and providing all the support for the massive works. I dropped suddenly and screeched, clutching the beam tighter. "Don't drop me, you assholes!"

"Sorry," Gryphon called. "My hand slipped."

Even after they took up the slack, I held onto the beam, my heart trying to punch its way out of my chest. "I'll forgive you once I'm back on the ground." A small, terrified laugh burbled out of my throat, and I choked it back.

"What the hell was that?" Anansi asked, happily spinning in his harness, arms thrown wide.

"I'm rethinking my life choices," I grunted, my arms beginning to ache. "One of those choices is about letting you figure this shit out on your own."

"No!" He straightened and stuck a foot out, catching the beam and stopping his spin. "I'll get back to work, but I need you to tell me what that is." He pointed to a section.

Having something else to focus on did help. He sketched and labeled everything we could see. Later, we'd sit down and figure out what needed to move in order to make the doors work. This was the first time we'd ever been able to get a bird's eye view of the damn doors and get a close-up view of the workings. There were some steel plates that blocked the gears from below. Probably protection, but it's hard to figure out how to fix something when you can't see it.

This was one of the rare moments I missed electricity. Not using a phone was a standard part of my workday, I was too busy to miss games, and I still had a few of my old paperbacks. I did miss my e-reader, because I didn't have the variety I was used to. Having a collector's bookshelf had given me a bit of reading material in the three seconds I got between jobs, and I'd read them so much I could recite each one from memory.

"Are we finally done?" I asked when Anansi's pencil finally stopped moving.

"Yeah...Can we come up here again soon?" He gave me beseeching, puppy-dog eyes. His black eyes were too sharp and intense to pull it off entirely, but he did look so cute.

I laughed, the sound still shaky, and nodded. "Okay, sure. Just don't tell your mom when we find her."

"You think we will?"

I scoffed. "Listen, if anyone makes it out of there whole and happy, it'll be your mom. She's a force of fucking nature, and don't you dare tell her I said that. She's already going to kill me."

"What makes you think my mom will kill you?"

"She asked me to keep you safe. Does this look safe to you?" I didn't even mention the tattoo he sported on his wrist. He'd asked Ink for another one, but she said she needed time to practice before she did anything fun, so I had a brief reprieve.

"Take us down, guys," Anansi called. He immediately started sinking and he stretched out, saying "Whee!" over and over, so soft I almost missed it.

My rope slacked off, and I clutched the beam tighter. "Sorry, guys," I croaked, squeezing my eyes shut. "I think I need another minute before I can come down." The slack disappeared, but I couldn't let go.

Mutters below me sorted themselves into broken phrases. "...Freaked her out too much...She's holding on like her life...You idiot, get her to let go!"

"Captain? Captain, can you hear me?" I cracked an eye open and tipped my head. Below me, too far below me, Archangel looked up, the first in line holding my rope. I nodded slightly. "I've got you," he said firmly. "I won't let you fall."

Do you trust me? I could hear the unspoken words as clearly as if he'd whispered them into my ear. Shutting my eyes again, I let go of the beam all at once. If I tried to go slowly, I'd never get down. As soon as I was away from the beam, I began moving. They lowered me quickly and smoothly. I kept my eyes shut until my boots touched the ground.

Breathing deeply, I flexed my knees, clutching the broad shoulders in front of me, feeling my way back to stability. Gentle hands began working the buckles of my harness. I opened my eyes to see Archangel's blond head bent in front of me. And my hands resting on *his* shoulders. Snatching them back, I rubbed my palms.

"Thanks," I said to him, then to the others, "And you're now forgiven for that little drop earlier."

"I honestly didn't expect you to have a problem with heights," Gryphon said. "You were a right proper maniac that day you rescued us, so..."

"I don't have a problem with heights." A couple of the men rolled their eyes, but I continued. "I have a problem with *falling*."

"I've seen her up in trees way higher than that," Anansi supplied helpfully. "Will you still go up with me next time? It's better when you're here."

Finally free of the harness, I threw an arm around his shoulders. He shied away from kisses when we were around the men, but he'd still let me hug him. "Yeah, I'll go up." I hugged the boy tighter. "I won't send you up alone."

We spent the rest of the day adding details to his drawings and drooling over the smell of fresh baked bread coming from the kitchens. All the flour we'd brought back needed to be sifted a few times, but it'd been stored securely enough to keep rodents out, and now baking happened daily.

"I just wish I could figure out how to bake," the boy muttered. "It's chemical reactions. That should be easy enough to do!"

I laughed and ruffled his tightly curled black hair. "I have a cousin who worked as a baker before she went into medical school, and from what she said, sometimes it takes a blood sacrifice to make things work."

He shook his head and went back to his drawings, while memories of my cousin flooded my mind. Mercy was a year younger than me, the same age as Faith, and the next closest to me in age. She should have left to go home to Australia right before this shit show started.

I hoped she was doing well. She'd probably be a resident by now. Thinking about her made me wonder about Faith, which brought me right back to all of my missing family. She was in central California and if she still lived, she was right in the middle of this, too.

Anansi asked a question, pulling me from useless musings, and I put my attention on things I could actually change.

***

With winter's early start and all the extra mouths, by midwinter we found ourselves...not running low on supplies, so much as feeling the need to constantly keep the pantry well-stocked. Which meant Eleanor finally let me go hunting.

I left with Sirius and Phoenix, who was barely well enough. We had to swear on a Bible (they borrowed it from our pastor, Shepherd) that we'd be careful with her before Doc and Eleanor let us leave and that we would *absolutely* return if it started snowing. Walking slowly for her sake, we spent more time reminiscing about our first (epically failed) attempt at bow hunting than actually hunting.

"If there's even a *hint* at a mountain lion, I'm leaving," Phoenix said.

"I'm not sure what your problem is," I grumbled. "*I'm* the one who got clawed." I rubbed my right thigh, where the claw marks went from hip to knee, then touched my left eye, where his teeth left me with thin scars narrowly missing the eye itself. If he hadn't had a badly injured back leg and been half-starved, he'd have killed us. Me, for sure.

Necessity was a great teacher, though, and we were much better at hunting now. I was still better at hunting people than game, but the principles were the same.

Eventually, the conversation turned to the new faces in the Lair. Sergeant Perry kept his men in line, and I'd miss him when he left. He was a good, steady man to have around. Archangel was sticking around, though, and he was looked up to by almost everyone within minutes of meeting him. It was uncanny, how the man did that. He was simply a good man to have around.

The celebrities we'd rescued were, for the most part, adjusting to a life where they had to work. The weatherman, I never bothered to remember his name, was an entitled little prick who wanted every woman he met to mother him. Fortunately, he was the worst of the lot, and after a few rounds of emptying the toilet buckets, he was learning to keep his head down and his mouth shut.

Amana was extremely effective at dealing with malcontents.

***

After cleaning up from our first kill, Obelix twisted, his ears flat to his skull, a quiet growl rumbling in his throat. Sirius motioned us down. I crouched, carefully setting down my end of the pole our kill was slung on.

Phoenix put her back to a tree, watching our backtrail while Sirius slipped after Obelix, following the dog into the thin underbrush. Looking around couldn't give any information. The area was hilly enough that an army could be half a mile away and we'd never know it.

Sirius returned as silently as she left. "Four Steve, three hundred feet that way." She pointed towards the ridge just south of us. "Unless they're the world's biggest idiots, they'll find our trail."

She described the landscape. I liked the fact that there was a bit more brush around them.

Grinning, I said, "Can't nobody raise the alarm if there ain't nobody left to raise the alarm."

"There might be more around," Sirius warned.

"So, we'll be quiet." Phoenix hefted her bow. "No guns."

"No guns," I agreed.

A short time later, I crawled through the bushes, moving from dead branch to dry, shallow gully. Picking a spot on Steve's route didn't take any guesswork. These guys were going straight uphill without deviating. Maybe we could have run back and hidden our sign, but really. That idea was so intelligent I hadn't even thought of it until I was nearly at my ambush site.

We'd even left our deer up a tree, hopefully out of reach of any bears while Sirius and Phoenix worked their way around the oblivious soldiers. Sirius stayed in the middle, her aim with a bow better than mine.

It was galling. The woman was nearly blind, now that her glasses were failing, and she still shot better than me. I couldn't figure it out. Phoenix would stay well back, picking off those who escaped the first attack.

Which meant I was the first attack.

Half behind a tree, half under a bush, I loosened my swords and waited. My eyes slid half-closed while I listened to Steve's stomping march up the mountain. Nearly there...Nearly...

I watched the first man pass, then the second. My heart, thundering away seconds before, slowed now that the fight was here. I rose silently.

The last man in line only had time to gurgle as he died.

***

I leaned forward, dragging the dead man by his feet to the edge of the gorge. Well, nearly to the edge. Steep hillside, lots of ferns. There wasn't an easy or safe way to get all the way to the edge.

"Took you long enough to get here," Phoenix said irritably, dusting her hands off.

"Well, maybe if you'd shot him a little sooner, instead of letting him run so far, I wouldn't have such a long ways to pull him," I shot back.

Shaking her head, Phoenix grabbed his shoulders, and I adjusted my grip on his feet. We swung him back and forth, counting.

"One...two...three!"

We let go on 'three,' watching the last man of the patrol tumble down the cliff. I held my breath until he disappeared into the narrow gorge.

"What's down there, anyway?" I asked as we gathered our things and headed back to help Sirius finish cleaning up the site of the battle.

Phoenix shrugged. "No idea. I really hope it's not a creek that's going to spit them out too soon."

"I dunno." I scratched Obelix's head. "If there is water, Steve'll never be able to figure out exactly where they entered it. It might even give them the wrong idea of what happened."

"Don't bet on it," Sirius said, sweeping the ground with a branch. "Grab those leaves and scatter them around, would you? We have no idea what kind of forensic ability they have."

"What kind can they have, with no access to a database and the internet?" I objected.

"Don't be so nearsighted." She swatted me with her branch.

"Hey!"

"For all we know, they have a room that's shielded from whatever-the-hell this is," she gestured vaguely around, "and they can check on everything."

"Nah." I waved that away. "If that were the case, Steve could've found us ages ago."

"Maybe they ship them back to Korea and perform autopsies there," Sirius continued stubbornly. "Basically, let's hope the water washes away the evidence."

"Either way, let's not tell Eleanor about this right away, okay?"

The others agreed, but I knew we'd have to tell Mouse.

***

I knelt in the damp earth over the dead deer, hurriedly gutting it before the cold seeped through my layers. The topic of the soldiers sat, abandoned in favor of butchering the deer as quickly as possible. Now, Sirius brought it up as if the conversation had never stopped.

"How many of them are taking those famous people out?" Sirius asked suddenly, hitching her pack into a more comfortable position. She talked to fewer people than I did, preferring the company of her dogs, and didn't bother to stay up to date with the people at the Lair if she didn't have to.

"Perry said he and six others will be finishing their mission." I stepped carefully over a downed log and paused, letting Phoenix use my shoulder for balance. It hadn't snowed yet, but I kept an eye on the clouds low in the sky. They had the look of snow clouds, and once it snowed, that was it, we were heading back. I didn't want to leave a trail leading right to our door.

"Get those whiny ones out of our hair," Phoenix muttered.

"Only problem," Sirius continued, "is that those men are under orders, aren't they? Military don't like men disobeying orders. So, is Perry planning on coming back here? How will they react when he doesn't show up with all his men *and* all the people he was sent to rescue? Like, do you think they'll send him back with more men and orders to get *everyone* he's supposed to?"

"You mean, do you think he'll be ordered to force people to go back with him?" I asked.

"Pretty much."

I nodded, considering her words while we forged upwards. "Government doesn't often pass up on an opportunity to be assholes, but Perry thinks they've got more important things on their plates right now."

Sirius suddenly hushed me, and crouched, pointing to our right. A deer, facing away from us, wiggled its short tail, a sign it was about to lift its head. As quickly as that, we were back to hunting.

The second morning out, we woke to discover a sea of white. Our lean-to was the only thing protecting us from the snow still drifting down.

"Well. Shit." I put my hands on my hips. "Time to pack it in. If we don't get back today, Eleanor's going to freak."

"I'm gonna freak." Phoenix pulled her hat lower, tucking her braid into her jacket. "If it's snowing, I want to be inside with something warm."

"Don't you mean some*one*?" Sirius suggested slyly.

I snickered.

Gryphon's determination to join the fighters could be a man trying to impress a pretty girl. But when you combined that with his decision to charge *into* gunfire to rescue said pretty girl, well, he already had her attention. As it was, they spent much of their free time together. The man wasn't stupid, though, and gave her her space.

He made no secret of his romantic interest in Phoenix—in a very respectful way, that had the other fighters nodding in approval—though the sniper hadn't yet weighed in with her feelings on the matter. He was also courteous to everyone he met and had Eleanor's blessing. Our den mother was fiercely protective of her chicks and had a hard time trusting men when it came to us, but she'd told me that he meant what he said about Phoenix, and he had her support.

Phoenix reddened at Sirius's teasing and finished packing with a scowl. However it went with Gryphon, I wasn't worried. She was perfectly capable of killing a man by herself. If she ended up wanting help, she knew all she had to do was ask.

***

Phoenix had gotten over giving us the silent treatment by the time we made it back to the Lair, not least because we were the ones doing the hauling. Me and Sirius carried a pole with a whole buck hanging from it, to go with the meat from our first kill. We brought back whole animals as often as we could because, like the native tribes, we used *everything*.

Hightide, Al, Nobody, and the other leatherworkers descended on the carcass, carrying it off to be skinned and butchered to keep the ligaments whole, chattering excitedly about what they'd make next. They'd hand the meat, innards, and bones over to the kitchen. The antlers would be given to those who liked working with their hands to turn into handles, buttons, and other useful objects.

Leather was a highly valuable commodity, being both sturdy and comfortable. The leatherworkers had gained a level of respect only equaled by the cooks—and far above that of the fighters—because those skills required more intense training than anything else in the Lair, including fighting.

Phoenix showed up as we were about to enter the Lair, missing all the commotion.

Walking into the common room, I shrugged, resettling my bra. The first one designed by Al, it was by far the most comfortable bra I'd ever owned. So hopeless that he'd been banished to the tannery where he couldn't break anything, Al finally found his calling. There, he'd designed the bra and lives were changed. Women no longer had to deal with boobs moving too much. He'd also caught Amana's eye.

Arching my back to ease sore muscles, Phoenix suddenly jabbed my side, hissing in excitement. "Did you see that?"

"See what?"

"The scout. Listen, if a man looked at a woman like that in a nightclub, you know they're going home together. I think he likes it when you do that. Do it again!"

My cheeks heated. "Fuck off. I'm not doing anything except warming up and eating," I grumbled. "So shut up about it." If there was one thing I'd learned in my twenty-seven years of life, it was that men who looked like Archangel didn't seriously look at women who looked like me.

"I bet you a candy bar he likes you," she murmured, giving me a sly grin.

That made me pause. Candy bars could be found, but they were rare now. They were the highest currency we had to bet with. "You're on."

As people disappeared with the game, Anansi strode through the thinning crowd with a purpose I wasn't used to seeing in the boy. He carried a rough folio in one hand, loose papers tied together with twine.

"We've made a breakthrough," he announced. My mouth dropped open, and he continued, "We need your help. There's a few bolts that need loosening, but I can't get leverage on my own. The other guys are either too heavy or can't figure out what I'm telling them." The faint note of exasperation in his voice said what he wasn't willing to about men who could bench press two of him.

Like Amana, Anansi often found himself ignored by older people when he had an idea and needed help implementing it. It helped that men like Driver, Dry Eyes, and Sarge listened to the boy, but the soldiers hadn't quite wrapped their heads around our little genius.

The possibility of having a working garage began trickling through my half-frozen brain. "Wait. We could actually get those doors open?" He nodded. "We could protect the vehicles?" Another nod. "I could work on them *inside*?"

He rolled his eyes. "*Yes,* already. We just need to get the guys."

Any desire for a bath and clean clothes vanished. "Hot damn! Later, people. I have shit to do." I swung past the kitchen and grabbed a mug of tea, then made a beeline for the door. Section Eight, here I come. I spotted a little tow-headed girl with black eyes. "Optimus, honey, you busy?"

"Got a minute for you, Captain," the eleven-year-old said.

"Could you please tell those soldiers who are helping with the garage doors that I need them in the garage? Thank you," I called to her retreating back.

Optimus Prime, the youngest person at the Lair, had decided that, as an orphan, she could make up her own mind about what she'd do. So far, I had to agree with her assessment of her own capabilities. She worked in the tannery, had significant standing in the Lair, and helped where she pleased in her spare time. Most often, I saw her with our herbalist, Wildwood. The little girl darted through the Lair, the patter of her moccasined feet fading away.

***

"Damn, this thing doesn't want to budge," I grunted, straining.

I had a meter-long wrench set around a huge bolt and my feet braced against the doors for leverage. Relaxing, I reset myself, hooking the toes of my left foot under a lip of metal. I grunted again, my face reddening with the effort, but the stupid thing refused to move.

"Have you guys found any WD-40 yet?" My plaintive question echoed through the room. "This bitch ain't moving without a bit of help."

"We're still waiting for..."

Anansi came running into the room, waving a can over his head, closely followed by the huge young soldier, Goliath. "It was behind the pump," he wheezed, passing the can over and resting his hands on his knees to catch his breath. "Last can. Need to find more."

Gryphon sent the can whizzing up to me in a bucket tied to a rope. I shook it experimentally. Hopefully it'd be enough. "Thanks, 'Nansi. Have Amana add it to the list."

We'd started the shopping list almost a year ago, filling it with all the things we were looking for. It evolved from a piece of paper into a dry erase board in the common room. The scavengers consulted it before leaving on each trip, and every time, they came back with less and less because they didn't dare go too far.

Some things were standard: Hightide always needed tools for leather-working, Doc had a general request for medical supplies and first-aid kits, and I always needed parts for cars.

Spraying the WD-40 onto the bolt and giving it time to soak in left me contemplating what it would be like to work on vehicles out of the elements. All of them would last longer if they had time away from the weather. Not having to hike for an hour carrying my tools would free up a lot of time, too. Maybe I'd finally get some sleep.

Then again, maybe I was better off not sleeping. Nightmares were a plague. The only thing that changed was the monster I faced each night.

I rubbed the spray into the bolt and set the wrench again. Bracing, I hauled until I thought I'd stroke out—but the damn bolt moved. Crowing, I threw one hand into the air, celebrating and stretching my shoulders.

"Did you get it?"

"Did she get…?"

"I think she got it!"

The men shouted and laughed as I dropped a couple inches. Screeching, I grabbed the beam with both hands and to hell with the wrench. "Don't you bastards drop me again!"

"Sorry," the men chorused.

"And the bolt's only moved. It's not fucking off yet."

Anansi had determined that this bolt and its mate on the other side would allow us to detach the gates from the old system and rig our own. This was barely the first step, but we expected a long, cold winter and snow was already here. What else did I have to keep me occupied?

Certainly not playing patty-cake with a handsome man who frequently looked at me twice.

***

I shuffled into the common room, rubbing a cloth over my face. I couldn't be sure, but judging by the grease on the cloth, I might have been smearing grime around instead of removing it. Phoenix confirmed there was something off with my looks.

She paused with her snack halfway to her mouth, her eyes traveling up and down slowly before the snack continued its journey. "What the hell happened to you?" she asked around her food.

I collapsed onto the bench with a groan. "You know our garage?"

"Everybody knows the garage. You and Anansi never shut up about it."

"We can use it now."

"What? That's all you're going to say about it?"

"That's about all I want to remember right now." I dropped my head onto my folded arms, relaxing into the table.

"Oh, no you don't, Captain." Lavender's strident tone jostled me out of my doze. "That table is clean. You, on the other hand, are not. Shower!"

"Can I have a hot one?" I begged, only gaining my feet with her help.

She perused me silently, taking in my greasy hair and going all the way down to my scuffed and filthy boots, cataloging every bruise and scrape in between. "I'll do you one better. A hot bath after your shower. You can soak in the distillery." She waved towards the back of the kitchen where Anansi had taken over a pantry and turned it into a science experiment.

"Deal." I limped towards my room while Lavender went to put a few pots on to boil.

"Wait, what about me?" Phoenix complained to the nearly empty room. "Don't I get a hot bath, too?"

I flipped her the finger without turning around. "When you open some goddamn big doors, you can have a hot bath, too. Until then, fuck off."

***

I giggled as I pulled a Chimera, one of Steve's mongrel, souped-up Hummers, into the garage and parked it amongst our fleet of mismatched vehicles, so disreputable next to the slightly dusty Jeeps left behind by the army. None of those Jeeps would ever run, courtesy of the extensive computer systems that were now fried by whatever the hell it was Steve had done.

Dereva hopped down from an ancient van, circa 1995, and watched me spinning in the center of the garage, her arms folded and shaking her head. Archangel walked over from the Chimera he'd brought in and stood by the bus with Sirius.

"Just the GMC left." Dereva surveyed the rest of the vehicles. "Thank goodness. I really don't want to go on another two-hour hike today."

To keep Steve from finding the Lair, we'd closed off the road leading to it and encouraged the growth and spread of blackberries. Parking was haphazard and most spaces were an hour or two's hike away. The garage would completely revolutionize exits and entries, and I couldn't wait.

"How about a victory hike to my baby?" I asked. "We need a few people in this one to cover our tracks and help the snow out."

We'd waited until snow clouds covered the sky so that we'd have a way to cover our tracks. At this altitude, it wasn't likely that the snow would clear until spring, and I really didn't want to wait that long to move into my new playroom.

"*My* baby." Dereva grinned at me. "She's mine now, and you know it. *I* drive her."

"Yeah, but I fix her." I threw an arm around her shoulders, bracketed by Sirius and Archangel. The scout ended up next to me. When we crossed the barrier and stepped outside, snow crunched and slid underfoot. "I'd totally forgotten about this road."

Dereva turned to look up at the cliff face. "Why would we remember it?"

The bunker was built inside of half a mountain. The road we walked on dead ended at the cliff, and there were signs at the turn saying it did and talking about construction that should've continued this year. I remember following the road one time and not seeing any signs of a door. There were even reflective barriers connected to the cliff to prevent accidents.

Grown men and women (myself among them) squealed in delight at the sight of the cliff face simply…opening. I hadn't known this level of camouflage even existed. It was flawless. Seahorse shook her head, muttering about abandonment and assholes in charge.

She was still sore about that.

Now, walking to get the last vehicle, my precious GMC, Sirius watched the ground pensively, her fingers fiddling and twisting around themselves. "Remember that time Lightning," her voice hitched, then continued, "that first time, when she got her hands on the machine gun and shot you guys up? I think that's the most damage your pickup ever got at one time."

I grinned. "Yeah. My baby got all kinds of holes in her. It was a real bitch to fix, too."

Lightning and Thunder, sisters, had just been freed from an outpost. Scared, traumatized, and then we had Steve chasing us. Thunder figured out the gun in the stolen Hummer, and Sirius drove and saved our bacon. Only problem was, once the bad guys were dead, she couldn't seem to take her finger off the trigger. She'd nearly killed us.

"You guys looked pretty funny, slipping around in the back of the truck." Dereva sniffed, tears bright in her eyes. "I thought I was going to get my head shot off." She smiled a little, remembering.

Archangel looked from one to the other of us, finally settling on me. "So...one of your own shot at you, and now it's a good story?"

I scrunched my shoulders. "In hindsight, it's pretty damn hilarious." The others nodded.

He smiled hopefully. "Any chance I can meet them? I don't think I've even heard of them."

"All hail the victorious dead." I smiled sadly.

"Oh." He bit his lip and looked down.

Grimacing, I opened my mouth and shut it again. How was he supposed to know the girls had died? And I'd just dropped it on him. Like a flipping bomb.

Surprisingly, it was Sirius who spoke up first. "You couldn't know. We remember the fallen, but we don't normally talk about them outside of memorials."

"It hurts less that way," Dereva explained. "We prefer living in the present instead of the past."

"The rest of the time, we can pretend they're in another room, or that they're with our families," I finished. "Most of us don't know where our families are, either. That's why, when we get whole families out, we make sure they stay together."

"I'd wondered why there were so many able-bodied men who weren't in the fighters." Archangel nodded. After a brief silence, he stopped abruptly. "Captain, can I ask you a question?"

Sirius headed off the road, onto a narrower track where we could only walk two across. Dereva picked up her pace and I motioned for Archangel to join me.

He waited until Dereva got a bit farther away and lowered his voice. "I've seen the rules, but do you have any extra advice for those wanting to get to know a fighter. I've got a young soldier..."

I grinned into the rising dusk, stepping carefully through the snow. "Keep it platonic for a while. If they decide to go further, like holding hands and shit, they have to talk to Eleanor and Kestrel. There's no way around it. We don't react well when we find people in corners randomly. As long as he follows the rules, it'll go fine for him."

Three boys decided that since the girls had been with the enemy—they ignored the fact that the girls weren't willing participants—they were available to all. They'd cost one young woman her life.

Archangel cleared his throat. "Okay. No funny business, no sneaking kisses. I'll let him know."

We'd drawn closer as we talked and fallen behind the others. I could barely make out Dereva's back through the dark. "Hot Fuzz already knows the rules, and he knows we're serious about people following them." He'd asked me two weeks ago about dating Dereva. Boy was no slacker.

Dereva had already spoken to Eleanor on the matter, too.

Archangel snorted a laugh. "Of course, you know who I'm talking about. How do you keep track of everything?"

"Can you keep a secret?" I lowered my voice dramatically and he leaned closer, until I could bask in the warmth radiating from him. "I don't have to. I keep track of four or five people. *They* stay on top of everything and fill me in. I talk to maybe six people a day." I held a finger to my lips and grinned.

He smothered a laugh and choked, leaning on me, wheezing. I patted him on the back, unable to look at him but unwilling to look away. His eyes crinkled at the corners, so close to my own.

Eventually, still gasping, he straightened slightly but kept leaning on me. "I'm okay," he croaked. He peered at me. I held my breath. I hadn't been this close to a man without kicking his ass in forever. "What are you trying to do, kill me?" His voice was rough and held a note I didn't recognize. That didn't stop my stomach fluttering. Traitorous stomach. "Woman doesn't know her own strength. While I normally wouldn't object to laughing as a way to die, right now, I've got too much to live for."

My breath whooshed out at that. And I'm supposed to concentrate? Not while he stood so close. Unable to respond, I took off after Sirius and Dereva, and he fell back into step beside me.

"Six people a day," he continued as if nothing had happened. "Six fuckin' people is how you stay on top of this beehive." He shook his head.

"It's called delegating," I said loftily, wiping damp hands on my pants. "Didn't you learn anything about that in the army?"

Archangel made a growly noise deep in his throat. "You're a brat, aren't you?"

My heart sped up. What was wrong with me? Sweating under my clothes but pasting a grin on my face, I walked backwards. "Not the first time I've been called a b-word. Usually, it's a different one. Bit more accurate, too."

"Got the car," Dereva called, breaking into...whatever this was.

A *crack* split the air, followed by two more, and Sirius walked back into the tiny clearing carrying three slender pine branches, needles thickly clustered on the ends. She settled her hatchet back into its belt loop with the other.

I sniffed the air. Snow was coming, hopefully before dawn, but brushing our tracks away as we went would help the weather hide our home.

"Read my mind," I said to my cousin, pretending to adjust the scarf around my neck. A good enough distraction, since nobody needed to know my inner babbling except me. Swiping the ground with the branch Sirius gave me, I shrugged. As good as it gets around here.

Dereva drove while the three of us laid across the box she'd put at the tailgate. Leaning over and swishing the crude brooms over the snow partially filled the tracks. The truck rumbled over the snow, lurching in the potholes that had been there since the dawn of time.

"This'll probably be the last snow year for a while," Sirius grunted. "Kinda amazed we got two in a row."

Oregon liked to cycle its winters. One or two white Christmases followed by a decade or more of straight rain for the whole winter. My parents had photos of me as a baby in snow up to my vertically challenged chest. Snow years had gotten fewer, but we did get more sleet and northern freezes, the perfect things to fuck with Steve.

"But we're in the mountains," Archangel puffed. "Shouldn't there be lots of snow?"

"You gotta be high for that," I gasped. Laying across a box sounds simple until your weight really settles on your chest. My back rose and fell with each breath, the motion...wrong. Strange. Glancing at the other two, I could see them struggling as much as me, though from Sirius's clenched jaw and flared nostrils, she'd die before being the one to call for a rest. "Break," I croaked, levering up.

Dereva slowed the truck to give us a chance to catch our breath. I slid down until I was on my back, gasping for air, icicles stabbing into my lungs until I tugged my scarf back up. Sirius flopped backward, unmindful of what was behind her, right into the machine gun stand.

"Motherfucker!" She rolled to her side, clutching her head.

I laughed. "Top...top of your hat has a hole in it."

"Better that than my head."

"Amen, sister."

Archangel huddled against the tailgate box, hiding from the wind but still able to keep an eye on our surroundings. It was empty, the snow covering the small bushes so all we could see were the pines and the occasional tree naked of its leaves. "Can we get going, already?" he asked plaintively. "It's cold."

"Aren't army guys supposed to be tough?" Sirius sat up gingerly, holding her head with one hand.

"Not anymore. I was supposed to be out by now. I'd already ditched my toughness and I sure as hell didn't pick it up when they shoved me back in."

Rolling over, I stretched to knock on the window, then went back to the box and swept snow while the first flakes of fresh snowfall dusted our backs.

***

Back in the garage, I ran giddily around the room. The absence of snow and wind gave the huge stone and concrete room the illusion of warmth. I popped hoods and removed panels, giggling madly. I only had to wear three layers on top instead of the four to five I usually had to outside.

I squealed at the block and chain setup. I'd nearly forgotten! I could lift engines out. I could move a good engine into a good-bodied vehicle! Swinging my arms, enjoying the space, I spun and froze.

Archangel stood in the doorway, supporting my brother while he exercised. The scout had a silly grin on his face.

"How long have you been there?" I asked, folding my arms.

"Long enough. What's so funny?"

"Not funny. Just…" I gestured around the room. "The luxury! There's a pulley system, so I can remove the whole engine! I can leave the hoods up as long as I need to. No more scrambling to finish. I can walk in here and start working without having to spend an hour to get here and twenty minutes setting up."

Hot Fuzz chuckled and shook his head. He'd been around me and cars since he was a tyke. I was the one who taught him to drive.

"Dinner!" echoed down the hall and into the garage, closely followed by Dereva dancing, high on her toes. "Dinner. Dry Eyes came back with an elk today!"

"Hot damn." I punched the air.

They boys looked between us, shaking their heads. "I can't get over how much you girls love your food." Hot Fuzz laughed, stretching his arm out to Dereva. "I thought *I* was supposed to be the one thrilled about food while girls watched what they ate."

Dereva slid under his free arm, taking his weight from Archangel. My brother was finally walking, but he needed a cane or a person to help him along.

He probably couldn't figure a cane out, if his latest brain fart was any example of his thought processes. We simply didn't have enough food to eat luxuriously. There were too many people, and a good chunk of our hunts were taken Home. Until they could harvest, they were low on food.

Which meant we were low on food. Here, hunger was a companion closer than a lover, and far more reliable.

"I do watch what I eat," Dereva informed my idiot brother as they slowly navigated the hallway. "I watch it very carefully to make sure I eat it before it runs away."

I cracked up, joined by Archangel, slumping against the rough wall for support while Dereva continued blithely down the hall, ignoring the howling laughter behind her. Wiping my eyes, I straightened, still giggling, to find myself almost nose-to-nose with Archangel. His eyes sparkled, the tip of his tongue caught between his teeth while his snickers slowly died.

I looked up to find him watching me, his eyes warm…my heart stuttered, and I turned away quickly, my face heating up. In silence, we continued down the hallway. After a couple minutes, he picked a safe subject.

"Finding enough food can't be that bad, can it?" he asked carefully.

I took the rope he offered gratefully. "We've got almost a hundred people here, no way to plant, and no grocery stores or warehouses. It's what we can hunt or steal from Steve. And Steve has an annoying habit of randomly loading the food trucks with explosives or soldiers. It's a bit of a crapshoot, stealing from their trucks."

"You know how you guys have a major advantage?"

"No."

"You're mostly women, so you eat less."

I burst out laughing again. "Have you not been paying attention?" He shook his head. I snorted. "Watch the room. You'll see."

***

"Holy shit," Archangel muttered from his seat next to me. Apparently, he finally watched the fighters and noted how much we ate. "Where are you ladies putting it all?"

I sniggered into my cup of water. "Told you. Though according to Doc, it's easier than if we were men. Something about how we store fat." Another bonus was that most of us were too thin to have regular periods anymore. Not having to deal with the diaper-like pads made me extremely happy.

"I heard my name." Two places down, Doc looked up from her stew. "Who said my name?"

"Sorry, Doc." I raised my hand. "Archangel was asking about the difficulties of keeping women at a healthy weight as opposed to men."

I sat back, grinning, as Doc started in on a topic that was near and dear to her heart with no more invitation than that. Amana, Wildwood, and Lavender also had input, valuable knowledge painstakingly learned through trial and error. I placidly chewed my stew as the debate raged on about which were the best staple foods.

Then, Anansi and Hot Fuzz got into the spirit but with a different topic. The boys began loudly proclaiming the best movies, which quickly turned into a quote duel. My brother laboriously clambered (with help) onto the bench, spouting dialogue from the movie that gave him his name. Not to be outdone, Anansi leaped onto the table. The shorter boy started with Shakespeare and finished with classic Mel Brooks, stepping down to scattered applause.

Peter, already back on the floor, gave him a short bow and I shook my head. When did that boy get so smooth? Leaning onto the table, I listened to the conversations flowing around me—Archangel laughing at something Gryphon said, Phoenix's green eyes sparkling with laughter, Sirius giving Fuzz a noogie—contentment a warm ball in my stomach.

CHAPTER 4

Man 1: How the fuck is banning the guns I make a good thing? The President's going too far!

Man 2: Shut up! I've brought you this far, haven't I? Think long-term. Cooper won't be in office forever, and I have just the man to help us out...

Transcript of phone recording, 11:23 pm March 23, 2049

A month after we'd moved the trucks into the garage, I leaned inside the engine block of an ancient minivan, socket wrench in one hand and the water-stained user's manual propped on the oil filter next to me. The parts in here weren't an exact match for what I needed, but with a bit of machining, I could make it work in a gray van that had a solid undercarriage.

With one finger marking the relevant passage, I found the part in the engine, then felt around for the bolt. I sighed, relaxing into the work. I hadn't lost my knack of getting the right sized socket on the first try.

Then I heard, "Captain. Ssst, Captain!"

Reluctantly, I levered up, hand still in the belly of the machine, prepared to glare unholy death at the unfortunate who'd dared disturb me.

Seahorse uncharacteristically raced in, weaving between the cars and thumping to a halt against the van I worked on, rocking it. I hissed as I fumbled the wrench. "What?" I snapped, leaning back into the block. Grunting, I stretched, trying to reach the stupid thing.

"Forget that. You'll never guess what I saw!"

"Right now, unless it has to do with imminent death, I don't care."

"Phoenix and Gryphon have been talking to Kestrel. Together."

I straightened up so quickly I whacked my head against the hood. Cussing and rubbing my head, I abandoned the wrench and gave her my full attention. Beautiful by all of society's standards, endlessly pursued by men Before, angry, nasty, gutter fighter Phoenix had let go of her rage enough to visit our shrink to make sure she was emotionally healthy enough to get into a relationship.

She'd dealt more black eyes and given more sore balls to the local men than anyone else here, but if she was giving that up for a man who'd saved her life, took her seriously, and listened when she talked...Brava, Phoenix.

"Go on," I urged her.

Knowing what another person is up to makes it easier to ensure they have privacy if they want it, and I was all in to ensure that Phoenix had the space she needed to get to know a hottie like Gryphon. For the sake of making sure they were compatible, of course. Yeah. Not like we were living vicariously. Nope. Not at all.

"They were definitely sneaking." Seahorse lowered her voice, clutching the van for support. "Like, stereotypical checking both ways, leaving one at a time, all of it. Do you think our girl's gonna score with an actual famous actor?"

I snorted. "If anybody could, it'd be her." If I'd met her in normal, day-to-day life, I'd have a small problem with jealousy. Green eyes, sandy blonde hair with natural red highlights (once her white-blonde dye grew out), petite, and curvy, Phoenix could give an inferiority complex to a model without trying. She made me feel like a gigantic freak. "You should've seen him rescue her. It was some movie quality shit and I'd be ga-ga over him if I were her."

"Hey!" Sirius hailed us as soon as she walked in. She must have come here straight from outside, because she had snow on her hat. Her younger dog, Obelix, trotted beside her. "Why are we in here? Phoenix won't talk to me, and..."

Seahorse waved her over frantically. "Get your ass over here! You're never gonna believe this."

By the time Seahorse filled her in, Sirius was leaning against the van, wheezing with laughter. "Remember what you said about the bras?" she gasped.

I frowned. "That Al did a damn good job?"

"No! About Tom Carrington holding your boobs."

I choked. "Oh, fuck. I'd forgotten about that. Shit. I need a drink."

She held up a hand. "Say no more." Sirius fished a flask out of her jacket, her wicked smile wide enough to show the gap in her teeth. "*Afya yako*," she toasted.

***

Later that day, I was stuck in the armory, taking stock of ammunition and captured weaponry. Normally, the job was frustrating because for me, two plus two doesn't always equal four, but today, my thoughts were racing. Mostly running in circles about how I could possibly look Gryphon in the face after Sirius reminded me of my comment, with generous amounts of speculation included.

"What the hell are you muttering to yourself about?" Phoenix demanded behind me.

Spinning around, I gave her a guilty smile. As in, I should never play poker. "Uh...nothing?"

"You are so full of shit, you know that?"

I giggled, then clamped a hand over my mouth, eyes wide, face turning red with the effort. My stomach hurt and my shoulders shook with the force of suppressing the laugh, not helped by her irritated grimace and folded arms. Losing the battle, I howled with laughter, sinking to the floor while she glared at me.

Phoenix stood over me, oozing disapproval. "Will you just spit it out?"

Screeching and gasping, I struggled upright and cupped my breasts. "What I said...about the bras and...Gryphon..." I wiggled my eyebrows suggestively, snorting and snickering. "Is it...true?"

Her eyes got huge, and she sucked in a deep breath when the object of our discussion walked through the door, Archangel hot on his heels. She turned bright red, and I made a sound like a balloon deflating and sank back to the floor, cackling. The two men joined Phoenix in staring down at me, though they were more puzzled than anything.

I squirmed, but couldn't catch my breath enough to get up, then Gryphon asked, "Does she do this often? Because I don't remember seeing this before and I'm fairly sure this isn't proper behavior for a rebel leader."

"This vocal? No." Phoenix glared down her nose at me, the blush crawling down her neck. "This stupid? Unfortunately, yes. All I can say is she lives in the gutter. So far down that even a rope and a ladder couldn't get her out."

"I...I wasn't..." I cracked up again. "Fuck it. Yes. Yes, I am."

Phoenix waited until I met her eyes. "I wish I could say I expected better of you, but this is par for the course where you're concerned." Just when I thought she was angry beyond belief, she gave me the tiniest wink and nod.

My jaw dropped. Did she...? She did! Too many things tried to tumble out at once and I choked.

Spinning on her heel, she faced Gryphon directly. "Did you need us for something?"

"Erm...Yes." Gryphon looked between us, completely lost, bless his heart. "Seahorse called a meeting in the Useless Room. Tracks in the area that aren't ours."

I leaned against the wall with a groan and a giggle. "No rest for the wicked."

"Or the filthy minded," Phoenix said loftily, marching to the door. Gryphon followed, giving me a confused, concerned look.

Archangel just grinned and reached down to help me to my feet. "Finally learned they're interested in each other, huh?"

I was still sputtering when he dragged me into the Useless Room where Seahorse was kicked back in a chair, stocking feet on the table. Sirius waited impatiently by the map.

"Mouse found tracks to the south and east," Sirius said without preamble. She referred to a small, teenaged rescue who had become the head of our perimeter guard until she got old enough that we'd let her into the fighters. We all drew the line at thirteen for being in the field. "Footprints. We backtracked them to tire tracks, two Chimeras. Thing is, there were more footprints than Steve usually puts in a truck. They're hunting on foot."

South and east was the Opal Creek area, where we'd had a fight with Steve last summer, right after Steve tried to use the sisters, Lightning and Thunder, to draw us out. The women had been captured after we'd gone into Salem to rescue our spy's daughter, Olivia. It turned into a cluster fuck, especially when they gave into revenge instead of pulling back.

Gryphon looked at our solemn faces. "What's so bad about that? Looks like there's a mountain between us and them."

"On foot, that's a good distance." Archangel leaned over to draw a line on the map with his finger. "But with cars, trucks, or long-range missiles? Nope. We don't want them anywhere close to here."

I sat forward, resting my forearms on the table. "The only question I see is whether it would be easier to convince them we're really south or north."

"I have a better question." Archangel grinned, pushing his hair back, off his forehead. "How many people should we bring to fuck Steve up?"

An answering smile pulled at my lips. "Keep them so busy on their turf they have no time to hunt for ours?"

He nodded. "You guys know what they generally carry, you're good at finding them, and you're better in winter conditions than they are. So, we go out in two small teams, twenty to thirty each, with a set area to cover. From everything I've heard, they don't do well in cold or altitudes, right?"

I nodded.

"And we won't have to deal with snow down there."

Sirius snorted. "I'd rather have snow. The mud gets everywhere."

"It can't be that bad."

Phoenix laughed and shook her head. "The Valley is different. Very different. Anyway," she limped over to the wall where we kept a list of potential sites and frequent patrol routes, "we've got more than enough to keep us busy."

"So, it's a question of who should be on the teams," Sergeant Perry said.

"Not really." I shrugged. "Even with your lot, it'll still take all of us to get to sixty."

Perry nodded and stood, pacing slowly around the table. "We'll need to talk to your quartermaster. Determine what supplies we can bring with us." He looked around and settled on Driver and Dry Eyes. "What is the state of the supplies here?"

Amana laughed. "Don' ask *them*. I think jour quartermaster is me."

I rolled my eyes. She really didn't need to lay the accent on so thick. Perry just goggled at the teenager, taken by surprise that she was also in charge of all the supplies. He looked from her to me and back again, trying to wrap his head around this new concept.

I waved a hand. "If you want to be called the quartermaster, fine. I have no idea what to call everything you do anyway."

"Chef, too."

I sighed. "Fine. Any other titles you'd like?"

"I will tell jou when I decide."

CHAPTER 5

I groaned, shifting uncomfortably. Grumbling, I tried to figure out where the hell…? Oh, right. I sat down on the couch for a minute in the common room. Must've fallen asleep. All the late nights prepping vehicles to survive a couple months of use, plus all the planning, were taking their toll on me. I tugged irritably at my collar, flinging off the blanket in the process. The wash of cool air hit me like a soothing balm.

Cracking my eyes open, I made out Sirius and Dereva talking to Archangel at the next table over. Pushing upright, fire lanced from my shoulder, down my shoulder blade, alongside the spine, and all the way up, through my neck and into my skull. I froze, gasping until the pain eased.

When I could see again, all three of them watched me with concern. Archangel had already risen, and he knelt next to me, helping to get me upright. "You are not okay," he said firmly.

"I didn't say I was," I grumbled.

"You were about to."

I glared at him, shoving a hank of hair back. "It's nothing a good massage couldn't fix." Probably.

"You could use more sleep, too," Sirius said. "You look like shit."

"Pot. Kettle."

"Hah! I'd have to stay awake for three days to look as bad as you."

The ache started up again and I supported my right elbow with my left hand. Archangel, the perceptive bastard, saw it. "Not only do you need a massage, you're getting one. And physio. Or else," he held up a hand to forestall my protests, his voice hard, "you're going to be a liability in the field."

"I got way too much to do." I pressed back into the couch even though he hadn't made a move towards me. "Besides, it's been plaguing me for ages and hasn't stopped me yet." I looked frantically around, hoping Sirius or Dereva would rescue me. My cousin just folded her arms and shook her head. Dereva wouldn't even look at me. "Traitors," I accused.

"I've never seen you support your shoulder before." Archangel was implacable. "Come on. We're going to see Doc. Maybe there's someone here who specializes in acupuncture. Barring that, I've spent some time in PT. I'll work on you if I have to."

"Oh, gee, thanks," I muttered as he pulled me off the couch. "Don't lay those compliments on too thick. You might turn my head."

He stepped aside to let me pass and dropped a large, warm hand on my shoulder, pressing firmly with his thumb. I gasped, pain flaring hotly. It subsided almost as quickly, a breath of relief, and I moaned involuntarily.

"Okay," I mumbled. "Maybe you're hired. On probation."

He chuckled and squeezed again. "That's the spirit."

***

After a round of what Archangel called a 'sports massage' and I called 'torture' the following day, I sat in the common room, maps spread on the table, a cup of tea at my elbow. I rolled my head around, rotating my shoulder. Damn the man, but he was *good*. It hurt like hell in the moment, but after a few exercises Doc prescribed, my shoulder felt better than it had in months.

Archangel's hands running over my bare shoulder and down my spine flashed across my mind, distracting me from my work. Wrenching my attention, I went back to the task at hand, studying maps.

Committing chunks of map to memory wasn't easy, and unfortunately, my favorite TV show walked in before I'd gotten very far. Phoenix entered first, marching to another table, laying her guns and cleaning supplies out.

Gryphon sauntered in after her, casually walking around the place before 'accidentally' finding himself in her vicinity. I kept one eye on them and held my breath so I wouldn't miss anything.

They started out with quiet chit-chat, all very boring except for their goofy smiles and giggling. Then, Gryphon sat down as coolly as if he hadn't just spent the last ten minutes setting this up.

Until he put his gigantic foot in his mouth.

"Why is it I always hear about women having a go at each other, backbiting and all that rubbish, but here, in the largest female to male percentage I've ever bloody seen, there's none of that?"

I snorted into my tea. He went there? What did he want? World War III? Oh, wait. We're already living that.

Phoenix rolled her eyes, sniggering. "Seriously?"

"Well, it's always on American shows, you know? I just figured different cultures because English girls aren't like that, but it's what you see, innit?"

"Women are women. And when there's men around who don't treat us nicely, we'll put aside any and all differences we might have to gang up on the bastards. It's scientifically proven." She smiled beatifically.

Shaking my head, I huffed a tiny laugh. Damn good job, that. She'd managed to stop a dangerous topic of conversation and divert him. I could only wish I'd be as smooth someday.

Gryphon grinned back at her, completely besotted. "Erm. No. It's not. Is it?"

I bit my lip, struggling to keep the laugh from escaping. Is this what being a balloon feels like, a whole bunch of air struggling to escape, barely held in? Their pause lasted so long I had to breathe or risk spotty vision. Couldn't let anything spoil the view of my favorite daytime romantic drama.

Her lips parted. He leaned in slightly.

And I lost the battle with my mouth. "Would you two get a room already?" I heckled. "You're making *me* sweat."

Phoenix whipped around, her eyes narrowing murderously as she slammed the bolt home on her rifle, threat implicit in every movement. Snatching up my mug and maps, I ran for the door laughing like a madwoman.

***

Preparations for the winter campaign kept the entire Lair in a flurry of activity, broken only once when I was called Home to deal with an ex-politician. I took Phoenix and Sirius with me because they tend to get into too much trouble if I leave them behind. Oh, and Eleanor made me.

Home was set high in the mountains, in the Jefferson Wilderness. I'd never seen it in winter snow, and we stepped carefully, lifting our knees high, snowshoes strapped to our feet.

The trees around the mountain grew thick, only thinning out in the higher altitudes. In the summer, the land was green and gold, but the winter...Oh, the winter, snow-covered evergreens made a gorgeous backdrop, the area around their trunks treacherous with snow pits.

The messenger from Home only said that Sophie—Oregon's sole surviving career politician—was stirring up trouble, causing problems best handled by me.

Olivia and her husband, Sam, ran the place, though their main duties were ensuring that all the children had a safe, home-like environment. Their secondary ones were ensuring that all the necessary chores were done.

I paused, looking at the low entrance. I still found it hard to believe Sirius had even found the place, considering the cave mouth was small and hidden by a jumble of rocks. I guess that's what rabbit hunting can do for you. Sighing, I bellied onto the cold ground, worming my way forward.

No sooner did I set foot on the floor of the extensive cave network than a woman in her fifties ambushed me. Sophie, a politician to her core, didn't know when to shut up. "You should have someone in charge who understands how people think and knows what they want," she said, scuttling through the first cavern of Home after me.

I had no idea how far the system went, but Olivia said they were working to widen smaller passageways to create more space. She planned on having enough space to fit hundreds of people. Maybe even a thousand. This first cave was the largest, thirty feet high and sixty long. All around the edges, families carved space into alcoves, blankets covering the openings for privacy and warmth.

"No." I breathed deeply. Sophie tried being the intermediary between Useless Room meetings and the civilians, but that ended due to her idiotic attempts at taking control and her penchant for incendiary talk that nearly caused a riot. "I should have someone in charge who knows what people need, and who cares about them. Which we do. And everyone except you and your three cronies agrees with me. Or they would if you'd shut up for five minutes."

The rope ladder shook when Sirius climbed the ten feet down to the cave floor, closely followed by Phoenix. They were mobbed by children, who appeared as if by magic, laughing and grabbing their hands, dragging them away. Phoenix waved, grinning. Sirius shot me a panicked look, her eyes wide, mouth open in a silent No.

Sophie's harangue never stopped. Listening to her was useless. It all boiled down to "Olivia's incompetent and I should be in charge." I had to give the woman credit for ignoring an insult for the sake of getting her way, but I'd seen her in control of civilians, and an innocent woman was nearly hanged for self-defense while three rapists would've gotten off scot-free.

"Captain!" A high-pitched shriek split the air and cut off that infernal woman. A second later, a tiny human cannonball collided with my legs. "You're back!"

"Little Cub!" I swung the girl up in my arms, grunting with the effort. "You've gotten so big! What are they feeding you?"

Cub and her sister, Moana, had run away from the North American Liberation Corps, or Dorothy as we called them, with their mother. We'd found them on their first night away, during our first trip into Salem. Their mother, Leo, had died in the escape, so we'd all adopted them.

The little girl giggled at my theatrics. "You're silly. I eat deer and sheep milk and potatoes and mushrooms."

"Wow." I nuzzled her downy blonde hair. "You eat better than me."

"You could stay here?" She looked up at me, her blue eyes beseeching. "I don't like her very much," Cub whispered loudly, looking directly at Sophie, her warm, moist breath puffing the hair around my ear.

I snickered while Sophie sputtered. Apparently, her tolerance for being insulted ended with toddlers. "I wish I could, baby, but then who would kick the bad guys out?"

She stuck her lower lip out and wrapped her arms around my neck. Her preference for me never ceased to amaze me. Too many people refused to look at me directly, or avoided me altogether, but this little girl liked me better than almost anyone else. It made me think that all the blood on my hands might be washed away someday.

"Where's Olivia?" I asked Cub.

"In the Mushroom Room." She giggled. "Mushroom Room," she repeated softly several times, savoring the words.

Numerous small caves and tunnels opened off the main cave. "And...which one is that?"

"That one, silly." The little girl pointed to a low, roughly oval tunnel topped with a broad ledge covered with used candles.

"Are there any other tunnels inside?"

"Nope." She stroked my hair, fascinated with it.

"Do you want to hang out with Sirius and Phoenix? I think the kids are feeding them."

They were. A little boy sat on Phoenix's lap, holding a piece of meat to her lips. No matter how she tried to avoid it, the boy tracked her, determined to feed the woman. Sirius had it worse. She was pinned to the ground, two kids sitting on her chest, one of them trying to push food past her lips.

Cub squealed, and I let her slide down my side. The moment her feet touched the ground, she hugged my legs and rocketed over to join the others in force-feeding my people. Adults lounged around, watching the kids indulgently, done with their work for the day and enjoying the entertainment.

Sophie backed away. "Well, then, I guess I'll let you..."

"Ah, ah, *ah*." I grabbed her arm. "You can come with me. I want to get this sorted ASAP. You're interrupting my fun."

"Captain!" she squealed. "Are you even doing anything for these good people? Having fun?"

"Sophie." I made a fist and relaxed. Taking a deep breath didn't help. Neither did the two after that. Taking one of the candles, I lit it with the firestarter I kept in one of the pouches hanging from my belt. I'd felt stupid wearing one, but this meant I could carry more than my pockets could hold without always needing a backpack. "Just...shut up and follow me."

I ducked into the tunnel, the stub of a candle barely lighting my way. Scuffling behind let me know exactly where Sophie was. Maybe this meant she was finally taking responsibility for her asinine behavior. One could only hope.

The flickering candle made monsters with the shadows, obscuring almost as much as it revealed. The tunnel was low enough it forced me to hunch over. Pain flared in my neck and shoulder, but nowhere near as bad as it was before I got regular massages. Twice, I scraped my head on the ceiling. Then the uncertain light revealed a raised ceiling. I straightened cautiously, stretching and rolling my head.

The blow came suddenly, catching me over my right ear. It knocked me forward and I dropped the candle, my head automatically tucking as I fell into a roll. Sophie screeched and my legs and back thumped into the wall, finding every jutting point on it in the process. Sophie stood over my upside-down self, a rock in hand, face white, lips drawn into a rictus of a grin.

She rushed in, screeching again, the rock raised high. I fell left, pushing into an awkward roll, landing on my belly. She struck the rock bare inches from my face. Lunging, I slammed into the smaller woman. Her shrieks filled the small tunnel as we hit the ground, Sophie on the bottom.

"She tried to kill me!" Sophie yelled.

Olivia had heard the fight and came running, just in time to see me sitting on Sophie, one hand pressing on her head to keep the bitch from biting me. Now, we were back in the main cavern with a nice audience. I got up and stood away from Sophie next to Olivia and her husband, Sam.

They were good people, and almost everyone up here knew it. I'd only met Olivia a few times. The first was when we went into Salem to meet her mother and accidentally ended up recruiting her mom into spying for us. The next time I saw Olivia, she'd been taken and locked in a closet in an effort to break her. It hadn't worked. When we'd opened the door, she tried to kick Phoenix in the crotch.

Olivia watched Sophie with a judgmental eye. "So. Who should tell her that if Captain wanted her dead, she would be?" Her sour expression was belied by the spark of laughter in her eyes. The woman was enjoying this!

Sam merely sighed. Olivia, from what I could tell, had always been acerbic, and her captivity hadn't changed that one bit. "It's your turn to deal with her."

"Excuse you?" Olivia set her hands firmly on her hips. "*I'm* the one who got her out here. Now it's your turn."

"I'll sort her out," I said before this could degenerate any further. "It's why you called me up here, isn't it?"

"Oh!" Olivia stopped me with a raised finger. "Quick note. If she gives you too much trouble, we can call it her third strike and banish her in the spring!" Sam covered his eyes and groaned. "What?" She shrugged. "I can hope."

"I would've thought a murder attempt would be enough to banish someone." Phoenix had come up on us unnoticed.

Sam snorted. "Normally, yes. But since it's Captain, I'm fairly sure you have to be more competent than that for it to count."

"Hey," I protested. "I'm people, too."

But Phoenix nodded as if that made perfect sense. "Good point. How do you want to handle her?" she asked me.

I shrugged. "Fuck if I know. I figured I'd just put the fear of me into her."

She nodded again. "Good idea. Can I help?"

"If you want. Play with a knife or something."

'Sorting Sophie' really meant shouting over her, looming slightly, and a bunch of thinly veiled threats. Phoenix lounged behind me, and I had a good idea what she was doing based on how green Sophie and her friends turned.

By the time we were done, Sophie slinked out of the cave and the lump over my ear throbbed badly enough all I wanted was to lie down and sleep, but Olivia wouldn't let me. "You might have a concussion."

"What's a concussion even look like?" I asked irritably.

"I don't know." She rolled her eyes. "But you got hit on the head, so you might have one. You can't sleep because you might not wake up."

"Then you can't sleep. If you leave me alone, I'm totally taking a nap and I don't care if I never wake up."

Olivia snarled quietly, suddenly furious. "Don't be such a baby. And don't you dare joke about dying in here. The kids might hear you, and as far as they're concerned, you're Batman. Or Superman. I'm not sure what Moana and Cub have told them about you today. You're their hero."

"Oh."

Sirius wandered by, leading a train of kids. "You tell her what we brought?"

"Heh." I smiled slowly at Olivia, who suddenly looked trapped.

"What did you bring?"

"Books on sheep care, wool, yarn, spinning, shears, and some drop spindles that Dry Eyes made from drawings. Good luck learning how to use them."

Rather than alarm, Olivia looked intrigued at the thought. They had several ewes and a single ram. Using them for meat was a last resort, since they produced so much else that people needed. Mostly, wool.

Since I couldn't sleep yet, Olivia decided to feed me. Phoenix and Sirius sat with us, and Sam joined as soon as the kids were tucked in bed. Cub was right, the food at Home was excellent. Simple, but fresh and good.

"I'm dunno how I feel about sheep's milk." Phoenix sipped it experimentally. Her sleeve slipped back when she raised her hand, revealing her inner wrist.

"Whoa! Wait, what?" Olivia snatched her hand, spilling some of the milk. "When did you get this?" She shoved the sleeve back farther to show an A+ tattooed on Phoenix's wrist.

"It's been a couple months, I think," Phoenix said. "One of the girls does tattoos and she found some ink."

"Did it hurt? Why an A plus? Seems like a weird tattoo to get."

"It hurt a bit," Phoenix admitted. "And it doesn't mean 'A plus.' It's A positive. My blood type."

I pulled back my sleeve so they could see the O+ I sported. Sirius showed her wrist, too. "Doc asked us to get them," I said. "We've all got them in the same spot so that she can find our types easier."

"Not everyone has one yet," Phoenix continued. "Some people don't know their type. She's trying to find more stuff so she can test the rest."

I laughed quietly. "My first, and currently only, tattoo, and it's for my blood type. Which I can live with. My problem is Anansi got a tattoo. Like, a real one, not just his blood type."

"Why is that a problem?" Olivia shook her head. "You go out and fight, and you're worried about a kid getting a tattoo? You really need to get your priorities straight."

"He's only fourteen or so. And you haven't met his mother. She's going to kill me."

Olivia burst into laughter. Genuine, head thrown back, unrestrained laughter. Sam watched her, drinking in her joy as if she were water in a desert. "I'll come to your funeral," she gasped when she could breathe again.

"Oh, thank you so much," I said sourly. "That's such a comfort. Thank you."

CHAPTER 6

"It's another round of LA TV! Streaming all day, every day. Let's look back on the highlights of the last 24 hours, for those of you who missed it. A fresh water war between the Bloods and the Hipsters in Whittier, and the Masters in Pasadena have just heard about the weapons supply the Protestants have stocked..."

Majordrama Channel

I sat in the Useless Room, poring over maps one last time. We were set to leave in the morning, and as always, I couldn't leave the maps alone.

A quiet, easily agitated man called Photograph found me there, knocking lightly on the door. His fingers danced restlessly over the camera hanging around his neck. Where he'd found it, I had no idea, but the thing used film. We didn't know where he'd gotten that, either. Amana just said he'd gone exploring in the Lair and come back with the camera, and I'd never seen him without film yet.

I watched him, leaning my hip against the table. I'd learned you couldn't rush him. He had to do things in his own time.

Finally, he found his voice. "Captain. We should take a photo. Of the fighters."

"Not a bad idea. Why?"

"We need. We need to remember. All of us. All of this. And. I want to go with you. Some day. Not now." He fidgeted, flipped some things on the camera and went still, watching me from the corner of his eye.

"Okay…" Deciding to leave his wish to go into the field aside for the moment, I picked the one I could handle. "When do you want to take this picture?"

"Today? Now?" He started towards the door. "Sun's out."

Well, in that case, everyone would probably be outside, already enjoying the sunshine. "Let's go," I said when it became apparent that he was absolutely going to get those pictures now.

Less than an hour later, everyone was piled into the meadow. Sunlight glittered on the snow, making me squint. Everyone treated this like a giant play date. Snowball fights broke out, and a group of younger ones, led by Mouse, began building a snowman on the mound.

Photograph decided he wanted pictures of each group. Scavengers, perimeter guards, hunters, and the essential non-combatants who stayed at the Lair. We had fun, teasing whoever was up for their group shot, making faces and trying to mess them up. Finally, it was the fighters' turn.

"Photo, you want us to split into our smaller groups?" Phoenix asked.

"What do you mean?"

"Well, we have the scouts, the snipers, the bashers, and explosives."

"Basher?" Driver asked. "How have I never heard of this before? I thought you all did the same thing."

"Bashers are people like Captain," Phoenix explained, grinning. "Basically, she hits men very hard until they fall down. You should see it sometime. It's a lot of fun."

"Wait," I protested. "We should get at least one with all of us together."

"All together, then," Photo said decisively. "Please."

We piled together at the edge of the meadow, on the slope, pine trees liberally covered in snow rising behind us. Someone—probably Phoenix—shoved me to the front of the group, and I slammed into Archangel. He grunted, stumbling a little.

"Sorry, sorry," I mumbled, turning pink.

"All good here." He smiled, those gorgeous, deep blue eyes so close.

The man was barely taller than me, which meant that all I'd have to do was lean forward a few inches to kiss him. I bit my lip to stop myself doing something I probably wouldn't regret that much and watched his eyes drop to focus on my mouth. Phoenix slammed into me, laughing and throwing me into Archangel's arms.

"Sorry," I gasped, clutching his jacket.

There were too many layers between us for me to feel his warmth, but who needed it when I was burning up inside? He kept one hand on my back as we turned to face the poor man trying to take a dignified photo of us.

There'd been several flashes already, and now he stood with a white-knuckled grip on his camera, his face twisted in a grimace. "Please stand still?"

"Oh, I don't know." Lavender watched us from the sides, her hands on her hips. "This seems entirely accurate to me. Unruly, unpredictable, and highly entertaining."

"Please?" Poor Photo looked so distressed.

"Okay, people," I called, taking pity on the man. "Straighten up."

Phoenix slung her arm over my shoulder and across my chest, her other one wrapped around Gryphon, laughing as she nudged me against Archangel. If I got any closer to him, I'd be crawling inside his clothes. Which was a very pleasant thought, in retrospect. Archangel slid his hand down to my waist and leaned into me, too.

Photograph brightened as he looked through the camera lens. "Look at me, please."

I focused on him, and the camera flashed.

***

"Knock their socks off," Phoenix whispered.

"Fuck you," I whispered back.

Everyone gathered in the garage, ready to go out for a couple months and draw Steve back into the Valley. I stood in the center of the group, panic sparking through my chest, making it hard to breathe. It being the first time going with both fighters and soldiers, I had to say something to them, and my brain wasn't coughing any ideas up.

How the hell had I ended up here? I'd barely graduated high school. Most of what I knew came out of books. *Fake it 'til you make it.* The words drifted across my mind, Kitten's voice sounding clearly. Terrible advice but the best I had under the circumstances.

The fighters slowly separated from their loved ones, tears giving way to restless energy. It needed to be directed, because this would be the longest we'd ever been away from the calm, steadying presence of the non-coms. I needed fighters to do what was right, not what was easy. I needed them to fight and kill. Mostly, I needed them to still be human at the end.

Half an idea flashed across my mind, and I went with it, not bothering to check and see where this might take me. "All in, all out," I shouted.

"One shot, one kill," they roared. "No luck, all skill!"

"The Old Constitution gave our founders the right to bear arms," I yelled when they'd quieted. "An armed, well-regulated, trained militia. It was to prevent any government from enslaving them. I reckon it's time to resurrect that." I had to raise my voice to be heard over the occasional whistle or cheer.

"We've got the training." I pointed to Seahorse, who gave a jaunty wave, and Sarge, who nodded. More cheers and whistles filled the garage, but they quickly quieted. "We have the arms." I pointed down the tunnels, to loud whoops. "Now. What are we fighting for?"

"To kick Steve's ass!"

"Kill Steve!" a woman shrieked. "Kill them all!"

"Kill! Kill! Kill!" It became a chant rising above the crowd.

I shook my head, but they weren't listening. Gryphon standing off to the right, gave me an inscrutable look, and Eleanor's dismay was unmistakable as she tried to calm the ones nearest her. The core group, Sirius, Phoenix, Driver, Lavender, Amana, and Seahorse, were trying to regain control, but it wasn't working.

They were turning into a mob.

Whoops.

I hunted frantically around the room, hoping for inspiration. I can do the shooty thing and the fighty thing, but apparently, my skills at the speechy thing were somewhat lacking. I found my anchor in Archangel. He watched me, dark blue eyes fierce, focused, and urging me on. He was tense, hands clenched as if willing me to figure it out. Exhaling, I gave him a quick nod. He could do this better than me, we both knew it, but these were my people.

"No!" I bellowed, leaping into the back of my pickup. "That's *not* what we're about." The ones nearest me slowly quieted, waiting to hear more. Some glared, as if not wanting to be all about killing people might make me a traitor. "If we fight only to kill, we're no better than Steve. They came to conquer and exterminate." A few still muttered, but the majority were listening. Thankfully. "We're fighting for our families, and to regain our homes. We're taking back what they stole."

I took a big breath and continued. "This shit's been happening for forever, people. Way back when this country was founded, they said they weren't afraid of the enemy's weapons. We're not afraid of a little fight, are we?"

"No!"

"Like them, back in the day, the only thing I'm afraid of is slavery. They did not fear death, and neither do I. Not fighting, not dying..."

"Hail the victorious dead!" Phoenix shouted to cheers.

"I'll happily die if it means everyone else is freed," I continued. Archangel frowned at my mention of death, but the crowd finally caught on. "I'm here to make sure as many of us as possible make it out of here, grow old, have kids, live like we're supposed to. I don't want to fight, but by all that's Holy, I will damn well do it if that's what it takes for others to live in peace because *I* don't fear death! Instead, we fight so that others can live in peace. We don't make war for war's sake. We're just finishing what Steve started."

"All in, all out," Phoenix cried, and let them do the rest.

"One shot, one kill. No luck, all skill!"

I hoped I had them on the right page, because I had no fucking clue where this would go when I started. The fighters streamed to the cars, and I moved back to make room for the others riding with me. My truck rumbled to life, Dereva's curly-haired silhouette a familiar, comforting sight in the driver's seat.

"Fuck me." Phoenix leaned her arms on the edge of the truck next to me. "You almost lost them."

"Next time, you're talking."

"Oh, *hell* no." She reared back, shaking her head violently.

Archangel and Gryphon silently joined me in the truck bed. Gryphon merely nodded, but Archangel rested a hand on my shoulder. I leaned into the warmth for a moment, hoping he didn't notice the pressure.

"Fine. Archangel can give the next one."

He grinned. "There's no way I'd have been able to bring them back from that."

"I don't believe you, but whatever. They would never have gotten that far if you did it."

Archangel shook his head, looking past me. "I don't know about that. They've dealt with experiences that I can't relate to. Those women were out for blood, but you brought them back to doing this for others, and peace. You got them where they needed to go."

The pickup rolled forward, gentle enough that I barely swayed with the motion. As quickly as that, we were off.

***

We spent one night together in a large, spread-out camp in the foothills to the north of the Lair. Eleanor settled next to me and pulled her latest project out of her satchel while I tended the stoves. Tiny little fires from stoves or open flame littered the hillside, most of them invisible unless you were within a few yards. We'd already gotten out of the snow, and everything here was cold and damp.

"Your speech was...interesting. I especially liked those elements from the Revolutionary War," she said, her hands moving quickly over her mending. "I especially noticed the bit where you paraphrased John Hancock."

"What?" I glanced up. "You got that?"

"You're not the only one who reads. I borrowed your books, remember?"

"Oh. Yeah."

After a long pause where all I could hear was water dripping from the trees and the occasional, small crack of a branch, she continued. "Did you know that people have been going to Ink with specific requests today? Tattoos they want to get when we're back at the Lair. The most common one," she paused to look at me directly, "is 'peace.'"

I let out a slow breath. "Not gonna lie, I wasn't expecting that."

"Between 'peace' and that whole 'All in, all out' stuff, we have a motto and a purpose. Don't you think it's time we had a name?"

"Shit." I scrubbed a hand over my face. "No. I mean, we're an irregular military unit. I think. Why do we need a name?"

"Solidarity. Aren't military units given names like 'Charlie Company?'" Finished mending the hat, she put it on and pulled out a sock with a hole in the heel and a pair of fine knitting needles.

"Hell if I know. We've got some soldier boys we could ask." I had a moment of inspiration. "You know what? Fuck—I mean fudge—tradition. Why don't you come up with a name?"

She nodded slowly, tucking away her knitting. "I think I'll ask for a bit of help, then." She smiled, rose, and wandered to another fire to continue being the mother we all needed right now.

When she returned, right before I turned in, she had a name. "We've decided on the Oregonian Irregulars," she told the small group in our circle. "And they want to keep that whole 'All in, all out' as our motto."

Shaking my head, I rolled up in my blanket. Just past midnight, I got up for my shift on guard duty. I'd managed to get Sirius to put me with my brother, and we walked the perimeter slowly, chatting quietly.

"I like the Irregulars," he said. "Though where did Eleanor come up with that?"

I shrugged, watching the forest. "Something about how the English were called Regulars, like, regular army, during the Revolution, and the American militias were irregular because they didn't follow the rules."

"We should just call ourselves the Irregulars. It's easier."

"Why not the Oregonians?"

"That's a newspaper. So, no."

I laughed quietly. "Fair enough."

"Though having two names might help confuse Steve. Make them think there's more of us than there is."

I snorted. Yeah, less than sixty fighters wasn't a scary amount by anyone's count. Then again, this time last year, we'd just been five. The rest of our shift passed quietly, talking about Grace and Charlie, and about what he'd been up to for the last year. The military was finally deployed on American soil, and it was as shitty as I'd always imagined it would be. They'd been brought in to help with the fallout from the bombings, relocating folks who were out of town when their homes were invaded or blown up.

Good times.

***

Once inside the Valley, we split into two groups, Seahorse and Sergeant Perry taking half the fighters south while I took the rest north. Down here, everything dripped. A light, misting rain drifted down, beading on clothing and hair. I had my beanie firmly pulled down over my ears. I was still dry, but then again, I had one of those rainproof jackets. We couldn't use too many of them, with their bright colors, but the ones that were nice and dark were used to augment the jackets left in our stores.

Seahorse's dark eyes were somber when she met me on foot, in between our two convoys. She looked comfortable in her too-big camo jacket, like the soldier she used to be.

"Give 'em hell," I said quietly. "But nothing too stupid. Run if you have to."

"Away, you mean?" She smiled slightly, her hands comfortably resting on her weapons. "Only if you promise to do the same."

"I don't know what you're talking about." I lifted my chin, looking down my nose at her. "I perform strategic retreats. Occasionally, screaming is involved."

Seahorse laughed. "Ah, so *that's* what that is."

We watched each other in silence for a moment before she leaned in. I pressed my forehead to hers, our thick knit hats protecting our heads. She rested her hands on my forearms. Mine cupped her elbows as we stayed there for a minute.

"Okay," she whispered, her breath puffing warm over my face.

"Yeah." I pulled away. "It's time."

After one last glance, she turned away and walked to her truck, circling her hand in the air. "Time to go, kids!"

I hopped in the back of my pickup at the front of the convoy. Dereva had the engine running, watching the southbound crew leave through her rearview mirror. "Do you think we'll see them again?"

"I reckon so." I watched them leave. Perry had my brother with him because he was too young to send with someone else. I couldn't say a damn thing about why I wanted to keep that particular soldier near me. Sirius had volunteered to go with the southern group, in part to keep an eye on him. "They know what they're doing." *Better than me, anyway.*

"Let's go," I called, waving for the whole convoy to see.

Behind me, vehicles rumbled to life while my little truck rolled forward.

CHAPTER 7

I walked at the head of an uneven line of fighters, following a grassy trail surrounding an overgrown cornfield. Scouts ranged to the sides, almost a mile out in some cases, watching our flanks and finding a route for us to follow. Reaching out, I trailed my fingertips over the rough, broad, yellow leaves of a cornstalk.

Left to itself, the corn surprised me. Most of it didn't—couldn't—re-seed itself, but the odd plant here and there managed, so the dead field had random clusters of newer corn interspersed with bushy weeds whose names I didn't know. The blue-green leaves provided a pretty contrast to the gold of the dead corn.

One benefit? We could see over the weeds, so Steve should be clearly visible. Bad news? Steve could see us, too. Hence the scouts.

After enduring three days of pouring rain, I enjoyed the watery sunlight, even if the breeze carried the promise of more rain by nightfall. Staying on the wet ridge of grass took some doing, but I really didn't want to slip into the thick mud again. I'd only just gotten the last of it off my boots.

We were deep in the Willamette Valley, farther than we'd dared go since the Invasion. There'd been sign of Steve out on foot. Maybe work details.

So, we'd left half the crew with the vehicles to see what chaos they could cause while we went out on foot just to fuck with Steve.

I cocked my head, something off about our surroundings, but unable to tell what it was. Holding up a hand to call a halt, I turned in a slow circle. No strange sounds. The few winter birds chirped and swooped, unalarmed by humans.

"What is it?" Sparrow, right behind me, whispered. Once the trophy wife of a wealthy judge or something, she'd since become our explosives expert.

It always fascinated me, how people developed interests far beyond what you'd expect. She looked like she'd been a model and had done what was expected of her during her marriage. Things like playing tennis, hosting parties, working out at the gym. Once free of those expectations, she'd become a satisfactory fighter and enthralled by making shit go boom. Flipping fantastic.

The entire line, which had been in relaxed silence, went tense and wary the instant I called a halt. Now, they crouched, peering across the fields, weapons in hand.

"Not sure." On my next breath, I caught a scent. Raising my head, I sniffed the air like a hound, following the smell to the south. Whatever it was, we were downwind of it. "Gunpowder." Finally, I had it.

"That could be any one of us, too," Sparrow murmured.

"Not like this. Not that direction." I waved, signaling them to hide. Now I knew why it took me so long to recognize the odd scent. I'd always smelled it freshly burned, right after firing a gun. This was...muted.

An ambush? Unlikely. Our purpose was to stir some shit and pull them away from our mountains. Steve couldn't figure out where we were headed to ambush us if we didn't even know where we were going.

"Do you believe Steve is close?" Sparrow fiddled with some small bottles and cloth.

"Probably. We should say hi."

Towards the back of the line, people began shifting. Storm soon came crawling to the front, her curly, strawberry blonde hair hidden under a knit cap to help her blend into her surroundings. Storm was the scout working the southern flank.

"How's Steve?" I asked. Her blue eyes widened in surprise. "Think we should pay 'em a visit?"

"I was just coming to tell you that Steve invited us." The young woman recovered quickly, a gleam of laughter in her eyes. "They're bored and lonely, just across the field there." She pointed slightly ahead and off to the south.

"Well. It'd be rude of us to come all this way and not stop by." Sparrow smiled at the younger woman, all sharp edges and anticipation.

I pulled the map out. "Tell me about the landscape. I need to see."

***

I bulled into an enemy soldier, knocking him flat and kicking him in the head before turning on a new victim. Their screams were muffled by the low clouds, and the familiar, burnt scent of gunpowder filled my nostrils. I spun, taking in the fight.

Smoke drifted across the field, created by Sparrow's tiny Molotov cocktails. We'd spread out, smaller, individual fights spawning off the first melee. Spotting Steve about to shoot one of my people, I palmed a compact pistol, firing rapidly, taking down as many enemies as I could before the fight shifted, swallowing me again. Forced back into close range, I holstered the pistol and switched back to two short swords.

The fight swirled and eddied, bringing me face-to-face with a soldier. I snarled into his bloody face, slashing high with my right, low with the left.

The man dropped with a scream, and I moved on, giving him a hefty kick as I passed. A rifle butt came out of nowhere, knocking my right sword out of my hand. Deadly silent, Archangel appeared next to me, slashing at Steve with his machete.

Ahead, a woman struggled amid a group of Steve, her hair obscuring her face. Howling, I abandoned the sword and slammed into the rear of the soldiers, Archangel right beside me. Fighting was never a blur anymore. I'd learned to see through the adrenaline, take advantage of weaknesses. Where to hit, when to stab...it wasn't long before I met the woman, Storm, halfway. She gave me a nod and turned to find a new fight.

Soon, I hunted for a fresh target and saw only my own people. Taking in my surroundings, the fight had trampled a circle in the corn and weeds, leaving it full of bloody mud and some bodies. All theirs, I noted. Archangel helped one of his own back up, a mid-twenties guy everyone called Gameboy for some reason.

"You alright?" he asked, coming over and putting a hand on my shoulder.

I nodded, snot running from my nose. I sniffed, coughed explosively, and wiped my nose to find it was blood. Shaking my head, I held a corner of my shirt to stanch the flow. After a minute I pulled it away and waited cautiously. Not running anymore. So much for a scent of fresh air. Might as well get back to the end of the fight.

"All right, sound off. Who's not dead?"

***

That night and now miles away from the ambush site, Archangel joined me at my tiny camp stove. "So. The way you rescued us is standard operating procedure for you, then?"

I gave him a guilty smile and hunched my shoulders. "Yes and no? I mean, we don't normally go running around in stupid little scraps of cloth. Are you telling me that flying by the seat of your pants and making shit up as we go isn't a good way to run things?"

After the fight, we'd bandaged our hurts, gathered the wounded, blessed the fact that no one was badly injured, and buggered off. We'd found a meadow near a river to spend the night. Now, most of us were spread out, eating and relaxing under cover. Without Sirius here, and Phoenix hanging with Gryphon, I spent most of my evenings alone, going over what limited information we had. Having company that didn't require anything from me was...wonderfully refreshing.

Archangel smothered a laugh.

"Don't get me wrong," I continued. "I'd love to have tons of info, know exactly where they are, and basically have the military might of the good ol' US of A behind us, but we work with what we got. If you have any ideas, I'm all ears, but in my experience, you can make all the plans you want, but fucking Murphy will ruin every single one."

"Who's Murphy?" he asked, bewildered. "Is there someone I missed?"

I giggled. "Murphy's Law. Though that would've been a good name for Steve, too."

"Gotta admit," Archangel got comfortable, pulling out his MRE, "it's pretty damn fantastic, having all the intel you need. So, what have you guys done? Lured them into an ambush?"

"Yep."

"And they're always terrible in the mountains?"

"When they're on foot for longer periods of time, yeah." I considered the ambushes. "Going back to setting lures, we've actually done a few different types. If you have women, though, they always follow. Maybe we should up the ante and make the women look less threatening. No obvious weapons or something."

The pot lid rattled, steam escaping its edges and temporarily distracting me with making tea to go with dinner. As soon as I poured the water, we got back to the discussion, talking all through the meal. Around us, the camp slowly settled as fighters found their beds, some of them—mostly female, with a couple of preapproved male/female pairings—doubling up to share warmth. The rain came back, and we wrapped up in blankets while we spoke.

Later still, after we'd nursed our tea for as long as possible, we continued talking. Silly stuff, like movies, books, favorite foods. I got hung up on desserts. I hadn't had a dessert in over a year. Canned peaches do not count. There was no responsibility, no reining in hotheads, or having to be seen as the fearless leader that Sirius liked to call me. We were just a man and a woman talking over a little fire.

Those times when you talk and can't see their faces...that's when it's easiest to share deep thoughts, but this time, we kept it light. I was free to study his face, the way his mouth quirked at the corner when he smiled, and I finally saw a tiny dimple, nearly hidden in his left cheek. His eyes were shadowed, occasionally revealed as a dark blue glint. He watched me just as intently, but there was no self-consciousness. There couldn't be, not at this tiny little fire in the early evening, not after the fight earlier.

A shadow loomed out of the dark, pale skin making her easy to see. "It's a school night," Phoenix whispered. "You both should be in bed by now." Half-seen hands rested on her hips while she scolded us.

"Yes, mom." Archangel grinned, his teeth white in the dark.

I clamped my hands over my mouth to muffle my shout of laughter, toppling slowly over to lie on the ground, squealing and snorting with glee.

Archangel looked from Phoenix to me, and back again. "I really don't think it was that funny." Confusion filled his voice.

"She gets weird when she's tired." Phoenix heaved a long-suffering sigh. "Just...go to sleep, both of you. Or she'll be useless tomorrow."

Bedding down was simple as pillowing my head on my pack. Archangel settled down facing me, a few feet away. The patter of droplets striking the leaves lulled me to sleep.

***

Two days later, I slid slowly down a steep slope, one hand trailing behind me for balance. All around, rustling in the underbrush and the occasional curse let me know nobody had lost control yet. I dug my heels into the loam to slow myself a little more, checking for landmarks on the hills around. My rifle, the strap securely over my shoulder and across my chest, caught the ground, the butt dragging and knocking against the swords crossed over my back, hitting my head.

I cursed, mouthing a whole string of words I didn't dare say out loud, not this close to our destination. We'd caught up with our trucks, driven a few more hours. Now, we'd hidden the vehicles and taken everyone except the drivers up and over two ridges to the main highway, 99E, somewhere near Oregon City.

This was one of the few roads still in good repair, which meant frequent use. The other side of the 99 was bordered by the Willamette River, and this side was a slope a few degrees away from a cliff, thickly covered in trees and bushes. Steve would never expect an ambush here, mostly because *I* wasn't sure we'd make it down without giving the game away.

I continued my walk/slide down, yanking on the bag in my left hand to unstick it from a bush. The contents clinked and when it swung back, the damn thing jabbed my leg. Again. Half the group remained higher, ready to rain fire down on Steve. A few of us were going all the way to the bottom to lay out a nail strip and landmines. I got the nail strip. At this point, I'd prefer the landmines.

My boots touched pavement seconds before the others in our advance group.

"Contact left!" Jewel, positioned on the southern edge, shouted.

So much for the plan, then.

The low-lying clouds muffled all sound until they'd gotten too close to avoid. Whoopee. Looks like the ambushers just got ambushed. Dumping the strip out, I flung it across the road while Goliath and Jewel opened fire. Steve returned our fire, the large caliber bullets putting holes in the hillside.

We backed into the bushes and the Chimera shot past, over the strip. It spun in a circle before slewing to a halt in the middle of the road, facing the direction they'd just come. In the precious time it took for their gunner to reorient himself, the Irregulars hurled themselves into the cover of the trees. Safely ensconced, I positioned myself in time to see another truck appear out of the fog.

"Well, fuck me," I commented, sighting on the second Chimera.

"Later, for sure." Archangel tossed me a quick grin and nestled his cheek against his rifle stock.

"What?" I choked, staring at him longer than I should have.

The second truck wasted no time, firing blindly into the trees—right at us. A barrage of gunfire strafed the air, forcing us to hunker down. I found myself belly down behind a tree, my rifle underneath me and no memory of how I'd gotten there. Then, I wished my tree was bigger, being barely ten feet from the road. Bullets whistled past and all I could do was stay as flat as possible and hope the other half of the Irregulars were still above the firing line.

A chunk of tree disappeared just above my head, and I flinched. The others. How were the others handling this? I hissed and slapped the ground to get the attention of those around me. "Sound off. How's everyone doing?"

"Still here."

"I don't like this!"

"No one does."

"Pissing my pants, ma'am," Grandpa admitted a few feet to my left. He looked barely old enough to drive, much less join the army. His brown hair, grown long since joining us, lay flat against his skull, but he was smiling as if he found all this fun.

"I never asked, Gramps, but did you lie to join the army? And if so, was it worth it?" Archangel called, grinning even as the bullets flew over his head.

Idiots.

The only injuries mentioned were caused by flying splinters, and no sooner had the last report come in than I started. A sliver the size of a small branch flew past, grazing the skin above my eye. "Fuck!" I clapped a hand to my eye, blood running between my fingers.

"Yo, Captain, coming in." Phoenix dashed in from the rear, going into a full baseball dive and sliding to a stop next to me. "How's your eye? Let me see it."

"It's fine," I grumbled. "What the fuck are you doing, leaving your cover like that? This is literally a scratch."

"Macho, macho man," she sang softly, pouring a bit of alcohol from a small flask onto my scratch. "Hold still," she scolded.

"I don't know if we really have time for this." I waved vaguely at the twigs and bits of evergreen falling around our heads, bullets still peppering everything. "You do know we're in the middle of something here, right?"

"Just gotta make sure your eye's fine." Phoenix stared intently at my eyebrow and face, turning my head gently and probing with her fingertips, her eyes fierce. "Won't do anybody any good if you're blinded, dumbass. Fucking hell." She shook her head. "Half an inch lower and you'd've lost it. Gonna have another nice scar through your eyebrow."

"At least it's the same eye." My left eyebrow had no luck at all. Or maybe, it had tons of luck. Two near misses.

Finally deciding I wasn't in danger of dying from the scratch, she slapped a bandage on it. "She's fine," she called, reassuring those who had the attention to spare.

Phoenix stayed, plastered to my side, while we waited for a lull in Steve's fire. I kept my face pressed against the base of the tree, one eye on the shapes barely visible through the fog. Finally, the moment we'd been waiting for happened. The barrage paused.

A quick twist and I had the rifle in front of me, stock firmly against my shoulder. I fired first, the others joining in. We didn't waste time shooting at the armored sides, no. We shot out their tires, radiators, and kept the gunners' heads down.

To my right and slightly forward, Archangel and Goliath sent short lengths of pipes skipping over the asphalt. An explosion forced me to duck, shielding my eyes, and when I could see again, one vehicle remained unharmed but the other had a scorch mark. Before Steve had a chance to react, the boys lobbed another set, going high this time.

The explosions cleared the fog, pushing it back, and I caught a glimpse of a butt snaking over the ground, the round cheeks sticking up a bit too high. Steve, heading for the river. I fired, aiming at the soldier's ass, and was gratified to see him shoot forward, splashing into the water. In these temperatures, they weren't likely to die of hypothermia unless they were stupid about the aftermath.

This lot managed to be sneaky, utilizing their limited cover to get to safety. Phoenix, next to me, kept the gunners' heads down, giving us a chance to actually implement part of our ambush, though she couldn't stop all the small arms fire.

Another pipe bomb flew high, this one aimed at the far side of the Chimeras, where Steve was trying to find safety in the water. The explosion pushed more fog away. Men, hidden by the slope, screamed, or whimpered, but the worst were the ones whose cries sounded...wet. Return fire from Steve kicked up a notch, forcing us down again.

"About time to go?" Phoenix asked, her head bare inches away as we shared the scant cover of a single tree.

"Fuck no. Not in this mess. Something has to change, though."

This explosion rocked the ground and a fireball rose where the second Chimera used to be. The heat of it flattened us to the ground, along with all the vegetation, removing our cover. It also cleared the last of the fog in our general vicinity.

I had seconds to gauge the situation. Half our advance group lost their cover in the bushes. To my right, Goliath was down and Archangel, his beanie knocked askew, struggled to lift the giant. Steve, seeing us like sitting ducks, lined up their sights.

The only thing I could think of to spoil their aim was to change the distance between us and them.

"Charge!"

Suiting action to words, I slung my rifle over my shoulder, drew a gun and one of the short, katana-style swords and barreled across the short distance between us, screaming the entire way.

***

Panting, I hauled ass up the hill in a fast bear crawl, hot on Archangel's heels, grief a tight knot in my chest. Death always came too suddenly. I was the last in a line of Irregulars, strung out up the hill. Ahead, I caught glimpses of Jewel's black hair, still in its battle braids, hanging down Gryphon's back. She'd been hit in the charge, dead before she touched the ground.

"Are they still following us?" Archangel gasped. He lugged the large Black soldier, Goliath, across his shoulders in a fireman's carry. Goliath was unconscious, but if we could get him to safety—to Eleanor and Squirrel—then he had a chance.

"Yes. But..." I checked the landmarks. "It's still a quarter mile to the second point."

"I really..." He paused, chest heaving while he struggled to catch his breath. "...wish we didn't...have to do this...blind."

Because if we'd had drones, unlimited resources, or even fucking radios, we'd have known that those two trucks were an advance for a full caravan heading north and not the usual one to two truck patrols. Shouts from our pursuers mingled with excited barking. Bastards were using dogs, just like Shrike had warned.

I bared my teeth and started up the slope again. "Yeah, well, you had intel when you first got here. Fat lot of good that did." We rounded a sharp bend. "Oh, give me a second. I just need to..."

Pausing briefly, I kicked some wooden chocks out from under a bunch of rocks, climbed above them and, gripping a sturdy branch overhead, stomped on the whole mass. I dangled from the branch when the pile gave way, watching the large rocks bounce and roll down the hill, tearing through Steve's lines. Hours to set up, seconds to dislodge.

I cast one more glance down the hill where Jewel—beautiful, bold, opinionated Jewel—had seen her last. I'd known her for over a year and now.... Biting my lip, the physical pain brought me back to the present. No time to give into grief here. When we were back at the Lair, then I could offer my tears up, that someone I'd known was gone.

Archangel waited on the path above me, his beanie askew, exposing one ear, reddened by the cold, to the winter air. Goliath's long legs hung around his right arm, and he leaned to the left to compensate for the weight. "It's always a crapshoot," he said quietly, offering his hand to help me up a steep section.

Grasping his hand allowed me to feel just how cold my fingers were. He held my hand a moment longer than necessary, waiting for me to find my footing. Balancing on the edge of the slope, I tugged his beanie back over his ears, then yanked my gloves out of the pouch and pulled them on.

"Don't wait around here. I can go faster than you. Get moving!"

He flicked a small salute and dug his toes into the earth, looking for purchase. Below, the screams and shouts were just beginning to die away. The whining and yelps from the dogs were the worst. I hated hurting them, but it was either that or be caught, which I'd hate even more.

A hundred yards up the slope and around another bend, fighters slowly exited the obvious trail wherever they could find a spot that wouldn't leave tracks. Every person hauling the injured or dead was accompanied by a second to act as a guard and backup. At the bend, I pulled my secret weapon out of my pack: a bag full of ground black pepper. Amana would be pissed when she discovered I was the one who'd taken it all.

Scattering the pepper generously over the path behind me, I followed Archangel as he continued past the exit points. I paused here and there, smudging a print and scattering some fir needles or more black pepper. Satisfied that I'd done what I could in the time I had, I gave it one last look to ensure I hadn't missed anything obvious before stepping through fragrant fir branches, onto a root, and disappeared off the trail.

***

That chase marked the true start to our campaign to pull Steve out of the mountains. For the first time, we ranged as far west as the coastal mountains, swung north, almost to Portland, and back east. Along the way, we fought everyone. Most encounters were hit and run, but sometimes we stopped a little longer, causing some serious damage, when we found captives.

Once, it was four families held at an outpost, working the land, plantation style. The overseers, white men wearing the red armbands that marked them as Dorothy (because 'North American Liberation Corps' is too fucking long to say), even carried whips, and they liked using them.

We left them hanging, overlooking the fields, and burned the buildings. All that, only to be confronted by the former captives, huddled together for safety.

"Why should we go with you?" asked their spokesman, a man in his forties. "Nobody helps anyone for free. Not around here."

I surveyed my fighters, all of us dusty, sweat stained, with dirty bandages peeking through torn clothing. Ah, yes. We were glowing examples of humanity. No wonder they didn't trust us on sight alone. The reason for the spokesman's distrust hid behind him—two teenaged girls trying desperately to avoid the gazes of the men.

"I get you don't trust us," I said, then waved at the black smoke billowing into the sky, "but you sure you wanna stay with this? Steve ain't exactly gonna be thrilled when they get here, y'know."

"Not helping," Eleanor murmured, stepping around me and walking slowing towards the families, her hands extended out from her sides, palms facing them. "I know what you're feeling," she said, her voice low and soothing. "Just a year ago, I was almost where you are now." Carefully, using only her thumb and forefinger, she pulled down her waistband, showing the letter K branded on her right hip. Every woman taken by Steve was branded. Over half the fighters had one.

I swung back to the vehicles, filled with produce from the small farm's cellars. A tiny group, four people total, were already herding the animals into the forest. They would take a long, slow route to the Lair and then Home, while we drew Steve's eye.

"Hurry it up," I called. "We've been here twenty minutes, which is fifteen too long."

"How would you know?" Dereva gibed. "Not like anybody has a watch."

I blew a raspberry at the driver. "Can it. You're just jealous."

"Of what?" she taunted. "Your looks? Nope. Driving? Still nope. The only thing you do marginally better than me is beat up poor, unsuspecting Steve."

"Brat!" We danced around each other until I got in a shot, smacking her butt hard enough for the crack to carry through the cold air.

"Captain!" Eleanor left off convincing the rescued to scold me, going so far as to shake her finger. "Some dignity, please."

"Are they coming, or not?" Phoenix shouted from her perch in the back of the GMC. "Because if we leave now, we have a chance of not being chased for two days."

Within two minutes, the families were loaded and we pulled out, taking the beat-up van Dorothy had been using with us.

**

"You know," Eleanor regarded me, her arms crossed, "if you could just stay civil and maybe *not* say everything that crosses your mind, we wouldn't have to work so hard to convince people to run away with us."

We squatted next to the pickup so she could chew me out in privacy. Our camp lay in the middle of a weed-strewn corn field, half a mile from a nice grove of trees. The vehicles were parked in the valley between two shallow hills, our camp spread all around. The dry corn stalks were barely tall enough to provide concealment, and best of all, you had to be in it to realize how much you could fit in there.

Good places to camp in the Willamette Valley were like hide-and-seek. Don't choose the obvious spot and try not to be camp shaped. Without fires, we simply ate and went to sleep, unless you were getting the third degree from Eleanor.

"Bold of you to assume that anything that comes out of my mouth crossed my mind in the first place." I cringed away from Eleanor's playful swipe. "But it's not fair! We'd just freed them *and* killed their captors. How much nicer do I need to be?"

Eleanor glared at me. Guess that wasn't very convincing.

I pouted. "I'll try to be nicer," I said grudgingly.

***

Three days and another skirmish later, the families didn't look any more comfortable, but they stopped flinching every time I looked their way. That was progress. They were a little happier when we took out a patrol keeping a young woman captive. The families opened their arms to her, and then they slowly warmed up to us.

We called the rescued teen Nebula, for the blue ends of her hair, and she became inseparable from Dereva, Hightide, and Sweetpea. Heaven help me, Dereva was building an army within an army. Before too long, every teenager would be her best friend and they'd all listen to her.

Maybe not such a bad idea.

The days blended into an adrenaline-fueled round of running, chasing, hiding, and fighting. Sometimes we had vehicles, sometimes we went on foot. We all suffered minor injuries and half the time, I couldn't tell where I'd gotten mine. The more seriously injured, like Goliath, were left with the vehicles until they could be taken back to the Lair.

Every day, we became a little more ragged around the edges, and the soles of our boots got thinner. The only thing still looking good were our weapons. The nights were spent sleeping on cold ground, without sleeping pads, until I could tell when someone was sleeping standing up. We had to double up, two people to a single blanket so that our...guests...could stay warm. Even with that, they still viewed us as dangerous animals.

I huddled over my stove one evening, forced into close proximity by the lay of the land. Around me, fighters snuffled, snorted, and coughed, making the kinds of noises that slowly drove me insane.

A hand on my shoulder startled me out of my building rage and crowded mind. I twisted, ready to lash out only to find Archangel.

"Come on," he murmured. "I need to get out of here, and so do you."

Gratefully, I ditched my dinner and left my tiny fire to burn itself out in the next minute. Away from the camp and its accompanying noises, the tension flowed out of my shoulders.

"That's better," he grinned. "I can see your ears, now."

"Thank you." I smiled slowly.

He spread a spare jacket on the ground and held out his hand to help me down. I didn't need it, but any excuse to feel human warmth...I bit my lip when he sat comfortably next to me. "Maybe I just wanted an excuse to get you alone."

He gave me a sideways glance and a quick smile. I ducked my head, grinning, and companionably bumped his shoulder. I couldn't resist leaning against him, trying to figure out how to lead into the question I wanted to ask.

"Will you spit it out?" he eventually said. "I can hear the gears turning and they're starting to smoke."

I blew out a breath. "Okay, but you asked for it." I watched the moon play peek-a-boo through the clouds. "Why is it that, for a mission this important, only six of you had any real experience while the rest were barely out of basic training? If this mission was so important, and considering how dangerous things are, I would've expected more."

He huffed a quiet laugh, shaking his head. "The million-dollar question. We don't know. Hendricks refused to say, but I'd bet an ice cream shop he didn't know. Orders are orders in the military, and we were pulled from different units. I know why I was sent in."

"Mm?"

"Let's just say I pissed the wrong person off," he said easily.

I waited, but he kept his mouth shut. I made a small, frustrated sound, but he didn't take the bait. "Fine. But it feels like, if we could get an answer to that, things would begin making a lot more sense. The more I learn, the more questions I have."

"You and me, both."

We sat in companionable silence until the cold became too much to ignore. He rose, helping me to my feet. We wandered back to camp, and I sighed. They were asleep. I found Dereva by the pickup and Archangel bid me goodnight before going to find his own bunkmate. Squirming down next to my driver, the blanket nearly covered me, but I'd long since learned that as long as my butt and back were warm, I could sleep.

***

The days rolled on.

Send the non-combatants and injured back to the Lair, skirmish, run, lure Steve into a trap, stand and fight, steal a car, steal some food. Nights on cold, lumpy ground, not enough blankets, rain, mud, and twice, snow in the Valley, though it never stuck.

I forgot what it was like to be warm. To go to bed without having to wear every item of clothing I'd brought with me. To be clean. Dry socks were worth a fortune, so it's a good thing there weren't any to be had.

Any time I looked at Phoenix, I could practically see her brain fry when she saw Gryphon. Who could blame her? The actor turned basher was hot, a good fighter, and kindness radiated off him. Until he got into a fight, then he turned stone cold.

The female fighters got leaner, meaner, and I saw familiar, angry, single-minded fire in their eyes. They seemed determined to finish the fight this winter. Willing to do anything if it meant ending the war right here, right now. Some of them were close to crossing a line they'd never be able to come back from, on the verge of a vicious disregard for the lives of the others.

So, I sicced Eleanor on them.

All I had to do was suggest someone might enjoy her company. Then Eleanor would brush their hair, help them with their meals, hold their hands and talk softly, slowly drawing them out. Eleanor has a capacity to care that is truly terrifying in a wonderful, incredible way.

During all this, Steve flailed around, a cumbersome machine that couldn't operate quickly enough to really deal with us. More troops flooded the Valley, to the point we knew they had to be pulling them out of the mountains.

Our methods were as odd as our names, and it drove the methodical, logical enemy nuts. Their answer was to make themselves more cumbersome. Now, they traveled in convoys, not in small patrols. We'd made too many disappear. Tanks rumbled over the roads daily, tearing up the asphalt and making them difficult to drive on.

Assholes.

I'd still take it, if it kept them away from the Lair.

CHAPTER 8

Man 1: I told you my man would win the election.

Man 2: So what? I've still had to scramble to keep my business going. Even producing those ridiculous EMs isn't enough to replace the revenue I've lost from firearms.

Transcript of phone call, January 6, 2053

I spun, looking desperately for a way out.

How had we gotten to this point? It'd all seemed routine. Well, as routine as we'd had on this trip. We'd spotted the same truck rolling down a small lane through hazelnut orchards, in and out, two days in a row. So, we went looking for their destination.

Like so many others, it was full of women. Their ages ranged from mid-teens to mid-twenties. They were clean, eyes dull, uncaring of what went on around them, completely disinterested in the world until we broke down their door. Outside, we'd left their guards lying where they fell. Steve could do whatever the hell they wanted with the bodies.

So many people kept in such depression leaves a mark, even in a house as spacious as this one, but that's not what made Phoenix's eyes burn with a feral light.

The two-story house could've fit my home inside it twice over with room to spare, but that's not what made me snarl.

Every window was barred, but that's not what made Archangel curse with a creativity that would've made a sailor proud.

All the doors were solid wood with strong locks, but that's not what made Eleanor breathe the Lord's name in a prayer of deliverance.

No. It was that every woman in the place was heavily pregnant.

So, in the finest brand-new traditions of the Irregulars, we packed them up, into a transport we'd found hidden in the barn, and burned the place to the ground. Maybe burning it wasn't our best idea, because it led us to where I currently sat: Trapped, with no way out.

I took in our location, calculating options. Steve had us pinned on the banks of a wide, deep river, unable to cross without exposing ourselves. The thick underbrush and a few downed trees provided some cover, enough to keep us from dying wholesale, but we were still fucked, our backs to a river that...

I grinned.

"What? What?" Phoenix edged closer. "I recognize that look. We're about to do something really stupid or really smart, depending on how it ends."

Those nearest us perked up at her words and a lot of people glanced at me as if I were about to sprout wings. "I need two groups. Soldiers stay here. I need you to start building." I grabbed a piece of driftwood and hurled it onto a downed tree. "You guys like digging, right?"

"What do you have in mind?" Archangel turned away from the forest. Lines of exhaustion showed at the corners of his eyes, a scratch on his cheek his only color, but he gripped his handgun, ready to march straight into Steve's lines if I asked him.

"Build a barricade. Your choice how it comes together. You guys are gonna be bait, so whatever keeps you breathing." Some of the men, needing no more than that, got to work. Tiny folding shovels were produced, and they got to work, moving dirt, rocks and wood around.

"Why bother?" A big soldier called Bruiser spoke up. "All we have to do is get rid of a little extra weight…" He shot a significant glance at the rescued women. "They'll lose interest in us."

"Shut the fuck up, Bruiser," Archangel snarled. "We already know you're a moron. You don't have to prove it."

"What about us?" Phoenix watched me, her eyes sparkling.

"We're going hunting."

"What? No." Gryphon edged over, keeping the bulk of his attention on the trees. "You should be sending the soldiers. They're trained for this."

"Not like we are." I dropped my pack, stripping to the bare minimum—pants, long sleeve t-shirt, and moccasins—and began putting my weapons back on, strapping everything down snugly. The other women and young Thorin followed suit.

Archangel grabbed the big man's arm. "She's right. In five minutes, it'll be more dangerous here. We draw their fire, keep their attention on us. How safe they are depends on how well we do our job. Besides," he glanced at the pregnant women huddled by the water's edge, "they need us."

"Hey." Sparrow opened her pack, pulling out little packages and fixing a small mess of wires to each one. "I'm staying here. These," she hefted the little bomb, "will be more useful to these guys. And I don't know if they can get wet," she added under her breath.

"I like the way you think." I finished the last of my checks. "Everybody else…" Fifteen women and one young man watched me expectantly. "Water looks deep, don't it?"

"Ah, fuck you, Captain." Phoenix scrunched her nose. "I hate cold water."

I flicked her butt. "Me too. Should be fun, eh? Listen up, guys, this is loosely what I hope happens…"

***

The water carried me quickly, dragging me along the river bottom. I snatched at rocks as I flew past, pulling myself lower. I had no idea how deep the river was, and the thought of my butt surfacing and getting shot was great incentive to stay down.

My lungs grew tighter, begging me to surface, aching for a breath. Occasionally, a hand grasped my ankle, or another body brushed mine as we crawled the river. Finally, I couldn't take it anymore, my lungs screaming for air. I'd rather be shot than drown.

Pushing off the riverbed, I shot for the surface, grabbing what I could of other people as I passed. I'd prefer staying close together, but however it happened, it happened. Surfacing, I gasped, sucking in lungfuls of sweet, sweet air.

No bullets peppered the water, and the sound of gunfire was loud, but muffled, the trees blocking some of the noise and the occasional deeper *boom*. More heads broke the surface, and I counted each one as we crawled onto the shore and into the trees.

"Thirteen, fourteen, fifteen..." I looked around anxiously. "Where's Feisty?" Shaking heads and muttering met my question. Stepping carefully over the river rocks, I hustled down to the water's edge. I spotted the girl's hair downstream, sleek and shining in the watery sunlight. Waving, I contemplated jumping to get her attention, but she spotted me before I made an idiot of myself and waved back just before disappearing around the bend.

"She good?" Phoenix asked, her breath puffing white in the chill air.

The fighters shivered while they readied weapons and I struggled to make numbed fingers work to loosen the straps on mine. "Apparently, she can hold her breath longer than the rest of us." I stripped off my shoulder harnesses to pull my shirt off and wring it out. It wasn't warm, but it had stopped dripping.

Phoenix laughed quietly. "You could go into a fight like that." She nodded at my leather bra, the lacings on the front revealing the only hint of cleavage I'd ever had in my life. "Steve would be so distracted they wouldn't put up a fight."

"Super comfy, aren't they?" I gave her a meaningful glance. "I just wonder how close it is to the real deal." It was a dick move, but I couldn't resist reminding her about our discussions about the bras, and a certain actor.

She flushed a deep, fire-engine red. I grinned, about to put my foot in my mouth, but her fingers were flexed into claws. Perhaps this one time, discretion was the better part of valor. We really didn't need her murdering me right now.

"We're ready to go, Captain." Evenstar, Thorin's mother, pulled me from my fun, her lips tightly compressed. "Any time."

Her husband had died in a failed ambush earlier this year. Or last year. We'd taken her off rotation since the Ridge, but she'd insisted on helping with this campaign. Kestrel had given her the okay to return to the field. So far, she'd performed all right, but her sharp edges only grew sharper.

I soon found myself shirted once more and creeping through the brush, stepping high over a fallen branch. To my left, Phoenix was little more than a shadow. Evenstar was the next fighter to my right.

Movement two dozen yards ahead. I crouched lower, moving cautiously. Making use of every bit of cover, I worked my way closer, scooping up a hefty rock along the way. Despite his role as lookout, Steve clearly had his attention on the fight behind him. A breeze kicked up, hiding any telltale movements in the foliage around me and cutting right through my wet clothes.

I shivered again and bit my lip, focusing. Rising from behind a tree, I raised the rock and stepped out while his back was turned. Some whisper must have given me away, because he turned and started at the sight of me, his rifle held low. We stared at each other a moment, me with my rock high, he with his rifle halfway to his shoulder.

"Awkward," I said.

The soldier gaped, gasped, and crumpled to reveal Evenstar with a bloody knife in her hand. "What?" she snapped. "Were you planning to stare at each other all day?"

I held my hands out helplessly, still gripping the rock. When she frowned at it, I dropped it and tried to kick it behind, but she'd already turned back to the fight.

What followed was bloody work. The bulk of the small army concentrated on our soldiers and the pregnant women. In our area, at Steve's rear, small fights broke out. The fighters teamed up in groups of two or three to take down a man, then moving on to find their next target, finding the battle partners they preferred. The fighting was all hand-to-hand in an attempt to stay quiet and get us closer before the majority of Steve noticed.

I hunted for fresh targets, short swords in hand, moving quickly through the woods. Wet hair, the same color as an otter's pelt, caught my eye about thirty feet away. Feisty tangled with Steve, darting in and out, knife low, then high, but the man held her off. His partner lunged at Ink, who stayed at her friend's side.

While the girls kept Steve busy, I sheathed the swords and drew a gun, checking the mag. Fully loaded, as it should be. Firing pin looked clear and in good order. I nodded. Feisty danced around the soldier, slashing and spinning, but she couldn't keep that up long. Another pair of soldiers, spotting the fighters, headed over.

I nodded again. Couldn't keep quiet forever and return fire from the riverbank was slowing, so it was time to switch it up. "Feisty, down," I bellowed.

The teenager dropped immediately. The moment she moved, I fired. He'd barely hit the ground when Feisty slipped behind Ink's opponent, neatly slitting his throat. I lined up on the two who were now running at the fighters and dropped them. Only three missed.

Not bad, me.

"That took you way too long," Phoenix shouted as she ran past, tackling a soldier hiding behind a bush. Trust Phoenix to count my shots in the middle of a fight.

"Fuck shit up, kids!" I waved to Ink and Feisty. Time for the bigger guns.

More and more Irregulars switched to firearms, Steve's rear finally becoming aware of our presence. Things turned into a regular firefight, although we were spread out enough that Steve didn't have anywhere near as many targets as we did.

"I hope you guys are ready," I muttered, wishing I could talk to our soldiers.

Once we had Steve's full attention and they began turning away from the beleaguered group trapped on the riverbank, I waved to Phoenix. She let out a piercing whistle and we slowly retreated towards the river, allowing Steve to push us back.

Storm dashed past me, turning on a dime to take cover behind a tree, her gun up and firing steadily. "Go," she barked.

I ran a dozen paces past her, finding myself a secure spot. "Go," I yelled, the word echoed up and down our line.

Steve formed a ragged line, an implacable march towards us. They were close enough I could see mouths twisted, but not so close I could make out the whites of their eyes. Enough distance, then. Sarge had drilled us on this very maneuver until we could do it in our sleep, covering each other so that no one was too exposed. I didn't like firing so rarely, but we had to make Steve think we were on the run.

"C'mon, guys," I whispered, firing carefully. "Where's my signal?"

"The river's just there," Phoenix shouted as she passed me. "Ten yards!"

"Get to it and wait for the signal." I zeroed on a flash of movement, waiting until I saw it again before firing.

Phoenix waved her arms. "The river!" she screamed, leading the way to find a spot to use as cover.

I waited for Phoenix to call the last line back before moving. Turning, I spotted someone who wasn't retreating. Evenstar.

"Hey!" I ran over. "Didn't you hear? Fall back."

Evenstar took a firmer grip on her handgun, leaning her left shoulder harder into the tree. "You go. Someone should stay and provide cover."

"That's what the fucking signal is for." I put my back to hers, peering around the other side of the tree. "Get moving!"

"No," she shouted. "They took Daniel from me." Her voice shook.

Ah, fuck. It was what I'd been afraid of. Fuckfuckfuckfuck. "What about Thorin?" I wished I knew the boy's real name. That might've gotten her attention.

"He's grown into a good man. He has friends and all of you. Daniel only has me." Her shoulders trembled, then squared resolutely.

"Fine." I slumped, then sighted at Steve. "I'm staying with you, then."

She jabbed me with her elbow. "Don't be stupid. They need you."

"Mom!" Thorin screamed from the river, crawling over the downed tree they hid behind. "What are you doing?"

"I'm avenging your father," she shouted back, never moving from her position. "Someone needs to."

"Mom, please! Please come with me," he begged.

"Your father needs me right now." Her voice shook and she shifted at my back.

I stepped forward slightly, firing rapidly, switching to a fresh gun as soon as I emptied one. Only one left. Boy better hurry up and convince her...

Footsteps could barely be heard over the gunfire, and then next time he spoke, he was mere feet away. "Mom, this isn't the time. If you come away now, you can get way more than if you stayed here."

Steve surged forward a dozen feet, bullets flying thickly. I fired as much as I could, more concerned with not dying this instant than the conversation now taking place somewhere around my knees. Suddenly, a hand tapped my thigh.

"Cap'n," Thorin said urgently. "Let's go."

I backed after them, swapping mags as I went. "Oh? How nice, we've all come to a logical decision. I didn't really feel like dying today, anyway."

Noticing that we'd barely returned fire after their last push, Steve went into an all-out charge. Sudden gunfire erupted behind me, cutting down the first row. I sprinted towards the river, right on mother and son's heels.

"Where's my damn signal?" I bellowed to the sky.

The signal began as a tremble through the earth, the force of the explosion growing until I staggered, lost my balance, and face planted. Hot wind gusted, blasting the light under brush, and taking all sound with it. Time passed. I lifted my head, blinking rapidly, swiping frantically at my eyes to clear the dust. I tapped my ears, clearing them out with a finger, but blood rushing was all I could hear. Hopefully, it'd be temporary.

Rolling over, I knocked into Evenstar, lying stunned next to me. Shaking her, I shouted (I hope), "Wake up!" My words came as if from underwater, murky, the consonants blurring.

She stirred slightly. Good enough. Dragging her up, I shoved her towards the water. She staggered a couple steps and bent suddenly. I paused, afraid she was about to puke, but she just pulled Ink to her feet, the two of them steadier together. Thorin, moving under his own steam, followed them, grabbing others as he went.

The river stretched in front of me, wide, deep, and absolutely beautiful—if we could cross before Steve got their shit together. I counted heads as the fighters waded into the water, and only once everyone entered did I follow. Panting, I squealed when the water touched my belly. Lunging forward, I swam towards the middle. The far bank was too steep to climb, but we might be able to find a low spot downstream...

A second explosion poured more smoke and flames into the sky, the column rising to the clouds. I breathed out in relief. My ears still worked. *How often can a person be deafened before it becomes permanent?* I wondered. "Downstream," I shouted, turning to watch the bank for any sign of movement. "Let's not wait for Steve to wake up."

A splash and a merry laugh brought a grin to my face. "Can I offer an alternative?" Dereva shouted. "We're already collecting the others."

Twisting, I saw Dereva standing atop the bank, her hands on her hips in a full-on Wonder Woman pose. The watery sunlight shone on the blonde streak running through her brown hair. I thought she'd never looked more beautiful. A rope trailed through the water, the other end disappearing behind her.

"You beauty!" I shouted, treading water. "Marry me!"

"How'd you manage to find us?" Phoenix asked. A good question, since the last we'd seen of her, we'd been thirty miles and a bunch of hills and trees away from here.

"Easily." She grinned while the first fighters hauled themselves out of the water. "I just followed the sounds of violence."

***

Dereva left two days later with all the vehicles again, taking the pregnant women, the dead, and the badly injured back to the Lair. We had no plans on when to meet up again. She would simply do the best she could.

"There's a lot less Steve in the mountains, but you're not done yet," she said regretfully, right before they left.

Ever since she'd gone, the rain had been constant. A classic Oregon winter. Wet. Everything was wet, all the way down to my underwear, and I hated it when that got soaked. I could stand a lot, if I had dry underwear. The only not-so-bad thing was that I didn't have to deal with a period. It completely passed me by. Pretty sure Doc wouldn't like that fact, but there you have it. Can't please everybody.

"Can we do something big?" Phoenix asked.

"What do you mean?"

"Big. You know, something that'll really draw Steve out and make him stay down here."

Gryphon, heading past with freshly filled canteens, paused. "I'm sorry? Big fucking explosions weren't quite enough? What would you consider being properly 'big'?"

She shrugged. "Hit a town?"

I wrinkled my nose. "We just stole a bunch of pregnant women. And I'm tired. Let's give them a chance to have that news get out. In the meantime, maybe a convoy will do? Otherwise, how much food we got, without hunting?"

Gryphon shook his head. "Perhaps a week. It's not good."

***

Two weeks later, I knelt in front of a tiny campfire, feeding it twigs and leaves until it was large enough to catch on sticks. I chewed a new mint leaf, ignoring my growling stomach. People were listlessly lying on the ground, huddling together for warmth, asleep if they were lucky. They still doubled up, two to a blanket. We never seemed to have enough. Dereva had all our spares in the tailgate's box. Not like we knew we'd need them.

"Eleanor?" I shifted, preparing to stand. My legs couldn't do it and I dropped abruptly onto my butt. "Shit! Ga…" I found myself looking into the liquid brown eyes of a toddler, clutching a raggedy teddy bear. She was part of a group we'd rescued five days ago. She stared at my lips intently, her mouth working. "Uh…ouch?"

"Captain?" Eleanor made her way through our cramped camp, stepping over sleeping adults. "Oh, there you are, honey." Cooing, she scooped up the baby, kissing her rosy cheeks, making the baby smile and gurgle. "What did you need, Captain?"

I shook my head, trying to clear the cobwebs. "What? Oh, right. Um. Food. How are people doing?"

"Despite our best efforts, they're about to starve," Eleanor said gently. "We can't keep running. We need food or a pickup."

We'd found ten more people, three adults and the rest barely more than kids, five days ago. Half-starved, they'd devoured what food we had, and the wildlife wasn't exactly teeming right now. A couple rabbits didn't go too far when you had nearly thirty people. For the last week, we'd been on strict rations and that, combined with our grueling pace, was taking its toll on everyone, including the fighters.

I sighed, reexamining our position. We'd set up in a fallow field, right next to a creek, hiding in the trees. The nearest road was over a quarter mile away. It wasn't great, especially if the creek rose any more from the rain, but it could work.

"We'll stay here for a few days, then. Tomorrow, those of us who can hunt will go out and see what we can bring back."

It'd been three days since we'd seen Steve, when they were closing in on an old shed they thought we were in. Sparrow, using some fertilizer and a few things I'd previously thought useless under the circumstances, left them a surprise. I hoped it'd keep them busy for a while. At the very least, there'd be injured, which should buy us time and space.

Through everything, Archangel was everywhere. Mostly, he had my back. Sometimes literally. I'd almost gotten used to turning and finding him behind me, scanning our surrounds to ensure we were safe. Right now, he scrounged for inner bark for people to eat. It wasn't much, but it worked.

The next morning, half the fighters headed out in different directions. I walked with Archangel until our trail split. One went north, towards small towns and scattered farms, the other east, back towards the mountains. That trail rose slowly, skirting the edge of the trees.

"You take the mountains," I said, my lips quirking wryly. "I shouldn't be left to go hunting on my own."

He cocked his head, blue eyes bright with curiosity. "Why not?"

"Eleanor said so." I stuck out my lower lip. Eleanor said so only because of the mountain lion attack, but that was hardly my fault. She still said no. "But I'm really good at ransacking houses, so I'll take that one."

He held out his right hand. I reached out, only for him to clasp my forearm. I gripped his in return, his skin so hot, strong muscles under my fingers. I forced my fingers to keep still when all they wanted was to stroke and explore.

He stood close, his eyes mere inches away. I'd had no idea all the benefits of crushing on a man barely taller than me. "Stay safe," he said quietly.

I took a shuddering breath, releasing his arm reluctantly. "See you back at camp. Good hunting."

Without further ado, we parted, each taking our path. In town, every house I passed I ransacked, even going around in the yard, hoping for the remains of a garden. Cutting across a field, a farmhouse, slowly being consumed by wisteria and weeds, lurked. It'd been run down Before and now was little more than a pile of junk topped with corrugated iron surrounded by piles of what could, with decent imagination, be called outbuildings.

The ground swayed and I knelt abruptly, my stomach cramping, drinking water and breathing until the pain passed. I wobbled as I stood, my rifle knocking against low-hanging branches, too hungry to care about the noise. I'd never be able to outrun Steve in this condition, so either they were here and I was dead, or they weren't. Either way, no point worrying about it.

I spent more time than I should've searching those excuses for buildings, but I'd hoped, as remote as it was, that Steve missed something. I came up empty. Steve picked everything clean. No edible plants, no old garden, nothing. I cursed, tears coming to my eyes. Going back without finding *something* was intolerable, but I wouldn't be able to keep going much longer, either. Some of the people at camp were *starving*, not just extremely hungry. If they didn't get something soon, they were toast. My shoulders slumped, I turned back to the forest, to see a dog sitting just outside the trees, patiently waiting to be noticed.

She was a mutt, too many breeds to guess at, thin, her ribs showing plainly above hanging teats. The old girl had short, brownish black fur with a bit of gray around her muzzle. When I saw her, her ears pricked up, tail thumping the ground. I knelt and held a hand low to the ground, talking softly. The poor thing, starved of human companionship, didn't need much encouragement, nosing around my hand before lunging at me, nearly knocking me to the ground.

I laughed quietly, rubbing her ears and scratching her neck and back. She quivered with excitement, little whimpers escaping her throat. "Poor baby," I murmured. "How long have you been alone, huh?" She thrust her nose up, under my chin, her tail wagging so hard her entire back half waggled with it.

Eventually, I rose, stretching my legs and giving her a few good pats to her side. "Sorry, darling, but I gotta go." I smiled down at her, unsure whether she'd even follow me as I left. "I've got starving people to feed..." I stopped, a grimace of pain and realization twisting my face. This friendly dog, so sweet and lonely, could be my answer.

I sat down heavily, setting the rifle next to me and the dog got as much of herself as would fit into my lap, licking my face. "No. No," I whispered thickly, tears choking me. "Don't be happy I'm staying. Don't."

Reaching behind me, I pulled out the knife I kept sheathed at the small of my back. Stroking her head, I brought it around. "Forgive me," I whispered, setting the blade against her throat. I grit my teeth, preparing myself.

***

The east glowed rose and gold, the sun not even cresting the mountains before I made it back to camp, an old, weighted feed sack slung over my shoulder. Some heads popped up, looking hopefully at the sack, the rescued not having the energy to do more.

"Get anything?" Phoenix, sitting on a log, watching three cooking pots.

"Yes." I set the sack down carefully and plopped on the log next to her. "You have no idea how hard it was."

"No shit, Sherlock. I found a bunch of stinging nettle, some dandelion, and three rabbits. We'll have stew shortly, but it's nowhere near enough."

"Who else is back?"

She ran through a list while I rubbed my bad shoulder. Everyone came back with something, though in many cases, it was still thin. There were only two still out, Archangel and Storm. I hoped they were okay. The best to come back so far was Gryphon, with a small, old sheep. "Gryphon is chopping it up to roast, though these guys," she nodded to the rescued, "would probably eat it raw. What'd you get?"

I reached into the sack between my feet. "First off, hold this." I set a wriggling puppy in her hands. She squealed, cradling the pup, kissing its soft fur. I pulled out two more warm, wiggly bundles and passed them to Feisty and Gramps, who'd wandered over to see what had Phoenix so excited.

"What about food?" a rescued woman asked.

"Got that, too," I said, pulling out a layer of grass and leaves. Didn't want the puppies sitting right on it. It just wouldn't be right. I grinned, pulling out a chicken, its head hanging limply. Phoenix laughed, the first one to see what came out of my magic bag.

Exclamations surrounded me while Phoenix passed her puppy to Ink and grabbed the first chicken, taking it to the field to gut it. I took out three more chickens and in the bottom were a dozen eggs.

"How did you find all this?" Phoenix asked from the edge of the field.

"I had help." I pointed to the bushes upstream. The dog, her gray muzzle barely standing out against the shadows, stood trembling, yearning for companionship and her pups but terrified to be so close to so many strangers. "This old girl's been following the chickens, eating some eggs, it seems. She also had to move her pups, though, so we owe her a leg, and a home."

One of the rescued, an older woman, protested at that. "You can't be serious! We're starving and you want to feed a *dog*?!"

I looked to the heavens for patience and sighed heavily. "Keep this up and she's gonna get a whole chicken. I don't know how to say this any clearer, but we wouldn't have any of this if it wasn't for her."

In the excitement for more food, Archangel arrived back in camp. "Hey." He grinned at me, holding up his pack. "I found stuff."

I smiled at him, my heart lighter already. Phoenix, back at the stoves with a plucked and gutted chicken, nodded to the ground next to her. "Whatcha got?"

He turned his bag over, emptying out two dozen potatoes and a whole bunch of cans. In the very bottom, wrapped in leaves, lay two rabbits. I caught a glimpse of cherry pie filling. Without being asked, Gramps came back with an armload of dry wood. "We're gonna need this, between chickens and a sheep."

"Who got the sheep?" Archangel asked.

"Gryphon," I said. "And weren't you going hunting? What do you call all this?"

He laughed softly. "This pie filling was sneaky. I had to sit still for over an hour before it came within reach."

I snickered. A cold nose thrust against the back of my neck, and I started. Twisting, I found the dog behind me, drawn into camp. I scratched her, rubbing her ears. "Who's my good girl?" I murmured. "You are! Yes, you are my good girl. You're the bestest good girl in the world."

A pup whined and the old girl immediately left me to take care of her babies. Phoenix watched her go. "You didn't think of...you know?" She drew her finger across her throat.

I hunched my shoulders. "I did. Nearly did. But in the end...couldn't. So, I let her go."

"And she led you to this?" Archangel waved, encompassing the chickens and eggs. I nodded. He shook his head. "You guys are the best good girls in the world."

CHAPTER 9

A week later, I walked out to the burial meadow, followed by everyone in the Lair. Even the children and the wounded came out, though some were on crutches and others had to be carried out. The clear air didn't freeze my throat, though our breath puffed white. Green showed through the expanding mud. Winter's hold had broken while we'd been in the Valley.

My brother walked near me, Dereva on his other side, the two holding hands. They'd had an emotional reunion when the southern group made it back a few days after we did. Tears welled in my eyes when I finally laid eyes on him. He'd lost some of his joy, some of his sparkle, though he wouldn't tell me what had happened. But I'd seen him entering Kestrel's room. I could relax, knowing our resident therapist could help where I couldn't.

My group had returned...thinner. Dereva and the others found us three days after we'd found the food, and none of us had recovered yet, despite best efforts. Amana kept more stew and bread than usual on hand and Wildwood hovered and poured fragrant, nutritional teas into every empty cup.

Amana walked on my other side. Her eyes lit up when we returned, and she'd walked straight to me for our customary greeting. She'd rested her forehead against mine longer than usual, her breathing ragged, relieved.

Now, she accompanied me to remember our dead.

Sirius was the last to arrive, carrying Cin in her arms. She'd made it back just in time to hold her dog while he died. Amana said he'd been holding on, waiting for Sirius. She'd lain on the floor next to him, giving him full-body pets. I'd knelt at his back, scratching his ears and stroking his head until his breathing just...stopped.

Obelix trotted at her heels, whining, following her to the only freshly dug grave in the meadow, a pile of rocks ready next to the dirt. I looked at all the graves, my face crumpling at the losses. In the field, it was easy to pretend someone was still here. They were just...away, and we'd see them when we got back to the Lair.

Here, there was no hiding from the truth, and the truth was, we'd lost people. One was too many, and now I looked at six fresh graves, two from mine, three from the south, and one a rescued girl. Her remaining loved ones gathered around her cairn.

A fresh breeze lifted, bringing chill air from the south, ruffling hair and causing many to pull their caps down tighter. Winter's last push. It was a toss-up whether it would be rain or snow, this late in the season.

Sirius laid Cin to rest to tears from those who knew him. The new civilians all respected the dog's funeral, even shedding tears for the good boy they hadn't known long. The new dog and her pups stayed close to the people they knew, but even they were here. Sirius cried quietly, sandwiched between me and Phoenix at Cin's grave.

When the last rock was laid, Shepherd stepped forward. He cleared his throat. "Sirius, I know you're not overly religious, but I was hoping you'd allow me to say a few words." He clasped a bible to his chest.

Sirius looked down at the half-filled grave and nodded, tears spilling down her cheeks. Emotions clogged my throat, looking down at Cin's growing cairn, Amana fixing a small wooden cross with his name into the ground.

When Shepherd finished, I raised my bottle. "Hail the victorious dead."

"Hail!"

And the memorial began.

***

I rolled over, grunting, my stomach attempting to crawl up my throat. Swallowing repeatedly, I cracked my eyes open, ready to shut them if that upset my stomach further. Blackness. I frowned. Ah! Shoving my hair back with a shaky hand, I tried again.

It took a few seconds to focus, but some light filtered through the vents in the room. Yes, it was a room. Definitely a bed. I moved my eyes cautiously, lest the sandpaper lining them rub my eyes raw. Map. When…?

"H-ow…?" I mumbled. What was the last thing I remembered? I scrunched my nose, the effort of thinking almost too much. Fresh air. A breeze. Outside? My brain finally registered the lump lying next to me. "S'rius? Watchoo doin' 'ere?"

She moaned. "What happened? Anybody get the plate of that truck?" She swallowed noisily and I winced, holding my head. Rolling over, she collided with me. "What you doin' in my bed?"

I covered one eye, hoping it would help me focus. "No. 'm pretty sure iss my room."

She glared, her bloodshot eyes mere inches away. Her hair was nearly out of its customary ponytail, hanging around her face in clumps. "Since when?"

"You gotta map on your wall?" I flicked a finger, that being as much as I dared to move.

A new moan filled the air. "My fault." The man's voice came from somewhere off the side of my bed.

Moving carefully, I inched to the side of the bed, rolling just far enough to see blond, messy hair and a long bundle next to the mattress. "Arch'ngel?"

He moaned again. "Why does it taste like something crawled into my mouth and died?"

"Moonshine," I grunted. Anansi's concoction went down smooth when you were grieving, but it packed a hell of a punch. It wasn't even Dirt Huggers, named for all the good people who'd had two drinks and woke up still in the dirt. What we'd had was his version of cheap shit.

A sudden pounding on the door made me cringe, covering my ears. Poor Archangel curled into a miserable ball, clutching his head. Moaning and groaning filled the air, more than could have come from just three people.

"All right," I whimpered. The mystery of who else was in my room could wait until the horrible pounding stopped. "We're awake. Please stop. I'd like to stop dying."

The door opened, revealing Eleanor. Her stern gaze dissolved into muffled laughter. She held up a handful of cups and a jug. I didn't have to see it to know it was thick, green, and tasted almost as awful as I felt.

"Who's we?" she asked. "Never mind, I don't think I want to know what happened. At least you didn't pass out on the mound!" she said cheerfully.

I whimpered. I had passed out on the mound before and woke up covered in mosquito bites.

"Make fun all you want," Sirius shifted, rocking the mattress. The motion roiled through my stomach, and I swallowed again. "Just do it quietly, please."

Eleanor's gaze softened. I knew she really didn't mind us drowning our sorrows. It moved us through grief so much faster when we didn't try to hold back and 'stay strong,' whatever the hell that meant. "Here." Setting the cups on the ground, she filled them and gently passed them out. I squinted. She walked to the other side of the room, handing out more.

How many people did I have in here? And how did we all get here?

Taking my own cup, I levered up onto my elbow. I hesitated for just a moment. "Bottom's up." I tipped it back, swallowing the sludge as quickly as I could. I had to wait a moment for my stomach to decide it wouldn't cast it back up. "Thank you." I inhaled, finding that helped keep everything down.

"How many people are in here, anyway?" I asked.

She smiled. "You've got six in here, though I am very curious why."

"You and me, both," I mumbled.

"Ugh..." Archangel gingerly sat up, leaning on the edge of the mattress, which sat directly on the ground. A hank of hair fell across his forehead, obscuring one bloodshot eye. "That was me. I couldn't find people's rooms, so I put...people in here?" He looked around. "Why did I bring people in here? What the hell?"

I shrugged. "Hey, I got my bed. Who else is in here?"

Three more heads popped up around the room, turning into Amana, Al, and Dry Eyes. They looked as miserable and confused as me, which made me feel a bit better about myself. Dry Eyes leaned against the wall, nursing his mug and refusing to look up. Al took it all with his usual chill. I guess when you were known as a bad luck charm, you learned to go with the flow.

Shaking with repressed laughter, Eleanor touched my foot. "I'd like a word with you in the common room once you've gotten yourself together."

I grunted. Setting my cup down on the stack of books that served as a nightstand, I slithered off the bed, too hungover to care that I crawled over my crush. At the door, I used it to get to my feet. Eleanor had already disappeared. Waving to the rest of the people occupying my room, I slowly followed.

It couldn't be that bad, could it? Usually, when Eleanor let me have it, we were in the Useless Room. The common room was more...casual. Safe. When I joined her, she passed a mug of tea over and set a plate of toast between us. She even let me take a couple bites.

"It's been a while since you've had that much to drink." She didn't beat around the bush. "What brought this on?"

"Burying Jewel, Cin, and the others isn't reason enough?" I bristled, muscles tense.

She laid a hand on my arm, petting until I relaxed. "We did a lot of good out there. I know you had to face far more than I did, especially since I kept coming back to the Lair, but don't forget how many people you helped."

I ran a hand over my hair and stopped. Maybe I shouldn't do that until I'd had a chance to wash. "We got people killed and hurt, too."

She observed me silently for a moment. "You should talk to Kestrel."

I grunted. "I'd love to. But she's got a waiting list two weeks long, dealing with trauma and relationships. I've gone through a lot less than most of these women. I'll make it."

Eleanor's eyes narrowed and her lips pursed. Uh, oh. I'd managed to piss her off. "*You* need it, you spoon. You need to talk to someone. Why not the pretty scout you have in your room?"

I wrinkled my nose. "You make it sound like it was only him and me, not enough people to have an orgy." I saw the merit of her suggestion. We all needed to talk sometimes, but my pool of people I was comfortable talking to was already abysmally small and busy. He'd probably find time, but...would he still like me after?

"Oh!" She huffed, smacking my arm lightly and pulling me from my thoughts. "Go talk to him. Or anyone. I really don't care. Now, finish your tea and toast." She rose, gliding to the door.

"'You spoon'?" I called.

Her laughter drifted back. "I may be spending too much time with Gryphon."

***

After breakfast, Perry caught me on my way to my room, announcing it was time for him and the remainder of his men to complete their mission. "Before they decide we've gone AWOL," he said, grinning. "I'd rather not get court martialed. It's a pain to deal with."

"Need any extra hands to get you to the border?" I asked.

He thought about that for a bit, pulling on his bottom lip. Finally, he shook his head. "We're not that big of a group. We might be able to sneak through where others would get captured. Plus, I don't know if they've decided to start patrolling inside the border. I'd hate for your people to be caught again. Sirius's vacation sounded like it sucked."

I smiled, a breath of laughter escaping. "Fair enough. Whatever you need, talk to Amana...No, wait. Talk to Lavender. She's probably in better shape."

He quirked an eyebrow. "Not Amana? What happened?"

"Hangover."

He cocked his head. "How...?"

At that moment, my door opened, and Amana slid out, the doorway taking most credit for her being on her feet. Her hair hung around her face, and she clutched her jacket and boots. Mumbling a greeting, she leaned on the wall. Al followed her out, still a little green.

Perry's mouth dropped open as they weaved down the hall to their room. Sirius wobbled out the door a moment later, her arm slung over Dry Eyes's shoulder, the two of them using each other as a walker. They didn't even see us.

"I don't want to know, do I?" Perry asked.

"Nope." I waited, afraid Archangel would wander out next. "Just talk to Lavender, please. Or wait until tomorrow to check over supplies."

I walked into my room, straight-backed, hoping I wouldn't run into any other guests. I relaxed a little at the empty room. I needed to brace myself before talking to Archangel. Even after all our late-night conversations, I was still afraid of talking to him. Would it be different, here at the Lair?

Caught up in my thoughts, I didn't even hear Perry leave.

In the end, I didn't have to track Archangel down. He found me in the garage. I'd been tinkering with the GMC. It'd seen a lot of hard use, and I finally had a good idea to improve the durability of the spark plugs, but I just needed time. Plus, I had some nice sheet metal to reinforce the sides. Might be able to prevent so many bullets from wandering through my precious engine.

"Captain?" He coughed, shifting nervously when I leaned into the engine block. "How's it going?"

I tensed, then forced myself to relax, straightening. I smiled, then frowned. Did I want him to know how happy I was to see him? Had Eleanor sent him? "Hey. I was planning to find you later. What do you need?"

He spun, holding his arms out, showing off a leather jacket before leaning his butt against the pickup next to me. "Al finished my new jacket! And I wanted to see if you needed to talk. I notice most people go to Kestrel. I've been to talk with her, too, but you haven't. What did you need to talk to me about?"

I eyed him suspiciously. "Did Eleanor send you here?"

"What?" He stared. His hair, clean now, shone in the natural light coming through the windows high on the walls and the candles I used for close-up work. "Why would Eleanor send me? For what?"

I relaxed, straightened and moved around to the side next to him. "Sorry, just something I'd talked to her about earlier. So...uh. Talking to you. Eleanor noticed I haven't really been to Kestrel, either. But she's so busy, and I don't know where to start," I burst out.

"I don't know." He grinned at me, his eyes sparkling, leaning against the truck, his shoulder brushing mine. "You didn't have a problem talking when we were on the trail."

"Yeah, and how many people did you see me talking to?" I groused.

"Are you saying I'm special?" His grin widened.

I frowned. "This is a trap. It doesn't matter what I say, I'm trapped. How dare you!" Mock irritation turned into giggles at his delight.

"See?" he said. "We're talking already."

My mouth dropped open. "You sneaky bastard!"

"Go on." He leaned in, bumping my shoulder companionably. "Ask me something."

I chewed on my lip, until I saw his gaze drop to my mouth. My heart beat quicker than the situation called for, and the adrenaline surged, as if I were heading into a fight. Not knowing what to say, I blurted out the first thing that crossed my mind.

"What's the stupidest thing you ever did?"

Blood surged to my cheeks. What kind of a dumbass question was that?

He laughed, leaning back a little, putting a modicum space between us. Okay. I could handle this distance. Too close and I might spontaneously combust.

"You mean, besides agreeing to come here?" He tipped his head back, revealing the chain that held his dog tags, disappearing into his collar.

"Probably messing with a cow when I was a kid. Me and my cousin wanted to see the new calf."

"That doesn't sound so bad."

"The problem is that once we realized she didn't like us near her baby, we kept trying anyway. And we tried to scare her away."

I snickered. "Are you crazy?"

He shrugged. "In our defense, we were like, five. Anyway, we barely made it out. I did a running dive through the stanchion to get away. I was grounded for two weeks. No games, no console, and I had to do all the dishes."

I eyed him skeptically. "No way that was the stupidest thing you've ever done. You're more than old enough to have that beat."

Archangel sighed, surprisingly wistful. "Maybe, but I'm not ready to go there yet."

I nodded slowly. "Okay. When you're ready, then."

The corner of his mouth quirked, and he gave me a sideways glance, kicking my hormones into high gear, reminding me all over again that all my parts were in working order. "Come on, I want to sit."

Leading me to the back of the pickup, he lowered the tailgate and made himself comfortable. I stood, fidgeting, wanting so badly to sit, but how close was too close...would he think I was hitting on him if I did...what do I do with my hands...

Smiling gently, he grabbed my shirt and tugged me down next to him. "So...what's the dumbest thing you've ever done?"

"Mmmm." I shifted to face him fully, resisting the urge to stretch luxuriously. Something about being near him made me want to be different. To move, rub against him, purring.

And his face...I loved watching his expressions. He didn't try to hide anything, and there was a physicality and confidence to him, even relaxed like this, that I couldn't get enough of. "The top, like, fifty, are all since the Invasion, so I think we can rule those out. So, probably hiking with my cousin."

The cousin had been Sirius, but we weren't at a point where I was willing to tell him who my relatives are. "We were a little ways south of here, around Opal Creek, coming down one of those steeper slopes. There was a spot with a three-foot drop, so instead of trying to climb down with my pack on, I got the brilliant idea to take it off, drop it down, and follow after."

He grinned, biting his lip to try and hide it, but he'd already begun sniggering.

I nodded. "My pack overbalanced and started this wonderful little cartwheel down what was almost a cliff." He stopped trying to hide his laughter, slowly toppling onto his back, whooping, his leg rubbing mine. I smacked his leg gently. "It's not *that* funny. Geez. And it could've been worse. Somehow, it stopped on a tiny ledge, part of a deer track, right before a gorge. Straight up, dumbest thing I did, Before."

"It's just...your face..." He slowly subsided into giggles. "Is that what you looked like?"

I rolled my eyes. "How the fuck would I know? I didn't have a mirror to know, did I?"

"What's the dumbest thing you've done since the Invasion?" he asked, suddenly serious.

"Nice segue." I slouched forward, elbows on my knees. He stayed lying down, but he stacked his hands behind his head, leaving himself completely vulnerable. Strangely enough, it made it easier to dredge something up. "The dumbest thing since is starting this little uprising. The worst, though..."

I took a deep, shuddering breath. This is what Eleanor wanted for me, I suddenly realized. Being safe with someone, able to unburden myself. "The worst is realizing that every time we hit Salem, or hurt Steve in some way, they take it out on people who didn't do anything. And I still do it. I still go in, still try to get a few out, still try to hurt Steve, even knowing there'll be reprisals. That's the worst."

He stared at the ceiling. For the first time, he refused to look at me. "The worst thing I ever did? I shot a kid. I keep telling myself I didn't know it was a kid, he had a gun, he would've killed me, but the truth is, I could see enough of him to know he was small. I knew it wasn't an adult. Maybe I could've done something, disarmed him..." His normally expressive face was curiously blank, still.

I rested a hand on his leg. "If there's one thing we've learned, it's you can't do that. Be sad that it happened, but don't hold onto it like that. Because the first people ever killed in a reprisal were a four-year-old kid and his mom. We talked to the kid, he told his mom, and she reported us. After we busted out of Salem, they were publicly executed as a warning."

I'd broken the day I'd heard, and it was only River, scared and determined, that got me thinking again. But I'd cried, later. Sobbed into my pillow.

He sat up slowly, scrubbing his hands over his face and hair, leaving bits of it sticking up all over his head. "You know what I learned? Sometimes, you gotta get hot and sweaty to get rid of certain memories."

My brain fried and my heart jumped just looking into those blue eyes so close to my own. My breath came short, and I leaned closer...

Five minutes later, I was in the gym, on the mat with Sarge, running through my stick kata. That rat bastard of a man.

But it worked.

FRESNO, CALIFORNIA

Faith bit her lip in concentration, scanning the report, flipping through pages rapidly. Occasionally, she checked out the office, but the others were all busily working away at their desks. The two guards, one at each door, watched the proceedings, but they were too far away to see anything except her industriously filing paperwork.

She took notes on a small pad of paper, using a shorthand code of her own devising. To the casual reader, it looked like a supply list.

The guards snapped to attention as Lieutenant Colonel Han strode into the office. Faith dropped the paperwork, placing her hands on her desktop, casually shuffling papers as she stood to attention with the other office workers.

Han, a man of middling height, looked about the room, his black eyes piercing. He meandered through the room, cursorily checking desks and paperwork. At Faith's desk, he paused. She smiled, keeping her expression open and friendly.

"Sir."

"Miss Wilkins," he said, his accent almost undetectable. "Report, please."

"Sacramento has ordered munitions, here is the list." Running through all the munitions ordered, Faith shoved all other thoughts out, wholly believing that she was a loyal citizen of the Liberated States.

***

At the end of the day, Faith walked down the road with her coworkers, talking quietly. At the corner, she lit up. "Lucas!" she cried, waving.

The young man leaning his shoulder against the side of the concrete warehouse on the corner straightened, grinning broadly as his eyes trailed over Faith. Tall and lean, his dark skin and sharp features showed his Latino heritage.

"Oh, my God," Samantha said quietly, fanning herself. "What would it take to get a man to look at me like that?"

Lying. Faith smiled, rushing to him, relaxing only when his arm slipped around her shoulders. Lucas pressed a kiss to her temple. Faith closed her eyes, leaning into his embrace. "We need to talk to Carter," she murmured. "Tonight."

He nodded and waved to another man further down the road, just exiting a munitions factory. "Jon!" he called.

Jon, slender, his brown hair falling softly to his shoulders, glanced their way. He smiled, waving back, waiting for them to catch up.

"We need to talk to Carter," Lucas said quietly.

"I'll send word." Jon veered off down the next alley, quickly disappearing in the growing dark.

***

"There was a report out of Oregon today," Faith began, glancing quickly around the small circle of listeners.

Besides herself and Lucas, Carter, Jon, and Alma had come, all that could be found on such short notice. They huddled in an intersection in the sewers. Faith kept her voice low, to keep from echoing.

"Why is that unusual?" Carter asked, his hand jerking impatiently.

"We've had hardly any word from them over the last year. And," Faith lowered her voice even more, the others leaning in, "there's an uprising in Oregon. The NKs caught two of them. Those people gave up names, but...not?"

"Spit it out," Carter whispered harshly.

"Names like Captain, Phoenix, Dereva, Storm. Weird names. Code. This Captain is their leader, apparently. He killed a whole patrol on his own!"

This caught everyone's attention. "What else did the report say?" Lucas asked, nearly vibrating with excitement.

"They're asking for more ammunition, mortars, whatever we can send them. Men, too. Patrols have gone missing, outposts demolished. Whole maternity wards are disappearing."

The men hissed, grinning and punching the air. Alma smiled, the first genuine smile Faith had ever seen on the woman's face.

"We have to help them," Faith concluded. "But how?"

"We can ruin gunpowder," Lucas whispered. "Not in everything, but in enough. Or, in the mortars, leave out the explosives. It'll fire, but it won't blow up on landing."

"We'll create delays," Carter continued, his dark eyes alight. "Can you adjust requisition forms?"

"As long as I do it before Han sees anything. Which I usually do." Faith shivered. Reading the occasional paper was far different to actually altering them, but if it helped someone fight back...

CHAPTER 11

Man 1: (snorts) Listen, Trembly will do whatever we need. He's a smart man,
he'll do as he's told.
Man 2: I know why I'm doing this. What are you getting?
Transcript of phone call, January 6, 2053

Gryphon breathed deeply as we walked through the forest. My pack, weighted down with food we didn't normally get, like mushrooms, sat comfortably on my shoulders. Phoenix watched the rear, I had the front, and Gryphon walked in the middle. He still had a tendency to get lost if left to his own devices out here.

We were returning from Home, having taken the pregnant women up there. While the Lair was more comfortable, Home was more peaceful. It also had a midwife. Well, she'd had a lot of kids in her time, which was good enough for us. Doc and Wildwood were staying for a few extra days with some of the fighters to go over midwifey stuff. Complications, nutrition, whatever.

Perry had taken the opportunity to go with us partway, then he and his men left, taking thirteen of the rich people Steve had in Mohawk.

Archangel had gone with him, just to see them over the mountains, along with Goliath and Chaos.

I mulled over what Perry had said before parting.

"It's a good thing you're keeping your real names out of this." He glanced up and down the trail, as if checking that we wouldn't be overheard. "I talked with Sirius, and from what she's said...If you make it out of this, there could be repercussions down the line. I'll tell them as little as I can. They'll jump to their own conclusions without questioning too much, especially if I appear to be fully cooperating, but there's no guaranteeing what the civilians will say."

"What about the rest of your men?" I asked.

"I'll take care of them," he said, a hard look in his eye.

I nodded, thinking about the long road ahead of us. And what the hell did he mean, 'there could be repercussions'? We were defending our homes, something this government liked to yap about excessively, calling it a good thing. Maybe that was until it wasn't.

By his grim expression, it wouldn't surprise me if he was expecting some consequences, too.

"I love the scent of pine in the spring." Gryphon pulled me from my thoughts. Glancing back, he looked around appreciatively. "I don't see much pine in England, but..." He broke off when Phoenix burst into laughter. "What? What did I say?"

"It's not spring," I explained, snickering.

"What?"

"This...this is..." Phoenix gasped and broke out into hiccups interspersed with giggles. "Cap-*hic*-tain?" she pleaded.

Watching Phoenix struggle, I leaned against a tree, shaking with silent laughter. What he said hadn't been too funny, but Phoenix's reaction? Priceless. Gryphon folded his arms, surveying us with stiff English dignity.

I wiped tears from my eyes. "It's a false spring. We're gonna get cold again. Woman, aren't you supposed to drink from the opposite rim?" I asked Phoenix, who was sipping from her canteen in an effort to still the hiccups.

"How the...*hic*...am I supposed to do that?"

"Damned if I know. Probably just invented for other's amusement, but whatever." Seeing Gryphon's patience slowly leaking out his ears, I straightened. "Right. Yeah. Oregon likes to do a false spring a couple times. We have, like, second and third winter. We're between second and third winter, which is why we brought the women up now, although it shouldn't be as bad. We could also call this early spring, I suppose."

"Even though it'll get cold, and we'll get tons more rain," Phoenix added, her hiccups slowing down after holding her breath.

We started down the trail again, picking up speed when we crossed gravel roads to disappear into the brush again. A few birds flitted through the forest. To the north, huge power lines cut through the forest. Usually, we'd be able to hear them humming, but they were silent, victim to Steve's tech.

"But I can smell pine," Gryph protested. "Which means it's warming up."

"Yeah, for like, three days." Phoenix walked closer to him when the trail widened enough. I glanced back occasionally, seeing their fingers brush, but they weren't at a point where they would hold hands.

Pretty sure they were doing more than that, but they were keeping it under wraps so far. Whatever it was, Eleanor was calm and happy with him, which meant it was all good. I smirked, remembering him meeting Olivia and Sam. Sam was a sweetheart, shaking his hand, clapping him on the back, all that man stuff. Olivia glared at him as if he were a fox stalking a chicken coop.

Gryphon smiled at everyone he met, played with the kids, and soon became a favorite with them. But Olivia...I'd lurked behind a rock outcropping, listening to the grilling. It started with "Who's your family?" and went all the way to "What's your occupation? Will you still have work when all this is over?"

At his response of, "I don't even know if I'll live to see the end of this. Why worry for something that far out?" and her dumbfounded expression, I stuffed my sleeve in my mouth, muffling the laughter, ducking away before she heard me. I didn't need Olivia raining hellfire on me. I was finally in her good graces.

"My aunt went to England for a couple years, ages ago," Phoenix commented. I remembered photos at her Aunt Mary's house. They'd been from all sorts of exotic locations I dreamed of seeing. Now, if I was lucky, I didn't dream. "She told me England was pretty dry, comparatively speaking. I guess the English are prone to over exaggeration." She smiled flirtatiously.

I breathed deeply of the pine scented air. "As much fun as it is to watch Gryphon's brain short-circuit, I'd really rather not see you two making googly eyes, so I'll just..." I pointed to myself then down the trail. "I'll see you later?"

Phoenix's ears and cheeks turned pink. Fucking hell. She even blushed beautifully. How annoying is that? "I...uh. No...I mean, we're not..."

I laughed. "You're so full of shit you can't even see the shore. But since Eleanor's cool with this...Although, shouldn't we have some kind of announcement, back at the Lair, so everyone knows if they find you necking, it's okay?"

Phoenix met my gaze and slowly, deliberately, drew a handgun, drawing back the slide. The ominous clicking was loud, unnatural, in the forest. I looked her straight in the eyes, grinned, turned my back, and walked down the trail.

***

"Captain!"

My name bounced off the high ceilings in the garage, filtering down to where I was working under a vehicle.

"Cap-taaain!"

"I'm under a truck, Eleanor," I shouted, sliding out from underneath the Chimera. The creeper rolled smoothly out, courtesy of the WD-40 I'd used generously. When the army boys bugged out, they'd gone in a hurry.

Bare feet pattered over smooth rock, preceding Eleanor, her skirts swirling with every stride. "There you are! You do realize that 'truck' is very generic, and there are many things in here that can be categorized as a 'truck'?"

I sighed. "What did I do now?"

She tried to laugh it off, but I saw the hurt in her eyes, and I cussed silently. "It's not you, honey," Eleanor said, striving for joy. "It's Phoenix and Gryphon. They've decided to make their relationship official. Kestrel has signed off."

Climbing to my feet, I stretched my arms overhead, loosening my back and shoulders. Then, I wiped the grease off my hands and gave Eleanor a hug. "I'm sorry," I whispered into her hair. "I'm a little bit grumpy lately."

Sirius was still sad about Cin, and her bad mood worried me. She usually recovered quickly from loss, a result of growing up around animals. This one hit her hard, but then again, Cin was special.

She hugged me back, her wiry arms holding me tightly. "I know. But you need to see the joy wherever it is and not get too bogged down. And," she held me away, hands on my shoulders, "I wanted to tell you specifically so that there's no...mistakes."

"What kind of mistake?" I protested, grinning. "It's not like I'm going to storm in there and kick him in the bal...Oh." I bit my lip and stared at the ceiling, rocking back and forth, hands clasped behind my back. "It was *one* time!"

"Which is why I'm telling you this. Amana still hasn't gotten over you bursting in because she got a little noisy."

"It's not like they had a towel on the door!"

She chuckled. "Listen, we don't want you to go accidentally kicking Gryphon in the family jewels. I know," she held up her hand, "you know that Phoenix can take care of herself, but you also spend your time protecting them. So, this is me, also protecting them." Her shoulders shook with silent laughter.

"Maybe. But Al and Amana still hadn't made it communally official, so as far as I'm concerned, it was justified." I rolled my head around, trying to loosen that one, stubbornly tight muscle. "Special dinner?"

"Dry Eyes is out right now with the hunters, looking for something we can turn into steak."

I laid back onto the creeper. "Yay," I said softly, sliding back under the truck. Nothing in here paused for long, not even for good news like this.

*****

In the days that followed, Gryphon moved out of the barracks and into Phoenix's room. None of the women said anything, but suddenly, more of them were cleaning their weapons in the common room whenever he was there. One, Gorgon, would mutter under her breath, and I don't think she wished him well.

More people qualified to join the fighters and we had over fifty women. It was odd. More women would join than men, by a large percentage.

"We were forced out of our comfort zone," Kestrel explained in one of the rare times I saw her outside of meetings or the gym. "Ripped out, really. Steve made this deeply personal in how we've been hurt. We understand how many more women are going through the same thing. Collectively, we're on a mission to save the women. That's really what it is. We're emotionally invested, and we have little to nothing to lose. Those men still have their dignity, their bodily autonomy, and their families. They don't want to risk it."

Her summation left me stunned. I was still sitting there when Sirius found me and dragged me to the armory for inventory.

"This keeps up," I said to Sirius, "we're gonna have to start actively stealing Steve's guns."

"Hm. Yes. Steal Steve's guns." She turned slowly, making a show of taking in all the weapons still hanging on the walls and filling the tables. "Yeah. We're gonna run out."

In the back corner, a husband/wife duo, Tabitha and Landon Speers ("Oh, honey, we're not from around here. We got caught in the Invasion on a visit. If people want to know our names, they're welcome to it."), worked to reload shells. Long-time hunters, they'd do their own shells to save a buck. Thankfully, because they knew what some weird tools in the armory were for.

I barely had time to see people, or get any downtime, because between every bit of necessary training, dealing with bull-headed people, or meals, I was in the garage, trying to fix vehicles with all the wrong parts. My only relief came when Archangel would bring me a snack or lunch on his way to the rolling garden beds he was building. A quick chat, and then I had to get back to the small forge, the grinder, the lathe...everything I was trying to manufacture parts with.

When we thought we were truly into spring, Oregon decided to dump four inches of snow on us. The sight of the expanse of unbroken white drove me mad. I jogged through the halls, back to the garage and a pretense of space when Phoenix hurtled around the corner. Stopping mere inches away, she bounced on her toes, unable to keep still.

"What?" I asked, looking around for the cause. Was there a fire? Had Steve finally found us?

"I'm getting married," she squealed.

"Whoa. Wait. What?" I reared back. "You guys just went official like...last week."

In an instant, she went from excited future bride to the threatening fighter I knew. "That was over two months ago! Try to keep up. Yeah, it's quick, but when you know, you know. Plus, Kestrel said we have as healthy a relationship as she's ever seen. We know it's fast," she repeated quietly, "but in this world, you have to take joy where it is, and hold onto it."

***

Two days after the engagement, the Lair constantly buzzed with the news. People even invaded the garage to talk about it. Random people, like Lavender, who only ventured to that section when we were leaving or returning.

Unable to take it any longer, I packed a bag, spoke briefly with Eleanor, and headed for the front door. Phoenix, spotting the pack, hounded me. "Where you going? Can I come?"

"No. I need you here."

"How come? I wanna go, too."

"I need you here," I said again.

"How come you can go and not me?"

I took and deep breath and reminded myself that murdering a bride is still outside what we consider okay behavior. "Because I'm about to shoot everybody and have done with this. You can't go because you and Seahorse get to be the ones to make sure everybody is fighting fit when the snow is gone."

"Maybe I need a break, too," she tried.

I stopped so fast she ran smack into my back. "You're playing patty-cake with the hottie who saved your life. You don't need a break. You need to get some for all of us who don't. Now, shut up and stay!"

"Woof!"

"Bitch."

"Asshole."

Archangel poked his head out of the common room. "What's all the fighting about? Should I make popcorn?"

"Captain's going out and she's not taking any backup," Phoenix said in her prissiest tone. "She shouldn't go alone."

"I can come." He stepped fully into the hallway, dressed in fatigue pants and a flannel shirt that displayed his broad shoulders to perfection.

I bit my lip, trying not to blush.

"That would be GREAT!" Phoenix practically shouted. I glared, willing her to be silent, pick a different topic, anything but this. "She's going on foot and she's leaving right now, but Gryphon keeps a bag packed and ready to go. One second."

She raced down the hall to her room, leaving us standing in awkward silence, broken only when she returned, the dark blue bag over her shoulder. "Here. Have fun, kids!"

"I still need my winter gear," he said mildly. "Give me five minutes, Captain."

"I hate you," I muttered once he was out of earshot. She grinned, batting her big green eyes. "Bah. I'm glad I'm getting out for a bit."

"Just be back in time for the wedding, okay?"

"Seven days, right?"

"Ten. Idiot."

Archangel emerged, buttoning his leather jacket over a few layers, a beanie already pulled down around his ears. Our conversation ceased. At least Phoenix had the decency not to embarrass me more.

Away from the Lair, I took what felt like my first deep breath in weeks. The freezing air cleared the cobwebs from my head and my lungs. I paused for a minute to enjoy the wind on my face. Taking the deer track passing near the bunker to hide our tracks, we headed out. Bird whistles flew around us, the perimeter guards passing the message: two heading out. Captain leaving.

Unable to whistle, I couldn't communicate with them, but I'd managed to learn some of their signals. I enjoyed listening to them, at any rate. Some of them were so skilled at mimicking birds, the only way to tell the difference was when the pattern was off.

"What was all that about?" Archangel asked eventually, jerking his head towards the Lair.

We'd been out for nearly an hour, keeping the pace slow to avoid sweating. The snow wouldn't last long, already thinning, mud patches showing through more frequently, and we'd only dropped a couple hundred feet, but sweating in this weather was no less deadly.

"Just Phoenix asking to be shot," I assured him.

"Okay...Every time I think I have you guys figured, you just get weirder."

I laughed. "We're not that bad. We're just..." I waved a hand, unable to find a good word.

"Exactly." Satisfaction rolled through every syllable.

"Takes one to know one. You and Gryphon have quite the bromance going," I teased.

He shrugged, the motion resettling his pack. "Gotta respect a man with guts. Not many people, much less the privileged, willing to risk life and limb for others."

"And sharing food off each other's plates?" I snickered.

"What?" He grinned, blue eyes glowing, highlighted by the brown beanie. "A man can't have food preferences?"

"Preferences are one thing, but you guys take food off each other's plates in sync. I've never seen you clash. It's so damn cute." I laughed when he turned pink, grinning. Finally, I wasn't the one blushing.

We continued in silence, comfortable together. He took the lead, leaving me free to look at him as much as I pleased, without anyone to see or comment. He strode purposefully along the deer track, confidently leading the way even though he didn't know where I planned to go. He knew downhill and north, so he followed that.

He constantly tracked the sounds around us, his head tipping one way or the other as he listened. After so long in these woods, I knew the usual sounds, but seeing his attention moving this way and that made me smile.

That evening, we made camp in the small hollow created when a giant tree had fallen, its roots forming a wall on one side. The snow thinned enough for us to easily clear space to lay out the blankets, hopefully staying dry, but even if not...

I closed my eyes, listening to the stillness.

We sat, wrapped in our blankets, making a cold camp. MREs aren't great, but I barely remember good food anymore anyway. I opened an insulated thermos taken from an outdoor store, steam rising from the mouth.

"Are we looking for anything in particular?" he asked. "Since you rarely do something without a purpose."

"Not shooting people isn't a purpose?" I asked dryly.

He chuckled. "You saying you only had one reason to leave that nice, warm, overcrowded Lair?"

"Maybe two," I admitted. He waited patiently, comfortable with silence. Laughing quietly, I leaned companionably against him, relaxed in a way I rarely experienced anymore. "Phoenix and Gryphon's wedding. I wanted them to have...something nice."

His shoulders shook in silent laughter. "We're going on a shopping trip?"

"A bride, even one in this world, needs a nice dress to get married in."

He ducked his head to see me better. "You're a good friend. Well, they also shouldn't wait longer, not now that they've made the decision. Live in the moment." He was quiet for a while, then said, "Good thing you didn't let her come. Don't want the bride to know of her present."

"Don't want the bride getting shot before her wedding," I said sourly.

We kept talking into the night, eventually moving to share blankets. In these temps, it was automatic to share. Archangel never said anything about it. My brother would've made jokes about sleeping together, others would turn complete prude. Never mind that this is the most sensible way to get a good night's sleep.

He pointed out some constellations while we lay on our backs, watching the stars turn. I told him what I'd learned about the edibility of the ferns that formed our mattress until we drifted off to sleep, our backs pressed together.

The four days it took to reach our destination were the most relaxing I'd had since this whole shit-show started. I didn't have to lead, babysit, or even talk.

The third evening out, we reached the outskirts of Molalla, my home-town. It sat forlornly in the midst of overgrown fields, no lights, no curls of smoke rising from chimneys. My throat tightened, seeing the familiar, low skyline dreary and gray under the clouds. Long grass poked through cracks in the sidewalks, the roads liberally coated in leaves and downed branches along with the snow and muck.

"Let's give it a couple hours and head in," I said. "I know where I want to go."

He dropped his pack and helped me with mine. It still boggled my mind, that he saw a need to take care of me, even though I'd been running like this for so long. Don't get me wrong, I liked it, but still…

"Why this town?"

Because I haven't seen home in over a year, I didn't say. *Because I hoped it would look safe in a dangerous world.* "It's the closest town with a bridal shop that hasn't been blown up."

He slanted a glance my way.

"We didn't blow it up!" I protested.

He shook his head, skeptical. "If you say so. Here, have some delicious MREs." He held out a package.

I wrinkled my nose. "You've been in the military too long. You shouldn't joke about shit like this."

"What are you talking about? These *are* delicious. Compared to when I first joined."

Laughing, we sat down to a meal and a nap before heading into town.

CHAPTER 12

A bullet ricocheted off the car we hid behind. *A Kia*, I noted. *Good riddance.* I knelt, bent over so far my chest pressed against my knee, waiting for an opportunity, but Steve had us trapped behind a podunk piece of shit car at a strip mall. Mere feet stretched between us and the crafts store in front of me, but it might as well have been miles for all the good it did now. The store even had a lovely counter two-thirds of the way back, making a cozy spot away from the firefight if we could get to it.

"Where the fuck did they come from?" Archangel asked, speaking loudly to be heard over the gunfire.

"Honestly, I'm just impressed they finally had a successful ambush," I said, showing my head for a second before pulling back right before a bullet went through it and cast another longing glance at the counter inside the store. "Though they've got a façade blocking their view of us. Shit spot for an ambush, really."

"Oh, I don't know." Archangel stuck a hand around the front and fired a couple rounds blindly, drawing them into shooting more. "They did surprise us. Hate to say it, but I have to give them points for that."

"But what are they doing? Setting up in every single town, hoping we show up? Or is this completely on accident and Steve's managing to improv for the first time, ever? Do you know, I think our little enemy's finally growing up." I wiped away an imaginary tear. A fresh barrage peppered the car, shattering the last bits of glass. "Also, I think we might be fucked."

"And they didn't even buy us dinner first," he shouted, firing again.

I stared, open mouthed. "For some reason, I wasn't expecting sex jokes."

He shot me a quick grin. "Get to know me a little."

Leaving him to keep Steve occupied, I sat comfortably down, keeping my head low, and assessed the situation. The stupid store I wanted was literally twenty feet away. I was so close! Sighing, I checked out the buildings.

"I wish I had some light..."

Whoompf!

The far side of the car went up in flames, the blast forcing us away from our cover. Diving back against its side, the car comfortably warm already, Archangel shook his head at me. "You had to ask!"

Steve picked up their speed, taking advantage of the light. I looked around, trying to spot a way out.

"Any time now," he said urgently.

"I'm thinking," I snapped. "There!" I pulled him down, pointing to what I'd seen: an open vent, hanging from the ceiling of the craft store. It was far back, in the corner, behind their beautiful countertop, out of Steve's sight. If we could cross the distance, we could do it. "We can go through there."

"Are you crazy? Half the time, those things aren't big enough for people. And all they'd have to do is blow up the building!"

"All they have to do is blow up the car, but they haven't done that, either. It's our best chance. These buildings don't have back doors."

"And getting there?"

"I'm waiting until they have to reload. Once you're in, go that way." I nodded towards a bridal store, which also happened to be towards Steve.

He stared at me, at a loss for words. Time slowed, his blue eyes glowing in the light. His skin, tanned and ruddy with cold, looked inviting, asking me to touch his cheek. He froze, staring at me, his eyes traveling over my face. Callused fingertips brushed my cheek, his warm breath puffing over my face as he leaned closer.

A bullet burst through the side of the car, just above our heads, breaking the moment. He gave me a crooked smile. I still stared at him wide eyed, unable to believe what nearly happened. He shook his head as if trying to clear it.

"Towards them? Are you crazy? Wait." He shot me a shaky grin. "Of course, you're crazy. I can't believe I said that. Why do I have to go first?"

"Because we're heading *towards* Steve." I croaked. "I don't want to be first in line for that."

Before he could answer, Steve's fire paused. Archangel shot upright, gun in each hand, firing as rapidly as he could. I raced into the store, pausing at the first bit of cover, a chair. "Go!" I shouted, covering him.

He dived past me, rolled, and hurtled the counter before swarming up the old shelving, some of it breaking under his weight. I ran to join him, sliding across the counter on my belly, tucking into a roll on the far side.

He yanked the vent off and shoved his pack inside, pulling himself after it, thumping and rattling, nearly tearing through the ceiling. I passed him my pack, then he reached down for me. I clasped his hand, using the shelves to help boost my ass up.

"Go, go, go," he hissed, pushing me forward.

"Why the fuck am I in the front?" I complained.

"Because we're going towards Steve. I don't want to be first in line."

"Sneaky, pretty boy," I muttered, wriggling forward as quickly as possible, pushing my pack ahead. Vibrations ran along the narrow shaft as the heavier Archangel followed.

"Move that ass," he whispered. "They'll figure out where—" Shouting erupted behind us, and the duct began shaking in earnest. "Aaand they've figured it out."

"Persistent bastards," I grunted, my chest tightening. I took short, shallow breaths. "Hey. I...uh. I ever tell you I don't like tight spaces?"

"Not right now you don't!" He shoved hard against my feet, sending me sliding.

There was no warning, no groaning of supporters pushed past their limits, nothing. Just the floor dropping out from under me, leaving my stomach behind. Only long habit kept me from screaming, and training put me into a roll, allowing me to land gently on my back. It took long seconds for me to realize what was right above me.

"Perfect-" I grunted, Archangel landing on top of me, flattening my face to the old linoleum.

"If this is how you shop," he gasped, scrambling to his feet, "remind me to never go with you again."

The banging in the duct got closer, the broken, hanging metal shaking like a leaf. Archangel yanked it down, pulled a grenade from his belt, pulled the pin and leaped, throwing it in the shaft in one smooth motion.

By the time the dust drifted out of the shaft, I had my find off its hanger and stuffed into my pack, ready to go. Grabbing his hand, I pulled him away from a display case, pack over my shoulder, to the new hole in the back wall.

"C'mon." I laughed, new energy rushing through me. "Time to get the hell outta Dodge!"

***

"So. Uh. You always carry landmines with you?" Archangel scrutinized me like he hoped he'd suddenly develop the ability to spot metal, wherever it was. "I was a bit...surprised...when you pulled that out."

"Not as surprised as Steve," I said smugly. "Just something I picked up from Phoenix."

"Wonderful," he muttered. "You're learning from Phoenix."

I stopped a moment to look back. Molalla was barely visible, only the smoldering fires left to tell anyone had been there. Would I ever see it like it had been? Would anybody even be left to remember it, or us?

He touched my shoulder and I started. "We should go," he said quietly. "Before someone comes to see what's happening." He adjusted his pack, and it made a suspicious clinking sound.

"Whatcha got in there?"

He grinned. "Wouldn't you like to know?"

I stuck my tongue out at him. "No, wait." He turned back, his eyebrow lifted. Blushing, hoping the darkness hid it, I reached out, straightening the collar of his jacket. "There. I didn't want it to, uh...give you a blister."

He smiled and brushed his thumb over my cheek. "You got a smudge there." Taking my hand, he led the way.

The morning sun was high before we finally made camp. I'd been deep in thought and memories when Archangel stopped in a hollow surrounded by thick bushes.

"I think it's easier for me," he said softly. "Not knowing what this place was before. What was it like?"

"This time of year..." My throat tightened. "This time of year, you'd be seeing people in farming communities in the fields. No singing, though. We're not a fucking Disney film. But people would be in their fields. Grass has been mowed for the first time in ages, and there's tons of lambs. Calves. This is the heart of lambing season."

His face softened and he looked around as if he might see lambs gamboling out here.

I stared blindly. "Summer times...those were the best for food. That highway back there, 214, it's a foodie's paradise. There's a farm stand every few miles. Self-serve. I got a box of strawberries once, this big," I measured out a foot and a half by one foot, "for twenty bucks. Best damn strawberries. It's..." My voice failed me. "I can't." I shook my head, pleading with him. "This isn't a great place to have a breakdown. Make me laugh."

He sighed, leaning against his pack, long legs stretched out in front of him. He nudged my foot. "It's really hard to come up with jokes on command," he said wryly. "I think I've forgotten them all. Who needs jokes when all you have to do for a laugh is watch your fighters and my boys trying to interact? Those women are ruthless."

I huffed, a tiny laugh that lightened the weight in my chest. "They're not that bad."

"That's because you don't have them dramatically clasping their hands to their chests, screeching 'My hero!' every time you do anything."

I shrugged. "Your boys wanted a bit of thanks when they first showed up. Kept saying something about being heroes and 'showing thanks'? So..." I grinned evilly.

"You need to go to sleep," he said, shaking his head, "if you think *that* is appropriate. The first time it happened I spewed stew. It wasn't comfortable," he finished darkly.

I giggled, sprawling against my pack and its precious burden. He grinned, shifting onto his side to watch me. "Okay, you're loopy, now." He got the blankets, spreading the bottom one out and rolling me onto it while I laughed, then laid down next to me. "Go to sleep," he whispered, settling his back against mine.

***

I knew we'd reached home territory when the bird whistles increased. The guards, passing messages. The snow was already melting, forming puddles in the low spots and raising the creeks.

We didn't have to worry about tracks. The next rain would take care of everything, and by the sky we were due for more soon. A little farther in, a slim teenager appeared, sliding down a rope to land lightly, her knees bent to absorb the pressure.

"Mouse," I greeted her, cupping her cheek to press our foreheads together. She sighed, tension flowing out of her shoulders. "How's things at the Lair?"

"All quiet, Captain. Preparations are well on their way for the wedding. Was the hunt successful?" Mouse, maybe fourteen years old, commanded the perimeter guards with a firm grip. We'd found her with three others in a hellhole of a brothel, and she never ceased to amaze me.

She garnered respect from everyone in her area through the innovations she implemented. Most of them were Anansi's ideas, but she took them and ran. Looking up, through the trees, I could barely make out ropes strung between them, providing easier travels and no chance Steve would find their tracks. The guards themselves had tiny platforms to sit on, each spot carefully chosen to provide cover to the guard and a good field of fire.

I already regretted the day she got old enough to join the fighters. The small girl would leave big shoes to fill, but I also understood her need to go out and do what she could for others in her situation. Her second in command, Moose, had no desire to join the fighting arm and would take over when Mouse moved on.

"I found what I was looking for, yeah." She walked beside us for a bit while we talked. Without warning, she disappeared up a tree as easily as she'd come down. A bit of mud at the base of the tree was the only sign she'd been there.

Archangel shook his head, watching her swarm up the tree. "How the hell did they ever come up with that?"

I held my hands up protectively. "I've learned not to ask. That opens a whole can of worms. You do not want a glimpse in their heads. Pick another topic."

"Fine." He grinned, mischief in his eyes. "You can thank me later for coming with you and saving your ass."

"What?" I laughed. "You? I'm sorry, but you make so much noise. There's absolutely nothing about this," I indicated all of him, "that says 'sneaky.'"

His mouth dropped open. "Excuse you? Ex-cuse *you*! Who cussed a blue streak because her favorite bookstore had broken windows?"

"Those books were destroyed," I protested. "We could've *used* them!"

"And the noise brought us to whose attention?" He folded his arms.

I pursed my lips, determined not to give him a smile, shaking with the effort of holding back the laughter. Chatter reached my ears, indistinct still, but we were almost there. Anansi was the first to reach us, crashing headlong into me, taking us both down. I yelped, breaking 'Nansi's fall, my arms and legs waving uselessly like a turtle on its back. Archangel bodily lifted the boy and set him on his feet, then reached down and pulled me up.

Anansi walked us back, moving lightly around. Instead of plodding through mud, having it caked on his boots, he found every patch to avoid it. He used his arms for balance and just...danced.

"He is beautiful," I whispered to Archangel. "How did he learn to move like that while the rest of us are a bunch of elephants?"

"To be fair," he whispered back, "he's not weighted down with a pack."

I stared straight into his deep blue eyes. "Well. As bad as I am, at least I'm not like a drunken cow."

He sputtered, outraged and laughing. "Drunken cow? I was trained by the best this country has to offer!"

"Not when it comes to sneaking around." I grinned, unrepentant.

"If you didn't have a present in that pack…" His hand snaked out, tugged a lock of my hair, and he pulled back before I could do more than turn my head.

I gasped. "Did you just pull my hair?"

We burst into laughter, snickering and sliding through the mud.

"What are you two talking about?" Anansi waited for us at the edge of the meadow. "What's so funny?"

"Nothing." Still giggling, I looked past him. "Uh oh." I sobered up. "Phoenix is coming, and she looks *pissed*."

Anansi got out of her way in a hurry, leaving me and Archangel to face the wrathful woman rapidly approaching. She positively glowed in the weak sunlight, her skin scrubbed smooth. She might've even used a nice lotion instead of grease, and I'd be willing to bet she'd gotten to shave her legs and armpits. I longed for the days when I had smooth legs. Everything itched less then.

"My wedding is in TWO DAYS!" She charged across the clearing and slid to a halt in front of us. "You've been gone, having fun *without me* for eight days? Where's the justice? I've been stuck dealing with wedding planning! Do you know how hard it is to plan a wedding when you haven't got the usual stuff and stores? Pretty easy, actually," she said, blowing on her nails and buffing them on her shirt.

During her tirade, I'd hunched my shoulders and at her last sentence, my mouth dropped open. "You asshole! For that, I don't know if I'm going to give you your present."

Her eyes narrowed. "You got me a present? Did she?" she asked Archangel.

He nodded. "Nearly got our heads blown off in the process," he said seriously.

She looked back to me, still suspicious. "May I still have it?"

A slow grin spread over my face. "Get the Fates. Meeting in your room."

"Yesss!" She punched the air.

"Find your joy where you can," Archangel said softly.

"She'd been through some shit. You'd never recognize her from a year and a half ago." I smiled. "I'd better go. If I'm late, she'll definitely hurt me."

I walked a few steps then turned back. "Thank you for coming with me. It was...fun."

He still had a silly grin on his face when I turned away.

***

I made it to Phoenix's room two steps before the Fates. The three women could make a woman look fantastic with nothing but spit and polish, but we also gave them any beauty products we ever found. While the only time the women ever came on a mission was when Hot Fuzz and Co were captured, anytime we went into Salem and we needed to blend in with the nicer side of the city, we'd go to them to get cleaned up.

Pulling the door closed, I made a show of unbuckling my backpack while Phoenix waited impatiently. I pulled my find out with a flourish, holding up a white wedding dress. The women gasped, Phoenix's eyes tearing immediately. The dress was simply made, a sheath top, full skirt, with spaghetti straps that crisscrossed down the back.

The Fates had Phoenix out of her normal clothes and into the dress in record time. Then they walked around her, gathering loose bits and talking clothes. Pins appeared from thin air. Phoenix looked down at herself, her arms held out from her sides, as if she couldn't believe this was really her.

When they finished pinning and stepped back, I covered my mouth, tearing up. "You look amazing!"

And she did. They'd hemmed it up so that the dress just brushed the floor. It flared slightly from the hips and when Phoenix turned, it swished around in a satisfying way. The back sat a bit low, but then again, Phoenix is short. It accentuated her muscular form and took her from 'Hulk, smash!' to 'I'll kill you, but look sexy while I'm doing it.'

The Second handed Phoenix a handkerchief to blot her tears before they fell on the dress. "You did well," she said to me. "I'm very impressed that you managed to find it."

"I sort of...fell into it." Suddenly exhausted, I excused myself, but not before a nearly naked Phoenix tackled me, sobbing and hugging me.

"I would've married him in a potato sack," she said, "but I'm so glad I'll get to look beautiful for him. Thank you."

I hugged her back. "You'd make a potato sack look good, and you know it."

***

The morning of the wedding dawned bright and clear, the second day of sun. The mud dried enough that Amana had no qualms about sending the gatherers out to find things to pretty up the common room. Wildwood, the herbalist, went with them, full of ideas on what they needed.

The hunters had come back yesterday with enough game to give us a feast that wasn't stew, and Lavender took charge of the kitchen. Delicious smells mixed with the banging and clatter of pots and pans while they worked furiously.

When the gatherers returned, I was volunteered—along with everyone else—into hanging garlands of evergreens, holly, and early flowers around the common room. The boys rearranged furniture, stacking the tables against the wall and lining the benches up so that everyone would be facing the back wall, their backs to the kitchen.

Amana covered the game tables with sheets stolen from cupboards, decorating a rough arch constructed from I-have-no-idea-what. I just hoped we still had all our toilets. The evergreens' scent filled the room. I closed my eyes, inhaling deeply.

Across the room, my brother flirted with Dereva, drawing a frond across her cheek. She blushed and gave him a look.

Eleanor swept into the room as we nearly finished decorating. "Captain, Phoenix would like to see you."

Casting Amana a worried glance, I followed her out of the room, potential problems running through my head.

"What's wrong?" I asked the moment I entered Phoenix's room.

"Why would you think something was wrong?" Phoenix turned. My mouth dropped open. She'd been completely transformed by the Fates. Light makeup accented her eyes and hid the tiny scars she'd acquired.

This was what she would've looked like before I'd ever met her, her skin smooth and clear. They put her hair up, trilliums carefully placed through the piled mass of curls. The dress fit her perfectly. As beautiful as she'd looked in it the other day, this was on a whole other level.

"You're gorgeous!" I blurted, tears forming. "Gryphon is going to lose it when he sees you."

I kept staring, completely forgetting that I'd been summoned until I reached Phoenix's face again and saw her own tears. She smoothed the fabric over her hips, a small smile trembling on her lips. "I wanted to ask..."

Wiping my tears, I took the handkerchief Eleanor offered and blew my nose. "What?"

"Would you be my maid of honor?"

My lip trembled and I bit it, my face crumpling. Eleanor, standing quietly to the side, rushed over, wrapping me in her arms, my adoptive mother to the rescue. I sobbed into her shoulder, clutching her tightly. Phoenix hovered around the edges, rubbing my back, apologizing.

"I want to," I bawled. "I just…" An unfamiliar emotion bloomed in my chest, squeezing and expanding simultaneously.

"I think she's happy," I dimly heard Eleanor say. "She did think there was a problem. It's okay, just give her a minute."

When I finally regained control, tears spent, the Fates were in the room. I stepped away from Eleanor, sniffling and wiping my nose while they clustered around, gently wiping my face with a cool cloth, and stroking my hair back. I stood quietly under their ministrations, enjoying the peaceful attention.

"So," the First smiled, mischief in her eyes, "you will be her maid of honor, yes?"

I nodded.

My weapons were laid respectfully in a corner (treated with more respect than me), and I found myself unceremoniously stripped and washed before being bundled in Eleanor's clothing. Eleanor was the only person in the Lair who regularly wore clothing the Fates deemed appropriate for a maid of honor.

They'd hemmed one of her skirts, bringing it to my knees, and I blissfully got to shave. I rubbed my legs together, enjoying smooth skin. The skirt was simple, black, one of the A-line skirts Eleanor favored. The blouse, a lovely midnight blue, was snug in the shoulders and the chest only fit because we left it unbuttoned enough to show cleavage.

The Third couldn't resist teasing me about my breasts, usually invisible under all my layers. Once dressed, I spun and twirled, enjoying the drape and swirl of fabric. I rarely wore dresses Before, and certainly hadn't since. The beautiful, drapey fabric was an entirely new arena.

"While I am glad you enjoy this," the First stepped forward, holding a bag of brushes, "there is still more to do."

Reluctantly, I sat down, closing my eyes or pursing my lips at their direction. The Third brushed and styled my hair, settling on battle braids that looked like a mohawk. They worked quickly, mindful of the time and updates Optimus Prime brought. Phoenix stood off to the side with Eleanor, quietly going over her vows one last time.

When they were done, the First Fate handed me a small mirror. I smiled, surprised. "I'm pretty! And not looking like a prostitute." I grinned slyly at the First and she laughed, reminded of the last time I wore a dress. Although calling that scrap of cloth a dress had been too generous.

"Pretty, hah!" the Second said. I braced myself for the usual round of "No, you're *very* pretty," and "Don't worry, you'll be next," accompanied by sympathetic pats. She continued. "'Pretty' is mild and boring. You are fierce, elegant. You wear a dress to show your lethality and athleticism. 'Pretty' is for those who lack the character to be more. It is...faugh!" She sniffed, her nose in the air that I'd insulted myself this way.

The First slipped her arms around the Second's waist, resting her chin on the other woman's shoulder, sighing as she looked at me and Phoenix. "I love weddings."

The Third smiled at them, love in her eyes. How did they do it? Stay so in love after all those years together?

"Ladies," Eleanor turned away from the door, where she'd been having a whispered conversation. "It's time."

At the door, we paused while Eleanor and the Fates slipped in and found their seats. Phoenix clutched my hand and whispered, "I'm the luckiest woman in the world."

"You bitch," I whispered back.

She laughed and pushed me gently towards the door.

When she entered, Anansi and Dereva sang a song I'd never heard before, sweet, old. Under the arch, Gryphon stood next to our preacher, Shepherd, Archangel at his back. Like grooms and best men throughout history, they were armed, which made me smile. Both men wore clean, white dress shirts. Archangel had his sleeves rolled up to his elbows and I discovered something new that could make me hot and bothered.

The scent of pine and spruce permeated the room, rich, heady, and so alive, just like the people filling the benches.

Archangel watched me, his eyes hot. They flickered away for just a second, taking in the woman entering behind before fixing on me again. Gryphon's eyes filled with tears, watching his bride, and I could barely tear my gaze from a man who openly cried at the sight of his love, but I did, for the brilliant, deep blue eyes that didn't look away from mine.

Reaching the end, I stepped back, taking Phoenix's bouquet of pine, spruce, and cedar, sprinkled with early flowers. Gryphon took her hand and they turned to Shepherd. He spoke simply, from his heart.

The wedding flew by. Weird. For Grace, we'd spent days, weeks, months, agonizing over decorations, dresses, color schemes. For something that was over in minutes.

Now, our focus was giving them a day of peace and joy, and about the rest of their lives, however long that might be. It changed...everything.

Then, Shepherd asked for the rings.

Phoenix turned to me, and I stared back, stricken. I hadn't even thought of rings. I'd just wanted a pretty dress for her.

"Uh, never mind," Shepherd stumbled.

But Archangel reached around Gryphon, a shit-eating grin on his face. Nestled in the center of his palm, two rings lay. Gryphon scooped them up, took Phoenix's left hand and slid a slender gold band onto her fourth finger.

"You didn't think I'd forget, did you?" he whispered, passing her the larger ring.

Phoenix gave a watery laugh, wiping her eyes. Eleanor hopped up, passing me a handkerchief for her. Everyone cheered when Shepherd announced that they could kiss. Gryphon swept her up, kissing long enough for the cheers to turn into laughter.

Photographer was everywhere, snapping pictures on his ancient camera. We even posed for some. Hordes of people shuffled benches and brought the tables back in, lining them up for Lavender to begin directing the meal.

Waiting for a space to be created, I found myself next to Archangel. "Rings, huh?"

He grinned. "Gryphon really wanted one. I found a few so he could choose."

"How did I not notice you grabbing them?"

"You were busy picking a dress." He shrugged, shifting closer to allow a table to make it past us. "On the plus side, there's more."

"...How many did you get? How many couples do we have?"

"A lot."

"A lot of what?"

He laughed. "Both. You really are oblivious to people, aren't you?"

"Hey!"

***

The only person not enjoying herself at the wedding was a new woman, Gorgon. She wasn't a part of the fighters yet. Kestrel wouldn't give her the all-clear. She lurked on the edges of the party, muttering to two more. I leaned over to point them out to Phoenix, then thought better.

Photographer steered clear of them, flinching when one stomped a foot in his direction. I frowned. Behavior like that was unacceptable. We'd seen too often what could happen when aggression snowballed under pressure and imagined power. No wonder Kestrel hadn't okayed them.

The food was plentiful and delicious, served family style. Platters came out and people helped themselves, filling and refilling plates and cups. Perimeter guards came and went, everyone getting a chance to drink to the happy couple and grab a solid meal. The hunters and scavengers rotated with them, giving everyone an hour or two at the wedding and reception.

Archangel brought his drink around and sat next to me. "I'm sorry, but I can't hear myself with them right behind me."

I laughed at the rowdy young fighters. They were well on their way to drunk, loud and animated. "Liar. You know you love it."

He grinned and leaned in to be more easily heard. "Penny for your thoughts?"

I grunted. "Not worth a penny." I looked to Gorgon again. She pushed one of Lavender's kitchen crew...right into Sarge. "I guess I'm torn between wanting everyone to be happy and wanting to take someone to the gym and work them over."

He followed my gaze to where Sarge lectured the young women, his finger moving from one to the other. I'd have to talk to him. My head spun pleasantly. When I remembered, because there was every probability that I wouldn't remember chunks of tonight.

"Sarge'll sort her out," he said confidently. I was less sure of that, but there wasn't anything to do about it now.

A hunter produced a guitar from nowhere and a spritely tune was plucked. Archangel grabbed my hand, pulling me onto a small, cleared space.

"Come on, Captain," he called. "Let's show the kids how it's done."

"I don't know how to dance," I protested, following reluctantly.

"Nobody ever does. Just...follow my lead."

He swung me around into a fast paced, spinning dance, the mutant child of a waltz and square dancing. More people joined us, the tables slowly being cleared to give us more space. A set of spoons and a harmonica sang and tapped a beat, calling more people to the floor.

He held me tightly, to keep us from careening into other couples, everyone out for a good time. We staggered out for a drink and a breath before barreling back in, cannonballing through the dancers. I laughed, spinning and gripping his shoulder for support and balance. Who would've thought dancing could be so fun?

The dancing slowed down as people got too drunk to move easily, and then another wedding tradition was remembered.

"Speech! Speech!" A drunken Storm pounded her table. "Izn 'ere s'posed t' be a speech?"

"You jzrunk?" Sirius asked, listing sharply.

"Nah!" She waved. "On'y had one!" She held up two fingers. The two of them fell over themselves, cackling.

"Uh, oh. They've pulled out the blend." I shook my head. They were going to have a hell of a hangover tomorrow. I sniffed my glass carefully. Pretty sure it was plain old vodka with a bit of tea, but it was hard to tell.

Archangel leaned hard against me. "W'ass it a blend of?" he asked, watching his glass carefully.

"You don't want to know. Is that what you're drinking?" Dirt Huggers was bad enough, but when Anansi blended it with the turnip stuff...It hit even harder.

Dereva and Hot Fuzz ignored everyone, pressing close together, giggling and whispering. I smiled, watching them. So innocent and oblivious. Until he bit her earlobe. Frowning, I glanced around to find Eleanor. She should really know about...

She was already watching them. Catching my eye, she nodded. I shrugged. Guess she had it in hand. Kioni might want to kill me when we found her, but she'd have to get in line. After all, she'd probably want to skin me just for Anansi and all the shit I'd let him do.

Some of the more sober people took up Storm's call.

"Speech! Speech!"

I nudged Archangel. "That's you, pretty boy."

"Dammit. I was hoping they'd forget the speech thing." He took a long swig of his drink.

"When did you write it?" We'd all been running for the last few days.

"About four hours ago." Standing up, he rested his hand on my shoulder, leaning a bit. Oh, shit. I hoped he made it through without falling or passing out.

"Ladies and gents, fighters and civilians," he began. I smiled into my cup. "When Gryphon asked me to be his best man—it seems like a lifetime ago, after only one shopping trip with our beloved Captain..." This got cheers and laughter. "I was honored. I was also bummed out because I have no dirt on the man whatsoever. No overly embarrassing stories. In fact, the first time I saw him he was so heroic *I* nearly fell in love with him."

For all that he'd had to drink, his speech went well. Slurring was down to a minimum, and he would pause occasionally to collect himself. He gripped my shoulder, slowly leaning harder but trying to hide it. They laughed with him, sighed when he described Gryphon's dramatic rescue of Phoenix, and a few shed tears when he mentioned their love.

Basically, they were eating out of his hand. Bastard.

He wrapped the speech up to laughter and applause. Downing his drink to cheers, he turned it upside down to show it was empty and sat heavily next to me. "Fuck," he muttered, leaning his forearms on the table. "I think I'm drunker now than when I started. Shit."

He began slipping to the side and I grabbed his arm, hauling him upright. The room swayed. "Whoa, big guy. Bedtime for you. And for me. I'm drunker than I thought."

We wouldn't be the first to leave. Amana and Al had already collected Storm and Sirius. A few people were sleeping where they sat, and Lavender went around with spare blankets, covering some and helping others lie down.

"Aw, c'mon," he protested while I got his arm over my shoulders. "Issa wedding! I'm s'posed to be drunk!"

"You pass out, I'm leaving you," I said. "I can't haul your ass to your room by myself."

"C'n haul my ass to your room," he muttered. My mouth dropped open, but he continued almost without pause. "Okay. Fine. Meanie."

We staggered and swayed towards the door, stepping carefully over and around people. He sagged a little more and I had to bend my knees to find a better level to support him. Getting him to bed would be my good deed for today. The rest could shift for themselves.

Driver and Lavender, apparently deciding they'd done what they could, were back on the dance floor, swaying to a slow tune. Phoenix and Gryphon had disappeared sometime between the end of the speech and now, and I was damned if I knew when it happened. Eleanor and Dry Eyes joined the other couple, enjoying the music and moving easily.

I puffed, hauling Archangel down the hall. Who would've thought a man this short would be so heavy? He was barely taller than me and Driver, and I'd carried Driver before. He couldn't weigh this much. Where did Archangel put it? He staggered, sagging a little more.

"No...!" I grunted. "You're supposed to be...oof!" I careened into the wall. We bounced off it, unsteadily weaving across the hall like a drunken bumblebee. "Never mind. New plan. We're not going to your room anymore."

I wouldn't make it that far, even on my own. No way I could do it with him.

"Mmmm?" he asked.

"My room." I groaned.

At my door, I had a frantic second where I had to let go of something to open it without dropping him. Once inside, we made the four steps from door to bed, and I simply dropped Archangel on it. I took a minute, hands on my knees, to breathe.

Dropping to my knees, I scrabbled for a match and a candle stub, lighting it carefully and spitting on the match to make sure it was out. It'd be embarrassing if I started a fire because I was drunk. Archangel sprawled across my bed, one arm outflung and his legs dragging on the floor.

I sighed. "Let's get you..." I grunted, lifting his legs and pulling them around, trying to straighten the man out. His face was buried in the blanket. I hurriedly rolled him over to clear his airways.

What else? Boots. Eleanor would never forgive me if I put someone to bed and left their boots on. I surveyed him. Holsters, guns, and harnesses were next. I struggled to move him, working stubborn buckles that became complex puzzles after a few drinks, pretending to not notice the firm muscles under my hands.

"Mmm...Nope. Don't know nothing," I muttered in a singsong. "No, Eleanor, I never felt him up. Nope, not accidentally groping an unconscious man, even if it is in the interests of getting him comfortable. Uh, uh. Oh, shit! I'm a creeper. I'm the creeper. How the fuck did that happen? I'm finally close to a man I'm attracted to, who I think is attracted to me, and I'm a creeper? My life sucks."

At one point, I had to stop to catch my breath, leaning heavily on his side, panting and dealing with my buzz, on top of his unconscious self. "Why are you so *heavy*?!" I gasped.

His stuff got dumped at the foot of the mattress, next to my gear. I surveyed him to make sure I hadn't forgotten anything. Nope. He was in shirt, pants, and socks, and he could stay like that. The blanket covered him, and he lay on his side, his tousled blond hair obscuring part of his face while he snored softly.

Now, what about me? "Fuck it, man," I told him. "I'm not sleeping on the floor of my own room, and I'm not wandering around, hoping to find an unoccupied bed, so you're gonna have to suck it up and share." I pulled on a pair of soft shorts, ditching the blouse and bra for a t-shirt. I don't care how comfortable a bra is, it's still not meant to be slept in.

Pushing him over, I crawled in, too drunk and tired to really care about the overall situation, and pulled the blanket up, over our shoulders. Tomorrow could sort itself out.

***

I groaned before my eyes even opened. How much had I had? Flashes of the wedding came through, and I relaxed. Not as bad as last time, then. Shifting slightly, I sighed. I'd slept unbelievably well. Having something warm to lean back against certainly didn't hurt. It was quite nice...

I bolted upright, twisting to see a blond head nestled on the pillow behind me. "Oh, shit. Oh, shit, ohshit, ohshit." Panic ripped through me. What the hell had I been thinking? I gaped at the man lying in my bed, remembering the last part of the evening.

Archangel stirred, flexing his hand. Which happened to be on my thigh. I froze, hoping he wouldn't notice, but he squeezed again, running his hand down, then up. I squeaked, grabbing his wrist. His eyes flew open, bloodshot but aware.

My stomach tightened as he slowly removed his hand, never breaking eye contact. I could swear he stroked my leg, but I didn't have the guts to ask. "So," he said. "It appears I'm not the only one who can't find another room when drunk."

"I'd say that at least it's my room, but somehow, that doesn't seem like much comfort right now."

"I didn't snore, did I?" He moved slowly, sitting up and stuffing the pillow behind his back. His shirt had come partially undone during the night and I wrenched my eyes away. "No, don't answer that. Do I need to worry about someone bursting in here to break my balls?"

I grinned. "No. No man has ever tried to get in my pants, and I'm pretty sure nobody expects one to."

"Wow..." He stared at me, shaking his head slowly.

"What?"

"Just...the number of idiots you've met."

"Not like I'm pretty. Pretty Boy." My lip curled in a poor attempt at a smile, but he just kept shaking his head.

"'Pretty' is what you call someone when they haven't got anything except passable looks to go on." He clambered off the bed, gathering his things slowly. At the door, he stood helplessly, unable to open it. He gave me a pleading look, still drunk. "Help?"

Sighing, I opened the door for him. Like a falling tree, he sagged, pinning me against the wall. He studied my face, then leaned in and kissed me. Slowly. Deeply. Lips and teeth and tongue. Pulling away, he shook his head again. "'Pretty' is so bland compared to what you are. Those men weren't just idiots. They were cowards, too."

I stared, wide eyed, while he ambled out the door, as if my world hadn't just turned upside down.

Chapter 13

Woman 1: We are not changing the timeline. It took me years to get Kim Soon
Ong ready to invade. Do your part!
Man 1: I just found out about those outposts along the coast! If we want this
to work, I need time to get the military out.
Recorded phone conversation, June 23, 2061

Over the next two months, Archangel's prediction about weddings proved correct. The snow melted fully, new, bright green leaves graced the trees, and we had half a dozen weddings. Each bride wore the same dress, adjusted by the Fates to fit them as well as it had Phoenix. Except Gameboy and Stretch, but then, neither of them *liked* dresses. And when Triskele and Kestrel got married, I regretted not having two dresses, but Kestrel made do with some things from the Fates and Eleanor, so it all worked out.

Anansi's still went full throttle, churning through the old root vegetables scrounged from valley gardens, until Doc banned drinking excessively after our second case of liver poisoning.

"No," she said, slashing a hand through the air. "I'm already up to my eyes with colds, flu, bruises, cuts, and punctures. I'm not dealing with any more self-inflicted shit. You all are done. Two drinks and that's it."

When Eleanor, Amana, and Lavender backed her up, I backed down. No one else was stupid enough to go against that lot, either.

Sirius hid behind me, stretching up to whisper, "We should let them loose on Steve. This'll be done inside a month."

"Stop hiding and tell them that yourself," I muttered from the corner of my mouth, never taking my eyes from the irate women descending on the hapless Dionysius. He'd gotten drunk to forget, and in response, Eleanor had him booked to see Kestrel, no complaints or he was off the Irregulars.

After Amana and Al's wedding, every woman wearing a bra designed by him got together to give him a whole tool kit: knife, leather punch, needles, scissors, tape measure, tons of scrap fabric, and sinew. We even cut the sinew to a good width, as decreed by Wisteria. It took us two scavenging raids and a run-in with Steve, but it was worth it to see his face when we presented the gift.

After spending somewhere around two months in the Valley, everyone needed a break, so we limited excursions during this time. We were twitchy, on edge, and burning out. Kestrel and Doc agreed we needed the break.

So, we finished building the mobile planting beds, filling them with compost and scraps from the kitchen. Various seeds and some old potatoes were the first things planted. Home had most of everything we'd ever found, but we did keep a few of each type of seed. The beds spent most of their time hiding next to the road, but occasionally, we'd bring them in or send someone out to water them.

The chores list was never ending. Training, hunting, cleaning, gathering, mending... We also took the opportunity to restock our larders.

And every vehicle got a major overhaul. I'd been tinkering for months, trying to keep these things running. Now, I selected the worst ones to be used for spare parts and expanded my forge, turning it into a decent workspace.

Shortly after Amana's wedding, my brother and Dereva made their relationship official. Most people were thrilled, but Anansi wouldn't stop glaring at Hot Fuzz. The teenager would visit me in the garage, complaining about how soppy his sister had gotten since she fell in love.

He left a bit before me for dinner one day, and as I approached the corridor, voices stopped me. I peeked around the corner to see Anansi barring the way, thin, wiry arms folded over his narrow chest, glaring up at Fuzz, who towered over him. "Dude, just because you're with my sister doesn't mean I have to like you. And knowing what you're getting up to..." He shook his head. "I'm scarred. Seriously. I had to see Kestrel to deal with it."

Hot Fuzz gave the teenager a condescending smile. "Listen, when you fall in love someday, you'll..."

"Understand?" Anansi scoffed. "Whatever. Just don't hurt her. If you do," his voice turned cold, a tone I'd never heard from him before, "I'll wait until you're asleep and set up an alcohol IV directly into your bloodstream. Once you've died of liver poisoning, I'll dissolve you in a tub of lime. Then, I'll help them look for you."

The level tone and absolute certainty with which the boy uttered those words made Fuzz lose his cocky grin. He rocked back on his heels, probably from the force of Anansi's iron will. My brother looked around the corridor, as if hunting for witnesses. Or an escape.

"Welcome to the family." The little shit grinned, punched Fuzz on the arm, and walked jauntily down the corridor, whistling.

Fuzz stared after him, frozen. I bit the meaty part of my palm to stifle the laughter, muffling squeals until he'd gone, trailing slowly after Anansi. Once he left, I hustled back into the garage, howling. Peter had been an overconfident little shit at a young age because he got tall fast.

Somewhere in that brain of his, he equated height with maturity, so shorter people were somehow not as aware of life. At six foot four, that was most people. The army had worn a lot of that arrogance out. Looks like Anansi just took care of the rest of it.

My legs gave out and I slumped on a bumper when Archangel walked in on me, mid-howl. The look on his face sobered me up.

"You," he jabbed a finger in my direction, "have been avoiding me."

"Whaaat?" I glanced away, the laughter gone. "No, I haven't. Honest."

"Bullshit." He stalked closer. "And you've been missing out on your doctor-mandated massages."

"I have not! Amana's been working on me." After what he'd said, I could barely be in the same room as him. Having him give me a massage? I'd go up in flames or do something embarrassing.

Hurt flashed across his face, gone so quickly I almost thought I imagined it. He moved closer. It was exactly the same as watching a wolf stalk a deer. "You. Are. Avoiding. Me. Why?"

I skittered back to avoid being cornered. "I haven't." Embarrassment gave way to something new. Focused. Intent. His slow advance continued until I came up against the wall.

I had been avoiding him. It was that damn kiss. I didn't know what to do with it. He'd been drunk. I'm an emotional mess. It wasn't the kind of thing that should mean anything, and yet... And yet. To me, it had. He'd acted as if nothing happened, and I had to wonder if he even remembered.

"Liar." A stray beam of sunlight glanced off his hair, cutting across his face, casting half of it in shadow. It illuminated one eye, practically glowing blue as if lit from within. "What happened? Tell me."

Disappointment lanced through me. He didn't remember, but...I watched him as intently as a rabbit watches a fox. Was that desire or anger? I didn't know enough about one to tell it from the other. He leaned in, so close I scented him with every breath. Pine, dirt, a hint of green, and underneath, sweat.

His pulse beat faster, and my breath hitched. His eyes darted to my neck, and he bit his lip. Unable to take the proximity, I slid sideways, only to find the way blocked by his arm. He watched me intently, a small smile playing over his lips.

Without passing through my brain at all to check on the wisdom of it, my mouth said, "Make me."

He grinned, his mouth a hair's breadth from mine. "If you insist."

An instant before he kissed me, I slid down the wall, rolling to the side and hopping to my feet. His eyes sparkled and he fell into a classic stance, feet shoulder width apart, one behind the other. I stayed just out of arm's reach, circling until my back was to the garage once more.

"You didn't think it would be that easy, did you?" I taunted.

He attacked in a flurry, so quick it was all I could do to block or deflect. It ended with him holding my right wrist, our arms high. Meeting his eyes, I smiled as sweetly as I knew how and, seeing his eyes narrow with suspicion, stomped on his foot.

I retreated, laughing as he growled and came after me, his teeth bared in a grin. Neither of us could gain the upper hand, but I'd seen him fight. He could pull a dirty trick or three that I wouldn't be able to fight off, but he didn't. He...played. Back and forth, we ranged over the garage.

I twisted, kicking from the hip, and he turned, catching it on his arm. Curling it, he captured my foot. Rotating on my standing leg, I fell into a forward roll, popping back to my feet and ran around my pickup for protection. I turned, just in time to see him slide across the hood.

"Shit!"

He caught my shirt, hauling me back, trying to trap me. I exhaled, raised my arms and dropped, sliding right out, leaving him holding an empty shirt.

"You know," he panted, "if you wanted to get naked, all you had to do was ask. Or answer the damn question."

He punched before he finished his last sentence. I blocked it, dancing away from the kick that soon followed. He pursued. I darted in, throwing a series of punches. Once his attention was on my hands, I kicked. He turned just in time to catch it on his thigh. I spun too far and he got behind me. Warm hands locked together against my stomach, holding me still.

"Tell me," he breathed against my ear. I shivered. "Why have you been avoiding me?"

"Gotta do better than that." I stomped on his other foot, making him howl, loosening his grip enough for me to get his arm over my shoulder, tucking myself tightly against him. Dropping, I used my body weight to bring him over, dumping him on his back.

Quick, quicker than I would've thought possible, he slapped the ground with his free hand, releasing the pent-up momentum. His other hand, the one I held, hooked into my bra strap, yanking me down. He rolled us until I was on my back. He was against my side, one arm hooked around my neck, the other holding my arm outstretched, trapped against his body.

To an ignorant onlooker, we appeared to be in an intimate embrace. To any fighter, we were in a hold that was damned difficult to get out of.

"If you try any monkey business," he ground out, a hair's breadth away, "I will kiss you."

Probably the only threat I would listen to, damn him. I ceased squirming. "You can't," I squeaked, bending my knees and adjusting my hips. "There's rules and we are nowhere near that."

"Everyone has broken those rules. Trust me." His dark blue eyes shone like an Oregon sky at the height of summer. A red spot on his cheek showed where I'd managed to clip him, but it didn't detract from the humor in his eyes. "Tell me. Please."

I shifted restlessly, hoping he didn't notice exactly what I was doing. "Since you asked nicely."

I wet my lips, searching for the right words. He slackened his hold slightly, and I seized the moment. Wrapping my arms around his middle, I pulled him tight to my hip. Pressing my heels to the ground, I arched, lifting him bodily and threw him over. He grunted but stayed down, watching me intently.

Instead of scrambling to put him in the same hold, I rolled to my feet. He'd said please. Time to go out on a limb like Eleanor was always urging me to do.

"You complimented me." I swallowed. "Kissed me. I don't know how to handle that. I just...I don't."

Unable to face him any longer, I snatched up my shirt. For the first time since all this shit started, I ran away, leaving him lying on the floor, a dumbfounded expression on his ridiculously handsome face.

***

"What do you mean 'for the first time'?" Phoenix asked a short time later. She'd cornered me and dragged me into my room. Mine, since hers had Gryphon in it. "We run away all the time!"

"Those are 'daring escapes.'" I rolled my eyes. "Or that's what I'm told. This time, I just...I ran. I couldn't..."

"So, what are you going to do next?"

"I don't know," I wailed. "I have no fucking experience with any of this. I've never had a boyfriend. I barely even *dated!*"

"Well." She stared at me, impassive. "It's not hard to see why he's falling for you..." I snorted but she ignored me. "While you may have the personality of an angry rhino, you've got a great ass and legs—which he's already seen, good for him—and you're passably pretty, though we might want to do something about how you dress…"

"How I dress is perfectly acceptable for these shit times!" I folded my arms.

"…which is okay, but it doesn't really show off your features. And by features, I mean your boobs." She scrutinized me like a choice piece of meat, her head tilted to the side.

I found I didn't mind her blunt assessment, if only because she didn't give back-handed compliments like "You could be so pretty, if only (insert bad fashion advice here)." Except… "Where are you going with all this?" I asked. "What's the point of having me dress up?"

"To get him to make a move." She gave me a 'duh' look, as if it was obvious.

I looked up, biting my lip. I still hadn't told her about the kiss. I probably wouldn't start now. "I already have his attention. The problem is I don't know what to do with it."

"Kiss him, idiot."

"Isn't there something else we could be talking about?" I asked desperately. "Some crisis? Steve encroaching on our territory again? Gorgon?"

"Nope!" She plopped down on the floor, leaning against the wall. "Amana and Lavender have this place running like clockwork, Eleanor and Kestrel are seeing to people's emotional wellbeing, and a hunting party left just this morning. We're all good." She grinned, terrifyingly evil in her delight.

I sighed. "Is it just me, or is this the first time we've really had a normal conversation? The kind we would've had Before?" I sighed again and slid down the wall. "I miss talking about guns, supplies, and raids. They were so much simpler. Can we have one of those?" I asked hopefully.

"No, dumbass. We need to talk about why you're so scared of this, all things considered."

I narrowed my eyes. "You just think this is funny, don't you?"

"Of course! But you're obviously an idiot about these things, so you'll never figure it out on your own and I'd hate to see you miss out on a good relationship because Kestrel is busy and you're stubborn." She stretched her legs out. "So, spill."

***

At dinner that night, Archangel didn't say anything, just sat next to me, immediately digging into his meal. I released my breath in a relieved rush. Apparently, he was more interested in dinner than me. Until he nudged me playfully with his foot. I started and he cast me a sly, sideways smile but his spoon didn't stop moving.

Words stuck in my throat until Lavender moved past with fresh bread. "Oh, bless you," I murmured, taking one. "I'm starving."

A large foot settled on top of mine, I kicked him lightly, carrying on with the business of eating. Like most of our meals, it was soup. Or stew. I'm still fuzzy on the difference. Chunkier? Meat? I called it whatever Amana told me to. Whatever it was, it had chunks of meat, but it was strangely light on potatoes.

I frowned at my bowl. "Are we running low on potatoes already? Do we need to go hunting for more?"

"More would always be nice," Lavender said. "Ah!" She lifted the tray of bread higher to keep it out of her husband's reach. "You've already had yours. Hands off."

"My own wife." Driver shook his head, patting her hip. "Won't bend the rules for me. What is the world coming to?" Grinning, he stood long enough to steal a kiss to a few random whoops and cheers.

Archangel, still smiling, answered my question while simultaneously beginning a war under the table. "What potatoes didn't fit into the garden beds, we chopped up and planted in the forest." The footsie war ended when his feet rested on mind again, pressing to keep me from knocking them off without causing a scene. "They're not that weird looking, so even if Steve comes close, they shouldn't notice."

I snarled slightly, unable to move now because he had both my feet trapped. "'Nansi! Stop making—and I can't believe I'm saying this—stop making alcohol."

"We are already doing this," Amana informed me. "Where jou live? Under a rock?"

"Ooohhhh!" The sound rose from so many throats I couldn't tell where it started. People looked between us, waiting for the next volley.

"Actually," I shouted, striving to be heard over the laughter, "I'm living under a few tons of rock."

Storm cracked up, thumping the table. "She's got you there!"

Amana huffed and shook her finger at me, but her smile lit up her dark eyes. Then Al leaned into her with a question and dinner went back to normal.

Archangel leaned closer. "Where's River?"

I stared at him mutely, wiggling my toes, reminding him they were still trapped. He waited, but I merely pursed my lips. He sighed and removed his feet. "She's in Salem, meeting her contacts. Time for another raid to Salem, I reckon. Just for shits and giggles," I finished grimly.

As much as I never wanted to see that city again, we couldn't leave people there. Not only that, but on every trip, I dreamed I'd find the rest of my family. While we never mentioned them in normal conversation, I'd seen a faraway look in people's eyes enough to know they dreamed, too.

***

Two days after my 'conversation' with Archangel in the garage, I still had no better idea what to do about a budding relationship. I sat alone at a trestle table, having just finished in the gym. It was time to sharpen my knives and oil them. Keeping weapons in top shape was a time-consuming business.

At the other end of the room, a few younger people played around the tables, letting off some steam and remembering their age. I smiled, my hands never stopping the smooth movement to sharpen the blade. Amana came over, a teapot in hand.

"What kind of tea today?" I asked.

"Is no tea, is herbal infusion," she replied with a slight smile.

I glared at the liquid as she poured it into my mug. "What's the difference? And thank you." Why did even tea have to be so complicated?

"No tea leaves, *hermana*." She turned back to the kitchen. I stuck my tongue out at her back. "Is no' nice to do that. Did jou *madre* never teach jou manners?"

"How the hell did you know what I did?"

She turned, smiling serenely. "Because jou are very simple, and very predictable."

She snickered in the face of my glare. "How does Al manage to live with this level of smart-assery?" I demanded.

Amana shrugged. "He loves me."

Those simply spoken words shook me to my core, and I looked down before she could see it. Part of me longed for love, but another part was terrified. I'd seen what it did to my dad, losing Mom the way he had. I'd rather walk into Steve's camp stark naked than risk myself that way.

Except...

Her quiet confidence, the knowledge that no matter what, she had a person in her corner...I'd seen her, several times, turn to Al without a second thought. Amana didn't have to say what bothered her; he simply gave without reservation. And vice versa.

I'd seen the same thing with Phoenix and Gryphon and with several other couples. I wanted it so badly, but how did they *know?* How could they be so sure of this one person and know they would never be abandoned or left behind?

I'd seen so many people leap before they looked, going from one relationship to another, outwardly confident that this was forever. Then, they'd be crushed when it wasn't. Such recklessness.

Fear twinged in my chest, worse than looking down the barrel of a gun. My life was easy to gamble. If I was dead, then nothing here mattered. But a wrong choice in love? Or, what if they died? In this world, that was increasingly likely. But what was life without love? What was the point, if all you did was hide your heart away?

I was so caught up in my head, I didn't even know Amana left until she was busy in the kitchen again.

***

River returned from Salem a week later, bearing news. Our usual suspects gathered in the Useless Room. Sarge, Seahorse, Driver, Lavender, Eleanor, Doc, Dereva, Archangel, Sirius, Phoenix, and Gryphon. Anansi and Hot Fuzz decided to join us today, sitting to the side.

"Captain." River addressed me directly, as usual, rarely speaking to the group in the Useless Room. "Shrike's noticed Steve's feeling pretty secure in Salem. Plus, they've managed to figure out the location of a bunch of pregnant women."

People sat up straighter.

"How accurate is this?" Seahorse demanded.

"Can they trust the source?" Archangel had different concerns. "Is it possible that this is bait for a trap?"

"Fairly accurate." River touched a spot on the map. "And unlikely that it's bait. They collect information and put it together. There is no single source, but gossip from a bunch of people." Spinning suddenly, she paced. Her namesake suited her. Sometimes, like now, her agitation was visible for all to see. Other times, she was the epitome of 'still waters run deep.' "It sounds like the women had been kept outside but were brought in to keep them from being found. Bad news? Not sure on their numbers, or how far along they are. Worse news? They're being held in the University."

"Ah, fuck." I sat back, my clasped hands resting on my head as I regarded the Salem map.

"Why is it bad?" Driver asked.

"Because that's Dorothy's barracks," Phoenix said grimly. "The Capitol is right next door, and it's being used as Steve's headquarters, so security around there is pretty heavy."

"Did Shrike have a rough location?" I rolled my chair to the next table over, the one with a detailed map of Salem on the top.

"So, Dorothy's at Willamette University, right?" River put a marker on the complex when I nodded. "But it's pretty big, made up of a whole bunch of smaller buildings, max two story." I nodded again. "As far as Shrike can tell, the women are in one of the buildings to the north, closest to the Capitol."

"Fuck me," I muttered, leaning in at the area she indicated. "A distraction won't work. Too close. They'll never take all the guards away anyway. A distraction'll just put them on high alert."

"Especially after some of our other shit," Sirius said, then laughed quietly.

"Any chance your contact will be able to get more accurate information before we arrive?" Archangel asked. His tone was brisk, professional, and I relaxed. We'd talked a few times over the last week, and he'd been keeping it more casual and friendly. I could handle that right now.

"No." River stared at the map. "This is the result of weeks of collating information. We do know they were all kept for pleasure until they became pregnant. Sutter," her lip curled, "apparently referred to them as 'breeders'."

Doc, our patient, feisty, sweet Doc, growled. "We'll need the steadiest people we've got. No cowboys, nobody who'll let anger get in the way."

"Stone cold fighters," Sirius said. "Gorgon and her friends are out."

I raised my eyebrows and Sarge explained, "Her and her friends were hoping to go out on our next run. If it was a smaller one, I'd say yes, but..." He shook his head. "Not to this. Not when so much is on the line."

"Bear's out, too," Eleanor said.

While Bear had settled some, she still had a wide streak of revenge running through her—barely held in check by her children, safely at Home. All of them got too hot in a fight. Screaming in your enemy's face is great and all, but not when you scream before the shooting starts.

I pulled a candle closer and had my nose nearly pressed to the map, tracing tiny alleys. "We need to decide how many we're taking in. The smallest group possible, which means guesstimating the max number of women. One to one, with five left over to run interference.

"I want another team outside the fence, with more vehicles than we think we need. River, what's the closest unlikely exit possible? I don't want to be inside longer than we have to, but I also don't want them to expect the direction we take."

River settled down at the map while Eleanor's pencil scratched, busily taking notes. I shook my head, suddenly angry. "That close to the Capitol, we don't get seen. Whatever it takes." I looked to Sarge. "We need those with the best knife skills."

He nodded.

Archangel came over and leaned on the table next to me, close enough to feel his warmth. "We'll get them out," he murmured. "You've got good people here. You've got me."

"I know," I said quietly. "But I wish..." I broke off. Then, louder, "River, make sure it's an area you know well. I want to know the terrain before we even get there. We can't have any mistakes, not with pregnant women..."

River pulled a notebook from her cargo pocket without looking away from the map. While she checked her notes, Phoenix stretched and stacked her hands behind her head, grinning. "We usually just...plan to fuck shit up..."

"Language!" Eleanor scolded without looking up.

"...and we're brilliant at it, but we don't generally need details to do it."

"I know." I narrowed my eyes at her as she continued.

"So this time, we're not flailing around in the dark anymore, flying by the seat of our pants. This is the first time we've actually got solid intel. This ain't like our last run on Salem." The time that Kitten, our last spy, died. The time that the sisters, Lightning and Thunder were captured and subsequently tortured. The time that Steve hunted us in our own mountains. "We can plan it out, this time."

"Is this going anywhere?" I snapped.

"I'm bringing this up because you're making it sound like we've been failing to plan. We haven't. We've planned as well as we could."

It's not your fault hung in the air.

"We can plan better this time," Seahorse said. "Stop regretting what we couldn't do. It's behind us. Done. Put it away. You know this already. You tell us often enough. We live in the present and we don't regret the past."

"Basically," Sirius finished, "stop being a lil' bitch."

I glared around the room at the fighters who'd been with me for so long, my eyes narrowed again. They were right, and they all knew it. Assholes. "Will you shits stop ganging up on me?"

"Nobody's ganging up on you, dear," Eleanor finally looked up from her notes. "They're just reminding you. You need to let go of the guilt. You're not God, you're not omniscient or omnipotent, but you are still enough.

"You are enough."

CHAPTER 14

The plan, the plan. Why did I even bother with a plan when it was prone to going to hell?

***

I walked boldly through the grounds of the former university, red armband high on my right arm, a black stain against my jacket in the dark. The moon provided the only illumination, more than enough to see by. Overhead, the Milky Way cut across the sky, a kaleidoscope reminding me how small our troubles really were.

This part of the plan sucked the most. We had to split up to find the women as quickly as possible. I'd brought twenty fighters into Salem, with the rest staggered along the escape route to provide support on our way out, so we couldn't cover ground too quickly.

From experience, River favored night maneuvers, what with Steve's curfew and Dorothy's nosiness. The American collaborators apparently couldn't resist sticking their noses in other people's business, bullying everyone more helpless than them. And our last hit, less than a year ago, had apparently made them all overly cautious and jumpy.

We moved in pairs, each pair having a person who could pick a lock in a pinch. Phoenix, to my irritation and everyone else's amusement, set the working pairs. She preferred pairing people who were in relationships or cared for each other, not just to be with her husband, but because she figured people would take greater care of their partner.

"You're an asshole," I muttered in her ear after she paired me with Archangel. "A genius, but an asshole."

"I know." She grinned.

Moving through the dark after Archangel, I kept my ears open, hoping to hear a chickadee's cheerful chirp, the signal the women had been found. At the next building, Archangel stepped aside for me to work the lock. He kept a hand on my back so that we knew exactly where the other was at all times. As soon as the tumblers clicked, and I eased the door open. Pulling a tiny can of WD-40 out of my belt pouch, I generously sprayed the hinges.

I wonder if Steve would notice they had a lot of doors opening quieter than usual?

Slipping into the room, I heard slight snoring. One man, dozing on a chair in the corner. Silently drawing the knife sheathed at the small of my back, I tapped Archangel's shoulder, the signal to stay.

I remained pressed up against the man, stilling his thrashing, until he went limp before cleaning my blade and sheathing it. Archangel slipped in as soon as I gave the all clear. "Next one's mine," he breathed near my ear.

"I can do this," I whispered roughly.

"I know." He stepped a bit closer. "But you don't have to."

A knot in my chest loosened and I swayed towards him. How seductive was it, having someone at your back like that? He wouldn't be like Phoenix in the beginning, wanting to kill just to kill. This offer was made with...concern?

"I'll keep that in mind." I turned my head, so close my nose brushed his cheek. We stayed like that for a moment before I stirred reluctantly. "We need to keep going."

He nodded, leading the way, catching my hand and placing it on his back for a follow. Upstairs, we cleared the rooms quickly, exactly how I'd been taught by our soldiers.

Nothing.

I hissed silently. There weren't that many buildings left, and dawn was closer than I'd like. If we didn't find them soon...Could our intel be wrong?

A rhythmic *chickaneeneenee* carried through the closed window and I cocked my head, tapping Archangel's back. He paused and I pulled him back when the sound repeated.

The women had been found.

***

Our way to the building was interrupted by a guard. Ducking into the bushes, we waited, but then the fucker began poking around through the fucking plants. Why the fuck was he so concerned with shrubbery? There couldn't have been that much shit going on this close to Steve's headquarters. He poked his head in too far and I looped my right arm around his neck, yanking him in and applying pressure until he went limp.

Irregulars cleared all the guards around the building in preparation of bringing the women out. Sixteen women, all in late stages of pregnancy, were enough to make us extra cautious. It also meant they'd never make the walk to our exit, so I sent Sirius and Seahorse to get us a ride. They were to meet us on the southern side of the complex, as far from the Capitol as we could get.

My right hand twitched at my side, a little shake, nerves finding a way out. Despite the warm air, I kept a bandana over my face, hiding pale skin while I hunted. Bushes rustled nearby and I froze until Archangel stepped out, his blond hair covered by a cap. Otherwise, it nearly glowed in moonlight, shining like a freaking beacon.

As soon as the perimeter was secured, I made my way back to the building. The sign on the door read *Daycare* in large, block letters. It had a series of medium sized rooms lining a hallway. Each woman was given her own room, and it looked like they were able to roam the building freely, though the ground floor had been heavily guarded.

Until Storm and Goliath came along, that is.

Inside, Doc had just finished checking the women, putting her stethoscope back in her messenger bag. "Ready to go?" I asked. "We need to meet our ride." This side of the university was way too close to Steve Central, so the trucks would meet us on the far side, hopefully without alerting anyone.

Doc nodded, getting to her feet. She normally wouldn't come on a mission like this, but with the pregnant women, we'd all decided it was best to hedge our bets and bring her along.

Chaos, the soldiers' demolitions man, lurked nearby. He was Doc's bodyguard tonight. Big enough to act as a shield and a damn good fighter, he could Bash with the best of us.

Doc and Eleanor got the women upright and moving, the Irregulars forming up on their perimeter as they left the building. The women held hands, moving in pairs while fighters stayed within arm's reach. Amazingly enough, we had enough fighters for one-to-one attention, with four left over.

I led the way, Archangel two steps ahead, clearing the path. Occasionally, a fighter would disappear into the dark, then I'd hear a dull thud or a gasp, and the fighter would return.

I paused for the umpteenth time, waiting for the women to catch up. Too used to working with people who can run a few miles, I suppose. Over halfway to the rendezvous, I hoped trucks were waiting for us. Security had definitely been beefed up since the first time we'd come to Salem, and I couldn't wait to get out.

"Help!" a woman screamed behind me.

"The fuck?" I spun back.

In the middle of the group, an older woman, her face tipped towards the sky, screamed again. "Help! They're kidnapping us."

"Shut her up," I hissed.

Evenstar, closest to her, shook her roughly. When she wouldn't be quiet, Evenstar slapped her across the face, but the damage was done. Doors slammed, men shouted, and small lights flickered to life around us. Simultaneously, without communication, we began moving again, shifting into a shambling run. I glimpsed Evenstar manhandling the woman, shoving her forward with the others.

Poor, stupid, Stockholmed woman was still crying out.

"Phoenix, Gryphon, incoming on the rear," I shouted. "Archangel, with me. We're the battering ram. Don't stop, people!"

Five Dorothys formed a line directly in our path, weapons held across their chests, ready to aim. Their stance was casual, arrogant. Archangel disappeared from the sidewalk, so I drew my swords, still hoping to keep the noise down.

I was ten feet away and accelerating before Dorothy decided I was a threat and began readying their weapons. From my right, Archangel hit them like a whirlwind, his machete put to deadly use. I followed in his wake, dealing with the detritus.

Before we knew it, we were through the line. Small skirmishes broke out behind me, but I trusted my people to deal with it. The screamer was finally silent, abandoned, gagged, or dead, I couldn't care which right now.

Whimpers and gasps, interspersed with thudding footsteps, marked our progress.

Archangel disappeared from my side. Where...? Two men, on the right. Ahead, a large, shadowy form loomed, half illuminated by moonlight.

"Ambrose, no!" Doc cried.

A moment of disconnect while I tried to place the name, then it dawned on me. Ambrose Sutter. Doc's abusive husband. The man who'd tortured Lightning and Thunder. Mutilated them so badly they'd begged for death.

The man we all hoped we'd meet one day.

Pulling down my bandana, I smiled nastily. "Hello, Ambrose."

"Get the fuck out of my way," the large man snarled, teeth showing dimly by the light of the waxing moon, the upper half of his face shadowed by a prominent brow. His hands were empty, but by the size of them, and the way his fingers flexed and clenched, he didn't need anything extra. "Where's that whore wife of mine?"

"Now, now. Is that any way to talk about your lovely wife?" I shifted, drawing his attention. "I'd say she missed you, but we all know that would be a filthy lie."

He finally focused on me, his lip curled. "Who the fuck are you?"

I bared my teeth in a semblance of a grin. "I've only ever had two names. The first wouldn't mean a damn thing to you," I said lightly, pacing, keeping his attention. Keeping him in my sight. "Most people these days call me Captain."

The change that washed over him was certainly gratifying. He'd heard my name, and often enough that the sound brought him to the edge of rage. He tensed, shifting onto his toes, fists clenched. The fight continued around us, oddly quiet. No guns were being used, my brain supplied helpfully. As long as no shots were fired, we had a chance.

Eleanor took the opportunity to guide the women through, with the Irregulars clearing a path. Phoenix and Gryphon followed them, mission first. That might change if Phoenix knew who I faced. Or Sirius. Please, don't let Sirius find out.

"You," he hissed.

I waggled my fingers. "Hi!"

***

I spun to the left, my mouth open, panting. For such a big man, he was abominably *fast*. Motherfucker. I couldn't get more than a glancing hit on the bastard. He was also fresher, more rested, better fed, and he had a knife big enough to be a sword.

Basically, I was fucked.

The fight raged around me in near silence. Grunts, squeals, and the occasional clash of metal on metal the only noises. Sutter charged in again, pulling my attention back. He held his knife low, waiting for a chance to gut me. I lashed out, but the wide leather cuffs on his wrists deflected the blade.

So, I danced around, swords weaving in a flashy routine Sarge taught me to improve my blade work. Virtually useless, it was nevertheless impressive and kept Sutter off me for a few seconds. Occasionally, he threw out a slur.

Bitch. Cunt. Whore.

"You're repeating yourself," I laughed breathlessly. "Pathetic. Can't even...insult a woman...with any originality."

Rage twisted his face into vicious lines. Teeth bared, he charged, growling. I laughed again. Finally. He was beyond angry. Feinting left, I moved right, catching a backhanded blow to the mouth but I was already moving in the same direction so it reduced the force. I slid inside his guard, one high, one low. Black lines appeared across his shirt and he sagged. Spinning out, I cut his hand on the way, knocking the knife free.

Archangel, in my face. Sudden, welcome. "They're out. It's time to go!"

Lashing out with one last kick, I caught Sutter on the knee before abandoning the fight as quickly as we picked it up, leaving Dorothy milling, confused, and shouting for backup and medics.

***

"You beautiful legend, you," I whisper shouted to Sirius. She'd pulled up in a big-ass troop transport. To me, it was a Mercedes, Cadillac, and classic Mustang all rolled into one.

The Stockholm woman had to be restrained, and our zip ties were put to a whole new use. Well, new for us. The rest of the pregnant women huddled together at the front, Eleanor and Doc with them. Doc herself didn't look too good, pale and shaky, but having people who needed her seemed to ground her.

Chaos stayed close to her, watching our back trail through the flaps. "How long do you think we have?"

"We usually go out through the gate," I replied, "so hopefully, that's where they head first."

Because Sirius, as soon as we piled in, drove off at a nice, sedate pace, for all the world like someone who was in the middle of a boring routine, heading west, the nearest gate behind us. Watching out the back, a Chimera roared to life, its tires squealing as it raced in our direction. Sirius casually turned a corner and the Chimera hurtled past, sure it was on the right track.

"Guess that answers that question," Archangel said, quickly tying the back closed.

Getting back to our vehicles was harrowing only because we had mamas. Their best pace was a waddle, slowing us even more. But the ditch River led us to provided enough cover to get through their lines, watched over by Anarchy, Gummy, Triskele, and Raven, who had already taken the towers.

When would Steve learn, those towers had holes?

I shed a tear, watching the transport burn. I liked that truck. Smooth ride, plenty of room. Its only problem was the canvas sides. No protection from the elements at all. From the trees, we began shooting at the towers, starting with the ones occupied by Irregulars.

"What's the point of this again?" Phoenix asked. She and Storm were the best snipers I had, so it was their deal, shooting to miss our people.

"Make them think their dudes died in a hail of gunfire," Sirius said, watching the show, hands on her hips. "They'll never guess we're already in and out and hopefully think they managed to drive us off."

"Well, until they talk to Dorothy later," I finished.

I could barely follow the progress of the fighters leaving the towers. Before we left the Lair, they'd painstakingly sewn fresh leaves and grass to blankets. An idea from an earlier ambush, those blankets got more use than I'd ever have thought. The fighters were four lumps crawling across the ground while the snipers kept Steve's heads down.

"Welcome back," I whispered to Raven, the first one to make it into the trees. The petite, black haired, gray eyed woman still didn't like me much, but she could work with me. The other three followed in short order, checking in then racing for the trucks that were filling fast.

"Let's go, kids!" Archangel called. "Steve's turning into a rude host, so it's time to leave."

The snipers snatched up their huge rifles and we headed for the last vehicle, an old van. Nine of us piled in, where Obelix greeted us. We left, peeling out after a Chimera. The armored bus sat in the middle of the cavalcade while my baby led the way.

"Wait!" I shouted. "Why the fuck is Sirius behind the wheel? She can't see for shit at night."

"I don't know," she shouted back. "It just…happened."

"I got out to open the doors," Nebula said apologetically.

"You couldn't have…I don't know…sat in the back?" I wrestled my way forward, kneeling between the bucket seats. Obelix barred the way, the dog already there, his chin resting on her knee, his tail wagging slightly. "Fine. Dawn's only a few hours away anyway."

She laughed, the little shit.

We followed the cavalcade south, then east, picking up speed once we got a tail. Sporadic gunfire peppered the van, but I'd prepared. Most of my spare time for the last few weeks had been spent…tweaking…the whole thing, adding plates for armor or filling the space between panels with old phone books. Why the army kept those around, I had no idea. Seahorse said they didn't like to throw things away.

We wound through the night, slowly widening the gap between us and the convoy, once coming close enough to the edge of the road to have me hanging onto the seats with a white-knuckled death grip.

"What the fuck, Sirius? Are you trying to kill us?" Phoenix braced herself against the dashboard, pressing away from the windshield.

My insane cousin just laughed, driving nearly blind at…I squinted. Either that speedometer was broken, or we were going sixty on roads meant for forty-five. Fuck me. On a brief straight stretch right before a series of curves, we slowed down. I glanced back at Gryphon and Archangel, lowering a landmine.

Shit. That time already

Through a hole in the roof I'd made just last week with a grinder and welder, Storm stood, setting up her rifle's tripod legs. It was chaos, complete and perfect chaos, as always.

"Go!" I yelled, tapping Sirius's shoulder. "They should have enough of a lead and it's getting too hot here."

A deep boom overrode all sound. Landmine success. After the first S-curve, I looked for the narrow dirt track heading straight into the mountains that the bus had taken, but they'd taken care to hide their tracks. I relaxed between the seats.

"Hey," Sirius shouted over her shoulder when the engine sputtered, "is this thing even going to make it back to the Lair?"

I laughed. "You really expected to be bait and still drive back? Hell no, it won't make it. That's why I picked this one."

"Motherfucker!"

It was just us and Steve now. All we had to do was keep them following our asses instead of noticing where the others had jumped off.

***

Late afternoon had come and gone, and we were, as usual, running. Upon reaching the top of a short, steep hill, I turned with Archangel to provide cover for Sirius, Sung Ki, and Storm, our rearguard. Scattered dark clouds dotted the sky, promising rain in the next few days. Trees behind us, trees in front, with this one hill the only thing we could scale quickly.

It'd been a tossup what would break first on the van, and it ended up being the radiator. I'm fairly sure the engine block was nothing more than a lump of melted metal and rubber by the time we stopped. Fortunately, Steve had taken the bait, hook, line, and sinker.

Unfortunately, there were fuckloads of them shooting from the trees. The scouts had given us cover to get over the hill. Bless Obelix. That dog's nose told us when Steve was getting too close, and we'd managed to turn aside before running into an ambush.

Steve flickered through the trees, whose foliage slowly turned to the darker green of summer. Sung Ki crested the hill in a headlong dive for safety. Over the gunfire, I heard Sirius scream, "Move your ass!"

Standing, I fired as rapidly as I could work the lever, dropping to my knees to reload while Archangel and Sung Ki kept shooting. Sirius had nearly reached the top of the hill and Storm was off to the right when I stood up again.

Sirius lurched, tripped, falling heavily, her arms outflung.

"What are you doing?" I bellowed. "Get moving."

Only then did I see the red stain spreading over her back. Obelix stopped at her side, barking and whining, pushing her with his nose. She didn't move, not even to twitch.

The bottom fell out of my world and my heart stopped. "Noo!" I screamed, my rifle dangling from nerveless fingers.

Dropping it, I slid the few feet to her side. Archangel lunged, trying to stop me but I slipped his grasp, stopping just past the dog. "Get up," I shouted, nudging her with my knee, firing a handgun down the hill. "Come on, you've gotten scratches worse than this..." My voice broke.

She just lay there, not moving. Clenching my teeth, I kept shooting. She was fine. She just needed a minute to recover. I knew it. She'd be fine. She had to be fine.

Archangel slid to a stop on her other side, swearing. Scooping her into a fireman's carry, he kicked me lightly. "Come on! Time to go."

I scrambled after him, the rest of the band coming back to provide cover fire for us. As soon as we passed them, Seahorse gave the order and they lobbed two grenades each, rocking the hillside. Archangel headed straight to the back where Eleanor gave basic first aid. He laid her down, but none of us needed to see Eleanor's tears to know.

Sirius was already gone.

I sat down abruptly, shaking. "Fuck! I...fuck! She...she was supposed to be the one who made it." I gasped, struggling to find enough air, sobbing with every breath. "Fuck."

"Hey. Hey." Archangel knelt next to me, shaking me gently at first, then harder, brushing the hair that had come loose from my battle braid back, behind my ear. "Your friend is gone. We need to worry about the living now."

I wiped my tears away to see Eleanor, her hair a mess, blood smeared on her shirt, sitting in the dirt next to Sirius, sobbing like a child. "Noo!" Phoenix darted past, skidding to her knees next to them. She patted and stroked Sirius, trying to wake her up.

Over the ridge, the gunfire increased, but it sounded like fewer guns. I frowned, absorbed in an abstract way. What a good way to avoid grief. Maybe the rest of them were rejoining the fight to find the pregnant women?

"Orders, Captain?"

I looked up to see Archangel in front of me, Gryphon scooping Sirius up, and Seahorse striving to hold the line. Archangel gripped my hand, his thumb making little circles on the back. I took a deep breath, blowing it out slowly. He nodded.

"Pack it up," I bellowed, allowing Archangel to pull me to my feet. "Stay with your buddy. Phoenix, you have the front, Gryphon has Sirius. Storm, I need you and Sung Ki..."

Sung Ki turned towards me, shaking her head. "I do not see her."

"Has anyone seen Storm?" I shouted.

A chorus of No's, some of them shouted over shoulders from where the Irregulars guarded the hill.

"Captain." Eleanor grasped my hand, her eyes wide, panicked. "She's not here."

"She's not in the bushes, either," Seahorse called. "She should've come up over here, and nothing."

"Seahorse," I shouted to the ex-soldier, "are there fewer Steve than there had been?"

She took a swift inventory over the hill. "I'd guess so."

"Change of plans. Sparrow!"

"Captain!" She snapped out a salute.

"We're heading back in. Clear the ground. Blow their asses to Kingdom Come."

"What about Sirius?" Phoenix cried.

I looked down at my cousin, her dark blue eyes closed for the last time, her dog curled next to her, crying and whimpering. Kneeling, I brushed a stray lock of hair back from her face, wiping away a smear of blood. My heart clenched, and I wiped away a fresh bout of tears.

I couldn't lose it yet. Storm needed us, and they needed me. "We'll come back for you," I whispered. Then, louder, "We'll leave her here. Find a place..." I raised my voice to be heard over the objections. "We can't carry her into this. Storm needs us to be fast. We need to be fast. Sirius won't mind. Do it!"

I slumped next to her, my head buried in my hands. How was I supposed to keep it together when all I got was shit? I couldn't...Shouting broke through my grief and I looked around to see Seahorse and Archangel marshaling all...eight of my people.

Oh, fuck.

We were running a rescue with only eight people? What the fuck is wrong with me? No wonder they were protesting. Until Seahorse harshly reminded them of our promise—All in, all out.

CHAPTER 15

Woman 1: You assured me your contact inside the Pentagon could do any-thing. I will hang your balls on my Christmas tree as ornaments if you fuck this up, Bryce, and you can kiss your unlimited terms in office and your cushy life goodbye. Don't disappoint me.

Recorded phone conversation, June 23, 2061

I stumbled into a run, resisting the urge to look behind. We'd found a shallow cave to bury Sirius in, managing to move a few large rocks and logs to block the entrance. Phoenix crowded behind, gently urging me on, occasionally using a firm nudge to keep me on the trail.

The thick green undergrowth left barely any room for us, and the first fighters had already disappeared from view. The trees, a mix of evergreens, towered above, their needles whispering in the wind, sounding like distant weeping.

There were very few directions Steve could take from here, but at the fork we stopped. We had a brief discussion to see which way we should go, until Seahorse shook her head. "There's too many trails around here. We need to track smart."

"Will they go for a building?" Archangel asked. "Or are they likely to just set up a random camp?"

"Either way, they'll need water," I said. "Which is...that way." I pointed west and south. "Archangel."

"Captain!"

"How's your climbing?" He gave me an odd look. I nodded to a tree. "I need two in the trees. Get as high as you can. See if you can spot smoke anywhere. Me and Phoenix will go down a path each, see what tracks we can find. We need a direction. The rest of you, get the maps out, see if there are any cabins, towns, whatever, where Steve might go."

My trail, the southern one, was a bust, the trail washed out, and I returned to the junction. My hands trembled while I automatically checked weapons and several times, I came to with a start, having been staring into space without moving.

When Phoenix returned, everyone stared at her hungrily, but she shook her head. Dammit.

Through it all, I couldn't stop remembering. Going to the Abiqua with all our siblings when we were kids. Or the time I taught her to hotwire a car. The time she tricked me into that damn shopping cart...

I squeezed my eyes shut, pressing my palms against my eyes in a futile effort to stem the tears. *Papa. I want my Papa.* The words never left my lips, but I wanted him more now than I had at any time since this shit started. I took slow, deep breaths, trying to calm myself. I could see the irritation written all over Sirius's face, that I was a wreck when I needed to be at the top of my game.

The sun was nearly to the horizon before a whistle carried through the air. A chickadee. They'd found something.

I shot to my feet, holstering the Glock. Sung Ki slid down from her tree, triumphantly pointing north of the northern trail. The rest of us gathered around her, pressing in eagerly for news.

"Smoke," she gasped. "Smoke there."

"Seahorse," I snapped, habit finally kicking in. "What's there?"

"Yes!" Seahorse crawled over her map. "There's some kind of spa or something. Mineral baths. A bunch of buildings and water! It's not the closest water, but who cares."

I circled a hand in the air. "Pack it up. We're going hunting. One thing." They stopped what they were doing to watch me. "These ones...these ones can disappear completely."

"Fuck yeah," Phoenix hissed, her eyes narrowed. "Let's go."

***

We slowly encircled the handful of buildings, working in pairs. Clearing their guards took more time than I liked, but the dark helped us more than it did them. The thickening clouds made it harder but did offer concealment. One soldier turned just in time to get a knife in his gut. I dropped him, barely pausing, following Archangel to the next one.

They used stationary perimeter guards, designed to stay hidden and be harder to spot as opposed to the roaming teams Steve usually liked to do. It'd taken us a few minutes to spot these boys. Some of them were even decently hidden.

Until you spotted the pattern.

The buildings were rustic, cute, an open log design with an intentional run-down look before they were abandoned. At the edge of the clearings, Phoenix hissed, pointing to the ground. Scattered by scavengers, there was still enough to recognize human bones and torn, degrading backpacks. One skull had enough together to make out a little bullet hole in the middle of its forehead.

There but for the grace of God...

Eleanor folded her hands, her lips moving until a shriek broke the silence. I snarled, turning immediately towards the rest of the buildings. It wasn't hard to tell which one contained Storm, but we had to make sure, nonetheless.

Empty building. Building with a few men sleeping. Sung Ki, Seahorse, Phoenix, and Gryphon took care of that, only a few muffled cries escaping. Empty building. Empty building...

One building left.

This one had lights, noise, men's laughter and a woman's cries of pain and rage. Storm's cries. We'd have to breach the room. Fuck. Fuck. Sarge had trained us on shit like this, but it wasn't a regular part of our day. I wished we had more soldiers with us right now.

Archangel took command, peeking through the window to see how many bad guys. Five. Then, he pointed to the order through the door. Him, then me, going to the left. Gryphon slightly behind me, Seahorse on his right, Sung Ki behind her, Phoenix last.

Nebula would stay outside, on the porch next door to get a bead through the windows. Sparrow passed a small bomb to Archangel, then took up a position guarding Eleanor. Storm would need her.

We gathered at the door, weapons ready, waiting for Archangel. He held three fingers up, counting down. On *one*, Gryphon kicked the door in, and we poured through.

It was over quickly. I fired two shots and suddenly, we were standing in a room full of dead men and one beautifully alive Storm. She was naked, her wrists bound together and tied above her head to a beam. She twisted slowly, coughing and crying, but alive. When she turned, I gasped. Gryphon leaned over, retching against a wall.

Her back was a bloody ruin, covered in lash marks. The blood shone, brought into stark relief by the candles lit on every flat surface. I leaped over a bench, stepping on a body to wrap an arm around her hips, the only spot relatively clear. Archangel reached up, slicing neatly through the rope tying her to the beam and I caught her over my shoulder.

Eleanor shoved her way through to us while the others checked to ensure Steve was dead. I lowered Storm carefully onto a narrow bench, since the bed had Steve in it. Her blonde hair hung limp, wet with blood and sweat. She leaned against me, clutching my jacket, shaking.

Seahorse cursed. She kicked a body several times, stomping on the whip he still held. Sung Ki collected spare weapons while Eleanor immediately began tending to Storm's back. Storm buried her head in my shoulder, her nails biting into my arms when Eleanor poured clean water over the wounds, whimpering.

"I'm sorry," I whispered. "We should've got here sooner."

"Knew you'd come," she rasped, pulling away slightly. "Knew if I held out long enough, you'd get here. They only beat me 'cause when one tried rape, I ripped his dick off. With my teeth." Storm grinned at me, a bloody, triumphant smile.

I shook my head, a reluctant grin answering her. "Fuckin' A, scout. We'll make a basher of you yet." The corners of my mouth turned down involuntarily. I pressed my forehead to hers when she gasped in pain again. "You should know that Sirius is..." I bit my lip, tears welling.

"She...she's...gone?" Storm whispered.

I nodded, cupping the back of her neck to hold her still for Eleanor. "It was quick. We had to leave her behind. We'll get her on our way back."

Storm jerked in my hold, biting back a cry. "What are you doing back there?" she rasped once she regained her breath.

"Cleaning it, dear." Eleanor's tone was ragged but stern. "We have to clean it now to prevent infection. Phoenix, love, can you help me?" Eleanor focused on Storm's back with fierce concentration, her hands shaking with the effort. Phoenix, snapped out of her funk, hustled to help, yanking her first-aid kit from her pack.

Heavy footsteps shook the floor as Archangel knelt beside me. "Captain. What kind of message you want us to leave? Bury them?"

"Leave them. Leave the doors open and let the animals have what's left. Maybe Steve will find them. Maybe not."

"Done." Standing in one smooth motion, he moved off, organizing our departure.

I watched him go, the candlelight burnishing his hair. We wouldn't go far tonight, not with Storm in this condition, but we couldn't stay, in case their buddies came back. Storm sniggered, drawing my attention. "What?"

"Nothing," she said innocently, drawing in a sharp breath and digging her nails in while Eleanor cleaned a deeper cut. "Just...you and the Avenging Angel, huh?"

Phoenix snorted. "If you've only just picked up on that..." She frowned in concentration, then pulled her belt off, folding it and passing it to Storm. "Here. It's time for Dirt Huggers."

"Oh, fuck," Storm whimpered, right before biting down on the leather. She wrapped her arms around me, under my arms. I clamped down to hold her still and got a good grip on the bench.

"On three," Eleanor said. "One, two..." She poured it all over Storm's back.

The woman screamed into the leather gag and my ear, jerking in my hold. I pressed down to keep her still, easing up when she went limp. Breathing hard, I checked out the room. The others had dragged the bodies out and were nowhere to be seen. Shaking my head, I leaned away from Storm to get a good look at her.

Sweaty, pale, she still had blood spattered over her face, but she looked calmer than she had. "Well, after that, the rest of it doesn't seem so bad," she murmured. Then she tensed when Eleanor began spreading a salve on. "I take it back," she grunted.

"What the hell gave you the idea there's anything between me and Archangel?" I asked, mostly as a distraction. Eleanor used a soothing salve Wildwood made that we all carried, but it was designed for small cuts and burns, not this. Still, when you haven't got anything else...

Phoenix laughed, choked, coughed, and kept laughing, staring at me incredulously. Even Eleanor cracked a smile, shaking her head.

"What?"

"You stare at him when he's not looking. When you're not watching him, he's watching you," Phoenix said. "And that little escapade to get the dress..."

"What about the dress?" I demanded. "I never said anything about that. What did Archangel say?"

"Nothing." Eleanor gave me a brief, reproving look, pausing in wrapping bandages around Storm's middle. "But you disappeared for around a week, return with a dress and a bunch of rings, minus a landmine? You know how the rumor mill works in the Lair."

"Um, no," I grunted when Storm squeezed again. "I don't talk to most people. If you, Amana, or Lavender don't tell me, I don't know it."

"Okay." Eleanor stepped back. "You're as done as I can get you. You really need rest and sleep, but..."

"But I'm not going to get it," Storm finished. "I'd rather not be here when Steve comes looking either. Where are my clothes?"

Phoenix found Storm's pack in the corner. It took all three of us to get Storm into spare clothes. Eleanor frowned at the leggings that were her backup bottoms. "She can't wear those," she said. "You need warm clothing, and heavy enough to protect you while you heal."

Shit. We didn't carry much by way of pants. Too heavy, too bulky. I had a pair of shorts at this time of year, mostly to wear on those rare occasions that I washed my pants. I knew Phoenix didn't have more than that, either.

Phoenix's hands went to her waistband, ready to pull her pants off, but I shook my head. "You're too short." She looked from herself to Storm, a good five inches taller than her. "Use mine," I said, suiting action to words and unbuttoning my pants. "I've got shorts. The biggest danger there will be…"

"Whoa!" Phoenix held up her hand. "Reflective, much?"

"So, I glow in the dark," I snapped, huffing and pulling my shorts up. "I need to shave." I rubbed my legs, the hair soft against my palm.

Thankfully, I had knee high moccasins, so that was some protection from bushes. And they couldn't see my whole hairy leg. It wasn't as bad as I'd always thought it would be, really. The worst part was that I always low-key itched, and sometimes, hair got caught and pulled. So, I had a lot of irritation around my bikini line, but overall, not bad.

"Nah, it's not too bad," Storm croaked, her hands on her mom's and my shoulders while Eleanor buttoned the pants up. "At least your leg hair is blonde."

"Pfft. So's yours," Phoenix said. "Mine, though…"

Someone coughed in the doorway before Gryphon walked in, closely followed by Archangel. "You know," Gryphon commented, "I've always wondered what my wife talks about when I'm not around."

"Weren't expecting a discussion about leg hair, were you?" Archangel grinned. "I mean, we could join in, if you ladies would like? Even have a rousing talk about armpit hair."

Outside, the others had a moment with Storm. "I bit a man's dick off," Storm announced, gripping Seahorse's arm. "I didn't freeze, I didn't give in. I did it."

Seahorse beamed, pressing their foreheads together.

I shook my head. That's why she looked odd. She was happy she'd passed a personal test. What a shit way to have to cross a hurdle. Phoenix, all of them, had had to go through something like this. Shit. Maybe Sirius…

"Captain?" Eleanor touched my shoulder. I started, seeing they were all staring at me, concerned and confused. "You all right?"

I shook myself, loosening tense muscles. "No, but that's never stopped us before. Let's go get Sirius and go home."

***

I walked slowly into the meadow, carrying the front corner of Sirius's bier. The open grave gaped in front of me, a foreshadowing of what was to come—the emptiness of not having my cousin nearby or in this world. Eleanor stood at the head of the grave next to Shepherd, her mouth turned down, wiping tears constantly.

I blinked furiously to hold back a fresh wave. While Sirius would think it hilarious if we tripped while carrying her, I'd be damned if it was me who did the tripping. My eyes went back to the grave. Next to the dirt, rocks were piled for her cairn.

It'd been a hellish few days, getting back. Steve was still active in the mountains, and we'd heard shooting several times. Thankfully, we'd returned to only find injured, no more dead. Storm developed a fever, so the men took it in turns to carry her while the rest of us worked in teams of two to bring Sirius back.

We'd stumbled in just this morning and had gone immediately to the meadow. Her body...her body wasn't in good shape, and we needed to get her in the ground. I probably should have left her in the cave. She wouldn't have minded, but I wanted her closer. Obelix needed her nearby, too. He'd never have left her, and I couldn't leave the dog.

At the grave, Phoenix, Seahorse, River, Kestrel, Dereva, and I set her down carefully. My legs failed and I stayed there, kneeling in the bruised grass, looking helplessly around at the people surrounding us. What was I supposed to do now?

Hot Fuzz managed to find a place behind Eleanor. His lean shoulders shook, his face buried in his hands. I gripped the bier to keep from leaping to him. His safety mattered more, now. Gorgon, in the middle of her cronies, watched, her lip curled. I had to stay away from him because she constantly watched. If she suspected, and she already hated men, what might happen to him?

Rocking, I looked down at her blanket-wrapped body. Pulling the blanket back for one last look, pain ripped through my stomach, and I curled over her, tears dripping from my face to land on her swollen cheeks. Obelix shoved his nose in, trying to get closer to her. I had to cover her face, but he wouldn't stop until I sat down, pulling him onto my lap while he cried.

I looked up at Eleanor and held my free hand up, unable to speak. *What now?* What now? She nodded to the others. Phoenix and Seahorse jumped into the grave, then the five of them carefully lifted her and set her gently down before helping the women back out. I rocked, holding the dog tightly while he struggled when they began shoveling the dirt in.

I honestly thought that if anyone could survive this, it was her. She was so strong, both physically and mentally. She could survive on her own, and regularly went out with just Obelix. She'd helped me keep an eye on Fuzz without being obvious.

Silence. When had it gone quiet? Were they done with the service already? I'd noticed the basics of the service when Mom died. How had I spaced for Sirius? Sonya. Today, she should be Sonya, even if it was only to me.

Wait. People were looking at me. Waiting for me to speak. What do I say? Right. One thing settled in my chest. Everything else was in turmoil, but this I knew.

"Hail the victorious dead."

CHAPTER 16

As the memorial progressed, I retreated. I wanted to speak so badly, but if I did, I'd never stop. I knew I'd spill the beans about Peter, what Grace was up to in Washington, who I was, what we used to get up to. I'd had too many drinks, cried too many tears, to be able to hold my tongue.

Suddenly hot, I staggered outside, looking for fresh air. The cold froze my tear tracks in place. I swigged from the bottle, weaving as I climbed the mound. I vaguely remembered my mom's memorial, and all the stupid platitudes people had spouted.

You could spot the ones who'd lost someone from those who hadn't easily, once you experienced it yourself. The ones who hadn't had a need to talk, constantly, when all I wanted them to do was shut up.

Here, everyone knew already. Stories were shared, but no one tried to come up with grand words. There was no way to explain this. It happened, we drank, we remembered them and all those who came before, we cried, laughed, and got on with living and fighting.

It still sucked.

The door swung open, showing a flash of candlelight before closing again. "Captain?"

Archangel. I'd half expected Phoenix, but then, she was in desperate need of comfort herself. Without waiting for an answer, Archangel unsteadily climbed the mound. He spread a blanket out and sat on it, patting the space next to him.

Well. My ass was freezing, so...I settled next to him, crossing my legs beneath me. Frowning, he took off his jacket, putting it around my shoulders.

"Thanks. Who told you I'd be up here?" Ignoring the slurring, I tried to conjure anger. Indignation. Irritation. Hard to do when he'd just given me his jacket. Bastard.

"Not that I needed it, but Eleanor, Amana, Dereva, Anansi, Phoenix, and Lavender." He ticked each name off on his finger. "Want me to go on?"

"Smart ass." An involuntary smile twitched my lips, dying swiftly by the image of Sirius falling that flashed behind my eyes. My guts twisted so sharply a quiet keen escaped my lips as I bent over, holding my stomach.

He shifted to face me. "Captain?" Concern and fear sharpened his tone, his hands hovering, barely skimming my arms.

"I don't know how much longer I can do this," I whispered, taking his proffered hand. "I keep seeing...her. Them. All of them. I can't..." I shuddered, dropping my head.

Slowly, cautiously, he rested a hand on the back of my neck. I shivered, goosebumps rising on my arms, sobbing. He didn't do anything else. Just sat, holding my hand, his other on the back of my neck, waiting with me while I cried.

When my crying finally eased enough for me to take another drink, he shifted. "You've taken Sirius's death harder than anyone else I've seen," he finally said. "Why?"

Bracing our linked hands on my knee, I pushed myself upright. I wanted to talk. Needed to. Eleanor kept encouraging me to open up. To talk to him. I'd trusted him so many times by now. To watch my back, to keep me safe. He'd done it every time without question.

I licked my lips. "Oh, fuck it. Swear you'll never repeat this."

"I promise," he said, his eyes never leaving mine.

Still, I hesitated. It'd been so long since I'd said this out loud. His silence was more encouraging than anything else could have been. Taking a deep breath, I let it out slowly. "Her name was Sonya." His hand jerked slightly in surprise. "She was my cousin."

"Oh. Oh, fuck," he breathed. "Shit. Captain." Gently, he pulled me forward, leaning in until he could press his forehead to mine. "Tell me about her. The real Sonya."

***

I stirred, wincing at the pounding headache already making itself known. Why had I gotten hungover this time? No sooner had the thought happened then an image, in full color, of Sirius lying face down on the grass crossed the backs of my eyelids, quickly followed by one of Obelix lying on a cairn, whimpering.

I buried my head in the pillow to catch the tears, my shoulders shaking. An arm, wrapped around my back, tightened. I frowned, distracted. Slowly, the rest of me chimed in, letting me know I wasn't alone in bed. Cracking my eyes open, I cringed at the candlelight filling the room.

The candle stood on the pile of books next to the mattress, illuminating the door with gear piled next to it and golden hair half covering Archangel's face. His arm was slung over my waist, and he stirred, blearily opening one bloodshot eye.

"We have really got to stop doing this," I mumbled, afraid if I spoke louder my stomach would crawl up my throat. My head threatened to explode at the slightest motion.

"You asked me to stay," he whispered. "You didn't want to be alone. Figured lighting a candle was a good idea, in case you woke up full of fire. Didn't want to end up shot or something because you forgot."

I pulled back slightly, to see him easier. "Who knows?"

His lips twitched at the corners. "Amana and Lavender both know I'm in here. Amana has already threatened me. Something about cutting my balls off if you weren't happy waking up. They're the ones who got you comfortable."

I ran a hand down my side. T-shirt and shorts, my usual pajamas. "And you came in here anyway?" I rested my hand on his. "Bold."

"You asked me to," he said simply. As if that one request was the most important thing in his world. As if it was worth any measure of danger and threats.

What a wonderful, novel concept.

My breathing hitched. Stupid nose. All the crying and it was beginning to leak. Slowly, to keep my head from falling off, I edged over Archangel, wrapping a leg around his for balance. He mumbled, rolling onto his back, keeping a steadying hand on my hip. Fumbling, I found a handkerchief. Eleanor had pressed one into my hands yesterday. My searching fingers found another piece of cloth. It seemed I had plenty.

Half draped over Archangel, I blew my nose noisily. Discarding it, I took the clean one, just in case I needed it again. I wriggled, scooting back. Except I didn't move.

I frowned. "I'm stuck," I complained, hanging over the side, my head almost touching the ground. "I can't get back in."

Groaning slightly, Archangel simply wrapped his arms around me and rolled over.

"Hhnngg," I mumbled, suddenly smothered. He lay, a heavy weight over my left side.

He shifted until my mouth was freed and I waited for him to move more, but he snored faintly. I stretched, pleasantly surprised at how comfortable this all was. One of his legs was draped over mine and we now shared a pillow. His breath wasn't the sweetest, but considering I had to give serious thought to whether or not something had crawled into my mouth and died, I could give him some leeway there.

And while he was here, I had something else to think about as I drifted back to sleep.

Like why he kept ending up in my room.

***

When I finally slouched out of my room, the Lair had been quietly humming for hours. It was always this way, the grieving left alone until they felt ready to face the day, but it was the first time I'd been the bereaved.

Everyone was at once busy, yet had enough time to offer a hug, a gentle touch, or a simple regret. Sirius and me had been here when every single person had arrived at the Lair. Now...I chewed my lip. Nobody bothered with the empty words showered on us at Mom's funeral.

Then, there'd been so many people who, stuck on what to say, decided to say everything. The worst was the psycho who told me that while Papa would someday remarry, his new wife would never try to replace Mom, and it would make everything so much better.

What a fuckwit.

Here, everyone had lost someone. Often, several someones. This was probably the world's largest group grief counseling session. The biggest relief was that any words of sympathy were brief, then people moved on.

Amana took one look at me and sat me down with a bowl of stew and Eleanor's cure. When Archangel wandered in, I made room for him on the bench. Amana gave him a sharp glance then nodded once. When she brought his stew and cure over, she put it within reach. Barely.

"She still thinks you're okay," I whispered.

"How can you tell?" He pressed his palms over his eyes. "I don't think I can stand up again."

"She knows. That's why she put it in reach. I've seen her just...take stuff away from people who pissed her off."

"Yippee."

Halfway through the stew and just finished with Eleanor's cure, Phoenix appeared out of nowhere. Guess my brain wasn't all back yet. Sitting across from us, she leaned forward, resting her forearms on the table.

"We've got a problem," she announced without preamble.

"Maybe not now." Archangel glared at her. "After everything..."

"Listen, pretty boy." Archangel scowled at the name, but Phoenix was relentless. "I know what they were to each other. I lost a woman who was more a sister to me than my own ever was, but," she transferred her attention to me, "this is important. One of the newbies—can't remember the bitch's name—wants to choose a new name."

"So?"

"She wants to be called Major."

I frowned. "Correct me if I'm wrong, but don't we tell people no military things unless agreed upon?"

"Yep."

Fuck. Was this a challenger, then?

Archangel looked between us. "Okay, anybody want to spell it out? Other than that choosing it sounds stupid."

Without taking her eyes off me, Phoenix explained, "She's going for a name of a higher rank. She wants to be the boss. I'd prefer it if she didn't. Captain, as annoying as she is, has been surprisingly good at this shit. Definitely better than this bitch will be. She's even offering a formal challenge. Wants you to meet her in the gym. Something about too many deaths."

"Well, she's not wrong there," I said. "Why now?"

"Pretty sure it's Gorgon."

"Aw, fuck," I complained. "All right, how old is this chick? Anybody gonna be pissed if she gets hurt?"

Phoenix shrugged. "Around your age."

Archangel watched us, utter fascination written all over his face. What a strange man.

"She's in the gym now." Phoenix ignored Archangel the way she ignored all men except Gryphon. "Keeps talking about how she's got 'training' and that your thuggish—I shit you not, she said 'thuggish'—ways might work on the average fighter, but she's a *black belt*. In karate. Oooh!" She wiggled her fingers, making faces.

I rolled my eyes. "How classy do you have to be, challenging someone the day after their best friend dies? Although..." I tapped my chin. "I have been heading into the anger part of the grieving process. She might be just what I need."

"When Hendricks tried to supplant you, everyone stopped him before you even heard about it," Archangel reminded me. "So, why aren't they stopping her now?"

Phoenix shrugged. "Kestrel had the same thought as Captain. She says it's therapeutic."

Amana set another glass of the cure down in front of me. "Jou will need this, then."

"*Gracias, hermana.*" I tossed the contents back, grimacing and shaking my head. "Gah! Yuck. Well. Don't want to disappoint her. Gotta go get my ass kicked by a...*black belt.*" We cracked up and I pushed myself to my feet. "Who wants to watch?"

***

Everyone, apparently.

I had an entire convoy following me, led by Amana. As soon as we arrived, she peeled off, heading straight for Dereva, who sat in the middle of a small crowd, notebook open, taking bets. Archangel headed to the soldiers. I watched him go, enjoying the way his shirt stretched across his shoulders.

Phoenix quickly wiped my chin. I looked at her, puzzled. "For the drool," she whispered, grinning. "And I know where he slept last night. You *definitely* owe me a candy bar."

My face heated up. "I hate you." I scanned the room, looking for the girl who would be Major. And every spot where Sirius would normally be—next to me, ruffling Anansi's hair, on the edges, followed by a group of dogs—was a gaping hole that constantly caught my attention.

"There she is," Phoenix pointed.

The woman was roughly my age and only a couple inches shorter. I eyed her speculatively. She was stocky where I was painfully lean, and her tank top revealed muscular arms. It's what we had when we were able to stay at the Lair, where meals were better, and the workload less. In the field...My stomach growled even though I'd just eaten. Patting it, I continued to peruse the newbie.

Brown hair, too far to see her eyes—not that I'd remember or cared—and a softness to her face that those who came from the brothels didn't have. Ah. She didn't have that anger driving her. Gorgon and a few others I didn't know well gathered around her, talking intently.

"Odds are on you, two to one." Anansi appeared at my side. "They figure you'll be off your game because of the funeral, but I think they miscalculated. You kicking her ass would make Sirius crazy happy, so you kinda owe it to Sirius."

I nodded. "You've got a point. I gotta do it for Sirius."

"For Sirius."

"What's for Sirius?" Hot Fuzz asked. He'd just arrived, his face tight with worry and grief. He held hands with Dereva, who'd tucked away her notebook until the next round of bets.

A knot in my chest relaxed. He was taken care of. I wished I could've done it, but even Before, I don't think I'd have had the emotional capacity for it. I didn't when Mom died, no matter how much I wanted to. Not for the first time, I wished he'd never come here. He could've been with Grace. Maybe not completely safe, but not in this shitstorm, either.

"What can I do?" he asked, raising his hand as if to touch me before dropping it helplessly.

"Put some bets on me," I grinned, turning my attention back to the newbie. "I gotta whup her ass for Sirius, so..."

"You shouldn't be so cocky," he said. "You've been through a lot, and..."

Dereva rolled her eyes, laughing. "We've all been through a lot. She handles it really good. Gorgon's probably hoping to rattle her by making the challenge while she's grieving, but Captain compartmentalizes better than most. Don't worry. She's got this."

Her confidence warmed my heart and while Fuzz didn't look reassured, he smiled and nodded at her. They moved aside, making space for Archangel, weaving through the quickly filling gym. Chatter and bets flowed, people jockeying for better positions to see. A group climbed on top of the benches lining the walls, while others tried to form the front line of the ring. Only my corner and the newbie's were quieter.

"The boys hear the girl is a figurehead," he said quietly. "She's pretty good on the mats, claims she's won a bunch of awards. Definitely the best fighter in Gorgon's lot."

"Probably why she was chosen to challenge, then," Phoenix interjected.

I nodded while Archangel continued. "She's a competition fighter. Follows the rules of engagement or some shit, but Gorgon's been giving her pointers on things to say to rile you up. Don't," he touched my shoulder to get my full attention, "let her. If she beats you, you won't lose the whole Lair, but there's a lot of newer fighters who haven't fully integrated. It'd likely split loyalties and plans."

"I know."

The newbie walked out, throwing warm-up punches in lightning-fast combos. Gorgon and her cronies cheered her on. Archangel caught my arm before I walked out, leaning so close our foreheads nearly touched. I could barely focus on those deep blue eyes, mere inches away. The darker blue rim around the edges, little flecks of gray and gold...He gripped my hand tightly, pulling me out of my reverie.

"Stay focused," he whispered under the cheering. "Gorgon hasn't got what it takes to lead five people, much less forty. You win, you'll save lives."

"No pressure, huh?" Taking a deep breath, I nodded, my hair brushing over my shoulders. "Ah, shit. My hair! Phoenix, got a hair tie?"

Phoenix laughed, undoing the knot holding her hair back and handed the tie to me. "Hold this. I can get it done faster." She pressed on my shoulders, and I knelt so she could reach the top of my head, quickly doing a battle braid. Taking the leather tie from me, she wrapped it around, tugging my whole head while she did it.

"Thanks," I said, walking out onto the mats.

"About time you got here," the newbie sneered. "Did you have to make sure your hair was all pretty?" Gorgon and company laughed raucously, patting her on the back. She bounced lightly on her toes, her fingers working to limber them up. Either that, or she was imagining my neck in her hands.

I pinched the bridge of my nose, but it was no use. There was simply no cure for stupid. "Yes," I said dryly. "That's exactly it. Considering it's customary for friends of the deceased to have time to mourn. Poor form to interrupt my hangover and then be mad I'm not ready 'on time.'"

Fighters and most of the non-coms sniggered at that, a few even *tsk*ing her.

The newbie's face reddened. "You should be crying! It's your fault she's dead!"

I flinched and turned it into a cringe. "Wow. What is this, a planned speech?" I asked, the words sticking in my throat. "You do realize that's not the best response, right? You're acting like you knew Sirius, but I know for a fact that if she wasn't dead, she'd be in here about to kick your ass. Actually, you're lucky you're getting me. Sirius would be mean."

More laughter. Even Fuzz smiled at that one.

"You're not fit to run this army!" she screamed, jabbing her finger at me. "It's always the leader's fault when their people die, and there's been too many dead already! You should've resigned when you let down the first person. Instead, you got drunk on your own power, and now you're trying to become a dictator. Forcing people to work for you, holding starvation over their heads if they don't. You won't let people join the fighters, even when they're better equipped than the average. You're incompetent, and you punish those who see you for the bitch you are!"

The lot in her corner cheered, punching the air. I couldn't count them all, but close to twenty. Amana probably had their names down in her notebook. Now I knew exactly who hated my guts. Yay.

I nodded, enjoying this now. There's just something about overblown accusations. Sirius was reflected in the mirth I saw all around, spurring me on. "Somebody got put on toilets a lot, didn't they?" Amana and the Lair crew howled. "How much did you have to practice that? It seems like a lot to remember."

I moved, stepping to my left, forcing her away from her supporters if she wanted to maintain distance. She ground her teeth, red creeping up her face while her mouth worked.

Finally, she spit it out, the family favorites I'd already heard. "I'm a karate champion. I've won so many, I have a wall of trophies. I'm also a chess master, so I understand both tactics and strategy better than you ever could," she screeched. "Plus, I've got friends who are intelligent and not afraid to tell me when I'm wrong. I can actually listen to them and take their advice into account."

"Are these the same friends who said this much talking was a good idea? 'Cause, I dunno." I shrugged. "I came here for a fight and all I'm getting is a lousy resume."

The newbie fell into a fighting stance. "Come on, then. Unless you're *scared*," she sneered.

Fighters, especially the veterans, gave her and her lot disgusted looks. A couple—cough, Phoenix, cough—stirred, looking ready to beat her on my behalf. Up until now, her temper tantrum was just that. Amusing, juvenile, and good for entertainment. But insulting a fighter with over a year and a half in the field?

I shook my head, sighing and started walking again, forcing her to move.

"Do you always smile before you get your ass handed to you? You must be all giggly in the field, then. You're so arrogant, I can't believe no one has stood up to you before now."

Sliding my hand into the back of my waistband, I whipped out the pistol I'd stashed there, lining it up right between her eyes. The *click* of the pistol being cocked was deafening in the sudden silence. She froze, staring, her mouth opening and closing like a fish's. Blood drained from her face while the room exploded with laughter.

Gorgon, suffused with rage, stepped forward, being careful to remain out of the line of fire. "That's not fair! You were challenged to a fight. Hand-to-hand. You can't bring a gun to this and expect to get away with it."

I grinned, waiting until the crowd calmed down. While I waited, I ejected the magazine, holding it up to show it was empty. Pulling back the slide, I confirmed for them that it was also empty. "You're walking around screaming about fairness, when 'fair' would've been to wait until I was through mourning. And, what the fuck makes you think fighting out there would be 'fair'?" I handed my pistol to Anansi, who still giggled. "You come to your senses yet, you expositioning idiot?"

The newbie, apparently fed up with being made fun of, screamed and charged.

Guess not.

***

This girl was *good*.

To an extent.

Her fists blurring, she hit me half a dozen times inside a minute. It was all I could do to protect my face and stomach while we moved around each other. She thought she knew it all because she'd been in competitions with *rules*. For her, winning was a point system, not life and death.

I grimaced, not sure how far to go. I didn't want to kill her, or even maim her. Fighting someone with so many rules was hard. With Sarge, Phoenix, Archangel, literally anybody else, I knew how far I could go because it was practice. This was a weird gray area. Don't kill her, but it's not just sparring...

She got in a headshot, sending me reeling. Gorgon and Co cheered when I staggered back, and I caught a glimpse of Eleanor's white face. Without thinking, I looked for Sirius, where she usually stood next to Phoenix. That empty space struck my heart, and I froze, searching for her.

The blow came from nowhere, knocking me sprawling to accompanying screams from her lot and boos from the fighters. Shaking my head to clear it, reminding myself the fight was where I needed to be right now, I wiped blood from my eye.

The newbie stood over me, her hands planted on her hips, smirking. "Had enough, bitch?"

I rose to my feet in one smooth move. No stupid fancy flips or legs swinging like you see in movies. Just...standing up. Sarge offered me a cloth to blot the blood running down my face. Wiping it away, I handed it back with a nod.

"Finish this," he said in a low voice.

"Fine." Looking back at the newbie, my lip curled involuntarily. "Fuck this. I'm done being nice."

When it was done, I left the girl crying on the floor with a broken nose, holding her arm. I'd felt something give in her wrist. Maybe Doc would be able to splint it so it healed correctly, maybe not. I wished it was Gorgon facing me.

The whole ordeal left a bad taste in my mouth. I'd played with her, slapping her around. Gorgon's lot was finally silenced, and even the Lair's crew—the scavengers, the hunters, all of them—were surprised by what happened here. The fighters watched grimly. They knew this was a lesson. They'd known from the start what it was. The soldiers were shocked, my brother's face pale when he looked at me.

I spat into the rag Sarge offered, clearing the blood out of my mouth. "Can I finish mourning now?" I asked plaintively.

As if it broke a spell, some people broke out in cheers while others groaned. Who bet for me, who bet against. Dereva ended up in the middle of the crowd, checking her notes and passing slips of paper.

Shaking my head, I stumbled. Amana appeared under my left shoulder and Archangel took my right arm.

"Come on, basher," he said. "Let's get you cleaned up."

Ahead, Eleanor supported Storm, who'd come to watch, disappearing around a corner. Phoenix and Gryphon walked behind them, swinging their linked hands, discussing the fight.

"I liked the bit where Captain kept the idiot looking at her hands, then kicked her in the kneecap," Phoenix said. "Solid basher tactic."

"I thought your favorite was when she kicked the idiot's feet out from under her, then landed on her with both knees."

"Yes, I did enjoy that, too." Phoenix smiled up at him.

"And then bit her."

Phoenix bumped him with her shoulder. "You know me too well."

"Jou know my favorite part?" Amana asked them.

Phoenix turned, walking backwards. "What?"

"When she fell, she tried to flip to her feet. Then *Capítan* did..." Amana mimed slamming an elbow down.

Shaking my head at their antics, the floor swayed under my feet. Archangel closed the last bit of distance between us, wrapping an arm around my waist. At my and Amana's astonished looks, he just shook his head, muttering, "Last thing we need is for you to faceplant. Gorgon'll jump on that like paparazzi on a sex scandal."

"Here." Eleanor reappeared, carrying a steaming mug. "Let's get her settled and then we could all use a nap."

Just like that, everyone else's joy at the fight took on a new light. They were trying to behave as if Sirius was still here. The tears I'd been holding back all morning came rushing up and I crumpled. Archangel caught me. Eleanor caught the mug.

"Whoa, there," he murmured, stroking my hair while Amana pet my back. "Let's get you more comfortable."

Phoenix led the way to my room and Archangel half-carried me there while I cried. Once in the room, the men were unceremoniously thrown out while the women got me into pajamas. Eleanor passed me the still warm mug, but my hands were shaking so much she cupped mine and helped bring the mug to my lips.

When the guys returned, they brought Storm and Al with them. I tipped my head, a question crossing my mind so fast I couldn't catch it. That simple tilt continued until I toppled onto the bed, burying my face in the pillow. Someone scooped my legs onto the bed and urged me towards the middle. I obligingly scooted over, then the mattress dipped as someone climbed on.

I cracked open one eye, temporarily brought out of my tears, startled to be face to face with Storm. She smiled, tears tracking down her own cheeks and snuggled against me. I froze, unsure what to do next. Amana crawled up from the foot of the bed, settling in behind me, draping an arm over my waist as if we did this every day.

I looked around the room, panic setting in. What do I do with this? What am I supposed to do? Phoenix didn't even bother trying to hide her grin.

"You have no idea how to handle cuddling, do you?"

"I don't exactly have a lot of experience."

"What kind of experience does it take?" Storm mumbled, taking one of my hands and draping around her waist. "We cuddle all the time."

"Not with me, you don't! When does all this happen?"

"When jou are out, being the *Capitán*. Jou need to learn to *relajarse*."

I looked wildly around the room, the others beginning to redistribute themselves. Gryphon settled between Amana and the wall. Phoenix crawled over him, sprawling like a cat. Archangel got comfortable at the end of the bed, some feet ending up in his lap, his legs bent over others. This was only a double mattress. How did so many people fit? "This is like that thing about how many angels and the head of a pin."

"Your bed is bigger than the head of a pin," Phoenix said dryly from her perch. "And none of us are angels."

"Speak for yourself," Archangel retorted, making himself comfortable.

"I thought I said that in my head," I protested.

Phoenix sniggered. "Hate to break it to you, but you've been saying everything that's crossed your tiny little mind for the last several minutes."

"Eleanor." I glared as best I could from the pile of people. She looked away. "What did you put in the tea?"

"Just a little something to help you relax. You woke up too early, and then the fight..." She bit her lip and glanced at me, pleading.

My sigh was lost in the tangle of Storm's hair. Her head was tucked almost beneath my chin, her breathing already soft and regular. My eyelids drooped, Amana wriggled, and sleep claimed me.

CHAPTER 17

Those of you who bet that Mercy would be raped…Too bad! She skillfully avoided it by secretly drinking something to make herself vomit! Now, let's go back the water war happening in Whittier…

Majordrama Channel

When I finally woke, my head was clearer than it had been since Sirius died. Mere inches away, Archangel lay, his face relaxed in sleep. I freed a hand and gently touched his cheek, unsure whether this was real. Squirming around, I identified the hard warmth at my back as Gryphon. Getting upright took more effort than I would've thought, more to pry myself out from between the two men.

They grumbled and Archangel's hand dropped to the mattress, fingers stirring slightly. Behind Gryphon, tangled, sandy blonde hair was just visible above the tumbled blankets. Phoenix. I shook my head, but it all stayed where it should be. No hangover, so I hadn't been drunk. A soft snore drew my attention to the foot, where Amana curled. And there was Al on a pile of blankets on the floor.

I rubbed the bridge of my nose and the door creaked open. Storm slid in, closely followed by Obelix. She smiled when she saw me sitting up.

"How are you?" she whispered.

I shoved my hair back and winced when my shoulder twinged. When had I done that? "Weird. I don't know..." Rotating my shoulder, I grimaced. "I remember going to bed. Why do I remember fighting?"

Yesterday wasn't a normal memory. It was too patchy. Too hit and miss. Kestrel, in a group session, said something about how grief can create gaps in memory because it was damaged, but this was weird. Maybe it felt different from Mom's funeral because there were things happening here that bore remembering.

Storm smothered a laugh as she pulled a chair close and sank into it gingerly. "Yeah, you got into a fight yesterday. Gorgon egged some idiot rookie into challenging you."

"Did I win?"

She rolled her eyes. "You won. By a landslide. Gorgon's implying you cheated somehow, which makes you unfit to lead. General consensus is that if you managed to cheat in a fight you didn't expect and didn't instigate, we're even closer to beating Steve than they thought." Storm paused a moment, considering. "She won't shut up, and her followers—sixteen girls as hardheaded as her—who haven't been cleared to fight, echo every stupid thing she says. It's all very vague so far, but Mom thinks it's only a matter of time before she pulls some other shit."

I sank down, dropping my head to rest on Archangel's arm, muttering. 'Fuckin' fuckwit doesn't fuckin' know when to fucking quit. Fuckin' idiot's gonna fuckin' get us all fuckin' killed 'cause she wants to go on a fucking bullshit power trip..."

Storm sniggered, shaking her head. I slid the rest of the way down. "I'm going back to sleep. When I wake up, it's time I have a chat with the Lair crew. Since they're the ones who deal with Gorgon and company the most."

***

Even though the meeting didn't have a damn thing to do with fighting Steve, habit had us gathering in the Useless Room. Amana, Eleanor, Lavender, Driver, and Sarge were the ones I needed to see, but Phoenix, Archangel, and Seahorse elected to attend as well.

"It's about time we talked about Gorgon." Lavender folded her arms over her chest. "That woman is a menace, even worse than Sophie."

"Ugh." Phoenix recoiled. "I'm not sure Gorgon's there, yet."

"She challenged Captain to a fight!" Lavender shrugged. "Well, she got a proxy to do it, but same thing."

Phoenix shook her head. "Nowhere near. Sophie tried to murder Captain. I think that's worse."

Everyone else stared at me. Eleanor's mouth dropped open. "When did this happen?" she demanded.

I squirmed. "Dunno. Few months ago? I think. I went specifically because Olivia requested it, to deal with Sophie."

"Why didn't you say anything!"

"Well..." I scratched my stomach. "I...forgot?" Eleanor glared at me, and I shrank back. "It was a really pathetic murder attempt! I'm in more danger when Amana is pissed. Seriously. It was nothing. Sophie's a politician, and she brought that to her wannabe murder spree."

"And what," Eleanor asked dangerously, stalking forward, "is that supposed to mean?"

"Um...she's incompetent?" I smiled hesitantly. When she didn't slow, I backed away. "Why aren't you mad at Phoenix? Her and Sirius..." I swallowed hard, then continued. "They were there, too."

"Hey!"

Eleanor didn't deviate, her full attention on me. I bumped into a table and scooted around it, too scared to take my eyes off her. She stalked me methodically, grim death in her eyes. Everyone else watched, grinning but quiet, unwilling to risk her wrath.

"Guys, help!" I stumbled over a chair and Eleanor pounced.

"Just because people keep trying to kill you is no excuse not to tell us about things like this," Eleanor shouted, hugging me fiercely.

I cautiously opened one eye, my shoulders slowly relaxing away from my ears. Groans and laughter filled the room.

"Do not interrupt me," Eleanor snapped, never loosening her grip. "I'm giving her life lessons! We care about you, and we should know when things like this happen so we can help you," she continued at the top of her lungs. "You don't have to go through everything alone!"

"No, ma'am," I said meekly, muffled against her shoulder.

Movement caught my eye and I saw Phoenix pout as Amana passed notes to Archangel. Little shits were betting on this, too?

***

Storm wandered through my garage, where I'd taken refuge after Eleanor chewed me out. I kept an eye on her, gauging her movements. There was some definite stiffness, but with the infection gone, she should heal within a few weeks. Even dealing with Sirius's death, she looked lighter than I'd ever seen her. Guess that's what happens when you face your personal demons and win.

She tried to act casual, barely stopping short of having her hands in her pockets and whistling. When she finally arrived at the truck I was elbows deep in, she did stick her hands in her pockets. I grunted when she stopped but didn't straighten. It'd taken me forever to get this piece to fit, and I was damned if I'd stop before it was finally connected.

"So..." she drew the word out. "Why is Mom so mad? Amana won't say, she just keeps laughing and says I should ask you."

"Why not ask your mom?" I grunted, tightening a nut. "Can't read your mom's mind."

"She's still a little...upset. Tell me."

"I'm working on a truck, you know!" She didn't move. Shifting to reach the other side, I panted when my weight settled on my stomach. "Archangel, Phoenix, Lavender, Seahorse...they were all there."

"I tried. Archangel kept giggling and Phoenix looked pissed. Lavender and Driver are apparently celebrating and not seeing people. But I was asleep when you had the meeting, otherwise I would've been there!"

I hunched my shoulders. "Fine. But you gotta get your mom to stop yelling at me. She found out Sophie tried to kill me a few months ago. Wasn't happy I forgot to say anything. Like, she thought I'd deliberately stayed quiet instead of just forgetting. She wants me to 'let people in'."

"Well, she's not wrong," Storm observed. "You barely talk to anyone."

"Hey! I talk. To four or five people. It works."

"So, what's up with the others? Since I couldn't get two sensible words out of any of them."

"Oh." I grunted again. "Yeah, pretty sure there were some bets running. Don't know what, since I was the subject. Again. Bastards. But Driver and Lavender are just happy we're kicking Gorgon and her lot out. We'll give them some weapons, enough to get them started, and some food. They can fight Steve however the hell they want."

Storm laughed, clapping her hands. "I wish Sirius had been here to see this!" She tilted her head, calculating. "Actually, I think she'd have gotten them out the door the minute the decision was made."

I smiled sadly. "Yeah, she would, wouldn't she?" I rubbed a hand over my face, brushing away fresh tears.

"No. Oh, no." Storm carefully made her way around the car, her back stiff. "I didn't mean to make you cry. I hoped it would be a good thought." She hugged me gently, laying her head on my shoulder.

I rested my cheek on her hair, laughter and tears mingling. "You know it'll be a while before those thoughts become happier."

"Yes...and no. I haven't lost anyone as close as you and Sirius were."

"What about Anna?" I asked. Eleanor's blood daughter had grown up side by side with Amana and Storm, Eleanor acting as a mother to all three girls, until Anna sided with Steve, turning in her mother and best friends. We knew she had the commander's ear, and that she had a cruel streak a mile wide.

Storm snarled, pulling away from me. "That's different. That was betrayal, not death. Death would've been better. I'll kill her if I ever get her in my sights again."

"I'll help," I said dryly. "But in the meantime, I need to fix the truck. Then, first thing in the morning, we're kicking Gorgon and company out. Amana's prepping a bit of food for them. Sarge is selecting weapons. We're not giving her time to throw a temper tantrum. I'm just too tired to deal with her, right now."

***

Gorgon took the news surprisingly well. She only called me four names. When she moved towards a table, looking like she intended to sit down, Amana stepped forward, her arms folded implacably and slowly shook her head. The short Latina had more threat to her in that moment than Gorgon at her angriest. Gorgon had enough brains to back up, trying to cover it with more swearing, blame, and bluster.

Amana didn't give her time for more than that, because she had their packs lined up, a pistol or knife hanging on the outside of each one. Sarge had chosen decent enough weapons, but things smaller or larger than the

Irregulars preferred to use. They'd also have a limited number of bullets, so they'd either have to head east or steal guns and ammo from Steve.

"But what are we supposed to *do*?" Gorgon shouted.

"What you've been saying you're going to do." I rolled my eyes. "Now's your chance to show us what you can do, how great of a leader you are, blah, blah, blah."

"You're sending us out to die!"

"You could make it to Idaho on what you've got and a bit of hunting or trapping."

Her face turned red, and her fists clenched. "You know what? Fuck you all! We'll finish this war before you know what hit you, you glow in the dark bitch."

I put a hand to my heart. "Ooh. Ouch. You almost hurt my feelings."

Phoenix sniggered. "Better hurry up and leave. You want to find a good place to spend the night. You should go east. This shit is too much for you. You're not ready for it." She kicked Gorgon's pack towards her, green eyes hard.

A few of Gorgon's followers looked scared, but they kept glancing to their leader and bracing their shoulders. The idiots didn't know enough to know how much they didn't know, and my heart hurt. I hoped they went east.

Sarge agreed to take some trainees and hunters to lead them away. The hunters knew every trail for forty miles. They'd get the girls thoroughly lost before setting them loose.

I jerked my head, indicating Sarge should meet me off to the side. "Take them over the ridge," I whispered. "Get them more east before you turn them loose. Maybe that'll help 'em get out of here."

***

Without the drama Gorgon brought, I struggled to find ways to keep my mind busy and off my loss. So I visited Doc to learn more about the women we'd brought out. Two of them had given birth at some point on their escape. Thankfully, they were healthy.

"One of them can't keep the baby." Doc pulled me to the side of the room. That one sat away, not looking at the baby.

I nodded. It happened. I'd find it hard to accept the product of rape, especially since having a kid wasn't on my radar. To suddenly be stuck with one, and under these circumstances…Instead, the women were offered a shot at joining the fighters. Those babies were simply listed as orphans and taken Home.

"Any health issues with either of them?"

"No. The baby's a bit small, but then, the women were never *that* well fed. He'll need to get a bit older, but the other mother is willing to nurse both."

"Okay, then."

After a bit more chat, I left when Tabitha arrived, her arms full of soft things for babies and women. The older women were constantly in and out, with Eleanor and Tabitha becoming grandmothers for the lot.

Kestrel had a different view.

Over tea, while I sharpened my blades, she told me a little of what it was like. Many of them were dealing with severe disassociation, unable to see the babies as anything other than the spawn of their rapists. Others saw the babies as theirs, and therefore okay. I found it interesting that the split was roughly fifty-fifty. She said there was no way to gauge in advance which way a woman would choose, only that it had to be *her* choice.

The new lot would be more of the same, except for the one who'd tried warning Steve. Severe Stockholm Syndrome, she said, and there was no telling if she'd get over it.

So far, we hadn't had any of the formerly pregnant women able to join the fighters yet, but several were in training. One woman, Deerskin, was out to get her brother. Literally, get her brother. He'd joined Dorothy. Then, he'd done unspeakable things to her, protected by his new station. Now, she was in the fight, and he'd better watch out.

In between, I spent a lot of time with Obelix. He slept on my bed, his head resting on my side. He'd play with the other dogs, but he didn't bond with them. And when I couldn't sleep, he walked with me. We'd always swing by the meadow, and he'd make a beeline for Sirius's cairn, curling up against it until I called him in.

The only other person he'd really spend time with was Storm, which made sense. The two of them often scouted together, so he'd gotten used to working with her. One night, about two weeks after the funeral, he didn't turn up at my door for bed.

I hunted through the common room and the gym, then checked the meadow. I stood at her cairn, chewing on my lip. "Where would he go?" And finally remembered he'd sat next to Storm during dinner.

Swinging around, I back inside to Storm's room. I knocked, hoping he'd be here, because if he wasn't, then I'd somehow lost him. Sirius would never forgive me for that. My right hand twitched at my side, waiting. I was about ready to give up when the door opened slowly.

"Shhh...Oh, it's you, Captain." Storm smiled but kept glancing back. "Sorry. Obelix just fell asleep, and I don't want to wake him."

I relaxed. "He's here? Oh, thank God. For a moment, I thought I'd lost him."

She grinned, opening the door wide enough for me to see the border collie curled on the bed. "Sirius would personally chuck you out of heaven if that happened."

I leaned against the doorframe, watching him sleep, his nose covered by his tail. Sighing, I touched her shoulder gently and turned to leave.

She hesitated. "Are you okay with him staying with me?"

"Of course. Why wouldn't I?"

"Well, it's just...you and Sirius were best friends. He's her other best friend. I didn't know if...if you wanted him to be your dog, now."

I shook my head. "She'll always be his human. And I don't know if he'll bond with me the way he did with her. But if he wants to spend more time with you, I'm okay with that. I don't..." I swallowed. "There are times when I don't think my life expectancy is all that great, you know? So, I'd like him to be around someone who has a good chance for survival."

She chewed on her lip, nodding. I smiled sadly and left her with the sleeping dog.

***

We stayed close to the Lair, acclimating the newly rescued, assisting Doc with births or childcare, and resting. Except River. It didn't matter the danger, she headed into the Valley with irregular frequency. Every time she returned, she carried news of troop movements. Once, she even had a map with major outposts marked.

"How the hell does she get this kind of intel?" Archangel demanded incredulously when we were alone in the Useless Room. "She's never gone that long and, however good she is, she's not that good at talking to people. How does she get them to spill?"

I shrugged, grinning slightly. "She's the messenger. The actual spy never leaves Salem. I don't know the details of their arrangement. Shrike agreed to work with us around the time our original spy was killed."

While I'd set up the initial meeting, I didn't know how things changed. Shrike was the only woman who'd ever refused outright to leave the brothel we'd found her in. I suspected a lot about her past, especially since she didn't decide to help us until she learned that children were being targeted by Steve for the brothels.

Either way, men talked to her, unaware of how much they actually told. The only thing that made me uneasy was that, as far as I knew, my entire network was two people long, and they were the only two who knew how this shit worked. Not my best idea, but we couldn't risk Shrike's identity getting out, and River was exceptional at getting in and out of Salem.

Archangel's mouth dropped open. "You have...one spy?"

"To be fair, Shrike does talk to multiple people every day, and all intel is pieced together from that."

"They're fucking good at puzzles, then," he said.

"Why?"

"I've seen intelligence reports in the past. Putting two and two together and actually getting four is genius level shit."

"That bad, huh?" I grinned up at him. He laughed, and I waited another second.

I didn't even realize I'd been waiting for Sirius to laugh, too. It'd been a month, and I still expected to see her in her chair in the Useless room, or in a crowd. I waited to hear her laughing in the hallways, and when it didn't come...

The corners of my mouth turned down. Archangel moved around the table and leaned against it. Reaching down, he pulled me up. He didn't have to do more than that, I immediately turned into his embrace, tucking my face into his shoulder. He rubbed my back, and I relaxed.

His arms were one of the few places where I completely let go, where I didn't have to worry about what kind of example I was making for others. I didn't have to worry about morale, or anything else. I could simply *feel*. He was silent, resting his cheek against my hair. The steady thump of his heart eventually calmed me.

When I pulled back, I wiped my tears away with my sleeves and he pulled out a handkerchief, passing it over without being asked. He left one hand on my hip, as reluctant to give up all contact as I was, studying me.

"You know what'll take your mind off things and make you feel better?" he asked. I smiled slightly and he continued, "Getting out those maps and figuring out how we can fuck with Steve some more."

I laughed, leaning in to give him a hug. He looped his arm around my shoulders, turning us towards the table with the latest maps spread over it. "Yeah...You know what I like."

Chapter 18

I missed Sirius's input and level head whilst planning hits on the outposts, but Archangel was right. It did help distract me. Then I had to wonder: Why do you have so many good times planning dumb shit?

This time, the idea was to completely wipe an outpost off the map. But we also didn't want to pick a place too close to us. Unfortunately, choosing a place would almost be easier if I hung the map on a wall and let the kids throw darts at it.

To keep us on our toes, the perimeter reported Steve wandering close to the Lair twice, but they never spotted any roads we used so they let them pass unchallenged. We'd finally gotten Steve out of the mountains, now we had to convince them we weren't where we were.

I was poring over the map in the common room over my late dinner when Anansi bounced in and plopped himself down next to me, his curly hair wild and bushy around his head. I shook my head. His sister kept her hair neater, pulling it back into a ponytail that looked like a bun. He left his wildly flying around.

I guess that's the difference between someone who regularly drove through fights and someone who spent his time coming up with new ways to make things we desperately needed out of random shit lying around.

"S'up?" he asked.

"Trying to figure out which outpost is hardest to hit without leaving us stranded in the middle of nowhere."

"Move over. Let me have a look at that."

I slid down, taking my bowl with me. I watched his face, scrunched in concentration while he traced his finger over various roads, tracing the route back to the Lair, over and over. Occasionally, he'd take the pencil and jot down notes, his tongue sticking out in concentration.

"I've got it," he shouted.

I jerked, choking on my stew. "What the fuck?" I had to sit for a few moments to let the adrenaline pass and my heart return to normal. "You nearly gave me a heart attack!"

He shrunk down, his shoulders around his ears. "Sorry." He giggled, the little shit, then shook it off. "Look. This one here." He pointed to a little dot north of us labeled Chehalem. "There are others further away, but this one's best, I think. There's no direct roads, so a navigator's even more important, but there's also no real outposts along the way that might set up roadblocks. What there is, we can avoid."

I shook my head dubiously. "That's closer to the Coastal Range *and* Portland than I really like."

"That's why it's perfect! Steve'll never suspect. Besides, these ones are inside our normal range, so they'd expect it more. These ones," he pointed to two others west of Salem, "won't work. I mean we could go south, but we've been really busy there."

Exhaling, I examined the map closely. He was right. "Smartass. All right. We'll run it by the others. I want you there."

He'd gotten tall enough that when he stood, it was a process of unfolding without knocking things over. When he made it to his feet, he grinned, resting a hand on my head. "You got it."

On his way out, he passed by my brother. Fuzz flitted in and out of my life, always on the edges no matter how much I wanted to spend more time with him. He and Dereva were joined at the hip, and tonight was no different. They cuddled on their favorite couch, reading dramatically to each other.

My brother had dyslexia, so he stumbled over some words, but Dereva watched him with stars in her eyes, only helping him when he passed the book to her, pointing at the offending word.

Anansi stuck his head back in the room. "Captain," he barked. "Get a move on. Nearly everyone is there already."

Sighing, I pushed to my feet, waving at the kids as I left.

***

"Anybody here familiar with 99W?" Phoenix asked, finger on the map, squinting as if, by force of will, she could make the map give up its secrets.

Driver held up a hand. "Little bit. But I don't know Chehalem. It's a blip. A main road, a couple of side streets. As far as I know, it was all about the wine. Near Newport, or something."

Phoenix looked up. "It's called Newberg," she informed him primly.

"Whatever." He waved. "The point is, the town's tiny. There's some small mountains—or tall hills, depending on how you look at it. You should be able to find a place to set up an overwatch."

"I'm on god duty!" Phoenix shot up, abandoning the map. "I like being god."

Eleanor rubbed the bridge of her nose, sighing heavily. She hated that one designation we'd learned from the soldiers, but nearly everyone else thought it was hilarious. "Why don't we just ask around here and see if anyone came from that area?" she asked. "We might get lucky."

"I get lucky *all* the time," Phoenix muttered, grinning and sliding a coy glance at Gryphon, who blushed.

To stop Phoenix before this turned into a riot, I stepped up to the table. "Eleanor, would you and Lavender ask around, please? Close is fine, I'll take what I can get. Driver, Dry Eyes, when the scavengers go out, can you have them hit auto stores and shops? I'll take any parts they can get me, especially since I'd like to take a few of the crappier cars. Having something we can throw away is always nice. Archangel..."

He stepped up smartly. "Yes, Captain?" The warmth in his voice was unmistakable, as was the roguish glint in his eyes. "Command me, Oh Captain, that we might fuck with Steve."

My heart thumped even as I laughed. "Weapons. Long range, explosives, things that can be set and left. Talk to Chaos and Sparrow. Prepare for the ridiculous. I've got a feeling about this one."

He nodded. "As you wish."

I glowed.

***

Three days later, Seahorse, Dereva, and Eleanor sat down with the five people we'd found who had even a vague idea of the region around Chehalem. Hightide, Nebula, and Porkpie, who'd lost part of his leg to blisters that went septic, were the closest to experts we could find.

Unfortunately, the region had gone through some devastating fires two years ago, so no one had any accurate information about the kind of cover we could expect or even hope for. Hightide argued that, going by previous fires, there should be a lot of ground cover but very little in the trees, so putting someone on overwatch might not be that viable.

Dereva busily drew features on a map as they were described to her. She was the most adept with paper and pencil, so I happily left writing to her. The one thing no one had ever mentioned about pens and pencils was how much lefties like me would smudge the writing. Half the time, what I wrote was nearly illegible because of it.

Instead, I plopped onto the couch with my own project, a rough net that needed to be covered with leaves. We'd used these things in a few ambushes last year and they'd done a damn good job of camouflage. If Chehalem only had bushes, then we'd be bushes again.

Phoenix dropped heavily onto the couch next to me, using one foot to pull a bench close enough to prop her feet on and set her bag of branches on the floor next to her. "Good thing Oregon's got basically the same plants across it, otherwise we'd be fucked."

"We hope." I squinted, threading the needle. "I sure as hell didn't pay attention to the plants last time we went to the coast."

"Who does?" she mumbled around the thread in her mouth. "As long as Steve doesn't notice, we're golden."

Silence filled the air between us, and I looked at her. She stared levelly back. "We're fucked," we said in unison and cracked up, laughing.

"What's so funny?" Gryphon swung a leg over the bench, sitting next to his wife's feet, a bowl of stew in his hand.

"Just discussing our chances of success, babe."

Archangel set his bowl and mug on the table. "How the hell do you do that?" he demanded, watching me sew another branch onto the net. "I tear shit every time. What kind of voodoo is this?"

"No," I said. "I won't sew your blanket."

"I didn't ask you to!"

I grinned wickedly. "You didn't have to. I can read subtext and the answer is no."

Wounded blue eyes met mine under a shock of blond hair that hadn't been cut in weeks. "Would I do that?"

Gryphon rolled his eyes and Phoenix stared at him, her eyes narrowed. "Yes!" they shouted, making Dereva startle so badly she nearly fell off the bench.

***

Weeks after Sirius fell, we left the Lair en masse. Warm air ruffled my hair on the drive into the Willamette Valley. I closed my eyes for a moment, enjoying being fully warm for the first time since the end of last summer. We rounded a corner and entered a wonderland.

Trees bloomed white and pale pink, interspersed with oaks, maples, and fir trees. I watched the left side, Gryphon the right, Phoenix had her large rifle set up on the cab, and Archangel had the machine gun. The Valley was beautiful, and we were the dark spot in it, leashed violence hanging over us like a cloud.

I breathed deeply of the lightly scented air when a thought struck me. "It'll be my birthday soon," I absently told the air.

Phoenix booted me lightly. "Why didn't you say something earlier?"

"I didn't know until I saw the cherry blossoms." We silently watched the scenery fly by. The deeper into the Valley we went, we saw fewer blossoms and more green fruits. Probably past my birthday, then. "It didn't seem important to keep track of," I said quietly.

She kicked me again, harder. "Celebrating shit is important, especially when it's about living another year."

"Then maybe we should start doing the New Year crap again, if weddings aren't enough." Since Sirius, I volunteered to go on the perimeter so that they could take turns attending weddings and having fun. Celebrating just wasn't my cup of tea right now, so best to leave it to those as would enjoy it.

"Bah!" I glanced around. Phoenix's lip curled. "You probably just don't want to tell us how old you are. You're probably fifty because you look nineteen."

I smiled. "I think I'm twenty-eight."

"You think?"

"It's all getting blurry."

That thought sobered us and we rode the rest of the way in silence. Dereva led the caravan off the broken road, onto a dirt track to an old farmhouse surrounded by overgrown orchards. In a couple weeks they should be filled with ripe peaches.

As soon as the truck slowed, we hopped out, spreading into the trees, checking the area for Steve. I ducked under a low-hanging branch loaded with green peaches and broke into a different section. The farmer had branched out—pun intended—planting some cherry trees. A few blossoms clung to them still, and I smiled, looking up at the silvery bark framing the tiny green cherries.

"Happy birthday to me," I sang softly. "Happy birthday to me..."

"Happy birthday, dear Captain..."

I turned to see Archangel straightening up. He brushed some twigs from his hair but didn't smile. "You heard?" I asked.

"You weren't talking that quiet." Now he did grin, crinkles forming at the corners of his eyes. He shook off the new leather jacket he wore. The tannery had done a damn fine job on it, and its natural color looked good against his tanned skin, making those deep, sky-blue eyes pop. "Though this whole song works better when you have a person's name."

I raised my eyebrows. "Bold, to ask a woman her name at a time like this."

A tide of red, partially obscured by his tan, climbed his neck and flushed his cheeks. He stepped closer but didn't quite meet my eyes. "People share names all the time."

Heat flushed my cheeks. "*Couples,*" I stressed the word, "share names."

"Maybe that's where I want to go. With you."

Sudden fury suffused me. "You're bringing this up *now?*" I punched him.

"Ow!" He rubbed his arm, scowling.

"We've been dancing around this for months. You've given me space to come to grips with all this—and I'm grateful—but then you decide to bring it up when we're going so far out of our territory it's probably a suicide mission?! What the fuck, man?"

Pushing off the tree, I stomped away from him, half hoping Steve was in the area. I needed a good fight. I snarled. "Does he say he wants to be a couple when we're getting wedding stuff? Noooo. Does he mention being a couple all those times we hung out? Nope! We've been practically glued at the hip, and he doesn't say a thing about wanting to be a couple!"

"Oh, please!" He moved lightly over the uneven ground, damn him. "As if you couldn't figure it out. I kissed you, and you sure as hell kissed me back, and we've shared a bed how many times, now? All the times spent talking, are you telling me you didn't feel something, too? Because if you didn't then maybe I should back way the hell off."

My mouth worked but no words came out.

A vein pulsed in his temple. "You're right, my timing isn't great, so let's compromise. No matter how bad this shit gets, we both survive because we *will* be having this conversation. Agreed?" He stuck out a hand.

Anger still pulsed through me, mollified somewhat by the fact that he had some good points. I grabbed his hand, shaking it once. "Agreed."

CHAPTER 19

"Despite our moral complications around LA TV, it's hard not to cheer when something goes right. How did the bondmaid, known as Prudence, suddenly end up outside the fundamentalist Christian compound? How did she escape? Did she do it on her own, or was there some compassionate soul inside who helped her?"

CSPAN, 2064

" and then we shook on it," I wailed, pacing through the trees well away from the camp. Night had settled over the valley so we didn't dare stray too far, and I hoped we were far enough away the fighters wouldn't hear me.

Phoenix laughed, choked, and coughed, waving me away when I moved to help her. "You fucking *shook* on it?" she said in between coughs, shaking and leaning weakly against a tree. She buried her head in her arms, howling.

After I'd left Archangel, I hadn't known what else to do, so I found Phoenix. I needed to talk to someone but now I doubted my judgment in bringing it to her. I paced up and down the row, waiting for her to get a grip, my right hand twitching.

Eventually, she looked up, her expression hidden in the dark, and whispered, "They *shook* on it" before dissolving back into laughter.

I rolled my eyes. No need to guess what her expression was, then. "I don't know why I talk to you. You're useless."

"No, no." She subsided into giggles, sinking weakly to the ground. "No. Don't go. I swear, I'm the perfect person to talk to. How else would I ever hear gold like this? I mean, I'm listening. No judgment. Promise."

Sighing heavily, I sat next to her. "Any advice?"

"What did you do after you shook on it?" A snort of laughter escaped with the question, and I smacked her arm.

"Nothing. He just...went back to camp and I found you."

"How the fuck are you planning to fight next to him after this?"

"The fuck should I know?" I whisper-shouted. "That's what I came to you for!"

"Oh, right." Phoenix sat up, crossing her legs, resting her hands on her knees and attempting to look solemn. She ruined it by giggling again. "I want to be a fly on the wall when you do talk about it."

"Tell me, oh gutter dweller, how am I supposed to see him over breakfast and act normal for the next few weeks?"

She pondered this before telling me, "Hear the wisdom of this idiot: act like you always do. Just pretend you're constipated. That should keep your face straight. Oh, I know!" She sat up straight. "Back when I tried public speaking, they said to imagine your audience naked."

I moaned, burying my face in my hands. Imagine him naked? I spent too much time memorizing the tendons in his neck already, wishing I could refresh my memory about what he tasted like. I cast a longing look at the mountains, wanting winter back. At least then, I could throw myself into a snowbank to cool off.

"Oh, right. Sorry." Finally figuring out the cause of my distress, Phoenix got serious. "You've been professional, or pretended to be professional, for over a year. You can do it for a few more days. You know what you're doing..."

"No, I don't," I mumbled.

"...So, you make it up really good," she amended, shrugging. "This is just another day, another mission. Focus on the mission."

I stared glumly up at the sky, hoping for some kind of intervention. Maybe for Steve to show up. Anything to take my mind off this, but nothing happened.

I pouted. "Fine."

***

The next day, Archangel didn't ride in the GMC like he usually did. He manned a gun mount in one of the Chimeras. I glanced over my shoulder all day, thinking he was right behind me. Every time he wasn't, I drooped.

We took every back road that could be found, Hightide keeping her nose glued to the map to see the thin lines. The early summer heat pressed in, the humidity so high I could almost get enough water from breathing, courtesy of the two puff ball clouds on the horizon.

I glanced back, looking for Archangel's blond hair, shining in the sun. He was looking in my direction, but as soon as he spotted me, he turned his head. My shoulders dropped. Phoenix, who'd seen the exchange, patted my back.

"It's okay," she said. "This is totally fixable. You didn't screw it up forever. He might be feeling a bit awkward over the handshake, too."

"Not. Helping," I grumbled.

That night, unable to sleep, I took first watch. The quiet night only let me run through the entire conversation, over and over. How irritated he'd been that I'd seemingly forgotten the kiss, and the shared times. I hadn't thought the kiss should count, considering we'd both been hung over and he'd done it to make a point, but he'd thought about it, too…

"Captain," Phoenix hissed a few yards away. "Where the fuck you hiding?"

"I'm not hiding," I said in a low voice. "I'm right here. Right next to a tree, in plain sight. Anyone could find me, all they'd have to do is use their flipping eyes for once in their lives."

Phoenix walked lightly toward me, neatly avoiding a low-hanging branch. "Shut up, you definitely want to hear this." She sat next to me, leaning close to prevent us being overheard. "During their watch last night, Archangel told Gryph he'd fucked up with you. He spent the whole watch moaning like he thought he'd messed up forever." She shook with silent laughter. "The handshake! You're both so hopeless, it's no wonder you guys haven't hooked up yet. Maybe I should hide nearby when you have this talk. You need the advice."

Her head dropped onto my shoulder while she laughed. I shrugged sharply to knock her off. "Fuck no!"

But my heart was lighter, knowing he'd been avoiding me because he thought he screwed up, too.

***

The next morning, I'd just finished my breakfast when Archangel walked past with Hot Fuzz. Taking a shaky breath, I caught up to them. Pulling him aside, my hands shaking, I led him to the edge of the clearing, watching the others gather and pack their things. In daylight, this forest was strangely devoid of undergrowth, making everything more open than it'd seemed last night.

Archangel moved restlessly, obviously wanting to be anywhere but here, but dammit! I'd worried myself sick over nothing, stupid stories in my head, and I wanted to get everything into the open.

"Listen," I said before he could come up with an excuse, "you didn't mess up." With that, I had his full attention, his blue eyes the color of a summer sky focused so intently I nearly flinched. "I have no idea what Gryphon might've told you, but if it was anything like the advice Phoenix gave me, we're better off ignoring them. Deal?"

His eyes narrowed. "Gryph told you what I said?"

"No, he told Phoenix," I said. "And she told me. Those two have no secrets, so remember that in the future. I don't know if Gryphon can keep his mouth shut, but on most matters, Phoenix absolutely can't."

He glanced quickly around the camp, which was nearly packed. Finally, he met my gaze. "So, we're still on for later?"

"Yeah."

"You're really ready to sit down and talk openly?"

The thread of hope in him made my heart contract. I put a hand on it to steady it. "Yes!"

His shoulders slowly relaxed and he grinned slowly. My heart stuttered again, for an entirely different reason. "Guess we'd better stick together, then. Watch each other's backs."

I nodded, heat working its way up my neck. He smirked, that asshole, leading the way back to camp. I watched his ass, his fatigues fitting perfectly. Once, I'd overheard Moose call them "tactical butt cheeks."

"Not a bad back to be watching," I muttered.

"Watch my back, Captain." He shot me a sly glance over his shoulder. "Not my ass."

"Fuck you!"

"Later, definitely."

My mouth dropped open. One little talk and all his sass came rushing back. "You lil' shit."

***

Two days of careful driving and one disappeared patrol later, we reached the edge of a forest. Sort of. Spread out before us, blackened, broken fingers stretched towards the sky. The ground was covered with new growth that was, at best, six feet tall.

I frowned. Not enough cover for the vehicles. Any idiot on a hill with a set of binoculars would be able to see them. Pacing, I pondered the different possibilities.

"Hightide, how far is it to town?" I asked abruptly.

"About four miles," she said after a moment's thought. "Less, if you leave the road."

I nodded. "Then that's what we'll do. Hide the cars. Drivers, you have the vehicles and our backs. Everyone else, you know the drill."

"All in, all out! No luck, all skill. One shot, one kill!"

"Aww." I grinned at the lot of them. "That's my beautiful babies."

Catching the pack Phoenix threw me, I slid it on, careful of the sword hilts protruding over my shoulders. Then, I slung my rifle over my left shoulder and lifted the net I'd spent so much time sewing greenery onto. It wasn't exact for the area, but good enough.

Once the trucks were emptied, the drivers took them back a ways. There was a clearing large enough to fit them. They had legit camouflage tarps with loose, leafy looking bits to cover them with, not like our Mickey Moused nets.

After draping my net over my head and shoulders, I checked the Irregulars out to make sure they were fine. Forty of us prepared to go in, and I hoped we all made it out. Doc, carrying her medical bag and a handgun, struggled when her net caught. Dionysius immediately moved to help her out.

I liked that kid. From the little he said, I had him down as a former frat boy and all-round himbo. Half the time I spent on watches was to let him attend the weddings. The party really started when he showed up.

Checking out the rest of the crew, I nodded. Forty fighters, no rookies, all looking mean as hell. As soon as the last bit of shine was covered, we headed out, leaving the road to follow a deer track into the brush.

We moved slowly over the rough terrain, but we had plenty of time before dark. It was approximately another mile to the town, but three feet away, the bushes ended. Beyond that, a gentle hill rose. At the top, a series of buildings sat clustered where they had great views over the Valley.

Peering through my scope, I counted five buildings of various sizes, one of them nearly hidden behind a large, barn-like structure. All the buildings were wanna-be Tudor style, very pretty, all together like that. An untidy vineyard covered the hills between us and the buildings, ending a few dozen feet from the closest building.

And everywhere I looked, I saw Steve, about twenty of them, entering or leaving buildings, standing guard, performing basic maintenance.

"Well, we found Steve," Phoenix said dryly.

Steve had built a decent perimeter, too. Rough fencing, topped with concertina wire and stakes facing outwards were fronted by a ditch. Impossible to say how deep. The best part was the general lack of cover.

"What a waste of a perfectly good winery," Gryphon mourned.

Nebula wrinkled her nose. "Wine. Blech. There's a buttload of wineries around here. Chances are good we'll find another one."

I grunted, squinting at the shadows to gauge the time. Just after noon. "There's a lot of damn buildings there. Seahorse, constant watch, please. Six shifts, minimum two people per shift."

She nodded. "They might have more sentries set further out. I would."

She began setting up shifts from those who hadn't had a watch the previous night while the rest of us pulled back, spreading out to look for spots to take a nap. A basic camp appeared in the middle of the bushes, two to three people here, more over there.

Once she finished with the shifts, she joined me, Archangel, Phoenix, and Gryphon around a tiny camp stove. I set a pot of water over the flames, checking that the handle was fully opened. Forgot that last night and nearly burned my fingers.

"There's still a partial moon tonight," Phoenix pointed out, lounging against Gryphon. He'd spread a blanket on the ground and leaned against their stacked packs.

"Good thing we've got those leafy blankets," Archangel said absently, pulling out a pouch of Wilder's tea and spooning some into his mug. He held the pouch up, checking if anyone else wanted some. I held out my mug and he dropped some in before doing the same for Seahorse.

"Thanks."

Gryphon rubbed his cheek against his wife's hair. "If we move fast, we might be able to make it to the top before the moon rises."

I shook my head. "Not too fast. We still need to see if Steve's gonna be a tricky little bastard or as unimaginative as they come."

Steam billowed around the pot lid. Snatching up the rag that did double duty as a cleaning cloth, I poured water into each mug, biting my lip in concentration. I've dumped dishes on the ground before, trying to serve, so I gave this my full attention.

Especially with my crush watching.

Sighing quietly when I was done, I set the pot aside to air dry for a while. The fire had already burned itself out and Archangel shook the ash into a small hole he'd scraped out, covering it completely. Sirius's insistence on hidden campsites, and the ways she went about it, were clearly visible in the small habits I saw all over the camp.

Gryphon, looking thoroughly comfortable with Phoenix in his arms and his eyes half closed, asked, "What's the plan, again? I'm having a hard time remembering it."

Archangel snickered when I rolled my eyes. "Bullshit."

"Yes," he admitted. "I just enjoy the simplicity of your plans. Please."

"The plan is, no one can raise the alarm if no one is alive to raise the alarm."

"Ah. Excellent. I'm glad I didn't forget any part of it."

Phoenix giggled sleepily while Seahorse ignored us, focusing on her tea. I took a sip, closing my eyes. Tea never tasted this good Before. Although, if I was being completely honest, my tastes had changed drastically, a result of not having any chocolate, ice cream, or sugar in general over the last year. I'd go back to those things in a heartbeat.

I stretched out on my own blanket, grimacing at the disgusting display of marital bliss nearby. Instead, I curled on my side, facing Archangel. He lay on his back, his hands folded over his stomach. I snorted softly. How these monsters managed to sleep on their backs was beyond me. Inhuman.

I traced the bridge of his nose with my eyes. It had a small bump, like it'd been broken. While trying to remember when that had occurred, I fell asleep.

***

As always, the last shift woke everyone up. The Celt preferred to use her foot, so the quiet yelps of hapless, heavy sleepers woke me long before she got a chance to use it on me. I shook Seahorse awake, and nudged Phoenix with my foot. The five of us made our way to the edge of the brush and the sentries made their reports, pointing to and describing locations.

Essentially, there were dugouts and hides all through the vineyards and in the brush about thirty yards downhill of the winery. The hides themselves were army camouflage like we used on the trucks, strung between gaps. Damn difficult to spot.

Unless you knew where to look.

"There's roughly fifty yards between each hide," the Celt finished, folding her arms, surveying the scene with a scowl.

"Wonderful." I sighed, slapping a flutter on my neck. Living outside, you learned to slap anything that brushed your skin without trying to identify it first. Possibly a mosquito, maybe a spider, and usually a hair. Still, better safe than sorry. Last thing I needed was to get sick from a skeeter bite.

But hey! We had a decent idea where Steve was, and they had as many sentries as we had people.

Shit.

"How do we keep to the plan, now?" Seahorse asked. "There's no way we'll get them all."

Archangel shook his head. "I'm more worried about *why* they have so many bodies here. What the hell are they guarding? Because chances are good, they'll fight to the death to protect it."

"Should we look for an easier target?" Hot Fuzz asked. By this time, everyone was up and ready to go, so they'd joined us, learning about the lay of the land.

"No!" Phoenix quietly burst out while women shook their heads, muttering.

I grinned. "If there's something in there they want to keep this badly, then they shouldn't have it. No." I chewed on my lower lip, thinking. "Buddy up, let me see where everyone is."

People paired up, choosing their battle partners. Checking them out, I nodded. "Seahorse, Chaos, Archangel, and me will take the four positions closest to us then head to the top. If you know or can see a position, take it out if you can, then head up. If you can't, wait until the party starts. Sentries'll make some noise when we do. Take them out and join us ASAP. Chances are good there'll be too many people for us to dance with them all."

Chaos raised his hand. I nodded at him. "Do you think we'll need a lot of explosives?"

I shrugged. "I haven't got a clue, but boom is always good."

Grinning, he dug into his pack, stowing a few items in outer pockets and belt pouches. Archangel leaned in. "You know he didn't choose that name, don't you? That's the nickname he was given while he was *in* the military."

"Is that bad?"

"It's certainly unpredictable."

"One more question," I whispered. He made an encouraging noise. "What was your nickname?"

He mumbled indistinctly.

"I'm sorry?"

"Mmfmanlemm..."

"Oh, come on! You said we could talk honestly."

"Angel," he finally grumbled.

Everyone looked at me strangely when I stuffed my mouth full of sweat-shirt, screeching.

PASADENA, CALIFORNIA

"Okay, everything looks good, Mary." Mercy washed her hands in the basin of water.

Mary sat up on the table, pulling her skirts down around her legs, smoothing the fabric over her large belly. "Is there any way to tell if it's a boy or girl? I hope it's a boy," she muttered under her breath.

Mercy shook her head, smiling faintly. "Despite what is said, there is no way to tell without an ultrasound."

"Hush!" Mary looked at the closed door, her eyes wide. "Do you want the Warriors to hear you? It's sacrilege, against the texts—"

"It's called the Bible," Mercy said dryly.

"—to speak of technology. You'll be stoned. I'll be stoned." Tears welled in the younger woman's eyes.

Mercy softened. "I won't say anything like that again, I promise. I'm sorry."

Nobody got sarcasm anymore. Everybody was so afraid. Mercy sighed. She'd gone beyond terror so long ago, but most of the bondmaids, Mary included, clung to life so tightly they'd put up with any indignity, any idiocy, to continue to exist.

Mercy's door burst open just as Mary gained her feet. Three men filled the doorway, two of them supporting the third, whose head rolled limply.

"Out, cow," one of the Warriors of Light snarled at Mary. Squeaking apologetically, she edged around them, hurrying as fast as her pregnant body allowed.

Mercy whipped a fresh sheet onto the table. "Here," she barked.

The Warriors laid out the third man on the table, blood from several open wounds quickly soaking into the sheet. Mercy cut away the rest of his clothing, revealing the injuries. "You can leave now," she said to the Warriors.

Stupid fights, all the time, over too few resources. Everyone left in the LA basin formed groups, to the best of her knowledge, all of them vying for the same limited resources: food and water. In the Master's compound, they were marginally better off, sitting on top of cisterns that refilled from an underground aquifer. She even had a water pump in her room/surgery, though use was limited to the bare essentials.

"Will he live?" the taller Warrior of Light snapped.

"Too soon to tell."

The Warrior loomed over her, a hand on the knife at his belt. "If he dies…"

Mercy closed her fingers over the scalpel on the table, biting her lip on the first words threatening to spill out, inhaling deeply through her nose. "Get. Out. You're dirtying my room and contaminating his wounds further. I report only to my Master. Not you. Now go."

Being the only medical person in the entire compound had its uses.

As soon as the men left, she cleaned, stitched, and bandaged. Before she finished, a timid knock sounded at the door.

"Enter," she called, her hands busy with needle and thread.

The door opened slowly, a kerchief-covered head peeking in. The woman's eyes widened at the sight of the man on the table, but Prudence entered, closing the door carefully behind her. "Is it still safe?" she whispered.

Mercy glanced up at her. "He won't wake up until sometime tomorrow. There is no other time. It must be now."

Prudence shifted, dropping a sack from between her legs. Shedding the skirt and blouse all bondmaids wore, she dressed quickly in the jeans and t-shirt she'd hidden. "How are you getting me out?" she whispered. "After the patrol was ambushed, there's guards everywhere."

Done with the wounded man, Mercy washed her hands. Going to her little pallet, in the corner in front of bookshelves loaded with medical texts, she rolled it up, revealing more concrete floor. Using a spatula, she levered up a section, showing it was nothing more than a board, carefully textured and painted to match the rest of the floor.

A dark hole yawned beneath, fetid air rising from it.

Prudence's mouth dropped open. "How—?"

"I've been here a long time," Mercy said grimly. "I can show you the way out, but I don't know what you'll find. Master keeps me on too short a leash."

Donning the trousers she kept hidden, she removed her sandals, preferring to go barefoot. Easier to clean. Tying a small lantern and a pouch with fire lighting tools to her belt, she slipped down, hanging by her fingertips for a moment before dropping.

Prudence followed as she lit the lamp, making sure the shade covered most of the light. "Quickly," Mercy whispered.

"How many..." Prudence swallowed. "How many have you helped this way?"

"Not enough."

"Stockholm syndrome?"

"And fear. Quiet! We're approaching the meeting hall."

CHAPTER 21

A light breeze provided cover as I crept up the hill, staying close to the bushes. Timing my movements to the rustling was slow, but better than getting my head blown off. The shrubby lump ahead and to my left set a slow pace that I matched.

Archangel took an irregular path following the edge of the vineyard, using every groove in the ground to stay low. Halfway up, the shift change happened. We didn't move until the relieved men were out of sight in the dark. Once we were within six yards, a red glow marked our target, the sentry taking a chance on a quick smoke. Right where our lookouts saw them set up, on the edge between bushes and vineyard.

The closer we got, the slower we went. Archangel stopped every time Steve faced our direction. I clenched my teeth. Only one man was visible, pacing in small half-circles. My lip curled in a snarl. The other bastard wasn't moving at all, which meant I had to go in after him.

Fuck.

Squeezing Archangel's leg, I let him know what I'd be doing. Well, I hoped that's what I told him. My Morse code skills are pretty shit. I could've told him I was going swimming or to jump off a cliff. Either way, the next time Steve turned away, I slid over the mounded dirt marking the edge of the vineyard and into the bushes.

Barely five feet into the bushes I hit a snag. Literally. My leafy cover caught on a branch, stopping my progress. Holding my breath, I waited to see if I'd been spotted. When nothing happened, I exhaled and wriggled forward, leaving it behind.

I made my way around the position, unsure whether I was giving it enough space or about to crawl in the middle. Once I could see Archangel's target's silhouette, I stopped. Barely breathing, I looked everywhere.

Move, motherfucker, move.

The hidden bastard was nowhere to be found, though I kept coming back to one bush. Something about it wasn't right. Tipping my head for a different angle, I saw it. Him. Sitting in the middle of the damn bush. The odd thing was his helmet, smooth where there shouldn't be smooth. If I'd been standing, I'd never have seen him.

I backed slowly into the bushes and went wide until I could stand. Outside Steve's bush, I breathed out slowly. No way to keep this completely silent. Knife in one hand, I lunged into the bush, wrapping my right arm around his face and stabbing up, under the chin.

When I made it out, Archangel had already dumped the other body into the bushes. Donning my retrieved net, we headed across the rows to the next target.

My victim this time was lively. He turned unexpectedly, and upon being confronted by a bush standing in front of him, didn't hesitate to try and stab me with his bayonet. I slid to the side, not far enough. A line of fire across my ribs made me hiss and I lunged before he could bring the bayonet around.

He thrashed while I punched anything that moved, too close to use the knife. Panicking, he squealed and bucked, throwing me off. Springing to his feet, he loomed over me. Rolling to my knees, I scrambled forward on hands and feet, lunging at his knees. He jerked a knee up, catching me on the cheek and knocking me aside. He followed me down, trying to land knees first.

Desperately, I rolled to the side, only to find him right over me. Spitting in his face, I took advantage of his shock and lunged, leading with my teeth. I bit his face even as I stabbed him. He managed one short, sharp scream before he died.

I paused on top of my kill, waiting and listening. A few shouts on the far side that quickly died out, but it wouldn't be long now.

"My bad," I hissed to Archangel.

He grabbed me, hauling me upright and into a run up the hill. It was a race against time. Could we get there before Steve fully mobilized?

Short answer? Yes.

Long answer? Not fast enough.

***

"Don't shoot!" the man screamed, holding his hands up. "Don't shoot. I'm not armed. I help! I help!"

I didn't lower my rifle, aimed directly at the man's head. We stood in a formerly locked room inside the winery. Pregnant women. There were so many pregnant women in here, keeping to the edges of the room, watching me curiously. Mattresses on the floor, but they had plenty of blankets, and there were actual toilets through one door, if the sign was any indication.

I'd zeroed in on the only man in the room, trying to lurk near the back, but the lantern light didn't let him hide. I'd barely stopped myself from shooting him on sight. Archangel stood just outside the door, watching outside. Every time he fired, the man in front of me flinched. Not a fighter, this one.

"Will anyone vouch for him?" I shouted. "Speak up! Do I let him live?"

A long pause in which the man gulped audibly, paling even more.

"Wait," one woman stepped forward, one hand on her protruding belly. "Don't shoot him. He's not bad."

Other women spoke up, and slowly, I lowered my rifle. I rocked back, as if punched, when I saw a woman bouncing a little bundle cradled in her arms. There were babies here.

Babies.

Shaking myself, I remembered the next step. "If you have any necessities, gather 'em up, ladies! We're getting the hell out, and we don't leave people behind." Questions and objections flew in thick and fast. I held up a hand. "We don't have time! Unless you want to stay here and be a part of the breeding program, get moving."

They moved reluctantly, though I figured it was all the guns I carried that prompted it and not any lack of desire to leave and head into the unknown. Archangel backed into the room.

"How's it going?"

"Well, I found out why there's so much security here," I said dryly.

"Captain!" Out of sight, Phoenix bellowed. "Where you at?"

Archangel stuck his head out, waving. "Yo! Get Eleanor, will you? We got civilians in here! And Doc."

"Excuse me, miss?" The man stepped forward, puffing out his chest. "I'll help. Give me a gun, and..."

"Nope." I turned away, more concerned with what was happening outside. "We don't give guns out. Stay close to your charges. Make sure they have what they need and keep them together."

As soon as Eleanor and Doc arrived, guarded by Stretch and Gameboy, we took off, back into the fight.

***

"Phoenix," I bellowed, striding to the door. Bullets peppered the walls, so I stopped just inside. "Found out why there's so many fucking Steve here."

"Civilians, I know."

I laughed. "Women. Kids." I nodded at her shock. "What's it like?"

"Fuck. Me. Shit." She shook her head, automatically reloading from the bandolier across her chest. "Our entrance is still good as an exit, sent Legs and Dionysius back to get the cars. And those motherfuckers are throwing everything they have at us. They're coming in on the road."

"Where?"

"Opposite side to the hill. They don't know our entrance, so...yeah."

"Right." I rolled my shoulders and jogged back inside. "Eleanor! We need to go!"

She appeared in the doorway, a baby in her arms. "When don't we?" Without waiting for an answer, she disappeared back into the room

Doc walked slowly, keeping an eye on several women but made her way over. "Some of them shouldn't be moved," she said in a low voice, keeping an eye on them.

"When should they ever?"

"They haven't had the exercise they need. Steve let them go for walks, but they're weaker than they should be. Stronger than the last lot," she amended.

"Good enough." I glanced back. Twenty-four, by my count, and Eleanor was the last one out. The man stayed with the group, providing a supporting arm to two women. "Hey, it's all downhill. Yo!" I shouted.

"Yo!" A variety of voices echoed back.

"Time to go! Pick a mama and move!"

Chaos made a new door in the wall, giving us an easier exit. As soon as the dust cleared, five fighters went first, then the mamas, each walking with a fighter. I held the rear guard with Archangel, Gryphon, and Sparrow.

Sparrow ran around inside the building, setting things in corners or in containers. Soon we'd have some boom.

Yay.

We fired as quickly as we could, but it wasn't long before things were desperate as Steve continued pouring into the area. Phoenix, standing in the new 'door,' waved when it was time to go.

"They're really not far enough," she said, "but there's too many Steve here. The building will slow them more than we can."

Sparrow ran around the building with a lit match, giggling madly. She left six burning fuses. Lord help me.

"Fancy sitting on the roof, Captain?" Gryphon called, laughing as he ran downhill with Phoenix.

"No." I stuck out my lower lip to hide a smile. "But I'll do it anyway."

"C'mon," Archangel teased. "It'll be fun." He fired three quick shots before we ran past the other two. "I promise I won't let you fall," he continued, as casually as if we were chilling in a cafe.

Why was that so hot?

"Oh, yes. Thank you so much." Sliding the pump, I smelled the heat as a spent shell flew past my face. My shots were barely slower than the boys,' even though they had semi-autos, so we kept up a good rate of fire, augmented by Phoenix's more accurate ones.

"Time's almost up," Sparrow shouted, bouncing on her toes. "We should go."

"Don't mind us," Gryphon shouted, hurtling past.

I turned to Archangel. "You know, if we want to make our ride, we'd probably better hurry."

He nodded seriously. "I do believe you're right."

"Hit the deck," Sparrow screamed.

My legs collapsed without conscious command. I'd long since learned, when Sparrow sounds like that, you do what she says. The concussion rocked the ground, the heat and blasting air brushing my skin. I looked up in time to see half the roof fly into the sky.

"Time to GO!" I bellowed, still looking skyward.

Archangel yanked me to my feet and like the terrifying fighters we were...we ran away.

***

The engines were running, all vehicles pointing *away* when we plunged out of the brush and onto the narrow road. The bed was loaded with fighters, piled in the back like puppies, all squirming for a more comfortable position. I leapt onto the running board, Archangel beside me, just before Dereva hit the gas.

That awful storm nearly two years ago kept flashing through my mind. We passed so close to trees I tried sucking in my butt, to no avail. My breath came faster, old memories piling up until a particularly brutal jolt had Archangel swearing as he scrambled for a better hold.

Grabbing his belt, I hauled him closer. "Here," I shouted. "Through the window there's a handle. I can spare some space."

In order to reach, he wrapped an arm around my waist. I found myself flattened between his body and the truck. Barely turning my head, I eyed him, then the truck, then back to him. Suspicion blossomed in my tiny brain, because I'd swear he could've reached in front of me.

I narrowed my eyes. "Are you sure you slipped?"

He grinned, bracing around me, his jacket taking the brunt of the tiny, myriad blows from the branches. "How do you feel now?"

Like I had other things on my mind than a nightmare of a drive from my past. That shit. It worked.

CHAPTER 22

"We're here to talk about the morality of not only watching LA TV, but how people are treating it. Are we forgetting that those are real people who are being tortured and murdered? And that's not even counting those who die through starvation or dehydration."

CSPAN, 2063

By noon, we were all dragging. We'd managed to resettle so that those of us in precarious positions were slowly absorbed by the puppy piles of fighters. I'd taken a turn driving while Dereva slept, but she was back behind the wheel when we stopped for a toilet break.

I spoke quietly to Doc and looked in on our wounded. No dead, thank God, but some bad gunshots. One of them had a broken thigh. Femur or something. Plus, Doc was increasingly worried about two of the women who had a...squishy...look to them. Something about retaining water to a dangerous degree.

"They need to lay down, feet up, and have some dandelions to start flushing things out. At their stage of pregnancy, this is ridiculously dangerous. Whoever Steve had looking after them should've known better."

"So...you want to be back at the Lair yesterday?"

She nodded.

I sighed, pressing against my eyebrows, trying to relieve the headache before it gained traction. "I knew the moment I saw them we weren't hitting any more outposts, but I'd hoped we could lie low and disappear for a bit."

Doc chewed her lip. "I know. But a firefight could raise their blood pressure, too. Last night was bad enough, but in the cars…"

"All right. Let me talk to the others." Doc went back to her charges while I approached the fighters. "Okay, children, listen up!" They didn't stop stretching, massaging, or moving, but I saw heads tipping in my direction. "Doc says we need to get back to the Lair ASAP. Which means we need to lose Steve or kill the ones after us. Suggestions?"

Phoenix raised her hand. "I vote kill them all."

"Yes, luv," Gryphon murmured, his eyes warm, "but I think she's asking for the best way to do it."

"Thank you!" I pointed at him. "C'mon. I came up with the last few plans. I mean, landmines behind us are a given. We can up the frequency if we have enough, and when we pass a good spot for an ambush, we can do that, too. Though we don't want the mamas getting too far ahead, because patrols. It'd suck if they got recaptured…"

"Not to mention, we'd probably be dead," Phoenix pointed out.

I ignored her. "I'd also like to bring down a hillside to block the road. There were a couple likely spots. Chaos, Sparrow, wanna talk with Hightide about that?"

Archangel started grinning long before I finished and at that last one, he laughed. "Sweet plan, Captain. I think we can do that, right?" He turned to the fighters when my jaw dropped. He was right, it wasn't completely shitty for our situation. "We probably want to pick a point before any side roads that easily connect to the other side of the Valley, too."

Hightide pulled map after map from her satchel before he finished speaking. She spread them out, weighing the corners with rocks, finding our location. A topographical map, a geological one, and a road map. Fuck, that girl had it all covered.

"Where did you get all that?" I asked.

"Useless Room," she said absently, tracing her finger over the road map. "It was a map room slash control Before."

We watched as she sorted through the information, switching from one map to another. Sparrow sorted through her bag, pulled something out, and, cupping it in her hand, licked it. I grimaced. Licking explosives?

"It's not explosives," she said, reading my expression. "Just damping down the cap. All the boom clay is stored in the vehicles, and we only take out what we need."

"Why the fuck am I just learning about this?" I demanded.

"To keep your blood pressure down, of course." She grinned.

"Got it," Hightide announced. We gathered around her. "Roughly ten miles down the road. It's that section of road that was blasted from two hillsides."

"You guys have enough?" Archangel asked.

Chaos shrugged and Sparrow nodded. "Although a drill of some kind to set it into the hillside would work better," she said.

Chaos opened the tailgate box on the GMC and dug under the clothes and blankets Dereva stored there for emergencies. "Here!" He pulled out a metal T with swirlies at the bottom. "Hand-powered auger," he explained to a bunch of blank faces. "We can make holes in the ground, but it'll be slow going."

I opened my mouth, shut it, then tried again. "And you just...carry it around?"

"Of course! You never know when you're gonna need an auger." He grinned. I shook my head. All that rough charm bottled up in a handsome man was a dangerous thing. Not as handsome as Gryphon, but that man had ridiculous good looks.

"No." I held up my hand. "No, I've decided I don't want to know. Take Dereva, Hightide, and the GMC and make it happen. We'll buy you time."

While they gathered their things, I walked to the cab of my pickup. Stroking the hood, I leaned down and planted a kiss on it. "You be careful with my baby," I said to Dereva.

"Aren't I always?" she asked jauntily, sliding into the driver's seat.

As they drove away, I turned back to the rest. "All right, kids. We need a spot for an ambush."

***

When the sun sat halfway between noon and the horizon, I lay face down in an open meadow by the road, fighters spread out all around. Some were in the trees, and a few were hiding in the bushes behind me, but most of us were in the grass.

In the distance, I heard another explosion as some poor bastard drove over a landmine. I nodded—I'd been counting them, and that was the last one. Next stop, us.

"You couldn't find shorter grass?" Phoenix muttered to my left. She was a disembodied voice as persistent and annoying as a mosquito in my ear, hiding in grass that barely reached my shins. "All I have to do is take a deep breath and they'll see me, but *nooo*. Captain is scrawny as fuck, so if she can hide in short grass, *everyone* should be able to hide in short grass."

The absence of Sirius's quick reply struck me, and I bit the meaty part of my hand. Physical pain was so much better than emotional. Then I giggled wetly. "Sirius would be proud of you. Carrying on her grand tradition of being a pain in my ass. Go bother Gryphon."

"Why would I bother him? I like him. You, not so much, since you picked a stupid place for an ambush. I've got ants, too. Other people better have ants. If I'm the only one who has ants, I'm gonna be so pissed off."

I buried my face in the crook of my elbow, silent tears shaking me. Missing Sirius was an ache that ebbed and flowed, and when it hit, I couldn't...

Taking a deep breath, I wiped my eyes and peered through the grass. Should be any minute now...Raven's caw echoed over the meadow. A former brothel prisoner, Raven joined the scouts. Last I'd seen her, she'd been perched high in a tree, her name well chosen. Her call meant Steve was close.

A faint rustle, like wind through the grass, drifted through the air as everyone readied their weapons. Vibrations ran through the ground, and I cursed under my breath. A Chimera rolled into view, then another, closely followed by a tank. I sighed. Sometimes, I hated being right.

Fucking tank, all because we'd stolen their baby mamas.

Rude.

The echoing gunshot from Phoenix's large rifle started the party. I grinned, sorrow taking a backseat. Her first shot took out the lead vehicle's front tire, causing it to slew to a stop, blocking the road. Being bulletproof doesn't mean much when you have a sharpshooter with an attitude and a Barret M82 sniper rifle. A .50 cal doesn't really care about bulletproof, especially when it's fired less than a hundred yards from its target.

Her second and third shots ruined the engine completely.

I chose softer targets, all of us providing cover for the two closest to the road—Archangel and Goliath. They popped up, lobbing hand grenades like bowling balls under the tank. Once their third volley was off, they abandoned their spots, racing away while the rest of us kept up withering cover fire.

When the explosions rocked the ground, I pushed to my feet, firing while backing away. I worked the pump as quickly as I could, backing after the fighters. Rifle emptied, I slung it over my shoulder and booked it after the rest. Around a bend, out of Steve's sight, several downed trees blocked the road, the waiting cars just past them.

Fighters made their way over as they could. Some hurdled the trees like track stars, some needed a hand over, and others dived down to crawl under. I hurdled the first tree, hopped onto the second, and leaped from one to the other, landing on the far side, knees bent to absorb the shock.

The engines were running, and fighters piled into the cars willy-nilly. The Celt skidded to a halt, waving. "Raven isn't here yet!"

Without thinking, I swerved to the rear of an old Suburban, already half-full. "'Scuse me." I reached in, pulling a box towards me. I flipped open the lid, giggling and running my hands over the bazooka inside. Grabbing it and one rocket, I grinned "Gotta go!"

Racing back to the trees, I hopped on the closest one for the best view. Steve's second Chimera, relatively unharmed, nudged the broken one out of the way, closely followed by the barely scratched tank. More Chimeras were behind those.

Something flickered through the trees to my left. There! Raven, maybe fifty yards away and running, but it was only a matter of time before Steve spotted her, too. Hopping the gap, I knelt on two trees and balanced the bazooka on my shoulder, peering through the sights.

"What are you waiting for?" someone screamed. "Shoot!"

Holding the bazooka firmly, I waited. Ignoring the shouts behind me, both encouragement for Raven and urges for me to shoot, I waited. My heartbeat slowed and I wet my lips with my tongue, wishing I had a moment for a drink. As soon as the tank made it past the downed truck and the parts I wanted to hit came into unobstructed view, I fired.

For a millisecond, nothing happened. Long enough for a flash of dread to shoot through me. Maybe it was broken? Then, the bazooka trembled, and the rocket went off with more force than I was prepared for. The shock pushed me sideways, my foot slipping. I shrieked, sliding between the trees, my world turning upside down. Literally.

"Captain!"

"Fuckin' 'ell!"

I clutched the bazooka for dear life and cautiously opened my eyes. "Save me," I yelled. My right leg twisted awkwardly above, caught between the trees. The bazooka formed a bridge over a wider gap, and only my grip on it kept me from hitting the ground.

Trees shook as people scrambled over and under. Archangel grasped my wrist, taking my weight while Phoenix untangled my leg. Someone took the bazooka away. When Archangel pulled me up, there was a wall of people and weapons between us and the smoking tank. The body was fine, but I'd blown it off its treads.

I whooped, then my world turned over again. Archangel scooped me over his shoulder, hustling away from the sporadic fire. "No time for that," he grunted.

"Clear!" Phoenix bellowed.

The fighters hopped back nimbly, collecting Raven along the way. The last truck was rolling before the fighter's got their feet off the ground. Archangel dumped me in the back of a Chimera. Hands caught me, lowering me gently to the floor. People pressed in on all sides while Archangel ran his hands over my leg, checking for broken bones.

I grunted when he squeezed, the pain shooting to my hip. I breathed in deep through my nose, letting it out long and slow, watching the clouds through the gun nest as we raced along the curvy road.

"Wiggle your toes," he ordered.

Reluctantly, I looked at my bare foot, cradled in his warm hands, but I obeyed. I melted into the floor, sweet relief flooding me. My toes moved. He sighed, too.

"It's fine," he reported. "Doesn't look like the ankle is damaged, but you should take it easy for the next few weeks."

I laughed. "How am I supposed to 'take it easy'? We're still outside the Lair."

"The other injured rest," Phoenix snapped. "Now, you have to, too. Suck it up, buttercup."

"If you try to walk too much," Archangel warned, "you could make it worse. Ruin your leg."

Goosebumps rippled down my arms. I didn't want to stay down, but I wanted a bum knee even less. Death didn't scare me. We looked into his eyes, laughing at the stupid shit we were about to pull every time we left the Lair. He was more like an old friend at this point. It might even be a relief. But an infection meant my friends would be at greater risk, trying to protect me.

Sighing, I nodded. "I'll be good."

Phoenix snorted. "As if. You're so full of shit it's coming out your ears. I'm just glad you didn't shatter your leg. If you'd done that," she continued, talking over me, "then we might've had to put you down. Which means that *I'd* be the one dealing with people's complaints, and that's a headache I don't need."

I stuck my tongue out.

Her grin widened. "You should've seen yourself. Screaming, sure. But you just held onto the bazooka like it was your lifeline. I don't think I've ever seen you hold onto anything so hard. You still looked like an idiot."

Shaking my head, laughter all around me, I closed my eyes. "I can do that just by waking up, so get fucked."

"Every damn day."

Whoops echoed off the mountains, the fighters enjoying this more than me. I cackled. "Bitch. You know what? Make yourself useful and watch the sides. See if there's another good spot for an ambush."

***

Two skirmishes later and my leg had stiffened up so much I could barely walk. Fuck my life. I crawled into the back of the truck slowly, psyching myself up before every move.

Done with me, Doc intervened. "You," she pointed at me. "Rest. Sleep is better, but close your eyes. Everyone who can, should."

I snapped at her finger, my teeth closing inches away. She didn't flinch, just watching me with implacable empathy. Archangel nodded. "I'll make sure she naps," he said.

"I'm fine," I said, watching Doc hustle back to her patients. "She shouldn't worry about—"

"Can it, Captain," he interrupted pleasantly. My mouth dropped open. "You're in so much pain I'm starting to feel it. So, shut up and close your eyes for five minutes, will you?"

"Don't I get a say in this?"

"No."

"Fine!"

CHAPTER 23

"Captain."

Someone shook my shoulders and rubbed my hands.

"Captain!"

I mumbled, burying my nose against smooth, warm skin. Dirt, grass, and gunpowder filled my nostrils and I sighed. Archangel. Nestling deeper into his embrace, I shook my head. Whatever it was could wait. This safety, this care, this was more important.

Archangel shifted under me, shaking with silent laughter. "You wanted to know when we got to the hill, remember?" he whispered against my hair.

Reason returned all at once and I sat up carefully, to avoid jostling my leg. Opening my eyes last, my first sight was deep, sky-blue eyes, with gold and gray flecks, enhancing the impression of sky. The corners of his eyes crinkled, though his lips barely curved.

"Fine." I slumped slightly and he leaned forward, gently pressing our foreheads together. We stayed that way indefinitely, his hands hot, one on my back, stroking softly, the other resting on my thigh while he waited. Sighing again, I straightened. "Okay, let's go make a hill fall down."

"That's the spirit." He grinned, but there was something in his eyes...I exhaled slowly. If he didn't stop watching me like that, I was about to give everyone something to look at. "Oh." He held up one finger. One of my hair-ties was looped around it. "You might want this."

I gathered the section back, twisting it into a braid down the side of my head. Most of the women sported braids from their crown to the ends of their hair in various styles that were collectively called "battle braids." I couldn't even remember where I first heard the term, but if it kept our hair back and away from the eyes, it was a battle braid.

"Ready to get up?" Archangel asked when I was done.

"Yo, Captain," Phoenix jogged over. "Can you even get up?"

I grimaced. "We're about to find out." Every tiny motion shot pain up to my hip, but I needed to get up at some point. Gripping the sides of the doorway, I panted, steeling myself. Pushing upright, I arched, levering myself out, keeping my right leg as straight as possible.

Archangel slid out the back and pulled me the rest of the way to my feet. "It's not too bad, once I'm up," I said. I put my full weight on it, pain free.

"It's probably muscular." Doc had come over to watch, too, her arms folded while she assessed me. "Walk a bit."

A small crowd gathered to watch. They treated the whole thing like an evening's entertainment, but once I was moving, Doc took over and peppered me with questions and commands: walk here, how does that feel, where does it hurt?

"Definitely muscular," she confirmed. "You'll need a good massage, and you need to take it easy."

"As soon as that hill comes down," I promised.

"No," she said sternly. "You keep your ass right here. If something is off, you're in no shape to run."

"I could run."

"You'll fuck your leg up even more. Shut up and stay put!"

"Fine." I drooped, turning to the others. "Go have fun without me."

Chaos, Sparrow, Archangel, Gryphon, and Phoenix trooped up the hill, to do whatever the hell it was that needed to be done to bring the hill down. I paced around the vehicles, continually glancing up the slope.

Finally, Doc had enough. "Join me," she invited. She lay on her belly, braced up on her hands in a yoga pose. She exhaled, moving to a classic position, Down Dog.

I shook my head, continuing to pace.

"You might as well do something useful with your time," she said irritably. "Plus, if you want to be able to walk later, you need to stretch it out now. This isn't a request!"

Snarling slightly because she was right, I grabbed my blanket from my pack. I knew most of the moves from cooling down after workouts, so I could follow along easily enough. Pigeon and Frog are weird names, but Frog made sense. I never could get what Pigeon pose had to do with actual pigeons.

"The fact that you can do these is a good sign." Doc settled into the pose, sighing with relief.

"I'm glad you think these feel good," I grunted. A muscle from my knee to my hip screamed at the motion but I kept breathing, relaxing a little after each exhale.

I'd gone through a full sequence of moves three times, pretending to enjoy the sun on my face while really listening for Steve, when Phoenix raced to the trucks like a bat out of hell. Wisps of hair flew around her face, a halo in the sun. They highlighted her red face, especially when she bellowed.

"Back in the trucks," she yelled hoarsely. "The fuses are lit, but we're not entirely sure when it'll, uh..."

I pulled myself up, easier now for the yoga. "Pack it up. Make sure all the mamas are in."

Gryphon raced in next, a wild look in his eyes. "We should hurry."

Some of the mamas began crying, in fear or frustration, and the fighters tending them gently urged them on. Half the people were loaded when Sparrow shot out of the trees, grinning madly. I eyed the hillside set to collapse. Almost half the trees on it were dead, burned in the fires a few years back, but there was plenty of short growth blocking my view.

Climbing awkwardly into the back of my pickup, I held onto the machine gun when Dereva goosed the truck to get it rolling. More fighters, including my brother, piled into the truck in a haphazard rush. Archangel appeared next, closely followed by Chaos, who laughed as he flung himself onto the pickup's running board opposite Archangel.

Seahorse, on the highest position, gave a final check. "Go!" she shouted. Then she pointed to her eyes and circled a hand in the air. *Watch all sides.*

The ground shook by the time the convoy lurched forward, and some of the fighters looked around nervously. The shaking forced me to sit on the tail box, and I couldn't resist watching. Dirt puffed into the air and the trees slowly folded into the ground. The entire hillside gave way, sliding into the narrow space cut out for the road.

Chaos whooped, punching the air, bouncing and rocking the truck even more until Hightide punched him through her open window.

"Knock it off," she shouted. "You're slowing us down."

He stopped bouncing, but he couldn't take his eyes off the destruction behind us. I shook my head. Archangel was right. Chaos personified his name in a way few of us managed.

***

As soon as we crossed the I-5, tension flowed out of my shoulders. Stupid, yes, considering there's just as many Steve *this* side as the other, but now, we were on our turf. The sun had long since set by the time we found a good campsite, though we couldn't rest immediately, first needing to make sure our guests were safe and comfortable.

I groaned, sitting and leaning back against my pack. The ground was finally still. Untying my blanket, I spread it without standing. My knee throbbed, and I grit my teeth, scooting slowly onto it, using my hands to lift and move the leg.

A dark shadow slowly made her way over, pausing to bend periodically. The fact that she made any noise at all marked her as Eleanor. "Let me see your leg," she murmured, setting her bag down.

I unbuttoned my pants, wiggling to get them down, my leg too swollen to pull the pants up over it. Eleanor's hands, cool against my right leg, helped get the cloth over the knee. Little plastic pots clicked dully, the noise barely carrying. She spread an ointment on my skin. My knee cooled, then heated, almost painfully, and I bit my lip, breathing hard through my nose.

"You," she said sternly, "need to work on your people skills."

"I don't have any. I thought you knew that."

The end of her braid brushed against my skin when she shook her head. "Do you know how long it took to soothe his hurt feelings?"

"Whose? I haven't upset Archangel or Gryphon today. Well, not that I know of."

"Not them. The man you found with the women."

I wrinkled my nose. "What man?"

"The one you wouldn't arm!" Though unseen, Eleanor's glare was perfectly obvious. It drilled through my forehead.

A large shape, Gryphon or Chaos, made his way over. "The beacons are lit!" he whispered theatrically when he saw me. "Gondor calls for aid!"

I snorted, clamping a hand over my mouth to stifle a laugh. "Har de fucking har. Fucking hell, Gryph."

He knelt. "Doc sent over some bandages. She says binding the knee will help with swelling."

He helped pull my pants off, over my moccasins, supporting my lower leg while Eleanor wrapped my knee and several inches above and below. I gripped the blanket, gritting my teeth. When she finished, I relaxed slowly, sighing in relief.

"It helps?" Eleanor whispered.

I nodded, then realized it was too dark for her to see. "Yes, thanks."

She helped me back into my pants. "You still need to talk to that man, and be nice."

"Wait," Gryphon said. "I thought the last time someone told her to be nice, she made a man cry."

"Hey!" I protested. "I *was* being nice! It was an accident."

"However it goes," Eleanor interrupted, before we could go off on a tangent, "just be nicer so that I don't have to spend so much time smoothing ruffled feathers."

By the time we got my pants back on, Gryphon had his and Phoenix's bed set up, and Archangel arrived. Without any more discussion, we bedded down. Those who'd slept during the day would take first watches. Our small group had the last one. Eleanor snored softly before I got my pack into a comfortable position, and I smiled, closing my eyes.

***

I watched the sun rise, closing my eyes when the sun crested the horizon. Its warmth existed only in my imagination, but I enjoyed it nonetheless. Archangel found me, slipping quietly out of the trees. I'd set up at the end of the driveway, where it wouldn't be so hard to walk.

When I opened my eyes, he smiled. "You usually only look that happy when it's raining. Which is when everyone else is about to murder you."

"Steve doesn't like rain," I explained. "Which means I love it. Sung Ki told me once that she thought her home rained a lot. Then she got here."

The conversation stayed light, but I caught myself leaning towards him. Once, almost without thinking, he reached out, tucking a stray lock back, behind my ear. My chest stilled, and I stared at him, unmoving. Realizing what he'd done, he froze, his fingers barely touching my skin.

My tongue flicked out, wetting my upper lip. His eyes followed the tiny motion. "Maybe we should have that talk now," I croaked.

His lips tightened and he dropped his hand. "We can't get distracted. And I'd find this...conversation...very distracting."

"Just...tell me what you want from it," I burst out. "The suspense is killing me."

"You," he said simply. "I want you. I want to know who you are, who you were, what you like, what you love...All of it."

"Oh, is that all?" I melted where I sat.

"Well, I think I'd like to marry you," he said reasonably. "But it's a bit too soon to be asking, so I figured I'd leave that till later." Then he headed out to check the perimeter.

I stared after him, open-mouthed. "WhatYou smooth motherfucker, you better come back, you hear me?"

When he came back, he leaned against a tree as if he hadn't said he'd like to marry me someday. I shook my head, amazed. "Tell me something. About you."

He nodded, pursing his lips. "I grew up in Michigan, and my parents are still there. I also have a brother, sister-in-law, two nieces, and three nephews living in the UP, plus a sister back East. People who live in north Michigan are Yoopers." I laughed and he continued, "it gets colder there, and we get more snow, but you guys have got a hell of a lot of rain here."

While he talked, he gave me little touches. His fingertips running down my cheek, holding my hand to point to spots on my palm in demonstration. Although, how he got the idea parts of Michigan looked remotely like a hand was beyond me.

When it was time to wake the camp, we walked slowly back. My knee, stiff at first, moved more easily as we walked. Phoenix and Gryphon were already shaking people awake, and Doc looked like she'd barely slept.

Eleanor caught my arm. "Heads up," she whispered. "It's the man I told you about last night. *You* can deal with him this time."

She disappeared as swiftly as she'd come, and I stared after her, confused. Looking around, I saw a thin, brown-haired man walking towards us, his nose wrinkled, and his lip curled back whenever he looked at the women. Not a woman, not carrying a gun, and I didn't know him...

The man Eleanor didn't like. Just call me Sherlock, deducing who he was. He stopped in front of us but looked at Archangel. "I'd like to put in another request to have a gun," he said, attempting to push out his skinny chest. "I have a gun license—I doubt anyone else here has one, yourself excluded, sir—and I've been training to fight since my teens! I think I'm more than qualified to have one, and then I can help you fight!"

Archangel glanced at me, the corner of his mouth kicking up. I shifted my weight to keep my knee from freezing up. "Where did you learn?" I asked.

He squinted at me, then spoke to Archangel. "I went to a dojo in Salem for like, eight months, then I continued with videos. Tons of people have said I'm super intimidating, too! I've shown up to a fight, and guys—big guys—have backed down. I'd like a Glock," he finished.

"No," I said. "Which I already told you."

"That's why I'm talking to him!" He pointed at Archangel. "He's the boss."

I stared up at the sky, shaking my head and begging for patience. "He's not, but I'm glad you've shown me how well you can make deductions. You are not getting a gun."

"But...but that's not fair!" he whined. Reaching out, fingers hooked like claws, I thought he might try to grab me, but he thought better of it and dropped his hand. "You have four guns. And a rifle! Who needs that many guns?"

"I do." I clenched my jaw to hide my distaste. "They do." I waved a hand to encompass the fighters. "If you want to try for the fighters, you'll have to go through training, and we'll talk to Sarge about that. When we get back to the Lair. Now, if that is all...?" I stared levelly at him until he looked away.

"I...you...Why...?" he sputtered, rage darkening his face, his fingers working into fists.

Big hands. I catalogued his response automatically. If he managed to hit me, he might hurt me. Especially since I couldn't move easily just yet. Archangel tensed, shifting his feet slightly.

"Listen, dude," I said, trying to follow Eleanor's instructions and be nice, "just keep doing what you're doing. Help the mamas. They trust you, and you're keeping them calm, which keeps them safe. Right now ain't the best time to try learning new skills."

"I'm trained in karate," he said, rolling his 'R's, defining each syllable. I rolled my eyes. Second person I've met who was trained in karate. I knew not everyone who trained in it was this big of a douchebag, but there was something about karate that drew a particular kind of person.

He shifted, one foot forward, the other back, and he held it for a second. Then, he stepped forward, one leg coming forward in a sloppy kick. I watched, shaking my head internally. Archangel didn't even move. He followed his miserable kick with a punch that lacked any sort of force or drive, shouting, "Kiai!"

"See?" he said. "I could be helpful. But if you don't want my help, then when things get tough, don't come looking for me!" He scowled. I think he meant to be threatening. He spun away, staggering when he hit a rock, ruining his attempt at an exit.

Nearby fighters didn't bother hiding their smirks, and one laughed outright, further wounding his fragile, over-sized ego.

"We should take bets," Phoenix said from behind me.

"On what?"

"How long he lasts before someone shoots him."

I nodded. "That's a good one. Open another for how long it takes him to cry."

"And how often he says he knows karate," she said. "I'm beginning to think we sent Gorgon away too soon. We could've sent this guy with them."

I shook my head. "She hates men. He wouldn't've made it out of the meadow."

"And this is a problem...why?"

"Good point. What about you, Archangel...Are you okay?" I asked him. He looked...odd.

"Sure." Then, he giggled. "His face...He honestly thought telling you he was intimidating would work. I can't..." He doubled over, wheezing slightly, shaking with laughter. "I've never...been...so ashamed...to be a man!"

"I think you're okay," I said dryly. "I don't think that qualifies as a man. Man-baby, maybe, so your masculinity should be fine."

"My masculinity is in no way threatened by him." Archangel looked up, his eyes wet with repressed laughter.

My breath caught at the sight of him. His hair gathered sunlight, shining like a halo. Another shard of light made his eyes glow. Noticing my stare, his grin died as he focused on me. I bit my lip to hold back a whimper and he watched me with an intensity that raised my heart. I found myself unable to catch my breath.

When he met my eyes, I forced myself not to look away. The intimacy of meeting his eyes like this...heat climbed my cheeks. His eyes, so much darker than mine, were lit with an inner fire I didn't know what to do with.

He leaned in. "When we're done here," he murmured. "Don't forget."

He left abruptly, weaving through people having breakfast. Sagging slightly, I saw Phoenix, her mouth open in a little 'o.' I shook myself. "That actually happened, did it?" She nodded. "You look about how I feel."

"No," she squeaked. "You definitely have more color." She fanned herself. "Holy shit. Holy shit. I thought I'd go up in flames and he wasn't even looking at me. Holy fuck."

"Captain." Seahorse stepped neatly over the rock that had tripped the whiner. "We've got a...what happened to you?"

"Girl!" Phoenix grabbed her arm. "Our girl's about to get some!"

I buried my face in my hands when Seahorse lit up. "*Tell me!*"

That's the problem with living with women. Sooner or later, for better or worse, everyone knew everyone else's business.

CHAPTER 24

Man 1: I set those soldiers up to be taken, I swear! I have no idea how they
escaped.
Woman 1: Stop your pathetic excuses, McKinney! I told you what would
happen if you failed me.
Transcripts, recorded December 28, 2062

Doc chafed every time we camped, which meant she chafed a lot. Our journey back to the Lair went slowly, since we spent more time hiding than moving. Apparently, Steve didn't like it when we took their stuff.

The roads crawled with patrols, to the point we camped during the day, only moving at night. The fighters, used to the vagaries of travel in our new world, took the opportunity to rest or do little projects.

I relaxed against my pack, sharpening my short swords. I frowned at one, examining the blade.

"What did that sword ever do to you?" Eleanor settled down, fishing her latest piece of mending out of her satchel.

"It's what it might do." Gently running my thumb along the edge, I hissed. It had a small chip, and I could not, for the life of me, remember when or how it happened. Definitely wasn't there the last time I sharpened it. Maybe during the fight at the winery? "What are you working on?"

"Mending socks."

I glanced up. "How do you do those? I've never figured it out."

"I'll let you know when I do." She worked away with tiny knitting needles, a sewing needle, and thin yarn.

"Why not grab another pair from stores, then?" My second blade moved smoothly and easily over the whetstone, the familiar rhythm calming.

"We have a very limited number of socks, even with what's been brought back." She bit her lip, concentrating on the task. "How's your knee?"

"Archangel gave me a massage earlier." Until I met him, I'd thought I was asexual, but no, turned out, my hormones and bits worked just fine. "I didn't know half those muscles were remotely connected, but it's doing better. Doc reckons another week and I should be good."

A small breeze kicked up, playing with the hanging yarn and bringing the scent of rain. I peered up. A few clouds on the southern horizon, but it's Oregon. Those could be over us in an hour. I grinned. Our luck might've finally changed.

"Seahorse!" I waved. "Get a whiff of that."

The soldier inhaled deeply, nostrils flaring. "Is that...moisture?"

My grin sharpened. "Oh, yeah. By those clouds, could be a good one. We need to be ready to move the moment it hits."

She nodded. "I'll pass the word to pack anything non-essential." She chuckled. "We might make some distance tonight."

***

Settling my goggles firmly over my eyes, I laughed into the storm. Instead of a steady, light rain, we were gifted with a glorious summer storm. Glorious, because visibility was damn near zero. Maybe we couldn't see shit, but neither could Steve.

I sat on the hood of my pickup, using hand signals to give Dereva directions and information. The bull bars I'd installed were coming in useful in a totally unexpected and delightful way. I shifted my shoulder, missing the weight of my rifle, but Phoenix had it tucked in the toolbox with hers.

People were crammed inside the vehicles, attempting to stay dry. Behind me, Dereva had managed to cram an extra two people in a cab built for two. As far as I was concerned, outside was the place to be. The cramped quarters inside weren't worth it, no, thank you. Soaking wet was much better, as long as my gear stayed dry.

Rain drummed on metal, and I tipped my head back, mouth open, tongue out. A vague thrum in the air pulled me out of my reverie and I cocked my head, listening intently.

There it was again.

I knocked on the windshield and Dereva slowed even more. Through the sheets of rain, a large, square shape emerged. I pounded the window. "Truck ahead," I called.

Seconds later, Steve spotted us, slewing to a halt. The top hatch flung open. Not waiting for them to get a damn big gun out, I launched off the hood, landing on my good knee and running for Steve.

"Get 'em!" I bellowed.

Swearing behind me, and Archangel shouted, "Wait!" but I had momentum.

Phoenix fired until I got too close and by that time, whooping behind let me know I wasn't the only idiot in the lot. I scrambled up, over the hood, and shot the head poking cautiously out point blank. Swiping the back of my gun hand over my eyes to clear the rainwater, I pulled a grenade off my belt, yanking the pin with my teeth.

Only one man threw open his door, but I'd already dropped the grenade in the hatch, slamming it shut...And froze. Behind this truck was another one, men spilling out into the rainy night.

Oh, fuck.

***

When the world returned, I lay on my back, rain pelting my face. Archangel stood over me, stepping smoothly over and around my body, twisting and turning as he dealt with the melee. Lurching upright, I staggered, nearly falling again when my knee gave out. He caught me in one arm, spinning us both, slashing wide with the machete he carried.

When the move finished, we stood back-to-back. He had a hand on my hip, tracking my position. I'd grabbed another gun, sword in my left, shaking my head to clear it.

"You good?" he shouted.

"Fucking A!"

Without giving us any more time than that, Steve closed in.

The melee moved with frenetic energy, Steve fighting with a desperation I rarely saw. They were usually more self-assured, confident they had more numbers, unlimited ammunition, and ready backup. Tonight, they were more like cornered rats, determined to win and live.

Twisting, I narrowly avoided a club, separated from Archangel for a moment. The club swung back and, holding the blade along my forearm, I blocked. The blade shattered, pain exploding in my forearm. Screaming, I shot him in the face.

Body slamming another, who crowded too close to Archangel, I pistol whipped the face appearing out of the rain. Lost my gun...lost my gun!

Wrapping my fingers around the hilt over my right shoulder, I whipped it out, slashing.

Archangel hauled me back, away from a sudden rush. A gang of Irregulars, led by Gryphon, barreled into the crush of soldiers around us, breaking the group apart. Gasping, I leaned against Archangel.

"Does this mean we won?"

"I think so."

Sticking my sword into the ground, I reached up, carefully feeling along his cheekbone. Blood covered half his face from a cut just under his eye. "Almost to the bone," I murmured.

He checked my arms. I gasped, flinching when he squeezed my left forearm. He returned to it, checking both bones and my wrist carefully while I shook, swallowing repeatedly to hold back the vomit. When he moved on, I checked over his shoulder, squinting at a darker spot on his chest.

Around us, similar ministrations went on. In the heat of battle, wounded were yanked back for Doc and Squirrel to deal with. The rest of us waited until after a fight to check.

I rubbed the dark spot on his shirt, feeling the fabric, then running my hand across the muscles of his chest, looking for any open wounds. His heart beat strong under my fingers, his chest barely moving. He squeezed my hip and my breathing hitched.

Desire roared to the surface, catching me by surprise. My legs nearly gave out from the force of it. I turned into him, intensely aware of the heat radiating from every inch of him, the rain running down my face. I licked my lips and his eyes tracked the motion.

He cradled my injured arm in his right hand, his left resting on my hip. My hand on his chest, barely an inch between us...Yanking my gaze away before I did something we didn't have time for, I saw several people hastily turn away. Phoenix watched openly, grinning and wiggling her eyebrows.

Get some, she mouthed.

Seahorse straightened. "Pack it up, people," she shouted. "Gather your things, little ones. It's time to ditch this joint."

"It's a shit hole, anyway," Gryphon shouted back to general laughter.

"We're definitely talking later," Archangel murmured. "And, if I'm a very good boy, maybe more?"

My heart stuttered. "Maybe," I whispered.

***

Later—how much it was impossible to know—I huddled in the back of the pickup, my injured arm strapped to my chest, zipped under my jacket. The rain had slowed slightly, but that didn't do anything for my mood. On my lap, I held the broken hilt of one sword, the other securely in its sheath.

"I can't believe it broke," I said for the umpteenth time.

"Better that than your arm," Phoenix growled. "Though if you bring it up one more time, I swear…"

"Fine." I stuck my lip out. Archangel dozed on my left, and Gryphon sat tightly against my right, while Phoenix had the machine gun. Stretch and Gameboy watched the sides, playing footsie around Phoenix when they could. And through it all, my arm throbbed, the pain streaking up to my shoulder and neck. "Distract me," I commanded. "Or else I'm gonna distract myself." I stroked the broken sword's hilt, glaring balefully at the men around me.

"Oh…fuck," Gryphon mumbled, straightening up. "Ehm…the weather? No, bloody hell, that's entirely too English." He went silent for a moment before bursting out, "What I really want to know is, what the fuck did Chaos do to get his nickname? Like, what's so crazy the craziest military in the world calls a man 'chaos,' and what was his?" He pointed at Archangel.

I bit my tongue to keep Archangel's old call sign in. Plus, I wanted to know the story behind Chaos's.

"C'mon, Stretch," I wheedled. "Tell us."

Stretch grinned, his teeth a momentary flash in the dark. "Well, it wasn't just one incident, y'see? Chaos has always had a healthy dose of 'fuck you' in his personality. Tell him something couldn't be done, and he'd do it just to prove you wrong. You'd think all the punishment would be enough to drub that kind of thinking out of him, but nope. Turned out, that made him damn fine at improvising. The event that got him his name involved blowing up a building with a homemade bomb. Army didn't like that he could do something like that so well. Nearly got tossed out, but they couldn't get it to stick."

He paused for a moment. "Well, no," he revised. "He did get tossed out, for the Major's wife. They brought him back for this mission, like our boy Archangel. It's partly because of Chaos that Archangel got his own callsign."

"And how was that?" Gryphon pressed.

Stretch chuckled. "Well, with both of them being blond and blue-eyed, looking as similar as they do, people thought they might be cut from the same cloth. But he's fairly quiet. Compared to Chaos, our boy here," he nodded to Archangel, who snored lightly, "looked positively angelic. So, they ended up calling him Angel."

Gryphon smothered a shout of laughter in his arms. "Angel? His name was Angel? Shite, woman," he said to me, "you gave him a right proper name."

The soldier shrugged. "The main point, though, is that Archangel could be just as much trouble as Chaos. He was just quieter about it. When we were cadets, someone broke into the staff sergeant's office and set up his entire office perfectly in the middle of the square. Except none of the locks showed signs of damage. They never could prove who did it, but the MPs looked hard at him. Then there was the time the bell—a hundred pounds if it's an ounce—ended up in the commander's chair, even wearing his dress hat..."

I leaned against Archangel, listening to Stretch's comfortable Southern drawl continued, telling stories of more innocent times.

CHAPTER 25

Archangel threaded his way through the crowded common room towards me. We'd arrived home without any casualties and spirits were high. People were drinking, the musicians had set up on top of a table, and all Lavender did was laugh.

Archangel passed so close our shoulders brushed. He barely slowed, just turned his head, whispering, "It's time."

My breath caught, but I turned and followed him without a word, tugged by an invisible rope, only the slightest limp slowing me. When the door shut behind us, all the laughter and chatter cut off abruptly. The sun stood two fingers above the final ridge, flooding the meadow with light and warmth. My heart pounded, blood throbbing in my neck.

He glanced back, raising one eyebrow, his eyes glittering, almost feral. I shrugged helplessly. He shook his head, a tiny smile quirking the corner of his mouth, but the intensity never faded. Instead, he grabbed my hand, leading me deeper into the forest.

Tension flowed out of my shoulders even as the butterflies ramped up in my chest. An odd juxtaposition to be sure, but the scout knew me well enough to take me outside for something like this. He led me to a wide, grassy spot alongside the river running past the Lair.

He dropped down, sprawling in the patch of sun, stacking his hands behind his head. I settled next to him, my right leg outstretched, my hip just brushing his side. He shifted, like he would touch me, but then he laid back. I relaxed a little more.

I finally broke the silence. "I don't know how to do...any of this."

He lay there for a while, mulling over my words. "Maybe it's not so much about doing anything. Maybe it's as much about...being. Together."

I cocked my head. "Being?"

"Not having to do anything, just enjoying each other's company. Getting used to this together."

I chewed on my lip, thinking about it, then nodded. "Talk to me. Tell me about growing up. About your old call sign."

"You already know about that." His eyes laughed at me, but his lips only twitched at the corners.

"You were awake?" He nodded. I smacked his ribs lightly. "You cheeky bastard."

He laughed openly now. "You've been spending too much time with Gryphon. But I can tell you more about growing up a Yooper."

He talked about kayaking on Lake Superior and Lake Michigan, even surfing on them in the winter. About watching for bears and visiting a little island that still used horses. His parents, and growing up with two brothers. And about his years in the army, but he still didn't talk about why he'd left, or why he'd rejoined.

Then, I talked about growing up dirt poor. My sister and brothers. Mom's death. My cousins, Grace's wedding, Search and Rescue, and being a mechanic.

Somewhere along the way, he took my hand, playing idly with my fingers. At first, I was stiff, uncomfortable, but he didn't seem to notice, just enjoying the feel of my hand in his until I relaxed. Rubbing his thumb across the backs of my knuckles, asking about the tiny scars on my hand, but I couldn't remember where I'd gotten them all. Most were a result of training or fighting.

When I got to the part about mechanics, he laughed softly. "You didn't learn tactics and strategy from mechanics, and we've been wondering. Where did you learn all this?"

I stared at him too long, suspicious of the question. "Who's 'we'? And why are people wondering? Why should they care?"

He rested our linked hands on his belly. "'We' is literally everyone. When the military got their hands on intel—I guess from Sirius's capture—they learned about you. Or Captain, really. The fact that you'd successfully rescued people and appeared to have a military-type operation had all the brass scrambling to figure out who was unaccounted for, and therefore running this joint. Hendricks was sure you were a classmate of his who lived somewhere out here."

"And he was disappointed to find lil' ol' me, huh?" My heartbeat quickened when he trailed his fingers up my forearm, gently tracing vines and circles on my skin. "He still didn't have to be such a dick about it."

Archangel shrugged, surprisingly sinuous for all his prone position. "And people are really curious because the politicians have no idea what to label you. They don't—or didn't—know much about what's happening in here, but they were told not to poke the bear and they knew just enough to know someone was poking it. So, they can't decide whether to hail you as an American hero or label you a national threat."

I stared dreamily up, through the leaves to a sky the same color as Archangel's eyes. "Imagine. Me, a national threat."

He choked, laughing and coughing. "What?"

I snickered, leaning sideways until I rested lightly against his chest. Running my fingers over the muscles that made intriguing dips and hollows, I shook my head helplessly.

"You little rat!" He slid his hand down to my thigh. "And you still haven't answered my question."

"What question?" I smiled blandly, making him laugh again.

"Where did you learn tactics and strategy?" he asked slowly.

I leaned in, grinning. "If I tell you, you have to promise to keep it a secret. People'd freak the fuck out if they knew. Well," I amended, "freak out *more*."

"Hand to my heart," he said dramatically, moving my hand to his heart.

"Close enough." I suddenly realized I was draped across his chest. How had this happened? He nearly purred when I settled against him, his hand stroking the small of my back, grinning when he encountered the knife I kept there. My thoughts scattered. "If you want an answer, you're gonna have to stop that," I informed him. "As much as I should probably be cutesy and whatnot, the fact is, I can't think when you do that."

He moved his hand away, resting it on my leg again. "Promise." He grinned wickedly.

My heart stuttered and I looked away, focusing on the scents filling the meadow. The green of things growing, and leaf mold, which smelled brown to me, the clear, crisp scent of water over it all.

"Tell me," he urged softly.

I bit my lip, struggling to gather my wayward thoughts. "Right. Well. If you must know..."

"I must, I must!"

"I read. A lot. Most of them are fantasy and sci-fi and have inventive and interesting ways of dealing with things. Oh, and sometimes, we get inspiration from movies. There. Happy now?" His mouth dropped open.

"What?" I snickered. "You think I went to school for this shit or something? We've already established I'm not one of your military school people."

He laughed. Dropping his head back, the grass framing his blond hair, he laughed until we shook with it. And while he laughed, he gathered me firmly against himself until he had me tucked against his side. "Are you telling me they're out there, holding their breath to see what happens next, and it's all based on *books*?"

"Age of the nerd, baby." He howled, tears running down his cheeks. As he laughed, I glanced around, in case someone showed up. Which would be worse, a newbie without two brain cells to rub together, or Steve? "Shut up," I hissed, grinning. "You want the entire Lair to show up? We've got entirely too many nosy bastards..."

"Yo, Captain." Phoenix sauntered out of the trees, smirking. "What's the ruckus..." She broke off when she saw us.

I jumped, trying to squirm away from Archangel, but he held on with negligent ease. "No," he said firmly. "She's not going to judge you. You're okay."

"Judge, no," she said, her eyes sparkling. "But I'm very glad you two have decided to have your...talk. Do you need anything? Drinks? Cigarettes? Romantic music?"

"Fuck. Off. Phoenix," I ground out, pushing up onto my hands.

"Yeah, yeah." She backed away, her hands up, palms towards us. "I'm going. I need to have a little chat with some of the girls anyway."

"No!" I scrambled out of Archangel's hold, but she bolted, racing for the Lair, cackling. Slumping down, I whimpered, "Oh, shit."

"What? It can't be that bad. Can it?"

"You've met her. What do you think?"

"Oh, fuck."

***

I cringed when I opened the Lair door, but nothing happened. No people gathered by the door, nothing. The party continued in the common room, filling the halls with singing and music, but that was it. I almost wished Phoenix had spilled the beans to the entire Lair instead of this odd normalcy.

My entire world just changed, so why didn't my surroundings reflect that?

Archangel didn't let go of my hand when we walked in. By now, I knew him well enough to know he'd release me if I insisted. I didn't want to let him go, part of me just thought I should, as the 'fearless leader' Sirius liked to call me.

At the thought of her, my heart weighed heavy in my chest. She'd've loved to see this, and that she didn't...tears welled in my eyes, and I walked a little closer to him, reaching over with my free hand to hold his arm. He glanced around, frowning slightly when he saw my face.

"Sirius?" he asked.

I nodded, and that was it. He knew. I wanted my cousin back. I could *see* her sly smirk at the sight of us, but when I looked for it, nothing.

"Do you want to leave?"

I opened my mouth, then shut it again, considering and shook my head. No, I didn't want to leave. I wanted to be around people who celebrated being alive.

He led the way into the common room. The music swirled like a living thing. Grinning, Archangel pulled me into the cleared space in the middle of the room, spinning us into a dance. Gasping and laughing, we emerged from the other side in the brief space between songs.

Plopping onto the bench next to Phoenix, I grabbed a plate and served myself from the nearest platter. Fresh greens and lettuce piled high on my plate, with carrots, zucchini, and even a few tomatoes and cucumbers.

Phoenix, her mouth full, pushed a small pitcher over. Drizzling it over the salad, I sighed, contentment seeping through me.

There were people missing, but in this very moment, life was good.

I hadn't had salad since Before. And now we had dressing, too? "It's hard to beat this," I said around a mouthful of delicious freshness.

Archangel, disdaining a plate, picked off Gryphon's until the other man swatted his hands away. "Keep your fuckin' hands off my courgettes, mate," he said. "Do you know how long I waited for these to be ready?"

"What. Are. Courgettes?" Phoenix asked with thinly veiled patience.

"This." Gryphon speared a zucchini, waving it around.

"Zucchini, babe. Those are definitely zucchini."

"Only to you Yanks, who've forgotten the finer points of English, luv."

I rubbed two fingers between my eyebrows. "Is this what happens to everyone after only three months of marriage?"

"Four," Gryphon said, threatening Archangel with his fork. "It's been four. Learn to bloody count."

"Speaking of..." Phoenix leaned towards her husband, wiggling her eyebrows. "Guess who finally 'talked' and didn't just shake hands?"

I turned red, Archangel grinned smugly, and Gryphon clapped Archangel on the shoulder. "About time! For a moment there, I thought you'd decided to take lessons from Jane Austen."

The three Americans just stared at the Brit, utterly confused.

"What?" he asked, leaning back. "Don't tell me you've never heard of her."

"Oh, I have," I said. "I'm just confused as to why you have."

He reared back, slapping the table. "How dare you? She's a national treasure, and I'll fight anyone who says otherwise. Plus," he shrugged, "I played Henry Tilney once."

I rolled my eyes. "English actors. There's five of them, thirty roles, and two props."

CHAPTER 26

*Man 1: That resistance in Oregon won't die! Kwan Jae hasn't been able to
root them out.*

*Woman 1: Tell them to try harder! Burn it if they have to. We need to move
onto the next phase. Do it, McKinney.*

Transcripts, recorded March 16, 2066

I had one glorious week of making out with Archangel in various corners of the Lair and woods. Twice, I happened to glance up in time to see a fascinated face pull hastily back, out of sight.

On an afternoon uphill run at the end of the week, I discovered something I wasn't supposed to see. Their blank expressions, the way Phoenix avoided my eyes. Archangel's lips, usually so full and soft, were compressed into a thin line, his eyes hard when he looked at Phoenix.

I'd stumbled across them just off the trail and Phoenix jumped a foot when I rounded the bend. Her shoulders hunched around her ears, and she wouldn't meet my eyes.

"Wassup?" I asked, breaking the tense silence.

Phoenix mumbled inaudibly, still not looking up.

"What's that, Phoenix?" Archangel cupped a hand around his ear. "I don't think she could hear you."

I looked between them. How had she managed to piss off the most level-headed man in the Lair? "What's going on?"

He shook his head, a small muscle jumping in his jaw. "I don't think so. Go on. Tell her. You didn't have a damn problem telling me."

Finally raising her head, Phoenix whispered, "I told him you were still a virgin."

"What the fuck...? Dammit, Phoenix," I exploded. "Do the words 'none of your fucking business' mean anything to you?" Heat rose in my cheeks, a combination of embarrassment and anger. "Wanna explain...No, you know what?" I raised a hand. "I don't want to hear it. I...just...go."

Without another word, she took off back to the Lair. Small, hunched in on herself, for the first time since I'd known her she looked her size. Tiny. My heart hurt, watching her go. She looked like a kicked puppy.

"Walk with me." Not waiting, I headed north, slightly downhill.

My feet found their own way. After almost two years of running these trails, they should know the way. Glancing back once, I almost missed Archangel, who walked twenty paces behind, far enough I couldn't hear his passage and it struck me. I, who fiercely held onto my distance from others for the sake of my sanity, missed physical closeness.

How odd.

How wonderful.

Soon, we entered a small deer track that widened slowly. The track wound through thinning trees until the land dropped sharply away and we emerged onto a precipice.

Archangel stopped abruptly. "Oh, my God," he breathed.

I walked further out, onto a rock jutting over a slope too shallow to be a cliff and too steep to be a hill. My private viewpoint looked out over a wide, tree-filled basin. Green overflowed the edges.

Bright green pooled in the bottom and the darker green of pines and fir trees marked the edges. Here and there, bright dots of color, bushes blooming with wild abandon, offered a contrast. To the west, directly across from us, a steep hill climbed, pines marching up its sides in uneven rows to a ridgetop. Over the ridge, I could just make out the rolling hills of the Willamette Valley. To the left, a hidden waterfall threw a fine mist into the air, fed by the creek that wandered past the Lair.

This was my secret spot, where I went when I needed peace and distance.

I broke the silence. "You're the only person I've brought out here." I glanced back. Archangel's mouth still hung open. Grinning, I took his arm, leading him to the rock I used as a seat. Pushing him down, I cuddled next to him. "You alright?"

Shaking himself, he found his tongue. "I don't..." He sighed, smiling at the little valley. "I don't think I've seen anything this peaceful since coming here."

Shoulder to shoulder, we sat in silence, watching the sun slowly make its way to the ridge. Leaning into him a little more, I bit my lip. Time to bite the bullet. "What, exactly, did Phoenix say to you?"

Taking my hand, he rubbed his thumb over my palm, tracing the lines and thin scars. "She was blunt. Told me you're a virgin. Then, she threatened me. Which I'm fine with," he added. "But she had no right to tell me something that personal about you. She should've let you tell me yourself."

"Um...yeah." I huffed a laugh. "Considering we've been making out in corners for a week and..." I shrugged helplessly. "I haven't been able to say anything, maybe she did me a favor." Glancing at him, I got lost in the intensity in his eyes.

"I'd still rather you were comfortable enough to have told me yourself," he said quietly. "What stopped you?"

"What?"

He smiled. "Why do you think you're not comfortable telling me?"

"I was scared," I blurted. On reflection, I realized it was true. "I was afraid that if you knew, it'd change how you saw me. Maybe change your mind."

He laughed, and I had just enough brains left to hear the incredulity. "Why the hell would I change my mind?"

"Do you know how weird people get about female virginity?" I demanded. "There's something about it...There was a guy, a few years ago, that I went on a few dates with. He kept pressuring for sex, so I finally admitted the whole v-card thing. And...he got freaky. Like..." I shook my head, baffled. "Something about purity and how I wouldn't be the same after he 'deflowered' me, but it was a super precious gift... I don't know, it was creepy as hell."

Archangel snorted. "Yeah, I've met the type. The one that always wonders why girls won't stay."

I nodded. "Flip side of the coin? My cousin, Toni, suggested I get laid 'just to get it over with.' Like being a virgin is stopping me from living my life." I curled my lip. "How dare they?"

"What did you tell Toni?" He laced our fingers together, bringing them up to his mouth. He pressed his lips to my knuckles, then bit one delicately.

I shuddered. "If you want me to remember how to talk, you really can't do that right now." He chuckled but lowered our hands to his lap. Swallowing, I looked away to gather myself and bring my heart rate down. "I told her being a virgin wasn't stopping me from doing anything I wanted. Besides which, sleeping with a guy I didn't have real feelings for? Yech. I'd feel so guilty. And thinking about a random dude touching me..." I gagged.

He growled. "Yeah. Nope, not happening like that for you."

"No?" I bit my lip, giving him a slow, sly smile. "How do you imagine it happening?"

He laughed, cupping my face. "Okay, one? Do that. You look evil. Adorable, sexy, and evil. And two, like this." He leaned forward and kissed me.

***

That evening, I found Phoenix in her room, red-eyed, lying on her back, staring at the ceiling. She shot up when she saw it was me. "I thought you were Gryphon!"

"You okay?"

"Yes...no," she admitted, looking down at her hands, twisting them into knots on her lap. "I'm sorry," she burst out. "Did I ruin things between you? I just wanted him to treat you right. I had an awful first time. Like, really bad, and so did most of my friends. You've got a chance to have a great first experience, and I just...and then you showed up, and it looked so bad...Did I fuck it up?"

Crying now, she used the blanket to wipe away the tears. Sighing, I sat next to her and nudged her gently. "You didn't ruin anything. We had a good talk. He was mad because you went behind my back, not because you said something. And I have to say thanks, because I'm not sure how long it would've taken me to say anything. Then, uh..." I couldn't stop a smile.

She looked up at me for the first time. "What...? Wait...You have stuff in your hair." She picked out a leaf, then some grass. "Did you...? Girl, what did you two get up to?"

I grinned wickedly. "I don't kiss and tell."

***

I met Archangel at our viewpoint. Well away from the perimeter, it was our new favorite place to cuddle, talk, and kiss. This time, I pushed for more.

Impatiently, I pulled his shirt over his head. My breath caught at the sight of him. Smooth skin, firm muscle. I stroked and petted, my lips following my fingers. His heart thundered and I pressed my lips against the swell of muscle.

My questing fingers found a long, straight scar from a blade along his ribs. A cluster of bullet scars dotted his upper right chest. I paused, covering the scars with my hand, as if by doing so, I could protect him from the pain and trauma it had caused.

"When did this happen?" I whispered.

He covered my hand. "A little over two years ago. Russia. Intel was bad, the op went sideways, and too many people, innocent civilians included, didn't make it."

"Was that why you were leaving the army?"

"Not...this specifically. My former CO..." He hesitated, pulling my hand so it rested over his heart. "He was a fucking idiot, to say it mildly. A glory-hunting narcissist who should never have been promoted. I can't speak for how it happened, but he was, until he got put in charge of this."

Shifting closer, asking for permission with every motion, I draped a leg over his and cuddled against his side, offering comfort and warmth. Slowly, he shifted until he could wrap his free arm around my shoulders. Sighing, I closed my eyes, waiting for him to be ready to continue.

"When I was well enough to be placed back with the remains of my unit, that fucking idiot showed up. There was something about duty, sacrifice, and necessities. I don't know. I punched that motherfucker so hard I broke his face. He needed a little surgery to fix his eye.

"But the army takes a dim view of grunts like me punching a commanding officer," he continued, his face curiously blank. "My CO demanded they court martial me and dump me in prison, but the brass didn't want news of what happened in Russia getting out. So, they slapped me with a dishonorable discharge, let me avoid prison, and were in the process of booting me out when this happened. My ex-CO requested I be put here. I think he has plans for me to go to prison after."

"Or he hoped you wouldn't come back," I growled. "I sincerely hope I meet that son of a bitch someday. Although calling him that is an insult to dogs. What's that motherfucker's name?"

He chuckled, the mask gone, thankfully. "Major Arnold Keller. Climbing the ladder on the backs of his dead men for over a decade."

Even knowing how useless the words could be, I couldn't hold them back. "I'm sorry," I whispered, kissing his chest. "I'm sorry," I repeated, kissing each of those scars. We lay there quietly until I snorted. "Well, I fucked the mood up, didn't I?"

He laughed, the action shaking me. "We are a hell of a pair, ain't we? Never mind. We weren't going to go as far as you wanted, anyway."

Sitting up, I shoved my hair back. "Why the hell not?" I glared at him.

"Because your first time will damn well be comfortable. Plus, we're not okay'ed by Kestrel yet, and *every* woman in that place and most of the men would geld me if we did." He cupped himself reflexively.

I sniggered. "Fine! Geez. Who'd expect you to be such a prude?"

Lunging, he flipped me over, pinning me to the blanket. "Prude, am I? Fine."

His hands roamed freely, investigating. I squirmed, squeaked, and a blush started at my collarbone, rushing north. He smirked. Bracing himself on one elbow let him explore further with the other. My breath hitched when he squeezed.

"You like that, huh?"

"No. Do it again."

Chapter 27

"**Y**ou are *not* getting married!"

My baby brother, my little angel, the only blood relative I had left here, found me cannibalizing parts from one of the vehicles. While I never spent anywhere near as much time as I wanted around Hot Fuzz—mostly for his safety, partly for my sanity—today, I was ready to panic and run away with his one simple sentence: "Dereva and I want to get married."

I dropped my wrench, whacked my head on the hood, suddenly in no mood for this.

"Why not?" he argued. "Tons of people have gotten married. None of them have known each other long, either."

"Well, for one, you're nineteen and she's seventeen! She needs a parent or guardian's consent." Feeling gingerly over my skull, I grimaced. The spot was tender, and any sort of poking made me wince. I hoped it wouldn't turn into a lump. "You've also never met her mother. The woman will assume it's all my fault—and she probably wouldn't be wrong—kill me, then she'd kill you. It's bad enough you're sleeping together..."

"We're not having sex!" Fuzz leaned away, maybe looking to escape my unholy thoughts. "We share a bed, yeah, but that's because you need to, with all this shit. She's not ready for sex."

"Oh, but she's ready for marriage?" Dismissing him offhand, I retrieved the wrench off the floor. "While I'm thrilled to hear you're not getting up to any shenanigans that'll get me hurt, I can't give consent for you to marry. Not yet," I finished, glaring at him.

"What would it take?" He folded his arms, his jaw tight.

"Keep the relationship going for a couple more years. Until she turns eighteen, at least."

"What?" A little muscle in his jaw jumped and his hands clenched.

Keeping an eye on him, I wiped the grease from my hands with a rag. I'd cared for him when he was little, and usually, that was enough to deter him from trying anything when I pissed him off. Not so with Sean, who didn't see me as a girl, so he had no problems punching me, especially once he got bigger than me. But now...I'd have to hurt him to win, but I figured I could take him in a fight, if I saw him coming.

"Listen, I've got girls too young to fight working perimeter, hunting, whatever, until they're old enough to join the fighters. I'm gonna do the same thing for you, relationship-wise. You've got to go slow. Both of you need a bit more emotional development. Because I'm betting Kestrel didn't give you the all-clear, did she?"

He looked away guiltily.

I snorted. "Yeah, that's what I thought. I don't know if you know this, but when it comes to relationships, Kestrel has the final word. So even if I'd said yes, if she said no, you're not getting married. I'm glad you're in love, I'm glad you've found each other, but you need to follow Kestrel's advice. We're all pretty fucked up right now, and it'd be too easy for things to go sideways. Keep dating, keep doing what you're doing, but no marriage vows until she says and Dereva's actually old enough. Okay?"

He glowered at me, his dark brown eyes not as warm and friendly as usual. "Fine. But then you have to take your own advice."

I laughed. "No, I don't."

"Hypocrite!"

"Don't you fucking dare, boy." I snarled, headache forgotten. He flinched, then rallied, his hands knotted into fists. "My situation is nowhere near the same as yours and you know it. Now, pull your head out of your ass and go work it off in the gym. I have work to do."

His mouth worked, but he kept whatever it was behind his teeth. Spinning on his heel, he marched out, his back rigid.

At dinner that night, I sat next to Phoenix, the men across from us. She leaned over and nudged me. "Why does Dereva look like she'd happily throw you off a cliff?"

Glancing at the driver, I muttered, "I wouldn't give her and Fuzz permission to get married."

"They're too young!"

"That's what I said!" I hissed. "And Kestrel hasn't given them the okay, either."

"I'll take care of this." Phoenix grinned, devilry dancing in her green eyes.

Sliding down the bench, she scooted next to Eleanor. I watched the whispered conversation and knew the exact moment Phoenix spilled the beans. Eleanor's head whipped around, latching onto the young couple. Nodding once, decisively, she began eating her stew with renewed vigor.

"You are so mean," I whispered when Phoenix returned. "I can't believe you did that. Even I wouldn't do that."

She sniggered. "Better Eleanor than Amana. She was my second choice. Eleanor will sort them out."

Eleanor wouldn't be cruel or hurtful. No, she'd be sad and upset, which was worse. No one wanted to disappoint her, and she had a knack for making you feel two feet tall when necessary. As soon as she finished, Eleanor approached the couple. A quick, whispered conversation ensued, then she left. Fuzz and Dereva downed their meals and followed her promptly.

Eleanor may have a vast reservoir of patience, but by all that you hold dear, you never kept her waiting.

***

A month later, Fuzz had mostly gotten over himself. Probably because I'd told him and few others to go over River's intel and brainstorm a big hit. Routes, equipment, time, the lot. I needed a break and I had too much to do in the garage, anyway. We'd gone on a few smaller raids into the Valley, in and out, and everything needed work.

With my bare toes gripping the rock floor, I leaned over the engine block of a Chimera, trying to loosen a stubborn clamp. "You mother...fuck-ing...son of a bitching, piece of shit!" I shouted. "I swear I'll turn you into spare parts. Give me half an excuse..." Grunting, I kept pressure on the bolt and sucked a scraped knuckle on my right hand.

"Captain!" Archangel shouted. "You in here?"

"Here!" I called, waving a greasy rag. I had this clamp right where I wanted it. Now, it was all about...leverage. Leaning in further, I raised one foot, extending it behind me for balance as I used both hands to work the clamp.

Footsteps preceded Archangel's arrival. "So." He leaned against the Chimera. "Is it sexist to say you look incredibly hot like that?"

"No? I mean, I thought you looked sexy fixing the water pump." He'd been drenched, wearing just a pair of wet pants in the tight confines under the gym, water beading over smooth muscles and scarred skin, muttering up a storm as he'd stuck his thumb in his mouth. "Fair is fair."

"Why, thank you, dear." He laughed.

I panted. It is, apparently, difficult to breathe whilst having most of your weight on your belly. Who'd a thunk? Finally, finally, the clamp began to give. I grinned, still taking shallow breaths.

He leaned his elbows on the truck, watching me loosen the clamp, and continued. "I gotta say, this whole faux damsel in distress look..."

"What?"

"You know, one foot up behind you, bent over the engine—your ass looks amazing from this angle, by the way. Except, this isn't distress, it's just you, doing your thing and looking...mmh." He shook his head.

"HaHAAA!" I straightened, raising the clamp triumphantly. Now, I finally saw how corroded the damn thing was. More importantly, I could fix the hose so the Chimera didn't leak like a sieve. "You do say the sweetest things." I blew hair out of my face, grinning at him.

Losing his grin, he straightened, suddenly serious. "Captain."

I frowned, watching him fidget, his hands moving from his pockets to his hips. Then clasped in front of him before being stuck back in his pockets. "I'm officially worried." I tossed the clamp in the trash bucket. "What's wrong?"

He cleared his throat. "Nothing. Um..." He half laughed, half sighed, running a hand through his hair, leaving it tousled. "I'd thought...Would you like to go for a walk?"

"Yes...?"

But my face pulled in some weird expression, and he grimaced. "I'm fucking this up so badly."

"What? What's even going on?"

"Fuck it." He dropped to one knee, reaching out and taking my hand. My eyes widened. "I'd wanted to take you to some romantic spot, but maybe this is more suited to who we both are." My jaw dropped but he continued, "Captain—because I still don't know your real name—will you marry me?"

Tears spilled over. I couldn't control it, but warmth—happiness and joy, all mixed—filled me. He looked up anxiously and I laughed, watery through the tears, but laughter, nonetheless. "Yes, of course I'll marry you!"

He lunged to his feet, wrapping me in his arms, and buried his face in my neck, laughing and crying. He pulled back just far enough to kiss me, small, biting kisses, then one deep one. They tasted of salt, and we giggled. I smoothed his hair back, stroking his cheeks and cupping his face. This was the face I'd wake up next to most days for the rest of my life, and I couldn't be happier.

"We'll need to choose out a ring," he said, lacing our fingers together. "All I know is that your hands always surprise me, and I'd never guess right."

"It's okay," I said dryly. "You can just say I've got fat fingers."

"You can just shut up about your fingers." He glared at me, bringing my hand to his mouth. "I love your hands. Wouldn't change a thing about them. They're not skinny, but then again, you're more solid than most people give you credit for. They're like you. Strong. Gentle. Elegant, in your own way. So, if nothing fits, I'll head back to the Valley to find you one that does."

My lower lip trembled at his words. As soon as he finished, I pulled him in for another kiss. When he let me up for air, he studied my face. "What was that for?" he asked. "Not that I'm complaining."

"You're one in a million, you know that?"

"Fuck yeah! I got you. Now," he tugged me towards the hall, "let's do some ring shopping, Irregular-style."

***

"Oh, please." I looked at the ring he showed me, some silver-colored thing with a massive diamond. "You're telling me this is solid gold and a real diamond?"

I'd already chosen a simple, narrow, silver colored band with a pretty floral pattern on it. I had no idea how they'd done it, but now we couldn't resist browsing the remaining rings, searching for something for Archangel.

For some reason, the rings ended up in the armory, in a cloth bag Eleanor made to keep them. There were fewer now, since we'd had so many weddings, but plenty more for all those to come.

"Babe." Archangel stared at me levelly. "We found them in a jewelry store. A *nice* jewelry store. They'd have access to good stuff."

"It was *Molalla*. Not a thriving metropolis. We were lucky to have a jewelry store at all. Here, what about this?"

I held up a wide band, half of it silver, the other third turquoise with a delicate band of gold between. He slid it on his ring finger, and grinned. Perfect fit.

"I'll take it," he declared. "And no." He rubbed his thumb over the diamond. "You see that color? That's quality shine right there. It's not quartz."

"As if you can tell!"

He growled. "You know what? Maybe you need to listen to others a little more."

"Make me."

Making a noise halfway between a growl and a purr, he scooped me up, one hand under each thigh. My legs automatically wrapping around his waist, I purred as he walked until my back hit the wall. Without giving me a chance to tease, his lips captured mine. My pulse raced when one hand slid up to cup my butt, squeezing and testing the feel. Giggling against his mouth, I adjusted my legs, pulling him closer, running my fingers through his thick, silky hair.

The door slammed open, bouncing off the wall. Jerking apart only as far as my legs would allow, my hand slapped the table next to us and the weapons on it while we glared at the hapless person framed in the doorway. Staring, his mouth open, Driver stood frozen.

"So...um..." Driver's eyes darted around, looking anywhere but at us, tangled and breathing heavily, pressed against the wall. "Uh. I just...needed to grab..." Walking jerkily, he passed us to grab a crossbow and bolts off its rack. "Going hunting. You kids...have fun." A bead of sweat ran down his cheek as he escaped.

As soon as the door closed, we burst into laughter. I buried my face against his neck, hoping to muffle the sound and not embarrass poor Driver anymore. Archangel had no such compunctions, leaning into me as he howled.

I flicked my tongue out, tasting his mirth and the light sheen of sweat over his skin, his laughter slowing to chuckles that vibrated pleasantly. Quickly diverted, he gave me quick, nibbling kisses, moving down my jaw to my ear.

"You know," he murmured, "you still haven't told me your name."

"You haven't told me yours, either," I retorted, biting his ear.

He shivered. "Mmm...Noah. Noah Sanders."

"Hope Wilkins." My tongue twisted oddly as I said it and it dawned on me. I hadn't said my own name in nearly two years.

"Nice to meet you, Hope." He kissed me deeply.

"Pleased to meet you, Noah," I whispered when he freed my mouth.

A knock sounded. Well, banging, more like. "I know you're in there," Phoenix shouted. "It's time to come out. We need the room and you guys have two to choose from."

When I threw the door open, she confronted us, leaning against the opposite wall, one bare foot tapping impatiently. Her censorious look was ruined by the gleeful glint in her eyes. A little ways down the hall, the hunting party broke into cheers and jeers when we emerged. I narrowed my eyes, wishing I could give them a collective kick in the ass. The cheers died down slowly, but the grins, winks, and nudges continued.

They were assholes, but they were my assholes.

"Have a good time, kids?" Phoenix sang. She waved and the hunting party filed past us, into the armory. Once inside, they all managed to look remarkably busy while staying near the door.

"Piss off," I told her, but a blush crawled up my cheeks.

Archangel merely lifted my left hand and kissed my knuckles. The delicate ring shone in the dim light of the corridor.

Her eyes got huge. "Whoa, what?" Snatching my hand, she examined the ring. "You popped the question?!"

Archer, one of the hunters, nearly fell into the hallway. "Hey!" He scrambled to stay upright. "Congratulations!" He pumped Archangel's hand and pressed a gallant kiss to the back of mine.

The rest of the party spilled back into the hall, shouting congratulations, slapping my...fiancé's back and gingerly patting mine. A few of the bolder ones took a cue from Archer and kissed my hand, an oddly sweet gesture. Although, by the time they were done, I really needed to wash my hands. Or rub dirt on them.

Slipping a few feet away, I huddled with Phoenix. "He asked in the garage, but my fingers are a little thick so he didn't have one picked out ahead of time."

Phoenix snorted, dragging me away. "I'll return her later!" she shouted over her shoulder. Pushing me into my room, she slammed the door. "Spill!"

"Captain!" Someone shouted, banging on my door. "You have a minute?"

Phoenix flung the door open, glaring at Sarge, who looked bewildered. "Is someone dead?"

"No."

"Is someone about to die?"

"No."

"Then it can wait twenty minutes. Archangel just got engaged. Go congratulate him," Phoenix said, shutting the door in his surprised face, then pressed her back to it, her eyes dancing. "You were saying?"

"I wasn't but..." I sighed, reliving the last hour. "He found me in the garage..."

***

I backed slowly away from the Three Fates, my hands up, pleading. But my cries fell on deaf ears. The Fates showed no mercy, particularly not to a woman on her wedding day.

"My dear," the Second addressed me sternly. "You will allow us to bathe you. Do you understand?"

"Perhaps she doesn't?"

The Third brandished a loofah, grown at Home, in a distinctly threatening manner.

"I can wash myself!" I said petulantly, but none of them looked impressed.

"You have nothing we haven't seen before," the First said, stalking me like a hunter on a deer.

"You ain't never seen mine before!"

"You have been assisted in the past, have you not?" The Second tried reason.

I dodged around the half-barrel bathtub taking up one end of my room, steam rising invitingly. "Listen, those were extenuating circumstances. I was half-dead for one reason or another. I'm much better now."

"That can be remedied," the First muttered grimly.

The door burst open without warning and Phoenix barreled in. "Captain! Why aren't you washed yet?"

We all started talking at once.

"They keep trying to wash me..."

"She refuses to be helped at all..."

"Stubborn, mule-headed woman..."

"Enough!" Phoenix slashed a hand through the air. "Captain, you will let them help you. I saw you helping with the hunt yesterday. Do you really want Archangel to find blood somewhere later?"

I stared down, scuffing the ground with my foot. "No," I mumbled.

"Then get in the damn tub! We have a timeline, and if you're late and the food is overcooked, Amana will be very disappointed."

I shuddered. She'd come after me. I knew it. Defeated, I stripped and climbed into the tub. I groaned, sinking into the still warm water. I hadn't had luxury like this in...months.

The Fates descended, wielding scrubbers, brushes, and soap. In short order, I found myself scrubbed to within an inch of my life, then they ordered me to lie down on a towel on the floor so they could paint hot wax on my legs.

"Motherfucker!" I yelped when the Third ripped a swath of hair out. "Why the fuck do I need to be waxed? Archangel is already more than familiar with me being hairy!"

"Do try for a little dignity, my dear." The Second Fate patted my cheek while she plucked my eyebrows. "I know it's difficult, but if you look *really* hard, you might be able to find some."

"*Fucking* hell!"

"No? Well, it was worth a shot, I suppose."

***

Late afternoon sunlight shone under the looming clouds, turning the air gold as I walked to the meadow where the ceremony would be held. The Fates had primped, lotioned, and scrubbed. I was now more presentable than I'd ever been in my life.

I carried a small bouquet of late summer blooms Wildwood had found, mixed with the evergreens that abounded in our mountains. The soft grass cushioned my bare feet, and the skirts of a dress worn by a dozen women before me flowed around my legs.

The lowering clouds trapped the heat, adding a layer of humidity. Sweat beaded in my cleavage and gathered on my upper lip, some caused by the heat, some the result of nerves. I licked my lips when all eyes turned to me. Phoenix reached the end of the short aisle and stood opposite Gryphon, who paled in comparison to Archangel.

I drank in the sight of him. He'd found a dark gray, button down shirt, setting off his bright hair. His sleeves were rolled up to his elbows and my stomach tightened. Love a man with rolled up sleeves. When I met his gaze, all the air in my lungs left in a whoosh.

I sucked in a quick breath, licking my lips nervously at what I saw in his eyes. Heat. Love. And lust. "Oh, my God," I whispered. My shaking legs barely carried me down the aisle. I couldn't have gone faster to save my life.

Tears gathered in his eyes as he looked me up and down. Reaching out, his fingers trembling, he took my free hand and drew me next to him. Together, we turned to face Shepherd.

I barely heard Shepherd, everything focused on the man next to me. When it came time for the vows, we turned to face each other. Warmth, the warmth of home, knowing, security, and love, spread through me. Finally, I could stare into his eyes all I wanted, watch his mouth, feel his warm hands engulfing mine.

Archangel's voice sounded clearly, the first thing I'd truly heard since walking down the aisle. He spoke surely, without hesitation or fear, but his hands still trembled slightly.

"Beloved, I seek to know you, and ask of God that I be given the wisdom to see you as you are, and to know you as a mystery.

I give to you all that which is mine to give.

I pledge to you that it will be your eyes into which I smile every morning.

I pledge to you my living and my dying, each equally into your care.

I shall be a shield for your back, and you for mine.

You are my friend, my lover.

Grow old with me, as I will do with you.

I love you. I adore you."

I bit my lip, tears sliding hotly down my cheeks.

My hands spasmed nervously, and he simply squeezed tighter, raising one to his mouth, kissing my scarred knuckles, his eyes never wavering from mine. I'd been so afraid I'd forget my vows, but they flowed naturally, without being forced.

"I choose you for life.

I give you my hand and my heart, as a sanctuary for all this life has to offer.

I didn't fall in love with you.

I walked into love with you, with my eyes wide open.

I promise you my deepest love, my fullest devotion, my tenderest care through the pressures of the present and the uncertainties of the future.

As I have given you my hand to hold, I give you my life to keep

I'd choose you.

In a hundred lifetimes, in a hundred worlds, I'd find you and I'd choose you."

Shepherd nodded to Gryphon. "Do you have the rings?"

I'd reluctantly given up my ring this morning for it to be presented to me again. Archangel slid the ring onto my finger as Shepherd said, "You are now married in the eyes of God. When this is all over, you'll have to deal with the laws of man. In the meantime, you may now kiss."

Archangel swept me into a kiss, dipping me low as the first drops of rain fell, quickly turning into a soothing summer rain.

The gentle strains of a folk song, timelessly voiced by a violin, a guitar, and a harmonica, filled the rain drenched meadow. Archangel swept me through the steps, sure and light on his feet.

I laughed, tipping my face up to the rain, feeling safe for the first time since this whole shit-show began. We spun through another turn and my new husband pulled me closer.

"How do you feel, Mrs. Sanders?" he whispered in my ear.

"Elated. Excited. And maybe a little..." I nipped his jaw. "Mr. Sanders."

He growled, holding me closer. "Soon."

And the song played on. I smiled, the world fading away until there was nothing but him and me, in this moment, the rain pattering down around us.

***

"How can you still worship a god who let this happen?!" Kathy screamed at Eleanor. "God should be ashamed of himself and beg our forgiveness."

I closed my eyes and sighed, pinching the bridge of my nose. Archangel buried his head in his arms, groaning. One day. We'd had *one day* before this lady busted out of nowhere, shrieking fit to wake the dead. And it only happened when we finally left the room. Yesterday, they'd left a tray at my...*our* door, but today, we had to surface.

Sighing, I propped my head on my hand. Fine. This could be my after-lunch entertainment. I watched Storm frown at Kathy (okay, I don't know her name, it just seemed to fit), one hand dropping to her gun before she snatched it away, eyes wide.

"Really?" Eleanor folded her hands in front of her, raising a questioning eyebrow.

"Yes! He let my daughter die, saw my family enslaved, our country be overrun. 'In God we trust' my ass." She spat.

"You'd better clean that up before Lavender finds out," I said mildly, but I was thoroughly ignored.

"And what did we do?" Eleanor replied with admirable calm. "We said God didn't exist, and even if He did, we didn't want to listen to Him. God," she raised her hand, forestalling Kathy, "God set up Adam and Eve in a garden with pretty clear instructions and a good life. They had no idea about things like 'good' and 'evil.' It all just *was*. And then one day, they were tempted and ate a forbidden fruit..."

"We *know* all this. God, you're so pedantic."

Storm frowned, running her fingers along the butt of the gun, head tilted to one side as she eyed the woman. The Irregulars in the common room gathered silently around this little tableau, not a friendly face among them.

"Yet you still call a name you don't believe in." Eleanor gave her a level look. "As I was saying, with the eating of the fruit, there came knowledge and suddenly, there was also choice. The choice to do something good, or something bad. They now knew the difference.

"We still have that choice today. To do good, or evil. So, when people look at terrible things that man has done to man, or at natural disasters, and the people who have lost everything, we like to say, 'God, how could you let this happen?' Maybe, we should be asking, 'Why did that person make that choice?' or 'What could I do to stop it?' Maybe even, "What can I do to help?' To lay all the blame on God says that you no longer want to choose, you want God to make all the decisions for you. I don't know about you, but if I had the chance to give up my choices, I don't think I would. Oh, look." Eleanor smiled. "Another choice."

Kathy screamed, Archangel sniggered, she stomped her foot and stormed out of the common room as abruptly as she'd entered. The Irregulars dispersed, a few of them looking disappointed. They were probably hoping Storm would intervene. I knew I was.

I sighed. "Do I even want to know?"

Eleanor chuckled. "Why don't you and your new husband go Home for a few days?"

"Do we have to take her?" For better or worse, all the people who became a hindrance at the Lair were sent Home and became Olivia's problem, poor thing. I think she enjoyed herself, though she'd never admit as much. However, I really didn't want to be trapped on the trail with that for the time it took to get Home.

"No." Eleanor grinned, displaying her teeth. "There's still a bit of work that needs to be done here. Composting needs to be turned and we need to make and fill a few more garden beds. I think she'll do nicely for that work."

I laughed. "You don't look like it, but you have an evil, devious mind. I like it."

"Get going, you." She swatted me, laughing.

CHAPTER 28

"We're back, with LA TV! We're heading straight for Pasadena, where a religious war has broken out between the Christians and the Catholics. Who do you think will win? Which side do you predict will have less mercy? Find out here!"

Majordrama Channel

Our week at Home was more peaceful than anything I'd experienced in months. For privacy, we camped outside the caves, but being in one spot for a while, we made our camp comfortable, even building a tiny shelter.

Our last day there, I reluctantly began packing, preparing for an early morning departure the next day. Archangel came up behind, wrapping his arms around me and resting his chin on my shoulder.

"We could stay," he whispered the words running through my mind.

Even as he said it, I knew we couldn't. He knew it, too. He was simply offering it as a choice. Choosing to leave, rather than feeling like I had to, made it more palatable. I leaned back, running my fingers over the backs of his hands.

"We could. But we won't. Which you already know. Asshole."

He laughed. "Make the most of today. And don't let Sophie get you alone. I don't want to deal with her drama."

"Nice way to say she tried to kill me!"

He shrugged. "I have to agree with Olivia. She's just not competent enough to really call it a murder attempt."

That afternoon, I sat cross-legged on the ground, surrounded by small humans. The kids giggled, covering their mouths with tiny hands to muffle the sound and avoid distracting the actors in the makeshift play. I bit my lip to hold back laughter, watching them. It was from some old sci-fi movie.

A tall guy covered in dried grass waved his arms, making weird noises. I think it represented fur, but at this point, I was just damn impressed they could put on a play.

Cub lay, a warm, heavy weight at my side, and on my other, a little boy casually rested a hand on my knee, slapping it lightly when he laughed.

I'd walked through Home with Olivia, going back and forth over specific supplies they needed, Sophie, and animals, when the kids ran past, shrieking about the play. Cub doubled back to grab my hand, digging her feet in, hauling.

"Go ahead," Olivia said. "I'm not sure where they're at right now, something about carbonite, but it's still fun. I'll tell Archangel where you are."

The lead man walked into the center of a circle, and it was all very poignant. She said she loved him, he said, "I know," then the curtain went down. A little girl, three or four years old, twisted around to look me up and down.

"Why don't you sit down?" she invited, her chubby face serious.

I looked down at my legs crossed neatly in front of me, my butt firmly planted on the floor, just like everyone else. "I am sitting down," I said dryly. "I don't think I can get any more sitting down."

At this piece of information, she surveyed me again, more slowly, her forehead wrinkled with deep thought. "Captain," she announced solemnly, "you're too tall!" She then turned around, ignoring me completely.

I stared desperately up at the ceiling, making a noise like a balloon slowly losing air, clenching my teeth and rocking with the effort of holding it all in. What the hell?

In camp that night, I giggled and gasped, trying to recount it to Archangel. That grave little face under thick brown bangs, trying to grasp that I was already sitting down...I slowly toppled sideways, giggling.

"Oh, you think you got a good one, huh?" He wiped tears away. "I played hide-and-seek with some of them, and I was It. I walk around a corner, and there's a girl standing in the middle of the room with a bucket on her head, hiding."

Eventually, we calmed down, crawling into our blankets. He curled around me, cupping one hand around my breast in a move that had already become familiar, comforting. "It's nice to see kids. Especially kids being kids," he murmured.

"Mmm..." I pressed my hips back, my eyes closed. "They're probably more kids than we were. I wish I'd had access to forests like this when I was little."

He leaned over me, tipping my face up for a kiss, long and slow. Paused, then kissed me again, moving slightly.

"Oh." I smiled up, his face a blurry light patch in the dark. "Not too tired then?" He chuckled. "Me neither."

***

Summer turned into fall, turned into winter and we raided, fought, buried our dead, and loved with the fierceness of those who know each day might be our last. And yet, we all also thought we were immortal. After all, we'd made it this far, hadn't we?

But the price of over two years of constant war could be seen all over the Lair. Bright laughter turning into a squabble that escalated into a fistfight because that was all we knew. Or civilians who didn't understand gallows humor becoming incensed and judgmental because we wouldn't—couldn't—stop. The best was the camaraderie, the ride-or-die mentality, the knowledge that no matter what, these people had my back and I had theirs.

But the nightmares. Dear God, the nightmares. I gave thanks every morning for waking up because some nights, I seriously doubted I would. Having a man—*this* man—in my bed and in my life kept me from avoiding sleep altogether, because who could say no when those blue eyes suggested bed?

One night, in the dead of winter, I started awake with a sob, heart pounding, my cheeks wet with tears. I fumbled around, pushing blankets aside impatiently, searching. For a moment, I couldn't find him. A small cry of panic slipped out and I twisted frantically.

The mattress shifted and Noah rolled over, trapping me against the mattress, throwing one leg over mine. The scent of dirt, paint, and *him* filled my nostrils, slowly thawing my body. My lips pressed against his neck, and I relaxed slowly.

"You're freezing!" He tucked my hands between us. "Bad dream?" he murmured, kissing my temple. I nodded. "The usual?"

The faces of the dead marching past, bodies clogging the forests, whispering...I shook my head. "No."

"Tell me?"

"I couldn't..." My breath hitched and I clutched him spasmodically. "I couldn't find you. Walking through molasses, and you were always...just out of reach. And just now, when I couldn't find you..." I stopped. I couldn't say it, couldn't even think it. How could one person come to mean so much in such a short time? Weren't there guidelines and rules about how quickly you could become attached? It seemed excessive, but my pounding heart and the sweat drying on my face called society's rules a lie.

"I'm here," he murmured, giving me more of his weight. "I'm right here, no matter what." He slid his hand into my hair, cupping my head, nuzzling my cheek.

Wrapping a leg around his, I fell asleep tangled so tightly I couldn't tell where I ended and he began, his heart beating strongly against my chest.

***

In the fourth spring since this shit-show started, I hustled through the corridors, hoping the freaking Kathy following me would get tired and quit. Instead, her self-righteous nagging, compressed in the limited space of the hallways, bounced, surrounding me, becoming the only thing I could hear.

"You can't send her out there," Kathy screeched. "Mouse is only fifteen!"

My patience snapped. "I'm not 'sending' her anywhere!" The fucking woman had been harassing me for days and I lost it. "The girl's volunteering. Hell, it's a fucking miracle we managed to keep her in the Lair as long as we have!"

"You should have forbidden her to go at all!" Kathy—I called every woman who acted like this Kathy, it just fit—continued, her voice rising higher.

I rubbed my forehead. "If I'd tried to forbid her, she'd have fucked off anyway," I ground out. "And quite frankly, she's been training for three years. She's better than half the people we've got. She told me she'd be damned if..."

"And *will* you stop cursing! There are children here. They're picking up all kinds of unsavory behaviors. I will not..."

"For fuck's sake, lady! Do you ever talk in anything except exclamation marks? I don't have to explain myself to you, and you are getting on my last fucking nerve. Fortunately for you, I'mma have someone explain some things to you. Amana," I bellowed, continuing down the hall. "Amana!"

Amana walked quickly down the hall, the fastest she was ever willing to move. "*Sí, Capitán?*"

"This one," I jerked a thumb over my shoulder, "needs to go Home. Now. Before Mouse and the others hear her talking."

Amana shook her head. "I keep telling her to leave jou alone. *Aseos, compostaje*, she still talk, talk, talk. Does she listen? Noooooo..."

I jogged towards the gym. I needed a workout. And Archangel. And with Archangel, we could combine the two. Yay.

Behind me, I heard Seahorse talking cheerfully. "Good thing Captain's sending you away. Protection, that's what she's giving you." Kathy said something indistinct. Seahorse replied, "They don't like to be called 'children.' And they can get creative."

***

The days sped up while the nights slowed down. Any time I could spend alone with Archangel stretched into an eternity I didn't want to end, but eventually, the sun rose, the Lair awakened, and the day flew by. Until we went out on the trail again.

On a raid, I curled on my side in front of a tiny fire. Archangel, curved around my back, radiated a steady heat greater than the fire itself. Periodically, I dropped a couple more twigs on, feeding the little fire.

He sighed, his chest pressing against my back. "Is it just me, or are we spending more time on the trail these days?"

I stretched and resettled firmly against him. "What are you complaining about? This was your idea!"

But he wasn't wrong. Steve, finally realizing we wouldn't randomly disappear, became more active. And there was a curious desperation to their movements. For the first two years, they acted like we were a nuisance, a gnat against their war machine. Now, they traveled in small packs wherever they went, not just occasionally.

By necessity, we had a larger presence in the Valley, stymying their movements. Half our forces spent their time running from our current location back to the Lair with people we found, food we'd stolen, and the injured and dead. Sometimes, they came back with fresh people who were just given the all-clear to fight.

This time, we'd been out long enough for the blossoms to fade and early fruits to ripen. Wild fruit abounded, and we ate as much as we could in between skirmishes with Steve.

He nuzzled my neck, biting down delicately. I shivered, moaning, the sound barely audible. "We never get any alone time anymore," he mourned.

I snorted. "What was last night, then? Or this morning?"

His lips curved against my neck, and he chuckled. The night deepened and an owl hooted. Out in the dark, a small creature squeaked when that silent death found it.

"Babe?" I whispered.

"Hmm?"

"You ever hear that thing about how relationships that start in dangerous situations never last?"

"We've been together two years and you still wonder if we can make it in the normal world?"

I nodded. "Honestly, I'm not sure I can do it regardless. Make it. Sometimes, I'm afraid I'll just be that drunk on the corner, unable to forget or accept what happened and move on from it."

His arms tightened. "We may have met in this shit, but what keeps me going is the knowledge that someday, we'll have more. I want to wake up next to you and just...stay in bed all day. I want to cook together. I'm terrible, and you're worse, but dammit, I want to try.

"I want to learn every last bit and nuance of you. Not just what pertains to this life. What do you look like when you're taking a shower? What's your favorite dessert? I want to learn how to cook decent food with you. I want to see you get fat and sassy, living an easy life." I sputtered a laughing protest, but he kept going.

"I want some pets. Maybe a couple of kids. Do you want kids?"

I squirmed around until I was facing him. Smiling, I brushed a lock of hair from his eyes, the firelight making them glow. "Haven't really had time to think about it, but yeah. Kids would be nice."

He kissed me deeply, sighing when he pulled away. "Okay. Couple of kids. Maybe we started out in dangerous times, but I'm dreaming of knowing you in peaceful times. Unless you only think I'm interesting when the shit hits the fan?"

"What?" I hissed, incensed. "Are you crazy? You're seriously lying here, thinking I'm only interested in your hot body? I can't wait until I cuddle your hot dad bod. Idiot."

He buried his face against my neck, muffling his laughter. "Sometimes," he wheezed, "you're just too easy."

"Asshole."

"Takes one to know one."

***

"Babe," Archangel whispered, holding me close, "it won't be long, and we have to try it."

I shook my head. "Send someone else."

He chuckled. "Is that what you'd do, in my shoes?"

I compressed my lips, glaring. He had me there. Bastard. We were on the edge of the foothills, saying our farewells. Around us, others took leave of the small group going their own way. Archangel had an idea that he wanted to test out. Instead of all of us working in concert on a single target, he thought we could send out loads of smaller groups, anywhere from four to eight people, whatever comfortably fit in a single vehicle.

Right now, we'd go out in force, starting with a convoy of roughly sixty that split up to attack a target from multiple directions. What Archangel proposed would be more like the early days, multiplied. Each group would have a target, but the overall aim was to cause chaos.

Basically, set the Valley on fire.

It meant that the moment you had a badly injured person, you were out of the game and needed to head back to the Lair, but it might also mean that we had more rest. Instead of needing to stay out for a month or two in order to cause trouble, we could send out seven to ten groups for a couple weeks and cover more ground.

It also meant that if you found a target too large, you had to leave it alone.

"But we never split up battle partners," I protested. "You know we don't." *It's bad luck,* I didn't say.

"I'll be extra careful," he promised. "But you know we have to try."

"Fine," I groused. Grabbing his ears, I pulled him in for a kiss. When he straightened, we were both breathless. "But if something happens to you, I'll strangle you."

"I'll hold you to it." He grinned, mischief dancing in his eyes.

The man drove me nuts, but when he did that...I could forgive him anything, even being apart. Having already talked to the other people going—Gryphon, Chaos, River, Gameboy, and Stretch—I held his hand in both of mine, waiting for the others to be ready.

When the small group climbed into their vehicle, my heart sank into my moccasins. Phoenix stood next to me, her lips pursed to hold back tears. Nudging her with my shoulder, we headed back to our own vehicles. Archangel's group headed south and east. Our targets were north.

***

Squinting in the bright sunlight, I raised my head, peering around the field. Nice and empty looking. Satisfied, I settled back down, pulling a couple of wild strawberries out of my belt pouch. Best place to set an ambush is the one place nobody thought it could be done, like a nice, wide-open field. You'd never guess there were nearly thirty people in here.

I closed one eye in a lame attempt to spare my eyes from the sun. No Oregonian managed to keep track of a pair of sunglasses through a single winter. Not a snowball's chance in hell I could do it through a war. Glaring at the brassy sky, I willed the two tiny puffball clouds on the horizon to spread.

Several minutes later, not a single cloud moved. Well, guess my weather powers still hadn't shown up. Sighing, I rubbed my face. We'd been out for weeks and when there was fighting, I was good. In the quiet moments, exhaustion hit me like a truck.

Out of the fifteen Irregulars out of commission, eight of them were due to stress and exhaustion. But we really needed the supplies this convoy supposedly carried, and Shrike said we needed to hit one more after this. The sooner the better, she said.

The Raven's caw snapped me back to the present. Stuffing the last strawberry in my mouth, I shouldered my rifle. Steve would be just around the bend. The scent of dust filled my nose, strawberry on my tongue, a last taste before gun smoke and blood. I pumped the rifle, preparing for the fight.

The first truck rumbled into view, a man in the gun turret. The windows were down, a forearm visible, fingers dancing in the wind. Sighting directly above the elbow, I waited for Phoenix to start the show.

***

I whooped, racing away from the ambush, the air filled with shouts of triumph, the entire crew tearing over the hill between us and our cars. My pack, loaded with liberated food, bounced around my shoulders as I leaped over a shallow gully, landing heavily on the far side.

"This is a good day," I shouted, laughing.

Cheers rang out, swallowed by the humid air. Hot Fuzz ran next to me, slowing to let me catch up.

"Wassup, kiddo?"

"How do you know how many of these to do before it's time to get out?"

"Now? Seriously?"

"If I want to lead a crew, I've got to step up, don't I?" He kept pace with me easily. The little shit wasn't even breathing hard. "You alright there? I know you're getting old, but damn..." He laughed, dodging away from my playful swipe.

"It's not hard to figure out." I huffed, running up a small slope. "When we're low on supplies, especially ammo, or if it's getting too hot. Why do you want to run a crew? It's not like there's a promotion and a pay raise involved."

"I just think it's time I took more responsibility," he said. "I'm getting married soon, you know."

Putting one hand on a fallen tree trunk, I vaulted it. My brother didn't need to bother with that, leaping straight over it, and then we were in the circle of trucks. Dereva put up her rifle, rushing to meet us with a glad cry. Except she ran past me, straight to Fuzz, leaping into his arms.

"Oh, yeah, nice." I rolled my eyes. "And what am I, chopped liver? Whoa, kids, leave something to the imagination, will you?"

"Ugh! Get a room," Phoenix shouted, laughing.

"Aaah! I've gone blind!" Sweetpea yelled.

The jibes flew thick and fast, and Fuzz flipped us off, grinning.

***

Two days later, I sat in a tree checking an innocuous farm out through my scope. A single house, a large barn, and two other outbuildings. Nice bunch of trees around and the road lay an easy walk away. If the drivers had to come get us, the lay of the land shouldn't cause too much trouble.

We'd been watching the place since last night. It looked like there were only fifteen guards for twenty prisoners. Those prisoners were locked in one of the outbuildings, a rickety old thing, at night. I liked that they were all in one place. Made it a bit easier.

Stuffing the scope in my pocket, I made my way down, trying to avoid branches and pointy sticks. "Gah! Motherfucking piece of..."

"Language," Eleanor scolded, smiling.

"Storm back yet?" I brushed debris off my head, squirming when something slid down my back.

"She's at the map."

Running my fingers around inside my waistband, I fished a twig out of my underwear. "Yech. Eleanor, have I got anything in my hair?" I bent over, hands on my knees as she picked delicately through my battle braids.

"Storm, dear," she called as she worked. "Captain would like a word."

"Yo, Captain." Storm came over. "Perimeter looks good. The trees are clear and no signs of Steve."

Straightening, I tucked loose hair behind my ears. "Tonight, then."

"Fuckin' A!"

"Language!"

***

"You can't go through the wall!" a prisoner hissed.

Getting to the outbuilding was easier than making pie. Seriously. Making pie is a bitch.

Testing the walls, we woke some of the prisoners and one of them promptly stopped us from breaking a board. The rest of the fighters spread out in a circle around the shed, on their bellies, facing outward. So far, all was quiet.

"Why not?" I asked.

"They've wired it. The last group out here didn't believe them."

"And you do?"

"We saw the remains."

I digested this. "Sparrow!" One figure wriggled backwards, only getting to her feet when she was close to the shed. "Can we cut the wires?"

She spent a few minutes asking questions and checking out the job while I knelt, rifle up. When she came back, she shook her head. "It's not a good idea, Captain. I couldn't tell exactly which one to cut."

"What about the roof?"

Another whispered discussion went on behind me. "That works," she whispered.

"The roof!" I called softly. "I need two inside to boost, two on the roof, two on the ground."

Bear and Kodiak immediately moved to the base of the wall, cupping their hands, ready to boost the rest up the wall. Gummy, Kodiak's brother, and Anarchy were the first up. While they tore at the roof, Grayman and Fuzz were tossed up.

"Quicker is better," Storm sang softly.

"Hatchet," Gummy whispered. "I can't get through this part."

Someone tossed a hatchet up and the others crowded around, struggling to muffle the noises, but it wasn't enough. Steve spilled out of the house, ready for a fight, even though we hadn't been that loud. Phoenix, in God position up a tree, fired first, dropping a man where he stood.

"Go, go, go!" I bellowed.

We opened fire, holding them back. Then Steve poured out of the barn. Far more than we'd ever seen in twenty-four hours of observation.

"What the fuck is that, a clown car?" Storm asked.

She wasn't wrong. A small army poured out, too many men for us to kill, even if every bullet hit a man. I didn't have to choose my targets, simply firing as fast as I could work the pump.

Nebula, the blue-haired teenager who'd gone straight into the bashers, paused her firing for a moment, surveying the scene. "It's getting a bit crowded here, don't you think?" she asked, before continuing to shoot.

"You know, I think it is. Time to thin the herd." A scream from my left caught my attention. One of the fighters was cut off from the circle. Firing rapidly, I took two down, then she dispatched a third. I aimed at one of the two remaining and...clicking. "Fucking hell!"

Shouldering my rifle, I snatched a handgun out, yanking a grenade off my belt with my other hand. Firing at the last man standing to my right, I yanked the pin with my teeth, twisting and lobbing the grenade overhand to the left, where Steve's main forces were.

"Grenade," I bellowed, hitting the ground, reloading awkwardly.

Everyone still on their feet dropped, a couple of them tackling the prisoners standing awkwardly by the shed. That one grenade was quickly followed by more.

"Grenade!"

"Grenade!"

"Potato!"

After the last concussion, I pushed up to my elbows, firing haphazardly, but Steve had begun to thin. Phoenix's rifle continued to speak and next to me, Storm lay on her back shoving a fresh magazine into her rifle.

"Did you hear someone yell 'potato'?" she asked calmly, cocking her rifle.

"Oh, you heard that, too?" I exhaled, relieved. "I thought I was going deaf."

Small fires from the explosions lit the area, the flickering light concealing as much as it showed. Bodies littered the ground, some of them in more than one piece. Black puddles filled the hollows in the earth and the wounded stirred weakly, crying out. Steve, forced down and decimated, was slow to move.

Time to capitalize on our breather. Rising and simultaneously drawing my smaller guns, I fired as quickly as I could pull the triggers. Across the field, the trucks raced in, bouncing over the uneven ground.

"Captain!" My brother, on the roof of the shed, shouted and waved. "More Steve incoming!"

"How many more to come out?" All I needed was for the last of the prisoners to get out of the damn shed. That's it.

"Eight!"

"Move faster! We're waiting on you."

A hand patted my calf none too gently. "They're afraid of the bullets flying," a woman barked.

"What? You think inside the shed is safer?" I snapped. Ignoring the woman's spluttering, I turned my attention to not dying.

Phoenix's rifle fell silent, and minutes later, she rejoined us. "Steve's acting like it's full of mamas," she commented, reloading her rifle. "I need a boost."

I glanced around quickly. Bear and Kodiak lowered the last of the prisoners. Putting my back to the shed, I laced my fingers together in a stirrup. She slung her rifle over her shoulder. Once I was ready, she took four light, running steps. Catching her foot, I tossed her up.

"You'll have to get yourself down," I called over my shoulder.

"As if I couldn't jump off this in my sleep. Why don't you make yourself useful?"

"Captain!" Seahorse shouted. "They're pouring in from the road!"

"Well." I switched magazines. "This turned into a cluster fuck in a hurry. Doc! How's it going?"

"They'll need help."

"They always do."

"But they're mobile. I don't think they can run."

"They only have to walk to the cars."

Which were still not here. Damn Steve. The machine gun on the pickup fired rapidly, but the bouncing meant Hightide probably missed as many as she hit. Dammit. We pulled slowly towards the back of the shed, away from the main driveway and Steve. A hand seized my arm, spoiling my shot.

"Hey," I snarled, pulling my elbow free.

"Oh, my God. It *is* you!"

Who...? I peered at the woman. Painfully thin, scars from a whip marking her arms and shoulders, she was recognizable, nevertheless. I'd only seen her features on her two children nearly every day for three years.

"Fuck me," I gasped. "Kioni. Is Walter here?"

Tears streamed down her gaunt cheeks as she called over her shoulder, "She's here. It's her!"

A bald man turned away from the woman he assisted. A patch covered one eye, a thick scar showing above and below. What remained of Walter's hair was snow white, and he was as thin as his wife.

He rushed over, clawing at my arms. Gathering them up, I shoved them back, away from the front line. Tears streaked his cheeks and questions rushed out of him, too many for me to follow.

Storm seized my arm. "Captain!"

Kioni gasped and Walter swayed. "*You're* the ghost Captain?"

I grinned. "You've heard of me? Gimme a sec," I said to Storm. Back to the Blakes, I lowered my voice. "We don't use real names. I need you to forget you ever knew me Before."

"What about our kids?"

Firing picked up from the front and I shook my head. Realizing they couldn't see, I grabbed their arms. "The kids are fine. One of them is back at the Lair—our basecamp—and you'll see the other in a few minutes. Meanwhile, I have shit to do."

Storm had rejoined the front. At the rear, the vehicles were almost to us. Steve, seeing our escape so close, charged. "Get to the trucks," I bellowed. "Stay low, move fast. Irregulars...One shot, one kill!"

Roaring, we braced to meet Steve.

***

Charging en masse like they did, we couldn't hold them back any longer. Through the chaos, I caught glimpses of their Chimeras, and one thing struck me. I saw it several times, brief flashes in the melee. They weren't using any heavier artillery like mortars or their machine guns.

Unable to concentrate on what that meant, I fought. The fighting swirled and eddied. Dust and smoke filled the air, the flames from a Molotov cocktail lighting the scene. Shouts, screams, hand-to-hand fighting all over the place. Sword in one hand, gun in the other, I spun, ducked, fired, and slashed.

To my left, Sparrow took a blow that knocked her off her feet. I shot her attacker and moved on. Slowly, to give the injured time, we backed towards the vehicles. I hit a person, knocking them down.

"Kioni!" Walter cried.

"Keep moving," I shouted, backing with them.

The Irregulars formed a rough circle that shrank rapidly, constantly shifting as the prisoners and injured were loaded into vehicles and we fell back. A soldier charged, bayonet fixed and aimed at my heart. I only had time to fire once before he was on me. Ducking, I let the blade go over my shoulder. Straightening, I slammed my knife up, under his chin.

When he fell, he took the knife with it, flopping limply to the ground. Spinning to my right, I fired, but the gun clicked. Dropping the gun, I hit him, left, right, knee to the groin then the nose, knocking him flat. Back to the Blakes...

Steve had Kioni by the arm, yanking her away from the cars. Walter held her other arm, struggling to hold onto his wife. Swooping down, I scooped up my empty gun and drew a fresh one simultaneously. No, too close. My own people were all over the place.

Holstering both thigh guns, I launched at the soldier holding Kioni. We went down, struggling in the dirt until I got a hand on my leg knife. Bellowing, I stabbed the body above me until he went limp.

When I got to my feet, I glanced wildly around. We were cut off from the rest of the Irregulars. "Fuck!"

Herding the Blakes in front of me, and occasionally behind as I turned to engage Steve, I threw elbows, kicked, stabbed, punched, and shot in a losing battle. The cars were too far away, and the Blakes were slowing, gasping and stumbling every step. Without them, I could make it. I knew it. With them...

My back to the Blakes now, I faced a small group of five Steve who were intent on capture. That could be the only reason they weren't shooting. Working in concert, they closed in, stabbing with their bayonets. Baring my teeth, I snarled. I could make it back, but could I look at the kids again, knowing I'd abandoned their parents?

My gun empty again, I worked back and forth with the knife and gun, desperately turning aside their blades, shifting and dancing to stay between them and the Blakes.

From the left, a man rushed into the group facing me, shouting, "'Nobody tells me nothing!'"

That quote did it. Hot Fuzz. "Fucking...fuck. Run!" I shouted over my shoulder to the Blakes.

A shot sounded, astonishingly loud in a sudden lull and Fuzz stumbled. My heart stuttered in my chest. Two of the men attacking me diverted to him, their rifles stabbing down. Screaming, I launched forward, taking out one before reinforcements arrived.

Dropping to my knees beside Fuzz, I struggled to lift him, a keening wail ripping from my throat. Light from the fires danced over his face and I pressed two fingers to his neck, praying to a God I didn't believe would listen to me, after everything I'd done.

But there, faint, but there, his pulse fluttered under my fingers. "C'mon, kiddo," I whispered, bending over him. "You can do it."

"Captain! Captain!" A hand struck me across the face and my eyes cleared. Phoenix knelt across from me, shaking me by the shoulder harnesses I wore. "Get up. Grab Fuzz, let's move!"

We flung ourselves into the last of the cars, Phoenix, Fuzz, and me ending up in my old pickup. Dust flew up like a rooster tail when Dereva gunned it. Leaning over Fuzz, I felt for his pulse.

"Papa?" he whimpered. "It hurts. Papa? Hope? I want Mama..." His head lolled, eyes rolling.

"Fuzz?" I patted his face frantically. "Kiddo, come back. Come back..."

Storm, manning the machine gun, cried out, her knees buckling. Phoenix pulled her back and took her place, firing behind us. His pulse returned, weaker than before. "We need..." Clearing my throat, I raised my voice. "We need to get Dereva back here, now. He hasn't....He's not..." I couldn't go on, tears choking me.

Phoenix pounded on the cab. Dereva got us on the road and slowed. "Hightide needs to drive," Phoenix shouted. "Now!"

The truck paused, the bed rocked and thumped when Dereva climbed in, and the truck screeched off before she even settled.

"What?" Seeing Fuzz, she gave a little shriek and sank down next to him.

I shifted back to give her space but kept my fingers on his neck, raising a hand to cover my mouth, sobbing. She whispered to him, stroking his hair back. Peter thrashed, cried out for Mom one more time, and slumped, his eyes fixed sightlessly at the sky.

Dereva screamed, clutching his shoulders, pressing frantic kisses to his face.

Squeezing my eyes shut, I swallowed my cries, wishing I could block the sound of her sobbing. Storm wept, pressing his free hand to her face. The Blakes had somehow ended up in the pickup with us and now they moved towards the sobbing young woman.

"No names!" I said harshly before they could open their mouths. "She is Dereva, now."

"What she will always be is my daughter," Kioni replied tartly.

"And he..." I nodded to my brother, lying so still in the bed of my pickup. I choked, pressing my lips together to hold back the sobs. "He was about two months away from being your son-in-law."

CHAPTER 29

Looking out over the gathering, I couldn't help but compare it to the first tiny funeral held on a frozen winter morning. Now, our funerals were full ceremonies where we—the originals—knew how to mourn.

Too bad that didn't make it any easier.

Four new cairns rested in the meadow and now...we remembered them. Dereva stood, talking about the young man she loved, pausing frequently to let the tears flow. Her parents sat nearby, but it was Sweetpea and Storm who offered the driver comfort in this time. Walter and Kioni offered what support they could, but they didn't understand this.

Anansi sat next to Kioni, his head resting on her shoulder. She stroked his hair, and whenever her fingers trailed over the tattoos on his arm, she sent me a dirty glare.

Listening to the others talking about their loved ones, I so badly wanted to be next. I wanted to let them all know he was my brother, that I loved him, that I missed him, and mourned his passing in a way none of them could.

But I didn't.

Was it safe to tell them? Would it harm anyone? It would confirm that I had family here, and I didn't know…My eyes wandered over the people, passing over the face of the whiny man-baby. My lip curled. No. I didn't trust everyone here. I couldn't…

But I wanted to.

Eleanor sank to the grass next to me, a cup cradled in her hands. "They were so young," she whispered. "It hurts, so much. I wish I could take this for them." She watched Dereva where the driver sat, surrounded by family and friends. "How are you?"

"I lost my sword," I said numbly. Stupid. I missed it. I could miss it. I could mourn for the sword because for that, I could stop crying. For Peter…

Unable to take it anymore, I stood abruptly, leaving the gathering. I couldn't. I couldn't. Not anymore. Stumbling away from Eleanor's confused look, I took the trail to my lookout. Blinded by tears, I crashed straight into a solid form, rocking him slightly.

"Babe?" He caught my shoulders, peering at my face.

Noah. Archangel. Crumpling, I buried my face in his shoulder, screaming my grief. Safety. Was anything safe? Yes. Yes, here, there was always safety, acceptance, and love. No matter what, he would always be here.

"I'm sorry," he whispered against my temple, his breath cool against my overheated skin. "Let it out. I've got you."

***

The worst part was that I didn't get a chance to rest and mourn like I had with Sirius. With her, everyone knew she was my friend, knew we were close. With Peter, they thought he was just a fighter that I knew slightly.

So, the day after the funerals, I ended up in the Useless Room for our usual debrief. Of particular interest to the others was why the fuck there'd been so much security at that little farm. There'd been even more than our last raid that pulled out a bunch of mamas-to-be.

To that end, Kioni and Walter were in, holding hands, watching us warily. I leaned back in my chair, wishing I was hungover. It'd feel better than this gaping wound in my chest, barely held together with duct tape and twine.

Archangel lounged next to me, looking sleepy and comfortable to the others. I noticed the slight tension, the leashed violence. The usual suspects of Gryphon, Phoenix, Eleanor, Storm, Driver, Sarge, Seahorse, and Lavender rounded us out. Eleanor leaned forward, resting her forearms on the table, radiating calm energy.

"What do you know about that place?" *Why was it so heavily guarded?* screamed silently around the room.

Kioni took a deep breath, sighing it out. "The Liberation Army wanted to get an energy source up and running. But because of what they did, they've effectively destroyed all the components you need to quickly and easily make a fusion reactor, and because it's still up and running, it slowly degrades parts..."

"Wait," Archangel interrupted. "Do you know what they've done?"

Kioni shrugged. "Well, I haven't seen it, if that's what you mean. We thought it was strictly theoretical. Besides, who'd want to take us back to the Dark Ages?"

She went silent for a beat, then continued. "As near as I can guess, it's a series of magnets that are operating together to create a...a force-field, if you will, that damages electronics. At the time it was unleashed, people with pacemakers and other such devices were affected, and it damaged chips, computer components, and even metal filaments. Prolonged exposure to the field doesn't appear to be damaging to humans, but I hypothesize that any new electronics brought in here would stop working, and that their parts would slowly degrade over time."

"Can confirm on the new electronics," Archangel said. "We brought things in. Couldn't say about their degradation, we don't have anything left."

"So, they brought us in to make a fusion reactor," Kioni continued, "which turned out to be extremely difficult when the finer components constantly degrade. We never managed to make a working model."

"What were they planning to do with it?" Eleanor asked.

Kioni shrugged. "Power the city? Make weapons? Honestly, despite what the government tells you, there's very little you can't do. Now that I know about you...It wouldn't surprise me if they were planning on weapons."

"I overheard two of the Corpsmen talking, once," Walter put in. "They were upset because they were suddenly limited on firearms. Something about problems with supply lines?"

Phoenix shrugged. "We've messed with them a little, but I don't think you could say we've really disrupted them, could you, Captain? Captain?"

When Archangel nudged me, I started, remembering who I was. The fearless leader. My lip curled unconsciously, and I smoothed my features. Archangel swung his chair closer, taking my hand. "What? Um...Right. Supplies. I wouldn't say we've done too much with that. Uh...Steve has a bad habit of randomly adding a lot of soldiers, so that's always a bit of a crapshoot."

Phoenix nodded. "Maybe there's another group operating that's messing with them?" We all paused, then she slowly continued, "You don't think...Gorgon?"

At that, I snorted. "As if. She'd have to pull her head out of her ego for five minutes for that one."

When the discussion turned to speculation on whether another group was accidentally helping, I tuned out of the conversation, sitting in a fog.

When I came out of it, people were pushing back from the tables and the meeting was over.

Kioni and Walter didn't move. "We'd like to talk to you for a minute, Captain, if that's okay," Walter said. "And…Phoenix, too."

Exhaustion hit me, leaving me unable to even think about standing. Archangel glanced sharply at me. "No," he said abruptly. "Not now."

Kioni's features tightened. "There are some things you need to answer to."

"Not now!" he barked, making Kioni flinch. Wincing, he softened. "The last raids were…difficult…" He trailed off when I put a hand on his leg.

"It's okay," I said. Explaining more would mean telling them about Peter, and I didn't think I could survive a discussion about my brother. "If not now, she'll just ambush me in the hallway, anyway."

His jaw clenched, a mulish expression on his face. I smiled. He was adorable when he was protective. His concern acted like a soothing balm to the raw grief circling and held it at bay for a moment.

Gryphon and Phoenix simply stayed in their seats, waiting. Looking around the table, the weirdness of it all caught me. I knew everyone's name. Phoenix knew mine and Gryphon's as well as the Blakes. Archangel knew mine, Gryphon knew Phoenix's…Who knew whose names, and who didn't…It was dizzying.

Phoenix came to the same conclusion, going by her wry smile as she looked around the table. "This could get confusing, so let me get a few things out of the way. Captain rescued me from being assaulted—" A mild way to describe rape, but okay. "—and at the Blakes' request, we took Anansi and Dereva out of town with us. She's the one I told you about," she finished quietly, just for Gryphon, who glanced up sharply.

Archangel looked at me, curious, but I shook my head. That was Phoenix's secret to tell. Thankfully, she'd told Gryphon about her son, Dylan. "So, now you know exactly who here knows our names," I finished.

"Yes, yes," Kioni said impatiently. "But there's a few things I want to know. Like, why did you put my children in harm's way? My daughter is barely eighteen!"

"Closer to nineteen," Phoenix interjected.

Kioni ignored her. "And from what people have let slip, you've had her driving since she was fifteen! In battle situations, no less!"

Unable to remain seated, she got up, pacing. A lot of people paced in this room. There was something about it...

"My son's tattoos!" She whirled to face me. "How can you possibly justify that?"

Archangel growled, bringing me back to the present. Tattoos. This, at least, I could follow. Pulling back my sleeve, I showed her my wrist. The other fighters did the same. "Doc needed to know where to find our blood types. It saves lives."

"Not that one! He has a *sleeve*!"

Needing more contact than just holding his hand, I left my chair and climbed into Archangel's lap. He immediately cuddled me, one hand stroking my thigh, glaring at the gaunt woman hurling accusations my way. Secure in his arms, I shrugged. "That's on him. I came back one day, and he had half the damn thing done. It's not like he needs my permission."

"And distilling alcohol?" she asked dangerously.

Phoenix giggled, and Kioni didn't even look at her. It dawned on me. It wasn't the issues. Those weren't important. What mattered was she needed someone to yell at and she'd decided I was it. Not too wrong, since technically, I led this group, but still. Being a whipping girl always sucked.

Throwing caution to the winds, I asked the big question in my mind. "Why don't you ask me what's *really* got you going? Don't skirt the issue. What are you *really* pissed off about?"

Her mouth dropped open, then snapped shut. Her nostrils flared and she glared at me, fury in every line. Inside, I smirked. Hit the nail on the head. She was mad about something else entirely. Without another word, she stormed out of the Useless Room, slamming the door behind her.

I blew on my nails and polished them on my shirt, not bothering to hide my grin. "Oh, yeah, I still got it."

"Got what?" Phoenix inquired. "The ability to drive people to the brink of murder? Because you never lost it."

Walter watched his wife leave, concern and humor an odd mix on his features. "She's felt terribly about sending the kids away. Even when we knew we'd done the right thing, never knowing what they were doing or how they were..." He sighed.

"And then seeing them and realizing they'd developed some bad habits..." I added.

"And seeing their heartbreak," he finished. "So, I wanted to thank you, instead."

I blinked, surprised. "Oh. Thank you."

"And also, how much of your reputation is real?"

"It's a bunch of lies," I assured him over the other's laughter. "Especially anything you heard here. They're all full of shit."

***

Two nights later, I left Archangel sleeping in our room and roamed the halls. I needed...I don't know. I needed to know my brother still breathed, but that would never happen again. Still, my feet took me outside, to the meadow. First, I stopped by Sirius's cairn. Sonya's. No, it hurt too much to remember her real name. Someone had left a dog treat on her cairn for Obelix to find.

Then, I went to Fuzz's cairn. Small wooden crosses with the fighter's names appeared on some of them, but my brother had a word carved in stone on his: Beloved.

Tears rushed in with the memories, choking me. Peter as a toddler, wearing his favorite red rubber boots. The number of people he'd upset during those months because he'd just...kick people's butts. It didn't matter that he was tiny. If anybody ever knelt or worked on something low to the ground that put their butt at his boot level, he'd kick them in the ass. Didn't matter who the ass belonged to.

When my tears turned into watery laughter, I headed back into the Lair. I needed sleep. If I woke Archangel up, he'd be happy to help me relax. I smiled, walking past the first side hall, then grunted when a small, solid shape slammed into me.

Reeling, I barely caught the wall before I fell.

"Shit!" was the only word I recognized in a stream of Spanish. Amana, then. A match snicked, and she lit a candle, looking sheepishly up at me. On the floor next to her rested The Book. Our only connection to the past, The Book was our record, where each fighter put down all their information. Real name, Social Security, family members, everything.

It contained everyone in the Lair, except the first two we lost, Leo and Jasmine. The Book was our way to contact families after this was over, to let people know what happened to their loved ones. To tell them how they died.

Amana looked at me with unexpected compassion. I said, "You've read his page, then?"

"*Sí.* You should have told someone you lost a brother."

Now she lost the accent. I sighed. "Archangel knows. That's enough."

"It's not. Are you sorry nobody else knows?"

The corner of my mouth kicked up and I huffed. "It seemed best. Considering my reputation."

"Is it hard, keeping a secret this big?"

"You tell me. You know all our secrets."

She sighed, staring into space. As The Book's keeper, she recorded every person's death on their page. "It's hard. But worth it, in the end."

"Yes."

We stood quietly at the intersection for a time, lost in our own thoughts. Finally, she shook herself. "Good night, *Capitán.* If you need talk..."

I nodded, touching her shoulder lightly, and walked away, resolutely not looking back. I didn't want to know where she went next. I didn't want to know where she hid The Book.

***

I circled Archangel on the mat, watching him warily. He stalked me, his face intent, watching my every move. I touched my tongue to my lips and his eyes flicked, following the move. Ah. Inside, I laughed. Shifting my feet, I let my hips swing and his eyes went down, then flew up. I didn't try to hide my grin anymore.

He'd dragged me out of bed and another bout of crying and into the gym, where he deposited me none-too-gently on the mats. He put Phoenix against me first, and she knocked me around enough to wake me up and get me pissed, then he stepped in before I let loose.

Clever man.

Other people sparred around us, but they slowly stopped and gathered as we moved, punches and kicks getting further away from fighting and closer to dancing. Bets flew around the group, people risking chores and treats.

The people around us faded and it was just him and me. I slid past his strike, so close his warmth brushed my lips. My heart lightened, and I spun away. When I stopped, I gave him a sideways glance and bit my lip. He growled, rushing in.

He deliberately let me slip through his grasp. I felt it in the fingers that loosened their hold enough to allow me to escape. Twisting, I ran my hand across his chest to hook his arm and his pulse leapt at my touch. He spun into my tug, and I laughed as we moved together, our chests mere inches apart.

His jaw tightened even as his eyes lit with an inner fire I well recognized after two years of marriage. The lust on his face raised an answer in me. When he lunged, I evaded to keep the chase going a bit longer. Now, he smiled, wolfish and excited.

My next punch connected, harder than I'd intended and he froze, blinking slowly. I gasped, my hands covering my mouth, eyes wide.

He bared his teeth. "Is that the way you want to play, pretty one?"

I gulped. My next decision didn't cross my brain at all. It rose from the most primitive part of myself and went straight to my legs. Spinning on one heel, I bolted. "Move," I screeched, tearing through a crowd that sprung up out of nowhere.

A tall, narrow, dark-haired man blocked my path momentarily and I picked up speed, willing to mow him down in my efforts to escape the people before Archangel caught me, but the man stepped aside at the last minute.

And Archangel would catch me. It was a foregone conclusion.

I wanted him to catch me.

I'd only made it around the first corner when a heavy weight hit me, spinning us both so that when we hit the wall, it was his shoulders that took the blow. I scrabbled, twisting, trying to escape, but it was useless. Archangel had me firmly, and by the time we stopped, my back was against the cold stone wall, and a very heated Archangel pressed tightly against my front.

I purred, arching into him. The contrast between cold wall and hot man was...delicious. It woke the last parts of me that had fallen numb after Peter's death. He chuckled, deep in his chest. Sliding his hands under my thighs, he pulled them high around his waist. I locked my ankles together against his tight butt.

Leaning close, he whispered in my ear, his breath puffing hot against tender skin, "Do you want me to take you right now?"

I moaned and nodded, nipping his ear. Purring, he straightened, his hands cupped under my butt and began walking down the hall. "As much fun as it would be," he said, "I'd rather not have an audience. Phoenix would find some popcorn if we did."

I snickered, but it ended on a whimper. Right now, I wouldn't mind as long as he got in my pants. Wrapping my arms around his shoulders, I levered myself higher. "Walk faster," I whispered, closing my eyes and resting my cheek against his.

I didn't open them until our bedroom door shut behind us and he had me pressed against the wall again. The immediate fire of desire turned into deep, glowing embers that would only need a tiny breath of air to turn it into a raging inferno, but before that happened, I needed to say something to my husband.

"I feel like I've barely looked at you," I admitted in a small voice.

He leaned against me, holding me in place so he could free one hand to roam over my side, hip, breast...I held my breath, only releasing it when he tangled it in my hair. "You haven't. And that's okay. I knew you'd find your way back to me."

Running my fingers through his thick hair, I admired the golden strands, so different from my own. People called me blonde, if they were being kind, but my hair was nowhere near the color of his. Mine was darker, honey blonde to those who liked me, dirty blonde to those who didn't. But both described by the same word...So strange, much like the incredible man who held me so carefully, who was so steadfast and sure of himself.

"You knew, did you?" I murmured, looking at him in awe, tears filling my eyes.

"You said it. 'In a hundred lifetimes, in a hundred worlds...'"

EASTERN WASHINGTON

"Wait for it," Grace whispered, one hand out to keep the DeGois family back.

Sure enough, the rumble of a vehicle preceded the thing itself. Grace held her breath, wide-eyed, watching the Humvee-like vehicle pass. Beyond the well-worn track, a chain link fence stretched, nearly invisible in the dark. Razor wire curled along the top, preventing anyone from going over.

Once the Humvee passed, Charlie urged the small family across the road. Grace, in the lead, ran quickly, dodging around a boulder. They'd chosen this spot because the boulder made both a good marker and a decent hiding spot.

"How...?" Carrie DeGois whispered, skidding down next to Grace, the last of the despair brought on by over two years in the occupied zone finally leaving at the sight of the narrow gap at the bottom of the fence.

"If there's one thing my sister taught me," Grace whispered back, "it's to think outside the box."

Clearing out the debris she'd placed the last time she and Charlie had come through, Grace helped Carrie through, then the children, followed by Frank DeGois. Charlie, the last to arrive, hunkered down beside her as the next patrol passed.

He shook his head. "Right on schedule," he muttered, giving his wife a quick kiss. "Off you go."

***

"How'd it all go?" Lieutenant John Sears, the shift commander, greeted them at the American fence.

His men hastily closed the gate, locking it once more. Medics ushered the DeGoises away, offering blankets and hot drinks. The children's exclamations at the hot chocolate were muffled when they entered the medical tent.

"Quietly enough," Charlie said, watching their ducklings leave. "Some new rumors from down south flying around. That guy, Captain—"

"We told you about him last year," Grace put in.

Charlie nodded. "The Captain and his team are ramping things up. It's impossible to tell truth from embellishment. Blowing up towns and mountains is pretty far-fetched, I know, but at the very least, the North Koreans are treating him like a serious threat. More troops have been sent south."

"Any news from D.C.?" Grace asked. "I was wondering if you heard anything about my brother, Private Peter Wilkins. Last time I saw him, he was on a classified mission. These days, that means here."

Sears hesitated. Then, glancing around, he jerked his head. They followed him into the trees surrounding the camp. Charlie took Grace's hand as they walked behind him, lacing their fingers together. Once they were far enough from the camp, Sears stopped.

"This is way above my pay grade," he began, "and I shouldn't have to tell you that this *never* leaves the forest."

They nodded. Fear lanced through Grace, and she leaned against Charlie, clutching his hand.

"I don't know much, just caught a glimpse of paperwork that I should not have seen." Sears stood at ease, hands behind his back, the familiar pose offering small comfort. "He was sent into Oregon. I don't know what for. Can't ask, either. Less than half the unit came back."

Grace gasped, sagging.

"What about Peter?" Charlie asked roughly, wrapping an arm around his wife's shoulders.

"Perry danced around what happened to the rest," Sears allowed, "but I got the impression they just didn't want to come back, not that they couldn't."

"Thank God." Grace closed her eyes, relaxing in Charlie's arms. He pressed a kiss to her hair, holding her tighter.

"Let's get you back to camp so you can rest." Sears gestured for them to lead the way. "When do you want to head out next?"

"We've been talking," Charlie said, his words drifting above Grace's head. "We're heading to D.C. first."

"I'd have thought you were done beating your heads against that wall." Humor laced Sears's voice.

"We have a contact we're overdue to meet," Charlie said.

Yes, they did. Hopefully, Constance had found some new information, something to give them a clue to how the invasion had happened. Who had dropped the ball this badly? The CIA said there hadn't been any rumors, but Grace, Charlie, and thousands of displaced, murdered, and captive Americans deserved to know the truth.

CHAPTER 31

*"We are conflicted, sure. As a Christian man, I find the fundamentalists'
behavior incredibly brutal, but at the same time, I can understand it. After
all, what else are they to believe but that they're being punished for the sins of
mankind? It makes sense to become stricter, and to try to continue their lines
by propagating..."*
Christian Channel TV

I sighed, leaning against Archangel's chest. We faced a tiny campfire, the chill evening air making me doubly grateful for his arms around me. I ran my hands up and down his thighs where they bracketed my hips. Sliding my hands down farther, I enjoyed the firm muscles under my palms, purring when he growled.

He shifted behind me. "If you don't stop that, I'm going to be embarrassed."

I snorted. "As if you're ever embarrassed. But fine. Distract me."

He nuzzled my neck. "Before you got me all hot and bothered, I'd been watching them." He jerked his chin to the camp spread out around us. The Irregulars were settling down for the night, people eating dinner, quiet talk, and the occasional snatch of laughter, all colored by the warm glow of little campfires.

"The resilience of the human spirit," he continued. "If you'd asked anyone four years ago if they could be happy like this, no phones, no TVs, nothing, it would've been a resounding 'hell, no.' But here we are. Laughing, loving," he squeezed me gently, "and generally enjoying life. What a thing."

Tipping my head back, I watched him from the corner of my eye. The firelight turned his blond hair red. He didn't say the obvious. We lived harder for those who couldn't anymore. It made us laugh louder, love more, and look for every opportunity to do and *be*, because we all loved someone who couldn't.

"And then there's me." He shook his head. "This is all just...*huge*. It's enough to make a man feel small. Give him some perspective."

I snorted. "Listen to the man," I said to the air. "He's talking like he's some schmuck who wandered in off the street. Well," I amended, "you did, but not like that. If there's one thing I've learned after being married to you for this many seasons, it's that you're up for the task. Most take one look at us and run screaming for the hills. Instead, you decided to join the lunatics trying to get their houses back. I mean, we're just a bunch of chicks trying to go home."

Now he snorted. "You're so full of shit it's a miracle the Valley hasn't flooded yet. 'Just' is a fucked-up word, you know that? It tries to take someone amazing and make it smaller. Just." His hand began exploring, snaking underneath my sweatshirt and harness. "You took a bunch of abused women and turned them into an effective, disciplined militia. Who else do you know has a regular army backing up and panicking over a ragtag bunch of guerilla fighters?"

"Second oldest story in the book," I assured him. "It's nothing new." I jerked slightly when his finger moved south, and my breathing hitched. "You shouldn't start something you can't finish, buddy."

He chuckled. "Who says I can't finish?" I waved around the clearing, and he laughed. "I already found a nice little spot, not too far, with some thick grass. If we're quiet and let Storm know…"

He bit my ear and I purred. "You're on. Wanna see who gets noisy first?"

Giggling, we crept through the camp as the rest of the Irregulars settled down for the night, stopping briefly to talk to Storm on our way out. Her lascivious grin belied her innocent looks when she told us to "Do things I wouldn't do."

Gotta take your opportunities where you find them.

***

Two weeks later, I leaned over the map, tracking our progress. Once out of the mountains, we'd split up into one- and two-vehicle groups—following Archangel's plan—and scattered, and now I tried to follow where we'd been.

As near as I could tell, we operated under the idea that Steve couldn't predict our movements if we couldn't.

"Someone's having a good day," Archangel commented, passing me his scope. "Southwest."

Peering in the direction he indicated, I grinned. "That's a lot of smoke. Do we know who went that way?"

He scoffed. "You're asking me? I still don't know how you've managed to track our progress."

"*I* haven't. Dereva and Hightide do that. I'm lost."

He leaned against the truck, his fingers playing with mine. "It's been a while," he murmured.

"It's been two days," I hissed, grinning. "You're incorrigible."

"We're honeymooners."

"We've been married nine seasons."

"We don't make love every day, anymore," he mourned.

I laughed, pleasure coursing through me. "Only when we're on the trail, and then you manage to make up for lost time when we're back at the Lair."

He snickered. "Whatever. Meet me in the trees before tonight's raid. It'll be the last chance we get on this trip."

I rolled my eyes. "Stop being so melodramatic..."

"You love it."

I did, but that didn't stop me. "Tonight's our last raid."

"Only because we ran out of shit to make bombs with," he pointed out.

True. And we were running low on ammo. Steve didn't have as much to steal as usual. We couldn't even depend on our invaders having enough shit to steal. What kind of losers were we dealing with?

***

Our return to camp before the raid wasn't as inconspicuous as I'd hoped. Poorly hidden smiles, open grins, and then, there was Storm. Who'd apparently been taking notes on indecent behavior from Phoenix.

"Well!" She looked at her bare wrist, then glared at us. Over at the sun, just below the horizon. Back at us. "*Where* have you been? No note! Just...gone. Right before a raid! I was worried sick!"

I growled.

Fighters sniggered.

"Don't you give me that, young lady," Storm said tartly. "At your age, you should know better."

Archangel mumbled under his breath, giving her the evil eye.

Storm cupped a hand around her ear. "I'm sorry? I didn't quite catch that."

Dereva choked on a laugh and my heart melted. I hadn't heard anything like that from her in a very long time.

"I said," he raised his voice, "you can tell Phoenix to shove it when she grills you on what we did."

"Oh, we know what you did." Eleanor gently untangled a twig from my hair. "You brought back half the forest."

"Shit."

"Language," Storm scolded.

After that, I couldn't keep a straight face anymore. Too bad we had a raid tonight, instead of sitting down for open mic. Storm was killing it.

***

I laid in the middle of the road, my ears ringing, struggling to remember what happened. Fighting. A raid. Our last? My side burned every time I breathed. My hand dragged across my front. Fine. Clean. Where…? I sucked in a breath and my back spasmed. I put my hand on the ground. It came away wet.

Screaming. Shouting. My name? What is my name? Gunfire. Shouting. So noisy…Shoving myself upright, everything swam and the ground swayed. Snarling, pushing against gravity, I got a knee up. Bright headlights hit me full in the face, a blow almost as grievous as the one that knocked me flat.

An engine roared, coming closer. The lights filled my world and screams filled my head.

"Captain! Captain..."

"HOPE!"

Shaking my head, I stumbled upright. I knew that voice, but it usually crooned, laughed, cajoled...loved. A dark shape split the light and memories of the last few minutes crashed through me, nearly bringing me down.

I'd been stabbed. A truck bore down, straight at me, and between me and it stood my heroic, idiotic husband, firing at a bulletproof windshield like it'd do something. The Chimera was close enough for me to see the spiderwebbed cracks covering the glass, and no matter how I struggled, I wasn't moving fast enough.

Still firing, he ran forward, leaping up onto the hood as lightly as a dancer, then slammed both feet into the windshield, jackhammering it into the car. I stared, open mouthed, as he sat on the hood, firing rapidly into the truck, then rolled backward, landing neatly on his feet.

Scooping me deftly over his shoulder, he raced away.

I grunted with every bouncing stride. "What...the fuck...was that?"

"It's what I'd been working on with Fuzz."

"You said it'd...probably never work! You said...it didn't have practical...applications!"

"For someone who just got stabbed and rescued from a Chimera about to run you over...you've got a lot of opinions about it."

Even upside down, I recognized my pickup truck. "Baby," I cried.

"Squirrel," he bellowed, lowering me gently. "I need Squirrel."

"I'm...alright." I smiled up at him, then gasped when he touched my back.

Squirrel appeared and the two of them talked too fast for me to follow. I looked back and forth, but everything went right past. "Rude."

"Look at her," Archangel finished.

They rolled me over, quickly cutting away my shirt. Squirrel pressed a flask to my lips. "Here. You don't want to be sober for this." After two swigs, the teenager pulled the flask away and pressed a thick piece of leather against my lips. "Bite down," she advised. "This is gonna hurt."

"Yaohaffabeshohaffpa," I mumbled through the gag.

Archangel tugged it out. "What's that, babe?"

"You don't have to sound so happy about it," I complained.

"Oh, for fuck's…" He stuffed the gag back in my mouth and laid next to me, throwing a leg over mine and wrapping his arms tight around me. "Do it," he said grimly.

I shrieked into the gag when the liquid hit my side and back, thrashing in Archangel's hold. When Squirrel pressed a pad to the wound, I sagged, too tired to protest the tightening bandage. Archangel cuddled me while she did this, helping shift me around. I protested half-heartedly, which they both ignored.

When she finished, he pressed his damp cheek to mine. "How bad is it?"

"She'll be fine," Squirrel said cheerfully. "It's a nasty gash, but she's short waisted so it bounced off her ribs and hit her hip. Don't worry, it just missed her ass. There's some muscles that'll need to heal, but no organ damage. Some blood loss. She'll fever, but if we're lucky, we can stay on top of it."

"Yay," I mumbled.

The pickup shook, fighters piling in. The engine rumbled to life, and I smiled up at Archangel. "Hear tha'? She's work…workin' lika scharm."

His laughter bounced pleasantly inside my head. "Nice to see you're feeling better."

"C'mon. Giz us a kiss." I puckered up, squinting to make him hold still. "Sssexy."

He kissed me on the forehead and adjusted me across his legs. I winced when the truck hit a hard bump.

"How is she?" Storm asked, balancing easily against the rocking truck.

"It missed my ass," I supplied helpfully.

Archangel shook his head. "Go to sleep. You're gonna feel like shit in the morning."

I sniggered. "Okay."

CHAPTER 32

I tossed restlessly, and every time I moved, I bumped someone new. "I hate this fucking truck," I grumbled, shifting. "And this stupid war, and this stupid road. I wanna lay down," I complained. "I'm thirsty."

Squirrel laughed, holding a canteen to my lips. "I swear, you complain more than any other patient I've had to deal with. And if you don't stop soon, we're taking a vote and I'm pretty sure it'll be all of us against Archangel to toss you out."

"Fine. Do it. At least it'll be still." Squirrel felt my forehead, her hand wonderfully cool. "Don't stop," I whimpered when she took her hand away.

Storm snorted. "Oh, great and terrible fearless leader."

"Fuck off."

Archangel chuckled, though he sounded worried. "As long as you respond like that, I know you're okay."

"Don't feel okay..."

I couldn't tell how much time passed. Interminable. Abominable. Slowly, and quickly, excruciating and dream-like. My side and back never stopped throbbing. Ages, days, minutes, or seconds later, grinding from the garage doors opening filled my ears as the blinding, aggravating sun finally disappeared.

Everything happened from a distance, people talking in shock, fear, worry. I rested my head against Archangel's shoulder, uncaring what happened out there. Someone else could deal with it. Archangel's chest vibrated when he spoke. I moved my hand up, over his chest, enjoying the sensation.

Archangel would take care of things.

I sighed, slipping into sleep once more.

***

Male voices spoke nearby. I smiled involuntarily at the sound. Archangel and Gryphon. My heart and my friend, going back and forth, sounding like they were right over my head. Archangel—it could only be him—stroked my hair back, tracing my ear. I sighed, turning into his hand.

"I can't believe that's the daft shite you'd been practicing with Fuzz," Gryphon said, sounding even more British than usual. "When I saw you jump on the windshield, I thought you were pisht in the middle of a bloody fight."

"It was just a stupid theory! I never thought it'd have a practical application. We were just...hanging out."

"I thought you were going to die, you git. All I could think was how was I supposed to explain this to your wife? You were so close to cocking that up. Don't do it again, mate."

Archangel's laughter filled the room, but his hand stayed gentle where he stroked my hair. "Why do you get more British when you're upset?"

"I am fucking British, you prick!"

Sleep pulled me back before Archangel answered.

***

The next time I woke, I managed to crack my eyes open. A single candle burned, sitting in a dish atop the stack of books I called a nightstand. I lay propped on my left side, my right...feeling carefully around, I discovered bandages and a good deal of soreness. My eyes burned slightly with every blink, like my eyeballs were covered with a light coating of sand.

My attempt to sit up ended as soon as I got to one elbow. I hissed, sinking down slowly. The mattress shifted behind me.

"What the hell do you think you're doing, woman?" Archangel asked, helping me back down. "The knife didn't go deep, but it did give you a hell of a long cut. You've been out for three days."

"Not too bad."

"No." He rested on one elbow, leaning above me, smoothing my hair. Reaching up to his face was almost too much effort, but I got my hand there, mesmerized by the sight and feel of his hair.

"How many did we lose?"

He hesitated, chewing on his lip, then went for it. "We lost Acorn, Manbat, Badger, and Grayman."

I closed my eyes. Manbat left behind a widow, Aspen. They'd been married shortly after Phoenix and Gryphon. Grayman and Badger were soldiers. Acorn, small, tough, yet so bright and hopeful for the future, was a basher.

But Archangel wasn't done there. "And Triskele..." My heart seized. Triskele was Kestrel's wife, her anchor in the midst of dealing with everyone's emotional hurts. "Triskele lost her lower leg to a bullet. It shattered the bone and by the time Doc got to her, there was no saving it."

"But she'll live?"

"She's not out of the woods yet, but Doc's hopeful."

Triskele might live, but we lost four. Four more down…The tears came thick and fast, and I let them flow. Holding them back only meant it hit you later, harder. He held me, careful of my side, while I cried into his chest.

When I settled, he pressed a damp cloth to my face, gently wiping the tears away. "Seventy-three people went out," he said quietly. "We lost four, but we managed to rescue thirty-one."

My lips twisted, bitterness a harsh bubble in my chest. "It's okay because we're refilling the ranks?"

"Shame on you, Hope." He nipped my ear.

"Ow!"

He readjusted his hold, easing the pillows further away and taking their place at my back. I let my head fall back and he pressed his forehead to mine. "Wouldn't you be willing to die to save people?"

"I don't know."

"Liar."

"Where are you in all this?"

"I'm the shield at your back."

I considered this. "And I wouldn't be leaving you behind?"

"As if you could."

I shrugged. "I'm surprisingly okay with this."

He chuckled. "Yeah. So why would you think everyone else in this mess doesn't feel the same?

"Don't use logic on me," I grumbled. "Pretty sure you're not supposed to use logic on a sick person."

"They rescued thirty-one people—quite a few kids, too—and went down fighting Steve. In this world, there isn't a better way to go."

My face crumpled as the tears renewed. "I know. I just don't want to keep losing people. It hurts."

He cupped my face, our foreheads pressed together. "I know. But you'll never be alone. I am the shield at your back."

"In a thousand lifetimes, a thousand worlds," I whispered against his lips, "I'd choose you."

***

After a week of bed rest, I was ready to crawl up the walls, but the best I could do was get Phoenix in. When Sirius died, my own mortality became even more real. Then with Peter, and now my injury...I needed to ask a favor.

She ribbed me gently, but I didn't respond. I needed to get this out, and it was hard enough. At my expression, Phoenix settled cross-legged onto the floor next to my bed, leaning her elbows on the mattress.

"When—*if* something happens to me..." I stopped blinking furiously. "I need you to be there for Archangel. You'll do it, won't you?" Phoenix opened her mouth, angry, but I held up a hand. "Don't argue the possibility. We both know the chances get higher every time we go out. I need you to say it. Please."

I couldn't hold the tears back any longer. I didn't want to leave him behind, and the thought of being without him was tearing me apart. I needed to know she'd have his back. Phoenix, blinking furiously, nodded.

"And," I cleared my throat, hating this next thought with every fiber of my being, "when he moves on, be kind to her, won't you?"

She covered her eyes, her shoulders shaking. "You bitch. You absolute bitch. How dare you!" I passed her a cloth to blow her nose. When she could speak, she leaned in close, her green eyes sparking angrily. "Fine, but only so you shut up about it. And if you think he'll move on from you, you're dumber than I thought. And most days, I think you're pretty stupid."

She bit her lips, staring up at the ceiling. A lone tear trailed down her cheek. "Not me. If I go and Gryph moves on, give the bitch hell. Make sure she's worthy of him. God knows I'm not, but the blessed man is too blind to see it."

"Deal," I choked out.

Unable to look at each other, we simply sat in silence. I hoped I'd never need to call in this favor, or respond to hers, but what were the chances?

I scrubbed my hands over my cheeks, unable to look this potential reality in the face. Knowing how unlikely it was that both of us would see the end was crippling, but knowing that Phoenix would keep an eye on Archangel for me helped.

***

Archangel entered our room, sitting next to me on the mattress. I put the book down, smiling up at him. "Get me out of here, will you?" Then his serious expression registered. "What is it?"

"River just got back. She didn't even wait for a Useless Room meet. Apparently, it's after we're active that Steve moves supplies. We need to hit them now."

I stared at him, mouth open in disbelief. "You're raiding without me?"

He shifted, resting a hand on my knee. "You have to admit, you're in no condition to go out. You've barely started physio."

I glared at him and unbidden, tears welled. "Who's going to watch your back? You can't go without me!" He gathered me close, careful of my back. I clung to him, my lips pressed against his neck. "We don't split up battle partners."

"Unless we have to," he said gently, warm breath fluffing my hair. "It won't be long, just a couple weeks. Just enough for them to think they haven't figured us out completely and grab some convoys."

My lips trembled and I pressed them together to stop it. We needed the gas, but still... "When are you planning to leave?"

"We thought tomorrow, but I wanted to check and see what you think."

"You mean I still get a say in all this?" I cursed silently. "I'm sorry, that came out cattier than I wanted it to."

He pulled back, just far enough to look at me. "If you were leaving without me, I'd be throwing a fit right now. Like, full-on, man-baby whining. Give me a good kiss before I go, and I think I can live with the cat."

I hissed like a cat, making him laugh. "About you leaving." He sobered, watching me intently. I sighed. I wanted to stay mad, but he was so adorable when he went serious. "As much as I hate to say it, leaving tonight would be better. There's enough moonlight to get you a good distance away so you can hit them sooner."

He smiled.

I narrowed my eyes. "You already wanted to leave tonight, didn't you?" I asked. "You just asked my opinion to make me feel better and like I still had some input."

His smile widened.

I grinned slowly and he looked worried. "This wouldn't be fair...if I didn't do this to *you* so often."

His mouth dropped open. "When the hell do you manage me?"

Sniggering, I leaned forward and planted a kiss on his lips. "Gimme a good kiss. You guys need to get going sooner than later." But even as I said it, fear and worry churned, a sticky morass of emotions I didn't like dealing with.

They were leaving me behind, and I didn't like it.

***

After their departure, I pouted for days, and it didn't matter because hardly anyone saw me. I moped around, limping with a cane until Kestrel took one look at me, grabbed my arm and dragged me to her room. She unceremoniously shoved me through the door and shut it.

"Here," she said through the door. "Keep each other company."

Turning, I found Triskele sitting up in bed, arms folded and a mulish expression on her face. The blanket lay over her legs, making it easy to see where one ended abruptly just below her knee. Sighing, I limped to the chair, slowly easing into it.

"Guess she needs a break from both of us, huh?" I said eventually.

"At least you're on your feet," she snarled.

"In my defense, they only just let me up. Not the same thing, I know." I raised one hand, half apologetic, half resigned.

She grunted, looking at the empty space on the bed morosely. "They're using the time to try to figure out a prosthetic. They've got 'Nansi on it."

I nodded. "Good person to have on it." We sat in silence for a time, and I kept staring at her foot until it finally dawned on me. "You lost the other leg. I mean," I hastily explained "the opposite of Porkpie. Between the two of you, you could wear a pair of shoes."

Her eyes narrowed, lips compressed. I'd put my foot in it again, hadn't I? And with someone trying to deal with the loss of a leg...I started to sweat. She grunted, huffed, then her shoulders shook until she burst into laughter.

"You're a bitch, but you should see your face," she cackled.

I slowly relaxed, sitting back in the chair. "Tell me something I don't know. Overall, how have you been, anyway? Sorry I couldn't come by sooner, but like I said, they only just let me up."

Shifting restlessly on the bed, she shrugged. "I don't know. How am I supposed to feel? I lost my damn leg and I can't go back in the field." Her gaze lowered. "Part of me is relieved. The rest of me is furious. I can't run anymore. I can't even walk!" She thumped the bed.

Her lips twisted and she pounded the bed with both fists. "I can't even walk!" she screamed. "They took it from me, and I can't take anything from them again. What the fuck am I supposed to do now? Who am I? I'm a scout. That's what I am. I go out, I scout, I keep you safe, and I kill Steve's scouts where I find them. Who am I now?"

I waited while she got it all out, and when she finally settled, too exhausted to continue, I passed her a handkerchief sitting on the nightstand and leaned forward. "You're Kestrel's *wife*," I said fiercely while she mopped the tears from her face and blew her nose. I waited for her to finish before continuing. "Above all else, no matter who else you may become, you'll always be her wife. Can that be enough for now?"

She heaved a great, shuddering sigh and nodded. "I guess that explains why Kestrel's been so happy most of the time. Because I won't be going out anymore."

I grimaced. "In her defense, her first time out was pretty rough. And she never went out enough to really use it as a coping mechanism."

Triskele snorted. "Have you been talking to her?"

"Of course I have. And even if I don't, Eleanor does and then talks to me. They're not wrong. We're not doing ourselves any favors, in the long run."

We kept talking quietly until the strain of sitting got too much for me. When I stood, Triskele sat up slightly. "Can I see it?" she asked.

Turning, I pulled up my shirt. I still didn't know the scope of the injury. They'd taken the bandages off to let it breathe. Triskele's fingers, warm with a lingering fever, traced over the scar. She had to tug my pants down slightly to reach the end. It stopped a couple inches into the curve of my butt.

She sighed, sitting back. "Nearly got your ass, there. Get your man to massage some oil or lotion into it. It'll help it heal so it won't be so thick.

Kestrel's already gathering some oils from the tannery and kitchen to use for mine."

I'd only taken a step towards the door when it flew open. Amana stood on the other side, her hair in a sleek black braid, her expression thunderous. "*Ai, Dios mio! Esta loca, que mierda una idiota, te arrojaré a los lobos!*"

I rocked back slightly. "What did I do?"

"Jou have been up too long! We tol' jou to be in bed!"

Kestrel walked up behind her, and I pointed. "Kestrel threw me in here! What was I supposed to do? I've been sitting—"

"Which you are no' supposed to do for too long," Amana interrupted. "Don't jou blame Kestrel. Come, nap time."

Taking my arm firmly, Amana led me from the room. I glanced helplessly over my shoulder, but Triskele shook her head, sinking down. "You're on your own," she said as Kestrel took my place in the room, shutting the door in my face.

"You know," I gasped, struggling not to flatten Amana with my weight, "this might be easier if you'd let me out of bed more often."

"No."

"Amana!" Eleanor's worried voiced bounced through the hallway. "Have you seen her?"

"*Si! Mama, ella esta aqui.*"

Eleanor ground to a halt when she saw me, her hand to her heart, skirts swirling around her legs. "What were you thinking, being up so long?"

"I got bored." We paused and I leaned against the wall, a sheen of sweat dampening my shirt. "It's not that bad of a cut. Why the hell is it knocking me sideways?"

Eleanor shook her head, taking my other side. We staggered down the hall, a drunken, six-legged monster, weaving across the hall. "Healing is hard work. I would've thought you'd know that by now."

"My last bad one was this." I stuck my right leg out, the scars from the mountain lion marring my thigh hidden under my pants. "I wasn't down that long."

Amana shook her head, breathing heavily. "Jou remember the snow? Nobody went anywhere. *Loca.*"

"I barely remember what I had for breakfast." We finally made it to my room and they eased me down. I groaned when my back moved. "I ain't falling asleep just yet. Distract me, Eleanor? Is the latest batch at Home already?"

Distraction was the only way to deal with pain. Doc needed what little magic potions she had for the bad injuries. Healing, especially pain brought on by overdoing it, didn't get the good stuff.

Amana huffed at me again, then left, her back ramrod straight.

"No, they're not." Eleanor straightened, arching her back, then sank gracefully to the floor, sitting cross-legged. "Some of them were in terrible condition and are still resting and healing. Oh, we did find a mechanic!"

I grunted, pulling my pillow to a more comfortable position. "Maybe I know them." That comment sank in, and my heart twisted. "Oh, shit, I might actually know them."

Eleanor pulled a needle and thread out, then a shirt. "How do you want to handle it, then?" Licking the thread, she threaded the needle and tied a knot.

I watched her working, the needle weaving deftly through the fabric, her stitches half the size of anything I managed. "Meet them in private, I suppose. We could bring them here..." I grimaced, shaking my head. "Nope. That'd look suss. Make it the Useless Room."

"Only after you have a nap," Eleanor said firmly without looking up.

I relaxed into the mattress, my eyelids heavy. "Okay."

"Humph. You should really rest for the remainder of the day and see them tomorrow."

"Uh, uh. I'd never sleep. Today. After my nap."

As if I'd be able to wait another day when a piece of my past might be in this bunker. I shifted slightly, trying to find a comfortable spot where my back didn't twinge or pull. Missing Archangel. The nights stretched out interminably without him near me. And without him, I had no way to allay my fears after the nightmares woke me.

But Eleanor's steady presence brought its own calm, and I drifted off, even knowing she wouldn't wake me.

***

Late afternoon, after sleeping longer than I'd intended, I sat in the Useless Room, poring over maps, bound and determined not to look nervous. Meeting someone without Archangel to talk to afterwards sucked ass, but at the same time, I couldn't risk running across someone I knew.

I had to know who it was.

When a tap sounded at the door, my heart leaped, then began beating heavily, my pulse throbbing. I fidgeted with the maps, then set my hands on it firmly. Pushing myself to my feet, I took one more deep breath.

"Come in."

The shadowed doorway only showed a shape, a tall man, thin to the point of gauntness. Eleanor hadn't been joking when she said people were too starved to be moved. The only light in the room belonged to a lamp in the center of the table, behind me.

He walked slowly, hesitant, a small hitch in his stride. Left side. I frowned. Nothing about him was familiar, not his shape or the way he walked. Maybe I'd gone through all this secrecy and anxiety for nothing.

Until he reached the lamplight. Turning to follow his progress, I saw the moment the light reached his eyes. His face had changed, his cheeks hollowed and his eyes haunted, but the rich blue couldn't be mistaken. The only person in this joint with eyes that shade of blue had been my cousin, Sonya.

I bit my lip, holding back the tears. "Will," I said, the slightest quaver in my voice. Will, Sonya's brother and my business partner. We'd owned a tiny garage in Silverton, scraping by, but it was ours. He'd been gone by the time we made it back to Silverton, never to be seen again.

Until now.

He jerked like he'd been slapped, then came closer, peering at me. I could've reached out and touched him by the time the spark of recognition crossed his face. His mouth worked, but no sound came out. He sank to the floor, tears spilling down his cheeks.

"Hope?" he croaked.

My legs gave out and I dropped into my chair, making it creak. "You're alive?"

"You're alive!" He toppled forward until his forehead rested on my knees, sobbing. "You're alive."

I bent as far as I was able, wrapping my arms around him. I don't know how long we stayed that way, grief at the separation, joy at the reunion, uncertainty, fear...It all swirled together in a maelstrom of emotion.

When we finally parted, Will had to help me upright, concern tightening his features. "What happened? Did they just bring you here? How did you get hurt?"

I wiped my eyes on my sleeves, laughing through the tears that refused to stop. "I'm okay. It happened around the same time you were rescued, I think. I've been here...a while. But where's your mom? Have you seen Jake? Your sisters?"

His face fell, his mouth working as he shook his head. I took his hand, hope dashed. "Okay. Tell me about that when you're ready." I bit my lip, terrified to ask, but at the same time, if I didn't... "What about Papa and Sean? Have you heard anything about them?"

He half laughed. "I forgot. You don't know."

"Know what?" I snapped.

He just shook his head, more tears falling, grinning. My hand twitched where it sat on the arm of my chair. I couldn't tell if this was good or bad. Maybe the pressure of seeing me made him crack? Then he stole my breath.

"Your dad and Sean are here. They were with me when we were rescued."

CHAPTER 33

I rocked in my chair, the stiffness in my back crawling up my spine, but I couldn't lie down yet. Will, perhaps wanting to bring some joy, insisted on bringing Papa and Sean to me right away. In truth, if he hadn't offered, I would have demanded. He probably remembered that about me, too.

I wanted to hunt them down myself, comb through the Lair until I found them. Instead, I was relegated to waiting—again—squirming, trying to relieve the pressure on my hip and lower back.

He had looked puzzled at my insistence that he not tell them about me, but he'd promised. Maybe he thought I wanted to surprise them.

The door opened behind me. Swiveling the chair, I waited, but the figures who walked through the door were even more unfamiliar than Will. Papa used to have salt and pepper hair, an increasing widow's peak, and a short beard. His hands were large, thick with muscle. He had a comfortable belly and he always smelled of grease and machine oil.

The man walking into the Useless room was bald, with just a fringe of white hair, and an unkempt beard. He was thin, almost skeletal, leaning heavily on a younger man...who was my other brother, Sean.

The main differences between Papa and Sean was that Sean had more hair and it was thicker, but not by much. He was taller, but just as thin. Sean's eyes burned with an inner light, an intensity that said he'd seen things he'd never be able to forget.

Will shut the door behind himself, urging them towards the table. Papa squinted, though I'd lit another lamp. Sean stopped abruptly, staring at me.

"Hope?" he croaked.

"Where?" Papa demanded. "Where is...?" He finally found me, but he squinted, struggling to see. "Is that you?"

"Papa?" My face crumpled and I leaned forward, a keening cry ripped from my throat.

"My girl!" He pulled forward and Sean hitched, trying to keep up.

I struggled to rise, but my legs failed me. Papa cried out, panicking. Making a last-ditch effort, I hauled myself to my feet, smiling and wiping the tears away. Papa crashed into me, his thin arms clutching me tight. I held onto him, pressing my face into his shoulder, shaking with the sobs.

I don't know how long it went on, but it ended with an arm around my waist. I jerked, an involuntary shriek ripping from my throat. I held them away, hand out, leaning against the table. The men circled me anxiously, as if a different angle would provide clarity. When I regained my breath, I lowered myself carefully into my chair and gestured them to some seats. Papa took my hand as soon as he could and held it gently, as if I were made of glass.

I smiled wryly, squeezing back. "I won't break, you know."

"What happened? Were you injured in your own rescue?"

I squinted at the table, hoping something would magically appear, at a loss for words. How to tell them? Scrunching my face, I shook my head. "What happened to you all?"

Yeah, redirect. Smooth, me.

Will sighed, rubbing a hand over his head. "You said you knew we were missing?" I nodded. "So you made it home." I nodded again. "We were taken. Mom...lost her temper."

I snorted a quiet laugh. Aunt Rose lost her temper? Say it ain't so.

He continued. "We were put to work in the sewers. All of us. Sophie..." He stopped swallowing. He'd only been married a couple years, but his wife brought a sophistication to the family the rest of us didn't have. "She was the first. The work and the plague got her. Mom, Dana, Trish...Jake was taken away. I haven't seen him since."

I closed my eyes. "Why did they do that?"

Papa snorted. "Do they ever need a reason?" he asked harshly. "All you have to do is look at them wrong. And the women..."

"What about you two?" I asked. "You look like..."

"Like we just got out of a gulag," Sean finished. "We know. When the first prisoners in the sewers died, they began grabbing anyone. We just so happened to be really fucking unlucky."

"Hope," Will sat forward, his hands clenched on the table, "where's Sonya? You two were out camping. Is she here, too?"

The corners of my mouth turned down and I looked away, all the pain rising as fresh as the day she died. He buried his face in his hands, shoulders shaking. Sean wrapped an arm around his shoulders, rubbing his back.

"How did it happen?" Papa asked. "And do you know anything about Peter and Grace?"

I cleared my throat, shaking my head. "Peter found me here."

"He's here?"

"Where's my boy?"

Even Will smiled. I hated it, but I shook my head. "No," I rasped. "And yes. He's...he's buried in the meadow."

I sat helplessly, watching my father cry, my brother moan, slumping against the table, and could give them nothing to ease the pain. I just held Papa's hand, waiting for them to get through the worst of it. When they calmed, I thought maybe we should break, but Papa wouldn't hear of it. He needed to know where I'd been, and what I'd been up to. I would've demanded the same.

"Well, to start," I smiled tremulously, "last I heard, Grace is alive."

"How old is this news?" Sean asked, rubbing at his red eyes.

I grimaced. "Peter told me. He'd seen her before being sent here. Although...um..." I scrunched my nose, bracing myself. "Her and Charlie were smuggling people out of Washington," I admitted in a rush.

"What?" Sean whisper-shouted, too weak to rage.

"Don't yell at me," I snapped. "I didn't put her onto it. She figured it out for herself."

"What do you mean, 'you didn't put her onto it'?" Papa asked. "And how did you end up here? What have they put my girl through?"

The sympathy in his eyes when he looked at me finally dawned. He thought I'd been amongst those raped. I shook my head. "Steve didn't do nearly as much to me as we've done to them. Their whole invasion was finished by the time we made it out of Opal Creek..."

I gave them the bare bones, and by the time I finished, Papa was even grayer and Sean buried his face in his hands, shaking his head over and over. "So," I finished, "if you want to know anything, ask them about Sirius and Hot Fuzz. Don't tell them you're related, just ask for stories. There's some good ones."

Will frowned, thinking, his fingers tapping on the table. "Wait...Sonya was Sirius?"

"Yep."

"I heard a rumor...only it wasn't a rumor, because some guys I worked with suddenly weren't there anymore. This guy, Sirius, stole a fleet of buses and broke like, a thousand people out in one night. Destroyed the gates and some guard towers on the way out. That was...Son?"

I nodded. The Great Bus-capade's legend had grown to a ridiculous degree.

"Hey," Sean rejoined the conversation. "Do you know Captain? Because that guy is nuts. Can we meet him? He's like, folk hero and legend rolled into one. They say he single-handedly killed a small army. Some people call him a ghost, because he walked through a whole encampment."

I shifted, frowning. My right hand twitched. "Um..."

Sean sat forward, his eyes blazing. "You do know him! I just want to meet him. Just once."

Papa and Will leaned forward, eager and excited by turns.

I squirmed. "Yeah, I'm..."

Before I could finish, there was a perfunctory knock on the door and Dereva stuck her head in. "Hey, Captain, it's almost..."

What she had to say was lost in the uproar. "Out!" I shouted. "Shut the door behind you, please!" She retreated, disappointed. Yeah, just missing out on all the drama. My patience wore thin long before the guys quieted. "Oi! Calm the fuck down!"

When they only got louder, I levered myself up. "Shut UP!" I bellowed.

Three men froze, wide eyed.

"Thank you so much for making this all really fucking weird," I growled.

"Why didn't you tell us you were Captain?" Sean demanded. "You give us this bullshit story and you don't even mention your new name?"

Papa sat silently, shaking like a leaf, mumbling, "No," over and over.

"Papa? Are you okay? Is he gonna be alright?" I asked the other two.

"You tell us all that, and you never said...?" Papa finally managed to get out.

I shrugged helplessly. "I didn't think you'd heard of me. So why mention it? I had a few other things to talk about, like the fact that you can't let anyone know we're family."

"Is there a danger of someone telling?" he asked.

"Nobody's gone running to Steve, if that's what you mean." Then I sighed. "But we've had people taken and tortured. Which is why the rule."

"Did you really kill all those soldiers?" Sean interjected.

"What about that town that got completely blown up?" Will added. "We were fighting fires for two weeks."

I wrinkled my nose. "Which town?"

There was a long pause. "How...how many towns have you blown up?" Will asked cautiously.

"Um..." I looked desperately around for an escape route. "More than one?"

"Have you blown up anything else?"

"Some cars. Maybe a mountain."

Papa moaned into his hands. "No. No. I can't take this anymore. My son, my daughters...No."

Another knock at the door, but this time it didn't open. "Give us one more minute," I called. I sat forward, trying to force them to recognize the importance of what I was about to say. "You really can't let on that we're family. I'd prefer it if you didn't let on that we knew each other Before, too. You can let them know you're Fuzz's—Peter's—family. That should be safe enough. But you've heard of me. You know, better than I do, what's being said.

"It sounds like I'm a hot commodity out there, which means you have to forget you ever had a sister, cousin, daughter, named Hope, and what she looks like. For all our sakes."

Chapter 34

Papa and Sean were to be sent Home as soon as they were strong enough for the trek. There were several others in bad shape who were taking their time, too. Will decided to stick around and help me with the vehicles, but he chose the dumbest name: Mechanic.

So, after getting permission from Eleanor and Amana, I took the newly named Mechanic down to the garage. But the name...

"What?" he asked defensively. "It's what I am. I'm happy I don't have to deal with computers anymore. Just good, old-fashioned auto work."

"Mood. Just...don't tell Anansi you studied chemistry, okay?"

"Why not?"

"Dude...The boy made Dirt Huggers using half-accurate formulas he found in a bunch of books the scavengers brought back. We didn't exactly hand him a book called *Everything You Need to Know to Make Booze*. He figured it out. And if his mom thinks you're leading her boy astray..." I shook my head. Will cringed and I laughed. "You met her."

We walked in silence for a while, and he kept glancing at me, his mouth working, but nothing came out. Finally, I sighed. "Will you spit it out already?"

"Why are you wearing guns in here?" he blurted. "Aren't we safe?"

I rubbed the shoulder harness where it buckled under my boobs. "Safe enough. We insist the newbies wear them to get used to them, and we do it to set an example. You're lucky I can't wear the thigh ones."

"Why can't you?"

"I can't wear a belt right now." *Duh.* We rounded the last corner, my cane thumping on the rough stone and I swept an arm out. "Here she is."

His lips pursed in a soundless whistle as he turned, surveying the space, my guns forgotten. The huge double doors, over fifteen feet tall, were against the wall catty-corner to us. The room itself was nearly two stories high, big enough to raise even the tallest vehicles up—if the hydraulics worked, and if the transports themselves hadn't been blown by Steve.

We only had twenty vehicles in residence, and most of these would never run again. All the best ones were out with Archangel and the rest. I used the ones here for spare parts. One corner held the small forge I'd made to fabricate what I couldn't find. Rolling toolboxes, work benches, and a board holding useless power tools neatly lined up took up the wall to our left.

He rested his hands on his hips. "I can tell it's your garage," he said. "It has that...tidy messiness you're so fond of. How do you have your list?"

"Things that need to be worked on go there." I pointed to the left, where a Chimera sat, hood raised. "Spare parts are there." I indicated the vehicles on our right. "All the good stuff sits in the middle, always facing the doors to make it easy to get out. Keys are left in the ignitions."

"Keys?" he interrupted. "Why do we have...Oh, right."

"Yeah, dumbass." I shook my head. "Anyway, I gotta go see about my physio. Try not to blow my shit up, alright?"

"That's your thing," he shot back. "I'm a perfectly respectable member of society."

"Hah!" I shouted, limping down the hallway. I turned back once to see him elbow deep in the engine. It was the most peaceful I'd seen him so far.

I slowed down, not eager for my session in the slightest. Kioni had taken over physical therapy, and she enjoyed it a little too much. Especially when I walked through the door. We'd made a rough peace, mostly because her kids chewed her out for chewing me out. Seeing them stand up to their mother...I shook my head. They were braver than me, but then again, she didn't want to murder them.

Still...I continued down the hallway, crossing the distance slowly. Barely inside Section One, I heard a commotion coming from the front door. I hissed, reaching for the left-handed gun. Steve couldn't have found us, could they?

The shouting increased and I eased to the corner, peeking swiftly around it. What I saw made me relax immediately and step out into the corridor, holstering the gun. Non-combatants filled the hall, flowing around the returning fighters, laughing and hugging them. I hitched along faster, looking for...

"Archangel," I cried, reaching the outer edges of the gathering.

His face lit up, changing in an instant from weary traveler to energetic lover. He pressed through the people, who parted easily. I liberally used my cane, thrusting it straight in front of me and pressing it against people to shift them.

The crowd parted and he stood before me, dirty, a bit ragged around the edges, unshaven, with his blond hair windswept and wild around his face, but *here*. Gasping, I dropped my cane, both hands reaching for him. He swept me into a tight hug, and I closed my eyes, sighing, finally content with my world.

He cupped the back of my head and my butt, careful to avoid the healing wound on my back, murmuring my name—my *real* name—over and over in my ear. "Hope. Hope. Hope..."

"You know," I whispered, "our room is literally *right* over there..."

We'd barely taken two steps when Seahorse breezed past, whacking his shoulder. "Stop it! Useless Room first. *Then*, you can get some nookie."

I sighed. "Fine. Where did you leave the cars? *Why* did you leave the cars?"

"It was getting too hot for Gryphon and Phoenix, so we took Steve for a run. Don't worry, your truck will be back soon."

We hadn't even made it to the Useless Room, trailing after Seahorse, when another group approached from the garage. No mistaking the tall, black-haired man at the front. Gryphon drew eyes no matter who he stood next to. Phoenix managed the same thing through sheer force of will, even when she was surrounded by taller people.

Phoenix hailed me. "You finally off the cane?"

"No. I ditched it. I'm tired of having to get around on my own, so when a hot man offers me his arm, you bet your ass I'm taking it."

Seahorse unceremoniously shoved the other two through the door. "Come on, people! I have a cold shower with my name on it. Let's get a move on."

Just before stepping through, I glanced down the hall and saw my dad, standing less than ten feet away. I nodded to Archangel, grinning. His eyes narrowed, then he shrugged. Guess one look wasn't enough for Papa's approval. Shaking my head, I let Archangel guide me through the door, back into the world of war.

***

"What do you mean 'nothing major'?" I demanded once they gave me a rough overview. "You came back on foot! You abandoned a vehicle."

"Yes." Archangel grimaced. "But it was that black truck you don't like. You said it was on its last legs. So, we figured, why not put it to good use?"

"That's not 'nothing major'!"

"Well…" Phoenix shrugged, holding up her hands. "When you think about our track record, it's pretty normal. Some injuries, sure, but we weren't looking for a full-on fight, so nothing too bad. We just needed to be a pain in the ass."

"Okay, so we're good, right?" Seahorse stood briskly. "I've got someplace to be."

"What? You got a hot date?" Phoenix asked. Seahorse froze and jaws all around the table dropped. Phoenix cackled. "You do? Go get 'em, girl! We can finish up here."

"One thing," River said after Seahorse left the room. "Shrike's been hearing some things about supply lines from the south. Like, staples are infested with vermin and there's been less ammunition. They've been having to piece it together, but they wanted to tell us good job on messing with that."

I frowned. "But we haven't. Unless there's been some lines hit and we didn't realize it?"

Phoenix shook her head. "We'd have noticed the food and bullets. No way we'd have missed that."

"Out of state," Archangel said. "My bet is out of state supplies. After all, you can't farm all year round here, but next door…"

"California." I arched my back. "Okay. Another operator. Farther south. What else from Salem?"

"Bad morale, the rumor mill is busy, and general unhappiness. Steve doesn't like leaving Salem. The last two weeks just blew their theory to hell and they don't like it." River scratched her arm. "Thing is, Steve doesn't want to stay. They've made the place a shithole to keep the residents in line, and they couldn't contain it as much as they wanted. Everything smells."

Phoenix moved to sit in Gryphon's lap. "They're nervous. We should hit them hard while they're off balance."

Gryphon shook his head. "No, luv. Think about it," he argued when she poked him. "Waiting will give them more time to stew in their own rumors. It's letting the whole mess ferment for a while."

"They can't stay put," I objected. "It'll make it harder for them to get moving later. If Kwan Jae is remotely competent, he needs a win. He'll send them out after us."

Archangel leaned forward, studying the map. "You're right. Some kind of big push..." He traced a finger over the roads around Salem.

My stomach dropped. "You think they'll try for the mountains again," I said flatly.

He shrugged. "Wouldn't you?"

"I'd have a fucking plan!"

He laughed. "I bet Kwan's got a plan. Last time they did a concentrated hit on the mountains, we were nearly trapped. So, we need to be a step ahead."

I sighed. "Looks like we'll be out of the Lair for a while, again."

He narrowed his eyes. "You're not ready."

"I nearly am. By the time we're ready to move out, I'll be fit. You're not leaving me behind again," I said when he opened his mouth to protest.

"You know what?" Phoenix hopped up. "I really don't need to hear the rest of this. I need this man," she hauled on Gryphon's jacket, "to tear my clothes off, then I'll find out how Seahorse's hot date went."

"Who is her hot date, anyway?" I asked

Archangel burst into laughter. Phoenix and Gryphon were already halfway to the door, in their own world. The others weren't far behind, but Eleanor chuckled, patting my shoulder gently as she passed. I turned to my husband.

"Are you done yet?"

"Yes. No…" He giggled. "You…are a wonderful woman, but you're blind as a bat," he said, once he'd caught his breath.

"Talk!"

Rubbing my thigh, he kissed my nose. "She's been seeing Sarge since forever."

My mouth dropped open. "The last time I heard Sarge say anything, he was a confirmed bachelor. Wife passed, he couldn't get over it, et cetera, et cetera. How the fuck did I not see this?"

"I love you," he said, pulling me into a kiss. "You're truly one-of-a-kind."

I sighed, my eyes slowly opening, pressing my forehead to his. We stayed that way for long minutes. He smelled like moist, growing things, dampness, and earth. I trailed my fingers over his chest. "I've already burned down a chunk of this part of the world. It's probably best there's not another me."

"You're not wrong. Now." He stood, pulling me to my feet. "I think it's time we had a real welcome, don't you?"

I laughed, but we were interrupted by a knock at the door. "Come in," I called.

Papa stuck his head in. "Are you decent?"

Without waiting for a reply, he entered, side-eyeing Archangel, closely followed by Sean. Archangel smiled politely. "Can we help you?"

Papa frowned. "Young man, is that any way to speak to—"

"I haven't told him yet," I protested.

"Why not?" Papa demanded.

"Oh, I don't know!" I threw up my free hand. "Maybe because he's just gotten back, and we've barely finished a meeting? I've hardly had time to say hi."

"Captain," Archangel said slowly. "Who are these people?"

He sounded suspicious, looking from Papa, to me, to Sean, and back. Once upon a time, it wasn't difficult to see the family resemblance. More than once, Sean and me had been mistaken for twins. We had the same dark blonde hair, light blue, almost gray eyes, and unfortunate nose. Now, he looked a good fifteen years older, his hair had thinned, and he'd begun going prematurely gray.

While we didn't share Papa's hair color—he used to have black hair—we did get our eyes from him. Now, in the dim light that was all we could manage inside the Lair, it was difficult to see them. Seeing my remaining family so weak and in pain just...hurt. My heart ached, and I wished Peter were still here, and Sonya, and everyone else we'd lost.

My breath caught and Archangel glanced sharply at me. I shook my head. He gave me a look that said we'd definitely be talking about all this later. "What haven't you told me?" he asked instead.

"Meet my dad." I smiled weakly. "And my other brother. Papa, Sean, this is my husband, Archangel."

"Mr. Wilkins." He immediately nodded to Papa but stayed by me. "You must be Sean. I'm glad to see you here."

"My cousin, one of Sirius's brothers, is here, too," I added. "Mechanic."

He nodded, his eyes crinkling at the corners. "Another mechanic is always welcome. Sirius's family, even more."

Sean frowned, folding his arms. He made a little moue of distaste, for what, I had no idea. Archangel was handsomer than a Greek god in my eyes, and he not only put up with me, he was delighted by my attitude and behavior.

"How long have you two been married?" Papa asked. "And why didn't you mention him yesterday?"

I laughed, my heart twisting. Why couldn't they just be happy for me? Papa had always wanted me to marry a good man, but Sean made it seem like he'd give me away to the first guy who'd look at me twice. I was happier than I had a right to be, even if not at this exact moment, and my brother hadn't had to go to any effort to get me married.

"We were a little busy catching up on the fact that I'm notorious and you can't know me."

After checking to see that I was okay, Archangel stepped forward, holding his hand out. "I wish I could really introduce myself, but you understand? Here, I'm known as Archangel."

Papa shook his hand, but Sean snorted, glaring.

"Sean," I rolled my eyes. "Knock it off. I've got ten year olds who'd see that look and wouldn't be able to resist beating you up."

The men flinched and Archangel shook his head. "Damn, woman," he murmured.

"What? You know it's true."

"Tell me about yourself," Papa offered, giving him a strained smile and ignoring me. "Where are you from?"

I winced. I'd told him we couldn't talk about the past, not ours, nor anyone else's. Archangel sighed, straightening his shoulders. Everything said he absolutely didn't want to stay, but he would.

"Papa," I protested gently. "First off, he's not telling you about his past. Second, he needs a bath and bed, not an interrogation. He's been out for nearly a month. I think."

"Bed with you?" Sean asked snidely.

"Damn straight," I snapped. "He's been away, or did you miss that part?"

"We haven't had you around for *years!*"

"I know that," I shouted, "but I'd rather..." I froze. *But I'd rather spend time with him than with you* hung in the air between us. "I'm sorry," I whispered, shrinking in on myself. "I don't mean that. I don't...I don't know how..."

I don't know how to be around you anymore. I don't know how to be with you and not think of how things were. I don't know how to be with you and not sob for those gone, because you remind me of what used to be.

Archangel rolled his shoulders. "Okay, everyone. To the table. We'll get to know each other for however long this candle lasts." He pointed to the shortest one. "After that, I get a bath and some time with my wife." His tone brooked no argument.

But Papa found one. "*My* daughter," he said sharply.

"Papa." I stared at him levelly. He rocked back slightly. "While I appreciate the protectiveness, it's not necessary. Especially with him."

Archangel sighed, rubbing his forehead. "Babe..."

"Let's just sit down," Papa said stiffly.

***

Later, back in our room, Archangel kept giving me weird looks, shaking his head while he undressed. The portion of the room not occupied by the mattress had been cleared and the half-barrel bathtub sat in the space, the water cooled but not freezing. I disarmed myself, hanging the harnessing and weapons on the hooks screwed into the door, right below Archangel's.

"What?" I asked.

"You gotta stop emasculating them," he said, gingerly sitting in the tub.

I knelt behind him, wielding a loofah. "I'm not! If they're emasculated, that's on them. I just said not to—"

"Not to bother trying to protect you," he finished, leaning forward, groaning when I scrubbed his back. "Which is implying they're not capable..."

"They're not. A good breeze could knock them over."

"...and if they can't protect you physically, let them protect you emotionally," he finished.

"Papa still asked that stupid question," I muttered.

He fell silent. What could he say? *Nobody* asked who they'd been or where they were from. The fact that Papa didn't know was a possibility, but...I blew out a breath in frustration. Then, the amount of naked man in front of me finally sank in.

"You know," I said conversationally, sliding my hand down his chest, lightly scratching him. "You're naked, in a tub, and we're talking about my dad and brother."

There was a loaded pause. "You know what?" he finally said. "You're right. You're not dressed for the occasion."

I laughed, leaning around to kiss him. He seized me, carefully pulling me around, into the tub. I shrieked, laughing.

***

Getting to the common room for breakfast, I used Archangel's arm instead of the stupid cane. Its constant *tap tap tapping* drove me nuts. Papa sat with Sean at one of the tables to the left of the entrance, where the newly rescued tended to congregate. The fighters and non-coms always sat to the right, closer to the kitchens, and the rescued didn't like to get too close.

What, were we scary?

Seahorse sat at the trainee tables with Sarge, which she often did, being an instructor when she was in the Lair. But now, I finally saw her easy smiles and the way she leaned into the big man.

"Someone had a good time last night," Archangel murmured in my ear, grinning wickedly.

I elbowed him sharply, snickering. He grunted, leaning dramatically on me. "Whoa! You do that, we'll both end up on the floor."

Chuckling, he straightened, placing a hand on my upper back until I got my balance back. Will—I sighed, mentally kicking myself—*Mechanic,* nodded as he passed us, headed to Papa and Sean with a plate. On the excuse of talking to the new mechanic, I towed Archangel over. Papa smiled tightly. He'd loosened up towards Archangel, but he griped that Archangel wouldn't answer his every question.

Especially not the one about how he planned to support me after this was over.

Part of me didn't want to see him at all, after the stabbing pain of a question we hardly dared contemplate. What would we do after the war? We'd talked about it once, but it was more like a pipe dream, something to imagine but never achieve. Other days, it seemed as though this current existence couldn't last much longer.

Having it thrown in my face, no matter how accidental, just rubbed salt in an open wound.

Sensing my stiffness, Archangel towed me away to our usual seats after a polite greeting and a few words.

"What's on the menu for you today?" Phoenix greeted us.

"Now that she's back in the Lair, I have an appointment with Doc. Hoping I get cleared for light training."

Archangel shrugged. "Cleaning and mending. I don't know why you bothered asking me."

"I bet I can finish faster and do a better job of it than you," Gryphon challenged him.

He snorted. "You're on."

CHAPTER 35

Doc's fingers were gentle on my back as she palpated the scar, checking for soreness and tearing. I sat in her infirmary in pants and bra while she examined that injury and a few of the others I'd sustained recently. After she'd cleared me for light training two weeks ago, she'd also insisted on more frequent check-ins to ensure I didn't damage it.

Gotta say, she knows her audience.

Small patrols went out to cause minor inconveniences to Steve, and they all reported Steve massing, ready to strike into the mountains. Usually, we'd hide in the Lair until they left. This time, we had other plans and I needed to be ready for it. Even Doc agreed.

"You're using that lotion daily, right?" she asked, straightening.

I grinned. "Oh, it's Archangel's favorite time of day. He's realizing there's *so* many places that really need it."

"Oh. Oh! Oh, my God," she groaned, smacking my shoulder. "I don't need to know that!" I looked over my shoulder to see Doc scrubbing her hands over her eyes. "I can't...Augh! It's in my head! Why, Lord? Why did you send her to me?"

"You're an atheist," I chided her, walking to the table to get my shirt. "And as I recall, I kidnapped you."

Doc laughed. "I'm grateful for it every day."

I'd barely picked up my shirt when the door opened without warning. A thin man stood in the doorway, black hair slicked down. He halted when he saw me shirtless, his eyes roaming over me.

"Oi!" Snapping my fingers to get his attention, I raised them to eye level. "I'm up here!"

"What," Doc interrupted, stepping between us and breaking his view, "the hell do you think you're doing?"

"I just...I came to see if you needed help with anything," he gabbled.

"Get the fuck away from my examination room!"

He left, but not before casting a last look over his shoulder.

I frowned. "Has he done that before?"

Doc shut the door, white with fury. "Once. I thought I'd made it clear then that he's never to enter when the door is shut without knocking."

"Who is he?"

"Remember that run on Chehalem?" she asked. I shook my head. "The winery. Pregnant women. Your knee?"

"Oh, right!" I scratched my cheek. "Where does he come into..." My eyes widened. "I remember, there was this dude who kept whining. Is that him?"

She nodded. "He's just...I can't put my finger on it. He's not bad enough to cut him loose, and I'd rather not have him around the children. He has some beliefs that I wouldn't want the kids picking up on...There's nothing concrete, I just don't like the guy. But he's useful, and he does the jobs he's asked to do."

I finished dressing. "What's his name?"

"Spartacus."

"You're shitting me."

"I wish I was." She shook her head. "I've overheard him talking to the injured about how he's going to be a fighter."

"Like hell!"

But after I left Doc's, I tracked down Amana to ask about Spartacus.

Her lip curled. "Faugh! *Es un complete gilipollas.* He thinks he should have the world. I think no."

"You want to get rid of him?"

She grinned evilly. "No. I make him clean *los inodoros.*"

I laughed. "Let me know if that ever changes. I don't think we'll find anyone willing to speak up for him."

***

When I found Archangel, I asked if he'd noticed Spartacus.

He frowned. "You mean that skinny dude who thinks he's God's gift to women, but at the same time, he's scared of you all?"

I cracked up. He waited patiently for me to finish, the corners of his mouth curling up when I finally straightened. "Yeah." I wiped my eyes, still giggling. "That sums him up nicely. What do you think of him?"

"He's a braggart. And he has an exaggerated sense of his own importance. None of which are crimes." He offered me his elbow and I took it, leaning into him as we walked down the hall. "On the one hand, he's making himself useful. On the other, no one really likes him. I can't help wanting to punch him every time I see him." He changed the subject. "How was your appointment?"

"I need to go to the yoga classes they're holding every morning in the gym. And I get another massage in two weeks. Oh, and she says we need to keep going with the lotion." I grinned up at him, biting the tip of my tongue.

He growled. "Then what are we still doing out here?"

***

Two weeks later, I'd finished my period. It'd been ages since my last one. By Amana's calendar, I reckoned my periods were coming every forty-five to sixty days. About as regular as any of the fighters, and a source of concern to Doc.

I figured it meant more time for bed play with my husband, which suited me fine.

I stretched my arms overhead, arching my back, groaning with the pleasure of moving without pain. He'd been so gentle with me, even when I begged him not to be, but today, we hadn't needed to hold back at all.

He stacked his hands behind his head, watching me through half-closed eyes. "Well," he murmured. "That's a sight a man can get used to."

I raised one eyebrow. "You mean you haven't?"

"Nope. But maybe you should keep moving around like that. See if I manage to get used to it. I think we should really give it a good try."

"Mmm." I rubbed my right leg, where the claw marks the mountain lion left me ached when the weather turned. "Scars and all?"

"Scars and all," he confirmed.

I followed the thin line of hair running from his chest, down his belly, then down further...I nodded. "I guess you really do want to give it a try," I said without taking my eyes from that one portion of his anatomy that couldn't lie.

He stood in one lithe move, his head cocked while he studied me. "You know...we're going to be out of the Lair for a while."

I tipped my head back the barest inch, until our lips were a breath apart. "We should make up for lost time. Before we lose it."

Crinkles appeared at the corners of his eyes when he smiled. "That shouldn't make sense. Is it bad that it made sense? Because yes." He scooped me up, walking until my back was pressed against the cold wall. "We really should."

***

Several days later, we gathered in the garage, preparing to leave for a month. With Mech's help, we had fifteen working vehicles of varying kinds, and two buses, one armored, the other reinforced. Not having to spend all my spare time in the garage was a blessing.

Except I had no way to avoid my father.

He stood off to the side with Sean, watching the proceedings uncomfortably. Yesterday, he'd tried to talk me out of going, saying I shouldn't put myself in danger. I'd nearly laughed in his face.

"You should leave this to the professionals," he'd tried next.

"As far as it goes, here, I *am* the professionals," I said, resisting the urge to roll my eyes.

Archangel sat in the corner of the Useless Room. The door was barred to prevent unexpected visitors. People would probably think it was just me and Archangel doing something kinky in the room, which was fine. As long as no one saw my family. Archangel leaned back in a chair, arms folded, biting the corners of his lips to hide a smile.

"He's a soldier!" Papa pointed. "You've got several more. Just...send them out."

Archangel laughed at that. When Papa spun on him, ready to chastise, the scout shook his head. "You got here all dewy-eyed about Captain, certain he was the biggest, baddest son of a bitch in the mountains. It was only when you found out Captain was your daughter you started doubting."

"You're right about one thing, she *is* my daughter, and I'll have you know…"

"That she's exactly the Captain you heard about. She earned her rep before I ever set foot in Oregon."

Once he realized he couldn't win that fight, Papa left in a huff, his eyes dark with worry. He wouldn't answer when I went knocking at his door to explain later. So today, I was simply glad he'd come to see us off.

Hopping into the bed of the pickup, the machine gun's barrel locked downward, the fighters gathered close. Outside their tight group, the non-coms of the Lair, the people who cared for us when we were hurt, mourned us when we died, who we lived beside and loved, formed a line encompassing the fighters.

As much as they cared for us, we protected them. We went out to try to win our homes and land back. Without them, we wouldn't be who we were. Instead, we'd be as bad as Steve, fighting because we were told to, or only doing it for the bloodshed.

Without them, we didn't have a purpose.

Warmth filled my heart, looking at them. Amana, standing arm-in-arm with Al. Driver and Lavender, hoping for a more peaceful world for their daughter. Eleanor, halfway between the fighters and the non-coms, the person I looked to when I couldn't see what was right. Kestrel, Triskele next to her, balancing on her crude crutches, looking both envious and relieved. Kestrel looked…lighter. Perhaps it was knowing her love was no longer in danger.

Papa, Sean, and Mech, more family here than I thought I'd ever see again. And the pain of being unable to acknowledge the relationship. The greater pain of knowing they didn't approve of the choices I'd made. Pointing out that they'd still be in Steve's hands if I hadn't didn't make them think any differently, but it had made Archangel facepalm at my lack of tact, so there's that.

"All in, all out," I called to the fighters.

"One shot, one kill. No luck, all skill!"

Still roaring, they piled into the vehicles, their farewells already done. I watched the battle partners piling into vehicles, shaking my head over how many of them were either married or together. It created a closeness in relationships that I'd never remembered seeing Before. Even Kestrel commented on it, getting all technical in the evening's quiet talks while we worked on little projects.

Archangel paused by Papa, exchanging a few quick words before jogging to the pickup and vaulting in, landing lightly. The GMC rumbled to life, moving out first. Under cover of the engine's noise, the scout leaned in.

"He said to tell you good luck. He's sorry he didn't say it to you himself. It seems they're due to go to Home in a couple weeks and…He didn't want to leave."

I nodded, leaning against him. "It's better for them to go Home," I said, more to convince myself. "They'll be able to rest, heal."

That didn't stop tears from gathering, and Archangel dropped his head, kissing my shoulder. "It's okay to miss them."

"If I miss them, I miss *all* of them." I wiped my eyes quickly, turning my face into the cold wind.

CHAPTER 36

T he season had turned while I'd been healing and recovering. Heading into the Valley showed just how far winter's grip had really gone. The frost covered trees flew past, white, brown, and green forming patterns that I could almost see, if only I had the mind to create.

The plan, like always, was to be a pain in the ass and fuck shit up. Dorothy, those collaborators who were on a massive power trip, and Steve had been sitting pretty in Salem for too long. This, supplemented with targets from Shrike, took us back to the city.

Time to fuck with Steve but *good*.

While I'd been down, smaller raids had gone out, to harass them and keep them on their toes, but it was time to make Phoenix happy and cause some havoc.

I knelt on a folded blanket, knees spread to maintain my balance over the broken roads, enjoying the chill air in my face. Until I didn't and pulled my scarf over my nose and mouth. I grinned, listening to the boys talk.

"I'm telling you, any good house should have a barbecue in the back-yard," Archangel argued.

"What? And ruin the view of the garden?" Gryphon returned. "Nah, mate. You have a nice little grill that you can roll back in the shed when you're done with it. Anything else ruins the look, mate."

"Not if you build it in right. Think of a raised section, built in benches on either side. You can put a grill on there, or even a stone to bake a pizza…"

"Pizzas need an oven! Are you completely cracked? My nan would be gutted to hear this kind of gibberish. Pizzas without an oven…" Gryphon shook his head, muttering.

"Either way," Archangel stubbornly argued, "it makes more sense than putting ketchup in salsa."

"Ew!" I interrupted. "Who does that?"

"My dearly beloved," Phoenix said dryly over my husband's laughter.

"It tastes good, and it doesn't turn your mouth into an inferno. You watch. We ever get some tomatoes, I'll nick some and make you try it that way."

"Not with the way you say tomato." Archangel said it the same way Gryph did, "toe-*mah*-toe."

"That's the proper way to pronounce it." He frowned down at Archangel from his position at the machine gun.

"Well then, answer me this: how do you say 'potato'?"

Gryph glowered and Archangel shouted with laughter.

"You know," Phoenix commented. "I think this is their first real argument as a couple. Is it possible the honeymoon's over?"

"Longest honeymoon *I've* ever seen. My honeymoon barely lasted a week before he threw me over his shoulder because I was about to talk some sense into that batshit crazy politician at Home. 'Bout time, if you ask me."

"We didn't!" both men chorused. Then they watched, thoroughly unimpressed, when we fell over ourselves laughing.

**

I basked in the sun, hidden from the breeze, watching Salem's perimeter through my scope, my right hand tucked under my chin, keeping my fingers warm. I relayed what I saw to Legs, who sat comfortably behind a bush, leaning against her pack. The scout had developed handwriting neat enough to be read by everyone, so she always got these types of jobs.

Pens were so...inefficient.

Hidden behind a hill and a thin line of trees, the Irregulars napped in the sun, went over their weapons for the millionth time, or snacked. Archangel was out with most of the scouts, checking the perimeter and our way forward.

Photographer, out on his first major foray, wandered around, snapping candid photos, fascinated with the minutiae of a large group out on a mission. It'd taken this long for him to learn the skills necessary to come out with us and stay safe, but if Sarge put his stamp of approval on a man, who was I to gainsay him?

"So far, there've been three watch changes, and that's the only time Steve's ever on the ground." I summed up the day, shaking my head.

"Up in their towers with their big guns..." Legs shifted, peering across No Man's Land. "Scared little men. Do you think they're...compensating?" she asked, extending and wiggling her pinky, grinning evilly.

I grunted. "Gates are opening...Aand it's Dorothy! Finally making an appearance!"

"Do you see my loser husband?" Doc called from where she stretched out on her bedroll. "If you do, I'll get Phoenix and that ridiculously big gun of hers."

"If I see a ginormous man, I'll let you know." I didn't take my eye from the scope, following the truck Dorothy drove on the dirt track around the perimeter, little more than two wheel ruts, disappearing into either direction. "Don't quote me on this, but I get the idea they follow that track a lot."

I shook my head. What was the point of driving around the perimeter? Added security? The illusion of doing something about us? Flushing us out of hiding? My bet was on the illusion. I yawned, gluing my eye back to the scope.

We'd reached this spot around midnight and had someone watching it constantly ever since. I wished—not for the first time—that I was a scout. Running around looking for a working bridge across the river like they'd been doing the last few days, or hunting for Steve and Dorothy through the underbrush like today was more fun than this.

"How do you feel about the plan?" Legs asked. "Think it'll still work?"

I shrugged, glancing over my shoulder at the fighter. "They're looking, but I don't think they're *seeing*. Too scared. And we already know they don't leave their safe zones at night. I'm still liking it. What do you think?"

Legs nodded thoughtfully, staring at Salem. "I think we'll have to go slow and careful, but we hunt a lot."

Phoenix came over with her rifle, kicking my feet lightly. "Your turn to take a nap, Captain. I've got this one."

I curled up in my bedroll, closing my eyes. Sleep was elusive, and I had other things on my mind anyway, mainly how many people we had who'd never hit Salem before. It'd been...ages. Seasons? Since we'd last hit the city. There was so much activity outside of it, so many things to mess with, especially once Steve began setting up their farms and taking pregnant women out of the city to keep them safe from disease and us.

Laughter nearby made me crack my eyes open. Mouse, sitting with her friends, Feisty, Squirrel, and Ink. This was Mouse's first big raid. She'd done well on the smaller ones, but these things were a crapshoot. You could do everything right and just be in the wrong place at the wrong time. Like Sirius, Fuzz, and Jewel...Like Acorn, Grayman, Badger, Manbat, and everyone else we'd lost.

So many people. So many fighters, lovers, *humans*.

I listened to the quiet chatter, the laughter, and as I drifted off to sleep, I couldn't help but wonder: Who would it be tonight?

***

A rustle in the early evening woke me just enough to smell sweat, green things, and dirt. I smiled. Archangel was back. He pulled his moccasins off and slid into our bedroll as I drifted back to sleep.

Footsteps rustling through dry leaves woke me next. The Celt hissed for the fighters to wake up. I shifted, smiling at the heat radiating from the man at my back. Turning over, I threw a leg over his, running my fingers through his hair, lightly scratching his scalp to wake him.

He mumbled a protest, pressing closer, our noses brushing. "Sorry, babe," I whispered in his ear. "But it's time."

"I just got here," he grumbled.

I bit my lip. Poor man. The scouts had all been on the run the last couple of days. Throwing back the blankets, I rolled up while he hissed, shivering at the sudden rush of cold air. Finally opening his eyes, he glared at me. The moon would be setting in the next couple of hours, but there was enough light for me to see him glaring balefully at me. Reaching for his moccasins, I handed them to him and pulled on my own.

Once everyone was up, things moved rapidly. We had our gear stowed within minutes. The moon moved another finger width closer to the horizon as we erased all signs of our presence and piled into the cars.

The vehicles started with barely a rumble, the repaired mufflers working like a charm. The buses and two Chimeras went directly north, angling for the eastern side of Salem. The bulk of our forces headed south and west, crossing the only bridge spanning the Willamette for fifty miles.

The bodies of the bridge guards were stowed underneath the thing they were meant to protect, and we rolled through with barely a pause. From there, we turned northwest, where the trees slowly gave way to farmland. Drivers kept their lights off and navigated by moonlight while we muffled everything in blankets to prevent sharp sounds from carrying through the air.

I knelt, shoulder to shoulder with Archangel, watching the city's few lights flickering. Clouds slowly built up overhead and I shook my head. Rain. It would help, but it still sucked. No way we'd keep everything dry tonight.

Dereva drove confidently through the country lanes, the roads changing from gravel to pavement and back again. The convoy followed, silent but for the gentle rumble of engines and tires crunching over gravel and broken roads.

Our destination was a stretch of road that didn't look much different from anything else until you walked through the thin line of trees. There, just past the trees, lay No Man's Land, the cleared space Steve had built around the city to prevent us from sneaking up on them again.

Mouse, stationed by the GMC, silently passed me the knotted end of a thick rope and began playing it out when I headed into the trees, the end of the rope slung over my shoulder. Archangel, at the next truck, took another rope from Feisty.

Three more pairs of vehicles were stopped behind us at two-hundred-dred-yard intervals. Other vehicles were scattered in between, the fighters slowly making their way into No Man's Land.

The ropes snaked through brush and grass, leaving a narrow trail. The clouds finally delivered on their promise and a light drizzle started. It was the kind that misted over clothing and took a while to soak in but could go on for hours. Some Irregulars slowly passed me up, though occasionally, my rope seemed to move of its own accord and the going got easier for a few yards.

Everyone headed towards the towers, evenly spaced two hundred yards apart. I slithered into a shallow gully, grass cleaning a bit of the mud from me before going back into mud. Crawling around a shallow rise in the ground, I nearly bumped into Archangel.

"How's it hanging, hot stuff?" I whispered.

"Well, the drizzle started at the right time. I might make it out of this with my ass in one piece."

I hitched my rope higher over my shoulder, freeing a hand to run down his back, patting his butt. "I certainly hope so. I like your ass just as it is."

Invisible in the dark, I'd seen his butt often enough in those pants to visualize it easily. The fabric cupped his round buttocks, giving lie to the belief that men couldn't move in snug pants. He could climb, crawl, and fight, and all that happened is that the tactical style pants outlined his ass. We called the phenomenon 'tactical buttcheeks.'

I halted, stopped by my rope. Digging my toes in, I heaved, keeping one hand on the rope. Still stuck. Cursing silently, I twisted, struggling to loosen it. Archangel paused, glancing over his shoulder, but I tapped his leg, signaling him to continue.

Loosening my belt, I ran the rope underneath, tightening it as much as I could. Using hands and toes, I lunged forward, the knot the only thing keeping the rope threaded under my belt. Gritting my teeth, I grunted, straining forward.

The rope gave way suddenly. I plowed face first into the mud, my eyes scrunched shut to protect them. I panted, face in the grass, catching my breath. When I started forward again, I glanced ahead. Only one hundred feet left.

So little.

So much.

Periodically, Steve shone their lights out, into the darkness, over the empty ground between city and forest. The ground was torn, pitted by shovel and axe, marked by two wheel ruts mere inches from my hand.

When the lights swung my way, I buried my head in my arms, thinking muddy thoughts, half in, half out of a hole. As soon as it moved, so did I, crawling as quickly as I could to make up for lost time.

The Irregulars distributed themselves around the base of the tower, hidden from prying eyes as lumps of dirt, scraggly grass, or in the shadow of the structure itself. Hands joined me in pulling a little more rope, just enough to reach the legs closest to the city. Once the rope was wrapped and tied, I planted a little something at the base, burying it like Sparrow told me to.

Archangel had already finished with his and waited for me, drawing me into the space between the struts. The rest of the Irregulars made their slow way towards the fence, spreading out, moving so slowly I could barely see them.

I wiggled in anticipation, my heartbeat speeding up. This and Archangel were what I lived for now, and Steve was about to get the surprise of their lives.

The steady drizzle soaked into my mud-streaked battle braids, trickling across my scalp in cool lines, warm by the time they reached my neck. Tipping my face back, I stuck my tongue out, catching a drop. The searchlight flashed overhead, sweeping across the ground. Archangel pressed me against the strut, his mouth by my ear.

Would they see the ropes through the mud and grass? They left suspicious lines in the ground, but at the same time, this was so audacious. I tensed, ready to leap into action, and Archangel leaned into me, shaking his head, his hair brushing my cheeks.

I gripped his sides, heat flaring through me. I could take him right here, right now, and the temptation was almost too strong. He squeezed my hips.

My breath caught in my throat. "If we weren't about to light this shit up..."
he whispered.

"I'd trip you and beat you to the ground."

The light returned to its original position, pointed at Salem.

"It's time," I murmured.

Reluctantly, slowly, he released me and wormed back to the other support. Pulling out the little lighter, I lit it, shielding its glow with my body and the support, lighting the short fuse. According to Sparrow, we had a quick count of five to get away. As soon as the fuse sputtered to life, I bolted towards the fence, angling away from the tower.

Everything happened simultaneously. Steve barely had time to notice us when two *pops* at the base of their tower lit up the night, swiftly followed by three more pairs at the next towers. The small explosion was the signal. Ropes tightened, springing up, out of the grass in straight lines. Two bashers knelt on the ground, aiming at the next tower over, squeezing shots off.

The timbers of the struts, cracked from the tiny bombs, groaned and gave way. The entire tower fell towards the fence, the men inside gripping the railing, their mouths open in screams lost in the noise. I screamed, punching the air when the tower took out the fence. We raced forward in an undisciplined mob, scrambling over the broken wood, into Salem.

Shouting from inside the fence added to the din as people woke, confused and...I cocked my head. Yes, definitely afraid. Sparrow, carefully climbing over with a crate in her hands, began passing out small bottles of Dirt Huggers. The little Molotov cocktails were immediately put to use, the fighters throwing them against any building.

Steve and civilians rushed out of buildings and the fighters began choosing their fights. I lit and hurled my little bottle, shrieking when it shattered, scattering fire over a wall. Grabbing a civilian woman, I shoved her back, towards the hole in the fence and away from the fighting. The rest of the Irregulars pushed civilians into buildings, to the ground, or out of the way.

Archangel bulldozed a man to the ground, snatching something up as he passed. When he reached me, he held out a machete, the blade wider than I was used to but unmistakable.

"Got you a present while I was out, dear," he shouted, grinning.

"Aw, honey! You're too sweet." Holstering one of my guns, I took it, swinging it experimentally. It'd take a bit of getting used to, but it had a nice heft and balance. Not as good as my swords, but it was truly sweet of him to grab it.

Putting a hand on my back to usher me forward, we headed out to our objective while around us, the city burned.

***

Shrike had given us an address and a name: Kwan Jae. The only other thing on the note was a request that we make it look like reaching it was an accident. The only way we'd come up with to achieve both was to hit Steve's Green Zone.

While the snipers scaled the taller buildings, guarded by their bashers, a small group of us headed deeper into Salem, creating an untidy line of fighting. Steve, thoroughly disoriented by being attacked on the safest ground they had, struggled to rally and organize.

Gryphon and Phoenix found us, falling in on one side. Then Gummy, Anarchy, and Goliath, followed by Ink and Nebula. We headed deeper into Salem, quickly making our way through the streets. Other Irregulars followed, more intent on causing as much chaos as possible.

If we did our job right, Steve and Dorothy wouldn't notice Eleanor, River, Evenstar, and the rest on the eastern side.

Smoke billowed into the damp air, most of it from the small bombs Chaos and Sparrow used generously. And whenever Steve saw Gryph or Archangel, they'd panic, shouting *"Seonjang yulyeong!"*

Sung Ki raced out of the darkness, laughing wildly. "Ghost Captain," she cried. "They are afraid of the Ghost Captain who kills in the night." Without waiting for a response, she disappeared, accompanied by Thorin.

They were the last two left from the small band that went to Idaho with Sirius and were inseparable. The young man had gotten some tattoos to commemorate those fallen, a practice spreading through the Lair as quickly as Ink could get her hands on more...well, ink.

Archangel shook his head, staring after them. "Sometimes those kids worry me."

"Really? *That* worries you? I'd worry more that someone's gonna shoot me, if I was you. Killing Captain would be a feather in their caps, and you look more like someone named Captain than I do."

"Well, yes," he said equably, shoving me against a wall, away from incoming fire, flattening me there with his body. He waited until the machine gunfire slowed. "But if they get me, they're not killing Captain, are they?"

A small group of Dorothy ran past, the American collaborators armed with cudgels. "Yes, they are. We made a promise, remember?" I fired three quick rounds, still shielded by Archangel's body. "Where you go, I go, too. Don't think you can hog all the stupid martyrdom."

Dorothy scattered and the Irregulars, staying with their battle partners, made short work of them. Poor bastards didn't think women could be a threat until it was too late.

"Found it!" Ink cried, her shout rising above the screams, shots, and small explosions filling the night.

Sure enough. A whole line of Steve, intermixed with Dorothy, formed a wall around a small group of big houses. The housing was new, with landscaping too short and immature to hide behind or provide any significant cover. A fence had been built around it, containing the members of Steve's government in there as thoroughly as they contained the people in Salem.

What did it say about them, to have fences within fences? Did that still make them the masters, or free?

Phoenix, spotting a suitable perch, flicked her fingers in a jaunty wave and disappeared, shadowed by Gryphon. I tilted my head, studying the lineup. Steve had guns, Dorothy had machetes and clubs. Their attention was on the havoc just a block away. I pointed to the north. Get around the side, maybe surprise them.

"At least Phoenix can't miss," Archangel murmured as we trotted down alleys and side streets to reach the new angle.

Once situated, Gummy and Archangel gathered everything combustible and throwable—six Molotov cocktails and eight grenades—and prepared to move in. Archangel took my elbow, pulling me to the side. I gripped his shoulder harness, tugging him closer.

"You better come back on your own two feet," I whispered, our noses nearly touching. "If you don't, I'm going in there to get you."

He kissed me, harsh, desperate, and I responded the same way, savoring the taste of him, his stubble rasping against my skin. "Watch my ass," he said when he pulled himself away.

"Best ass in the militia." I grinned tightly, forcing my fingers open. And watched him walk away, his shoulders squared, a jaunty bounce to his step that disappeared the moment they left deep cover and he switched into stealth mode.

He and Gummy wormed their way closer, not having to worry about staying quiet. The Irregulars made way too much noise for that to be an issue. The women disappeared, finding another angle, while I sighted down my rifle. Goliath, his dark skin providing all the camouflage he needed, grinned and hefted a bazooka onto his shoulder, ready to fire once he had a target. Anarchy stayed by him, ready with a single reload.

I grit my teeth, swiping rainwater from my eyes with my sleeve. "Do me a favor. Don't shoot my husband." I swallowed the lump in my throat, watching him crawl towards the enemy. "I'd like to keep him a while longer, please."

I wasn't just talking to Goliath, there, but pleading with a higher power that I hoped still listened. Before I could continue, Phoenix's big gun spoke, and the game was on.

***

We raced away, several plumes of smoke billowing up despite the rain. Goliath managed to put a hole in a house, Archangel and Gummy decimated the guards around the perimeter, and we were all getting away in one piece.

Gummy's accuracy with a throw was remarkable. His lanky form, distinctive from Archangel's sturdier frame, had risen when Goliath put a hole in the house, and he'd landed a grenade right in the middle of the living room. The level of damage was invisible, but he still grinned as we ran away.

The women joined us along the way to collect Phoenix and Gryph, while Steve and Dorothy scrambled to get their shit together. Glancing back, I spotted a small group, maybe ten men, running after us and more organizing.

"Run faster," I cried.

Archangel slowed to clap Gryphon on the back when bullets started flying around us. When a man grunted, I turned back to see both men tumble to the ground. "Archangel!" I screamed, whirling.

"Gryph, baby!" Phoenix was hot on my heels.

The few feet between us seemed to stretch into infinity, my feet never carrying me closer. Neither of them moved and my heart climbed into my throat until suddenly, I was at his side, sliding in on my knees. The rest laid down cover fire and I grabbed Archangel's shoulder, pulling him roughly back, my breathing ragged.

Struggling to speak without crying, I patted his cheeks, then ran my hands over him, looking for an injury. His eyes fluttered open as I pulled his beanie aside, revealing a dark patch in his light hair. Touching it gently, he groaned and my fingers came away wet.

"Oh, my God," I bent over him, relief coursing through me. A graze, very shallow. He'd have a hell of a headache, but he was already recovering.

I spared a glance at Phoenix and the blood froze in my veins. She rocked Gryphon's still body, keening, pressing one hand futilely to a wound in his side. "Sorry, babe," I whispered to Archangel, sliding out from under him. Stripping off my harness, sweatshirt, and t-shirt, I bunched the shirt, pressing it against Gryph's front. My tank top went over the entry wound in his back. Phoenix desperately held them down, sobbing now.

Rolling the sweatshirt up, I wrapped it around his middle, pulling it as tightly as I could and tying it with the arms. Goliath, abandoning the bazooka, scooped Gryph over his shoulder while I slid the harness back on over my bra. Ink and Nebula guarded him and Phoenix in their wild run back to the fence.

Spinning on my knees, I snatched my rifle up, firing as rapidly as I could work the pump. Anarchy picked their shots more carefully while Archangel stumbled to his feet, grabbing the back of my shoulder harness, pulling me up. He wobbled on his feet. Getting his arm over my shoulder, casting one last backward glance, I caught a glimpse of a huge man with a buzz cut.

Fucking Sutter.

I owed him for Lightning and Thunder. If this cost us Gryphon, I'd never beat Phoenix to the man. I wouldn't collect this round. I watched Sutter run into the dark, following a small band clustered around a slender couple.

Me and Anarchy practically carried Archangel through the war zone, hustling back to our lines. At the fence, most of the buildings had been reduced to rubble. The few still standing showed the occasional, anxious face that quickly disappeared. Bodies lay scattered, most moving feebly, none of them mine.

"Seahorse," I bellowed, striding through the hellscape.

"Captain!" She popped out from behind a wall. Joining her, I found people using the wall as a cover to evacuate from Salem. "Nearly all out," she reported. "Waiting on three. Haven't spotted them yet, but I'm hearing gunfire from over there."

Gently depositing Archangel down, I checked his head. Shallower than I'd thought. I relaxed slightly, finally reloading my rifle. "Babe," I glanced up. He swayed slightly. "Back to the vehicles."

"I'm not leaving you," he said stubbornly.

"You're in no shape to come with me," I snapped, worry making my voice sharp. Head wounds could be so unpredictable, and I couldn't risk him.

"Then I'll wait for you here" He folded his arms, glaring, the motion ruined when he winced, pressing a hand to his head.

"He was grazed," I informed Seahorse. "Get him out when you can. I'll go after the kids."

Racing around the wall, I followed the noise to find Feisty supporting the Celt while Mouse provided cover fire. I shouted, letting them know who I was as I ran to them. Unslinging my rifle, I bent, ready to lift the Celt.

"What? No, I can do it," she said determinedly.

"No time," I snapped. "We need to move."

Mouse, just a few feet away, jerked, collapsing bonelessly, a hole appearing in the side of her head. Feisty screamed, lunging. Catching her belt, I pulled her back. "Get the Celt."

She snarled at me, tears in her eyes, but obeyed, getting the Celt's arm over her shoulder. I tossed her my rifle and she left, half carrying the Celt away. No way was I letting her go on what would become a suicide run. Not losing another fighter, not today.

Firing continuously with a handgun, I paused only long enough to go into a diving roll, scooping Mouse over my shoulder in the process.

Drawing a fresh handgun, praying it still had bullets in it, I retreated with Mouse over my shoulders. Little Mouse, just a teenager. The best commander of the perimeter guard we'd ever had and a solid member of the Irregulars.

I gasped, half sobbing, as I ran back to the fence. Ahead, Seahorse, Archangel, and a few others provided cover fire. My entire body demanded I sit down and howl my grief to the skies. And Mouse jolted and bounced against me, never protesting, relaxed in death as she had never been in life.

Chapter 37

"We're at a rally being held in front of the White House. People are holding signs calling for the President to take action to free Los Angeles. But we have to wonder, what kind of repercussions will we face if we do? The last time we fought back, first Georgia was bombed, then Maine. The country can't take another blow like that..."

The Morning Show

The vehicles had long since abandoned the relative safety of the trees to give us less distance to cover, pulling up just outside the mess left by the tumbled towers. As each vehicle filled up, it took off into the trees, carrying the fighters to safety.

The last few fighters at the fence parted to let Feisty and the Celt through, closing ranks as soon as I passed. The corners of Seahorse's mouth turned down when she saw Mouse and the blood. I shook my head, and she pressed a hand to her stomach, her face twisting with pain.

Archangel placed a hand on my lower back, ushering me through the tangled remains of the fence and tower. My GMC, the hospital van, and a Chimera were the last ones waiting, their engines running and facing away from the city.

Doc knelt in the van, straddling a wounded Dionysius, her and Squirrel fitting one last badly wounded person inside, their face obscured by a bandage.

"I don't have more space," Doc said grimly without looking up.

"Mine doesn't need your help." I continued past, to the pickup, only brought up by Doc's question.

"Who?"

"Mouse."

She swore softly but her hands never hesitated, deftly putting the last five stitches into Dionysius's side. As she moved on, Squirrel replaced her, wielding bandages. Seahorse, after a quick check, slid the door shut and rapped on the roof. The driver, mindful of the injured, took off for the road.

The last of us piled into any spare space, dirt flying as we raced away, right before a fresh wave of Steve poured into the hellscape we'd created.

Laying Mouse down in a corner of the pickup, I turned to see if there was anything I could do to help the living. Gryph lay sprawled, so tall they'd draped his legs over the tail box. Hightide, instead of riding shotgun and navigating like usual, worked feverishly over the injured man, assisting Goliath while Phoenix kept her fingers pressed against his neck, desperately reporting on his pulse.

Nothing I could do there, so I went to Archangel next. He sat on the toolbox, leaning against the cab and holding his head, squinting through one eye. Painkillers, ointment, and a bandage later, all he needed was to stay awake and rest.

The pickup roared over a pothole, and everyone caught air. Mouse, tucked in the corner, flopped oddly, her arm landing on the edge of the bed, her fingers dangling.

The sob caught me by surprise, and I sank slowly to the floor, gasping and crying, clutching Archangel's knees, searching for anything solid to anchor myself. Archangel stroked my head, finally working his way down to sit with his back against the toolbox, holding me with my back to his chest.

Pulling away for a moment, I opened half the tail box, pulling out extra blankets. Wrapping Mouse in one of them took some careful maneuvering, but the knot in my chest released a little with the small attempt to make her comfortable.

The rest went to the exhausted people who finished working over Gryphon, and for the wounded basher himself. Phoenix curled against his side, her fingers still pressed against his neck, constantly monitoring his pulse. Hightide and Goliath slumped against the tail box, leaving barely enough space for Archangel and myself.

We curled together, Archangel resting his head against my shoulder. I stroked his hair back, running my fingers through the wet strands, the rain mingling with the tears running down my cheeks. Gratitude that he was fine, sorrow at those we'd lost, and jubilation over the mission roiled together, a mess I couldn't deal with, so I picked one.

I pressed my lips to my husband's forehead, grateful he rested in my arms.

***

The truck stopped, the lurch waking me from a light doze. I checked Archangel, then Gryphon and the others, who'd fallen into an exhausted sleep. Stars winked in a narrow strip of clear sky above us, the earlier clouds too far north. To the south, a fresh batch of storm clouds covered the sky.

Dereva hopped out of the truck, pausing with her hands on the sides of the bed, examining all of us. I barely made out her features in the early dawn light. The bags under her eyes were pronounced but her movements were quick and smooth.

"Wassup?" I asked quietly.

"Gas stop. Even we're running a little low," she replied, jerking her head towards the trees. "How is...everybody?"

"They're gonna be okay." I shifted Archangel and he grumbled, cracking open one bloodshot eye before closing it and curling up with his head in my lap. I shook my head. How a man as broad as him managed to curl so tightly was both a marvel and adorable. Gently scratching his scalp with my nails, I watched him settle back into a deep sleep.

The few people still able to move quickly hopped out of the vehicles, heading into the trees. They refilled vehicles under Dereva's watchful eye. The dilapidated farmhouse was set well off the road, easy to forget and perfect for our needs. It was one of many cache sites around the Valley.

"That's the last barrel," Dereva said, siphoning the last bit of gas out.

"Any food left?"

She shrugged. "Six buckets. Mix of dried and canned."

Checking the sky again, I nodded. "Let's take it all and close this site. Steve's probably hunting us now anyway." Closing my eyes, I pictured our location. "There's a nice barn about forty minutes away, right?"

She squinted up, checking out the visible stars. "There is, but it's south of here."

"Good. Steve'll have to start looking for us when we don't cross their blockades. We're looking at a good storm, so sooner is better than later. You want me to spell you at the wheel?"

She put a hand to her heart, a wounded expression on her face. "You want to take my baby away from me? Never!"

I snorted, a quiet laugh escaping. "What a brat. Just trying to help."

The corners of her mouth turned up. "Not happening. You can't drive for shit."

Dereva slid into the driver's seat, leaving me sputtering in the back. I smiled up at the stars. Our little exchange had livened and lightened her up and her shoulders were straighter as she threw the pickup into gear.

"Do you know," Archangel murmured from my lap, "that I have no idea how well you drive? I don't think I've ever seen you."

I stroked his hair back from his forehead, tracing his eyebrows and cheekbones with my fingertips. "She won't let me. How are you feeling?"

After some reassurances from him, he moved so I could rise to my knees, carefully checking Gryphon and Phoenix, who slept with her head over his heart. His pulse was a bit thready, but there, his chest rising and falling rhythmically.

Grimacing, I sat back down. Gravity worked and I was suddenly, acutely aware that I needed to pee. Except I wasn't getting one. My chance had been back at the farmhouse, and I'd lost it. I'd have to wait until our next stop.

***

I crouched next to a tree, my eyes closing in bliss at finally being able to relieve myself. A number of people immediately headed into the trees, so I hadn't been the only one. Men went north, women south. No matter where we camped, we kept it that way. It prevented anyone from accidentally wandering where they shouldn't and made life easier.

Resettling my belts and holsters while I walked never worked well, but that didn't stop me from trying. I'd just managed to get the left holster clipped around my thigh by the time I made it to the edge of the clearing.

"Captain!" Squirrel hailed me from the hospital van.

"Yo." I jogged over. "What's up?"

"Doc's looking for you." She jerked her head towards the barn. Her eyes were red-rimmed, exhaustion making her voice crack. She hefted two packs out of the van, turning that direction herself.

"Gimme those." Shaking my head at her stubbornness, I took the packs from her, despite her protests. "You've been up longer than I have. I'll give these to Doc. You need sleep."

The first drops of the coming storm hastened our steps. Herding her along, we made it just as the deluge started. I sighed on entering the barn. The rain drumming on the tin roof was sweet, restful music to my ears.

The wounded lay in orderly rows at the back of the barn, interspersed with their healthier battle partners. Everyone was wrapped in sleeping bags and blankets, packs nearby. The lightly wounded pairs all slept near the doors, weapons handy. Some of the fighters were still up, inhaling a quick meal before collapsing into their bedrolls.

My eyes burned every time I blinked. Rolling my head around loosened my neck and shoulders but did nothing for the exhaustion. I'd caught a bit of shuteye, but the thought of actually laying down had me near to tears. I ached for it, almost as much as I needed Archangel.

Dereva slept curled on her side, only the top of her head visible above her blanket, in a row with the other drivers and navigators. Over there were the basher/sniper pairs, then the scout and basher pairs...Shaking my head, I laughed a little at how everyone grouped together.

Doc was easy to find. All I had to do was look for the only person still on their feet. She went from one injured to another, giving them a sip of water and checking their vitals. Dropping the packs, I untied the pouch of pemmican I kept on my belt.

"Doc." I held out the open bag. "Eat something before I fall down on your behalf."

Squirrel, right behind me, fished out a canteen and began giving water to the injured. Doc mechanically checked the next patient. I followed, taking my own advice and eating some pemmican.

"Doc. Seriously. I'll trade you the water bottle for the food."

Chaos walked past me and unceremoniously took the canteen from her, plucked the pouch from my hand and set it in hers, and passed me the canteen. Then, he half carried her to the wall, setting her down on a blanket spread on the floor.

She stared at him, the food in her hand, then me and Squirrel, tending to the wounded. Her shoulders slumped and she finally ate. Apparently, Chaos had a way with the good doctor. He joined us, the work going faster.

We finished tending the wounded in silence, too tired to talk. The rain on the tin roof drowned out the little sounds people make when they're settling into sleep. Seventeen grievously injured, even more with minor wounds, and countless scrapes, bruises, and cuts.

The dead lay peacefully inside one of the Chimeras, protected from the weather and animals, until we could bury them with their comrades in the meadow.

I groaned when I straightened from the last woman, arching my back. Squirrel snuggled next to the Celt, sharing a portion of her blanket, asleep before her head hit the pack. Sighing, I shook a blanket over her. I frowned. I'd come back here for a reason...

The lightbulb went off. "Doc," I said, then cleared my throat. "Doc," I said a little louder.

Doc, sitting on the floor with her legs stretched out in front of her, looked up at me blearily. "What?"

"You wanted to see me, earlier."

"Yes, I..." She put a hand to her forehead, rubbing the spot between her eyebrows. "Supplies? Yes. I'm running low. I had to amputate a hand. I need enough to make it back to the Lair."

Chaos, finished with his last person, crawled over to Doc and curled next to her, looking so much like a cat, his head on her thigh. A gentle snore reached me over the din of the rain. She rested a hand on his shoulder, stroking lightly.

This meant something, but my foggy brain couldn't process. Only one thought at a time could exist in my head, and it was supplies. Going to one of the packs I brought in, I knelt clumsily, pulling a blanket out of the bottom pocket. Grunting with the effort, I climbed to my feet and shook it out over Doc and Chaos.

Stumbling to the front, I found Archangel checking Gryph's wound and applying a dry bandage. Next to them, Photograph slept, his camera cradled in his arms.

"How's Gryph?" I whispered.

"Doc said nothing major was hit. He's got a light fever, though." Archangel looked at the injured man, his brows furrowed with concern.

I nodded. These days, infection was the worst thing to deal with. We had one man lose a leg from a blister that went septic. Splinters, cuts, scrapes...all the things that used to be considered nothing more than irritants now had the potential to kill if not treated correctly.

Which is why everyone went out with their own fully stocked first-aid kit.

"What about you?" he asked.

"Patients are all watered and resting. Doc needs more supplies. I'll take ours over, leave them for her." He nodded, tying the last bandage in place while I dug through our packs. "I'd forgotten Photograph," I admitted. "I'm glad he's okay."

Archangel shot me a quick grin. "The man's already gone through eight or nine rolls of film. He's in seventh heaven right now. He's got a good one of you I'm going to get." *Eventually.* When the war ended, and Photograph could develop them. In a future where peace settled over our valley once more and we all lived.

He smiled at me, sitting back on his heels, his blue eyes soft. "C'mere," he whispered, holding out his hand.

Taking it, I dropped to my knees in front of him, leaning wearily against him. He ran his hands over my back, down my sides, around my waist, and up, under my jacket, leaving trails of fire in their wake as he checked for sore spots and injuries. Closing my eyes, I rested against him, running my hands under his shirt, my nails scoring his skin lightly, ostensibly checking for other wounds.

"If it weren't raining outside," he groaned against my throat.

"Even with the rain," I whispered, inhaling slightly. Gunpowder, blood, and sweat, his scent served as a further reminder that we *lived*.

"Get a room." Phoenix deliberately bumped me as she squeezed past, knocking me into Archangel. We went sprawling across his bedroll. Sniggering, she watched us try to untangle ourselves without waking the entire building.

By the time we made it back up, I was breathing hard, and Archangel had red flags across his cheeks. She smirked. I shook my head. "I wish there were ghosts. Then Sirius could haunt you. Maybe clank chains or some shit."

Archangel pulled me to my feet, grinning, though he was still tense.

Phoenix snorted. "As if. She'd be egging me on. Hell, I could say she possessed me and that's why I knocked you down and no one would argue 'cause it's *exactly* what she'd do."

"Fuck." She was right. Sirius wouldn't've been as subtle as Phoenix, either. She'd have just shoved me into him for shits and giggles.

Archangel chuckled. "Let's just drop off the kits and go see if there's someone on watch who'd like to catch a bit of shut-eye." He raised one eyebrow and slowly bit his lip.

"For God's sake." Phoenix shook her head. "Go away so I don't have to see this anymore, will you? You're hornier than teenagers."

My husband snorted, grinning widely. "Don't give me that. I practically needed a bucket of water for you two last month and you've been married longer."

Phoenix laughed silently up at us, not denying it at all. "Shoo. I need my beauty sleep and you're radiating so much sexual tension you'll wake someone up."

Snickering quietly, I padded through the sleeping fighters and set the kits next to Doc. A little more awake, I studied the tableau in front of me. Doc had scooted down and now Chaos curled around her protectively. When had that happened?

Deciding it was a matter for another day and I had more important things to look forward to, I made my way back to Archangel. He caught my hand, leading me outside, into the rain. I sighed, content in this moment.

Chapter 38

The garage doors yawned open ahead, the Lair inside dark and welcoming. The non-coms waited within, already warned by the perimeter guards of our arrival. Eleanor stood at the front, her hands outstretched as Dereva maneuvered the pickup around until it faced the door.

I sighed, rolled my head around, loosening my neck. Eleanor didn't look overly upset, so the wounded had made it back safely. We'd drawn Steve off, using a damaged vehicle as a decoy and now, all I wanted was a bath and bed.

Stepping onto the edge of the truck bed, I dropped down, landing lightly despite my weariness. Amongst the crowd, I spotted Papa and Sean assisting the lightly wounded out. They looked better than when I'd last seen them, healthier. Wildwood and Amana knew how to feed people.

Archangel grunted when he landed on the ground, one hand going to the side of his head. I tucked myself under his shoulder. Seeing this, Eleanor hurried to his other side, her skirt flaring around her feet.

"Let's get you to your room," she said. "The others are resting comfortably. Gryphon, too." She smiled at me, her eyes sad. "We had the funerals two days ago."

Archangel's arm tightened around my shoulders as I squeezed against him. "I need to see them."

"Have a bath after the briefing," Eleanor said firmly. "You can pay your respects once you're clean."

The camera flashed nearby, and I huffed a quiet laugh through the welling tears. "Photo thoroughly enjoyed himself. You'll have to get him to tell you about the pictures he took."

We passed Amana, standing in the center of the room, marshaling her troops with more efficiency than a general. After all these seasons, she didn't waste a breath or a gesture, already knowing where to direct people, and only giving it if they needed direction. The non-combatants took their role seriously, and without them, we would've given in to despair and exhaustion ages ago.

***

I sat back in my chair, my eyes feeling like they were filled with sand after all the tears. Reliving Mouse's death allowed me to grieve, and now I wanted to sleep, but first, Storm stood, restless energy in every movement.

"We managed to clear five towers. You guys made enough noise that there were hardly any soldiers. They knew you were the main threat."

"Maybe they were worried about us making it to Kwan's house," Archangel murmured.

She shrugged. "Either way, it gave us space to cut a section of fencing out. We were able to pick off anyone who tried to stop us. A lot of people left on foot. There are Chimeras out now, hoping to find them and bring them in."

"We brought out one hundred and fifty-nine people," Eleanor continued. "Over one hundred of them are children fifteen and under. Severely malnourished, of course, but in good spirits."

"I hope Home is ready for an influx this big," I said.

Dry Eyes nodded. "They've got some food put away, and they save a lot by not having to hunt."

"How do they skip that?" Phoenix asked, sitting forward.

"All those animals have been breeding for a few years, now," he said dryly. "The shepherds had an excellent flock of lambs last year. They're planning to butcher the young rams this spring."

"That doesn't cover right now."

My comment sparked a discussion, but it ended when Eleanor pointed out that we didn't know enough about Home's resources and supplies.

"We'll have to send a couple people up to give them warning," she finished.

Driver and Dry Eyes took the task on, as well as organizing more hunting parties to go further afield to find game. "Sure, ask if any fighters want to go." I nodded. "The more the merrier, I guess. And now," I placed my hands on the table, "I need a bath."

"Yes, you do," Lavender said firmly, smiling when Archangel rose, offering me his hand. "But you'll also need to deal with the Wilkins men."

My hand jerked inside Archangel's grasp, but he was the only one who knew it. "Why's that?"

"The father's not improving. Even the younger one is exhausted after an easy task," she said bluntly. "Honestly? I'm afraid of working them to death by asking them to walk across the room. They need sunlight, lazy days, and no stress. So do the Ortizes, and all of them are being very stubborn about going Home."

I nodded. "I'll talk to them tomorrow. Get some rest, people."

***

"Papa." I rubbed my forehead. "This came from people here. You need rest and the Lair can't give you that. You both need to go Home."

Tomorrow had come too soon, and now I tried to convince my stubborn family to leave before I had to strong-arm them. Papa sat in the chair he'd found and brought to their room, frowning. Sean sat on the bed while I paced, Archangel leaning a shoulder against the door jamb.

Papa had tried to insist I take the chair, but the pained way he moved showed he'd already done too much by helping the injured yesterday. To say it made them more receptive to the idea of leaving would be like saying women actually calm down just because a man says, "Calm down."

"But you'll be alone," Papa repeated. "I've heard Home is days away. We'll hardly see you."

Archangel stared at him levelly, one hand turned up as if to say *What am I, chopped liver?* I coughed to hide a laugh.

"Water?" Sean offered me the glass by the bed.

Shaking my head, I covered my mouth. Once I had myself under control, I faced my dad, struggling not to roll my eyes. "I'm not alone. And I'd rather you both got healthy. You're less likely to do that here."

"But what would I do there?" Papa fretted. "I'm a machinist. I should be making parts for you."

"Will and me got that covered. But Home could really use someone like you." He gave me a look of disbelief and I nodded. "They need grand-fatherly and fatherly types. Someone to listen, give advice, and help out. There's a ton of jobs to do. Olivia and Sam would fill your schedules in no time. Bonus, there's no guns, fewer funerals, and nobody coming in with bullet holes."

Sean frowned. "It's still not fair. You've got thirteen-year-olds running around here, but I'm being sent away?"

"That thirteen-year-old didn't go through hard labor that killed most people put in it." Archangel hooked his thumb in his belt, shifting his weight onto his other foot.

I narrowed my eyes. How dare he make me hot when my dad was in the room? His eyes crinkled just a bit at the corner. That bastard knew full well what he was doing to me.

"Going Home doesn't have to be permanent," Archangel continued. "It's just until you're healthy and strong again."

He and I knew they were unlikely to ever get their full strength back, but it was a lie they needed to hear right now. And I needed it, too. Needed to believe that things could be normal someday.

"I'm not going to win this, am I?" Papa asked the air.

"Nope!" I said cheerfully. "But that's because I'm not the one making the request. When it comes to the Lair, Amana's word is law. I'm just the muscle."

Sean snorted. "About that. What's the deal with giving control of this place to a little girl?"

Pursing my lips, I inhaled strongly, staring at the ceiling. I loved my brother, but he could be the biggest idiot, sometimes. Turning, I caught Archangel glaring, tapping his fingers mere inches from his gun. He wouldn't, but the temptation to knock sense into someone could just...

"What?" Sean asked defensively, folding his arms. "What's happening here?"

Papa rubbed his head, running his hand over his thin hair. "I think—I could be wrong, but—I *think* they're trying to keep their tempers. Don't quote me on this. But maybe. I don't know, I'm just...reading the room. You should try it."

The laughter caught me by surprise and I snorted, degenerating into giggles. "So that's where you get it from," Archangel murmured.

"What are you getting mad at me for?" Sean didn't know when to shut up.

"Do I really have to explain this again?" I asked the air. "Where did I go wrong with you? I know Mom died when you were thirteen, but...damn. I've been here. How did I fail so miserably?"

Archangel shook his head. "Want me to try?"

I threw up my hands. "Why not? Maybe he'll listen to a man."

Papa snorted. "He didn't listen to me." He watched the proceedings with interest, his blue eyes bright, flicking back and forth.

"Okay." Archangel shifted. "Let's see...It's the year twenty sixty-something, right?" Sean shrugged. "Women are people, right?" Sean nodded. "Women can drive, shoot, cook, fight, clean, so we can assume they're, you know, capable." Sean nodded again. "So why isn't that enough? She runs a tight ship. People get fed, chores get done. Why isn't that enough to show you she's competent?"

"Because there's...older people." But Sean sounded a little uncertain, hallelujah.

"We all know that doesn't mean wiser. This war was started by older people."

"Guilty!" I waved.

"So why the fuck are you worrying about her age and gender?"

"Who said I had a problem with her gender?!"

"You called her a 'little girl'," I reminded him.

"It'd be like telling your sister she needs to step down because she's a woman," Archangel finished, as if that explained everything.

"He already tried to convince me to step down and let a man take over," I said evenly. "But Peter didn't have a problem with me and what I do. Didn't even pretend to cooperate when his CO tried to take over. He had my back. You're trying to stab me in it."

Sean clenched his jaw, glaring at me.

"Okay!" Papa stood suddenly. "Thank you for this. Now, why don't you let him think this over...Captain."

We found ourselves deposited gently but firmly outside, the door closed in our faces. "Were we ganging up on Sean?" I looked from the door to my husband.

He shrugged, taking my hand and tucking through his elbow, leading me down the corridor. "We might not have changed his mind, but hopefully, he'll think twice before saying something that stupid again."

"You know," I said after a few minutes. "I can't wait to introduce him to Olivia."

***

I didn't get to go.

"Every time you do, it just stirs Sophie up and it won't make the Wilkins or Ortizes feel any safer to see another murder attempt," Eleanor said with finality.

After privately saying goodbye to Papa and Sean, I sulked in the gym. Sarge worked me through a series of exercises to get me more comfortable and familiar with the machete. Well, with sticks the same shape and weight as the machete, anyway.

"Listen," he twirled his stick deftly in figure eights, "you're not going to be able to do fancy moves like you're used to. You've got to stop trying to go from the wrist and use your shoulder and elbow more."

"That's no fun," I complained. "I thought I'd be able to work up—"

"En guarde!" Sarge charged, stick whirling.

Dancing back, I narrowly beat off his attack, acutely aware he *let* me. Growling, I spun to the side, putting my shoulder into it. He barely blocked, beaming at me.

"Good!" He swung, a haymaker that could take a person's head off.

Falling backwards, I rolled to my feet. "How's things with Seahorse?" I swiped at his shins and he leaped back, incredibly quick for such a big man. "And how come you get the double whammy of size and speed?" My eyes widened as realization hit. "Is that why Seahorse likes you so much?"

He blushed and slowed for a second. Coming in low, I slipped to his left and whacked his ass. "C'mon, Sarge," I laughed. "You're really that shy about it?"

"My kids are here!"

***

"You have some kind of death wish." Archangel took my hand, drawing it through his elbow. By habit, I leaned against him as we walked, reaching around to rest my free hand on his forearm. We walked slowly towards the common room for dinner, training done for the day.

"What do you mean?" I smiled up at him, my bad mood at not being able to escort my family Home long since burned off.

"Well, I didn't see what started it, but I've never seen Sarge chase anybody with that much determination. The fact that you were laughing like a maniac does make me a little concerned for your mental health. As in, I think you enjoy danger a bit too much."

"I just asked about Seahorse." His sidelong glance clearly said he didn't believe me. "I may have made a comment that could be seen as a bit...dirty? But really, you'd have to be in the gutter for that one."

He laughed. "And you live there. Yeah, that makes sense."

Archangel tensed slightly when the tall, slightly greasy looking Spartacus passed us, glowering at...I cocked my head. He was glaring at Archangel. "Gah, it's the creeper, again."

"What?"

"He walked in on me when I was in Doc's office."

"What?!" He stopped abruptly, half turning back.

I tugged him forward. "It was worth it to see Doc toss him out on his ass, let me tell you. Now that I think about it, he lurked around a lot while I was recovering. But why was he glaring at you?"

Archangel stared ahead. "He wouldn't listen to Sarge about joining the fighters, so Sarge asked me to show him what a fight is like. He didn't care for it," he added neutrally.

We crossed into Section One. "Is that it? Geez. He's as bad as Gorgon."

Except Archangel remained tense. I kept quiet, hoping he'd say something, but whatever bothered him, he preferred to keep it to himself. "Are you talking to anyone about whatever this is?" I waved.

"Gryphon knows."

As long as he talked to someone. Guess guys have some things they didn't like sharing with us, just like we kept some things amongst the women. Shrugging, I kissed his cheek. "Whatever's for dinner smells good."

His shoulders relaxed. "Yeah. They did good on the soup today." We rounded the last corner and the scent of roasted meat greeted us. He laughed. "We should've made a bet on what dinner would be."

"Why?" I smiled up at him. "They always end the same way." Naked and sweaty, whether I won or not.

He swatted me on the butt when I entered the door, laughing, his concerns regarding Spartacus forgotten.

Phoenix threw her leg over the bench, her sandy hair glowing in the candlelight. A little knot in my chest released. If Phoenix stepped away from Gryphon, he was on the mend.

We served ourselves and sat on either side of her, Eleanor and Storm sitting opposite. "Where did we get all this from?" Phoenix asked, her mouth full.

"Extra hunting parties for all the new people," Eleanor replied, digging in. "And Lavender says they've finally gotten the sunlight to heat ratio right to grow veg later in the season."

"Does potato count as vegetables?"

"Turnips, sweet potatoes, and rutabaga do."

"*Si!*" Amana said cheerfully, setting her plate next to Storm. "*Todos son vegetales.*"

I covered my face with my free hand, practically crying but unwilling to put down my fork. "Why do you keep doing this to me?" I wailed. "It's been *years!*"

She stared at me levelly. "How many languages to jou speak?"

I shrugged. "English?"

"*Si. Uno.* I speak six."

Every jaw except Eleanor and Storm's dropped. "What are they, then?" I challenged her.

"English, *idiota,*" she muttered to herself. Then, "Portuguese, French, *Espanol*, Italian, *y* German."

I stared, completely at a loss.

"Well." My husband grinned at me. "She told you."

"Fuuuuck." I frowned. "Wait. What about that time with the noose? You didn't drop a hint of Spanish there!"

"I was very motivated!"

CHAPTER 39

That's very true, Wayne. Already, Europe has severely limited its ties to the US. England and Australia take in very few American expats as well, and Canada is allowing some refugees in, but they're very much against the current core American beliefs. What will the President do next?

The Morning Show

The next few months passed quickly, most easily tracked by Gryphon's improvement. Phoenix's mood improved at the same rate as her husband's health, and we needed all hands on deck.

In late winter, I paced the Useless Room, listening to more reports. Scouts went out daily, scouring the mountains and foothills for signs of Steve, and every day, they returned with fresh news.

Storm rested one hand on the map table, leaning over. "I was too far away to get a good count," she said, "but there were a fuck-ton of them all along here." She placed a line of flags along the foothills to the north.

"Is there a chance Steve's putting on a good show? Trying to look like there's more than there really is?" Eleanor asked.

Storm shrugged.

I snorted. "Unlikely. We haven't managed to kill that many of them. Even with Opal Creek." The Opal Creek fight had happened right after Lightning and Thunder died, and by my best remembrance, that was the most Steve we'd ever killed at one time.

Archangel, just entering the room, heard my comment. "Maybe not, but they're not being reinforced, either."

"Explain," I demanded, all of us giving him our full attention.

"Ink just got back." We'd sent her south with Nebula and two others to watch the southern passes to see how things were. He continued. "Passes are full of snow, nothing cleared. They also saw two major rock falls across the freeway. One of them completely blocked it. Looks like it's been there for a while. Since spring, at least."

"You think that's why they're so active now?" I mulled it over, staring at the map without seeing it. They had been acting more desperate.

"Could be," he allowed. "Valley's full of mud, too."

"True," Storm said. "It's been raining for a week or so."

Taking two big strides to the table, I stabbed my finger down on the map, at the edge of the Valley. "We can totally fuck with Steve. Small group, fifteen to twenty, based here. From there, we go out in smaller groups, three to five. Foot only, straight up, old fashioned guerilla shit."

"They're spread out too far for just one group," Storm objected.

"So we put three or four groups out." I looked up at them. "We'll leave fewer tracks, keep them out of the mountains, take some strain off the Lair."

Archangel nodded. "I like it."

***

"This sucks," Archangel grumbled, sneezing. "Everything's wet, even my underwear."

"I know for a fact you don't have any."

Motioning for him to be quiet, I pointed. Birds exploded from the trees. Steve was close. We sat at the top of a tall oak tree surrounded by younger firs and maples above the road. I didn't know what road and didn't care. All that mattered was Steve was coming and landmines were set.

I couldn't even remember how long we'd been out of the Lair. It was definitely mid-spring, by all the rain and mud, and we'd left at the end of winter. Beyond that...the days blurred together.

The low rumble of a Chimera reached my ears first. Breathing lightly, I leaned forward, waiting. Gripping the branch, I held my rifle loosely in my left, ready if I needed it. The truck rolled cautiously forward, but too many sections were broken by the tanks.

The explosive concussion rattled the trees and my teeth.

"Yes!" Whipping my rifle up, I peered through the scope.

A door creaked and Archangel fired once. Then, we waited. The smoke cleared and birds began singing. My eyes half closed, I smiled, tipping my face towards the watery sunlight. At this point, I'd take what I could get.

"You think they're all dead?" I murmured eventually.

"Hm?" Archangel shook himself, smiling down at me from his higher perch. "Oh. Don't know. Do we need to kill them all?"

I shrugged. "Guess not."

"Good. I'm hungry."

***

Another day, another landmine, another truck. Running down deer trails, chased by men in heavy gear. Steve began lighting fires in the forests. Wrong fucking season. Who tries lighting forest fires when it rains five hours a day?

Returning to the small cave system that served as a camp, I dropped my pack in the small hollow we used as a room, arching my back. Warm hands slid around my front, pulling me against a firm chest and I smiled. I'd know those hands anywhere. Broad, gentle, firm, his dexterous hands looked more suited to woodworking or gardening than fighting.

The days might be monotonous, but the nights were worth remembering.

Remembering we were living people, not machines. Remembering why we did all this. Remembering gentleness, passion, pleasure.

Archangel sighed, the motion rising and falling like a wave. "What are we doing tonight?" he murmured, biting my ear gently.

I shivered, dropping my head to the side to give him better access. Before I managed to gather my scattered thoughts, there was a commotion at the cave entrance. Archangel released me even as I spun, putting my back to a wall, a small, compact Glock in each hand. Archangel had a knife drawn, ready to snatch the first person to cross that threshold.

Peering around the corner, I recognized the faces. Immediately relaxing, I nodded to him, holstering my weapons. We were safe for another day.

The cave was too narrow to walk side-by-side, but Archangel stayed close enough for me to feel the heat radiating from him. Sparrow stood just inside the entrance, speaking to the two men, men I recognized as scavengers.

My lip curled at the second man. The creeper, Spartacus, had come to visit. Archangel wrapped an arm around my waist, pulling me back against him. Probably to keep me from kicking the creeper's ass. Still, I sighed, melting against him.

It was so good to not be alone.

"Amana sent some fresh supplies." The other scavenger, Respecty, lowered a massive backpack, leaning it against the wall. "Hope it's enough."

Sparrow smiled, her face lighting up. "Anything new is fantastic, thank you."

Ink and Nebula slipped into the cave behind the men. Spartacus immediately focused on the young women. Nebula glared back at him.

"What are you looking at, asshole?" she demanded.

"You shouldn't be so rude," he admonished.

She never stopped, just flipped him the finger over her shoulder. I smirked, and his eyes flitted over me before skittering away. He shifted, obviously uncomfortable.

"You should make them be nicer to me," he said without looking at me. "I'm a nice guy, all I want is for them to be happy and safe. I'd help with—"

"No," I interrupted. Archangel tightened his grip slightly. Yeah, no starting fights here, when Steve might hear. "No. They're fine. Respecty," I looked to the other man, the one who didn't make my skin feel like I'd accidentally walked into insulation, "you guys staying the night?"

Please say no.

"Thanks, Captain, but no." I relaxed a little. "It's too hot. We've got a ride waiting a couple hours away, so we need to get moving."

"Take the creek to the south," Archangel offered. "There's more cover and Steve just cleared that area yesterday, so they won't be looking there."

"Here." Sparrow dragged the pack a little deeper into the cave. "Let's empty this out."

"Unless you need an extra pack?" Respecty asked.

"No," she replied. "We're good. This would just get in the way."

They passed Gummy and Anarchy, just returning from their rounds. Archangel sighed, giving the fighters a fist-bump as they passed. Respecty nodded to the two, and Spartacus just looked uncomfortable.

"What's wrong with him?" I muttered to Anarchy.

"He doesn't care for anything he doesn't understand," they replied.

I gave them a confused look. "What?"

Anarchy grinned. "Me. He doesn't get me."

"What's there to get?"

They laughed, grabbed the packages Sparrow threw to them, and headed down the corridor. Anarchy was born female, we found them in the same 'play pen' as Nebula and several others, but they really didn't care for the whole gender thing. And really, who paid any attention to that shit these days, anyway? We all wore the same clothes, regardless. What was so difficult to get about that?

"Later, Captain." Respecty nodded, barely stopping short of a salute.

"Tell Amana we're all good, and thanks for the food," I said, shaking his hand.

The creeper just slunk out after him. I shook my head. "What a weird little man."

"He's taller than me," Archangel pointed out, amusement crinkling the corners of his eyes.

"He's little on the inside."

Sparrow snorted. "You're not wrong there. Maybe he'd be better if we could get him high." She clapped her hands briskly. "Now, don't forget to take some of this back with you."

"Yes, ma'am." Archangel smiled fully, showing off even teeth. "Then it's off to bed for us."

***

I started awake, my heart pounding, memory and nightmares a jumbled mess in my head. Blood spatter, dead babies, shouting, screaming, and deceased family members marching past, their empty eyes glaring accusations at me. That last image made me reach out, looking for Archangel, but my hand touched cool blankets.

A cold sweat broke out over my skin. Frantically, I patted the ground, searching for him. "Babe, are you here?" Silence. "Noah?"

Hunching over my knees, I rocked, choking back the whimpers. Were my nightmares true? Were my memories of happiness and marriage the lie? Where was he?

Warm hands ran down my chilled arms, pulling me back against his firm chest, Archangel's familiar scent welcoming and soothing. "What is it?" he murmured, stroking my hair. He tucked us under the blanket, pulling it high around my shoulders, holding me tightly.

I shook, silent tears streaming down my cheeks, the nightmare reluctant to give up its hold.

"Another nightmare?" he asked.

I nodded.

"Tell me about it."

I shook my head. He waited patiently, rocking us. Finally, the tremors eased, and I warmed up. I choked on the words at first, but once I started, I kept on until it was out. "I was alone, in the dream. And when I woke, I couldn't find you. I guess..." I gave a short laugh. "I guess my brain just took it to mean that this, us, was the dream and my nightmares were the reality. I didn't...I don't mean to freak you out..."

I relaxed, now that those fears were in the open and waited for his reaction.

He snorted gently, rolling me onto my back and settling half over me, fisting a hand in my hair. "I don't like the thought of you alone either," he murmured against my cheek. I felt his lips curve into a little smile. "Guess I'd better make sure you're not."

The knot in my chest released completely, and it was my turn to snort. "That didn't sound like it should have been comforting, but it was. Fuck."

"You're *my* weird." He nipped my jaw, my ear, and moved down. "Now," he said from around my collarbone, "how about we put a few other memories in that head of yours?"

"Mmm…" I stretched, my fingers finding his thick hair. "Yes, please!"

***

A few days later, smoke billowed through the trees and drifted across the road. The burnt hulk of a Chimera blocked the road, two more fast approaching.

"Time to go," I bellowed.

A few soldiers, barely escaping the burning truck, scattered into the bushes. The oncoming trucks screeched to a halt, disgorging more Steve. My lip curled. We didn't have enough people for the shitstorm forming on the ground.

Archangel and Sparrow headed for the trees while I covered them. At Archangel's shouted "Go!" I slid down from my perch and raced after them.

We ran north, switching between a jog and a run while the sun slid towards the horizon. It had moved a full finger's width before we cut east, passing an apple tree on the edge of a field, the swelling buds showing bright green tips. The land rose and fell, slowly climbing higher. We stuck to the trees wherever possible, never straying far from cover.

It's hard to say who was more surprised, us or Steve, when we barreled into their midst as they took a break. They stared at us for precious seconds, but we barely slowed. I whipped my rifle up, pumping the slide, screaming, while two handguns miraculously appeared in Archangel's hands. Sparrow was the fastest, flinging a little packet into their fire which exploded, spewing smoke, before we booked it through the camp.

I didn't care if I hit anyone, just sowing confusion and giving us a chance to escape. We departed their camp as abruptly as we entered, leaving chaos in our wake. Archangel took us north again. Steve to the south was already pissed off with us—now we had more to join them.

A mile down the new route, Sparrow pointed to a tree ahead. "Do we have time to booby-trap things?"

I shrugged, panting. "I guess."

"Good."

The tree she'd chosen had flexible, strong branches with enough brushy coverage to hide the limb bent backwards. Using the machete, I trimmed a stake while she rigged a lever and Archangel got the branch ready. We had the first trap done in under ten minutes.

As we went, we continued setting quick traps, even ones as simple as a tripwire with nothing to kill a man.

"That's so mean," Archangel said the first time we left a simple rawhide tripwire across our trail. "They're totally going to think there's more to it than this."

"Yay," I said, watching the rear.

***

We stumbled back into the cave well after dark. Close to the entrance, Archangel whistled like a chickadee and was answered by an owl hooting.

"Tell me there's hot water somewhere," Sparrow whispered in my ear. "My feet are killing me."

"Mine, too," I moaned, limping slightly. Somewhere back there, there'd been a rock and my foot found it with incredible precision.

Ink met us inside the cave mouth with jerky and fresh water. Following us to the fire, she continued to pass out food as we walked. I eyed her suspiciously. Normally, we found our own food. What had brought on this level of solicitousness?

"We had word from the Lair," she said.

Ah. I nodded. Archangel had already seated himself, pulling off his moccasins and checking for blisters. I gently rolled my foot around, stretching sore muscles. "How bad is it?"

She opened her mouth, reconsidered, and shut it again. Taking a deep breath, she let it out slowly, the firelight playing across the tattoos visible on her wrist. "There's a lot of action with Steve across the board. Some have returned due to injuries. Not too many Steve in the mountains anymore. The fires were a bit close at times."

I circled my hand, urging her on. I needed to hear this before I fell asleep where I sat.

Ink paused, her jaw working. "Chaos's group disappeared. Lookouts saw fire. When they went to investigate, they found the camp trashed. Steve had definitely been there. No bodies. No sign anywhere. And..." She looked away. "Doc was in camp at the time."

"Ah, fuck." My chest tightened, memories of the last time people had gone missing. Archangel growled, straightening, suddenly alert. Damned if I wanted to have to kill more of my own. I already had too many dead faces parading through my dreams. I didn't need more.

"All gone?" Sparrow whispered, stunned.

"Who brought the news?" I demanded. Maybe the scavengers weren't that good at tracking. Maybe Chaos and company were injured in the woods, waiting to be found. Not...not captured.

"Feisty found the camp. Dereva's waiting for you. Everyone figured you'd head south to search." Ink paced slowly, and for the first time, I noted the full packs sitting against the back wall. "We have one question: do you want the rest of us to stay here, head back to the Lair, or go to another camp?"

Huffing a humorless laugh, I shook my head, glancing at Archangel. He shrugged infinitesimally, giving me a small nod. I nodded back. "Go to Seahorse and Sarge's camp." It was the nearest one to ours. "I'll be borrowing them and Storm. Keep Steve busy for a few more days. Sparrow, you're with me."

Moving to stand next to Archangel, I leaned on him, his shoulder solid against my thigh. He ran a hand up my calf, squeezing. "We'll get them back," he said. "No worries."

I nodded, rubbing my mouth to hide its tremble. Eight people had been with Chaos. Eight. I couldn't lose eight at once. Add in Doc, and it could be enough to finish us. I didn't have it in me to start fresh, find a new doctor, struggle to fill the void left by so many people.

I *needed* them to be alright.

Ink called the others. Within minutes the fire was dampened, and we had our packs. Ink had been very thorough in her planning. The young woman had fantastic attention to detail, probably why she was such a good tattoo artist.

***

Driving through the night, we slept fitfully, eight of us crammed in the back of the truck, Dereva and Hightide in the cab. I sat on the toolbox with Feisty, rifle at the ready, going over what she'd found at the empty camp. Archangel, temporarily on the machine gun, cocked his head, listening in.

"Nothing was standing," Feisty said, pressing her back firmly against mine so we could stay balanced. "Those fuckers ran over everything fifty million times. You'd have to go a mile or more out to find any tracks. There were some burn marks, dunno if it was Chaos or Steve that left them, though."

"How long has it been?"

The young woman shook her head. "They'd been resupplied about a week ago. I was on watch, saw the smoke. Eventually checked it out, but it was about two days before I went." She was silent for a moment, then, "Maybe if I'd checked it out sooner..."

"No," I snapped. "Never second guess yourself. You went. Most people wouldn't have done that. They'd have figured it was Steve, the end. If you'd gone sooner, you might've been captured, then we wouldn't know about this at all. Maybe, maybe, maybe. We can't know what it was. You took the best possible course of action at the time, and I'm damn glad it didn't turn out another way."

"What if they're dead?" she whispered.

"Then we bury our dead, remember them, and hit Steve harder than ever," my mouth supplied while my heart quailed. Where the fuck did my mouth get all this bravado from? It certainly hadn't checked in with anything else first, otherwise a sob would've come out.

"Who took them the last batch of supplies?" Archangel asked.

Feisty shifted at my back, her shoulder blades pressing against me. "No idea." She sounded a bit watery, but whole. "We'd need to ask Lavender."

We passed the rest of the night quietly, switching out to have a rest ourselves. It was near dawn when we arrived at Seahorse's camp. Gummy, Anarchy, Nebula, Ink, and Feisty stayed. They'd spread word to the rest of the camps, cause havoc for a few more days, then bug out.

"Sorry, Sarge," I said without remorse. "You're not going back to the Lair just yet."

"Fucking Steve," he grumbled. "Still, Driver and Lavender have got my older ones, so..."

So, if the worst should happen, he knew his kids would be loved and cared for. I nodded. People who had kids in this shit were so much worse off. I couldn't imagine having kids. And those who got pregnant? Insanity.

"Just the eight of us?" Sarge asked, also indicating the driver and navigator, who were taking the opportunity for a nap.

Seahorse laughed. "Of course, that's...Oh, wait..." Her grin widened. "You've never seen her in the field. This'll be fun."

Archangel snickered.

"What?" Sarge looked between all of us, a worried crease between his eyebrows. "What?!"

Shaking my head, I turned Archangel around by the shoulders, marching him towards the truck. "Get in the truck. Stop worrying the poor man. He knows how I fight. He trained me."

Archangel lifted me into the pickup. "Don't ruin my fun. You should hear how cryptic he is about you to the rookies."

Turning, I knelt, taking a moment to cup his face in my hands, tracing my thumbs over his familiar, beloved features. The wide mouth with its full lower lip, high, flat cheekbones, square jaw, and deep set, dark blue eyes. He had a stubble of a blond beard, slow to grow, that rasped pleasantly under my hands. He looked up at me quizzically.

"You okay, babe?"

I dropped a quick kiss on his mouth. "Just taking a moment to admire my husband, that's all."

"Well." He grasped the side of the pickup and slowly lifted himself in, showing off. "Admire away."

"What aren't you telling me about how she fights?" Sarge asked again.

I heard Seahorse laugh harshly. "Remember that newbie Gorgon set on her?"

"Yes..."

"She was being nice."

Rousing herself, Dereva turned the key and my baby purred to life. I settled in facing forward, rifle at the ready. Time to pay attention. Storm steadied her larger rifle at the rear and Seahorse took the machine gun while Dereva rolled out, heading for the hills and backroads.

***

Late afternoon sun peeked through the thin clouds, warming my skin. It'd been so long since I'd been truly warm anywhere outside of Archangel's arms, I almost forgot what it felt like. Hightide let us know we weren't far from the camp and I rolled my head, shrugging to loosen the muscles for whatever lay ahead.

Dereva stopped a quarter of a mile from the site, and we walked the rest of the way. They'd set up in a long-abandoned hunting cabin in the middle of thick brush and forest. I surveyed the scene. It *used* to sit in the middle of a forest.

A wide swathe of broken trees and bushes, bracketed by deep treads, left a pit in my stomach.

I hated those tanks.

Over everything, boot tracks hid any sort of sign the Irregulars might've left. Storm and Archangel pulled on dull colored beanies to hide their bright hair. Storm shouldered her rifle and scaled a tree as nimbly as a squirrel, on God today. The rest of us split up, staying within shouting distance.

The sun had moved a hand's width closer to the horizon when Seahorse shouted, "Here!"

Abandoning my fruitless search, I raced over, running along a downed tree, leaping off the end. Sarge was already there, and Sparrow arrived when I did. When Archangel reached us, we followed the faint tracks Seahorse found.

They regularly disappeared when rocks and logs were around. No wonder Steve missed them. From the direction, we were able to figure they were heading for a nearby gully.

"I'm counting five sets of tracks," Archangel said.

"Six." Sparrow stood. "I've got another set here."

Two missing. Fuck.

At the gully, the tracks disappeared and didn't reappear on the other side. We examined up and down the gully without luck. Until Sarge hissed, waving us back. He pointed to what was either a large hole or a tiny cave.

"Smudged earth right here," he whispered. "I think they went in."

Kneeling, I tried to see down the hole. Shaking my head, I backed up. "Is it possible?"

Seahorse snorted. "Probable. All yours, Captain."

Shuddering, I crawled closer. "Guys? You in here? Please don't shoot me. And don't make me come in there. I really don't want to."

"Captain?" I sagged in relief. The Celt's voice echoed oddly out of the hole, but it was definitely her. "We're coming out."

Even expecting it, watching six women appear was miraculous. They were filthy, mud in their braids, coating their bodies, but whole. Seeing us staring, dumbfounded, they straightened, smirking.

"We opened it up more inside," the Celt said. "Chaos figured it'd be a good hidey hole."

Sarge kept shaking his head. "Nope. Nope, nope, nope. He wasn't wrong, but oh, hell no. I'd rather get caught."

"Speaking of," Doc interrupted, her voice tight. "Have you found Chaos and Goliath?"

I shook my head. "No sign. We barely found you. What happened?"

"A couple days after we got resupplied, just before dawn, the ground started vibrating." The Celt shook her head, disgusted. "Steve was already in the forest. Those fuckers knew exactly where we were. The scavengers must've given our position away, not been careful enough, whatever. Chaos and Goliath stayed behind to give us a chance to get out."

Doc flung her hands up. "We need to check the secondary spot, see if they made it to hiding! Unless..." she trailed off.

"No bodies," I said gently.

Doc sagged, clutching Seahorse's arm for support.

A check of the secondary location proved fruitless. No sign of them anywhere, which left one other option.

"They've been taken," I said grimly.

"That's what I've been saying!" Doc shouted.

I gently took her forearms, dropping my head. Eventually, she rested her hands on my arms, stretching up to press her forehead to mine. "We will find them," I whispered, "but we can't go off. We have one chance, and we have to do it right."

She heaved a shuddering sigh, her breath washing over my face. "I know. I just...I keep remembering last time..."

Lightning and Thunder.

"I know. But they'll treat them differently. They're men. We have a chance. You with me?"

She nodded, her head pressing hard against mine. "I can do this. *We* got this."

Lifting my head, I squeezed her arms. "All right," I said, raising my voice. "Let's get Dereva and Storm in here. And a map. Get your supplies, people! We've got damsels to rescue."

"We have no idea which direction they went," the Celt said, kneeling on the other side of the map I spread on the ground.

"So, which areas did you notice butt-loads of Steve at?" I asked. "Which areas were too hot to handle?"

Archangel disappeared into the trees while the Celt studied the map, pulling on her lower lip. "This area, here." She circled a section with her finger, the beads in her hair clicking when she moved.

My heart sank. The area she indicated had a slew of names, towns, inside it. How could we narrow it down? There were too many to search individually.

"Most of these places are barely two streets. We'd hit and run." She shrugged and pointed to the southern end of the circle. "We'd ambush here, so Steve didn't stay there..."

"Which town is bigger than the others?" I asked, reining in my impatience. To the north was Cascadia, but we'd burned that town when we left. Unlikely. Tracing the highways, I shook my head. It was impossible to tell from a map which of these was bigger.

What could Steve be looking for? Would they have gone all the way back to Salem? Not too far in peacetimes, but right now, with the roads and us lurking everywhere, it was less likely.

"Here." The Celt traced a smaller circle. "These two," she pointed to Sweet Home and Liberty, "are a bit bigger than the others. We never went inside, but we did watch them sometimes. Steve was in Sweet Home, but I don't know if they still are."

A low rumble filled the air while she talked, and I recognized the sound of my pickup. "Sweet Home is a good place to start," I said. "And if they're not there, it's on the way to Liberty."

"Yo, Captain," Storm hailed me as she ran up. "Saw a Chimera just a minute—"

"Where was it going?" I demanded, stabbing a finger at the map. "This is us. Which way?"

"West and north."

I bared my teeth in a grin. The direction of Sweet Home. "We have a heading."

***

The sun hung just below noon before we were able to leave, the original eight of us and Doc taking the pickup while the rest of the fighters would make their way back on foot by way of the Pacific Crest Trail.

The Celt was cool, taking everything in stride. The only thing that upset her was when I said she had to go back, but she was the one I trusted to get the others to the Lair in one piece.

"I don't like it," she informed me, "but I got it. See you in a few. Bring the boys back."

They disappeared quickly into the foothills while we turned our nose into the flatlands of the Valley, where the trees grew sparse.

Hightide drove most of the way, giving Dereva a chance to sleep, her head resting against the passenger side window. In the back, we set up two-person shifts while the rest slept, piled like kittens, in the bed. No one protested the grueling pace, none of us happy about having two of our own in Steve's hands.

For some of us, waking nightmares kept trying to surface, and when it was my turn to rest, Seahorse and Storm were right there, already awake. I was afraid I wouldn't be able to sleep, but resting my head on Archangel's chest, listening to his heartbeat, I drifted into a light sleep.

We passed through a series of small towns on our way to Sweet Home, each more a collection of houses than a town. No signal lights, few large buildings, and everything falling apart.

We reached Sweet Home shortly before dawn was even a light in the eastern sky. Dereva parked on the outer edges of town, behind a trailer house. Splitting into three teams, we began canvassing the town.

Jogging down a narrow lane whose sign was long gone with Archangel, I couldn't help but see how much nature had reclaimed. Gardens gone wild, mint waging war with strawberries, both vying for limited resources like sunlight. A lone tulip struggled to rise above the battlefield, the unopened flower heavy, ready to bloom.

A tall maple tree, its green a strong promise in the bright buds, rose in the yard next to the war zone. Giving a quick yip to catch Archangel's attention, I jerked my chin towards the tree. He nodded, putting his back to the yard, watching the street.

No need to check the house. The roof had fallen in, and vines climbed the walls. Slinging my rifle over my back, I scaled the tree, gripping the trunk between my knees and pushing upward from there. The branches were big and well-spaced, but easy enough to climb. Near the top, I slid my rifle around, examining the town through the scope.

Two streets over, Sparrow and Storm had the same idea, with Storm climbing a roof. Continuing on, I searched for any signs of life.

"How's it going?" Archangel called quietly.

"Sparrow, Storm, and a feral cat, so far."

A whistle pierced the air. Swinging round, I saw Storm waving, pointing. Following her gestures, I snarled softly. A Chimera headed away from the mountains on a three-lane road. West and north.

"We've got them," I said. "Bearing north on a larger road."

When I made it to the ground, Archangel already had a map out. "Only big road here is the 20. It goes past the edge of Liberty on its way to Salem."

"Good enough. Call the kids. It's time to go."

He put two fingers in his mouth, whistling loud enough that I cupped my near hand over my ear. He paused, then whistled again, the signal to return to the truck. Another whistle rent the air, the signal being passed along.

We jogged slowly through the crumbling remains of the empty town. "Looks like it was a nice place to live." Regret panged through my chest, and a surprising sense of loss. For the first time in my life, I was sorry I couldn't settle down. I didn't want to live like this forever.

I didn't want to always be on the run, hunter and prey. I wanted the chance to live in a house with Archangel, go back to our own names, and have a family. I wanted a quiet, normal life. My breath caught in my chest with the yearning.

"I want it too." Archangel pulled me to a stop just around the corner from the pickup. "You said that and I just..." He stepped closer, his blue eyes hot. I flushed and he smiled slightly, but that look never left his eyes. "I know we never talk about this, but dammit, I *want* to."

"Tell you what," I said breathlessly, still caught in his gaze, "once we find Chaos and Goliath, we can tempt fate and dream. Now, they're waiting on us."

"Just a minute." He dipped his head an inch, until our noses brushed. "I just need this, first..." His free hand cupped my head and my eyes slid closed when his warm lips covered mine. We stayed like that, barely touching, his mouth moving leisurely over mine. Finally, he pulled back the barest millimeter. "Okay. Let's get the guys."

***

Storm knelt on the toolbox, her rifle's tripod nearly on the windshield, her upper body supported on her elbows. I took my turn at the machine gun while Archangel and Sarge stayed low, watching the sides.

Storm hissed, tapping on the cab. Dereva immediately slowed. "Movement ahead and to the west," Storm called through the open window.

Dereva pulled off the highway onto one of those side streets that's entirely too easy to miss. The sign hung by one bolt, the rest of it nearly obscured. I caught a glimpse of an 'I' as we passed. Or a worn out 'T.'

Seahorse woke when the truck slowed. Glancing at me quickly, she relaxed and sat up slowly. I huffed a small laugh. Had she just used me as a shit-storm gauge?

Without taking my eyes off our surroundings, I leaned to the side. "Any buildings marked on the map?"

I heard rustling and muted voices in the cab, then Hightide stuck her head out the window. "I can see a fodder store and a school. Fodder store is closer."

"I can see houses," Storm reported. "Spread out neighborhood."

"Find us a house, Dereva. After all, Steve likes bigger buildings."

"Think they're compensating?" Archangel wiggled his pinky, eliciting some laughter.

Dereva, knowing the drill better than anyone, started moving before I finished talking, rolling forward cautiously.

"Oh, God," Doc whispered. "Please let them be here."

Seahorse wrapped an arm around her shoulders, holding her tight. Running her other hand down Sarge's back, she sighed. I shifted until my knee pressed against Archangel's side.

He dropped one hand, squeezing my ankle through the moccasin. "You good?"

"All in, all out, babe," I said.

"No luck, all skill. One shot, one kill," we all finished together.

Leaving Dereva and Hightide with the pickup, the rest of us went our separate ways. Sarge and Seahorse went to get Storm situated as God. The rest of us stayed to the sides of the only road around here, heading straight for the fodder store.

Looking around, I shook my head. Liberty could only be considered a town when compared to the speed bumps to the south of us. Yards and fields were indistinguishable, fences nearly non-existent, and both the houses we passed sported sagging roofs.

Then again, it'd been a few years since the Invasion, so there was that.

Archangel swore suddenly, dropping to one knee, whipping his rifle up. I immediately followed suit, looking for anything out of the ordinary. "Tank treads," he said, indicating with his chin, continually scanning our surroundings.

I hissed, my heart beginning a slow, heavy beat, nervousness and excitement warring. The promise of a fight just...I grinned, looking eagerly for Steve. The tracks came through a field scattered with trees, from the highway.

"Steve's going cross-country, huh?" I muttered. "Bastards. Follow the tank."

"Wonderful." Sparrow rolled her eyes and yanked a bandana out of her pocket. "Follow the tracks left by an unstoppable machine. Great idea, Captain." She pulled a grenade off her belt, wrapping the bandana carefully around it.

"Sarcasm, Sparrow?" I raised my eyebrows, glancing at her from the corner of my eye.

She looked at me innocently, the laugh lines around her eyes showing faintly. "I'm just a ray of sunshine when I'm instructed to follow the boom car, Captain."

"I would've thought it would be your favorite," Archangel said, standing and leading the way, his rifle snug against his shoulder. "Going boom and all."

"Only when I'm inside it," she said dryly.

"That's what he said," I murmured.

Archangel snickered, shooting me a glance. Even Doc cracked a smile.

We spread out, staying close to the trees. We only noticed the store location because it was a large open space. The building itself was gone, just cement foundations left.

"School it is," Archangel said tightly.

Roughly three hundred yards from the school, the trees thinned. At a hint of movement from the corner of my eye, I dropped, taking aim. Archangel promptly followed suit. An indignant "Hey!" from Doc followed by a thump told me Sparrow had Doc covered.

Literally.

We didn't relax until Sarge came into view, followed shortly by Seahorse. "Nice to see your reflexes haven't suffered," Seahorse said when they got close enough. "I really appreciate the Death Squad look when it's on my side."

"Hey, it's not a look everyone can pull off," Archangel said, scanning our backtrail while I checked out the school three hundred feet away.

The single-story building was covered in peeling, light blue paint. A few shabby outbuildings of varying colors surrounded it. I frowned. All the windows were covered, and it looked like there'd been some effort to prop up a sagging roof. Panning over the building, movement to the back caught my eye.

A blind at a rear window moved, but the window was closed.

"You see that?" Seahorse asked.

"Yep." Checking out the rest of the grounds, I scowled. At the far end of the school, leaves fluttered where there wasn't a tree. "Found the tank."

"Do you think Chaos is here?" Doc crawled forward, desperate hope in her face.

"Steve is, so that's a good sign."

"Fuck!" Seahorse angled up. "Dorothy's on the roof."

Doc paled, leaning forward, one hand going to her mouth. "Do you think...Is it possible...Ambrose?"

Leaving the rear watch, Archangel's mouth was set in a grim line, his lips flattened. Just having Dorothy here at all showed this was an outpost for Steve. It was the best chance we had. My gorge rose when an image of Lighting and Thunder, right before their deaths, flashed across my mind.

We were pretty sure Sutter had done that. If he was here...It wouldn't be good for our men.

Shuddering, I straightened my shoulders. Time to woman up. Archangel leaned in, brushing my shoulder. He knew my nightmares about that, and the reality. He knew what I'd do to prevent that happening again.

"We only need one, in case our boys aren't here," I said.

They nodded. We only needed to keep one man alive for questioning. Everyone else...well, no one would really miss them.

Sarge looked at Seahorse quizzically. "What am I missing?"

Seahorse smiled without humor. "Keep the first one alive. Everyone else dies as fast and quietly as possible."

Sarge shifted uncomfortably. "I know you don't have orders from officers, but it still..."

"Yeah." Archangel punched his arm lightly. "We're used to following orders and only going in hot with information. Out here, the rules are a little simpler. Kill them before they kill you."

"And, we are the reinforcements," Seahorse added.

"Where's Storm set up?" I asked.

"There." Seahorse pointed to the west, to a lone fir tree rising above a dilapidated house.

Using Sarge for cover, I grabbed a compact mirror and flashed a message to Storm. *Move closer. Going in at dark.* Seahorse had taught us Morse code and several words, but I rarely used it myself. The scouts and perimeter guards used it more, to relay information quickly.

Trusting that Storm got the message, I turned back to the school, examining it again. Sunset was less than an hour away. We'd wait for full dark and move in before the moon rose.

Nature hit and I grabbed my pack. "Gonna find a tree," I said. I wasn't the only one to disappear. You had to go pee while you could around here. "I gotta go."

Washington, D.C.

Her breaths coming in short, sharp pants, Constance glanced nervously around, smoothing her hands over her slacks, wishing for the fiftieth time that she had something a little more...*dowdy* in her closet. Lurking in dark alleys didn't work very well when all she had to wear were black slacks, stylish, ankle high boots, and a black cashmere turtleneck, and the people around her were dirty, their faces thin and hungry.

Too many of them had bald patches on their heads, the effects of radiation. Homeless, starving, the survivors of Georgia's population had come to D.C. in trickles, then hordes, seeking help from a government that promised much and delivered nothing.

Thoughts and prayers. She snorted, then flinched when the sound caught a ragged boy's attention.

"Spare any change, miss?" he whispered hoarsely, holding a shaky hand out.

Constance shook her head. She never carried money these days, relying entirely on her digiwallet. It was safer, with all the refugees flooding the area, but regret still twinged in her heart.

"Get out of here!" A rough voice broke in. "Go on, get!"

The boy scuttled off when a man in a trench coat entered the alley. Constance surveyed him slowly. And she thought *she* was poorly dressed. This man was a walking cliché, with his collar turned up and a fedora casting a shadow over his face.

Then again, she'd never be able to identify him again, so maybe he wasn't so crazy after all.

Putting his back to the wall, he faced her, his hands in his pockets. A sudden thought made her grip her EM tighter. What if he had a real gun? They'd been illegal for years, but in this place, every illicit thing seemed entirely plausible.

"What day did I first contact you?" he asked her abruptly.

"Wha—?" Shutting her mouth, Constance thought furiously. "Christmas day, last year. But it was dated the twenty-eighth."

It had confused her, why he'd gotten the date wrong, but now, her contact, known to her only as Amos, nodded. "Correct. You've been digging into how the invasion happened. Making some noise. If you don't quiet down, you're likely to go missing, Miss."

Constance shook her head. "Only if they catch me. They still need proof I've done something illegal. It hasn't degenerated that far."

Amos chuckled. "Yet."

When he offered nothing further, she ground her teeth. Damned if she'd leave here with nothing but a useless warning. "Do you have it?" she asked, more sharply than she'd intended.

"It's not here."

"Then why...?"

"It's in the Capitol's Archives."

She sucked in a breath. Knowledge of how North Korea had managed to catch the entire United States with its collective pants down, tucked away in the Capitol. Which meant the government had to know about it.

Or at least, some of them did.

"Why didn't you bring it here?"

He shook his head. "Too risky. If you want it, you'll have to do it yourself."

"How the hell do you expect me to do that?"

"You're Senator McKinney's aide, aren't you? Use that. I can give you codes, tell you exactly where to go, but I'm not taking that out. It's a treason charge if you're caught."

"No heroes here," Constance mumbled, pulling out her tablet. "Okay, what are the codes?"

"What the hell are you doing?" Amos snarled, shrinking against the wall, glancing furtively up and down the alley. "Are you trying to get arrested?"

"What?"

"No tech! You gotta go old school from here on out. They can't hack a piece of paper and a pencil."

"It's not connected. I made sure of that."

"And when you do? They'll have access to everything!"

She sighed, slipping the tablet back into her pocket. People still had pencils and paper, it was a popular aesthetic amongst the university crowd, but nobody took it seriously as a form of communication. She hadn't used one since her own craze a few years ago. Hopefully she could still remember—

Amos shoved a folded piece of paper at her. "Everything's on there," he muttered, already backing away.

"Wait!" she reached out, almost snatching his sleeve. "Who is 'they'? You keep saying 'they.'"

Reluctantly, he turned back. Weak light from the street showed her a chubby cheek between the upturned collar and the hat. "Whoever it is that planned this whole thing. They were in our government."

Chapter 41

Clouds rolled in as the sun set, allowing us to move earlier than planned. The wind kicked up, providing both sound cover and distracting movement. For us and Steve.

We gathered briefly for one last check, preparing to move. Archangel, warm and comforting at my back, nuzzled my ear. Turning my head slightly, I found his mouth. Sliding my fingers over his jaw, the rough texture of his short beard a delicious counterpoint to the softness of his lips, I smiled.

Sighing as we parted, I opened my eyes to see Sarge and Seahorse taking a moment together. Walking silently to the edge of the trees, we gave them an extra second.

Going low, I crawled across the open meadow towards the former school. Imagine crawling like Spiderman, hands and feet, to keep from flattening too much grass and leaving a trail, but needing to keep your butt low, and sometimes hovering just above the ground.

Yeah, there's a reason yoga is the second most popular exercise in the Lair.

Pausing every time the wind hit a lull, or one of the guards on the roof shifted too much, progress was slow. Halfway across, I flattened completely behind a low clump of grass, holding my breath when one of the guards stood up. Closing my eyes, I listened, waiting for them to spot us, my heartbeat slow and steady.

Instead, I heard a distant cough, followed shortly by the thud of a body hitting the ground, barely audible over the wind. Lifting up slowly, I peered around the grass. Another cough, another thud. This happened twice more.

I grimaced. Four guards on the roof? A bit much. This was either very bad, or very good.

At the short, chain link fence, I paused to adjust my pack and machete. Holding my rifle in front, I cleared the fence in a long, low roll, coming up on one knee, rifle aimed at the building. The others landed quietly around me, all of us waiting for the other shoe to drop.

Joy surged through me. As much as I hated the thought of having to fight, actually being in a fight or creeping through the dark like this was still *fun*. It did worry me, when I had time for introspection.

Heading to the back at a crouching run, Archangel took the lead. As soon as Seahorse tapped my shoulder, I patted his, and he moved out silently. The double doors sat in the middle, barely twenty feet away, guarded by two men looking half asleep.

Holstering his handgun, Archangel drew a knife, the blade carefully blackened to prevent any hint of shine. The minutes ticked away in silent agony until one finally looked away.

Archangel took out the first guard and I went past him, tackling the other to the ground. Sitting on his back to keep him from escaping, squirming, or even breathing, I quickly bound him using zip ties, then gagged him. Best invention in the world, zip ties.

Stuffing our captive in the overgrown flower garden, we took up positions around the door. Doc stayed behind Sparrow, holding onto her belt.

Sparrow had a lighter in one hand, her other filled with something that would undoubtedly go boom shortly after being lit.

Seahorse, one hand on the door, held her free hand up, slowly counting down. As soon as she reached zero, she opened the door, then Archangel, Sarge, and me spilled through.

***

We didn't clear rooms. It was too easy to hear snoring, farting, and men turning over in restless sleep. Each door we listened at held multiple men. Sweating lightly in the cool air, I crept down the hall, searching for some clue to where our men were.

In the center of the school, open to the hallway by large windows, lay the office. The windows were broken, the sills filled with jagged shards of glass. Skylights above dimly illuminated the scene inside.

My breath caught in my chest. The desks and chairs had been pushed to the edges, leaving the middle of the room clear. What lay there...

Doc gave a raw, strangled cry. I clapped a hand over her mouth to muffle the rest of it. Her eyes bulged and she clawed at my hand. "I'll kill them," she whispered, her nails digging into my skin.

Both men were naked. Goliath, a dark shape against the white floor, lay curled on his side, unmoving. Chaos was on his back, spreadeagle, tied wrist and ankle to railroad nails hammered into the office floor.

Seahorse tested the door. "It's stuck."

Archangel stripped off his jacket while Sarge carefully picked shards of glass out of the windowsill. When he had enough space, Archangel threw his jacket over the frame. Placing one hand on the jacket, I hopped up, catching one foot on the sill and stepping through, onto the desk pushed there.

Pulling Doc through, I set her on her feet. She immediately rushed to Chaos, placing her fingers against his neck. Nodding sharply, she checked Goliath next. Hopping down, I went to Goliath, gently checking him over.

As near as I could tell by feel, Goliath had been whipped, carefully, the marks crisscrossing his back, all the way down to his knees. Then they'd gone to work on his front. Goliath groaned, flinching when I found a particularly sore spot.

"Sorry, sorry," I whispered over and over. "It's me. Captain. You're okay. You're safe, now. I've got you."

His lips moved, but no sound came out. Grabbing my canteen off my belt, I held it to his lips. He drank thirstily, water spilling down his cheek. I hovered over him, fluttering uselessly. I didn't know how to help someone hurt like this. I couldn't even touch him.

How were we going to move him? "Have we got something to wrap him in?" I asked. Seahorse presented me with two dingy white sheets. "Where the hell did you find these?"

"Hall closet." She squatted on her heels, laying one hand on his head, stroking his curly hair. "We're gonna need a lot of Dirt Huggers."

Stripping off my pack, I fished out my little flask while Seahorse got hers. Laying one sheet on the ground next to him, I straightened it carefully. Seahorse held the flask to his mouth, encouraging him to drink as much as possible. Then, she took off her belt, folded it, and put it between his teeth.

Sarge rested a hand on the side of Goliath's neck, his other tucked under Goliath's arm, curving over his shoulder. Then, he leaned over, preparing to put all his considerable weight on the wounded man. I knelt, my feet crossing his. Then I sat.

When I nodded, Seahorse gave me one short, sharp nod in return, bit her lip, and poured the remains of her flask and most of mine across the wounds on his front. Goliath jerked so hard I fell forward, bracing my hands on his knees, struggling to hold him still.

Then she moved to his back. This time, I didn't even pretend. I straddled his legs, pressing down, while Seahorse doctored his back as best she could. Then, we carefully wrapped him in the sheet, turning him into a Goliath burrito.

"How ironic," Goliath whispered hoarsely, "that fucking Dorothy whips the black man but gives the white guy a whole different type of torture."

"Dorothy?" Seahorse asked, leaning close. Doc looked up briefly, listening intently. "Do you have a name?"

"Fucker...fucker..." He lapsed back into unconsciousness.

Sarge cradled Goliath, surprisingly gentle as he supported the unconscious man's head on his shoulder. Glancing over at Archangel and Sparrow, I hissed. When he looked over, I held up a hand, asking if anyone was coming. He shook his head, then indicated Sparrow, who was working on the door. She raised a fist triumphantly, delicately pulling the door open.

One thing going right, then. I crawled over to Doc to see if she needed help. She worked frantically over Chaos, her mouth set in a hard line of concentration.

"How is he?"

She shuddered. "I'll know more when I can *see* him, but it could be worse. Couple broken ribs. A few missing nails. I think these are burns on his chest. I can't tell what kind yet. I think..." Her voice broke. "I think they used slow slicing."

I snarled silently, rage surging.

"Goliath?"

"They whipped him. He can't walk. I have no idea how we're going to get him back to the pickup."

Sarge shifted. "I can carry him."

I scoffed. "The man's like six foot five and solid muscle. I've met bulls that weighed less than him."

"I can do it," he said stubbornly. "I'll need help to get him over my shoulders, but I can carry him."

"Then load him up." Doc interrupted my train of thought. "I can't do anything else here. I need to get Chaos out."

"Babe," I said softly to Archangel. "We need you."

Working swiftly, they got Goliath across Sarge's shoulders, his arms and legs reaching Sarge's knees. I helped Doc get Chaos situated on Archangel.

"Let's go," he whispered.

I shook my head. "Me and Sparrow are gonna do something about this shithole."

His mouth tightened but he nodded. "One shot, one kill, you hear me?"

I gave him a quick kiss. "Yessir. No luck, all skill. Seahorse, take the lead. Sparrow, with me."

At the first corner, Seahorse paused. My eyes half closed, I listened. A little *click* sounded, then Seahorse disappeared briefly. A quick scuffle and she was back, waving the line forward.

When the front door shut behind them, I breathed into Sparrow's ear, "I've got three grenades and two flashbangs. What are you holding?"

She unzipped her jacket and put my hand on her belt. Grenades lined it as neatly as peas in a pod. I huffed quietly. "Is everybody here a pyromaniac?"

"Um...yes?"

I quivered with restrained laughter. "One per room. Don't look, just toss and go. Ready?"

She nodded, the fine hairs that escaped her braids brushing my lips and put a grenade in my hand. "We can go every other," she whispered. "These walls are thin. They won't hold the shrapnel. Make sure you're not standing in front of it when it goes off, too."

Okay. Was not expecting that warning.

She plopped two grenades in my hand and moved to the right. One door each side in this section, then we'd have to run around the corners. The classrooms lined the outside edges of the school, the office in the center.

I took a couple deep, fast breaths, pumping myself up, and grasped the doorknob. Yanking the pin with my teeth, I glanced across the hallway. Sparrow held a hand up, counting down. On *three*, we wrenched the doors open just enough to toss the grenades, slammed them, and bolted.

Shrapnel punched through the wall even as screams filled the night.

Shouts and slamming doors said the rest of them were waking up. At the next door, I tossed the second grenade she'd given me, and ran like my life depended on it, skipping the door in between. Pistol suddenly in my left hand, I fired at the few people foolish enough to enter the hallway and made it to my third room.

Too many men in here, now. Where the hell had they all come from? Why the fuck were they even in this podunk town?

"Flambe!" Sparrow screamed from the other side of the office.

Flames lit the hallway on that side, men screaming as they burned. I threw my next grenade into the growing crush in front of me and dived headfirst through the office window, turning slightly to skid across the desk on my shoulder instead of my face, and land on my upper back, barely turning it into a tumble.

Racing through the now-empty office, I vaulted onto the table, kicked out the glass, and leaped down, grabbing Sparrow's arm even as she prepared to throw another cocktail.

"Time to go!" I wrenched my second to last grenade off my belt, dragging her towards the exit, yanking the pin and tossing it over my shoulder in one move.

Diving around the corner to hide from the explosion, I cupped my hands over my ears, wishing their screams weren't echoing in my head. I accidentally caught a glimpse of the carnage in our wake. A man's desperate, reaching hand, struggling to escape and frozen in death...

Once we made it outside, Sparrow doubled over, puking into the bushes. I held her battle braids away from her face, rubbing her back. My mouth worked and I scraped my face over my shoulder, trying to dislodge one of my smaller braids caught in the corner of my mouth.

"I know," I soothed. "I know. But we can't stay here, hon."

"I know," she gasped, rinsing her mouth. When she tried to stand, her legs wouldn't hold her.

Getting one of her arms over my shoulder, I led her to the north side, where the tank sat. She was so slight, even after all her training, that I barely noticed her weight. Half carrying her, half trying not to hear the groans and sobbing from inside, Oregon then decided to start a heavy drizzle.

I sighed, suddenly exhausted.

A faint scrape on concrete that didn't even register, and I was moving without fully knowing why. Shoving Sparrow behind me, I crouched just as a man howled, his fist thudding into the siding above me.

The howling formed words. "You bastard! You murdered my men. Do you know what I'll do to you, you son of a bitch?"

I straightened, stepping away from Sparrow. "Technically, I'm the bitch, not the son of," my mouth supplied, without consulting my brain first.

He paused. "Fucking bitches," he snarled. He continued hurling epithets, each one less imaginative than the last.

I frowned. Something about this sounded familiar. "Sutton, is that you, you mealy-mouthed, wife-beating wannabe?"

I'd had a run in with Doc's husband in Salem...oh, who knew how long ago. Before I got married. At my words, he froze, his big shoulders scrunching up. It was too dark to see his face, which was a shame. It would've been priceless. One to tell the family about.

Well, considering Papa and Sean, maybe not.

He sucked in a breath. "*You*! Captain." He roared my name.

I sniggered, bowing slightly. "You tell your masters it was a woman that kicked your ass?"

"Fuck you, cunt!" He stretched and flexed, cracking his knuckles. His massive silhouette looked more like a mountain shifting. "Let's go for round two. I'll teach you how to treat your master. You'll even enjoy it when I'm fucking you."

I yawned, patting my mouth. "Bo-ring!"

He roared, lurching forward, gaining momentum with every step. Finally remembering the other three pistols on my person, I drew, but only had time to fire a couple times before he reached me. Sidestepping, I tripped over a rock, and he mowed me down, his hands reaching for my throat.

Abandoning the guns, I yanked the small knife at the top of my moccasin, plunging it into his side frantically, hoping one of them would make it past his ribs.

"Captain!" Sparrow shrieked.

The weight on me doubled, Sutton going limp, then lessened when Sparrow rolled him off me. "Captain, talk to me," she gasped, patting my face.

I wheezed, gasping and coughing, my heart thundering out of my chest. "I don't...I don't like not being able to breathe."

Seeing I was okay, she rounded on Sutton's body. "You. Don't. Talk. To people. Like. That!" she sobbed, punctuating each word with a kick.

Crawling to the side, I coughed, struggling to breathe normally. I found one gun. The little knife went back into its sheath. Still crawling, I made my way around the body, which Sparrow had left off kicking. Instead, she pulled her knife out of his back, wiping it on his jacket. "Thanks," I wheezed.

Using the wall, I made it to my feet. Sparrow handed me my other gun. My rifle hung half off my arm, so I hadn't lost that. "I'm so fucking done with this shit," I rasped, my throat raw, recent events draining what little strength I had left. "Let's blow the fucking tank and leave."

After she'd set...something, in and around the moving bits in the tank's treads, she pulled me back. She eyed it for a moment and moved back further, behind a huge old oak. "Okay," she said. "Shoot it."

I glanced at her. "That's it?"

"It'll do."

Leaning against the trunk, I braced. Taking a deep breath, I let it out slowly, squeezing the trigger.

Whatever I did was good enough, because pieces of tank went pinging away, into the forest, the ground, even the shed off to the side. Sparrow laughed, clapping her hands.

"Boom," she whispered.

***

Walking back to the truck, my legs refused to work, fatigue crashing down. We leaned on each other, weaving drunkenly down the middle of the road.

"Which house?" I mumbled, squinting, my eyes going blurry.

Sparrow groaned. "I have to check every parking row to find my car. There's a reason I chose demolitions and not scouting."

"Yeah, because you're fucking crazy." A familiar purr reached my ears, one of the most beautiful sounds I'd ever heard.

Sparrow began crying. Blackness crawled in around the edges of my vision. The ground swayed and I couldn't find my footing.

"Captain," Archangel shouted just before everything went black.

***

The first thing I noted were the vibrations running through me. My baby. My pickup. Frantic hands running over me, delving under my harnesses, skimming over skin. Archangel's hands.

"Where is she hurt?" he asked urgently. "We heard gunshots. What happened, Sparrow?"

"We were fine until we ran across Sutton..."

"Oh, God," Doc moaned.

"He's dead."

"Oh, yay."

I mumbled something unintelligible, even to me. Archangel gently lifted me, cradling me close. I sighed, content for the first time in hours, burying my face against his shoulder.

"You passed out," he whispered.

"I don't pass out." I let out a shuddering breath, grimacing at the pain in my throat. Sutton had managed to get a good grip for a time. "I'm just tired."

"Sutton did land on her," Sparrow said apologetically. "And he...choked her a bit."

Archangel swore, a stream of inventive invective. No wonder I loved him. The man could be creative. "If he wasn't already dead, I'd kill him. Who did it?"

"It was a group effort," Sparrow murmured.

"She stabbed him in the back while he was choking me," I mumbled.

"Good for you."

"Here." Doc shifted to see around Archangel. "Let me check..." Flicking a lighter, she brought the flame closer, examining my eyes, then listened to my heart and breathing. "Well," she eventually said, "you don't look like you have a concussion. You're talking clearly. I'll need to see you for a full checkup to figure out why you passed out."

"I don't faint," I protested. "Never have before. Except for the time I passed out from getting stabbed."

"You're coming in."

"Don't worry, Doc," Archangel assured her. "She'll be there."

"Traitor," I whispered.

He pressed his cheek to mine. "Payback's a bitch."

I gasped. "I made you get a physical *one time*!"

"Now, I'm making you get one." By this time the sky had lightened enough to see the tightness around his mouth and the worry in his eyes.

Sighing, I sagged in his hold, tracing a finger down, over the bridge of his nose, lips, and stopping at his chin. "You win."

"It's not a matter of winning or losing." Doc looked up from Chaos. "I say you have to come in. The end. It's either that or I tell Amana you're refusing a doctor's visit."

My mouth dropped open even as exhausted laughter bubbled up while groans filled the truck. No one messed with Amana.

Dereva turned onto a side road, climbing slowly. Storm, watching the back, shook her head, her braids sliding over her back. "There's a fuck-ton of trucks and tanks converging on that school."

Archangel lifted me enough to see. Wisps of smoke still rose from the tank, the area buzzing with men and vehicles. I nestled back against Noah's shoulder, content with the previous night's work. Hopefully that was a spanner in their works.

CHAPTER 42

More importantly, what will Captain, the so-called leader of the uprising inside the occupied zone, do next? He puts us at risk every time he fights back, yet some are hailing this stranger as a hero. How do we know he has our best interests at heart?

The Morning Show

I sat in Doc's exam room, elbows on my knees, chin resting on my hands, contemplating the results of the meeting in the Useless Room. A hunter named Speakeasy had done Chaos's last supply run with the weasel, Spartacus. They said they'd never seen Steve, or even sign, but something felt off.

Sitting straight when Doc returned, I watched shuffle her notes, avoiding my gaze. I pursed my lips, watching her, and folded my arms. "Spill."

She chewed her lip, then huffed a breath. Fidgeted with her pencil, then set it aside. "You're pregnant," she blurted.

My mouth dropped open, all thought of Spartacus gone in an instant. "What? How?"

That drew a laugh out of her. "If you don't know that, then I'm not sure what you've been doing with that husband of yours these last several seasons."

Rolling my eyes, I snapped, "I know *how*, but you've been complaining for ages that we don't have enough fat or something. I barely have periods!"

"That may be true, but you've managed it anyway." There'd been a few other women who'd gotten pregnant with their partners. The one thing they had in common is they were immediately benched. They were all Home now, raising their kids. "I don't know how far along you are, but you know the drill."

Yes, and I didn't want to get benched. I ran my hands over my hair, pressing them against my mouth to hold back hysterical laughter. I'd never even thought of kids beyond a few pipe dreams with Noah...Oh, God. "How do I tell Archangel?"

Doc coughed to hide her laughter. She did a shit job of it. Then again, she'd been so much lighter in spirit without the threat of her husband hanging over her head. "I don't know. Gently?"

"Will you quit laughing at me?"

"It's hard not to. I rarely see you so...human. It's refreshing."

"Fuck off."

Now she laughed outright. "Good luck. Now, go away. Come see me next week. We'll need to set up prenatal care."

***

I hid in the garage with Mech. My cousin didn't question my presence. He simply grunted and pointed to a car. We worked quietly together, getting back to old, familiar rhythms while one thought echoed through my mind.

I'm pregnant.

I still hadn't grasped it when we broke for dinner, and I was no closer to a plan to break the news to Archangel.

He was seated with Phoenix and Gryph when I entered, and I smiled, momentarily distracted at seeing Gryph on his feet.

The distraction didn't last long, and I fiddled with my spoon through dinner, stumbling whenever someone spoke to me, wanting desperately to blurt my news out just to get it over with.

Archangel touched my knee. "You alright?"

I nodded and gave him a tight smile, but I didn't feel it. I didn't want to leave the fight. From a distance, I hated it, but in the middle...Oh, the rush, the exhilaration. And they needed every fighter out there. How could I leave?

I could try to abort, but I immediately shied away from that. A little piece of us both...Oh, no, I wanted this baby. I just didn't want it right now.

Archangel hauled me out when he realized I wasn't eating, straight to our room. "What is it?" he demanded. "Did Doc give you bad news?"

"What?" My hands went to my guns, then my belt, fluttering, a physical manifestation of the turmoil within.

He pointed at me. "You've barely said two words all through dinner. I've never seen you so distracted. What did Doc say?"

My legs gave out and I sat abruptly on the bed. My heart pounded, enough to leave me short of breath. Was this a panic attack? What should I say? Like all my life these days, the only way out was through. "Noah..." His eyes widened in alarm at his real name. "I'm pregnant. Doc reckons three months. Maybe four."

He sagged against the wall, his eyes blank, sinking slowly to the floor. "You sure?" he croaked.

"She seemed pretty certain," I said grimly.

"How?"

I laughed, but there was little humor to it. "How do you think?"

"But...but you barely have periods. I'd have noticed..."

The corners of my mouth turned down and I covered my mouth to hide it. "Are you...happy?"

He half laughed, half sobbed. "Happy. Terrified. I don't know...What the hell? How are we supposed to do this?" My heart sank with every word. "I..." He finally looked at me. Holding out his hand, he whispered, "Come here."

Lunging across the room, I curled in his arms, sobbing. He held me tightly, as if he'd never let go, stroking my hair while I cried. "I don't know what to do," I said. "What kind of world are we bringing a baby into?"

He kissed my forehead, resting his mouth between my eyebrows until I calmed. "It's a shitty world. I guess we have to make a better one for our baby. We'll figure this out. Together."

***

I would've ignored my pregnancy until I was in labor, but rumors began flying the third time I missed a mission, even a small one. Eleanor—working on the tiniest piece of knitting I'd ever seen—sat with me while the others were out.

"I don't want *everyone* to know," I protested. "We've got some people who are heading Home soon. I'll tell the fighters after they leave."

"In that case," Eleanor paused while she adjusted her yarn, "you have three days."

"And I'm waiting until Archangel's back."

He'd begun sticking to a schedule. Instead of leaving for an indeterminate time, he'd stay out for a max of seven days. And he had to go out often, because fucking Steve was operating around here. Our months living in a cave to draw them away hadn't worked for long. Steve poured back into the mountains in greater numbers.

"Which should be tomorrow," Eleanor said placidly. "So you can tell people in three days."

"Shit."

***

Three days later, I climbed onto the bench. It'd been somewhere around six weeks since Doc diagnosed me as pregnant. My waist had begun to thicken, but it was nowhere near noticeable yet. I placed a foot on the table.

"No." Amana shook her head slowly. "*Capitán,* don't jou dare."

Staring right into her eyes, I stepped up. In a couple minutes, she'd forget all about this. I cupped my hands around my mouth and shouted, "Oi! Shut it, you lot!"

Gryphon nudged his wife. "She got that from me, you know."

He wasn't wrong. We'd been spending a lot of time together while he recuperated, playing cards. He told me about England and Scotland. I'd never been, but it was on my list. I talked about Oregon Before.

"You may have noticed..." I cleared my throat. "You may have noticed I haven't been going into the field lately."

Nods, shrugs, a couple of irritated faces.

"I can't," I said baldly.

"Why not?" The Celt shouted. "You know you miss it."

"We made the rules...By all the rules..." I bit my lip, surprised by a sudden rush of tears. I looked down at my husband. "Help?"

Archangel hopped up on the bench and wrapped his arm around my hips. "She's pregnant."

Those two words ripped through the fighters, leaving absolute silence. A second later, the room exploded, everyone shouting questions, congratulations, and I don't know what else. Archangel pulled me off the table. Amana's mouth hung open, more than worth whatever punishment she'd mete out for standing on the table.

Phoenix gripped my hand. "You are?"

I nodded.

They kept shouting, until a loud clanging overrode them. Amana stood in front of the serving window, enthusiastically banging a metal ladle on the huge pot.

"*Silencio!*" When Amana raised her voice, people listened. "*Capitán.*" She nodded respectfully. "Jou will not be fighting, *sí*?"

"*Sí.*"

"Will jou go Home?"

"I don't know. Yet."

She nodded, rubbing the ladle absently. "Will you return to the fight, after?"

"I don't know."

"Okay, *hermano y hermanas*. Jou have the answers. Now, *callate!*"

They went back to their meals, but I saw many thoughtful faces and a small measure of worry.

Or maybe that was just me.

***

I groaned, sitting on the edge of our bed, arching my back. "I know they said back aches are normal, but they never said it would be this bad," I complained.

It was early summer outside, the cherries blossomed, and my belly ripened at a similar pace. The only reason I didn't waddle when I walked was my height. Instead, according to Phoenix, I swayed majestically through the Lair, but I felt like a barge.

The mattress shifted, a foot appearing on either side of me, then more leg as Archangel scooted closer. Strong fingers kneaded my lower back. My groan of pain turned to one of appreciation and relief. Spreading my knees to make room for my growing belly, I leaned forward to give him better access.

"And I don't like being fat," I continued. "How do women go through this more than once? Why did my mom do this four times?"

My husband bit my shoulder, letting me feel the sharpness of his teeth. "You're not fat." Reaching around, he stroked my belly, then ran his hands down my thighs. "You're just used to being really skinny. Trust me, there's plenty of muscle here. Anyway, I like you fat." He pressed against my butt, showing he really did like me this way.

"Well." Sliding off the mattress, onto the floor, I faced him. "It'd be a shame to let this go to waste."

Laughing, he helped me up, sinking slowly onto the bed, pulling me with him.

***

Anansi perked up when he saw me swaying down the hall to the Useless Room. River was back and it was time to decide where and how to hit Steve to get them to stop burning the hills.

Running ahead, 'Nansi cupped his hands around his mouth. "Everybody MOVE!" he bellowed, throwing his hands out. "Wide load, coming through!"

My jaw dropped. Fighters giggled or stared in shock, depending on how well they knew me. Dereva, leaning against the wall, grinned insolently, anticipating my reaction.

I couldn't disappoint her. "Anansi, you little shit," I yelled. "Get your ass over here so I can whup it good."

Cackling, the young man ran off. I heard a yelp and the boy reappeared, frog-marched around the corner, his ear held in his mother's firm grip.

"Oh, look." I grinned evilly. He gulped. "You're back."

I left his mother putting the fear of her into him and his abject apologies as I continued to the Useless Room.

After River presented us with the information and we heard from the recently returned scouts, the entire table looked to me. Continue with the small groups or send out one large one, more like a small army?

My mouth dried up and tears prickled my eyes. I couldn't think of anything. When had this ever happened? Archangel took my hand, lacing our fingers together. I studied his hand, the long fingers, broad palm with golden hairs sprinkled over the back.

His nails, square-ish, light pink, the nails kept short, had dirt underneath and around the edges. More than usual, so he'd been in the garden beds recently.

Slowly exhaling, I looked up. All eyes were focused on me. "I'm inclined towards slightly larger small groups. Something big enough to deal with a two to three truck patrol from Steve, but not too big to disappear. You guys?"

While Phoenix still preferred to hit them like a sledgehammer, she agreed that this could work for a while to push them out. We adjusted the size, deciding to go for twenty-five person teams. Then they said they'd leave in two days, and I had to accept that I'd be staying behind.

Again.

***

Afterwards, I went to check on Chaos and Goliath. Goliath, temporarily quartered next to Doc, lay half on his side, propped up with pillows. It was only by curling up that he was able to get his feet on the bed, and he looked comfortable enough, considering.

He immediately tried to sit up. "Whoa, whoa!" I hurried over. "Don't be struggling so hard, man. You're gonna tear something. Physio's no joke."

More than two months since the torture, and he still got winded easily. Weak as a kitten, by his own admission, he relaxed against the pillows, smiling slightly. "I hate not being able to move," he admitted.

I rubbed my belly. "Tell me about it. In another couple months, I won't be able to tie my shoes. How's things going with you?"

He shook his head, smiling, but the expression was hollow. "Nothing's changed since last week." His broad forehead wrinkled. "Or was it a couple days? Time crawls when you're stuck."

Except he didn't stop frowning. His fingers convulsively plucked at the blanket, and he wouldn't meet my eyes. Kestrel had told me something was up, but patient/doctor privilege meant all she could do was tell me to see him soon.

"It wasn't that long," I admitted. I sighed, unable to come up with a decent segue. "All right, spit it out. I can see something bothering you, and you being twitchy is making me twitchy."

He chewed on his bottom lip, tucking his hands under the pillow, looking like the biggest lost child I'd ever seen. Abandoning the chair, I sat on the edge of his mattress, resting my hand on his shoulder. "Dude...Goliath, you can ask me anything." The implications of that flashed across my mind, and the caveat slipped out before I could stop it. "Except about my sex life."

That got a laugh out of him, and he finally looked at me—in startled horror. "No! Gross! I can guess how your sex life is." He shuddered, reminding me that he was barely more than twenty. "I can't believe I just said that. Ew."

"Then what is it?" I asked gently.

He took a shuddering breath, letting it out slowly, struggling to keep his lips from trembling. I waited for him to speak, content to sit next to him until he was ready. Finally, he spoke. "I don't remember what happened. I know I was whipped, I can see and feel the evidence of it, but why can't I remember anything until I woke up here?"

"Trauma can do all kinds of weird things. You're not the first to lose their memory."

"Will I get it back?"

"Do you want to?" I chewed on my lip. "Some do, some don't. And you didn't just have a traumatic experience, you had to witness Chaos's torture, too." I rubbed his shoulder. "But if you want to know...We found you in an old school building. Steve had been using it as a major base. They had a lot of Dorothy there, too. Including that bastard, Sutton."

He flinched, burying his head a little deeper into the pillow. "I think I remember him. He said...he called me names. Nothing I've never heard before, but then, I wasn't chained..." A tear dropped onto the pillow. "I remember that, too. They chained me up. Put a dog collar on me for a while."

"We doctored you as best we could," I continued after a while. "Sarge carried you out. He looked like he was about to pull a muscle, but he did it. Archangel got Chaos. Me and Sparrow stayed behind to fuck shit up."

"And did you?"

"Fuck yeah!" I rubbed a hand over my mouth, trying to banish the scent of smoke, blood, and death that had been so strong I could taste it that night. "Sutton ambushed us outside." Goliath tensed. "He went for me, and while he was distracted, Sparrow stabbed him in the back."

"Did she really?" He smiled through the tears. "I owe her. And you. Big time."

Leaning down, I kissed his cheek. "You can repay us by getting better and talking to Kestrel. She's the best equipped to help you heal."

"Yes, ma'am." He yawned suddenly. He clapped a hand over his mouth, his eyes flying to my face, alarmed.

Smiling, I rose. "Now, you need your rest."

"Thank you, Captain. And…" I paused, turning back from the door. He looked unbearably young, lying there. "You won't stay Home, will you? You'll come back?"

I smiled, but it didn't reach my eyes. "I won't be going anywhere just yet. I'm not due until fall. Okay?"

He nodded, his eyes already closing. "Thank you, ma'am."

"And don't call me ma'am."

He grinned as I closed the door.

***

I lay awake in the dark room, Archangel sleeping peacefully next to me. My fingers drummed on my belly, the conversation with Goliath rolling around in my head. What should I do with a baby in this world? Could I take myself out of the fight? And what about Archangel? We tried not to split up families. Usually, the father would go Home, too.

We couldn't take both of us out of the fight. The truth was, we were too valuable. We had people who could lead, sure, but when it came to the actual fight, he was the best. I was the meanest, but he was better, hands down.

I shifted, trying to find a position that didn't put pressure on another part. And my body…I didn't recognize it anymore. I couldn't get comfortable, my legs were swelling, my belly seemed to get bigger by the day, and I'd had the joy of popping early. As near as we could guess, I was roughly five months along, and my stomach looked like a child's basketball.

Then there was Steve. Kwan Jae must've put the fear of God into them, because they were all over the foothills. So, I had to send my husband off again, without his battle partner.

A tear rolled down the side of my face, dropping onto the pillow. I squeezed my eyes shut to hold back more, until a distinct bump somewhere around my sternum took my breath away. No tiny flutter, this was thrown with some force.

I pressed a hand down, waiting for the next one. When it happened again, I reached awkwardly behind me, shaking Noah's hip.

"Noah," I hissed. "Babe. Wake up."

He exploded upright, weapon in hand. "What?"

I snorted, barely muffling the giggles that vibrated through me. "Sorry. Sorry. Here." Taking his hand, I pressed it to the spot.

His irritation vanished when the baby kicked again. He whistled quietly. "That's a basher, right there. Phew!"

Wrapping himself around me, he put both hands on my stomach, exploring gently. I moved his hand with the tiny thumps. He sighed, melting against my back. "That's our baby," he whispered, awed.

"Baby's gonna turn me black and blue," I said ruefully, grunting slightly when it hit a new spot. The tears hit again. "I don't know what's wrong with me. One minute I'm crying, the next I'm laughing, then the waterworks start again. This sucks so fucking much."

He kissed the back of my neck, right at the base. I shivered, like he knew I would. "Since I can't help with this part of it, maybe I can give you a distraction."

Right at that moment, the baby took the opportunity to dance the salsa low down. "Dammit, not my bladder. Shit. Babe, help me up." Sighing, he rolled to his feet, hauling me out. As soon as I made it upright, gravity worked in earnest, and I hustled from the room. By this time, I knew exactly where the nearest toilet was at all times, and I barely made it.

When I returned, Archangel sat on the side of the bed, waiting for me.

"Little twerp's been taking lessons from Anansi and Phoenix," I murmured, standing gingerly. "I guess this little one's going to be interrupting things fairly often."

He laughed quietly, pulling me to stand between his knees, speaking directly to my belly. "Mama and me are going to have times when we throw you outside, little one. Don't think that we don't love you, because we do, and we will even more as we get to know you. But once you're old enough, I will be making up for lost time with your mom. So, fair warning, kid."

I ran my fingers through his thick hair, smiling down at him. "Oh, is that right?"

"Yes, ma'am. And, by my reckoning, we have some lost time to make up for right now." He helped me back into bed, his hands and lips no more eager than my own, my laughter filling the little room.

***

"*Capitán,*" Amana called when I waddled into the common room. The fighters were due to leave today, and depression at having to say goodbye to them pulled me down, only lightened by the Latina's smile of greeting. "*Todo bien?*"

"*Sí,* Amana. I'll be alright. Just hungry."

"Ahh, jou are lucky. We have our very famous soup!"

I maneuvered onto the bench, aware that I wasn't fat enough to have *that* much trouble moving, but I'd lost all sense of my dimensions in the last few months. I had bruises over my hips from bumping into things, and I regularly knocked things over with my stomach. Plus, my breasts were sore all the time.

Basically, this trimester sucked.

"*Gracías.*" I smiled up at her when she set a bowl in front of me. "Thanks for not making me get up again."

She laughed. "Eat," she commanded, rubbing my shoulder before heading back to the kitchen.

Storm strode past the door, then backtracked. "Captain!" She wove through the tables with a speed and agility I envied. "How's it going?" She plopped onto the bench next to me.

"Baby's pretty active today." Taking her hand, I pressed it to my right side, where the baby practiced its running technique.

Her eyes widened and a huge grin spread over her face. Bending down, her curly golden hair falling across her face, she whispered, "Hey, you. You know, we're all pretty glad you're coming. Your parents are awesome people. We really miss having your mom in the field. Especially your dad. I know you'll need her, but we need her, too."

She glanced up at me, tucking her hair behind her ear, and shrugged. "Hate to break it to you, but it's different, not having you in the field."

"Oh, *sí,*" Amana put in. "It must be very hard, not having *tu comediante* with jou."

Ignoring her, I gently traced a finger down the scar running from her temple to her jaw. "I ain't going far. The kid'll simply have the proverbial village to raise 'em."

"So, you'll be back in the field?"

I shook my head. "Not sure yet. But I'm not staying Home, either."

Storm smiled, relief shining in her eyes. Rubbing my belly one last time, as if it were a lucky charm, she dropped a kiss on my cheek and breezed out.

Over the next few weeks, that scene played out many more times, with small variations, each person looking for reassurance that I wasn't leaving permanently.

***

I waddled down the corridor, frowning. Pregnancy created all kinds of extra problems that were pushed aside until they couldn't be ignored anymore. I'd spent so much time either fucking uncomfortable or amazed at the sensations of the baby moving around that I ignored some things.

Archangel's voice floated down the corridor. I couldn't see him, but I'd bet he was in the armory. Gryphon's deep, British accent reached me next. Yep. Definitely griping.

My heart plummeted to the soles of my feet. He wanted me to go Home. Now. Yesterday. Steve was near, slowly homing in on the Lair, and he worried they'd find us. They were sniffing around the right wilderness area, too close for comfort.

I didn't want to go, and every time I spoke to someone alone, all I heard was relief that I stayed.

"What are you going to do?" He'd leaned in, hissing, his face tight with anger. "Bump them away with your stomach? You're not Superman!"

"In their eyes, I damn well am!" I snapped. "What do you want me to do, abandon them?"

"Yes! If it keeps you and the baby safe, HELL YES!"

"So what?" Unable to pace, I threw my hands into the air. "'Abandon all hope, ye who enter here?'"

He whipped around, jabbing a finger in my direction. "You are the most pig-headed idiot I've ever met. 'Fake it 'til you make it' is fucking stupid advice. It wasn't meant to be the creed you died by." He rubbed a trembling hand over his mouth.

"Are you going to make me bury you and our baby?" he whispered.

Unable to take it, I'd fled before I broke down.

Now, I leaned against the wall, wanting to tell him I'd go Home right now. Another part of me seized at the thought of leaving the fight. What if all I was good for was fighting anymore? Taking care of a baby required reliability. Steady emotions. Someone who didn't hover on the edge of violence as a matter of course.

Anybody who wasn't me.

Archangel and Gryph suddenly rounded the corner, Gryph's head bent close to Archangel's. My husband's face was dark, he spoke intensely, his hands gesticulating, the motions sharp, abrupt.

His jaw tightened when he saw me, but he gave me a short nod. Gryphon, putting preservation ahead of the bro code, disappeared. Straightening, I reached out, running the backs of my fingers over his hand. He froze. Without volition, his hand twitched, catching my fingers.

I sighed, relaxing. "We should go talk to Eleanor," I said quietly. I hadn't planned it, the words just slipped out, but I knew as soon as I said it that it was the right course. She could help.

He nodded shortly, but when he fell in beside me, he didn't let go of my hand. Reaching over with my free hand, I took his arm, leaning against him slightly. "I'm sorry I yelled at you, earlier."

"Me, too." He relaxed a bit more. "Eleanor is a good idea."

"Better than Amana," I said dryly. "She'd just yell at us in Spanish. Maybe throw in a few other languages if we really piss her off."

At Eleanor's door, he knocked lightly.

"Just a minute," she called. "When she opened the door, she had a sleeping puppy cradled in the crook of her arm. "Don't wake him. Poor baby isn't feeling good."

"Whose is he?" I eyed the little one, mostly black, with white paws and a hint of white on his chest.

"Obelix and Lily's." One of the pups I'd found in the Valley years ago. They had the run of the Lair and had been adopted by various people. Mostly perimeter guards and hunters, but the next generation hadn't been spoken for yet, apparently. She smiled softly at the pup. "He's the runt, but the smartest one of the litter."

She looked back up, then did a double take. "What's up?"

"We've been arguing," Archangel said bluntly.

"I see." Stepping back, she motioned us in.

Once the door was shut, it all spilled out.

"He wants me to go Home—"

"—stubborn woman thinks she's fucking Superman—"

"—keep me locked in a tower if he had his way—"

"—pig-headed *idiot!*"

"—doesn't want me around anymore!"

He fell silent at my final outburst, his mouth hanging open. I was gasping, red-faced, more of those abominable tears streaming down my face. Eleanor watched us, her eyes bright with laughter or concern. Hard to tell at this point.

Archangel was the first to break the silence. "What. The fuck. Is. *Wrong.* With you?"

"Well, it's not like you're offering to come Home with me!"

"I would if I had to!"

I folded my arms, really just resting them on my stomach, glaring. "Really? You'd just...leave the fight? Leave all these poor shmucks to deal with Steve on our doorstep? Abandon them?"

He squirmed, then scowled. "I'm not pregnant!"

"And what if one person was the tipping point? What if, by leaving, they're short-handed? What if this becomes permanent and I have to raise our kid in occupied Salem? 'Sorry, kid, but me and your dad dropped the ball to raise you in a cave, now almost everyone we know is dead and we're in this shithole.'"

"That's not realistic," he pointed out, the corner of his mouth twitching in a tiny smile.

"Maybe not, but then again, *this*," I waved to indicate the whole situation, "wouldn't have been considered realistic ten years ago, either."

"Eleanor." He turned to her, his hands out in appeal. "Kids come first, right? That's who we're supposed to look out for most, right?"

She shrugged. "For the happiest, most successful marriages I've seen, it was higher calling, spouse, then children. I put my daughter first and look what happened there."

I winced. Yeah. Having your daughter turn you in and join an invading enemy ain't a sign of a healthy mind.

Eleanor turned to me. "Mind you, Captain, everything you said is a fear and a hypothetical."

"Is it, though? Call me crazy, but I feel like I might have been just the *slightest* bit integral to the success we've had so far. And the losses." I looked down. Tears threatened again.

"And then," Eleanor continued, "we have to ask, what would happen to the babe if you died in childbirth?"

Archangel snarled, blue eyes fierce. "Don't you even think it!"

"We have to," she said calmly. "Childbirth is dangerous, too."

I shrugged. "Me dying is different to me quitting. I quit, what's to stop them from losing hope? If I die...Well. Revenge is one hell of an incentive, ain't it?"

Archangel rounded on me, his eyes blazing. "I really..." He swallowed, wilting. "I really need you to stop talking about dying right now."

"Two more things," Eleanor said. "We do have a lot of women who could take care of another baby, quite easily, if something does happen to you. And, if Captain's Home and things go wrong, and Doc's here and you're not with her..."

His nostrils flared. "Fine, you stay until the baby is born. Then we can revisit this."

He left the room abruptly, shutting the door gently behind him. I grimaced, but Eleanor just laughed. "Oh, sure, you can laugh," I grumbled. "I'm the one who'll have to soothe an overwrought man. Thank God we can still..." I cut off abruptly, my eyes huge at what I'd nearly said.

She laughed harder, waking the puppy. She stroked his head, apologizing. He grumbled, wriggling in her arms until he found a new comfortable position and went back to sleep. "You can say 'sex' to me, you know."

"No, I can't." I squirmed. "You're like my mom. There's some things you don't talk to your mom about."

"Well, be that as it may, it sounds like you have a busy afternoon ahead of you."

"Eleanor!"

***

Much, much later, I lay on my side, Noah at my back. I sighed, my head resting on his arm. He ran his fingers lightly up and down my side, the cool air washing over my damp skin, making me shiver pleasantly.

"I am sorry," he whispered against the side of my throat.

"Me, too." I lay comfortably in the dark, floating in a cloud until my stomach growled.

He chuckled against my back, shaking us both. "We missed dinner."

"Amana has food somewhere. You're gonna have to pull me out." Still, I groaned when he got up, taking that exquisite heat with him. "I'm like a beached whale. Goddamn."

"A fierce, beautiful beached whale, babe. Never forget that."

"Only when I'm armed." Which was still all the time. I only used my guns on the practice range, but Steve was close enough I didn't dare go unarmed. I couldn't move fast enough to get to a weapon if they did breach the perimeter.

In the common room, Archangel lifted the lid on the big stew pot that never turned off. "Plenty left," he said quietly, smiling. He was more relaxed than he'd been in a while.

This relaxation spread to our walks, too. Doc prescribed walking as well as yoga to keep me fit for birth, but my hips had shifted enough that walking was no longer the easy, comfortable activity I was used to. Yet another reason to not go through pregnancy again, which I duly informed my husband about.

"Oh, come on." He playfully ran a hand down my back, even as his eyes tightened with worry. "It's not that bad."

"I haven't seen my feet in two months!"

He laughed, but my size was another reason for concern. This one, I did not share with him. No reason to cause him extra worry. He had enough on his plate, going out for short raids to try to draw Steve away from our wilderness area.

So, we walked together, and I leaned comfortably against him, giggling and whispering as we wandered the hallways of the Lair.

All this screeched to a halt when River returned from her latest trip to Salem. She'd begun taking more time, going slower, and having to be on foot for most of it. She'd take two others with her to watch her back, leave them at the edge of the city while she met Shrike, then they'd begin the laborious return trip.

We met the morning after her return, once she'd had a chance to rest and clean up. The late summer dust coated everything in a thick layer, ready to turn to mud at the first hint of moisture.

"We need to start planning how to pull Shrike out," River said without preamble.

I rocked in my chair while Driver and Gryph protested removing our best—and only—spy inside Salem. "Why?" I asked.

The older woman, hardened by years of solo missions into the city, chewed her lip. "Steve's getting suspicious. It's only a matter of time before they look at Shrike. And Kwan Jae's harpy…Well, she's more than happy to crucify anyone who gets in her way, and Shrike has begun running in the same circles."

Eleanor flinched at the veiled mention of her daughter, Anna, who'd sold her mother and two best friends into slavery in order to attain a position in Steve's occupation.

I shifted, pressing on my belly. "You didn't mention they were out and socializing. You'd given us the understanding that they learned everything through their work."

"It wasn't important how they learned it. It simply meant more cover for them because they talk to so many Steve. Regardless, we need to get Shrike out. It's been months since we were able to meet in person. They're being watched almost constantly. Steve's calling it a 'protection detail.'"

"Then we'll get planning." River relaxed at my easy agreement. "We'll need everything you know on their movements, accommodations, and any…social events that might be upcoming. In the meantime, what's up with Steve here? We need to get them out of the area if we're gonna do a Salem run."

Her mouth quirked sardonically. "Kwan Jae's in the field is what's up."

Gasps and low whistles greeted that comment. We hadn't seen hide nor hair of Kwan Jae since the sisters' deaths seasons ago. We could finally have a chance at the leader of the invaders.

"You're certain?" Archangel demanded, leaning forward.

"As certain as I can be. Shrike watched him leave. It would've been about two days before I read their missive. Just under a week ago. And," she stared grimly around the room, "he had barrels of accelerants. If we don't do something soon, he's going to burn everything."

CHAPTER 43

Days passed as we searched for Kwan Jae in the foothills and the edges of the Valley. Confined to the Lair by my ever-expanding stomach, I paced the hallways.

Archangel, deciding to sit the hunt out, stayed close. He met with the scouts, listened to the information, and marked the maps. We didn't know when my due date was, but sitting, standing, laying, and walking were all increasingly uncomfortable.

I'd spend what time I could in the Useless Room, but I cycled through positions, and when I had to lie down...I had to lie down.

Archangel hid his restlessness at staying out of the field, but it was mitigated somewhat when Gryphon returned to full activity. He and Phoenix scoured the landscape, searching not just for signs of Steve, but Kwan Jae himself.

This was increasingly difficult because fucking Steve made good on their threat. Black smoke filled the sky, flames sweeping through the mountains. The scent of smoke and burning pine clung to the fighter's clothes whenever they returned.

Tensions ran high inside the Lair, all of us wondering when the other shoe would drop, when we'd finally find Kwan Jae. It ramped higher when the skinny creep, Spartacus, returned from a trip with another scavenger, Craven.

"We found them," Spartacus gasped, dramatically staggering into the common room during dinner, throwing his chest out.

"Found who?" Amana asked, her lips making a little moue of distaste.

"Kwan Jae!"

That got everyone's attention.

Archangel and Amana got everyone seated and calmed so we could hear the story. Apparently, the two men had been wandering around and accidentally stumbled across a huge camp—several hundred soldiers, at least.

The central tent had a flag flying, he said, the same one every soldier wore on their shoulder. When asked where it was, he said he'd only show us if I was in the room.

"I wanted to show you how nice I am, Captain," he said, looking sideways at me.

Archangel growled quietly. If he'd had hackles, they would've been standing upright. Something about this man...

"And," he continued, "since Archangel isn't helping you out, I thought I should do something good for you."

My jaw dropped. It was the only reaction I was physically capable of. The man wasn't too bright, either, completely oblivious to the threat of imminent violence that immediately filled the common room.

I leaned against Archangel, pressing down on his tensed leg. Nothing about my current condition could stop him, but he listened to my silent wishes and stayed put. "Let's get to the Useless Room," I whispered. "I want to know where Kwan Jae is before someone kills him. Please?"

Nodding tightly, he stood abruptly, but his hands were gentle as he helped me out from the bench. *What the fuck,* Phoenix mouthed to me. I shrugged, hand splayed at my side. What the hell kind of idiot tried to impress a happily married person who was also hugely pregnant? Like, what part of any this said, 'Take me, I want someone else?'

Spartacus had an odd, burning light in his eyes whenever he looked at me, glancing back frequently over his shoulder as he led the way to the Useless room.

"You know something else about him," I murmured to Archangel. "No way he'd be able to rile you this easily."

"Not now," he breathed, his hand firm on my non-existent waist.

Inside the Room, Spartacus strutted and preened, pointing to a spot on the map. Seahorse and Dereva hauled out topographical maps while Storm questioned him, asking about landmarks and how he could be so certain that was Kwan Jae's exact location.

As the Useless Room became a hive of activity, people planning how we should approach the point, weapons, and who was fit to fight, I caught a glimpse of Spartacus off to the side. His lip protruded like a pouting child, yet the corner of his mouth quirked up, a self-satisfied smirk.

Then he glanced my way.

Something about him was off, and I couldn't place it. Then my belly tightened, and I sucked in a breath, pressing a hand to my stomach.

Archangel immediately stopped, turning fully to me, his hands hovering, his eyes worried. I smiled, relaxing as the mild contraction passed.

"It's just a Braxton-Hicks." I stroked his arm. "Doc said it's not uncommon. I'm big, but she reckons the kid still has a bit more growing to do."

"I should stay here, with you, just in case."

Phoenix glanced up. "We're going to need everybody." She sighed, studying me. "But no one will hate you for staying."

"We can talk about it later," I said. "Right now, we need to plan."

But even with Phoenix's words, people gave him worried glances. It was obvious that having the avenging angel along would ease people's minds. Hitting Kwan without either of us would deal a blow to morale before they even made it to the camp.

"How about I promise not to have the kid until we're together?" I said, smiling. "You will definitely be there."

"Deal." He held his hand out and we shook. Phoenix cracked up, immediately telling everyone about the beginning of our relationship and another handshake.

***

I paced restlessly through the nearly empty Lair. Even the non-combatants and lightly injured fighters had left to provide backup, first aid, or to act as drivers. Our entire existence hinged on this. If we could get Kwan, it could immediately turn the tide.

Who knew if we could even survive inside if the entire mountainside burned? While Anansi thought it probable, no one wanted to test the theory.

My cousin, Mech, remained in the garage, working on some dirt bikes the scavengers brought back for no reason they could explain other than it'd be 'fun.' Amana, Al, Optimus Prime, who was still too young to go out, Porkpie, the Three Fates, and a skeleton crew of perimeter guards were all that remained.

And Spartacus, who'd injured himself sometime during the two days of planning.

Sarge had curled his lip muttering, "Coward," when the other man turned up with a nasty cut. Apparently, he'd been begging to go into a fight for ages, but when the opportunity presented itself, he was 'hurt.'

No one really protested. A man who begged and whined, full of empty boasts, was not a man people wanted at their backs in a fight.

Until a full twenty-four hours passed and Amana found me in the Useless Room, staring at the maps as if I could see what was happening, share in the struggle at our doorstep.

"Have jou seen the little man?" she asked.

I shook my head, not looking up, my mind still on our parting. I'd kissed Archangel good luck, he'd held me tight, whispered to the baby, and then he was gone. And the stupid Braxton-Hicks contractions kept coming and going, preventing me from concentrating...

Another one tightened my belly, and I gripped the table, breathing deeply like Doc taught me until it passed. "Why do we care?"

"I asked him to do something, and it is not done."

"Amana," I said when she would have left the room. "Why on earth do none of the other Latins use Spanish names like you?"

At that, she laughed. "Because with English names, everyone expect to see a white man. Is another level of disguise."

"Damn." I inhaled sharply. "I should've thought of that. I could've picked a name in Spanish. Or Chinese, or something."

"You didn't pick jou name, remember?"

"Oh, right." Yeah. They had. Had it really been that long? While I stared down, lost in the past, Amana slipped quietly out.

I don't know how much time passed when she burst into the room again, this time pale and agitated, holding shreds of paper in her hands. "*Capitán!* See this?"

Alarmed at her tone, I sat up when she spilled them out onto the table, hastily rearranging them. Dread and panic clawed their way up my throat. Notes. Plans. Instructions. The exact information Spartacus had given us about Kwan's location, right down to the description of the tent.

"Where did you find this?"

"When I can't find him, I search his room. These were inside a book. He also has other papers—" She dropped a slim journal on the table, "where he calls Kwan Jae colonel. Is all very respectful. Also," she flipped through to an earlier entry and held it up.

There was a detailed map of the exact location for Chaos's camp, the one that had been raided and destroyed barely five months before.

"Ambush," I whispered.

She leaned down. "*Qué?*"

"Ambush." I said louder, my heart pounding. "It's an ambush. We have to warn them!"

"How? Is a long way. They will be there tonight."

I drummed on the table, my eyes darting around the room without seeing anything in front of me. "There are shortcuts in the mountains, if you know the trails. Those dirt bikes Mech has been working on will do the trick."

"Who knows the trails?"

"I do."

"Who is not you."

"I don't know," I shouted, slamming my hands on the table. "Ask. Please?" I bit my lip, struggling to hold back tears. "Hurry."

An hour later, Amana had gone through the entire Lair and not a single person left behind knew those trails. Not one.

They gathered in the Useless Room with me while I scrabbled through every map I could find, hoping one of them had the trails marked on it.

Nothing.

"What can we do?" The First Fate asked, breaking through my frantic searching.

I rested my hands on the table, my fingers tracing the familiar lines and ridges of the map rising from it. "I can do it."

Protests filled the room, a rising babble that I couldn't—wouldn't—sort through. The fighters had to be warned.

Archangel had to be warned.

"The plan is to attack tonight, before Steve has a chance to do any more damage." I waddled around the room, one hand on my back, one on my belly, thinking out loud. "We still have a bit of time."

Not much. Not with the sun more than halfway across the sky and sunset happening earlier every day. Fuck.

"None of you know the trails, and I don't know exactly how many trails you have to pass. I know the route, I can't describe it, which means unless we want literally *everyone* to die, I have to go, and none of you can say a damn thing about it.

"Your only choice here is which one of you will go with me. Because these stupid fake contractions are coming often enough that it's distracting, and it'll probably hit at least once along the way." I said this last bit harshly, truly angry with my pregnant body for the first time.

"We only have one dirt bike working," Mech protested.

"Then whoever goes with me better be skinny with long arms, because I ain't riding behind," I snapped.

If I hadn't been like this, pregnant, I'd have been out in the field. Maybe I'd see something the others would miss. Maybe an extra gun could make all the difference in the fight. Maybe, maybe, maybe.

I looked up, my lips curled back in a snarl at all the people standing frozen. "Listen!" I met each of their eyes. "Either help or get the fuck out of my way."

Al nodded once, sharply, and came forward, kneeling at my feet. I felt his fingers around my knee, retying the moccasin, my view blocked by my oversized belly. "Get her rifle, my love," he said over his shoulder. Amana opened her mouth to protest. "Please," he added quietly. "What would you do if it was me?"

She lowered her head and disappeared out the door. I had my thigh holsters strapped down, the belt running under my stomach, and the shoulder guns, but no extra ammunition.

"I need magazines," I said. "Armory, 9 mm, please. At least four."

The Third Fate left at a run. Mech still hadn't moved, his arms crossed over his chest. "Can I have a minute?""

"No. They don't have time."

Leaning close, he hissed, "What am I supposed to tell your dad? That you were stupid when you're eight months pregnant? He's nearly a grandfather and you're going to get yourself and the baby killed."

"Not if I'm careful, lucky, and good. And so far, I've more or less been all three."

"Bullshit!"

I rolled my eyes, biting back panic. "Okay, I've been lucky and good. Sue me."

Amana entered with my rifle and ammo belt over her shoulder, closely followed by the Third carrying four mags. The mags looked too big for her small hands. I took them with a grateful smile.

Mech planted himself in the doorway. "No. I'm not letting you risk your life and the baby's. They're good. They'll be fine."

My nostrils flared. "I've been fighting for I can't remember how long. It feels like forever, and if there's one thing I learned, it doesn't matter how good you are, you can still die. They need to know. Now, get out of my way before I hurt you."

He folded his arms.

Standing in front of him, I tilted my head back, glaring. Without looking, I stomped his instep. When his arms loosened, I swooped in. Grip, slide, twist, turn... Before he knew what hit him, I was in the doorway and he stood in the room, holding his wrist.

"Try to stop me again, I'll kick you so hard, anytime your balls itch you'll have to scratch your throat," I snarled.

Paling, he stepped back, one hand dropping to cup himself.

"Al." The younger man flinched, looking up. "Let's go."

Chapter 44

Woman 1: You will be a hero, honey. Mother's taken care of everything.

Man 1: We were supposed to be rescuing them by now!

Illegal wiretap on Keller mansion December 14, 2065, impermissible in court.

The ride down passed like a nightmare.

I sat in front, bracketed by Al's slender arms. I steered carefully while he maintained our balance through the sharp turns while I grit my teeth through the damn Braxton-Hicks. I'd barely had a period for the last few years, and these weren't worse than those cramps, but still...I'd gotten used to not having to deal with it.

The trees changed from thin and dry to lush evergreens interspersed with burnt sections and finally turned into brightly colored deciduous. The last vestiges of the sun sank below the horizon before we made it to the fall colors. Letting the engine idle, I raised my head, questing in the air like a hound for the scent or sound of a fight.

The distant *rattatat-tat* of gunfire reached my ears. Snarling, I took us down.

Halfway down, we ran across the first of the fighters. "Captain coming through!" I shouted.

"Captain, what the fuck?" Deerskin, one of the newer fighters, stared, her mouth open. "You shouldn't be out here!"

"Ambush," I snapped.

"No, it's just a patrol. We'll get 'em before they can warn the rest of 'em."

"It's an ambush," I snarled, hunching around another cramp, squeezing the handlebars. "Start the retreat. Get to the vehicles and send them in. It's gonna be hot."

She froze for another half second, then snapped into gear, spinning on her heel and racing away.

At the base of the hill, a highway ran north to south. Trees covered the hillside all the way to the edge of the road with little underbrush on this side. In the distance, dark green tents, one of them topped by a flag, rose above the thick brush carpeting the far side of the road.

Explosions rattled the ground. At my back, Al flinched but warned about the ambush. I looked frantically around at the fighters scattered over the ground, making their determined way forward, the few visible faces hard, focused, determined, searching for a bright yellow head of hair.

Al continued to shout at the fighters, telling them they had to leave. One look at my heavily pregnant presence was enough to convince the more experienced fighters that shit had well and truly hit the fan.

There! Finally spotting the one person I searched for, we reached tree ruts too high to drive over. Archangel was *right there* and I couldn't...Turning the bike sharply, we slid sideways a few feet to a stop. Awkwardly climbing off, I ordered Al back to help coordinate and continued down the hill, shouting at them to retreat.

At the road, Gryph broke cover, firing, drawing Steve's eyes. A flicker across the road, invisible from his level, and something flew through the air, directly toward him. I shrieked, my voice lost in the cacophony of gunfire and shouting.

The scene played out in slow motion, forever etched into my mind.

Archangel raced out, grabbing Gryph and whirling him around, physically body-checking the larger man into the ditch. The object landed behind him as he threw Gryphon down.

Another contraction, stronger than anything I'd yet experienced, ripped through me. I stumbled, hitting a tree, using it to keep on my feet. My heart stopped with the next explosion. I clutched the tree, my mouth open, no sound emerging.

At the road, so close, too far, the explosion flung Archangel forward like a rag doll. He landed by the ditch in an untidy tangle of limbs and red splotches.

I stumbled down the hill, only brought up by hands on my shoulders, Seahorse's furious face in mine, her mouth moving.

Eventually, I made out sounds. "What the *fuck* are you doing here, you lunatic?" she screeched.

"Archangel," I cried, pushing her hands away. "It's a full ambush. Get them out of here."

Bits of asphalt flew into the air as bullets hit around him every time Gryphon reached out. Remembering the rifle strapped to my back, I knelt, pulling it over my head. Swearing, Seahorse turned, screaming at those nearest to "Fall back, get the fuck out! Steve's here in force. Move!"

Working the pump, I fired into the bushes on the far side without bothering to aim. Another cramp, then I had the sudden urge to pee. As quickly as the urge came, warmth gushed down my thighs, too thick to be piss.

I fumbled my rifle, panting. It was too soon, too much. Glancing up, I saw Gryphon tumble out of the brush, rolling over Archangel and scooping him neatly over his shoulder, racing back into the forest.

"Not now, kid," I whispered, grunting with the next contraction, my eyes firmly on my husband's limp form, slung over Gryph's shoulders.

More shooting and hands were under my arms, lifting me to my feet. "I told you to fall back," I snarled.

"Not without Archangel," Storm snapped back.

Shouts of agreement? Glancing down, I spotted Seahorse, Sarge, River, Goliath, Grandpa, Ink, and Chaos with Storm. Tears prickled my eyes.

Below, Gryphon charged up the slope, joined by Phoenix, who tumbled down a fir tree, watching his back. I squeezed my eyes shut, knowing that when I opened them, Archangel would lift his head, call to me, speak, something...

"Shoot Spartacus," I choked out through the tears. Archangel would be fine. He'd need a fuck ton of physio, but payback's a bitch.

"Wha—"

"Motherfucker sold us out to Steve. Kill the fucker."

Gryphon ran past, chest heaving like a bellows, Archangel's hand dangling limply down, his back a bloody ruin. Chaos left the line, going to help him while at the bottom of the hill, Steve charged.

Abandoning thoughts of the fight to those who had the will for it, I stumbled after the men. "No. No, no, nonononononono," I keened, dropping to my knees under another contraction, clawing my way after them.

Swearing, Storm and Phoenix got hands under my arms as the GMC barreled down the hill, taking out bushes and a few small saplings, closely followed by another vehicle. Dereva pulled around in a spray of dirt mere feet from Chaos and Gryph.

Dereva stuck her head out the window. "Get moving! There's thousands of Steve coming. Last chance for a lift, people!"

Everything moved too quickly for me to follow. The ground swung away, arms around me, then the ribbed bed of my pickup under my butt and a hard chest at my back as Chaos lowered me down. "Archangel?" I gasped, the weight lifting from my heart. "Babe?"

Legs on either side of me, too long to be Archangel's. I groaned, deep in my throat, the next contraction bowing my back and a large hand took my left in a firm grip. Twisting, I caught a glimpse of Gryphon's strong profile, tears leaving silver tracks down his cheeks.

Gently taking my right hand, he lowered it, until my fingers met soft cloth and still flesh. The contours were familiar, yes, but they didn't have life, vitality. Surely, he was wrong. There's no way...

Hands tugged at my pants, cold metal drawing a line up my leg, cool air flowing over newly exposed skin. I stubbornly refused to look away from Gryph until a small lantern flickered to life and my eyes were drawn down.

A sob caught the back of my throat.

Noah lay on his back, his legs over the tail box, his hands folded peacefully over his chest, as if he were sleeping.

His bloodless lips and too pale skin gave lie to my hope. Leaning over Gryphon's leg, I stretched, sliding my hand over his rapidly cooling skin, up to his hand. Sobbing, I took his hand, bringing it to my lips.

"I didn't mean to keep the promise like this," I cried. "I didn't mean it like this."

When the next contraction hit, I opened up, screaming to the sky, uncaring that I gave away our position, that Steve was close, that we were running away. What did any of it matter anymore?

Word passed overhead, barely glancing off my ears.

"—need to get her ready—"

"How are we supposed to—"

"—can't do this—"

"How close are the contractions?"

"—think I can concentrate enough to count?"

"Wha...Why? Baby's here." I rolled my head around, indicating the baby. The only thing not limp was my grip on Archangel's hand. That, I clutched tight. "Don't have to wait too long, babe," I mumbled.

"There's another one, you idiot!" Phoenix shouted. "So fucking *push!*"

This contraction spread to my shoulders, my neck. Bearing down took every bit of strength, every last muscle I had. Clenching the leather between my teeth, I screamed.

Through the haze, frantic voices shouted. Hands patted my cheeks, my legs.

"Don't you dare die on me! You're too much of an asshole to go out like this."

***

Trees against the night sky. Red leaves. Dark green needles. A tiny, flickering fire. A hand wrapped around mine. Archangel? I smiled.

I woke next surrounded by Archangel's scent, and I smiled, rubbing my cheek against the buttery smooth leather of his favorite jacket. Overhead, a canopy hid the sky, as if I was in a bubble of leaves. I half laughed. Bubble of leaves.

Good one.

"She's awake."

The corners of my mouth turned down. Everything hurt. When had I been injured? It all concentrated between my legs...One hand went to my belly, soft now. People clustered around, talking quietly. A gentle hand stroked my hair back and tears immediately gathered.

I remembered.

"Leave me alone," I croaked.

"Not happening," Doc said, leaning over so I could see her. She was haggard, her lips compressed and her large brown eyes worriedly looking me over. "It was touch and go for a while. We nearly lost you."

"Should've let me go."

"No. You've got babies to take care of."

"Seems like you're all old enough to take care of yourselves."

"Not what I meant. Boys?"

"Look here," Gryphon said gently.

Turning my head took monumental effort. When I did, Gryphon and Chaos knelt side by side, little bundles of clothing in their arms. Except those bundles squirmed, tiny grunting noises emerging from the sweatshirts.

"Twins," he said gently. "You've got two boys. They need you."

Bracing one hand on the ground, he lowered the baby enough for me to see his little face, all red and wrinkly. His little rosebud mouth worked. Chaos carefully showed me the other one. Unless my eyes deceived me—a distinct possibility—I thought they might be identical.

"We had to put them onto you while you were unconscious," Eleanor said apologetically. "They needed to eat and you...Well. You were out. I'm sorry, but we had to. We also put a bracelet on the older one."

So, they were identical. Grandma was a twin. Guess the gene was still there.

"Now." Doc sat next to me, folding her arms across her chest, face like thunder. "Would you care to explain why the *fuck* you came riding out in your condition?"

My lip curled in a silent snarl, but there was no strength behind it. I had none left. It lay in a pickup, not too far away.

"We only just unplugged you from Hightide," Doc said. "You lost so much blood."

"Doc," Eleanor said, laying a hand on her arm. "She did save the fighters. Your warning came before they sprung the trap," she said to me.

"How many…" I cleared my throat and Doc held a canteen to my lips so I could drink. "How many did we lose?"

"One."

Fresh tears welled up, slipping down my temples, into my hair. "I want to see him."

Babies were passed and the men left, returning shortly with a blanket wrapped bundle that they carried as gently as a mother with a sleeping baby. Laying him next to me, I rolled clumsily onto my side, aided by Eleanor. Gryphon pulled the blanket back from his face.

Keening softly, I rested my head on his shoulder, my hand over his heart, hoping—praying—that it would miraculously start beating. Waiting, straining, aching, for something, anything.

Dawn lightened the sky before I spoke again, every word rasping through my throat. "Tell me the rest."

"I got Spartacus," Storm said baldly, satisfaction in every word. "The others are preparing for Steve to hit the Lair, but we're not sure if he said anything. Otherwise, why the setup? The ambush? Why not just hit us when we're least expecting it?"

"I'd love to know why," Phoenix said, violence lacing her words. They'd nearly killed her husband. Only mine had stopped it.

Lucky her.

I closed my eyes while Phoenix continued. "They did bring out nearly every soldier they have. So, we sent River and a small force to hit Salem, just to be shits about it. They won't do much, just cause a bit of havoc and mayhem."

Perhaps we'd find out. Perhaps not. Right now, his motivation didn't interest me, only the consequences of his actions. I wished Spartacus were still here so I could kill him again. Exhaustion won the morning, however, and even grief wasn't enough to keep me awake. Sleep claimed me, and all I could do was wish it was more permanent.

Why didn't you wait for me?

CHAPTER 45

The morning dawned cool and crisp, the air slightly smoky but not too bad after the torrential downpour. Low mist snaked over the ground, avoiding the gaping hole at my feet.

I had absolutely no fucks to give for the weather, all my attention on the pallbearers slowly walking towards me. The men had their hands linked under Noah's body, Gryphon and Chaos at the front, not even trying to keep the tears from their eyes. My heart and my mind refused the information my eyes sent, that I did know the person wrapped in that sheet, that he was...

No!

Eleanor and Phoenix stood on either side, their hands on my elbows the only things keeping me upright. The birth had left me drained, and now...

My right hand twitched at my side, gasping and shuddering. This couldn't be happening. It couldn't. Just last week, he'd wrapped himself around me, both hands smoothing over my belly as we lay in bed in a rare quiet moment before a mission like every other time. He'd kissed the back of my neck. I still felt the pressure of his lips.

When Gryphon, Chaos, Sarge, and Goliath laid his sheet-wrapped body in the shallow grave, my knees gave out completely. I sank down, bringing Phoenix and Eleanor with me, gasping for air, digging my fingers into the cold, damp earth.

I studied his face, still visible, the sheet carefully folded away, terrified the moment it was taken from my view I'd forget what he looked like. Praying he'd suddenly open his eyes, that this was all a huge mistake.

Gryphon knelt opposite me, sympathetically gazing at me. Reaching out, spanning the narrow grave, he gripped my arm. I focused on his grip, each individual finger digging into my arm.

"I'll never be ready," I whispered. "You'll have to do it."

Nodding, he released me, gently pulling the cloth over my husband's face, tucking him in like a parent cares for their child. Rising, he knelt by his wife on my right and spoke. "He was a brother to me from the moment we met. In the end, he did for me what my own brothers would never have done. Everything I do from here, brother, is because of you." His voice breaking, he held a knife to his palm, twisting the point just enough to draw a few small drops of blood. "I will be worthy of this sacrifice. I swear it."

"I swear it," Chaos said, marking his own palm, dripping blood into the grave, then raising his fist.

"I swear it," others echoed, beyond my sight.

Drawing my own knife, I bent low, bringing my mouth to the edge of the soil. "I swear it." Three bright red droplets marked the white sheet.

"All hail the victorious dead!" Gryphon shouted.

A song rose up as they covered Archangel with dirt. Words slowly formed through the haze in my head.

Spinning 'round the dance floor
Spinning with my lover
Open my eyes, you aren't really here
Hold my hand, won't you wait for me

Why was it so familiar? I knew this tune. I clung to the melody like a lifeline as the soldiers piled rocks into a cairn.

Running through the forest

Running with my lover

Look ahead, you disappear so quickly

Hold my hand, won't you wait for me

Dancing in the rain flashed through my mind. I rocked in Eleanor and Phoenix's grip.

My wedding day. The musicians had played this on our wedding day.

Lips pressed together so tightly

Kiss me warm and wet and wildly

Breathe me out, breathe you in

Hold my hand, won't you stay with me

I keened to the gray sky.

Why did you take him from me?

***

Time passed.

Seconds, minutes, hours, days. All of them without him. How could time do this? Why didn't it stop? All the rest of me had. I sat in my room, frozen in time, waiting, wishing, unable to grieve, unable to move.

Lavender and Amana brought the babies. I fed them, but even holding these remnants of Archangel couldn't suffice. I'd never dreamed of being a mother before. It only sounded like a wonderful thing when he was here to share it with me. What could I be to them as I was?

A violent, bloody woman. That was me. So little softness, so little gentleness...Did I even have enough?

Wandering out to the meadow just before dawn, Archangel's leather jacket thrown on, my bare feet leaving tracks in the frosty grass, I stumbled across Obelix, curled up on Sirius's cairn as he preferred. Kneeling stiffly, I scratched his neck, only the white parts visible against the dark stones.

"You and me both, it seems," I whispered to the border collie. Continuing on, my toes numb, I made my way through the numerous cairns dotting the meadow.

Would I lie here someday? It would be a relief. Releasing all these emotions, leaving all this behind. I wouldn't see our babies grow up, but they'd be cared for. Would their foster parents love them as much?

At a slight motion ahead, I slowed, instinct taking over. Drawing a gun, I crept closer. A fight, a fight. This could be my chance, but if it were an enemy, I had to win...Had Spartacus told them where we were after all?

Maybe all our preparations and worry hadn't been in vain. But how had he breached the perimeter without a warning being given? Impossible for Steve to have seen all our guards. They lived in the trees, having built a network of ropes and tiny platforms over the years.

The figure straightened, pulling off a beanie as the moon emerged from behind a cloud, revealing the balding pate of Walter Blake. He started when he saw me, clapping a hand over his own mouth to hold back a cry.

"What the fu—" Straightening slowly, I holstered the gun. So, no release today. "What brings you out so early?" I asked.

He shrugged. "I couldn't sleep until I finished."

Lighting a tiny lamp, he set it by his feet, revealing what he'd been working on. A wooden cross, placed at Noah's head, his name—the only name they knew—inscribed on it, beautifully decorated with vines and leaves.

Kneeling, I gently traced his name, admiring the work Walter had done. "How...?"

the pages. Our names inside hearts, imaginary conversations, this journal had it all.

Then Archangel's name caught my eye. He'd spotted the creep watching me and had words, but in Spartacus's mind, Archangel had kept me away from him. Archangel was the barrier, and if he were gone, Spartacus could sweep me off my feet.

His first meeting with Steve, where he promised to help them in exchange for my life. The one where he betrayed Chaos's location, the one that led to his and Goliath's capture. He spewed admiration for Kwan Jae and Sutton and bragged about the plan for the ambush.

My stomach heaved and I flung the book away, bending forward, my head hanging, gasping for air. Phoenix rubbed my back in little circles, pulling my hair back from my face.

"Saying he fancied you doesn't even come close." I looked up to see Gryph paging through the book, shaking his head. "I vaguely remember your first conversation with him. How did him getting humiliated turn into this level of obsession? No." He held up a hand. "Don't answer that, I don't want to know."

"Captain." Eleanor spoke up for the first time in a while. "You need to rest."

"No," I snapped. "We need to plan how to hit Steve and get Shrike out of Salem."

"You're swaying where you sit," she retaliated. "You're still recovering from a difficult birth, and you won't be any good if you relapse, to us or to Michael and Gabriel." I'd named our sons after their father by giving them the names of archangels. Every time I heard their names, a pang of loss shot through my chest. "Our wounded need time to heal as well. So, go sleep and we'll fill you in when you wake up."

"Will you?" I asked snidely, looking pointedly around the room.

Phoenix stared at me defiantly, Gryph had so much compassion I nearly wept, and the rest avoided my gaze. It took me two tries to get to my feet, and I snarled.

"Fine. But the moment we're ready, I'm through playing games."

"Is that what we've been doing?" Driver asked quietly right before I shut the door. "What'll she do, then?"

I'll kill them all.

***

Archangel nuzzled my ear, the wedding in full swing around us, and I dropped my head to the side to give him better access. "How 'bout we ditch this party?" he whispered.

Triskele glowed in the same gown I'd worn, and Phoenix, Amana and every other bride aside from Kestrel. Kestrel stood, equally radiant in her borrowed clothes, the darker colors setting off her reddish-brown hair.

More people headed to the dance floor, and I frowned. Something was odd.

But Archangel nibbled on my neck, driving out all other thought. I laughed when he tickled me. "We can't! There's toasts and speeches..."

The room flickered, turning dark, blood pooling in pine needles, then it went back to the wedding and Archangel laughing into my hair.

"You know what?" I whispered, dismissing it all. "They won't miss us, will they?"

Taking my hand, he pulled me off the bench. "Nope. Let's go, woman."

Giggling, we tumbled into our room, the sounds of the party barely muffled when the door shut. He pushed me against the wall, his hands busy with my pants. I ran my hands up, under his shirt, laughter giving way to murmurs and kisses.

Over his shoulder, Sirius sat on the bed watching us, her eyes empty, mouth smiling. I froze, dread building, but Archangel continued kissing his way up my neck. By the time he reached my chin, she'd disappeared, and I smiled again.

"Captain!" he called.

I frowned. Noah never called me that when lovemaking. It was the only time my real name passed his lips. So why...?

"Captain!"

A nagging thought surfaced. Kestrel and Triskele got married before us... The voice called again, and he began to fade, only his eyes alive and vibrant.

"No," I gasped. "Don't leave me. Not again! You promised!"

"I'm here," he whispered. "You only have to listen."

I snapped awake when a hand touched my shoulder, bolting upright, my knife already out. Phoenix sat slowly back on her heels, her hands held up and out from her body, my knife poised at her throat. The trees surrounding us provided a quiet susurrus, a gentle wind rustling their branches.

"It's okay," she said, soothing. "It's just me."

I pressed my lips together, the grief filling every part of me. Lowering the knife, I rubbed my free hand over my face. "What is it?"

Rising to her feet, she held out a hand to help me up. "We found someone."

Leading me through the camp, she spoke rapidly. "Scouts found a woman. Storm barely recognized her."

All around us, fighters geared up, cleaned weapons, or caught a quick nap after being on watch. The thickly forested area in the foothills north of Silverton was laced with overgrown dirt tracks that connected to the gravel roads of the backcountry, perfect for our needs. It was time to cause a ruckus, draw more Steve out, then swing south and get Shrike out of Salem.

"She's one of Gorgon's crew," Phoenix continued, taking me outside the camp's limits. "Chick named Switchblade."

"And we care because why?"

"Look."

We entered a small meadow bordered by thick brush. The woman sat in the center, guarded by Storm and Sweetpea, her head bent, but she looked up when we arrived. I inhaled sharply when I got closer. Black eye, her lip split, and blood around one iris. She'd been struck, multiple times.

Kneeling, I gently tipped her head to the side, towards the weak sunlight. "Who did this to you?"

***

Peeking around the tree, I caught a glimpse of my prey. The man wore non-military camouflage gear, the kind favored by over-enthusiastic preppers from the days Before. He sat in a deer hunting thing—a blind!—with a few wilting branches on the outside to muddle its outline. He watched the forest intently, a high-powered rifle poking out the narrow window.

I shook my head infinitesimally. He saw forward, but completely ignored the sides, especially behind him. Careless, but that matched what Switchblade had said, which sounded like something from a dystopian nightmare.

This group of preppers saw Steve's coming as a chance to live out their dreams of isolation in the mountains. The group comprised solely of men then proceeded to 'rescue' people, bringing them back to act as slaves. Women, of course, were there for sex and children. The half-starved men who couldn't fight were castrated and turned into general labor.

Upon being banished from the Lair, Gorgon decided to head north. They had one successful encounter against Steve, then lost another and were forced to flee into the hills. They were captured here and there, a few at a time, over a period of seasons.

Instead of fighting entitled foreigners, they began waging war against entitled Americans, with disastrous results.

Switchblade barely escaping their clutches, making her way south. "You should come at them from the east," Switchblade said earnestly. "There's no road on that side and enough cover for you to make it. The rocks made it hard for them to clear as far out. The other sides have a much wider killing zone. They'll see you and raise the alarm if you try any other side."

Phoenix just laughed. Storm grinned, checking her rifle, and Switchblade looked between them, utterly confused. "What?"

"Can't raise the alarm if there's no one left *to* raise it," Phoenix said, smiling wickedly.

Which is what led to me hiding in the forest in the evening hours, tracking an idiot with a big gun. A breeze rustled the boughs and I moved low, the dry twigs scratching my face as I slid through the brush. Outside the blind, I paused, glancing over my shoulder to ensure Archangel was in position—

My breath caught, grief swamping me like a tide. Closing my eyes, I waited until it receded enough to let me breathe without crying. His spot at my side remained cold and empty, though I felt like I should be able to see him, if only I looked hard enough.

Inside the blind, the man sniffled. Again. Grinding my teeth to keep my patience, I eased to my feet, testing the doorknob. Unlocked. Drawing a knife, I held it low at my side, shoulder braced against the door in case he'd put something in front of it.

Three... Two... One.

Flinging the door open, I rushed in, knife held along my arm.

***

Wiping the blade off, I rifled the dead man's gear, shifting when his blood neared my foot. A bit of jerky, ammunition, water, a tarp, iodine pills, another water filter, first aid kit with more things in it than I knew how to use, and toothpaste—toothpaste? I hadn't had that in years. Wilder made tooth powder, and that was it.

By the time I sorted his pack, I had a little pile next to me. It didn't end with toothpaste. He had enough supplies to last him several days, which seemed a bit long for a perimeter guard. Still, the supplies would be welcome, especially the overstocked first aid kit. Repacking and slinging the bag over my shoulder, I headed out, hunting my next target.

Once I'd hunted far enough to meet more Irregulars, I returned to the little camp I shared with ten others, the fighters taking the prepper's places. Our camps spread out all around the compound, small groups of ten to fifteen, picking off the slavers and replacing them with our own.

Switchblade paced under Nebula and Ink's watchful eyes. She spun when I entered camp, her eyes wild. "You have to attack from the east," she insisted. "That's the only way you'll take them. They have men all around..."

I dumped the extra bag on the ground. "Do they carry something like this?"

She trailed off, noticing the blood on my hands and clothes, shutting her mouth when she took a good look at the bag. Switchblade nodded infinitesimally.

I sighed heavily, squatting on my heels. "What did they offer you?"

"What?" She paled, her eyes darted around the forest, her hands spasming. "I—I don't know..." She cleared her throat. "I don't know what you're talking about."

Nebula sniggered and Ink rolled her eyes. I pinched the bridge of my nose. "Okay, it's official. I've finally met a worse liar than me."

Switchblade stuttered, shifting. She barely took two running steps when Nebula took her down with a wonderful throw, our captive's feet flying high before she slammed to the ground. In an instant, Ink had a blade at her throat, *tsking* at her.

"How about we try this again?" I settled on the ground, my legs stretched in front of me. I punched the stolen pack into a more comfortable position and leaned back. "What did they offer you to lead us into a trap?"

She began to cry. "I couldn't go through it again. I couldn't. So...when they said they'd leave me alone if I brought them more women, I thought..."

"You figured you'd offer us."

Ink's lip curled, then her face softened. "And this is why we don't use names."

"When do they expect us?" I asked.

Switchblade's sobbing eased slightly, tears and snot running down her face. "I couldn't give them a time. But they're holding my sister as a hostage."

"Well, fuck me." Nebula rocked back slightly but didn't loosen her grip. "Captain? I'd seriously consider betrayal to protect my sister."

I grunted, running over the implications. They were probably thicker around the eastern side, hidden behind the first line of guards. Going by the supplies...there shouldn't be a shift change anytime soon. Less movement, meant to lull us into a sense of security?

Shrugging, I rose. It was almost time to begin. "Take her back to the vehicles and tie her up, then get back here ASAP."

Nebula and Ink nodded, going about their work with business-like efficiency.

"No!" Switchblade gasped when they zip-tied her hands behind her back. "I have to know how it goes."

"You will, after we're done here. I can't risk you running into the middle of this and fucking it up."

The two fighters hauled her off, Switchblade unable to protest through the gag they'd stuffed in her mouth. Scaling a tree, I cocked my head, examining their encampment.

The original basement still existed but a crude cabin had been built above it. A series of smaller cabins encircled that. On the outer edges, sheds and pens contained the men and women not deemed worthy of a bed. A palisade fence roughly eight feet high surrounded the entire compound, preventing any escape.

Movement on the western side showed Chaos and Sparrow busily preparing the fence. Within moments, the last light disappeared, leaving the small valley in darkness. The moon wouldn't rise for a couple hours, perfect for my needs. Swinging out of the tree, I landed lightly on the balls of my feet.

I bared my teeth. Time to fuck shit up.

"Watch over us, Archangel."

***

The gun I aimed at the leader's head was rock steady. The man, in his forties, a comfortable belly protruding over his belt, knelt at my feet, a mad light in his eyes.

"Whores need to know their place," he raged. "The Lord sent me to show you cunts the error of your ways—"

Eleanor slapped him across the face, her face white, teeth clenched. "How *dare* you speak such filth?"

The Irregulars rocked back, myself included. I had never seen such fury, such uncompromising rage, on her face before. I'd never known her to be violent, either. She alone, of all of us in the field, did not give into anger.

Around us, the newly rescued gathered, all of them thin, the men skeletal, some missing fingers, eyes, ears...The rage, never far from the surface these days, rose higher. To one side, a woman I barely recognized as Gorgon gathered her fellow exiles together. They were bruised and battered, several of them missing.

Sullen anger smoldered in Gorgon's eyes. If she was pissed now, she'd be even more pissed at the deal I was about to offer.

The leader started, "God and Jesus were—"

"Enough! I will not have you continue to pervert a faith based on forgiveness and grace with this...this...ugh!" Eleanor threw up her hands, unable to find the words.

"You heathen lesbians should be grateful true men will even deign to sanctify you!"

The lesbians in the group laughed. Nebula and Ink, who'd returned in the middle of the fight, made it a point to get extra touchy for his benefit, causing his face to turn red while he sputtered.

"All right, people." I shook my head at their antics. "You've got one chance, asshole. One opportunity. You're gonna take your shitheads into the Valley and—"

"*You?!*" Spittle flew from his lips as he screamed. "You *dare* tell me, a prophet of God, what to do? I will fuck your cunt until it—"

I pulled the trigger, ending his tirade with a spatter of blood and bone, tired of his fanaticism. Turning my gun on the next man, I continued, "You're gonna attack Portland instead of farting around up here. These good people will be watching you—"

"You can't," Gorgon shouted.

"We will not be dictated to by women," the man screamed.

Sighing, I pulled the trigger again, and he slumped to the ground. This was getting old. Next man. "As I was saying, you'll be attacking Portland. My people will be watching you, and any man who tries to run will be shot. If you don't like this deal, we will geld you for the crimes you've committed against humanity in general and women in particular."

"Fucking bitch!" he yelled.

I shrugged. "All right. Plan B," I shouted to the fighters.

Within minutes, we had half the men on their backs, held down by four people each. The rest were herded into a pen to wait their turn. I pulled a knife and flipped it to grasp it by the blade, offering the hilt to the nearest woman.

"Would you like first honors?"

***

Eleanor found me by the tiny creek, washing blood spatter off my face and hands. The remaining men were guarded by their former slaves, who carried a mix of expandable batons, knives, and clubs. The preppers huddled together, shrunken shadows of their former bravado.

"Why didn't you punish the first three men this way?" she asked eventually.

I shrugged. "I had hopes they'd willingly fight. I guess this'll work as well, in the end."

"As cannon fodder?"

"It's not like we can let them go and trust they won't try to butcher women for this. Taking their balls doesn't eliminate the ideologies that prompted all this. We have nowhere to hold them, so..."

"And how are you?"

Biting my lip, I looked away. "I'll live. Unfortunately. Now, we've got to move. Shrike still needs an exit and I mean to give her one."

At the intersection halfway down the mountains, I stopped to talk with Stretch and Gameboy, the soldiers heading to Portland. "Keep those assholes moving, keep 'em in front, and don't be afraid to shoot a few."

Stretch nodded, still pale from last night's retribution. "Yes, ma'am. How long do you want us to keep it up?"

I snorted. "As if all our plans don't go to hell." He grinned. "Go as long as you can but try for a lot of hell the first week. Hit them hard, disappear. You know what to do better than I do."

"I seriously doubt that," he muttered, but snapped a crisp salute at odds with his motley clothing. Jeans, a camo jacket, bandana around his neck, and a knit cap to keep his ears warm was an Irregular standard.

"You know you don't have to salute," I reminded him.

"Ma'am, all due respect, but yes, I do. What you did last night was hard, but it was justice, not revenge. I can't help but respect that."

"Fine, but we'll say 'later' our way, too." I extended a fist. Startled, he bumped it with his own, grinning. "Now, go blow some shit up."

Laughing now, Stretch circled a hand in the air, signaling his people to head out. When their dust settled, I thumped the cab of the pickup and Dereva took us south, using Old Sawtell Road, a straight shot along the Cascades, deep enough in the mountains you had to know it was here to find it.

Chapter 46

Illegal wiretap on Keller mansion December 14, 2065, impermissible in court.

I stalked through Poor Town, Salem, walking right up to a man with a red armband who looked startled when I didn't cross the street. He reared back, one hand falling to the baton at his side.

"Hey, what are you doing...?"

I kneed him in the crotch, then slammed my elbow between his shoulder blades and moved on. Deerskin, smaller and less skilled but no less nasty, struck while he was down before scampering after me.

Irregulars spread through the streets, simply snatching men off the sidewalks. Storm, at the corner ahead, stomped up to another Dorothy, who grinned and rubbed himself at the beautiful, angry blonde rapidly approaching. She decked him without slowing and Sweetpea, hot on her heels, finished him off with a knife and darted after.

Behind us, at the fence, a tower collapsed, sending a brief plume of flames that quickly died down, eventually followed by the *whump* of an explosion. Well, that should get their attention.

Somewhere to the south, River was crossing into Salem to retrieve Shrike. With no way to know how long she needed, our plan was simply chaos and mayhem. Then I learned we had a new fighter named Mayhem. I threw up my hands and left.

At the mouth of a narrow space between cars, I stretched out, snatching a man walking past. One quick jerk and we stuffed him under a car. Then we found two Dorothy watching a house, catcalling and shouting for someone named Aria to come out and 'play.'

Both men were tall and heavily built. The taller one had a slight pooch, looking a bit older. I stopped a few feet away, Deerskin hiding in the bushes with my rifle, and flipped them the finger.

"What? Can't do anything except harass some poor girl? What are you, too afraid to even step on the lawn?"

They smirked, nudging each other. "Don't you know, little girls shouldn't poke sleeping lions?"

I clapped. "Oh, very good! You managed a two-syllable word! Honestly, I figured it'd all be single syllable, but there you go. Surprises around every corner."

"You slut—"

"Maybe, but still too good to sleep with you."

"Bitch!" said the other one.

"How'd you know?"

Snarling, the larger man charged, his thick, meaty hands clenched into fists. I squared up in a boxing stance, making the other man howl with laughter.

"I'm gonna have fun with you, cunt," the charging man growled. "I'll fuck your—"

With his eyes fastened on my hands, I kicked him in the nuts. In the distance, I heard a bark of laughter while the man in front of me doubled over, clutching himself. A quick stomp/kick combo later, and the bigger man was laid out, a tooth on the ground, blood pouring from his mouth.

"Come on." I waved the shorter man closer. "Or are you scared?"

Bellowing, he charged.

***

"You know," Gryphon said, leaning on the fence, "you can be a bit of a nutter, taking on two men alone. Though," he kicked one of the downed men, "you didn't have to embarrass the plonker that badly."

"All she did was trip him," Phoenix argued.

"Yeah, in the middle of his dramatic entrance. Absolutely ruined the moment, you know."

The door to the house, once yellow, but now the paint barely held on at the corners, creaked open and an older woman stuck her head out. "You that uprising? Irritated, or something?"

"We're the Oregonian Irregulars," Phoenix called. "What's it to you?"

"One minute," she shouted before disappearing back into the house.

We looked at each other, confused. Down the street, a lone Dorothy ran towards us, brandishing a baton, shouting. When he passed a thick lilac bush, a pair of hands reached out, yanking him sideways. The bushes rustled, there was a thump followed by a grunt, then Chaos stepped out, brushing off his jacket, tugging it down.

"Your hat's a bit crooked, mate," Gryph called.

"Thanks." He tugged it down and disappeared back into the bushes.

The door opened and the woman stepped out, brandishing a cooking pot, closely followed by three children. "Stay close," she ordered, holding the smallest one by the hand.

The last one was a pretty girl in her early teens holding a kitchen knife. "I'm Bronwen. My daughter, Aria," the woman pointed, "has been trying to avoid those men for..." She shook her head.

Deerskin straightened up after wiping her blade on a man's shirt. "You're alright now," she said, smiling at the younger woman.

With the small family in tow, we continued down the street. To our left, an older man, the evening sun gleaming on his balding pate, emerged onto the porch, adjusting his belt. When he saw us, his eyes went wide, then he opened his mouth. The door swung open and a frying pan took him out. He collapsed bonelessly.

A young woman, early twenties, stepped over him, carefully hitting him one more time for good measure. Then she lifted two small kids over him and waved to us. Bronwen waved back. Shrugging, Phoenix and Gryph headed over, leading her back to our growing group.

"You seem awfully sure we're safe," I said to Bronwen.

Laughing, almost carefree, Bronwen waved her pot. "You're clearing the streets. What else do I need to know? Actually...Who are you?"

The corner of my mouth lifted. "I'm Captain. I—"

"Oh, my God," Aria squealed. "My friends and I love you! I...Wait." She frowned. "We thought you were a..."

"A what?"

"A man." Bronwen laughed. "They all have crushes on you," she explained. "I'd hear them speculating about what Captain looked like, how handsome he is..."

"Mom!"

At that moment, another tower toppled, the crash muffled by the suburb and distance. Then a child cried out before clamping her hand over her mouth, pointing down a side street. A transport rumbled down the road, honking.

Deerskin tossed me my rifle and Phoenix had hers up before I managed to line up the sights, but I relaxed as soon as I saw the driver. Bear stuck her head out the window, waving.

"Look what I found!"

***

I leaned over the engine block of my pickup, undoing a clamp as quietly as possible. On the road, twenty feet away and ten feet below, a parade of Steve and Dorothy—on foot and in vehicles—passed by, hunting for us.

We had vehicles all over these mountains. The fighters took more random paths, intersecting with Steve, drawing them in, while a few transports took the most direct route available back to the Lair.

After picking up River and Shrike, we'd hit a rough section of road too fast. Dereva reported an unidentified odd sound. We'd barely made the hills when something burst. Phoenix and Gryph vaulted out of the pickup, running down the side of the road to hold Steve off long enough for us to hide, and now I found myself performing mechanical repairs to the tune of a dozen vehicles rumbling below and at least fifty men marching.

Dereva hovered nearby, wringing her hands. "What's wrong with her?" she whispered.

"Busted radiator hose," I whispered back. "The one I got out of that Toyota."

It didn't fit. Nothing fit, but I made it work. Until it didn't. Fuck.

A wave of longing for Archangel, for his steady presence and surety hit me. Closing my eyes, I bent my head, waiting for the worst of it to pass. So many memories tied to the vehicles...

"Captain?" Dereva laid a hand on my arm, her blue eyes, so bright against her dark skin, close to mine. "Are you okay?"

"No, but gimme a minute and I'll function."

Biting my lip, the physical pain pulling me back into my body, I continued working, whispering requests to Dereva. Phoenix wandered by to let me know they'd returned. The next time I lifted my head, I saw her curled against Gryph, her head resting on his chest.

As soon as I finished and the parade passed, we loaded up, coming up on Steve from the rear. Then it was attack, run away, attack, hide, run…It blurred together, and all I could feel was the yawning hole in my chest, back every time we were away from a fight.

When we did rest, it was in fits and starts. River curled around Shrike, her dark hair mingling with Shrike's blonde strands. Somehow, through letters and occasional meetings, they'd fallen in love. It was the one thing that brought a smile to my lips, the bright spot.

We hadn't lost anyone the last I'd heard, we'd gotten a bunch of people out of Salem, and River could rest easier, knowing she'd been able to rescue the woman she loved.

At the Lair, I left while Shrike still stared around, open-mouthed at the size of our home. Normally, I might enjoy watching the former spy gape, but not now. Now, I headed through the corridors on a mission.

Going straight to the common room, I cut through it to the kitchen. "Where are my babies—?"

My smile died when I didn't spy their cradles. My heart stopped. Spinning, I didn't see Lavender or Amana. "Where are they?" I roared at the nearest cook, Tabitha.

She squeaked, shrinking away. Snarling, I went to my room next. Also empty.

Fighting back panic, I raced through the Lair, shouting. How could I have lost Archangel's babies? My babies. The last piece of him I had.

"Where are Michael and Gabriel?"

CHAPTER 47

I sat in the common room, hunched over, my head hanging between my knees. Eleanor rubbed my back in soothing circles that did nothing for the inner turmoil.

Oh, we'd found Amana and Lavender. Or rather, we found someone willing to spill. Moose, who'd replaced Mouse as commander of the perimeter when Mouse moved to the fighters, shifted from one foot to the other, stumbling her way through the story.

"We caught them trying to exit," she began. "We knew it was suss because rookies never try to leave the area. They're too afraid of the deep woods. Turned out they had your babies under their jackets."

"And who are these walking dead?" I asked, clenching my hands.

"A man and a woman from the prepper's camp. They attacked when it was only Lavender watching—she's fine," Moose said hastily. "She's got a lump the size of an egg and she's madder than a hornet, but she's fine. They figured they'd take your kids to Steve and use them as leverage to save themselves."

"And where are my children now?" I choked out.

"Everyone figured it'd be safer if we took them Home and told people the boys were orphans." The usual story when a woman couldn't accept the result of her rape. It was the kindest story we could come up with for when those kids were older. "Amana planned to tell Olivia and Sam and swear them to secrecy. And Kioni and Walter will stay there until the boys are used to the new people."

"How..." I cleared my throat. "How long ago did they leave? Why didn't you wait for me?"

Moose shrugged helplessly. "They left a little over a week ago. Steve had briefly cleared out of the mountains and we weren't sure how long the window would be, so they took it. I'm sorry. I...I just..." She spread her hands, the corners of her mouth turning down.

I rocked on the couch, my hands clamped over my mouth, terrified that if I removed them, I'd start screaming and never stop. Gentle hands rubbed my back while words flew over my head. Only one thought percolated through the grief squeezing the breath out of me:

What goes around, comes around. Sometimes, you get what's coming around, sometimes you *are* what's coming around. If I wanted to hold my boys again, be a part of their lives, and see them grow up, then it was time to pull my head out and be what's coming around for Steve.

Noah would want me to be there for the boys.

I rubbed my face, pushing the never-ending grief away, and looked up. Talk ceased immediately. Eleanor continued rubbing my back, making me want nothing more than to lean into her and cry like a baby. Straightening my shoulders, I rested a hand on her knee, then rose.

"We're going to expand training. At least four people to support Sarge. We're going to get Tabitha and Landon some support and apprentices to make more bullets and up production." I took a deep breath and let it out slowly, turning to look at all of them. Driver, Dry Eyes, Phoenix, Gryphon,

Eleanor, Storm, Moose, Dereva, and Anansi. "We're driving Steve into the fucking ocean."

"Fucking A!" Phoenix punched the air.

Eleanor chewed on her lip. "Are you sure this is the best way...? What we've been doing—"

"Isn't working fast enough." The corners of my mouth turned down. We'd lost too many. *I'd* lost too many. It was time to ensure those deaths meant something, that their sacrifice hadn't been in vain. "We're growing, but I've been keeping us small, unwilling to try tactics necessary for something larger scale. But the people are willing. Bronwen and the others we took from Salem are proof of that. I can't take care of my kids with Steve everywhere."

"We're with you, Captain," Gryphon said earnestly. "We'll hit those fucking wankers where it hurts—"

"Right in the nuts," Phoenix finished, still grinning.

The fighters practically vibrated with pent-up excitement while the older folks gave each other troubled looks. I shook my head, proud of us. Now was not the time to hold back or hesitate.

"Not in vain. I swear it."

Chapter 48

Woman 1: If you go now, you'll look like you're assisting that stupid little uprising. We need the people there to be completely hopeless so that they hail you as their savior.

Illegal wiretap on Keller mansion December 14, 2065, impermissible in court.

The wind ripped down from the north, chilling my ears where I sat on the western side of the foothills. At the bottom, seemingly close enough to touch, the ocean stretched away to the horizon, its gunmetal gray waters tossing and churning.

It'd taken us two long years to get here. To take Portland and Salem, train the remaining residents to fight, all while continually pushing Steve and Dorothy west.

The low Coast Range rose behind me, thick evergreens hiding us from Steve's sight. They'd tried to burn the range, but by the time they realized they couldn't hold us back, the rainy season had begun. They'd caused avalanches in some passes and set ambushes in the remainder, but we didn't use the roads.

They had no idea how many ways there were over these mountains, but they were learning.

I flipped the collar of Archangel's leather jacket up to protect my neck and fished a beanie out of my pack. I smelled ice in the air, each breath freezing my nose, and glared at the clouds. Oregon wasn't content with rain this time. No, tonight it seemed she'd bring us sleet.

Maybe she'd wait until tomorrow, but I doubted it.

Raising my scope, I examined the beach below. Men and boxes were thick on the ground, covering the sand, barely out of the water. Lining their perimeter, barbed wire stretched over trenches gouged into the rocky portions of the beach.

I counted mortars and cannon, noting them down in a little notebook I carried in an inner pocket, tucking it back just before the first drops fell.

So much for waiting until tomorrow.

Steve milled around when the sleet hit, tiny men waving their arms, their voices lost to the distance. And there, to the south of their entrenchment, I spotted what I really wanted: a broad arm of the hill extending out, right to the edge of their fortifications, just wide enough for a small vehicle. Smirking, I slid back into the trees and set off down the deer track towards our camp.

Inside the camp, made up of low shelters built from downed branches and tarps, I ducked into the largest one, a tarp strung between three trees and a stick, with two more tarps forming the sides. Inside, TK, a young artist who'd volunteered to fight but turned out to be far more proficient at creating maps, worked steadily.

She was surrounded by Phoenix, Gryph, Eleanor, and a trickle of scouts bringing additional news and numbers from up and down the coast. I studied the map while pulling out my own notes and passing on the information therein.

TK jotted down troop locations and numbers, and it was grim. Steve was spread thinly along the coast, and we camped above the largest concentration. They worked as hard as they could to clear more ground. They'd learned not to enter the woods. Too many of them never came out.

Even as TK finished a section, Legs entered.

"Forget that." She pointed to a camp to the north. "They've abandoned it and are heading here, gathering others along the route. Looks like Steve's recalling the northern camps."

"Well, that sucks," the artist muttered, scrubbing out the northernmost camp. "I just put that in."

Anarchy showed up next, with similar news from the south. "They were decently dug in," they said. "It was a small area, but well-fortified. They had a lot of munitions."

"Fuck." Phoenix shook her head. "Steve's bringing in all the weapons and ammo."

"Anarchy, any chance we can intercept?" I asked.

They bit their lip before shrugging. "They're moving from camp to camp, but there is a spot where an arm from the mountain goes nearly to the water. There's not much space to walk, but plenty to hide."

"What? They haven't burned all the trees yet?" Phoenix asked sarcastically.

Anarchy laughed. "No, they did. There's just lots of rock."

I nodded, checking the other map, the one we'd brought from the Lair. For a moment, longing panged through my chest. The Lair was home, and we'd been away for…for months. I hadn't been to sit beside Noah, nor had I seen our boys.

They hadn't known me as anything other than 'Captain' the last time I'd been Home, hanging back, watching me with wide eyes, their father's eyes, thumbs in their mouths. They'd gone running when Olivia called them to dinner, as alike as two peas in a pod. Except Michael's hair fell differently, and Gabriel was slightly more outgoing, though Olivia said they took turns every few months on who was the outgoing one.

I shook my head, bringing myself back to the present, to the scent of loam, smoke, and ice, the sleet falling more heavily. "I need Seahorse and Sarge," I decided. "And Triskele."

Triskele lost a leg several winters ago, and she'd been forcibly grounded. However, on freeing the cities, we now had access to people and supplies previously denied us. We couldn't do much for the ones who lost their arms, but those who were missing legs, like Tris and Porkpie, were able to retake the field.

Triskele limped up first, rifle over her shoulder, beanie pulled down firmly over her ears. "Wassup?" She threw me a small salute, flicking her fingers from her forehead.

I nodded and pointed her to a couple of stacked up bedrolls. She waved it away. "It's easier if I stand."

Sarge and Seahorse joined us, both still flushed. "You, uh, you got something in your hair, there." Phoenix delicately picked a twig out, grinning wickedly.

Seahorse blushed but Sarge simply smiled widely, radiating contentment. "Whatcha need, Captain?" he rumbled.

"I need you two to go south. There's an encampment making their way north and they're loaded for bear. Your aim is to not only stop them but steal their shit. Legs pegged this as an obvious spot for an ambush." I pointed to locations on the map.

Sarge nodded. "Which means we need a point north of there, where they're not expecting it. Legs?"

Taking them aside, she began filling them in on everything she remembered in the region.

"What about me?" Tris asked.

"You're taking command of the bulk of the army," I said. Her mouth dropped open. "You've got a solid head, you're calm, and your sense of timing in these matters is exquisite."

"Timing for what? What the fuck, Captain? Where will you be?"

"She'll be doing the dumbest shit she can find, of course." Phoenix rolled her eyes. "Which is what, exactly?"

"You're not going to like it," I assured her.

"That's nice. As long as I'm not in it..." She trailed off. "Goddammit! Why me?"

"Because you like making shit go boom, and Sparrow will be busy up here."

"What about Chaos? He's crazy and stupid enough."

"Oh, he's coming, too. I need ALL the idiots. You included."

She stuck her tongue out and I laughed.

"Captain," Tris broke in desperately, "you can't leave me in charge. I can't move fast, my leg..."

"Tris." I set my hands on her shoulders. "You are the best person for this. I need you high up, barking orders and having them followed, and you do that very well. The newbies know you and they trust you. The vets trust you, too. Now, there's one other thing, and I need you to really hear me. You listening?" She nodded. "Good. I do what I want, and I want you to lead."

***

I dogpaddled through the ocean, the only stroke I could maintain for longer than two minutes. Sometime after midnight, the frozen rain still fell, coating everything on land in ice. I shivered inside the dry suit, struggling to keep my head above the waves.

We'd only found four dry suits without holes, so my force was considerably smaller than what I'd wanted to field. So, I brought the four stupidest, most reckless people I knew: Chaos, Gryphon, Phoenix, and me.

Yeah, I was just attacking the largest concentration of Steve we'd ever seen with four people. Great. At this moment, I wished there was a hospital so I could have myself committed.

The entire last dozen or more seasons, all the people, all the lives lost, all the people's freedom, everything, hinged on four people not getting caught in the next few hours. And the best I could do was dogpaddle.

Fuck me and this Oregon life.

We came in on the tide, mingling with some driftwood we'd shoved into the ocean with us. Steve barely paid attention to the ocean—and why should they? It's the middle of winter. Only morons would be in the ocean, even with dry suits.

The machete shifted, the handle digging into my side. I rolled onto my back, feeling my side, my fingers numb inside the gloves, adjusting the blade, allowing myself to be carried in on the tide. Last thing I needed right now was the handle bumping the package taped to my belly.

Sand scraped under my back and a piece of driftwood rolled against my leg. Sighing in relief, I crawled onto the beach, barely resisting the urge to kiss the sand with every step. The suit squeaked slightly where my thighs rubbed together.

I froze, listening intently, but no alarm was raised, no voices shouted warning.

To my left, Steve's tents marched along the beach in neat rows, lanterns placed every other tent. More lanterns were scattered through the encampment and bonfires sent sparks into the sky along the perimeter. Anyone trying to approach from land would be seen before they could get close enough to engage, much less surprise them.

Water lapped around my hands and knees, erasing my tracks. I paused next to a boat, scanning the beach, searching for the others. South, a large figure, one I couldn't identify, clung to the seaward side of a rock while a pair of sentries marched past, one gingerly holding a lantern high while the other held his rifle at the ready.

Wriggling farther up, I tucked myself against a rubber boat, thinking boat thoughts to blend in. My breath caught. North of my position, a slender shape emerged from the ocean, obviously clumsy. I stared from Phoenix to the soldiers, willing her to see them.

Apparently exhausted, she collapsed at the edge of the surf, allowing the water to lap around her. It flowed around her while she shivered and...I frowned, rubbing my eyes. Were they not working? She appeared to be shivering and...sinking into the sand?

Steve closed in on her position and what she'd done dawned on me. She'd half buried herself in the sand and let the ocean do the rest, hiding in plain view, nearly invisible now.

As soon as they passed, I started up, but a log washed in and a large shape detached from it, seizing Phoenix's dry suit and bodily hauling her from the sand and onto slightly drier ground. Slinking from one shadow to the next, I made my way to their position, the sleet making little difference to me in the suit.

"Captain," Phoenix whispered without looking up, rubbing her torso vigorously, her suit already down, around her waist. "You gotta lose the suit. You squeak."

Huffing, I sank down next to their hiding spot, a pile of crates covered with a large green tarp. "Gimme a hand and I will. Who's with you?"

"Me," Chaos whispered.

"Have you seen Gryph?" Phoenix scanned the beach, half-rising.

I pulled her back down. "He's a little south. Avoided the sentries, no worries."

She sighed, her shoulders relaxing. "Good. If he'd managed to get lost here, I couldn't have let him forget it."

If he'd died, she meant.

Chaos's struggle caught my attention. He was trapped, the suit's water-tight neckline halfway across his face, his nose smashed flat. Sniggering, I grabbed the edges of his suit nearest the neck.

"Wait for it..." Phoenix watched the camp, her hand raised. "Okay...go!" She dropped it and I yanked sharply.

He grunted but emerged in one piece, his hair sticking up around his head, his battle braids loosened by the rough treatment. "Your turn," he said.

No wonder they called putting a dry suit on and off 'birthing.' Removing it was slower, scraping hair and skin up, towards the scalp.

"Will Gryph be okay?" Phoenix chewed her lip, peering down the beach where I'd last seen him.

"If anybody could land on an occupied beach in the middle of a sleet storm and finish out with a glass of whiskey and a fine suit, it'd be him," Chaos murmured, raising a pendant to his lips and kissing it before dropping it back into his shirt.

I'd never seen him do that before. "What's that?"

"Little something from Doc." He hesitated, then fished it out. My fingers made out the shape of a heart with a tiny catch on the side. Gently placing it back in his hand, I closed his fingers around it.

Shoving the suits under the tarp, we took a moment to rearrange weapons. Untying the rawhide strings took too long, so I whipped out the knife from the small of my back, catching the rifle before it clattered against the boat.

Beanies down tight, weapons loose in holsters and sheaths, ready to use, nothing that would reflect or rattle on our persons. One last thing. Tonight, neck gaiters acted as masks to hide both breath and skin.

Before we parted ways, there was only one thing to say.

"All in, all out. One shot, one kill. No luck, all skill."

We bumped fists and that was that. I left the shelter of the crates first, crawling towards the camp.

"Not in vain," I whispered, watching Steve. Sudden warmth radiated on my shoulder. Closing my eyes, I turned my head, imagining a kiss brushed across my lips. "I swear it."

***

Setting charges with sketchy timers was always an adventure. Would it blow up in my face? Could I finish the job with all my fingers? Who knows? I passed near the perimeter, pausing and planting charges wherever would cause havoc.

After setting the last charge, I slipped through the shadows, holding my breath, leaning against a rock when a pair of Steve passed so close I could've reached out and touched them. Their hoods were up, obscuring their peripheral vision, the men muttering to each other.

I didn't understand Korean, but "Fuck this shit, I hate my life" sounds the same in every language.

Once they passed, I crawled to the largest pile of crates in the center of their camp. Gaining my feet, I edged towards the ocean side. At the corner, a faint sound made me freeze. Moving infinitesimally, I raised my hand to cover my masked mouth with my sleeve to further muffle my breathing.

The game, called *The First One to Move, Dies*, had begun.

The sleet soaked my beanie and mask, and I rubbed my nose, suppressing the urge to sneeze. Archangel's leather jacket wrapped around me, keeping the freezing rain off the rest, and I waited.

Closing my eyes helped me concentrate while I searched for the source of the sound. The sound repeated, revealing itself as metal on metal. But grating. A clank rather than a chime. Then a man's rhythmic, harsh breathing interspersed with a woman's quiet moans.

Peering around the corner, the couple was little more than shadows, even to my eyes. The woman held onto the soldier, one leg hitched high around his hip, her expression curiously still, chin tipped towards the sky so the rain fell on her face. It must hurt, and yet...

Dispassionate. That's what it was. She made noise, her fingers clutched him, but there was nothing behind it. An act designed to make him think she wanted it. And still that faint clank continued periodically, though I could see no source for it.

Gliding away from the crates, I went wide to come directly at the man's back, drawing my knife. The woman saw me, her dark eyes widening enough to show white at the edges. I tugged my mask down, holding a finger to my lips.

The man moved quickly now, nearing the end. Seeing no reason to inflict this on the poor woman any longer, I took two long strides forward, looping my arm around his neck, yanking him backwards, thrusting quickly between his ribs.

Letting the man drop, I held my hands up, the knife dangling between my fingers to show I was harmless. The woman shook her skirts over her legs, buttoning her blouse up, her wary eyes never leaving my hands.

"It's okay," I whispered. "I won't hurt you."

She shrugged. "Not a lot you could do that he," she nodded to the body at our feet, "hasn't already."

Curling my lip at the dead man, I cleaned the knife on his clothes and put it away before rolling him as far under the tarp as I could. I'd just kicked sand over his body when Chaos appeared around the corner.

The woman started, her hands flying up to cover her face, mouth open. I clamped a hand over her mouth, pressing her against the crates. "No!" I hissed. "He's okay. He's with me. It's okay. He won't hurt you, either."

Chaos pursed his lips, shaking his head. "Starting the show without me? How dare you."

"Look less threatening, will you?" I kept my attention on the woman. When she stopped struggling, I slowly removed my hands, ready to leap on her if she even inhaled sharply.

When she remained calm, her mouth closed, I relaxed. "FYI, there's two more of us, so I'd appreciate it if you didn't scream."

"Are you the Ghost Captain?" she asked Chaos.

"No," he replied.

"What's your name?" I asked her.

"Starlight."

I snorted. "Your real name."

Most newbies still chose a name and set aside their real ones, but that was more tradition than necessity, now. Sure, there'd been a few people running away to tattle to Steve, but ever since we'd taken Salem, Steve assumed any American except those they personally knew was one of us. It meant we didn't have to be quite so on guard.

Nobody wanted to tattle to people who'd torture you for fun, first.

"Aanisah," she whispered, tensing for a blow.

"Ready to ditch this shithole, Aanisah?"

In reply, she lifted her skirt slightly, wiggling her left foot. Manacles connected her ankles, the source of the clanking.

"I'mma take that as a yes. Well, you're in luck. All you have to do is sit tight and move when we tell you it's time."

"In the meantime," Chaos knelt, gesturing to her foot.

Aanisah shook her head. "They're hammered in. You'll need a file."

"Then we'll stuff cloth in between to muffle the sound and spare your ankles."

She squared her shoulders. "I would prefer if a man did not touch me right now. And...Do you have a scarf or anything I can use to cover my hair?"

"Oh!" Chaos rocked back, scrambling to his feet. "I'm so sorry." He turned his back.

Yanking off my neck gaiter, I passed it and a spare leather tie to her, then knelt at her feet. Cutting my shirt into strips while I wore it, I stuffed it between the links while she covered herself.

I was barely half done when Chaos hissed. "Phoenix, incoming."

Phoenix slid in, holding a whispered conversation. I couldn't hear what they said, but in her shoes, I'd have been asking about my husband, too. When I'd done as much as I could for Aanisah, she touched my shoulder gently.

"Thank you," she whispered, her hair now fully covered by the neck gaiter. "I haven't been properly dressed for...so long."

I patted her hand, then slid around to check on Phoenix. A whispered word and Chaos took the other side. We had maybe an hour until dawn, which is when the attack was set to begin. Phoenix fidgeted, picking at her nails and my right hand unconsciously twitched at my side, the tension building, Gryphon still in the wind.

Flexing and relaxing my legs didn't take the place of pacing, but it was the best I could do under the circumstances. Abruptly, the sky on the far side of our shelter lit up, the *whump* of an explosion blowing sand around our hiding spot, quickly followed by a wave of heat.

"Gryphon!" Phoenix cried, lunging out.

"Fuck," I snarled, catching her before she got too far.

She fought hard. It only ended when I sat on her.

The camp exploded like a kicked anthill. Steve charged out of their tents, twenty or thirty feet away, clothes flapping as they ran, boots barely laced up. Guards ran screaming, some in flames. Only the sleet prevented the whole camp from going up in smoke.

Seconds after the first, another explosion rocked the earth. This fireball reached so far, I could see it around the crates, swallowing men whole. Bodily hauling Phoenix back to the west side, I peered above the crates. On the hillside above, a flaming van raced down the hill, bumping crazily until, launched by an unseen rock, it crashed into Steve's perimeter.

The fires continued in a slightly curving line to the north and south, completely enclosing the camp. "Chaos!" I pointed.

Coughing, he wiped his eyes, squinting. "Oil," he rasped. "Oil in a ditch."

Fucking assholes. Sure, our trucks had three times the impact they'd have had without, but it meant the fighters would have to find a way over those fucking ditches. More, smaller, explosions joined the cacophony sporadically around the camp.

Phoenix screamed, twisting in my hold. "Let me go, you heartless bitch! I could lose him. Don't you care?"

I gasped, my grip loosening. Stricken, one hand went to her mouth, the other reaching out to me. Pushing her away, I stumbled, falling to my knees, retching. The screams, flames, bullets flying…The scent of blood strong in my nose, the cold sand under my hands suddenly felt like Archangel's lifeless body.

Unmoving and still.

Any apology was immediately lost when a very British voice cussed in extreme detail. "Fucking wankers couldn't find their fucking pricks with both hands and a dog, but they find a fucking bomb hidden under three bloody layers, what a load of fucking useless twats…"

Gryph coalesced out of the smoke and flames of another small explosion, soot-blackened and coughing. He didn't stop his litany until his wife grabbed his ears and hauled him down for a deep kiss.

That voice was what pulled me out of my memories and back into the present. Shaking, I crawled back to the dubious shelter of the crates to check on Aanisah and Chaos.

"Miss. Miss!" Aanisah grabbed my arm. "Look."

Dragging me down, she lifted the tarp, the burning camp providing sufficient illumination. She'd pried a crate open. Inside, neatly nested in individual compartments, rested glass bottles with two different colored liquids inside.

"Okay, so..." I shrugged. "Craft projects?"

"Acid bombs," she whispered. "I heard them talking about it. This was brought in recently. They have a ship out there, though it was returning to Korea."

"Oh, fuck." I sat back, nearly falling from shock. Then the potential uses struck me, and I grinned. Aanisah leaned away, looking alarmed. "Guys!"

Reluctantly, Gryph and Phoenix pulled apart and came over, preceded by Chaos. "'Sup?"

After showing them, I looked around the small circle. "Either we bug out, or we use it."

And I was all for using it.

I wished Eleanor were there. Or that I could call her. This shit was nasty, eating away at soft tissue. We'd run across it once just this side of the Coast Range and I'd had a first-hand look at its effects. So, I needed Eleanor to tell me whether it was moral and okay to use it. Because, surrounded by Steve, I *wanted* to.

And, since the fighters hadn't crossed into the camp yet, now was the best time...

The conversation flowed on around me, finally trickling through now that I'd made my decision.

"*She's* the Ghost?"

"Honestly, that's a way cooler name than Captain." This from Chaos.

"Takes too long," Phoenix retorted. "With Captain, we can shorten it down."

"'Hey, Bonehead' is not shorter," Gryph said dryly.

"Will someone tell me what a living legend is doing in the middle of this?" Aanisah demanded, a hysterical edge to her voice.

That's what it took for her to crack? Fuck, people are weird.

"Where else would I be?" I asked. "Okay, people. Time to be stupid."

"Yay! That's the best." Phoenix grinned up at me, her green eyes sparkling. "What are we doing?"

"Using those." I nodded to the bombs, and they all went silent. I licked my dry lips, salt from the ocean fresh on my tongue. If I died doing something as terrible as this, would I still see Archangel?

Who was the bigger monster, Steve in their attempts to subjugate, or me in my attempts to win free?

CHAPTER 49

Smoke billowed into the sky, blocking the view of the sunset and blurring the outlines of the three ships sitting in the bay. They rode low in the water, and I saw another small boat pull alongside a ship, disgorging soldiers who swarmed up the sides.

One ship listed badly, a hole in her side. Lights sparked against her side as sailors attempted to repair the damage. Turns out, Anansi's head for numbers was good for more than inventing. He'd calculated a trajectory and I don't even know what else off the top of his head, enough to put a series of shots in her—enough to threaten the ship.

Setting down my scope, I sagged against the pine tree I sat in, rubbing my face. It'd been two days since the fight. Two days of frantic activity, meetings, veiled and not-so-veiled threats. Negotiations that finally ended with some Navy bigwig agreeing to take Steve out of Oregon.

"I cannot speak for the rest," he warned. "But we will leave this forsaken place and its incessant rain."

Good enough. Fuck off and never come back.

I'd never gotten to kill Kwan Jae. Sung Ki pointed him out on the deck of a ship, the Navy guy stripping him of his rank. It'd been a sweet sight.

In the edges of the trees, the few uninjured fighters left manned anything that could launch explosives. Which meant a lot of inexperienced people under the tired eye of someone nursing their wounds. Neither of our primary trainers was available.

Sarge lay in the hospital area, Seahorse constantly by his side. He was expected to live, but we had no idea how long it would be before he recovered. Hightide...Hightide should even now be laid to rest in the Meadow, next to Fox. We'd found her in a bloody embrace with a beautiful, auburn-haired woman who bore a striking resemblance to Eleanor.

I would've expected Hightide's face to be twisted in a snarl, facing the woman who'd been responsible for so much hurt and destruction. Instead, there was a hint of joy, as if, at the moment her soul left her body, she saw paradise.

Perhaps she saw Fox, the girl she'd never stopped loving.

Eleanor sank to the ground next to her daughter, tears rolling down her cheeks. She'd carefully straightened the woman's limbs, arranging her hair around her face. Storm knelt opposite, stone-faced as she stared down at her one-time friend.

The rest of our dead waited to be laid to rest in a mountain meadow overlooking the ocean. After so many years of burying our people in the high mountains, away from Steve's sight and reach, it now felt...wrong, to bury them in the valleys. Up there, they could be free and at peace.

"Captain?"

I turned at the raspy voice. Eleanor stood at the foot of my pine, her eyes red with weeping. Despite everything, she mourned her daughter. Or perhaps, she mourned who Anna could have been and would now never be.

I climbed down, stretching when I reached the bottom, picking absently at some sap on my palm, content to wait for Eleanor to continue.

"They've loaded the last of their men and will leave with the next tide," she eventually said.

I nodded.

"Will they come back?"

"Shrike says that when they give their word, they mean it. I think they'll only go as far as Washington or California. We'll be seeing them again."

"We will?" She looked up at me, her forehead furrowed. "I thought...I'd hoped we were done."

I rubbed my mouth, unsure whether I wanted to laugh or cry. "You can go Home, Eleanor. You can take a break any time you need."

"What about you?" she asked sharply.

I shook my head. "This is only the beginning. I have family in both states. I can't..."

She nodded, understanding softening her features. "When do we leave?"

"As soon as Phoenix and Gryph are able."

EPILOGUE: THE PRESENT

Hope paced across the stage, rubbing her mouth. The inconspicuous wedding band on her finger took on new meaning to the watching crowd. The lowering sun lit her honey-blonde hair with strands of fire and ice, making her light eyes glow.

"It's funny," she mused, almost to herself, "how the mind works. During those years, I stopped thinking in terms of months and years. I can't...I can't put it together. I know my sons are sixteen, I know the Invasion happened in 2061, but I can't make time fit. I can't remember what year they were born. I can't put events that happened there into years, much less months.

"Memory is...fluid. A sound, a smell and suddenly, I'm back in those woods, carrying these things." She gestured to the worn weapons she carried. "Like I never stopped. And then I can smell his scent and..." She trailed off, her eyes closed.

"I feel his touch, the warmth of his body, his skin against mine..." Unconsciously, Hope tipped her head as if an invisible hand cradled her cheek.

"Is it odd that the first time I've been able to really talk about him in sixteen years has been to an auditorium full of strangers?" Humor filled her voice, tinged with sorrow. Her blue-gray eyes were blind to the present, to the cameras that hung on her every word, look, gesture. "He was my world, and I was his hopes and dreams. The day he died, my worst fears happened. After that…"

She sighed heavily, facing the crowd, her head bowed. "I had to speak, to ensure they wouldn't be forgotten. They didn't die in vain. I swear it."

She fell silent, one hand pressing against her heart, too full to continue.

A smattering of applause sounded around the stadium, dying out when the rebel leader didn't move. The lights dimmed, but she still didn't move. People murmured and shifted, the susurrus filling the arena. It wasn't until another voice spoke, the first new voice in hours, that she finally looked up.

"They are never forgotten." Alex Carrington's quiet words stilled the people. "Look up, Captain. Look up and see the people who are alive because of Archangel. Look and see the ones who are here because of you."

Hope wiped her eyes with a trembling hand and walked to the edge of the stage. All around, climbing high into the stands, tiny lights shone like stars that fell to earth. The TV screens surrounding the crowds touched on them, showing her the faces of her past.

So many who'd survived, and some few children. Seahorse. Sarge. Dereva. Anansi. Stretch. Goliath. Doc. Chaos. Amana. Olivia.

And right at the front, her sons sat next to Alex and Tom. Her sons, who had her dark blond hair and their father's eyes. Noah's straight nose and his smile. Wonderful young men, Hope gave all the credit to those who'd raised them and stayed in their lives all these years.

"As long as their names are remembered, they're never truly gone," Alex whispered through a tight throat. "We remember. Hail the victorious dead."

Hope held an imaginary glass high as the mass of people responded. "Hail!"

Tom Carrington, aka Gryphon, took the mic from his wife. "Now, tell them how it ended," he commanded. "Tell them the truth. It's time."

What's Next?

**The third and final book of The Northwest Uprising, The Fire-
brands, arrives in August 2025!**

Sign up to my 1-2 times a month newsletter for exclusive sneak peeks,
cover reveals, book launches, and more! Get the first 2 chapters of my new,
modern Arthurian retelling when you do! Scan the QR code to get started
or click here.

A Note from Nadya

I f you enjoyed The Irregulars, I would love it if you let your friends
know so they can experience the thrills of life with Hope, Sirius, and
Phoenix, too!

And as always, please leave a review! It helps other readers find or avoid
my books. Thank you!

ACKNOWLEDGMENTS

This book happened with the support and love of many people. My family and friends have been here every step of the way.

My beta readers gave me the best feedback I could have hoped for. Tan stalked into the room, informed me she'd finished the book, then proceeded to yell at me for making her feel things. Olia dropped the last stack of papers onto the table next to me, said, "I hate you," and went to bed. Thank you, Cicily, for listening while I was on a drunken ramble about my book and offering an amazing idea that changed...everything.

My editor, Dave Pasquantonio, is incredible. These books wouldn't be the same. Dave, these books would never be published so easily without you.

Thank you.

And finally, I have a special thank you to everyone who pledged to my Kickstarter and supported the publishing process. You are why I write, and I'm so grateful!

Thank you:

Katy, Olia Baghdanov, Hanya, Cynthia Coffman, Tatiana Baghdanov, Hillary Stone, Andreah Barker, Mania Siapin, Joanna Siapin, Jessica

Efsaeff, Suzanna Kudryashov, R Tolmachoff, Sarah Baghdanov, S Belia, Kendell Macomber, Cicily Wall, Jennifer Homutoff, Nemo Omnis, Chrystal, Andrew Lazootin, Joshua C. Chadd

You guys rock!

About Author

Nadya Siapin is the author of The Northwest Uprising trilogy and is now moving into Arthurian myths with The Dragon Queen Cycle.

An avid traveler and story lover, she mixes what she knows with what she imagines and is always on the lookout for slightly insane, definitely chaotic quotes for some characters 2 series into the future. (Sometimes, she manages to plan ahead.)

A dual citizen of the United States and Australia, Nadya uses her travel and backpacking experience extensively in her writing. She splits her time between the US and Australia. She can (occasionally)be persuaded to wear shoes. You can check out her other work or follow her on social media here.

instagram.com/nadya_siapin/

facebook.com/nadya.siapin.author/

tiktok.com/@nadyasiapin.author